John Irving was born in Exeter, New Hampshire in 1942, and he once admitted that he was a 'grim' child. Although he excelled in English at school and knew by the time he graduated that he wanted to write novels, it was not until he met a young Southern novelist named John Yount, at the University of New Hampshire, that he received encouragement. 'It was so simple,' he remembers. 'Yount was the first person to point out that anything I did except writing was going to be vaguely unsatisfying.'

In 1963, Irving enrolled at the Institute of European Studies in Vienna, and he later worked as a university lecturer. His first novel, *Setting Free the Bears*, about a plot to release all the animals from the Vienna Zoo, was followed by *The Water-Method Man*, an hilarious tale of a man with a complaint more serious than Portnoy's, and *The 158-Pound Marriage*, which exposes the complications of spouse-swapping. Irving achieved international recognition with *The World According To Garp*, which he hoped would 'cause a few smiles among the tough-minded and break a few softer hearts.'

The Hotel New Hampshire is a startlingly original family saga, and *The Cider House Rules*, is the story of Doctor Wilbur Larch – saint, obstetrician, founder of an orphanage, ether addict and abortionist – and of his favourite orphan, Homer Wells, who is never adopted. John Irving's masterly new novel, *A Prayer for Owen Meany*, features the most unforgettable character he has yet created.

John Irving has a life-long passion for wrestling, and he plays a wrestling referee in the film of *The World According to Garp*. He now writes full-time, has two children and lives in the United States.

Author photograph by Marion Ettlinger

Also by John Irving

THE 158LB MARRIAGE
THE CIDER HOUSE RULES
THE HOTEL NEW HAMPSHIRE
SETTING FREE THE BEARS
THE WATER METHOD MAN
THE WORLD ACCORDING TO GARP

A PRAYER FOR OWEN MEANY

John Irving

BLACK SWAN

A PRAYER FOR OWEN MEANY

A BLACK SWAN BOOK 0 552 99369 7

Originally published in Great Britain by
Bloomsbury Publishing Ltd.

PRINTING HISTORY
Bloomsbury edition published 1989
Corgi edition published 1989
Corgi edition reissued 1990
Black Swan edition published 1990
Black Swan edition reprinted 1990

A signed first edition of this book has been privately printed by the Franklin Library.

Grateful acknowledgement is made for permission to reprint from the following:

'Four Strong Winds' by Ian Tyson. Copyright © 1963 by Warner Bros., Inc. All rights reserved. Used by permission.

'The Gift Outright' by Robert Frost. From *The Poetry of Robert Frost*, Edward Connery Lathem, ed. Copyright © 1969 by Holt, Rinehart and Winston, Inc. Used by permission.

The first chapter of this book first appeared in *The New Yorker* in a slightly different form.

This book is set in 9/10pt Mallard
by Busby Typesetting, Exeter.

Corgi Books are published by Transworld Publishers Ltd., 61–63 Uxbridge Road, Ealing, London W5 5SA, in Australia by Transworld Publishers (Australia) Pty. Ltd., 15–23 Helles Avenue, Moorebank, NSW 2170, and in New Zealand by Transworld Publishers (N.Z.) Ltd., Cnr. Moselle and Waipareira Avenues, Henderson, Auckland.

Printed and bound in Great Britain by
Cox & Wyman Ltd., Reading, Berks.

'I am doomed to remember a boy with a wrecked voice – not because of his voice, or because he was the smallest person I ever knew, or even because he was the instrument of my mother's death, but because he is the reason I believe in God; I am a Christian because of Owen Meany.'

In the summer of 1953, two eleven-year-old boys – best friends – are playing in a Little League baseball game in Gravesend, New Hampshire; one of the boys hits a foul ball that kills his best friend's mother. The boy who hits the ball doesn't believe in accidents; Owen Meany believes he is God's instrument. What happens to Owen – after that 1953 foul ball – is extraordinary and terrifying.

THIS BOOK IS FOR
HELEN FRANCES WINSLOW IRVING &
COLIN FRANKLIN NEWELL IRVING,
MY MOTHER & FATHER

ACKNOWLEDGEMENTS

The author acknowledges his debt to Charles H. Bell's *History of the Town of Exeter, New Hampshire* (Boston: J. E. Farwell & Co., 1888), and to Mr Bell's *Phillips Exeter Academy in New Hampshire: A Historical Sketch* (Exeter, N.H.: Wiliam B. Morrill, News-Letter Press, 1883); all references in my novel to 'Wall's *History of Gravesend, N.H.*' are from these sources. Another valuable sourcebook for me was *Vietnam War Almanac* (New York: Facts on File Publications, 1985) by Harry G. Summers, Jr; I am grateful to Colonel Summers, too, for his helpful correspondence. The Rev. Ann E. Tottenham, headmistress of The Bishop Strachan School, was a special source of help to me; her careful reading of the manuscript is much appreciated. I am indebted, too, to the students and faculty of Bishop Strachan; on numerous occasions, they were patient with me and generous with their time. I am a grateful reader of *Your Voice* by Robert Lawrence Weer (New York: Keith Davis, 1977), revised and edited by Keith Davis; a justly respected voice and singing teacher, Mr Davis suffered my amateur attempts at 'breathing for singers' most graciously. The advice offered by the fictional character of 'Graham McSwiney' is *verbatim et literatim* to the teaching of Mr Weer; my thanks to Mr Davis for introducing me to the subject. I acknowledge, most of all, how much I owe to the writing of my former teacher Frederick Buechner; especially *The Magnificent Defeat* (New York: Harper & Row, 1977), *The Hungering Dark* (New York: Harper & Row, 1969), and *The Alphabet of Grace* (New York: Harper & Row, 1970). The Rev. Mr Buechner's correspondence, his criticism of the manuscript, and the constancy of his encouragement have meant a great deal to me: thank you, Fred. And to three old friends – close readers with special knowledge – I am indebted: to Dr Chas E. ('Skipper') Bickel, the granite master; to Col Charles C. ('Brute') Krulak, my hero; and to Ron Hansen, the body escort. To my first cousins in 'the north country,' Bayard and Curt: thank you, too.

CONTENTS

Have no anxiety about anything, but in everything by prayer and supplication with thanksgiving let your requests be made known to God.

– *The Letter of Paul to the Philippians*

Not the least of my problems is that I can hardly even imagine what kind of an experience a genuine, self-authenticating religious experience would be. Without somehow destroying me in the process, how could God reveal himself in a way that would leave no room for doubt? If there were no room for doubt, there would be no room for me.

– *Frederick Buechner*

Any Christian who is not a hero is a pig.

– *Leon Bloy*

1 : THE FOUL BALL

I am doomed to remember a boy with a wrecked voice – not because of his voice, or because he was the smallest person I ever knew, or even because he was the instrument of my mother's death, but because he is the reason I believe in God; I am a Christian because of Owen Meany. I make no claims to have a life in Christ, or with Christ – and certainly not *for* Christ, which I've heard some zealots claim. I'm not very sophisticated in my knowledge of the Old Testament, and I've not read the New Testament since my Sunday school days, except for those passages that I hear read aloud to me when I go to church. I'm somewhat more familiar with the passages from the Bible that appear in The Book of Common Prayer; I read my prayer book often, and my Bible only on holy days – the prayer book is so much more orderly.

I've always been a pretty regular churchgoer. I used to be a Congregationalist – I was baptized in the Congregational Church, and after some years of fraternity with Episcopalians (I was confirmed in the Episcopal Church, too), I became rather vague in my religion: in my teens I attended a 'non-denominational' church. Then I became an Anglican; the Anglican Church of Canada has been my church – ever since I left the United States, about twenty years ago. Being an Anglican is a lot like being an Episcopalian – so much so that being an Anglican occasionally impresses upon me the suspicion that I have simply become an Episcopalian again. Anyway, I left the Congregationalists and the Episcopalians – and my country once and for all.

When I die, I shall attempt to be buried in New Hampshire – alongside my mother – but the Anglican Church will perform the necessary service *before* my body suffers the indignity of trying to be sneaked through U.S. Customs. My selections from the Order for the Burial of the Dead are entirely conventional and can be found, in the order that I shall have them read – *not* sung – in The Book of Common Prayer. Almost everyone I know will be familiar with the passages from John, beginning with '. . . whosoever liveth and believeth in me shall never die.' And then there's '. . . in my Father's house are many mansions: If it were not so, I would have told you.' And I have always appreciated the frankness expressed in that passage from Timothy, the one that goes '. . . we brought nothing into this world, and it is certain we can carry nothing out.' It will be a by-the-book Anglican service, the kind that would make my former fellow Congregationalists fidget in their pews. I am an Anglican now, and I shall die an Anglican. But I skip a Sunday service now and then; I make no claims to be especially pious; I have a church-rummage faith – the kind that needs patching up every weekend. What faith I have I owe to Owen Meany, a boy I grew up with. It is Owen who made me a believer.

In Sunday school, we developed a form of entertainment based on abusing Owen Meany, who was *so* small that not only did his feet not touch the floor when he sat in his chair – his knees did not extend to the edge of his seat; therefore, his legs stuck out straight, like the legs of a doll. It was as if Owen Meany had been born without realistic joints.

Owen was so tiny, we loved to pick him up; in truth, we couldn't resist picking him up. We thought it was a miracle: how little he weighed. This was also incongruous because Owen came from a family in the granite business. The Meany Granite Quarry was a big place, the equipment for blasting and cutting the granite slabs was heavy and dangerous-looking; granite itself is such a rough, substantial rock. But the only aura of the granite quarry that clung to Owen was the granular dust, the gray powder that sprang off his clothes whenever we lifted him up. He was the color of a gravestone; light was both absorbed and reflected by his skin, as with a pearl, so that he appeared translucent at times – especially at his temples, where his blue veins showed through his skin (as though, in addition to his extraordinary size, there were other evidence that he was born too soon).

His vocal cords had not developed fully, or else his voice had been injured by the rock dust of his family's business. Maybe he had larynx damage, or a destroyed trachea; maybe he'd been hit in the throat by a chunk of granite. To be heard at all, Owen had to shout through his nose.

Yet he was dear to us – 'a little doll,' the girls called him, while he squirmed to get away from them; and from all of us.

I don't remember how our game of lifting Owen began.

This was Christ Church, the Episcopal Church of Gravesend, New Hampshire. Our Sunday school teacher was a strained, unhappy-looking woman named Mrs Walker. We thought this name suited her because her method of teaching involved a lot of walking out of class. Mrs Walker would read us an instructive passage from the Bible. She would then ask us to think seriously about what we had heard – 'Silently and seriously, that's how I want you to think!' she would say. 'I'm going to leave you alone with your thoughts, now,' she would tell us ominously – as if our thoughts were capable of driving us over the edge. 'I want you to think *very* hard,' Mrs Walker would say. Then she'd walk out on us. I think she was a smoker, and she couldn't allow herself to smoke in front of us. 'When I come back,' she'd say, 'we'll talk about it.'

By the time she came back, of course, we'd forgotten everything about whatever *it* was – because as soon as she left the room, we would fool around with a frenzy. Because being alone with our thoughts was no fun, we would pick up Owen Meany and pass him back and forth, overhead. We managed this while remaining seated in our chairs – that was the challenge of the game. Someone – I forget who started it – would get up, seize Owen, sit back down with him, pass him to the next person, who would pass him on, and so forth. The girls were included in this game; some of the girls were the most enthusiastic about it. Everyone could lift up Owen. We were very careful; we never dropped him. His shirt might become a little rumpled. His necktie was so long, Owen tucked it into his trousers – or else it would have hung to his knees – and his necktie often came untucked; sometimes his change would fall out (in our faces). We always gave him his money back.

If he had his baseball cards with him, they, too, would fall out of his pockets. This made him cross because the cards were alphabetized, or ordered under another system – all the infielders together, maybe. We didn't know what the system was, but obviously Owen had a system, because when Mrs Walker came back to the room – when Owen returned to his chair and we passed his nickels and dimes and his baseball cards back to him – he would sit shuffling through the cards with a grim, silent fury.

He was not a good baseball player, but he did have a very small strike zone and as a consequence he was often used as a pinch hitter – not because he ever hit the ball with any authority (in fact, he was instructed never to swing at the ball), but because he could be relied upon to earn a walk, a base on balls. In Little League games he resented this exploitation and once refused to come to bat unless he was allowed to swing at the pitches. But there was no bat small enough for him to swing that didn't hurl his tiny body after it – that didn't thump him on the back and knock him out of the batter's box and flat upon the ground. So, after the humiliation of swinging at a few pitches, and missing them, and whacking himself off his feet, Owen Meany selected that *other* humiliation of standing motionless and crouched at home plate while the pitcher *aimed* the ball at Owen's strike zone – and missed it, almost every time.

Yet Owen loved his baseball cards – and, for some reason, he clearly loved the game of baseball itself, although the game was cruel to him. Opposing pitchers would threaten him. They'd tell him that if he didn't swing at their pitches, they'd hit him with the ball. 'Your head's bigger than your strike zone, pal,' one pitcher told him. So Owen Meany made his way to first base after being struck by pitches, too.

Once on base, he was a star. No one could run the bases like Owen. If our team could stay at bat long enough, Owen Meany could steal home. He was used as a pinch runner in the late innings, too; pinch runner and pinch hitter Meany – pinch *walker* Meany, we called him. In the field, he was hopeless. He was afraid of the ball; he shut his eyes when it came anywhere near him. And if by some miracle he managed to catch it, he couldn't throw it; his hand was too small to get a good grip. But he was no ordinary complainer; if he was self-pitying, his voice was so original in its expression of complaint that he managed to make whining lovable.

In Sunday school, when we held Owen up in the air – especially, in the air! – he protested so uniquely. We tortured him, I think, in order to hear his voice; I used to think his voice came from another planet. Now I'm convinced it was a voice not entirely of this world.

'PUT ME DOWN!' he would say in a strangled, emphatic falsetto. 'CUT IT OUT! I DON'T WANT TO DO THIS ANYMORE. ENOUGH IS ENOUGH. PUT ME DOWN! YOU ASSHOLES!'

But we just passed him around and around. He grew more fatalistic about it, each time. His body was rigid; he wouldn't struggle. Once we had him in the air, he folded his arms defiantly on his chest; he scowled at the ceiling. Sometimes Owen grabbed hold of his chair the instant Mrs Walker left the room; he'd cling like a bird to a swing in its cage, but he was easy to dislodge because he was ticklish. A girl named Sukey Swift was especially deft at tickling Owen; instantly, his arms and legs would stick straight out and we'd have him up in the air again.

'NO TICKLING!' he'd say, but the rules to this game were *our* rules. We never listened to Owen.

Inevitably, Mrs Walker would return to the room when Owen was in the air. Given the biblical nature of her instructions to us: 'to think *very* hard . . .' she might have imagined that by a supreme act of our combined and hardest thoughts we had succeeded in levitating Owen Meany. She might have had the wit to suspect that Owen was reaching toward heaven as a direct result of leaving us alone with our thoughts.

But Mrs Walker's response was always the same – brutish and unimaginative and incredibly dense. 'Owen!' she would snap. 'Owen Meany, you get back to your seat! You get *down* from up there!'

What could Mrs Walker teach us about the Bible if she was stupid enough to think that Owen Meany had put himself up in the air?

Owen was always dignified about it. He never said, '*THEY* DID IT! THEY *ALWAYS* DO IT! THEY PICK ME UP AND LOSE MY MONEY AND MESS UP MY BASEBALL CARDS – AND THEY *NEVER* PUT ME DOWN WHEN I ASK THEM TO! WHAT DO YOU THINK, THAT I *FLEW* UP HERE?'

But although Owen would complain to us, he would never complain about us. If he was occasionally capable of being a stoic in the air, he was always a stoic when Mrs Walker accused him of childish behavior. He would never accuse us. Owen was no rat. As vividly as any number of the stories in the Bible, Owen Meany showed us what a martyr was.

It appeared there were no hard feelings. Although we saved our most ritualized attacks on him for Sunday school, we also lifted him up at other times – more spontaneously. Once someone hooked him by his collar to a coat tree in the elementary school auditorium; even then, even there, Owen didn't struggle. He dangled silently, and waited for someone to unhook him and put him down. And after gym class, someone hung him in his locker and shut the door. 'NOT FUNNY! NOT FUNNY!' he called, and called, until someone must have agreed with him and freed him from the company of his jockstrap – the size of a slingshot.

How could I have known that Owen was a hero?

Let me say at the outset that I was a Wheelwright – that was the family name that counted in our town: the Wheelwrights. And Wheelwrights were not inclined toward sympathy to Meanys. We were a matriarchal family because my grandfather died when he was a young man and left my grandmother to carry on, which she managed rather grandly. I am descended from John Adams on my grandmother's side (her maiden name was Bates, and her family came to America on the *Mayflower*); yet, in our town, it was my grandfather's name that had the clout, and my grandmother wielded her married name with such a sure sense of self-possession that she might as well have been a Wheelwright *and* an Adams *and* a Bates.

Her Christian name was Harriet, but she was Mrs Wheelwright to almost everyone – certainly to everyone in Owen Meany's family. I think that Grandmother's final vision of anyone named Meany would have been George Meany – the labor man, the cigar smoker. The combination of unions and cigars did not sit well with Harriet Wheelwright. (To my knowledge, George Meany is not related to the Meany family from my town.)

I grew up in Gravesend, New Hampshire; we didn't have any unions there – a few cigar smokers, but no union men. The town where I was born was purchased from an Indian sagamore in 1638 by the Rev. John Wheelwright, after whom I was named. In New England, the Indian chiefs and higher-ups were called sagamores; although, by the time I was a boy, the only sagamore I knew was a neighbor's dog – a male Labrador retriever named Sagamore (*not*, I think, for his

Indian ancestry but because of his owner's ignorance). Sagamore's owner, our neighbor, Mr Fish, always told me that his dog was named for a lake where he spent his summers swimming – 'when I was a youth,' Mr Fish would say. Poor Mr Fish: he didn't know that the lake was named after Indian chiefs and higher-ups – and that naming a stupid Labrador retriever 'Sagamore' was certain to cause some unholy offense. As you shall see, it did.

But Americans are not great historians, and so, for years – educated by my neighbor – I thought that sagamore was an Indian word for lake. The canine Sagamore was killed by a diaper truck, and I now believe that the gods of those troubled waters of that much-abused lake were responsible. It would be a better story, I think, if Mr Fish had been killed by the diaper truck – but every study of the gods, of everyone's gods, is a revelation of vengeance toward the innocent. (This is a part of my particular faith that meets with opposition from my Congregationalist and Episcopalian and Anglican friends.)

As for my ancestor John Wheelwright, he landed in Boston in 1636, only two years before he bought our town. He was from Lincolnshire, England – the hamlet of Saleby – and nobody knows why he named our town Gravesend. He had no known contact with the British Gravesend, although that is surely where the name of our town came from. Wheelwright was a Cambridge graduate; he'd played football with Oliver Cromwell – whose estimation of Wheelwright (as a football player) was both worshipful and paranoid. Oliver Cromwell believed that Wheelwright was a vicious, even a dirty player, who had perfected the art of tripping his opponents and then falling on them. Gravesend (the British Gravesend) is in Kent – a fair distance from Wheelwright's stamping ground. Perhaps he had a friend from there – maybe it was a friend who had wanted to make the trip to America with Wheelwright, but who hadn't been able to leave England, or had died on the voyage.

According to Wall's *History of Gravesend, N.H.*, the Rev. John Wheelwright had been a good minister of the English church until he began to 'question the authority of certain dogmas'; he became a Puritan, and was thereafter 'silenced by the ecclesiastical powers, for nonconformity.' I feel that my own religious confusion, and stubbornness, owe much to my ancestor, who suffered not only the criticisms of the English church before he left for the new world; once he arrived, he ran afoul of his fellow Puritans in Boston. Together with the famous Mrs Hutchinson, the Rev. Mr Wheelwright was banished from the Massachusetts Bay Colony for disturbing 'the civil peace'; in truth, he did nothing more seditious than offer some heterodox opinions regarding the location of the Holy Ghost – but Massachusetts judged him harshly. He was deprived of his weapons; and with his family and several of his bravest adherents, he sailed north from Boston to Great Bay, where he must have passed by two earlier New Hampshire outposts – what was then called Strawbery Banke, at the mouth of the Pascataqua (now Portsmouth), and the settlement in Dover.

Wheelwright followed the Squamscott River out of Great Bay; he went as far as the falls where the freshwater river met the saltwater river. The forest would have been dense then; the Indians would have showed him how good the fishing was. According to Wall's *History of Gravesend*, there were 'tracts of natural meadow' and 'marshes bordering upon the tidewater.'

The local sagamore's name was Watahantowet; instead of his signature, he made his mark upon the deed in the form of his totem – an armless man. Later, there was some dispute – not very interesting – regarding the Indian deed, and more interesting speculation regarding *why* Watahantowet's totem was an armless man. Some said it was how it made the sagamore feel to give up all that land – to have his arms cut off – and others pointed out that earlier 'marks' made by Watahantowet revealed that the figure, although armless, held a feather in his mouth; this was said to indicate the sagamore's frustration at being unable to write. But in several other versions of the totem ascribed to Watahantowet, the figure has a tomahawk in its mouth and looks completely crazy – or else, he is making a gesture toward peace: no arms, tomahawk in mouth; together, perhaps, they are meant to signify that Watahantowet does not fight. As for the settlement of the disputed deed, you can be sure the Indians were *not* the beneficiaries of the resolution to that difference of opinion.

And later still, our town fell under Massachusetts authority – which may, to this day, explain why residents of Gravesend detest people from Massachusetts. Mr Wheelwright would move to Maine. He was eighty when he spoke at Harvard, seeking contributions to rebuild a part of the college destroyed by a fire – demonstrating that he bore the citizens of Massachusetts less of a grudge than anyone else from Gravesend would bear them. Wheelwright died in Salisbury, Massachusetts, where he was the spiritual leader of the church, when he was almost ninety.

But listen to the names of Gravesend's founding fathers: you will not hear a Meany among them.

Barlow
Blackwell
Cole
Copeland
Crawley
Dearborn
Hilton
Hutchinson
Littlefield
Read
Rishworth
Smart
Smith
Walker
Wardell
Wentworth
Wheelwright

I doubt it's because she was a Wheelwright that my mother never gave up her maiden name; I think my mother's pride was independent of her Wheelwright ancestry, and that she would have kept her maiden name if she'd been born a Meany. And I never suffered in those years that I had her name; I was little Johnny Wheelwright, father unknown, and – at the time – that was okay with me. I never complained. One day, I always thought, she would tell me about it – when I was old enough to know the story. It was, apparently, the kind of story you had to be 'old enough' to hear. It wasn't until she died – without a word to me concerning who my father was – that I felt I'd been cheated out of information I had a right to know; it was only after her death that I felt the slightest anger toward her. Even if my father's identity and his story were painful to my mother – even if their relationship had been so sordid that *any* revelation of it would shed a continuous, unfavorable light upon both my parents – wasn't my mother being selfish not to tell me anything about my father?

Of course, as Owen Meany pointed out to me, I was only eleven when she died, and my mother was only thirty; she probably thought she had a lot of time left to tell me the story. She didn't *know* she was going to die, as Owen Meany put it.

Owen and I were throwing rocks in the Squamscott, the saltwater river, the tidal river – or, rather, *I* was throwing rocks in the river; Owen's rocks were landing in the mud flats because the tide was out and the water was too far away for Owen Meany's little, weak arm. Our throwing had disturbed the herring gulls who'd been pecking in the mud, and the gulls had moved into the marsh grass on the opposite shore of the Squamscott.

It was a hot, muggy, summer day; the low-tide smell of the mud flats was more brinish and morbid than usual. Owen Meany told me that my father would know that my mother was dead, and that – when I was old enough – he would identify himself to me.

'If he's alive,' I said, still throwing rocks. 'If he's alive *and* if he cares that he's my father – if he even *knows* he's my father.'

And although I didn't believe him that day, that was the day Owen Meany began his lengthy contribution to my belief in God. Owen was throwing smaller and smaller rocks, but he still couldn't reach the water; there was a certain small satisfaction to the sound the rocks made when they struck the mud flats, but the water was more satisfying than the mud in every way. And almost casually, with a confidence that stood in surprising and unreasonable juxtaposition to his tiny size, Owen Meany told me that he was sure my father was alive, that he was sure my father knew he was my father, and that *God* knew who my father was; even if my father never came forth to identify himself, Owen told me, *God* would identify him for me. 'YOUR DAD CAN HIDE FROM YOU,' Owen said, 'BUT HE CAN'T HIDE FROM GOD.'

And with that announcement, Owen Meany grunted as he

released a stone that reached the water. We were both surprised; it was the last rock either of us threw that day, and we stood watching the circle of ripples extending from the point of entry until even the gulls were assured we had stopped our disturbance of their universe, and they returned to our side of the Squamscott.

For years, there was a most successful salmon fishery on our river; no salmon would be caught dead there now – actually, the only salmon you could find in the Squamscott today *would* be a dead one. Alewives were also plentiful back then – and still were plentiful when I was a boy, and Owen Meany and I used to catch them. Gravesend is only nine miles from the ocean. Although the Squamscott was never the Thames, the big oceangoing ships once made their way to Gravesend on the Squamscott; the channel has since become so obstructed by rocks and shoals that no boat requiring any great draft of water could navigate it. And although Captain John Smith's beloved Pocahontas ended her unhappy life on British soil in the parish churchyard of the original Gravesend, the spiritually armless Watahantowet was never buried in *our* Gravesend. The only sagamore to be given official burial in our town was Mr Fish's black Labrador retriever, run over by a diaper truck on Front Street and buried – with the solemn attendance of some neighborhood children – in my grandmother's rose garden.

For more than a century, the big business of Gravesend was lumber, which was the first big business of New Hampshire. Although New Hampshire is called the Granite State, granite – building granite, curbstone granite, tombstone granite – came after lumber; it was never the booming business that lumber was. You can be sure that when all the trees are gone, there will still be rocks around; but in the case of granite, most of it remains underground.

My uncle was in the lumber business – Uncle Alfred, the Eastman Lumber Company; he married my mother's sister, my aunt, Martha Wheelwright. When I was a boy and traveled up north to visit my cousins, I saw log drives and logjams, and I even participated in a few log-rolling contests; I'm afraid I was too inexperienced to offer much competition to my cousins. But today, my Uncle Alfred's business, which is in his children's hands – my cousins' business, I should say – is real estate. In New Hampshire, that's what you have left to sell after you've cut down the trees.

But there will always be granite in the Granite State, and little Owen Meany's family was in the granite business – not ever a recommended business in our small, seacoast part of New Hampshire, although the Meany Granite Quarry was situated over what geologists call the Exeter Pluton. Owen Meany used to say that we residents of Gravesend were sitting over a bona fide outcrop of intrusive igneous rock; he would say this with an implied reverence – as if the consensus of the Gravesend community was that the Exeter Pluton was as valuable as a mother lode of gold.

My grandmother, perhaps owing to her descendants from *Mayflower* days, was more partial to trees than to rocks. For reasons that were never explained to me, Harriet Wheelwright thought that the lumber business was clean and that the granite business was dirty. Since my grandfather's business was shoes, this made no sense to me; but my grandfather died before I was born – his famous decision, to *not* unionize his shoeshop, is only hearsay to me. My grandmother sold the factory for a considerable profit, and I grew up with her opinions regarding how blessed were those who murdered trees for a living, and how low were those who handled rocks. We've all heard of lumber barons – my uncle, Alfred Eastman, was one – but who has heard of a rock baron?

The Meany Granite Quarry in Gravesend is inactive now; the pitted land, with its deep and dangerous quarry lakes, is not even valuable as real estate – it never was valuable, according to my mother. She told me that the quarry had been inactive all the years that *she* was growing up in Gravesend, and that its period of revived activity, in the Meany years, was fitful and doomed. All the good granite, Mother said, had been taken out of the ground before the Meanys moved to Gravesend. (As for *when* the Meanys moved to Gravesend, it was always described to me as 'about the time you were born.') Furthermore, only a small portion of the granite underground is worth getting out; the rest has defects – or if it's good, it's so far underground that it's hard to get out without cracking it.

Owen was always talking about cornerstones and monuments – a PROPER monument, he used to say, explaining that what was required was a large, evenly cut, smooth, unflawed piece of granite. The delicacy with which Owen spoke of this – and his own, physical delicacy – stood in absurd contrast to the huge, heavy slabs of rock we observed on the flatbed trucks, and to the violent noise of the quarry, the piercing sound of the rock chisels on the channeling machine – THE CHANNEL BAR, Owen called it – and the dynamite.

I used to wonder why Owen wasn't deaf; that there was something wrong with his voice, and with his size, was all the more surprising when you considered that there was nothing wrong with his ears – for the granite business is extremely percussive.

It was Owen who introduced me to Wall's *History of Gravesend*, although I didn't read the whole book until I was a senior at Gravesend Academy, where the tome was required as a part of a town history project; Owen read it before he was ten. He told me that the book was FULL OF WHEELWRIGHTS.

I was born in the Wheelwright house on Front Street; and I used to wonder why my mother decided to have me and to never explain a word about me – either to me or to her own mother and sister. My mother was not a brazen character. Her pregnancy, and her refusal to discuss it, must have struck the Wheelwrights with all the more severity because my mother had such a tranquil, modest nature.

She'd met a man on the Boston & Maine Railroad: that was all she'd say.

My Aunt Martha was a senior in college, and already engaged to be married, when my mother announced that she wasn't even going to apply for college entrance. My grandfather was dying, and perhaps this focusing of my grandmother's attention distracted her from demanding of my mother what the family had demanded of Aunt Martha: a college education. Besides, my mother argued, she could be of help at home, with her dying father – and with the strain and burden that his dying put upon her mother. And the Rev. Lewis Merrill, the pastor at the Congregational Church, and my mother's choirmaster, had convinced my grandparents that my mother's singing voice was truly worthy of professional training. For her to engage in serious voice and singing lessons, the Rev. Mr Merrill said, was as sensible an 'investment,' in my mother's case, as a college education.

At this point in my mother's life, I used to feel there was a conflict of motives. If singing and voice lessons were so important and serious to her, why did she arrange to have them only once a week? And if my grandparents accepted Mr Merrill's assessment of my mother's voice, why did they object so bitterly to her spending one night a week in Boston? It seemed to me that she should have *moved* to Boston and taken lessons every day! But I supposed the source of the conflict was my grandfather's terminal illness – my mother's desire to be of help at home, and my grandmother's need to have her there.

It was an early-morning voice or singing lesson; that was why she had to spend the previous night in Boston, which was an hour and a half from Gravesend – by train. Her singing and voice teacher was very popular; early morning was the only time he had for my mother. She was fortunate he would see her at all, the Rev. Lewis Merrill had said, because he normally saw only professionals; although my mother, and my Aunt Martha, had clocked many singing hours in the Congregational Church Choir, Mother was not a 'professional.' She simply had a lovely voice, and she was engaged – in her entirely unrebellious, even timid way – in training it.

My mother's decision to curtail her education was more acceptable to her parents than to her sister; Aunt Martha not only disapproved – my aunt (who is a lovely woman) resented my mother, if only slightly. My mother had the better voice, she was the prettier. When they'd been growing up in the big house on Front Street, it was my Aunt Martha who brought the boys from Gravesend Academy home to meet my grandmother and grandfather – Martha was the older, and the first to bring home 'beaus,' as my mother called them. But once the boys saw my mother – even before she was old enough to date – that was usually the end of their interest in Aunt Martha.

And now this: an unexplained pregnancy! According to my Aunt Martha, my grandfather was 'already out of it' – he was so very nearly dead that he never knew my mother was pregnant, 'although she took few pains to hide it,' Aunt Martha said. My poor grandfather, in Aunt Martha's words to me, 'died worrying why your mother was overweight.'

In my Aunt Martha's day, to grow up in Gravesend was to understand that Boston was a city of sin. And even though my mother had stayed in a highly approved and chaperoned women's residential hotel, she had managed to have her 'fling,' as Aunt Martha called it, with the man she'd met on the Boston & Maine.

My mother was so calm, so unrattled by either criticism or slander, that she was quite comfortable with her sister Martha's use of the word 'fling' – in truth, I heard Mother use the word fondly.

'My fling,' she would occasionally call me, with the greatest affection. 'My little fling!'

It was from my cousins that I first heard that my mother was thought to be 'a little simple'; it would have been from *their* mother – from Aunt Martha – that they would have heard this. By the time I heard these insinuations – 'a little simple' – they were no longer fighting words; my mother had been dead for more than ten years.

Yet my mother was more than a natural beauty with a beautiful voice and questionable reasoning powers; Aunt Martha had good grounds to suspect that my grandmother and grandfather spoiled my mother. It was not just that she was the baby, it was her temperament – she was never angry or sullen, she was not given to tantrums or to self-pity. She had such a sweet-tempered disposition, it was impossible to stay angry with her. As Aunt Martha said: 'She never appeared to be as assertive as she was.' She simply did what she wanted to do, and then said, in her engaging fashion, '*Oh!* I feel *terrible* that what I've done has upset you, and I intend to shower you with such affection that you'll forgive me and love me as much as you would if I'd done the right thing!' And it *worked*!

It worked, at least, until she was killed – and she couldn't promise to remedy how upsetting *that* was; there was no way she could make up for that.

And even after she went ahead and had me, unexplained, and named me after the founding father of Gravesend – even after she managed to make all that acceptable to her mother and sister, and to the town (not to mention to the Congregational Church, where she continued to sing in the choir and was often a participant in various parish-house functions) . . . even after she'd carried off my illegitimate birth (to everyone's satisfaction, or so it *appeared*), she *still* took the train to Boston every Wednesday, she *still* spent every Wednesday night in the dreaded city in order to be bright and early for her voice or singing lesson.

When I got a little older, I resented it – sometimes. Once when I had the mumps, and another time when I had the chicken pox, she canceled the trip; she stayed with me. And there was another time, when Owen and I had been catching alewives in the tidewater culvert that ran into the Squamscott under the Swasey Parkway and I slipped and broke my wrist; she didn't take the Boston & Maine that week. But all the other times – until I was ten and she married the man who would legally adopt me and become like a father to me; until then – she kept going to Boston, overnight. Until then, she kept singing. No one ever told me if her voice improved.

That's why I was born in my grandmother's house – a grand, brick, Federal monster of a house. When I was a child, the house was heated by a coal furnace; the coal chute was under the ell of the house where my bedroom was. Since the coal was always delivered very early in the morning, its rumbling down the chute was often the sound that woke me up. On the rare coincidence of a Thursday morning delivery (when my mother was in Boston), I used to wake up to the sound of the coal and imagine that, at that precise moment, my mother was starting to sing. In the summer, with the windows open, I woke up to the birds in my grandmother's rose garden. And there lies another of my grandmother's opinions, to take root alongside her opinions regarding rocks and trees: anyone could grow mere flowers or vegetables, but a gardener grew roses; Grandmother was a gardener.

The Gravesend Inn was the only other brick building of comparable size to my grandmother's house on Front Street; indeed, Grandmother's house was often mistaken for the Gravesend Inn by travelers following the usual directions given in the center of town: 'Look for the big brick place on your left, after you pass the academy.'

My grandmother was peeved at this – she was not in the slightest flattered to have her house mistaken for an inn. 'This is *not* an inn,' she would inform the lost and bewildered travelers, who'd been expecting someone younger to greet them and fetch their luggage. 'This is my home,' Grandmother would announce. 'The inn is further along,' she would say, waving her hand in the general direction. 'Further along,' is fairly specific compared to other New Hampshire forms of directions; we don't enjoy giving directions in New Hampshire – we tend to think that if you don't know where you're going, you don't belong where you are. In Canada, we give directions more freely – to anywhere, to anyone who asks.

In our Federal house on Front Street, there was also a secret passageway – a bookcase that was actually a door that led down a staircase to a dirt-floor basement that was entirely separate from the basement where the coal furnace was. That was just what it was: a bookcase that was a door that led to a place where absolutely nothing happened – it was simply a place to hide. From *what*? I used to wonder. That this secret passageway to nowhere existed in our house did not comfort me; rather, it provoked me to imagine what there might be that was sufficiently threatening to hide *from* – and it is never comforting to imagine that.

I took little Owen Meany into that passageway once, and I got him lost in there, in the dark, and I frightened the hell out of him; I did this to all my friends, of course, but frightening Owen Meany was always more special than frightening anyone else. It was his voice, that ruined voice, that made his fear unique. I have been engaged in private imitations of Owen Meany's voice for more than thirty years, and that voice used to prevent me from imagining that I could ever *write* about Owen, because – on the page – the sound of his voice is impossible to convey. *And* I was prevented from imagining that I could even make Owen a part of *oral* history, because the thought of imitating his voice – in public – is so embarrassing. It has taken me more than thirty years to get up the nerve to share Owen's voice with strangers.

My grandmother was so upset by the sound of Owen Meany's voice, protesting his abuse in the secret passageway, that she spoke to me, after Owen had gone home. 'I don't want you to describe to me – not ever – what you were doing to that poor boy to make him sound like that; but if you ever do it again, please cover his mouth with your hand,' Grandmother said. 'You've seen the mice caught in the mousetraps?' she asked me. 'I mean *caught* – their little necks *broken* – I mean absolutely *dead*,' Grandmother said. 'Well, that boy's voice,' my grandmother told me, 'that boy's voice could bring those mice back to life!'

And it occurs to me now that Owen's voice *was* the voice of all those murdered mice, coming back to life – with a vengeance.

I don't mean to make my grandmother sound insensitive. She had a maid named Lydia, a Prince Edward Islander, who was our cook and housekeeper for years and years. When Lydia developed a cancer and her right leg was amputated, my grandmother hired two other maids – one to look after Lydia. Lydia never worked again. She had her own room, and her favorite wheelchair routes through the huge house, and she became the entirely served invalid that, one day, my grandmother had imagined she herself might become – with someone like Lydia looking after her. Delivery boys and guests in our house frequently mistook Lydia for my grandmother, because Lydia looked quite regal in her wheelchair and she was about my grandmother's age; she had tea with my grandmother every afternoon, and she played cards with my grandmother's bridge club – with those very same ladies whose tea she had once fetched. Shortly before Lydia died, even my Aunt Martha was struck by the resemblance Lydia bore to my grandmother. Yet to various guests and delivery boys, Lydia would always say – with a certain indignation of tone that was borrowed from my grandmother – 'I am *not* Missus Wheelwright, I am Missus Wheelwright's former maid.' It was exactly in the manner that Grandmother would claim that her house was *not* the Gravesend Inn.

So my grandmother was not without humanity. And if she wore cocktail dresses when she labored in her rose garden, they were cocktail dresses that she no longer intended to wear to cocktail parties. Even in her rose garden, she did not want to be seen underdressed. If the dresses got too dirty from gardening, she threw them out. When my mother suggested to her that she might have them cleaned, my grandmother said, 'What? And have those people at the cleaners wonder what I was doing in a dress to make it *that* dirty?'

From my grandmother I learned that logic is relative.

But this story really *is* about Owen Meany, about how I have apprenticed myself to his voice. His cartoon voice has made an even stronger impression on me than has my grandmother's imperious wisdom.

Grandmother's memory began to elude her near the end. Like many old people, she had a firmer grasp of her own childhood than she had of the lives of her own children, or her grandchildren, or her great-grandchildren. The more recent the memory was, the more poorly remembered. 'I remember you as a little boy,' she told me, not long ago, 'but when I look at you now, I don't know who you are.' I told her I occasionally had the same feeling about myself. And in one conversation about her memory, I asked her if she remembered little Owen Meany.

'The labor man?' she said. 'The unionist!'

'No, *Owen* Meany,' I said.

'No,' she said. 'Certainly not.'

'The granite family?' I said. 'The Meany Granite Quarry. Remember?'

'Granite,' she said with distaste. 'Certainly not!'

'Maybe you remember his voice?' I said to my grandmother, when she was almost a hundred years old.

But she was impatient with me; she shook her head. I was getting up the nerve to imitate Owen's voice.

'I turned out the lights in the secret passageway, and scared him,' I reminded Grandmother.

'You were always doing that,' she said indifferently. 'You even did that to Lydia – when she still had both her legs.'

'TURN ON THE LIGHT!' said Owen Meany. 'SOMETHING IS TOUCHING MY FACE! TURN ON THE LIGHT! IT'S SOMETHING WITH A TONGUE! SOMETHING IS LICKING ME!' Owen Meany cried.

'It's just a cobweb, Owen,' I remember telling him.

'IT'S TOO *WET* FOR A COBWEB! IT'S A *TONGUE*! TURN ON THE LIGHT!'

'Stop it!' my grandmother told me. 'I remember, I remember – for God's sake,' she said. 'Don't *ever* do that again!' she told me. But it was from my grandmother that I gained the confidence that I could imitate Owen Meany's voice at all. Even when her memory was shot, Grandmother remembered Owen's voice; if she remembered him as the instrument of her daughter's death, she didn't say. Near the end, Grandmother didn't remember that I had become an Anglican – and a Canadian.

The Meanys, in my grandmother's lexicon, were not *Mayflower* stock. They were not descended from the founding fathers; you could not trace a Meany back to John Adams. They were descended from later immigrants; they were Boston Irish. The Meanys made their move to New Hampshire from Boston, which was never England; they'd also lived in Concord, New Hampshire, and in Barre, Vermont – those were much more working-class places than Gravesend. Those were New England's true granite kingdoms. My grandmother believed that mining and quarrying, of all kinds, was *groveling* work – and that quarriers and miners were more closely related to moles than to men. As for the Meanys: none of the family was especially small, except for Owen.

And for all the dirty tricks we played on him, he tricked us only once. We were allowed to swim in one of his father's quarries only if we entered and left the water one at a time and with a stout rope tied around our waists. One did not actually *swim* in those quarry lakes, which were rumored to be as deep as the ocean; they were as cold as the ocean, even in late summer; they were as black and still as pools of oil. It was not the cold that made you want to rush out as soon as you'd jumped in; it was the unmeasured depth – our fear of what was on the bottom, and how far below us the bottom was.

Owen's father, Mr Meany, insisted on the rope – *insisted* on one-at-a-time, in-and-out. It was one of the few parental rules from my childhood that remained unbroken, except once – by Owen. It was never a rule that any of us cared to challenge; no one wanted to untie the rope and plunge without hope of rescue toward the unknown bottom.

But one fine August day, Owen Meany untied the rope, underwater, and he swam underwater to some hidden crevice in the rocky shore while we waited for him to rise. When he didn't surface, we pulled up the rope. Because we believed that Owen was nearly weightless, we refused to believe what our arms told us – that he was not at the end of the rope. We didn't believe he was gone until we had the bulging knot at the rope's end out of the water. What a silence that was!

– interrupted only by the drops of water from the rope falling into the quarry.

No one called his name; no one dove in to look for him. In that water, no one could *see*! I prefer to believe that we *would* have gone in to look for him – if he'd given us just a few more seconds to gather up our nerve – but Owen decided that our response was altogether too slow and uncaring. He swam out from the crevice at the opposite shore; he moved as lightly as a water bug across the terrifying hole that reached, we were sure, to the bottom of the earth. He swam to us, angrier than we'd ever seen him.

'TALK ABOUT HURTING SOMEONE'S FEELINGS!' he cried. 'WHAT WERE YOU WAITING FOR? BUBBLES? DO YOU THINK I'M A *FISH*? WASN'T ANYONE GOING TO *TRY* TO FIND ME?'

'You scared us, Owen,' one of us said. We were too scared to defend ourselves, if there was any defending ourselves – ever – in regard to Owen.

'YOU LET ME DROWN!' Owen said. 'YOU DIDN'T DO ANYTHING! YOU JUST WATCHED ME DROWN! I'M ALREADY DEAD!' he told us. 'REMEMBER THAT: YOU LET ME DIE.'

What I remember best is Sunday school in the Episcopal Church. Both Owen and I were newcomers there. When my mother married the *second* man she met on the train, she and I changed churches; we left the Congregational Church for the church of my adoptive father – he was, my mother said, an Episcopalian, and although I never saw any evidence that he was a particularly serious Episcopalian, my mother insisted that she and I move with him to *his* church. It was a move that disturbed my grandmother, because we Wheelwrights had been in the Congregational Church ever since we got over being Puritans ('ever since we *almost* got over being Puritans,' my grandmother used to say, because – in her opinion – Puritanism had never entirely relinquished its hold on us Wheelwrights). Some Wheelwrights – not only our founding father – had even been in the ministry; in the last century, the Congregational ministry. *And* the move upset the pastor of the Congregational Church, the Rev. Lewis Merrill; he'd baptized me, and he was woebegone at the thought of losing my mother's voice from the choir – he'd known her since she was a young girl, and (my mother always said) he'd been especially supportive of her when she'd been calmly and good-naturedly insisting on her privacy regarding my origins.

The move did not sit well with me, either – as you shall see. But Owen Meany's manner of making and keeping a thing mysterious was to allude to something too dark and terrible to mention. *He* was changing churches, he said, TO ESCAPE THE CATHOLICS – or, actually, it was his father who was escaping and defying the Catholics by sending Owen to Sunday school, to be confirmed, in the Episcopal Church. When Congregationalists turned into Episcopalians, Owen told me, there was nothing to it; it simply represented a move *upward* in church formality – in HOCUS-POCUS, Owen called it. But for Catholics to move to the Episcopal Church was not only a move *away* from the hocus-pocus; it was a move that risked eternal damnation. Owen used to say, gravely, that his father would surely be damned for initiating the move, but that the Catholics had committed an UNSPEAKABLE OUTRAGE – that they had insulted his father and mother, irreparably.

When I would complain about the kneeling, which was new to me – not to mention the abundance of litanies and recited creeds in the Episcopal service – Owen would tell me that I knew nothing. Not only did Catholics kneel and mutter litanies and creeds without ceasing, but they ritualized any hope of contact with God to such an extent that Owen felt they'd interfered with his ability to pray – to talk to God DIRECTLY, as Owen put it. And then there was confession! Here I was complaining about some simple kneeling, but what did I know about confessing my sins? Owen said the pressure to confess – as a Catholic – was so great that he'd often made things up in order to be forgiven for them.

'But that's crazy!' I said.

Owen agreed. And what was the cause of the falling out between the Catholics and Mr Meany? I always asked. Owen never told me. The damage was irreparable, he would repeat; he would refer only to the UNSPEAKABLE OUTRAGE.

Perhaps my unhappiness at having traded the Congregational Church for the Episcopal – in combination with Owen's satisfaction at having ESCAPED the Catholics – contributed to my pleasure in our game of lifting Owen Meany up in the air. It occurs to me now that we were all guilty of thinking of Owen as existing only for our entertainment; but in my case – especially, in the Episcopal Church – I think I was also guilty of envying him. I believe my participation in abusing him in Sunday school was faintly hostile and inspired by the greatest difference between us: he believed more than I did, and although I was always aware of this, I was most aware in church. I disliked the Episcopalians because they appeared to believe more – or in more *things* – than the Congregationalists believed; and because I believed very little, I had been more comfortable with the Congregationalists, who demanded a minimum of participation from worshipers.

Owen disliked the Episcopalians, too, but he disliked them far less than he had disliked the Catholics; in his opinion, both of them believed *less* than he believed – but the Catholics had interfered with Owen's beliefs and practices *more*. He was my best friend, and with our best friends we overlook many differences; but it wasn't until we found ourselves attending the same Sunday school, and the same church, that I was forced to accept that my best friend's religious faith was more certain (if not always more dogmatic) than anything I heard in either the Congregational or the Episcopal Church.

I don't remember Sunday School in the Congregational Church at all – although my mother claimed that this was always an occasion whereat I ate a lot, both in Sunday school and at various parish-house functions. I vaguely remember the cider and the cookies; but I remember emphatically – with a crisp, winter-day brightness – the white clapboard church, the black steeple clock, and the services that were always held on the second floor in an informal, well-lit, meetinghouse atmosphere. You could look out the tall windows at the branches of the towering trees. By comparison, the Episcopal services were conducted in a gloomy, basement atmosphere. It was a stone church, and there was a ground-floor or even underground mustiness to the place, which was overcrowded with dark wood bric-a-brac, somber with dull gold organ pipes, garish with confused configurations of stained glass – through which not a single branch of a tree was visible.

When I complained about church, I complained about the usual things a kid complains about: the claustrophobia, the boredom. But Owen complained *religiously*. 'A PERSON'S FAITH GOES AT ITS OWN PACE,' Owen Meany said. 'THE TROUBLE WITH CHURCH IS THE SERVICE. A SERVICE IS CONDUCTED FOR A MASS AUDIENCE. JUST WHEN I START TO LIKE THE HYMN, EVERYONE PLOPS DOWN TO PRAY. JUST WHEN I START TO HEAR THE PRAYER, EVERYONE POPS UP TO SING. AND WHAT DOES THE STUPID *SERMON* HAVE TO DO WITH GOD? WHO KNOWS WHAT GOD THINKS OF CURRENT EVENTS? WHO CARES?'

To these complaints, and others like them, I could respond only by picking up Owen Meany and holding him above my head.

'You tease Owen too much,' my mother used to say to me. But I don't remember much teasing, not beyond the usual lifting him up – unless Mother meant that I failed to realize how serious Owen was; he was insulted by jokes of any kind. After all, he did read Wall's *History of Gravesend* before he was ten; this was not lighthearted work, this was never reading that merely skipped along. And he also read the Bible – not by the time he was ten, of course; but he actually read the whole thing.

And then there was the question of Gravesend Academy; that was the question for every boy born in Gravesend – the academy did not admit girls in those days. I was a poor student; and even though my grandmother could well have afforded the tuition, I was destined to stay at Gravesend High School – until my mother married someone on the academy faculty and he legally adopted me. Faculty children – faculty brats, we were called – could automatically attend the academy.

What a relief this must have been to my grandmother; she'd always resented that her own children couldn't go to Gravesend Academy – she'd had daughters. My mother and my Aunt Martha were high-school girls – what they saw of Gravesend Academy was only at the dating end, although my Aunt Martha put this to good use: she married a Gravesend Academy boy (one of the few who didn't prefer my mother), which made my cousins sons of alumni, which favored their admittance, too. (My only female cousin would not benefit from this alumni connection – as you shall see.)

But Owen Meany was a legitimate Gravesend Academy candidate; he was a brilliant student; he was the kind of student who was *supposed* to go to Gravesend. He could have applied and got in – and got a full scholarship, too, since the Meany Granite Company was never flourishing and his parents could not have afforded the tuition. But one day when my mother was driving Owen and me to the beach – Owen and I were ten – my mother said, 'I hope you never stop helping Johnny with his homework, Owen, because when you're both at the academy, the homework's going to be much harder – especially for Johnny.'

'BUT I'M NOT GOING TO THE ACADEMY,' Owen said.

'Of course you are!' my mother said. 'You're the best student in New Hampshire – maybe, in the whole country!'

'THE ACADEMY'S NOT FOR SOMEONE LIKE ME,' Owen said. 'THE PUBLIC SCHOOL IS FOR PEOPLE LIKE ME.'

I wondered for a moment if he meant, *for small people* – that public high schools were for people who were exceptionally small – but my mother was thinking far ahead of me, and she said, 'You'll get a full scholarship, Owen. I hope your parents know that. You'll go to the academy absolutely free.'

'YOU HAVE TO WEAR A COAT AND TIE EVERY DAY,' Owen said. 'THE SCHOLARSHIP DOESN'T BUY THE COATS AND TIES.'

'That can be arranged, Owen,' my mother said, and I could tell that she meant *she'd* arrange it – if no one else would, she'd buy him every coat and tie he could possibly have use for.

'THERE'S ALSO DRESS SHIRTS, AND SHOES,' Owen said. 'IF YOU GO TO SCHOOL WITH RICH PEOPLE, YOU DON'T WANT TO LOOK LIKE THEIR *SERVANTS*.' I now suppose that my mother could hear Mr Meany's prickly, working-class politics behind this observation.

'Everything you need, Owen,' my mother said. 'It will be taken care of.'

We were in Rye, passing the First Church, and the breeze from the ocean was already strong. A man with a great stack of roofing shingles in a wheelbarrow was having difficulty keeping the shingles from blowing away; the ladder, leaning against the vestry roof, was also in danger of being blown over. The man seemed in need of a co-worker – or, at least, of another pair of hands.

'WE SHOULD STOP AND HELP THAT MAN,' Owen observed, but my mother was pursuing a theme and, therefore, she'd noticed nothing unusual out the window.

'Would it help if I talked to your parents about it, Owen?' my mother asked.

'THERE'S ALSO THE MATTER OF THE BUS,' Owen said. 'TO GO TO HIGH SCHOOL, YOU CAN TAKE A BUS. I DON'T LIVE RIGHT IN TOWN, YOU KNOW. HOW WOULD I GET TO THE ACADEMY? IF I WAS A DAY STUDENT, I MEAN – HOW WOULD I GET THERE? HOW WOULD I GET BACK HOME? BECAUSE MY PARENTS WOULD NEVER LET ME LIVE IN A DORMITORY. THEY NEED ME AT HOME. ALSO, DORMITORIES ARE EVIL. SO HOW *DO* THE DAY STUDENTS GET TO SCHOOL AND GET HOME?' he asked.

'Someone drives them,' my mother said. '*I* could drive you, Owen – at least until you got a driver's license of your own.'

'NO, IT WON'T WORK,' Owen said. 'MY FATHER'S TOO BUSY, AND MY MOTHER DOESN'T DRIVE.'

Mrs Meany – both my mother and I knew – not only didn't drive; she never left the house. And even in the summer, the windows in that house were never open; his mother was allergic to dust, Owen had explained. Every day of the year, Mrs Meany sat indoors behind the windows bleared and streaked with grit from the quarry. She wore an old set of pilot's headphones (the wires dangling, unattached) because the sound of the channeling machine – the channel bar, and the rock chisels – disturbed her. On blasting days, she played the phonograph very loudly – the big band sound, the needle skipping occasionally when the dynamite was especially nearby and percussive.

Mr Meany did the shopping. He drove Owen to Sunday school, and picked him up – although he did not attend the Episcopal services himself. It was apparently enough revenge upon the Catholics to be sending Owen there; either the added defiance of his own attendance was unnecessary, or else Mr Meany had suffered such an outrage at the hands of the Catholic authorities that he was rendered unreceptive to the teachings of *any* church.

He was, my mother knew, quite unreceptive on the subject

of Gravesend Academy. 'There is the interests of the town,' he once said in Town Meeting, 'and then there is the interests of *them*!' This regarded the request of the academy to widen the saltwater river and dredge a deeper low-tide channel at a point in the Squamscott that would improve the racing course for the academy crew; several shells had become mired in the mud flats at low tide. The part of the river the academy wished to widen was a peninsula of tidewater marsh bordering the Meany Granite Quarry; it was totally unusable land, yet Mr Meany owned it and he resented that the academy wanted to scoop it away – 'for purposes of recreation!' he said.

'We're talking about mud, not granite,' a representative of the academy had remarked.

'I'm talkin' about us and *them*!' Mr Meany had shouted, in what is now recorded as a famous Town Meeting. In order for a Town Meeting to be famous in Gravesend, it is only necessary that there be a good *row*. The Squamscott was widened; the channel was dredged. If it was just mud, the town decided, it didn't matter whose mud it was.

'You're going to the academy, Owen,' my mother told him. 'That's all there is to it. If any student ever belonged in a proper school, it's you – that place was made with you in mind, or it was made for no one.'

'WE MISSED DOING A GOOD DEED,' Owen said morosely. 'THAT MAN SHINGLING THE CHURCH – HE NEEDED HELP.'

'Don't argue with me, Owen,' my mother said. 'You're going to the academy, if I have to adopt you. I'll *kidnap* you, if I have to,' she said.

But no one on this earth was ever as stubborn as Owen Meany; he waited a mile before he said another word, and then he said, 'NO. IT WON'T WORK.'

Gravesend Academy was founded in 1781 by the Rev. Emery Hurd, a follower of the original Wheelwright's original beliefs, a childless Puritan with an ability – according to Wall – for 'Oration on the advantages of Learning and its happy Tendency to promote Virtue and Piety.' What would the Rev. Mr Hurd have thought of Owen Meany? Hurd conceived of an academy whereat 'no vicious lad, who is liable to contaminate his associates, is allowed to remain an hour'; whereat 'the student shall bear the laboring oar' – and learn heartily from his labor!

As for the rest of his money, Emery Hurd left it for 'the education and christianization of the American Indians.' In his waning years – ever watchful that Gravesend Academy devote itself to 'pious and charitable purposes' – the Rev. Mr Hurd was known to patrol Water Street in downtown Gravesend, looking for youthful offenders: specifically, young men who would not doff their hats to him, and young ladies who would not curtsy. In payment for such offense, Emery Hurd was happy to give these young people a piece of his mind; near the end, only pieces were left.

I saw my grandmother lose her mind in pieces like that; when she was so old that she could remember almost nothing – certainly not Owen Meany, and not even me – she would occasionally reprimand the whole room, and anyone present in it. 'What has happened to tipping the hat?' she would howl. 'Bring back the bow!' she would croon. 'Bring back the curtsy!'

'Yes, Grandmother,' I would say.

'Oh, what do you know?' she would say. 'Who are you, anyway?' she would ask.

'HE IS YOUR GRANDSON, JOHNNY,' I would say, in my best imitation of Owen Meany's voice.

And my Grandmother would say, 'My God, is *he* still here? Is that funny little guy still here? Did you lock him in the passageway, Johnny?'

Later, in that summer when we were ten, Owen told me that my mother had been to the quarry to visit his parents.

'What did they say about it?' I asked him.

They hadn't mentioned the visit, Owen told me, but he knew she'd been there. 'I COULD SMELL HER PERFUME,' Owen said. 'SHE MUST HAVE BEEN THERE QUITE A WHILE BECAUSE THERE WAS ALMOST AS MUCH OF HER PERFUME AS THERE IS IN *YOUR* HOUSE. MY MOTHER DOESN'T WEAR PERFUME,' he added.

This was unnecessary to tell me. Not only did Mrs Meany not go outdoors; she refused to *look* outdoors. When I saw her positioned in the various windows of Owen's house, she was always in profile to the window, determined *not* to be observing the world – yet making an obscure point: by sitting in profile, possibly she meant to suggest that she had not entirely turned her back on the world, either. It occurred to me that the Catholics had done this to her – whatever it was, it surely qualified for the unmentioned UNSPEAKABLE OUTRAGE that Owen claimed his father and mother had suffered. There was something about Mrs Meany's obdurate self-imprisonment that smacked of religious persecution – if not eternal damnation.

'How did it go with the Meanys?' I asked my mother.

'They told Owen I was there?' she asked.

'No, they didn't tell him. He recognized your perfume.'

'He would,' she said, and smiled. I think she knew Owen had a crush on her – all my friends had crushes on my mother. And if she had lived until they'd all been teenagers, their degrees of infatuation with her would doubtless have deepened, and worsened, and been wholly unbearable – both to them, and to me.

Although my mother resisted the temptation of my generation – that is to say, she restrained herself from picking up Owen Meany – she could not resist touching Owen. You simply had to put your hands on Owen. He was mortally cute; he had a furry animal attractiveness – except for the nakedness of his nearly transparent ears, and the rodentlike way they protruded from his sharp face. My grandmother said that Owen resembled an embryonic fox. When touching Owen, one avoided his ears; they looked as if they would be cold to the touch. But not my mother; she even rubbed warmth into his rubbery ears. She hugged him, she kissed him, she touched noses with him. She did all these things as naturally as if she were doing them to me, but she did none of these things to my other friends – not even to my cousins. And Owen responded to her quite affectionately; he'd blush sometimes, but he'd always smile. His standard, nearly constant frown would disappear; an embarrassed beam would overcome his face.

I remember him best when he stood level to my mother's girlish waist; the top of his head, if he stood on his toes, would brush against her breasts. When she was sitting down and he would go over to her, to receive his usual touches and hugs, his face would be dead-even with her breasts. My mother was a sweater girl; she had a lovely figure, and she knew it, and she wore those sweaters of the period that showed it.

A measure of Owen's seriousness was that we could talk about the mothers of all our friends, and Owen could be extremely frank in his appraisal of my mother to me; he could get away with it, because I knew he wasn't joking. Owen never joked.

'YOUR MOTHER HAS THE BEST BREASTS OF ALL THE MOTHERS.' No other friend could have said this to me without starting a fight.

'You really think so?' I asked him.

'ABSOLUTELY, THE BEST,' he said.

'What about Missus Wiggin?' I asked him.

'TOO BIG,' Owen said.

'Missus Webster?' I asked him.

'TOO LOW,' Owen said.

'Missus Merrill?' I asked.

'VERY FUNNY,' Owen said.

'Miss Judkins?' I said.

'I DON'T KNOW,' he said. 'I CAN'T REMEMBER THEM. BUT SHE'S NOT A MOTHER.'

'Miss Farnum!' I said.

'YOU'RE JUST FOOLING AROUND,' Owen said peevishly.

'Caroline Perkins!' I said.

'MAYBE ONE DAY,' he said seriously. 'BUT SHE'S NOT A MOTHER, EITHER.'

'Irene Babson!' I said.

'DON'T GIVE ME THE SHIVERS,' Owen said. 'YOUR MOTHER'S THE ONE,' he said worshipfully. 'AND SHE SMELLS BETTER THAN ANYONE ELSE, TOO,' he added. I agreed with him about this; my mother always smelled wonderful.

Your own mother's bosom is a strange topic of conversation in which to indulge a friend, but my mother *was* an acknowledged beauty, and Owen possessed a completely reliable frankness; you could trust him, absolutely.

My mother was often our driver. She drove me out to the quarry to play with Owen; she picked Owen up to come play with me – and she drove him home. The Meany Granite Quarry was about three miles out of the center of town, not too far for a bike ride – except that the ride was all uphill. Mother would often drive me out there with my bike in the car, and then I could ride my bike home; or Owen would ride his bike to town, and she'd take him *and* his bike back.

The point is, she was so often our chauffeur that he might have seemed to her like a second son. And to the extent that mothers *are* the chauffeurs of small-town life, Owen had reason to identify her as more *his* mother than his own mother was.

When we played at Owen's, we rarely went inside. We played in the rock piles, in and around the pits, or down by the river, and on Sundays we sat in or on the silent machinery, imagining ourselves in charge of the quarry – or in a war. Owen seemed to find the inside of his house as strange and oppressive as I did. When the weather was inclement, we played at my house – and since the weather in New Hampshire is inclement most of the time, we played most of the time at my house.

And *play* is all we did, it seems to me now. We were both eleven the summer my mother died. It was our last year in Little League, which we were already bored with. Baseball, in my opinion, *is* boring; one's last year in Little League is only a preview of the boring moments in baseball that lie ahead for many Americans. Unfortunately, Canadians play and watch baseball, too. It is a game with a lot of waiting in it; it is a game with increasingly heightened anticipation of increasingly limited action. At least, Little Leaguers play the game more quickly than grown-ups – thank God! *We* never devoted the attention to spitting, or to tugging at our armpits and crotches, that is the essential expression of nervousness in the adult sport. But you still have to wait between pitches, and wait for the catcher and umpire to examine the ball after the pitch – and wait for the catcher to trot out to the mound to say something to the pitcher about how to throw the ball, and wait for the manager to waddle onto the field and worry (with the pitcher and the catcher) about the possibilities of the *next* pitch.

That day, in the last inning, Owen and I were just waiting for the game to be over. We were so bored, we had no idea that someone's life was about to be over, too. Our side was up. Our team was far behind – we had been substituting second-string players for first-string players so often and so randomly that I could no longer recognize half of our own batters – and I had lost track of my place in the batting order. I wasn't sure when I got to be up to bat next, and I was about to ask our nice, fat manager and coach, Mr Chickering, when Mr Chickering turned to Owen Meany and said, 'You bat for Johnny, Owen.'

'But I don't know when I bat,' I said to Mr Chickering, who didn't hear me; he was looking off the field somewhere. He was bored with the game, too, and he was just waiting for it to be over, like the rest of us.

'I KNOW WHEN YOU BAT,' Owen said. That was forever irritating about Owen; he kept track of things like that. He hardly ever got to play the stupid game, but he paid attention to all the boring details, anyway.

'IF HARRY GETS ON, I'M ON DECK,' Owen said. 'IF BUZZY GETS ON, I'M UP.'

'Fat chance,' I said. 'Or is there only one out?'

'TWO OUT,' Owen said.

Everyone on the bench was looking off the field, somewhere – even Owen, now – and I turned my attention to the intriguing object of their interest. Then I saw her: my mother. She'd just arrived. She was always late; she found the game boring, too. She had an instinct for arriving just in time to take me and Owen home. She was even a sweater girl in the summer, because she favored those summer-weight jersey dresses; she had a nice tan, and the dress was a simple, white-cotton one – clinging about the bosom and waist, full skirt below – and she wore a red scarf to hold her hair up, off her bare shoulders. She wasn't watching the game. She was standing well down the left-field foul line, past third base, looking into the sparse stands, the almost-empty bleacher seats – trying to see if there was anyone she knew there, I guess.

I realized that everyone was watching her. This was nothing new for me. Everyone was always staring at my mother, but the scrutiny seemed especially intense that day, or else I am remembering it acutely because it was the last time I saw her alive. The pitcher was looking at home plate, the catcher was waiting for the ball; the batter, I suppose, was waiting for the ball, too; but even the fielders had turned their heads to gape at my mother. Everyone on our bench was watching her – Mr Chickering, the hardest; maybe Owen, the next hardest; maybe me, the least. Everyone in the stands stared back at her as she looked them over.

It was ball four. Maybe the pitcher had one eye on my mother, too. Harry Hoyt walked. Buzzy Thurston was up, and Owen was on deck. He got up from the bench and looked for the smallest bat. Buzzy hit an easy grounder, a sure out, and my mother never turned her head to follow the play. She started walking parallel to the third-base line; she passed the third-base coach; she was still gazing into the stands when the shortstop bobbled Buzzy Thurston's easy grounder, and the runners were safe all around.

Owen was up.

As a testimony to how boring this particular game was – and how very much lost it was, too – Mr Chickering told Owen to swing away; Mr Chickering wanted to go home, too.

Usually, he said, 'Have a good eye, Owen!' That meant, *Walk!* That meant, Don't lift the bat off your shoulders. That meant, Don't swing at *anything*.

But this day, Mr Chickering said, 'Hit away, kid!'

'Knock the cover off the ball, Meany!' someone on the bench said; then he fell off the bench, laughing.

Owen, with dignity, stared at the pitcher.

'Give it a ride, Owen!' I called.

'Swing away, Owen!' said Mr Chickering. 'Swing away!'

Now the guys on our bench got into it; it was time to go home. Let Owen swing and miss the next three pitches, and then we were free. In addition, we awaited the potential comedy of his wild, weak swings.

The first pitch was way outside and Owen let it go.

'Swing!' Mr Chickering said. 'Swing away!'

'THAT WAS TOO FAR AWAY!' Owen said. He was strictly by the book, Owen Meany; he did everything by the rules.

The second pitch almost hit him in the head and he had to dive forward – across the dirt surrounding home plate and into the infield grass. Ball two. Everyone laughed at the explosion of dust created by Owen whacking his uniform; yet Owen made us all wait while he cleaned himself off.

My mother had her back to home plate; she had caught someone's eye – someone in the bleacher seats – and she was waving to whoever it was. She was past the third-base bag – on the third-base line, but still nearer third base than home plate – when Owen Meany started his swing. He appeared to start his swing before the ball left the pitcher's hand – it was a fast ball, such as they are in Little League play, but Owen's swing was well ahead of the ball, with which he made astonishing contact (a little in front of home plate, about chest-high). It was the hardest I'd ever seen him hit a ball, and the force of the contact was such a shock to Owen that he actually stayed on his feet – for once, he didn't fall down.

The crack of the bat was so unusually sharp and loud for a Little League game that the noise captured even my mother's wandering attention. She turned her head toward home plate – I guess, to see who had hit such a *shot* – and the ball struck her left temple, spinning her so quickly that one of her high heels broke and she fell forward, facing the stands, her knees splayed apart, her face hitting the ground first because her hands never moved from her sides (not even to break her fall), which later gave rise to the speculation that she was dead before she touched the earth.

Whether she died *that* quickly, I don't know; but she was dead by the time Mr Chickering reached her. He was the first one to her. He lifted her head, then turned her face to a slightly more comfortable position; someone said later that he closed her eyes before he let her head rest back on the ground. I remember that he pulled the skirt of her dress down – it was as high as midthigh – and he pinched her knees together. Then he stood up, removing his warm-up jacket, which he held in front of him as a bullfighter holds his cape. I was the first of the players to cross the third-base line, but – for a fat man – Mr Chickering was agile. He caught me, and he threw the warm-up jacket over my head. I could see nothing; it was impossible to struggle effectively.

'No, Johnny! No, Johnny!' Mr Chickering said. 'You don't want to see her, Johnny,' he said.

Your memory is a monster; *you* forget – *it* doesn't. It simply files things away. It keeps things for you, or hides things from you – and summons them to your recall with a will of its own. You think you have a memory; but it has you!

Later, I would remember everything. In revisiting the scene of my mother's death, I can remember everyone who was in the stands that day; I remember who wasn't there, too – and what everyone said, and didn't say, to me. But the first visit to that scene was very bare of details. I remember Chief Pike, our Gravesend chief of police – in later years, I would date his daughter. Chief Pike got my attention only because of what a ridiculous question he asked – and how much more absurd was his elaboration on his question!

'Where's the ball?' the police chief asked – after the area

had been cleared, as they say. My mother's body was gone and I was sitting on the bench in Mr Chickering's lap, his warm-up jacket still over my head – now, because I liked it that way: because *I* had put it there.

'The ball?' Mr Chickering said. 'You want the fucking *ball*?'

'Well, it's the murder weapon, kind of,' Chief Pike said. His Christian name was Ben. 'The instrument of death, I guess you'd call it,' Ben Pike said.

'The murder weapon!' Mr Chickering said, squeezing me as he spoke. We were waiting for either my grandmother or my mother's new husband to come get me. 'The instrument of death!' Mr Chickering said. 'Jesus Christ, Ben – it was a *baseball*!'

'Well, where *is* it?' Chief Pike said. 'If it killed somebody, I'm supposed to see it – actually, I'm supposed to *possess* it.'

'Don't be an asshole, Ben,' Mr Chickering said.

'Did one of your kids take it?' Chief Pike asked our fat coach and manager.

'Ask *them* – don't ask *me*!' Mr Chickering said.

All the players had been made to stand behind the bleachers while the police took photographs of my mother. They were still standing there, peering out at the murderous field through the empty seats. Several townspeople were standing with the players – mothers and dads and ardent baseball fans. Later, I would remember Owen's voice, speaking to me in the darkness – because my head was under the warm-up jacket.

'I'M SORRY!'

Bit by bit, over the years, all of it would come back to me – everyone who was standing there behind the bleachers, *and* everyone who had gone home.

But then I took the warm-up jacket off my head and all I knew was that Owen Meany was *not* standing there behind the bleachers. Mr Chickering must have observed the same thing.

'Owen!' he called.

'He went home!' someone called back.

'He had his bike!' someone said.

I could easily imagine him, struggling with his bike up the Maiden Hill Road – first pedaling, then wobbling, then getting off to walk his bike; all the while, in view of the river. In those days, our baseball uniforms were an itchy wool, and I could see Owen's uniform, heavy with sweat, the number 3 too big for his back – when he tucked his shirt into his pants, he tucked in half the number, too, so that anyone passing him on the Maiden Hill Road would have thought he was number 2.

I suppose there was no reason for him to wait; my mother always gave Owen and his bike a ride home after our Little League games.

Of course, I thought, Owen has the ball. He was a collector; one had to consider only his baseball cards. 'After all,' Mr Chickering would say – in later years – 'it was the only decent hit the kid ever made, the only real wood he ever got on the ball. And even then, it was a foul ball. Not to mention that it killed someone.'

So what if Owen has the ball? I was thinking. But at the time I was mainly thinking about my mother; I was already beginning to get angry with her for never telling me who my father was.

At the time, I was only eleven; I had no idea who else had attended that Little League game, and that death – and who had his own reason for wanting to possess the ball that Owen Meany hit.

2 : THE ARMADILLO

My mother's name was Tabitha, although no one but my grandmother actually called her that. Grandmother hated nicknames – with the exception that she never called me John; I was always Johnny to her, even long after I'd become just plain John to everyone else. To everyone else, my mother was Tabby. I recall one occasion when the Rev. Lewis Merrill said 'Tabitha,' but that was spoken in front of my mother *and* grandmother – and the occasion was an argument, or at least a plea. The issue was my mother's decision to leave the Congregational Church for the Episcopal, and the Rev. Mr Merrill – speaking to my grandmother, as if my mother wasn't in the room – said, 'Tabitha Wheelwright is the one truly angelic voice in our choir, and we shall be a choir without a soul if she leaves us.' I must add, in Pastor Merrill's defense, that he didn't *always* speak with such Byzantine muddiness, but he was sufficiently worked up about my mother's and my own departure from his church to offer his opinions as if he were speaking from the pulpit.

In New Hampshire, when I was a boy, Tabby was a common name for house cats, and there was undeniably a feline quality to my mother – never in the sly or stealthy sense of that word, but in the word's other catlike qualities: a clean, sleek, self-possessed, strokable quality. In quite a different way from Owen Meany, my mother looked touchable; I was always aware of how much people wanted, or needed, to touch her. I'm not talking only about men, although – even at my age – I was aware of how restlessly men moved their hands in her company. I mean that *everyone* liked to touch her – and depending on her attitude toward her toucher, my mother's responses to being touched were feline, too. She could be so chillingly indifferent that the touching would instantly stop; she was well coordinated and surprisingly quick and, like a cat, she could retreat from being touched – she could duck under or dart away from someone's hand as instinctively as the rest of us can shiver. And she could respond in that other way that cats can respond, too; she could luxuriate in being touched – she could contort her body quite shamelessly, putting more and more pressure against the toucher's hand, until (I used to imagine) anyone near enough to her could hear her *purr*.

Owen Meany, who rarely wasted words and who had the conversation-stopping habit of dropping remarks like coins in to a deep pool of water . . . remarks that sank, like truth, to the bottom of the pool where they would remain, untouchable . . . Owen said to me once, 'YOUR MOTHER IS SO SEXY, I KEEP FORGETTING SHE'S ANYBODY'S MOTHER.'

As for my Aunt Martha's insinuations, leaked to my cousins, who dribbled the suggestion, more than ten years late, to me – that my mother was 'a little simple' – I believe this is the result of a jealous elder sister's misunderstanding. My Aunt Martha failed to understand the most basic thing about my mother: that she was born into entirely the wrong body. Tabby Wheelwright looked like a starlet – lush, whimsical, easy to talk into anything; she looked eager to please, or 'a little simple,' as my Aunt Martha observed; she looked *touchable*. But I firmly believe that my mother was of an entirely different character than her appearance would suggest; as her son, I know, she was almost perfect as a mother – her sole imperfection being that she died before she could tell me who my father was. And in addition to being an almost perfect mother, I also know that she was a happy woman – and a truly happy woman drives some men and almost every other woman absolutely *crazy*. If her body looked restless, she wasn't. She was content – she was feline in that respect, too. She appeared to want nothing from life but a child and a loving husband; it is important to note these *singulars* – she did not want children, she wanted me, *just* me, and she got me; she did not want men in her life, she wanted a man, the *right* man, and shortly before she died, she found him.

I have said that my Aunt Martha is a 'lovely woman,' and I mean it: she is warm, she is attractive, she is decent and kind and honorably intentioned – and she has always been loving to me. She loved my mother, too; she just never understood her – and when however small a measure of jealousy is mixed with misunderstanding, there is going to be trouble.

I have said that my mother was a sweater girl, and that is a contradiction to the general modesty with which she dressed; she did show off her bosom – but never her flesh, except for her athletic, almost-innocent shoulders. She did like to bare her shoulders. And her dress was never slatternly, never wanton, never garish; she was so conservative in her choice of colors that I remember little in her wardrobe that wasn't black or white, except for some accessories – she had a fondness for red (in scarves, in hats, in shoes, in mittens and gloves). She wore nothing that was tight around her hips, but she did like her small waist and her good bosom to show – she *did* have THE BEST BREASTS OF ALL THE MOTHERS, as Owen observed.

I do not think that she flirted; she did not 'come on' to men – but how much of that would I have seen, up to the age of eleven? So maybe she did flirt – a little. I used to imagine that her flirting was reserved for the Boston & Maine, that she was absolutely and properly my mother in every location upon this earth – even in Boston, the dreaded city – but that on the train she might have looked for men. What else could explain her having met the man who fathered me there? And some six years later – on the same train – she met the man who would marry her! Did the rhythm of the train on the tracks somehow unravel her and make her behave out of character? Was she altered in transit, when her feet were not upon the ground?

I expressed this absurd fear only once, and only to Owen. He was shocked.

'HOW COULD YOU THINK SUCH A THING ABOUT YOUR OWN MOTHER?' he asked me.

'But *you* say she's sexy, you're the one who raves about her breasts,' I told him.

'I DON'T *RAVE*,' Owen told me.

'Well, okay – I mean, you like her,' I said. 'Men, and boys – they like her.'

'FORGET THAT ABOUT THE TRAIN,' Owen said. 'YOUR MOTHER IS A PERFECT WOMAN. NOTHING HAPPENS TO HER ON THE TRAIN.'

Well, although she *said* she 'met' my father on the Boston & Maine, I never imagined that my conception occurred there;

it is a fact, however, that she met the man she would marry on that train. That story was neither a lie nor a secret. How many times I asked her to tell me that story! And she never hesitated, she never lacked enthusiasm for telling that story – which she told the same way, every time. And after she was dead, how many times I asked *him* to tell me the story – and he would tell it, with enthusiasm, and the same way, every time.

His name was Dan Needham. How many times I have prayed to God that *he* was my real father!

My mother and my grandmother and I – and Lydia, minus one of her legs – were eating dinner on a Thursday evening in the spring of 1948. Thursdays were the days my mother returned from Boston, and we always had a better-than-average dinner those nights. I remember that it was shortly after Lydia's leg had been amputated, because it was still a little strange to have her eating with us at the table (in her wheelchair), and to have the two new maids doing the serving and the clearing that only recently Lydia had done. And the wheelchair was still new enough to Lydia so that she wouldn't allow me to push her around in it; only my grandmother and my mother – and one of the two new maids – were allowed to. I don't remember all the trivial intricacies of Lydia's wheelchair rules – just that the four of us were finishing our dinner, and Lydia's presence at the dinner table was as new and noticeable as fresh paint.

And my mother said, 'I've met another man on the good old Boston and Maine.'

It was not intended, I think, as an entirely mischievous remark, but the remark took instant and astonishing hold of Lydia and my grandmother and me. Lydia's wheelchair surged in reverse away from the table, dragging the tablecloth after her, so that all the dishes and glasses and silverware jumped – and the candlesticks wobbled. My grandmother seized the large brooch at the throat of her dress – she appeared to have suddenly choked on it – and I snapped so substantial a piece of my lower lip between my teeth that I could taste my blood.

We all thought that my mother was speaking euphemistically. I wasn't present when she'd announced the particulars of the case of the *first* man she claimed she'd met on the train. Maybe she'd said, 'I met a man on the good old Boston and Maine – and now I'm pregnant!' Maybe she said, 'I'm going to have a baby as a result of a fling I had with a total stranger I met on the good old Boston and Maine – someone I never expect to see again!'

Well, anyway, if I can't re-create the first announcement, the second announcement was spectacular enough. We all thought that she was telling us that she was pregnant again – by a *different* man!

And as an example of how wrong my Aunt Martha was, concerning her point of view that my mother was 'a little simple,' my mother instantly saw what we were thinking, and laughed at us, very quickly, and said, 'No, no! I'm not going to have a *baby*. I'm never going to have another baby – I *have* my baby. I'm just telling you that I've met a man. Someone I like.'

'A *different* man, Tabitha?' my grandmother asked, still holding her brooch.

'Oh, not *that* man! Don't be silly,' my mother said, and she laughed again – her laughter drawing Lydia's wheelchair, ever so cautiously, back toward the table.

'A man you *like*, you mean, Tabitha?' my grandmother asked.

'I wouldn't mention him if I didn't like him,' my mother said. 'I want you to meet him,' she said to us all.

'You've dated him?' my grandmother asked.

'No! I just *met* him – just today, on *today's* train!' my mother said.

'And already you *like* him?' Lydia asked, in a tone of voice so perfectly copied from my grandmother that I had to look to see which one of them was speaking.

'Well, yes,' my mother said seriously. 'You know such things. You don't need that much time.'

'How many times have you *known* such things – before?' my grandmother asked.

'This is the first time, really,' my mother said. 'That's why I know.'

Lydia and my grandmother instinctively looked at me, perhaps to ascertain if I'd understood my mother correctly: that the time 'before,' when she'd had her 'fling,' which had led to me, was *not* a time when my mother had enjoyed any special feelings toward whoever my father was. But I had another idea. I was thinking that maybe this *was* my father, that maybe this was the first man she'd met on the train, and he'd heard about me, and he was curious about me and wanted to see me – and something very important had kept him away for the last six years. There had, after all, been a war back when I'd been born, in 1942.

But as another example of how wrong my Aunt Martha was, my mother seemed to see what I was imagining, immediately, because she said, 'Please understand, Johnny, that this man has no relationship whatsoever to the man who is your father – this is a man I saw for the first time today, and I like him. That's all: I just like him, and I think you'll like him, too.'

'Okay,' I said, but I couldn't look at her. I remember keeping my eyes on Lydia's hands, gripping her wheelchair – and on my grandmother's hands, toying with her brooch.

'What does he *do*, Tabitha?' my grandmother asked. That was a Wheelwright thing to ask. In my grandmother's opinion, what one 'did' was related to where one's family 'came from' – she always hoped it was from England, and in the seventeenth century. And the short list of things that my grandmother approved of 'doing' was no less specific than seventeenth-century England.

'Dramatics,' my mother said. 'He's a sort of actor – but not really.'

'An unemployed actor?' my grandmother asked. (I think now that an *employed* actor would have been unsuitable enough.)

'No, he's not looking for employment as an actor – he's strictly an *amateur* actor,' my mother said. And I thought of those people in the train stations who handled puppets – I meant street performers, although at six years old I hadn't the vocabulary to suggest this. 'He *teaches* acting, and putting on plays,' my mother said.

'A director?' my grandmother asked, more hopefully.

'Not exactly,' my mother said, and she frowned. 'He was on his way to Gravesend for an interview.'

'I can't imagine there's much opportunity for *theater* here!' my grandmother said.

'He had an interview at the academy,' my mother said. 'It's a teaching job – the history of drama, or something. And the boys have their own theatrical productions – you know,

Martha and I used to go to them. It was so funny how they had to dress up as girls!'

That was the funniest part of those productions, in my memory; I'd had no idea that directing such performances was anyone's *job*.

'So he's a teacher?' my grandmother asked. This was borderline acceptable to Harriet Wheelwright – although my grandmother was a shrewd enough businesswoman to know that the dollars and cents of teaching (even at as prestigious a prep school as Gravesend Academy) were not exactly in her league.

'Yes!' my mother said in an exhausted voice. 'He's a *teacher*. He's been teaching *dramatics* in a private school in Boston. Before that, he went to Harvard – Class of Forty-five.'

'Goodness gracious!' my grandmother said. 'Why didn't you begin with Harvard?'

'It's not important to him,' my mother said.

But Harvard '45 was important enough to my grandmother to calm her troubled hands; they left her brooch alone, and returned to rest in her lap. After a polite pause, Lydia inched her wheelchair forward and picked up the little silver bell and shook it for the maids to come clear – the very bell that had summoned Lydia so often (only yesterday, it seemed). And the bell had the effect of releasing us all from the paralyzing tension we had just survived – but for only an instant. My grandmother had forgotten to ask: What is the man's name? For in her view, we Wheelwrights were not out of the woods without knowing the name of the potential new member of the family. God forbid, he was a Cohen, or a Calamari, or a Meany! Up went my grandmother's hands to her brooch again.

'His name is Daniel Needham,' my mother said. Whew! With what relief – down came my grandmother's hands! Needham was a fine old name, a founding fathers sort of name, a name you could trace back to the Massachusetts Bay Colony – if not exactly to Gravesend itself. And Daniel was as Daniel as Daniel Webster, which was as good a name as a Wheelwright could wish for.

'But he's called Dan,' my mother added, bringing a slight frown to my grandmother's countenance. She had never gone along with making Tabitha a Tabby, and if she'd had a Daniel she wouldn't have made him a Dan. But Harriet Wheelwright was fair-minded enough, and smart enough, to yield in the case of a *small* difference of opinion.

'So, have you made a date?' my grandmother asked.

'Not exactly,' my mother said. 'But I know I'll see him again.'

'But you haven't made any plans?' my grandmother asked. Vagueness annoyed her. 'If he doesn't get the job at the academy,' my grandmother said, 'you may never see him again!'

'But I *know* I'll see him again!' my mother repeated.

'You can be *such* a know-it-all, Tabitha Wheelwright,' my grandmother said crossly. 'I don't know why young people find it such a burden to plan ahead.' And to this notion, as to almost everything my grandmother said, Lydia wisely nodded her head – the explanation for her silence was that my grandmother was expressing exactly what Lydia would have expressed, only seconds before Lydia could have done so.

Then the doorbell rang.

Both Lydia and my grandmother stared at me, as if only *my* friends would be uncouth enough to make a call after dinner, uninvited.

'Heavens, who is that?' Grandmother asked, and she and Lydia both took a pointed and overly long look at their wristwatches – although it was not even eight o'clock on a balmy spring evening; there was still some light in the sky.

'I'll bet that's *him*!' my mother said, getting up from the table to go to the door. She gave herself a quick and approving look in the mirror over the sideboard where the roast sat, growing cold, and she hurried into the hall.

'Then you *did* make a date?' my grandmother asked. 'Did you invite him?'

'Not exactly!' my mother called. 'But I told him where I lived!'

'Nothing is *exactly* with young people, I've noticed,' my grandmother said, more to Lydia than to me.

'It certainly isn't,' said Lydia.

But I'd heard enough of them; I had heard them for years. I followed my mother to the door; my grandmother, pushing Lydia in her wheelchair in front of her, followed me. Curiosity, which – in New Hampshire, in those days – was often said to be responsible for the death of cats, had got the better of us all. We knew that my mother had no immediate plans to reveal to us a single clue regarding the first man she'd supposedly met on the Boston & Maine; but the second man – we could see him for ourselves. Dan Needham was on the doorstep of 80 Front Street, Gravesend.

Of course, my mother had had 'dates' before, but she'd never said of one of them that she *wanted* us to meet him, or that she even liked him, or that she knew she'd see him again. And so we were aware that Dan Needham was special, from the start.

I suppose Aunt Martha would have said that one aspect of my mother being 'a little simple' was her attraction to younger men; but in this habit my mother was simply ahead of her time – because it's true, the men she dated were often a little younger than she was. She even went out with a few seniors from Gravesend Academy when – if she'd gone to college – she would have been a *college* senior herself; but she just 'went out' with them. While they were only prep-school boys and she was in her twenties – with an illegitimate child – all she did with those boys was dance with them, or go to movies or plays with them, or to the sporting events.

I was used to seeing a few goons come calling, I will admit; and they never knew how to respond to me. They had no idea, for example, what a six-year-old was. They either brought me rubber ducks for the bath, or other toys for virtual infants – or else they brought me Fowler's *Modern English Usage*: something every six-year-old should plunge into. And when they saw me – when they were confronted with my short, sturdy presence, and the fact that I was too old for bathtub toys and too young for *Modern English Usage* – they would become insanely restless to impress me with their sensitivity to a waist-high person like myself. They would suggest a game of catch in the backyard, and then rifle an uncatchable football into my small face, or they would palaver to me in baby talk about showing them my favorite toy – so that they might know what kind of thing was more appropriate to bring me, next time. There was rarely a next time. Once one of them asked my mother if I was toilet-trained – I guess he found this a suitable question, prior to his inviting me to sit on his knees and play bucking bronco.

'YOU SHOULD HAVE SAID YES,' Owen Meany told me, 'AND THEN PISSED IN HIS LAP.'

One thing about my mother's 'beaus': they were all good-looking. So on that superficial level I was unprepared for Dan Needham, who was tall and gawky, with curly carrot-colored hair, and who wore eyeglasses that were too small for his egg-shaped face – the perfectly round lenses giving him the apprehensive, hunting expression of a large, mutant owl. My grandmother said, after he'd gone, that it must have been the first time in the history of Gravesend Academy that they had hired 'someone who looks younger than the students.' Furthermore, his clothes didn't fit him; the jacket was too tight – the sleeves too short – and the trousers were so baggy that the crotch flapped nearer his knees than his hips, which were womanly and the only padded parts of his peculiar body.

But I was too young and cynical to spot his kindness. Even before he was introduced to my grandmother or to Lydia or to me, he looked straight at me and said, 'You must be Johnny. I heard as much about you as anyone can hear in an hour and a half on the Boston and Maine, and I know you can be trusted with an important package.' It was a brown shopping bag with another brown paper bag stuffed inside it. Oh boy, here it comes, I thought: an inflatable camel – it floats and spits. But Dan Needham said, 'It's not for you, it's not for anyone your age. But I'm trusting you to put it somewhere where it can't be stepped on – and out of the way of any pets, if you have pets. You mustn't let a pet near it. And whatever you do, don't open it. Just tell me if it moves.'

Then he handed it to me; it didn't weigh enough to be Fowler's *Modern English Usage*, and if I was to keep it away from pets – and tell him if it moved – clearly it was *alive*. I put it quickly under the hall table – the telephone table, we called it – and I stood halfway in the hall and halfway in the living room, where I could watch Dan Needham taking a seat.

Taking a seat in my grandmother's living room was never easy, because many of the available seats were not for sitting in – they were antiques, which my grandmother was preserving, for historical reasons; sitting in them was not good for them. Therefore, although the living room was quite sumptuously arranged with upholstered chairs and couches, very little of this furniture was usable – and so a guest, his or her knees already bending in the act of sitting down, would suddenly snap to attention as my grandmother shouted, 'Oh, for goodness sake, not there! You can't sit *there*!' And the startled person would attempt to try the next chair or couch, which in my grandmother's opinion would also collapse or burst into flames at the strain. And I suppose my grandmother noticed that Dan Needham was tall, and that he had a sizable bottom, and this no doubt meant to her that an even fewer-than-usual number of seats were available to *him* – while Lydia, not yet deft with her wheelchair, blocked the way here, and the way there, and neither my mother nor my grandmother had yet developed that necessary reflex to simply wheel her out of the way.

And so the living room was a scene of idiocy and confusion, with Dan Needham spiraling toward one vulnerable antique after another, and my mother and grandmother colliding with Lydia's wheelchair while Grandmother barked this and that command regarding who should sit where. I hung back on the threshold of this awkwardness, keeping an eye on the ominous shopping bag, imagining that it had moved, a little – or that a mystery pet would suddenly materialize beside it and either eat, or be eaten by, the contents of the bag. We had never had a pet – my grandmother thought that people who kept pets were engaged in the basest form of self-mockery, intentionally putting themselves on a level with animals. Nevertheless, it made me extremely jumpy to observe the bag, awaiting its slightest twitch, and it made me even jumpier to observe the foolish nervousness of the adult ritual taking place in the living room. Gradually, I gave my whole attention to the bag; I slipped away from the threshold of the living room and retreated into the hall, sitting cross-legged on the scatter rug in front of the telephone table. The sides of the bag were almost breathing, and I thought I could detect an odor foreign to human experience. It was the suspicion of this odor that drew me nearer to the bag, until I crawled under the telephone table and put my ear to the bag and listened, and peered over the top of the bag – but the bag inside the bag blocked my view.

In the living room, they were talking about history – that was Dan Needham's actual appointment: in the History Department. He had studied enough history at Harvard to be qualified to teach the conventional courses in that field at Gravesend. 'Oh, you got the job!' my mother said. What was special in his approach was his use of the history of drama – and here he said something about the public entertainment of any period distinguishing the period as clearly as its so-called politics, but I drifted in and out of the sense of his remarks, so intent was I on the contents of the shopping bag in the hall. I picked up the bag and held it in my lap and waited for it to move.

In addition to his interview with the History Department members, and with the headmaster, Dan Needham was saying, he had requested some time to address those students interested in theater – and any faculty members who were interested, too – and in this session he had attempted to demonstrate how the development of certain techniques of the theatrical arts, how certain dramatic skills, can enhance our understanding of not only the characters on a stage but of a specific time and place as well. And for this session with the drama students, Dan Needham was saying, he always brought along a certain 'prop' – something interesting, either to hold or focus the students' attention, or to distract them from what he would, finally, make them see. He was rather long-winded, I thought.

'What *props*?' my grandmother asked.

'Yes, what *props*?' Lydia asked.

And Dan Needham said that a 'prop' could be anything; once he'd used a tennis ball – and once a live bird in a cage.

That was it! I thought, feeling that whatever it was in the bag was hard and lifeless and unmoving – and a birdcage would be all that. The bird, of course, I couldn't touch. Still, I wanted to see it, and with trepidation – and as silently as possible, so that the bores in the living room would not hear the paper crinkling of the two bags – I opened just a little bit of the bag within the bag.

The face that stared intently into mine was not a bird's face, and no cage prevented this creature from leaping out at me – and the creature appeared not only poised to leap out at me, but eager to do so. Its expression was fierce; its snout, as narrow as the nose of a fox, was pointed at my face like a gun; its wild, bright eyes winked with hatred and fearlessness, and the claws of its forepaws, which were reaching toward me, were long and prehistoric. It looked like a weasel in a shell – like a ferret with scales.

I screamed. I also forgot I was sitting under the telephone table, because I leaped up, knocking over the table and tangling my feet in the phone cord. I couldn't get away;

and when I lunged out of the hall and into the living room, the telephone, and the phone table, and the beast in the bag were all dragged – with considerable clamor – after me. And so I screamed again.

'Goodness gracious!' my grandmother cried.

But Dan Needham said cheerfully to my mother: 'I told you he'd open the bag.'

At first I had thought Dan Needham was a fool like all the others, and that he didn't know the first thing about six-year-olds – that to tell a six-year-old *not* to open a bag was an invitation to open it. But he knew very well what a six-year-old was like; to his credit, Dan Needham was always a little bit of a six-year-old himself.

'What in heaven's name is in the bag?' my grandmother asked, as I finally freed myself from the phone cord and went crawling to my mother.

'My *prop!*' Dan Needham said.

It was some 'prop,' all right, for in the bag was a stuffed armadillo. To a boy from New Hampshire, an armadillo resembled a small dinosaur – for who in New Hampshire ever heard of a two-foot-long rat with a shell on its back, and claws as distinguished as an anteater's? Armadillos eat insects and earthworms and spiders and land snails, but I had no way of knowing that. It looked at least willing, if not able, to eat *me*.

Dan Needham gave it to me. It was the first present any of my mother's 'beaus' gave me that I kept. For years – long after its claws were gone, and its tail fell off, and its stuffing came out, and its sides collapsed, and its nose broke in half, and its glass eyes were lost – I kept the bony plates from the shell of its back.

I loved the armadillo, of course, and Owen Meany also loved it. We would be playing in the attic, abusing my grandmother's ancient sewing machine, or dressing up in my dead grandmother's clothes, and Owen would say, out of nowhere, 'LET'S GO GET THE ARMADILLO. LET'S BRING IT UP HERE AND HIDE IT IN THE CLOSET.'

The closet that housed my dead grandfather's clothes was vast and mysterious, full of angles and overhead shelves, and rows upon rows of shoes. We would hide the armadillo in the armpit of an old tuxedo; we would hide it in the leg of an old pair of waders, or under a derby hat; we would hang it from a pair of suspenders. One of us would hide it and the other one would have to find it in the desk closet with the aid of only a flashlight. No matter how many times we had seen the armadillo, to come upon it in the black closet – to suddenly light up its insane, violent face – was always frightening. Every time the finder found it, he would yell.

Owen's yelling would occasionally produce my grandmother, who would not willingly mount the rickety staircase to the attic and struggle with the attic's trapdoor. She would stand at the foot of the staircase and say, 'Not so loud, you boys!' And she would sometimes add that we were to be careful with the ancient sewing machine, and with Grandfather's clothes – because she might want to sell them, someday. 'That sewing machine is an antique, you know!' Well, almost everything at 80 Front Street was an antique, and almost none of it – Owen and I knew perfectly well – would ever be sold; not, at least, while my grandmother was alive. She liked her antiques, as was evidenced by the growing number of chairs and couches in the living room that no one was allowed to sit on.

As for the discards in the attic, Owen and I knew they were safe forever. And searching among those relics for the terrifying armadillo . . . which itself looked like some relic of the animal world, some throwback to an age when men were taking a risk every time they left the cave . . . hunting for that stuffed beast among the artifacts of my grandmother's culture was one of Owen Meany's favorite games.

'I CAN'T FIND IT,' he would call out from the closet. 'I HOPE YOU DIDN'T PUT IT IN THE SHOES, BECAUSE I DON'T WANT TO STEP ON IT BEFORE I SEE IT. AND I HOPE YOU DIDN'T PUT IT ON THE TOP SHELF BECAUSE I DON'T LIKE TO HAVE IT ABOVE ME – I HATE TO SEE IT LOOKING DOWN AT ME. AND IT'S NO FAIR PUTTING IT WHERE IT WILL FALL DOWN IF I JUST TOUCH SOMETHING, BECAUSE THAT'S TOO SCARY. AND WHEN IT'S INSIDE THE SLEEVES, I CAN'T FIND IT WITHOUT REACHING INSIDE FOR IT – THAT'S NO FAIR, EITHER.'

'Just shut up and find it, Owen,' I would say.

'NO FAIR PUTTING IT IN THE HATBOXES,' Owen would say, while I listened to him stumbling over the shoes inside the closet. 'AND NO FAIR WHEN IT SPRINGS OUT

AT ME BECAUSE YOU STRETCH THE SUSPENDERS IN THAT WAY . . . *AAAAAAHHHHHH!* THAT'S *NO* FAIR!'

Before Dan Needham brought anything as exotic as that armadillo or himself into my life, my expectations regarding anything unusual were reserved for Owen Meany, and for school holidays and portions of my summer vacation when my mother and I would travel 'up north' to visit Aunt Martha and her family.

To anyone in coastal New Hampshire, 'up north' could mean almost anywhere else in the state, but Aunt Martha and Uncle Alfred lived in the White Mountains, in what everyone called 'the north country,' and when they or my cousins said they were going 'up north,' they meant a relatively short drive to any of several towns that were a little north of them – to Bartlett or to Jackson, up where the real skiing was. And in the summers, Loveless Lake, where we went to swim, was also 'up north' from where the Eastmans lived – in Sawyer Depot. It was the last train station on the Boston & Maine before North Conway, where most of the skiers got off. Every Christmas vacation and Easter, my mother and I, and our skis, departed the train in Sawyer Depot; from the depot itself, we could walk to the Eastmans' house. In the summer, when we visited at least once, it was an even easier walk – without our skis.

Those train rides – at least two hours from Gravesend – were the most concrete occasions I was given in which to imagine my mother riding the Boston & Maine in the *other* direction – south, to Boston, where I almost never went. But the passengers traveling north, I always believed, were very different types from the citybound travelers – skiers, hikers, mountain-lake swimmers: these were not men and women seeking trysts, or keeping assignations. The ritual of those train rides north is unforgettable to me, although I remember nothing of the equal number of rides back to Gravesend; return trips, to this day – from anywhere – are simply invitations to dull trances or leaden slumber.

But every time we rode the train to Sawyer Depot, my mother and I weighed the advantages of sitting on the left-hand side of the train, so that we could see Mt Chocorua – or on the right-hand side, so that we could see Ossipee Lake. Chocorua was our first indication of how much snow there would be where we were going, but there's more visible activity around a lake than there is on a mountain – and so we would sometimes 'opt for Ossipee,' as Mother and I described our decision. We also played a game that involved guessing where everyone was going to get off, and I always ate too many of those little tea sandwiches that they served on board, the kind with the crusts cut off; this overeating served to justify my inevitable trip to that lurching pit with the railroad ties going by underneath me, in a blur, and the *whoosh* of rank air that blew upward on my bare bottom.

My mother would always say, 'We're almost at Sawyer Depot, Johnny. Wouldn't you be more comfortable if you waited until we got to your Aunt Martha's?'

Yes; and no. I could almost always have waited; yet it was not only necessary to empty my bladder and bowels before encountering my cousins – it was a needed test of courage to sit naked over that dangerous hole, imagining lumps of coal and loosened railroad spikes hurtling *up* at me at bruising speed. I needed the empty bladder and bowels because there was immediate, rough treatment ahead; my cousins always greeted me with instant acrobatics, if not actual violence, and I needed to brace myself for them, to frighten myself a little in order to be ready for all the future terrors that the vacation held in store for me.

I would never describe my cousins as bullies; they were good-natured, rambunctious roughnecks and daredevils who genuinely wanted me to have *fun* – but fun in the north country was not what I was used to in my life with the women at 80 Front Street, Gravesend. I did not wrestle with my grandmother or box with Lydia, not even when she had both her legs. I did play croquet with my mother, but croquet is not a contact sport. And given that my best friend was Owen Meany, I was not inclined to much in the way of athletic roughhousing.

My mother loved her sister and brother-in-law; they always made her feel special and welcome – they certainly made me feel that way – and my mother doubtless appreciated a little time away from my grandmother's imperious wisdom.

Grandmother would come to Sawyer Depot for a few days at Christmas, and she would make a grand appearance for one weekend every summer, but the north country was not to Grandmother's liking. And although Grandmother was perfectly tolerant of my solitary disruption of the adult life at 80 Front Street – and even moderately tolerant of the games I would play in that old house with Owen – she had scant patience for the disruption caused in any house by *all* her grandchildren. For Thanksgiving, the Eastmans came to 80 Front Street, a disturbance that my grandmother referred to in terms of 'the casualties' for several months after their visit.

My cousins were active, combative athletes – my grandmother called them 'the warriors' – and I lived a different life whenever I was with them. I was both crazy about them and terrified of them; I couldn't contain my excitement as the time to see them drew near, but after several days, I couldn't wait to get away from them – I missed the peace of my private games, and I missed Owen Meany; I even missed Grandmother's constant but consistent criticism.

My cousins – Noah, Simon, and Hester (in order of their ages) – were all older than I: Hester was older by less than a year, although she would always be bigger; Simon was older by two years; Noah, by three. Those are not great differences in age, to be sure, but they were great enough in all those years before I was a teenager – when each of my cousins was *better* than I was, at everything.

Since they grew up in the north country, they were fabulous skiers. I was, at best, a cautious skier, modeling my slow, wide turns on my mother's graceful but undaring stem Christie – she was a pretty skier of intermediate ability who was consistently in control; she did not think that the essence of the sport was speed, nor did she fight the mountain. My cousins raced each other down the slopes, cutting each other off, knocking each other down – and rarely restraining their routes of descent to the marked trails. They would lead me into the deep, unmanageable powder snow in the woods, and in my efforts to keep up with them, I would abandon the controlled, conservative skiing that my mother had taught me and end up straddling trees, embracing snow fences, losing my goggles in icy streams.

My cousins were sincere in their efforts to teach me to keep my skis parallel – and to *hop* on my skis – but a school-vacation skier is never the equal to a north-country native. They set such standards for recklessness that, eventually, I could no longer have fun skiing with my mother. I felt guilty that I made her ski alone; but my mother was rarely left alone for long. By the end of the day, some man – a would-be ski instructor, if not an actual ski instructor – would be coaching her at her side.

What I remember of skiing with my cousins is long, humiliating, and hurtling falls, followed by my cousins retrieving my ski poles, my mittens, and my hat – from which I became inevitably separated.

'Are you all right?' my eldest cousin, Noah, would ask me. 'That looked rather harsh.'

'That looked *neat*!' my cousin Simon would say; Simon loved to fall – he skied to crash.

'You keep doing that, you'll make yourself sterile,' said my cousin Hester, to whom every event of our shared childhood was either sexually exhilarating or sexually damaging.

In the summers, we went waterskiing on Loveless Lake, where the Eastmans kept a boathouse, the second floor of which was remodeled to resemble an English pub – Uncle Alfred was admiring of the English. My mother and Aunt Martha would go sailing, but Uncle Alfred drove the powerboat wildly and fast, a beer in his free hand. Because he did not water-ski himself, Uncle Alfred thought that the responsibility of the boat's driver was to make the skier's ride as harrowing as possible. He would double back in the middle of a turn so that the rope would go slack, or you could even catch up to the rope and ski over it. He drove a murderous figure 8; he appeared to relish surprising you, by putting you directly in the path of an oncoming boat or of another surprised water-skier on the busy lake. Regardless of the cause of your fall, Uncle Alfred took credit for it. When anyone racing behind the boat would send up a fabulous spray, skimming length-wise across the water, skis ripped off, head under one second, up the next, and then under again – Uncle Alfred would shout, 'Bingo!'

I am living proof that the waters of Loveless Lake are potable because I swallowed half the lake every summer while waterskiing with my cousins. Once I struck the surface of the lake with such force that my right eyelid was rolled up into my head in a funny way. My cousin Simon told me I had lost my eyelid – and my cousin Hester added that the lost eyelid would lead to blindness. But Uncle Alfred managed to locate the missing eyelid, after a few anxious minutes.

Indoor life with my cousins was no less vigorous. The savagery of pillow-fighting would leave me breathless, and there was a game that involved Noah and Simon tying me up and stuffing me in Hester's laundry hamper, where Hester would always discover me; before she'd untie me, she'd accuse me of sniffing her underwear. I know that Hester especially looked forward to my visits because she suffered from being the constant inferior to her brothers – not that they abused her, or even teased her. Considering that they were boys, and older, and she was a girl, and younger, I thought they treated her splendidly, but every activity my cousins engaged in was competitive, and it clearly irked Hester to lose. Naturally, her brothers could 'best' her at everything. How she must have enjoyed having me around, for she could 'best' me at anything – even, when we went to the Eastman lumberyard and the sawmill, at log-rolling. There was also a game that involved taking possession of a sawdust pile – those piles were often twenty or thirty feet high, and the sawdust nearer the bottom, in contact with the ground, was often frozen or at least hardened to a crusty consistency. The object was to be king of the mountain, to hurl all comers off the top of the pile – or to bury one's attackers in the sawdust.

The worst part about being buried in the pile – up to your chin – was that the lumberyard dog, the Eastmans' slobbering boxer, a mindlessly friendly beast with halitosis vile enough to give you visions of corpses uprooted from their graves . . . this dog with the mouth of death was then summoned to lick your face. And with the sawdust packed all around you – as armless as Watahantowet's totem – you were powerless to fend the dog off.

But I loved being with my cousins; they were so vastly stimulating that I could rarely sleep in their house and would lie awake all night, waiting for them to pounce on me, or for them to let Firewater, the boxer, into my room, where he would lick me to death; or I would just lie awake imagining what exhausting contests I would encounter the next day.

For my mother, our trips to Sawyer Depot were serene occasions – fresh air and girl-talk with Aunt Martha, and some doubtless needed relief from what must have been the claustrophobia of her life with Grandmother and Lydia and the maids at 80 Front Street. Mother must have been dying to leave home. Almost everyone is dying to leave home, eventually; and almost everyone needs to. But, for me, Sawyer Depot was a training camp; yet the athleticism was not – all by itself – what was most thrilling to me about the time spent with my cousins. What made these contests thrilling was the presexual tension that I always associated with the competition – that I always associated with Hester in particular.

To this day, I still engage in debate with Noah and Simon regarding whether Hester was 'created' by her environment, which was almost entirely created by Noah and Simon – which is *my* opinion – or whether she was born with an overdose of sexual aggression and family animosity – which is what Noah and Simon say. We all agree that my Aunt Martha, as a model of womanhood, was no match for the superior impression my Uncle Alfred made – as a man. Felling trees, clearing the land, milling lumber – what a *male* business was the Eastman Lumber Company!

The house in Sawyer Depot was spacious and pretty; for my Aunt Martha had acquired my grandmother's good taste, and she'd brought money of her own to the marriage. But Uncle Alfred *made* more money than we Wheelwrights were simply sitting on. Uncle Alfred was a paragon of maleness, too, in that he was rich *and* he dressed like a lumberjack; that he spent most of the day behind a desk did not influence his appearance. Even if he only briefly visited the sawmill – and not more than twice a week did he actually venture into the forests where they were logging – he looked the part. Although he was fiercely strong, I never saw him do an ounce of physical labor. He radiated a burly good health, and despite how little time he spent 'in the field,' there was always sawdust in his bushy hair, wood chips wedged between the laces of his boots, and a few fragrant pine needles ground into the knees of his blue jeans. Possibly he kept the pine needles, the wood chips, and the sawdust in his office desk drawer.

What does it matter? While wrestling with my cousins and me, Uncle Alfred was an ever-friendly bruiser; and the cologne of his rough-and-ready business, the veritable scent of the woods, was always upon him. I don't know how my Aunt Martha tolerated it, but Firewater often slept in the king-size bed in my uncle and aunt's room – and that was an even further manifestation of Uncle Alfred's manliness: that when he wasn't snuggling up to my lovely Aunt Martha, he was lolling in bed with a big dog.

I thought Uncle Alfred was terrific – a wonderful father; and, for boys, he was what today's idiots would call a superior 'role model.' He must have been a difficult 'role model' for Hester, however, because I think her worshipful love of him – in addition to her constant losses in the daily competitions with her older brothers – simply overwhelmed her, and gave her an unwarranted contempt of my Aunt Martha.

But I know what Noah would say to that; he would say 'bullshit,' that his mother was a model of sweetness and caring – and she *was*! I don't argue with that! – and that Hester was *born* to her antagonism toward her mother, that she was *born* to challenge her parents' love with hostility toward *both* of them, and that the *only* way she could repay her brothers for outskiing her (on water and on snow), and for hurling her off sawdust piles, and for cramming her cousin into a basket with her old underwear, was to intimidate every girlfriend either of them ever had and to fuck the brains out of every boy they ever knew. Which she appeared to do.

It's a no-win argument – that business of what we're born with and what our environment does to us. And it's a boring argument, because it simplifies the mysteries that attend both our birth and our growth.

Privately, I continue to be more forgiving of Hester than her own family is. I think she was up against a stacked deck from the start, and that everything she would become began for her when Noah and Simon made me kiss her – because they made it clear that kissing Hester was punishment, the *penalty* part of the game; to have to kiss Hester meant you had lost.

I don't remember exactly how old we were when we were first forced to kiss, Hester and I, but it was sometime after my mother had met Dan Needham – because Dan was spending Christmas vacation with us at the Eastmans' in Sawyer Depot – and it was sometime before my mother and Dan Needham were married, because Mother and I were still living at 80 Front Street. Whenever it was, Hester and I were still in our preadolescent years – our presexual years, if that's safe to say; perhaps that is never safe to say in regard to Hester, but I promise it is safe to say of me.

Anyway, there'd been a thaw in the north country, and some rain, and then an ice storm, which froze the slush in deep-grooved ruts. The snow was the texture of jagged glass, which made skiing all the more exciting for Noah and Simon but made it entirely out of the question for me. So Noah and Simon went up north to brave the elements, and I stayed in the Eastmans' extremely comfortable house; I don't remember why Hester stayed home, too. Perhaps she was in a cranky temper, or else she just wanted to sleep in. For whatever reason, we were there together, and by the end of the day, when Noah and Simon returned, Hester and I were in her room, playing Monopoly. I *hate* Monopoly, but even a capitalist board game was welcome relief from the more strenuous activities my cousins subjected me to – and Hester was either in a rare mood to be calm, or else I rarely saw her without the company of Noah and Simon, around whom it was impossible to remain calm.

We were lounging on the thick, soft rug in Hester's room, with some of her old stuffed animals for pillows, when the boys – their hands and faces bitter cold from skiing – attacked us. They trod across the Monopoly game so effectively that there was no hope of re-creating where our houses and hotels and tokens might have been.

'Whoa!' Noah yelled. 'Look at this hanky-panky going on here!'

'There's no hanky-panky going on!' Hester said angrily.

'Whoa!' Simon yelled. 'Watch out for *Hester the Molester*!'

'Get out of my room!' Hester shouted.

'Last one through the house has to kiss Hester the Molester!' Noah said, and he and Simon were off running. In a panic, I looked at Hester and took off after them. 'Through the house' was a racing game that meant we had to travel through the back bedrooms – Noah and Simon's room and the back guest room, which was mine – down the back stairs, around the landing by the maid's room, where May the maid was likely to shout at us, and into the kitchen by May's usual entrance (she was also the cook). Then we chased each other through the kitchen and dining room, through the living room and the sun room, and through Uncle Alfred's study – provided he wasn't *in* his study – and up the front stairs, past the front guest rooms, which were off the main hall, and through my aunt and uncle's bedroom – provided they weren't *in* their bedroom – and then into the back hall, the first room off of which was Hester's bathroom. The next room that we came to was the finish line: Hester's room itself.

Of course, May emerged from her room to shout at Noah and Simon for running on the stairs, but only I was there on the landing to be shouted at – and only I had to slow down and say 'Excuse me' to May. And they closed the swinging door from the kitchen to the dining room after they ran through the doorway, so that only I had to pause long enough to open it. Uncle Alfred was not in his study, but Dan Needham was reading in there, and only I paused long enough to say 'Hello' to Dan. At the top of the front stairs, Firewater blocked my way; he'd doubtless been asleep when Noah and Simon had raced by him, but now he was alert enough to play. He managed to get the heel of my sock in his mouth as I attempted to run around him, and I could not travel far down the main hall – dragging him after me – before I had to stop to give him my sock.

So I was the last one through the house – I was always the last one through the house – and therefore I was expected to pay the loser's price, which was to kiss Hester. In order to bring this forced intercourse about, it had been necessary for Noah and Simon to prevent Hester from locking herself in her bathroom – which she attempted – and then it was necessary for them to tie her to her bed, which they managed to do after a violent struggle that included the decapitation of one of Hester's more fragile stuffed animals, which she had futilely ruined by beating her brothers with it. At last she was strapped prone to her bed, where she threatened to bite the lips off anyone who dared to kiss her – the thought of which filled me with such dread that Noah and Simon needed to use more mountain-climbing rope to tie me on top of Hester. We were bound uncomfortably face-to-face – and chest-to-chest, hips-to-hips, to make our humiliation more complete – and we were told that we would not be untied until we did it.

'Kiss her!' Noah cried to me.

'Let him kiss you, Hester!' Simon said.

It occurs to me now that this suggestion was even less compelling to Hester than it was to me, and I could think only that Hester's snarling mouth was about as inviting as Firewater's; yet I think we both realized that the potential embarrassment of being mated to this conjugal position for any duration of time, while Noah and Simon observed our breathing and minor movements, would perhaps lead to even greater suffering than indulging in a single kiss. What fools we were to think that Noah and Simon were dull enough fellows to be satisfied with one kiss! We tried a tiny one, but Noah said, 'That wasn't on the lips!' We tried a small, close-lipped one, on the lips – so brief that it was unnecessary to breathe – but this failed to satisfy Simon, who said, 'Open your mouths!' We opened our mouths. There was the problem of arranging the noses before we could enjoy the nervous exchange of saliva – the slithery contact of tongues, the surprising click of teeth. We were joined so long we had to breathe, and I was astonished at how sweet my cousin's breath was; to this day, I hope mine wasn't too bad.

As abruptly as they had conceived of this game, my cousins announced that the game was over. They never marshaled as much enthusiasm for the many repeats of the game called 'Last One Through the House Has to Kiss Hester'; maybe they realized, later, that I began to intentionally lose the game. And what did they make of the time they untied us and Hester said to me, 'I felt your hard-on'?

'You did not!' I said.

'I did. It wasn't much of a hard-on,' she said. 'It was no big deal. But I felt it.'

'You didn't!' I said.

'I did,' she said.

And it's true – it was no big deal, to be sure; it wasn't much of a hard-on, maybe; but I had one.

Did Noah and Simon ever consider the danger of the game? The way they skied, on water and on snow – and, later, the way they drove their cars – suggested to me that they thought nothing was dangerous. But Hester and I were dangerous. And they started it: Noah and Simon started it.

Owen Meany rescued me. As you shall see, Owen was always rescuing me; but he began the lifelong process of rescuing me by rescuing me from Hester.

Owen was extremely irritable regarding the time I spent with my cousins. He would be grouchy for several days before I left for Sawyer Depot, and he would be peevish and aloof for several days after I got back. Although I made a point of describing how physically demanding and psychologically upsetting the time spent with my cousins was, Owen was crabby; I thought he was jealous.

'YOU KNOW, I WAS THINKING,' he said to me. 'YOU KNOW HOW WHEN YOU ASK ME TO SPEND THE NIGHT, I ALMOST ALWAYS DO IT – AND WE HAVE A GOOD TIME, DON'T WE?'

'Sure we do, Owen,' I said.

'WELL, IF YOU ASKED ME TO COME WITH YOU AND YOUR MOTHER TO SAWYER DEPOT, I PROBABLY WOULD COME – YOU KNOW,' he said. 'OR DO YOU THINK YOUR COUSINS WOULDN'T LIKE ME?'

'Of course they'd like you,' I said, 'but I don't know if you'd like them.' I didn't know how to tell him that I thought he'd have a *terrible* time with my cousins – that if we picked him up and passed him over our heads in Sunday school, it was frightening to imagine what games my cousins might devise to play with Owen Meany. 'You don't know how to ski,' I told him. 'Or water-ski,' I added. 'And I don't think you'd like the log-rolling – or the sawdust piles.' I could have added, 'Or kissing Hester,' but I couldn't imagine Owen doing that. My God, I thought: my cousins would *kill* him!

'WELL, MAYBE YOUR MOTHER COULD TEACH ME HOW TO SKI. AND YOU DON'T HAVE TO DO THE LOG-ROLLING IF YOU DON'T WANT TO, DO YOU?' he asked.

'Well, my cousins kind of make everything happen so fast,' I said. 'You don't always have time to say "Yes" or "No" to something.'

'WELL, MAYBE IF YOU ASKED THEM NOT TO BE SO ROUGH WITH ME – UNTIL I GOT USED TO IT,' he said. 'THEY'D LISTEN TO YOU, WOULDN'T THEY?'

I could not imagine it – Owen together with my cousins! It seemed to me that they would be driven insane by the sight of him, and when he *spoke* – when they first encountered that *voice* – I could visualize their reaction only in terms of their inventing ways for Owen to be a projectile: they would make him the birdie for a badminton game; they would bind him to a single ski, launch him off the mountaintop, and race him to the bottom. They would make him sit in a salad bowl, and tow him – at high speeds – across Loveless Lake. They would bury him in sawdust and lose him; they'd never find him. Firewater would eat him.

'They're sort of hard to *control* – my cousins,' I said. 'That's the problem.'

'YOU MAKE THEM SOUND LIKE WILD ANIMALS,' Owen said.

'They *are* – kind of,' I said.

'BUT YOU HAVE FUN WITH THEM,' Owen said. 'WOULDN'T I HAVE FUN, TOO?'

'I have fun, and I don't have fun,' I told him. 'I just think my cousins might be too much for you.'

'YOU THINK I MIGHT BE TOO MUCH OF A WIMP FOR THEM,' he said.

'I don't think you're a wimp, Owen,' I said.

'BUT YOU THINK YOUR COUSINS WOULD THINK SO?' he said.

'I don't know,' I said.

'MAYBE I COULD MEET THEM AT YOUR HOUSE, WHEN THEY COME FOR THANKSGIVING,' he suggested. 'IT'S FUNNY HOW YOU DON'T INVITE ME OVER WHEN THEY'RE STAYING HERE.'

'My grandmother thinks there're too many kids in the house already – when they're here,' I explained, but Owen sulked about it so moodily that I invited him to spend the night, which he always enjoyed. He went through this ritual of calling his father to ask if it was all right, but it was always all right with Mr Meany; Owen stayed at 80 Front Street so frequently that he kept a toothbrush on my bathroom, and a pair of pajamas in my closet.

And after Dan Needham gave me the armadillo, Owen grew almost as attached to the little animal – and to Dan – as I was. When Owen would sleep in the other twin bed in my room, with the night table between us, we would carefully arrange the armadillo under the bedside lamp; in exact profile to both of us, the creature stared at the feet of our beds. The night-light, which was attached to one of the legs of the night table, shone upward, illuminating the armadillo's chin and the exposed nostrils of its thin snout. Owen and I would talk until we were drowsy; but in the morning, I always noticed that the armadillo had been moved – its face was turned more toward Owen than to me; its profile was no longer perfect. And once when I woke up, I saw that Owen was already awake; he was staring back at the armadillo, and he was smiling. After Dan Needham's armadillo came into my life, and the first occasion for me to travel to Sawyer Depot arose, I was not surprised that Owen took this opportunity to express his concern for the armadillo's well-being.

'FROM WHAT YOU TELL ME ABOUT YOUR COUSINS,' Owen said, 'I DON'T THINK YOU SHOULD TAKE THE ARMADILLO TO SAWYER DEPOT.' It had never occurred to me to take the armadillo with me, but Owen had clearly given some thought to the potential tragedy of such a journey. 'YOU MIGHT FORGET IT ON THE TRAIN,' he said, 'OR THAT DOG OF THEIRS MIGHT CHEW ON IT. WHAT'S THE DOG'S NAME?'

'Firewater,' I said.

'YES, FIREWATER – HE SOUNDS DANGEROUS TO THE ARMADILLO TO ME,' Owen said. 'AND IF YOUR COUSINS ARE THESE RUFFIANS, LIKE YOU SAY, THERE'S NO TELLING WHAT KIND OF GAME THEY MIGHT THINK UP – THEY MIGHT RIP THE ARMADILLO TO PIECES. OR LOSE IT IN THE SNOW.'

'Yes, you're right,' I said.

'IF THEY WANTED TO TAKE THE ARMADILLO WATERSKIING, COULD YOU STOP THEM?' he asked.

'Probably not,' I said.

'THAT'S JUST WHAT I THOUGHT,' he said. 'YOU BETTER NOT TAKE THE ARMADILLO WITH YOU.'

'Right,' I said.

'YOU BETTER LET ME TAKE IT HOME. I CAN LOOK AFTER IT WHILE YOU'RE AWAY. IF IT'S ALL ALONE HERE, ONE OF THE MAIDS MIGHT DO SOMETHING STUPID – OR THERE COULD BE A FIRE,' he said.

'I never thought of that,' I said.

'WELL, IT WOULD BE VERY SAFE WITH ME,' Owen said. Of course, I agreed. 'AND I'VE BEEN THINKING,' he added. 'OVER NEXT THANKSGIVING, WHEN YOUR COUSINS ARE HERE, YOU BETTER LET ME TAKE THE ARMADILLO HOME WITH ME THEN, TOO. IT SOUNDS TO ME LIKE THEY'D BE TOO VIOLENT WITH IT. IT HAS A VERY DELICATE NOSE – AND THE TAIL CAN BREAK, TOO. AND I DON'T THINK IT'S A GOOD IDEA TO SHOW YOUR COUSINS THAT GAME WE PLAY WITH THE ARMADILLO IN THE CLOSET WITH YOUR GRANDFATHER'S CLOTHES,' he said. 'IT SOUNDS TO ME LIKE THEY'D TRAMPLE ON THE ARMADILLO

IN THE DARK.' Or else they'd throw it out the window, I thought.

'I agree,' I said.

'GOOD,' Owen said. 'THEN IT'S ALL SETTLED: I'LL LOOK AFTER THE ARMADILLO WHEN YOU'RE AWAY, AND WHEN YOUR COUSINS ARE HERE, I'LL LOOK AFTER IT, TOO – OVER NEXT THANKSGIVING, WHEN YOU'RE GOING TO INVITE ME OVER TO MEET YOUR COUSINS. OKAY?'

'Okay, Owen,' I said.

'GOOD,' he said; he was very pleased about it, if a trifle nervous. The first time he took the armadillo home with him, he brought a box stuffed with cotton – it was such an elaborately conceived and strongly built carrying case that the armadillo could have been mailed safely overseas in it. The box, Owen explained, had been used to ship some granite-carving tools – some grave-marking equipment – so it was very sturdy. Mr Meany, in an effort to bolster the disappointing business at the quarry, was expanding his involvement in monument sales. Owen said his father resented selling some of his best pieces of granite to other granite companies that made gravestones, and charged an arm and a leg for them – according to Mr Meany. He had opened a gruesome monument shop downtown – Meany Monuments, the store was called – and the sample gravestones in the storefront window looked not so much like samples as like actual graves that someone had built a store around.

'It's absolutely frightful,' my grandmother said. 'It's a cemetery in a store,' she remarked indignantly, but Mr Meany was new to monument sales; it was possible he needed just a little more time to make the store look right.

Anyway, the armadillo was packed in a box designed for transporting chisels – for something Owen called WEDGES AND FEATHERS – and Owen solemnly promised that no harm would come to the diminutive beast. Apparently, Mrs Meany was frightened by it – Owen gave his parents no forewarning that the armadillo was visiting; but Owen maintained that this small shock served his mother right for going into his room uninvited. Owen's room (what little I ever saw of it) was as orderly and as untouchable as a museum. I think that is why it was so easy for me to imagine, for years, that the baseball that killed my mother was surely a resident souvenir in Owen's odd room.

I will never forget the Thanksgiving vacation when I introduced Owen Meany to my reckless cousins. The day before my cousins were to arrive in Gravesend, Owen came over to 80 Front Street to pick up the armadillo.

'They're not getting here until late tomorrow,' I told him.

'WHAT IF THEY COME EARLY?' he asked. 'SOMETHING COULD HAPPEN. IT'S BETTER NOT TO TAKE A CHANCE.'

Owen wanted to come over to meet my cousins immediately following Thanksgiving dinner, but I thought the day after Thanksgiving would be better; I suggested that everyone always felt so stuffed after Thanksgiving dinner that it was never a very lively time.

'BUT I WAS THINKING THAT THEY MIGHT BE CALMER, RIGHT AFTER THEY HAD EATEN,' Owen said. I admit, I enjoyed his nervousness. I was worried that my cousins might be in some rare, mellow condition when Owen met them, and therefore he'd think I'd just been making up stories about how wild they were – and that there was, therefore, *no* excuse for my never inviting him to Sawyer Depot. I wanted my cousins to like Owen, because *I* liked him – he was my best friend – but, at the same time, I didn't want everything to be so enjoyable that I'd have to invite Owen to Sawyer Depot the next time I went. I was sure that would be disastrous. And I was nervous that my cousins would make fun of Owen; and I confess I was nervous that Owen would embarrass me – I am ashamed of feeling that, to this day.

Anyway, both Owen and I were nervous. We talked on the phone in whispers Thanksgiving night.

'ARE THEY ESPECIALLY WILD?' he asked me.

'Not especially,' I said.

'WHAT TIME DO THEY GET UP? WHAT TIME TOMORROW SHOULD I COME OVER?' he asked.

'The boys get up early,' I said, 'but Hester sleeps a little later – or at least she stays in her room longer.'

'NOAH IS THE OLDEST?' Owen said, although he had checked these statistics with me a hundred times.

'Yes,' I said.

'AND SIMON IS THE NEXT OLDEST, ALTHOUGH HE'S JUST AS BIG AS NOAH – AND EVEN A LITTLE WILDER?' Owen said.

'Yes, yes,' I said.

'AND HESTER'S THE YOUNGEST BUT SHE'S BIGGER THAN YOU,' he said. 'AND SHE'S PRETTY, BUT NOT *THAT* PRETTY, RIGHT?'

'Right,' I said.

Hester just missed the Eastman good looks. It was an especially masculine good looks that Noah and Simon got from my Uncle Alfred – broad shoulders, big bones, a heavy jaw – and from my Aunt Martha the boys got their blondness, and their aristocracy. But the broad shoulders, the big bones, and the heavy jaw – these were less attractive on Hester, who did not receive either my aunt's blondness or her aristocracy. Hester was as dark and hairy as Uncle Alfred – even including his bushy eyebrows, which were actually one solid eyebrow without a gap above the bridge of the nose – and she had Uncle Alfred's big hands. Hester's hands looked like paws.

Yet Hester had sex appeal, in the manner – in those days – that tough girls were also sexy girls. She had a large, athletic body, and as a teenager she would have to struggle with her weight; but she had clear skin, she had solid curves; her mouth was aggressive, flashing lots of healthy teeth, and her eyes were taunting, with a dangerous-looking intelligence. Her hair was wild and thick.

'I have this friend,' I told Hester that evening. I thought I would begin with her, and try to win her over – and then tell Noah and Simon about Owen; but even though I was speaking quietly to Hester and I thought that Noah and Simon were engaged in finding a lost station on the radio, the boys heard me and were instantly curious.

'What friend?' Noah said.

'Well, he's my best friend,' I said cautiously, 'and he wants to meet all of you.'

'Fine, great – so where is he, and what's his name?' Simon said.

'Owen Meany,' I said as straightforwardly as possible.

'Who?' Noah said; the three of them laughed.

'What a wimp name!' Simon said.

'What's wrong with him?' Hester asked me.

'Nothing's wrong with him,' I said, a little too defensively. 'He's rather small.'

'Rather small,' Noah repeated, sounding very British.

'Rather a wimp, is he?' said Simon, imitating his brother.

'No, he's *not* a wimp,' I said. 'He's just small. And he has a funny voice,' I blurted out.

'A funny voice!' Noah said in a funny voice.

'A funny voice?' said Simon in a different funny voice.

'So he's a little guy with a funny voice,' Hester said. 'So what? So what's *wrong* with him?'

'Nothing!' I repeated.

'Why should anything be wrong with him, Hester?' Noah asked her.

'Hester probably wants to molest him,' Simon said.

'Shut up, Simon,' Hester said.

'Both of you shut up,' Noah said. 'I want to know why Hester thinks there's something wrong with everybody.'

'There's something wrong with all of *your* friends, Noah,' Hester said. 'And every friend of Simon's,' she added. 'I'll just bet there's something wrong with Johnny's friends, too.'

'I suppose there's nothing wrong with *your* friends,' Noah said to his sister.

'Hester doesn't have any friends!' Simon said.

'Shut up!' Hester said.

'I wonder why?' Noah said.

'Shut up!' Hester said.

'Well, there's nothing wrong with Owen,' I said. 'Except he's small, and his voice is a little different.'

'He sounds like fun,' Noah said pleasantly.

'Hey,' Simon said, patting me on the back. 'If he's your friend, don't worry – we'll be nice to him.'

'Hey,' Noah said, patting me on the back, too. 'Don't worry. We'll all have fun.'

Hester shrugged. 'We'll see,' she said. I had not kissed her since Easter. In my summer visit to Sawyer Depot, we had been outdoors every waking minute and there'd been no suggestion to play 'Last One Through the House Has to Kiss Hester.' I doubted we'd get to play that game over Thanksgiving, either, because my grandmother did not allow racing all over the house at 80 Front Street. So maybe I'll have to wait until Christmas, I thought.

'Maybe your friend would like to kiss Hester,' Simon said.

'I decide who kisses me,' Hester said.

'Whoa!' Noah said.

'I think Owen will be a little *timid* around all of you,' I ventured.

'You're saying he wouldn't like to kiss me?' Hester asked.

'I'm just saying he might be a little shy – around all of you,' I said.

'*You* like kissing me,' Hester said.

'I don't,' I lied.

'You do,' she said.

'Whoa!' said Noah.

'There's no stopping Hester the Molester!' Simon said.

'Shut up!' Hester said.

And so the stage was set for Owen Meany.

That day after Thanksgiving, my cousins and I were making so much noise up in the attic that we didn't hear Owen Meany creep up the attic stairs and open the trapdoor. I can imagine what Owen was thinking; he was probably waiting to be noticed so that he wouldn't have to announce himself – so that the very first thing my cousins would know about him wouldn't be that voice. On the other hand, the sight of how small and peculiar he was might have been an equal shock to my cousins. Owen must have been weighing these two ways of introducing himself: whether to speak up, which was always startling, or whether to wait until one of them saw him, which might be more than startling. Owen told me later that he just stood by the trapdoor – which he had closed loudly, on purpose, hoping that the *door* would get our attention. But we didn't notice the trapdoor.

Simon had been pumping the foot pedals of the sewing machine so vigorously that the needle and bobbin were a blur of activity, and Noah had managed to shove Hester's arm too close to the plunging needle and thread, so that the sleeve of Hester's blouse had been stitched to the piece of sample cloth she'd been sewing, and it was necessary for her to take her blouse off – in order to free herself from the machine, which Simon, insanely, refused to stop pedaling. While Owen was watching us, Noah was whacking Simon about his ears, to make him stop with the foot pedals, and Hester was standing in her T-shirt, tensed and flushed, wailing about her only white blouse, from which she was trying to extract a very random pattern of purple thread. And I was saying that if we didn't stop making such a racket, we could expect a ferocious lecture from Grandmother – regarding the resale value of her antique sewing machine.

All this time, Owen Meany was standing by the trapdoor, observing us – alternately getting up the nerve to introduce himself, and deciding to bolt for home before any of us noticed that he was there. At that moment, my cousins must have seemed even worse than his worst dreams about them. It was shocking how Simon loved to be beaten; I never saw a boy whose best defense against the beating routinely administered by an older brother was to adore being beaten. Just as much as he loved to roll down mountains and to be flung off sawdust piles and to ski so wildly that he struck glancing blows to trees, Simon thrived under a hail of Noah's punches. It was almost always necessary for Noah to draw blood before Simon would beg for mercy – and if blood was drawn, somehow Simon had won; the shame was Noah's then. Now Simon appeared committed to pedaling the sewing machine into destruction – both hands gripping the tabletop, his eyes squinted shut against Noah's pounding fists, his knees pumping as furiously as if he were pedaling a bicycle in too-low a gear down a steep hill. The savagery with which Noah hit his brother could easily have misled any visitor regarding Noah's truly relaxed disposition and steadily noble character; Noah had learned that striking his brother was a workout requiring patience, deliberation, and strategy – it was no good giving Simon a bloody nose in a hurry; better to hit him where it hurt, but where he didn't bleed easily; better to wear him down.

But I suspect that Hester must have impressed Owen Meany most of all. In her T-shirt, there was little doubt that she would one day have an impressive bosom; its early blossoming was as apparent as her manly biceps. And the way she tore the thread out of her damaged blouse with her teeth – snarling and cursing in the process, as if she were eating her blouse – must have demonstrated to Owen the full potential of Hester's dangerous mouth; at that moment, her basic rapaciousness was quite generously displayed.

Naturally, my pleas regarding the inevitable, grandmotherly reprimand were not only unheeded; they went as unnoticed as Owen Meany, who stood with his hands clasped behind his back, the sun from the attic skylight shining through his protrusive ears, which were a glowing pink – the sunlight so bright that the tiny veins and blood vessels in his ears appeared to be illuminated from within. The powerful morning sun struck Owen's head from above, and from a little behind him, so that the light itself seemed to be presenting him. In exasperation with my unresponsive cousins, I looked up from the sewing machine and saw Owen standing there. With his hands clasped behind his back, he looked as armless as Watahantowet, and in that blaze of sunlight he looked like a gnome plucked fresh from a fire, with his ears still aflame. I drew in my breath, and Hester – with her raging mouth full of purple thread – looked up at that instant and saw Owen, too. She screamed.

'I didn't think he was *human*,' she told me later. And from that moment of his introduction to my cousins, I would frequently consider the issue of exactly how human Owen Meany was; there is no doubt that, in the dazzling configurations of the sun that poured through the attic skylight, he looked like a descending angel – a tiny but fiery god, sent to adjudicate the errors of our ways.

When Hester screamed, she frightened Owen so much that he screamed back at her – and when Owen screamed, my cousins were not only introduced to his rare voice; their movements were suddenly arrested. Except for the hairs on the backs of their necks, they froze – as they would if they'd heard a cat being slowly run over by a car. And from deep in a distant part of the great house, my grandmother spoke out: 'Merciful Heavens, it's that boy again!'

I was trying to catch my breath, to say, 'This is my best friend, the one I told you about,' because I had never seen my cousins gape at anyone with such open mouths – and, in Hester's case, a mouth from which spilled much purple thread – but Owen was quicker.

'WELL, IT SEEMS I HAVE INTERRUPTED WHATEVER GAME THAT WAS YOU WERE PLAYING,' Owen said. 'MY NAME IS OWEN MEANY AND I'M YOUR COUSIN'S BEST FRIEND. PERHAPS HE'S TOLD YOU ALL ABOUT ME. I'VE CERTAINLY HEARD ALL ABOUT YOU. YOU MUST BE NOAH, THE OLDEST,' Owen said; he held out his hand to Noah, who shook it mutely. 'AND OF COURSE YOU'RE SIMON, THE NEXT OLDEST – BUT YOU'RE JUST AS BIG

AND EVEN A LITTLE WILDER THAN YOUR BROTHER. HELLO, SIMON,' Owen said, holding out his hand to Simon, who was panting and sweating from his furious journey on the sewing machine, but who quickly took Owen's hand and shook it. 'AND OF COURSE YOU'RE HESTER,' Owen said, his eyes averted. 'I'VE HEARD A LOT ABOUT YOU, AND YOU'RE JUST AS PRETTY AS I EXPECTED.'

'Thank you,' Hester mumbled, pulling thread out of her mouth, tucking her T-shirt into her blue jeans.

My cousins stared at him, and I feared the worst; but I suddenly realized what small towns are. They are places where you grow up with the peculiar – you live next to the strange and the unlikely for so long that everything and everyone become commonplace. My cousins were both small-towners and outsiders; they had not grown up with Owen Meany, who was so strange to them that he inspired awe – yet they were no more likely to fall upon him, or to devise ways to torture him, than it was likely for a herd of cattle to attack a cat. And in addition to the brightness of the sun that shone upon him, Owen's face was blood-red – throbbing, I presumed, from his riding his bike into town; for a late November bike ride down Maiden Hill, given the prevailing wind off the Squamscott, was bitter cold. And even before Thanksgiving, the weather had been cold enough to freeze the freshwater part of the river; there was black ice all the way from Gravesend to Kensington Corners.

'WELL, I'VE BEEN THINKING ABOUT WHAT WE COULD DO,' Owen announced, and my unruly cousins gave him their complete attention. 'THE RIVER IS FROZEN, SO THE SKATING IS VERY GOOD, AND I KNOW YOU ENJOY VERY ACTIVE THINGS LIKE THAT – THAT YOU ENJOY THINGS LIKE SPEED AND DANGER AND COLD WEATHER. SO SKATING IS ONE IDEA,' he said, 'AND EVEN THOUGH THE RIVER IS FROZEN, I'M SURE THERE ARE CRACKS SOMEWHERE, AND EVEN PLACES WHERE THERE ARE HOLES OF OPEN WATER – I FELL IN ONE LAST YEAR. I'M NOT SUCH A GOOD SKATER, BUT I'D BE HAPPY TO GO WITH YOU. EVEN THOUGH I'M GETTING OVER A COLD, SO I SUPPOSE I SHOULDN'T BE OUTSIDE FOR LONG PERIODS OF TIME IN THIS WEATHER.'

'No!' Hester said. 'If you're getting over a cold, you should stay inside. We should play indoors. We don't have to go skating. We go skating all the time.'

'Yes!' Noah agreed. 'We should do something indoors, if Owen's got a cold.'

'Indoors is best!' Simon said. 'Owen should get over his cold.' Perhaps my cousins were all relieved to hear that Owen was 'getting over a cold' because they thought this might partially explain the hypnotic awfulness of Owen's voice; I could have told them that Owen's voice was uninfluenced by his having a cold – and his 'getting over a cold' was news to me – but I was so relieved to see my cousins behaving respectfully that I had no desire to undermine Owen's effect on them.

'WELL, I'VE BEEN THINKING THAT INDOORS WOULD BE BEST, TOO,' Owen said, 'AND UNFORTUNATELY I REALLY CAN'T INVITE YOU TO MY HOUSE, BECAUSE THERE'S REALLY NOTHING TO DO IN THE HOUSE, AND BECAUSE MY FATHER RUNS A GRANITE QUARRY, HE'S RATHER STRICT ABOUT THE EQUIPMENT AND THE QUARRIES THEMSELVES, WHICH ARE OUTDOORS. ANYWAY. INDOORS, AT MY HOUSE, WOULD NOT BE A LOT OF FUN BECAUSE MY PARENTS ARE RATHER STRANGE ABOUT CHILDREN.'

'That's no problem!' Noah blurted.

'Don't worry!' Simon said. 'There's lots to do here, in this house.'

'Everyone's parents are strange!' Hester told Owen reassuringly, but I couldn't think of anything to say. In the years I'd known Owen, the issue of how strange his parents were – not only 'about children' – had never been discussed between us. It seemed, rather, the accepted knowledge of the town, not to be mentioned – except in passing, or in parentheses, or as an aside among intimates.

'WELL, I'VE BEEN THINKING THAT WE COULD PUT ON YOUR GRANDFATHER'S CLOTHES – YOU'VE TOLD YOUR COUSINS ABOUT THE CLOTHES?' Owen asked me; but I hadn't. I thought they would think that dressing up in Grandfather's clothes was either baby play, or morbid, or both; or that they would surely destroy the clothes, discovering that merely dressing up in them was insufficiently violent – therefore leading them to a game, the object of which was to rip the clothes off each other; whoever was naked last *won*.

'Grandfather's clothes?' Noah said with unaccustomed reverence.

Simon shivered; Hester nervously plucked purple thread from here and there.

And Owen Meany – at the moment, our leader – said, 'WELL, THERE'S ALSO THE CLOSET WHERE THE CLOTHES ARE KEPT. IT CAN BE SCARY IN THERE, IN THE DARK, AND WE COULD PLAY SOME KIND OF GAME WHERE ONE OF US HIDES AND ONE OF US HAS TO FIND WHOEVER IT IS – IN THE DARK. WELL,' Owen said, 'THAT COULD BE INTERESTING.'

'Yes! Hiding in the dark!' Simon said.

'I didn't know those were Grandfather's clothes in there,' Hester said.

'Do you think the clothes are haunted, Hester?' Noah asked.

'Shut up,' Hester said.

'Let Hester hide in there, in the dark,' Simon said, 'and we'll take turns trying to find her.'

'I don't want you pawing around in the dark for me,' Hester said.

'Hester, we just want to find you before you find us,' Noah said.

'No, it's who touches who first!' Simon said.

'You touch me, I'll pull your *doink*, Simon,' Hester said.

'Whoa!' Noah said. 'That's it! That's the game! We got to find Hester before she pulls our *doinks*.'

'Hester the Molester!' Simon said predictably.

'Only if I'm allowed to get used to the dark!' Hester said. 'I get to have an advantage! I'm allowed to get used to the dark – and whoever's looking for me comes into the closet with no chance to get used to how dark it is.'

'THERE'S A FLASHLIGHT,' Owen Meany said nervously. 'MAYBE WE COULD USE A FLASHLIGHT, BECAUSE IT WOULD STILL BE *PRETTY* DARK.'

'No flashlight!' Hester said.

'No!' Simon said. 'Whoever goes into the closet after Hester gets the flashlight shined in his face before he goes in – so he's blind, so he's the *opposite* of being used to the dark!'

'Good idea!' Noah said.

'I get as long as I need to get myself hidden,' Hester said. '*And* to get used to the dark.'

'No!' Simon said. 'We'll count to twenty.'

'A hundred!' Hester said.

'Fifty,' Noah said; so it was fifty. Simon started counting, but Hester hit him.

'You've got to wait till I'm completely inside the closet,' she said.

As she moved toward the closet, she had to brush past Owen Meany, and a curious thing happened to her when she was next to him. Hester stood still and put her hand out to Owen – her big paw, uncharacteristically tentative and gentle, reached out and touched his face, as if there were a force in Owen's immediate vicinity that compelled the passerby to touch him. Hester touched him, and she smiled – Owen's little face was level with those nubbins of Hester's early bosom, which appeared to be implanted under her T-shirt. Owen was quite accustomed to people feeling compelled to touch him, but in Hester's case he retreated a trifle anxiously from her touch – though not so much that she was offended.

Then Hester went clomping into the closet, stumbling over the shoes, and we heard her rustling among the clothes, and the hangers squeaking on the metal rods, and what sounded like the hatboxes sliding over the overhead shelves – once she said, 'Shit!' And another time, 'What's that?' By the time the noises quieted down, we had Simon completely dazed under the flashlight's close-up glare; Simon was eager to be first, and by the time we shoved him into the closet, he was certifiably blind – even if he'd been trying to walk around in the daylight. No sooner was Simon inside the closet, and we'd closed the door behind him, than we heard Hester attack him; she must have grabbed his 'doink' harder than she'd meant to, because he howled with more pain than surprise, and there were tears in his eyes, and he was still doubled over and holding fast to his private parts when he tumbled out of the closet and rolled upon the attic floor.

'Jesus, Hester!' Noah said. 'What did you do to him?'

'I didn't mean to,' came her voice from the dark closet.

'No fair pulling the doink *and* the balls!' Simon cried, still doubled up on the floor.

'I didn't mean to,' she repeated sweetly.

'You bitch!' Simon said.

'You're always rough with *me*, Simon,' Hester said.

'You can't be rough with balls and *doinks*!' Noah said.

But Hester was not talking; we could hear her positioning herself for her next attack, and Noah whispered to Owen and me that since there were two doors to the closet, we should surprise Hester by entering from the other door.

'WHO IS *WE*?' Owen whispered.

Noah pointed to him, silently, and I shone the flashlight into Owen's wide and darting eyes, which gave his face the sudden anxiety of a cornered mouse.

'No fair grabbing so *hard*, Hester!' Noah called, but Hester didn't answer.

'SHE'S JUST TRYING TO CONCEAL HER HIDING PLACE,' Owen whispered – to reassure himself.

Then Noah and I flung Owen into the closet through the other door: the closet was L-shaped, and by Owen's entering on the short arm of the L, Noah and I figured that he would not encounter Hester before the first corner – and only then if Hester managed to move, because her hiding place would surely be nearer the top of the L.

'No fair using the other door!' Hester promptly called, which Noah and I felt was further to Owen's advantage, since she must have given away her position in the closet – at least, to some general degree. Then there was silence. I knew what Owen was doing: he was hoping that his eyes would grow used to the dark before Hester found him, and he wasn't going to begin to move – to try to find her – until he could see a little.

'What in hell's going on in there?' Simon asked, but there was no sound.

Then we detected the occasional bumping of one of Grandfather's hundreds of shoes. Then silence. Then another slight movement of shoes. As I learned later, Owen was crawling on all fours, because he most feared – and expected – an attack from one of the large, overhead shelves. He had no way of knowing that Hester had stretched herself out on the floor of the closet, and that she had covered herself with one of Grandfather's topcoats, over which she'd positioned the usual number of shoes. She lay motionless, and – except for her head and her hands – invisible. But her head was pointed the wrong way; that is, she had to roll her eyes up into the top of her head and watch Owen Meany approaching her by staring at him upside down, looking over her own forehead and her considerable head of hair. What Owen touched first, as he approached her on all fours, was that live and kinky tangle of Hester's hair, which suddenly moved under his little hand – and Hester's arms reached up over her head, seizing Owen around his waist.

To her credit, Hester never had any intention of grabbing Owen's 'doink'; but finding it so easy to hold Owen around the waist, Hester decided to run her hands up his ribs and tickle him. Owen looked extremely susceptible to tickling, which he was, and Hester's gesture was of the friendliest of intentions – especially for Hester – but the combination of putting his hand on live hair, in the dark, coupled with being tickled by a girl who, Owen *thought*, was merely tickling him *en route* to grabbing his doink, was too much for him; he wet his pants.

The instant recognition of Owen's accident surprised Hester so much that she dropped him. He fell on top of her – and he wriggled free of her, and out of the closet, and through the trapdoor and down the stairs. Owen ran through the house so fast and noiselessly that even my grandmother failed to notice him; and if my mother hadn't happened to be looking out the kitchen window, she would not have seen him – with his jacket unzipped, and his boots unlaced, and his hat on crooked – mounting his bicycle with some difficulty in the icy wind.

'Jesus, Hester!' Noah said. 'What did you do to him?'

'*I* know what she did to him!' Simon said.

'It wasn't that,' Hester said simply. 'I just tickled him, and he wet his pants.' She did not report this to mock Owen, and – as a testimony to my cousins' basically decent natures – the news was not greeted with their usual rowdiness, which I associated with Sawyer Depot as firmly as various forms of skiing and collision.

'The poor little guy!' Simon said.

'I didn't mean to,' Hester said.

My mother called to me and I had to go tell her what had happened to Owen, whereupon she made me put on my outdoor clothes while she started the car. I thought I knew the route Owen would take home, but he must have been pedaling very hard because we did not overtake him by the Gas Works on Water Street, and when we passed Dewey Street without sighting him – and there was no sign of him at Salem Street, either – I began to think he had taken the

Swasey Parkway out of town. And so we doubled back, along the Squamscott, but he wasn't there.

We finally found him, already out of town, laboring up Maiden Hill; we slowed down when we saw his red-and-black wool hunter's jacket and the matching checkered cap with the earflaps protruding, and by the time we pulled alongside him, he had run out of steam and had gotten off to walk his bicycle. He knew it was us without looking at us but he wouldn't stop walking – so my mother drove slowly beside him, and I rolled down the window.

'IT WAS AN ACCIDENT, I JUST GOT TOO EXCITED, I HAD TOO MUCH ORANGE JUICE FOR BREAKFAST – AND YOU KNOW I CAN'T STAND BEING TICKLED,' Owen said. 'NOBODY SAID ANYTHING ABOUT TICKLING.'

'Please don't go home, Owen,' my mother said.

'Everything's all right,' I told him. 'My cousins are very sorry.'

'I PEED ON HESTER!' Owen said. 'AND I'M GOING TO GET IN TROUBLE AT HOME,' he said – still walking his bike at a good pace. 'MY FATHER GETS MAD ABOUT PEEING, HE SAYS I'M NOT A BABY ANYMORE, BUT SOMETIMES I GET EXCITED.'

'Owen, I'll wash and dry your clothes at our house,' my mother told him. 'You can wear something of Johnny's while yours are drying.'

'NOTHING OF JOHNNY'S WILL FIT ME,' Owen said. 'AND I HAVE TO TAKE A BATH.'

'You can take a bath at our house, Owen,' I told him. 'Please come back.'

'I have some outgrown things of Johnny's that will fit you, Owen,' my mother said.

'BABY CLOTHES, I SUPPOSE,' Owen said, but he stopped walking; he leaned his head on his bike's handlebars.

'Please get in the car, Owen,' my mother said. I got out and helped him put his bicycle in the back, and then he slid into the front seat, between my mother and me.

'I WANTED TO MAKE A GOOD IMPRESSION BECAUSE I WANTED TO GO TO SAWYER DEPOT,' he said. 'NOW YOU'LL NEVER TAKE ME.'

I found it incredible that he still wanted to go, but my mother said, 'Owen, you can come with us to Sawyer Depot, anytime.'

'JOHNNY DOESN'T WANT ME TO COME,' he told Mother – as if I weren't there in the car with them.

'It's not that, Owen,' I said. 'It's that I thought my cousins would be too much for you.' And on the evidence of him wetting his pants, I did *not* say, it struck me that my cousins *were* too much for him. 'That was a very mild game for my cousins, Owen,' I added.

'DO YOU THINK I CARE WHAT THEY DO TO ME?' he shouted; he stamped his little foot on the drive-shaft hump. 'DO YOU THINK I CARE IF THEY START AN AVALANCHE WITH ME?' he screamed. 'WHEN DO I GET TO GO *ANYWHERE*? IF I DIDN'T GO TO SCHOOL OR TO CHURCH OR TO EIGHTY FRONT STREET, I'D NEVER GET OUT OF MY HOUSE!' he cried. 'IF YOUR MOTHER DIDN'T TAKE ME TO THE BEACH, I'D NEVER GET OUT OF TOWN. AND I'VE NEVER BEEN TO THE MOUNTAINS,' he said. 'I'VE NEVER EVEN BEEN ON A TRAIN! DON'T YOU THINK I MIGHT LIKE GOING ON A TRAIN – TO THE MOUNTAINS?' he yelled.

My mother stopped the car and hugged him, and kissed him, and told him he was always welcome to come with us, anywhere we went; and I rather awkwardly put my arm around him, and we just sat that way in the car, until he had composed himself sufficiently for his return to 80 Front Street, where he marched in the back door, past Lydia's room and the maids fussing in the kitchen, up the back stairs past the maids' rooms, to my room and my bathroom, where he closed himself in and drew a deep bath. He handed me his sodden clothes, and I brought the clothes to the maids, who began their work on them. My mother knocked on the bathroom door, and, looking the other way, she extended her arm into the room, where Owen took a stack of my outgrown clothes from her – they were not baby clothes, as he had feared; they were just extremely small clothes.

'What shall we do with him?' Hester asked while we were waiting for Owen to join us in the upstairs den – or so it had been called, 'the den,' when my grandfather was alive; it was a children's room whenever my cousins visited.

'We'll do whatever he wants,' Noah said.

'That's what we did the last time!' Simon said.

'Not quite,' Hester said.

'WELL, I'VE BEEN THINKING,' Owen said when he

walked into the den – even pinker than usual; he was spanking clean, as they say, with his hair slicked back. In his stocking feet, he was slipping a little on the hardwood floor; and when he reached the old Oriental, he stood with one foot balanced on top of the other, twisting his hips back and forth as he talked – his hands, like butterflies, flitting up and down between his waist and his shoulders. 'I APOLOGIZE FOR BECOMING OVEREXCITED. I THINK I KNOW A GAME THAT WOULD NOT BE QUITE AS EXCITING FOR ME, BUT AT THE SAME TIME I THINK IT WOULD NOT BE BORING FOR YOU,' he said. 'YOU SEE, ONE OF YOU GETS TO HIDE *ME* – SOMEWHERE, IT COULD BE *ANYWHERE* – AND THE OTHERS HAVE TO FIND ME. AND WHO-EVER CAN FIND A PLACE TO HIDE ME THAT TAKES THE LONGEST TIME FOR THE OTHERS TO FIND ME – WHOEVER THAT IS *WINS*. YOU SEE, IT'S PRETTY EASY TO FIND PLACES IN THIS HOUSE TO HIDE ME – BECAUSE THIS HOUSE IS HUGE AND I'M SMALL,' Owen added.

'I go first,' Hester said. 'I get to hide him first.' No one argued; wherever she hid him, we never found him. Noah and Simon and I – we thought it would be easy to find him. I knew every inch of my grandmother's house, and Noah and Simon knew almost everything about Hester's diabolical mind; but we couldn't find him. Hester stretched out on the couch in the den, looking at old issues of *Life* magazine, growing more and more content as we searched and searched, and darkness fell; I even expressed to Hester my concern that she had put Owen somewhere where he might have run out of air, or – as the hours dragged on – where he would suffer severe cramps from having to maintain an uncomfortable position. But Hester dismissed these concerns with a wave of her hand, and when it was suppertime, we had to give up; Hester made us wait in the downstairs front hall, and she went and got Owen, who was very happy and walking without a limp, and breathing without difficulty – although his hair looked slept on. He stayed for supper, and he told me after we'd eaten that he wouldn't mind staying overnight, too – my mother invited him to stay, because (she said) his clothes hadn't completely dried.

And although I asked him – 'Where'd she hide you? Just give me a clue! Tell me what part of the house, just tell me which *floor*!' – he wouldn't disclose his triumph. He was wide awake, and in no mood to sleep, and he was irritatingly philosophic regarding the true character of my cousins, whom he said I had failed to present fairly to him.

'YOU HAVE REALLY MISJUDGED THEM,' he lectured me. 'PERHAPS WHAT YOU CALL THEIR WILDNESS IS JUST A MATTER OF LACK OF DIRECTION. SOMEONE HAS TO GIVE ANY GROUP OF PEOPLE DIRECTION, YOU KNOW.' I lay there thinking I couldn't wait until he came to Sawyer Depot, and my cousins got him on skis and simply pointed him downhill; that might shut him up about providing adequate 'direction.' But there was no turning him off; he just babbled on and on.

I got drowsy, and turned my back to him, and therefore I was confused when I heard him say, 'IT'S HARD TO GO TO SLEEP WITHOUT IT, ONCE YOU GET USED TO IT – ISN'T IT?'

'Without what?' I asked him. 'Used to what, Owen?'

'THE ARMADILLO,' he said.

And so that day after Thanksgiving, when Owen Meany met my cousins, provided me with two very powerful images of Owen – especially on the night I tried to get to sleep after the foul ball had killed my mother. I lay in bed knowing that Owen would be thinking about my mother, too, and that he would be thinking not only of me but also of Dan Needham – of how much we both would miss her – and if Owen was thinking of Dan, I knew that he would be thinking about the armadillo, too.

It was also important: that day when my mother and I chased after Owen in the car – and I saw the posture of his body jerking on his bicycle, trying to pedal up Maiden Hill; and I saw how he faltered, and had to get off the bike and walk it the rest of the way. That day provided me with a cold-weather picture of how Owen must have looked on that warm, summer evening when he was struggling home after the Little League game – with his baseball uniform plastered to his back. What was he going to tell his parents about the game?

It would take years for me to remember the decision regarding whether I should spend the night after that fatal game with Dan Needham, in the apartment that he and my mother had moved into, with me, after they'd married – it was a faculty apartment in one of the academy dormitories

– or whether I would be more comfortable spending that terrible night back in my old room in my grandmother's house at 80 Front Street. So many of the details surrounding that game would take years to remember!

Anyway, Dan Needham and my grandmother agreed that it would be better for me to spend the night at 80 Front Street, and so – in addition to the disorientation of waking up the next morning, after very little sleep, and gradually realizing that the dream of my mother being killed by a baseball that Owen Meany hit was *not* a dream – I faced the further disorientation of not immediately knowing where I was. It was very much like waking up as a kind of traveler in science fiction, someone who had traveled 'back in time' – because I had grown used to waking up in my room in Dan Needham's apartment.

And as if all this weren't sufficiently bewildering, there was a noise I had never before associated with 80 Front Street; it was a noise in the driveway, and my bedroom windows didn't face the driveway, so I had to get out of bed and leave my room to see what the noise was. I was pretty sure I knew. I had heard that noise many times at the Meany Granite Quarry; it was the unmistakable, very lowest gear of the huge, flatbed hauler – the truck Mr Meany used to carry the granite slabs, the curbstones and cornerstones, and the monuments. And sure enough, the Meany Granite Company truck was in my grandmother's driveway – taking up the whole driveway – and it was loaded with granite and gravestones.

I could easily imagine my grandmother's indignation – if she was up, and saw the truck there. I could just hear her saying, 'How incredibly tasteless of that man! My daughter not dead a day and what is he doing – giving us a tombstone? I suppose he's already carved the letters!' That is actually what *I* thought.

But Mr Meany did not get out of the cab of his truck. It was Owen who got out on the passenger side, and he walked around to the rear of the flatbed and removed several large cartons from the rest of the load; the cartons were clearly not full of granite or Owen would not have been able to lift them off by himself. But he managed this, and brought all the cartons to the step by the back door, where I was sure he was going to ring the bell. I could still hear his voice saying 'I'M SORRY!' – while my head was hidden under Mr Chickering's warm-up jacket – and as much as I wanted to see Owen, I knew I would burst into tears as soon as he spoke, or as soon as I had to speak to him. And therefore I was relieved when he didn't ring the bell; he left the cartons at the back door and ran quickly to the cab, and Mr Meany drove the granite truck out of the driveway, still in the very lowest gear.

In the cartons were all of Owen's baseball cards, his entire collection. My grandmother was appalled, but for several years she didn't understand Owen or appreciate him; to her, he was 'that boy,' or 'that little guy,' or 'that voice.' I knew the baseball cards were Owen's favorite things, they were what amounted to his treasure – I could instantly identify with how everything connected to the game of baseball had changed for him, as it had changed for me (although I'd never loved the game as Owen had loved it). I knew without speaking to Owen that neither of us would ever play Little League ball again, and that there was some necessary ritual ahead of us both – wherein we would need to throw away our bats and gloves and uniforms, and every stray baseball there was to be found around our houses and yards (except for *that* baseball, which I suspected Owen had relegated to a museum-piece status).

But I needed to talk to Dan Needham about the baseball cards, because they were Owen's most prized possessions – indeed, his only prized possessions – and since my mother's accident had made baseball a game of death, what did Owen want me to do with his baseball cards? Did they merely represent how he was washing his hands of the great American pastime, or did he want me to assuage my grief by indulging in the pleasure I would derive from *burning* all those baseball cards? On that day, it would have been a pleasure to burn them.

'He wants you to give them back,' Dan Needham said. I knew from the first that my mother had picked a winner when she picked Dan, but it was not until the day after my mother's death that I knew she'd picked a smart man, too. Of course, that's what Owen expected of me: he gave me his baseball cards to show me how sorry he was about the accident, and how much he was hurting, too – because Owen had loved my mother almost as much as I did, I was sure, and to give me all his cards was his way of saying that he loved me enough to trust me with his famous collection. But, naturally, he wanted all the cards back!

Dan Needham said, 'Let's look at a few of them. I'll bet they're all in some kind of order – even in these boxes.' And, yes, they were – Dan and I couldn't figure out the exact rules under which they were ordered, but the cards were organized under an *extreme* system; they were alphabetized by the names of players, but the hitters, I mean the *big* hitters, were alphabetized in a group of their own; and your golden-glove-type fielders, they had a category all to themselves, too; and the pitchers were all together. There even seemed to be some subindexing related to the age of the players; but Dan and I found it difficult to look at the cards for very long – so many of the players faced the camera with their lethal bats resting confidently on their shoulders.

I know many people, today, who instinctively cringe at any noise even faintly resembling a gunshot or an exploding bomb – a car backfires, the handle of a broom or a shovel *whacks* flat against a cement or a linoleum floor, a kid detonates a firecracker in an empty trash can, and my friends cover their heads, primed (as we all are, today) for the terrorist attack or the random assassin. But not me; and never Owen Meany. All because of one badly played baseball game, one unlucky swing – and the most unlikely contact – all because of one lousy foul ball, among millions, Owen Meany and I were permanently conditioned to flinch at the sound of a different kind of gunshot: that much-loved and most American sound of summer, the good old crack of the bat!

And so, as I often would, I took Dan Needham's advice. We loaded the cartons of Owen's baseball cards into the car, and we tried to think of the least conspicuous time of day when we could drive out to the Meany Granite Quarry – when we would not necessarily need to greet Mr Meany, or disturb Mrs Meany's grim profile in any of several windows, or actually need to talk with Owen. Dan understood that I loved Owen, and that I wanted to talk with him – most of all – but that it was a conversation, for both Owen's sake and mine, that was best to delay. But before we finished loading the baseball cards in the car, Dan Needham asked me, 'What are you giving *him*?'

'What?' I said.

'To show him that you love him,' Dan Needham said.

'That's what he was showing you. What have you got to give him?'

Of course I knew what I had that would show Owen that I loved him; I knew what my armadillo meant to him, but it was a little awkward to 'give' Owen the armadillo in front of Dan Needham, who'd given it to me – and what if Owen didn't give it back? I'd needed Dan's help to understand that I was supposed to return the damn baseball cards. What if Owen decided he was supposed to *keep* the armadillo?

'The main thing is, Johnny,' Dan Needham said, 'you have to show Owen that you love him enough to trust *anything* with him – to not care if you do or don't get it back. It's got to be something he *knows* you want back. That's what makes it special.'

'Suppose I give him the armadillo?' I said. 'Suppose he keeps it?'

Dan Needham sat down on the front bumper of the car. It was a Buick station wagon, forest green with real wooden panels on the sides and on the tailgate, and a chrome grille that looked like the gaping mouth of a voracious fish; from where Dan was sitting, the Buick appeared ready to eat him – and Dan looked tired enough to be eaten without much of a struggle. I'm sure he'd been up crying all night, like me – and, unlike me, he'd probably been up drinking, too. He looked awful. But he said very patiently and very carefully, 'Johnny, I would be honored if anything I gave you could actually be used for something important – if it were to have any special purpose, I'd be very proud.'

That was when I first began to think about certain events or specific things being 'important' and having 'special purpose.' Until then, the notion that anything had a designated, much less a special purpose would have been cuckoo to me. I was not what was commonly called a believer then, and I am a believer now; I believe in God, and I believe in the 'special purpose' of certain events or specific things. I observe all holy days, which only the most old-fashioned Anglicans call red-letter days. It was a red-letter day, fairly recently, when I had reason to think of Owen Meany – it was January 25, 1987, when the lessons proper for the conversion of St Paul reminded me of Owen. The Lord says to Jeremiah,

> Before I formed you in the womb
> I knew you,
> and before you were born
> I consecrated you;
> I appointed you a prophet to the
> nations.

But Jeremiah says he doesn't know how to speak; he's 'only a youth,' Jeremiah says. Then the Lord straightens him out about that; the Lord says,

> Do not say, 'I am only a youth';
> for to all to whom I send you you
> shall go,
> and whatever I command you you
> shall speak.
> Be not afraid of them,
> for I am with you to deliver you,
> says the Lord.

Then the Lord touches Jeremiah's mouth, and says,

> Behold, I have put my words in
> your mouth.
> See, I have set you this day over
> nations and over kingdoms,
> to pluck up and to break down,
> to destroy and to overthrow,
> to build and to plant.

It is on red-letter days, especially, that I think about Owen; sometimes I think about him too intensely, and that's usually when I skip a Sunday service, or two – and I try not to pick up my prayer book for a while. I suppose the conversion of St Paul has a special effect on a convert like me.

And how can I *not* think of Owen – when I read Paul's letter to the Galatians, that part where Paul says, 'And I was still not known by sight to the churches of Christ in Judea; they only heard it said, "He who once persecuted us is now preaching the faith he once tried to destroy." And they glorified God because of me.'

How well I know that feeling! I trust in God because of Owen Meany.

It was because I trusted Dan Needham that I gave the armadillo to Owen. I put it in a brown paper bag, which I put inside another brown paper bag, and although I had no doubt that Owen would know exactly what it was, before he opened the bags, I gave brief consideration to how shocked his mother might be if *she* opened the bags; but it was not her business to open the bags, I figured.

Owen and I were eleven; we had no other way to articulate what we felt about what had happened to my mother. He gave me his baseball cards, but he really wanted them back, and I gave him my stuffed armadillo, which I certainly hoped he'd give back to me – all because it was impossible for us to say to each other how we really felt. How did it feel to hit a ball that hard – and then realize that the ball had killed your best friend's mother? How did it feel to see my mother sprawled in the grass, and to have the moronic chief of police complain about the missing baseball – and calling that stupid ball 'the instrument of death' and 'the murder weapon'? Owen and I couldn't have *talked* about those things – at least, not then. So we gave each other our best-loved possessions, and hoped to get them back. When you think of it, that's not so silly.

By my calculations, Owen was a day late returning the armadillo; he kept it overnight for two nights, which in my view was one night too many. But he *did* return it. Once again I heard the lowest-possible gear of the granite truck; once again, there was an early-morning drop-off at 80 Front Street, before Mr Meany went ahead with the rest of the day's heavy business. And there were the same brown paper bags that I had used on the step by the back door; it was a little dangerous to leave the armadillo outside on the step, I thought, given the indiscriminate appetites of that certain Labrador retriever belonging to our neighbor Mr Fish. Then I remembered that Sagamore was dead.

But my greatest indignation was to follow: missing from the armadillo were the little animal's front claws – the most useful and impressive parts of its curious body. Owen had returned the armadillo, but he'd kept the claws!

Well – friendship being one thing, and the armadillo quite another – I was so outraged by this discovery that I needed to talk to Dan Needham. As always, Dan made himself available. He sat on the edge of my bed while I sniveled; without its claws, the beast could no longer stand upright – not without pitching forward and resting on its snout. There was virtually no position I could find for the armadillo that did not make the creature resemble a supplicant – not to mention, a wretched amputee. I was quite upset at how my best friend could have done this to me, until Dan Needham informed me that this was precisely what Owen *felt* he had done to me, and to himself: that we were both maimed and mutilated by what had happened to us.

'Your friend is most *original*,' Dan Needham said, with the greatest respect. 'Don't you see, Johnny? If he could, he would cut off his *hands* for you – that's how it makes him feel, to have *touched* that baseball bat, to have swung that bat with those results. It's how we *all* feel – you and me *and* Owen. We've lost a part of ourselves.' And Dan picked up the wrecked armadillo and began to experiment with it on my night table, trying – as I had tried – to find a position that allowed the beast to stand, or even to lie down, with any semblance of comfort or dignity; it was quite impossible. The thing had been crippled; it was rendered an invalid. And how had Owen arranged the claws? I wondered. What sort of terrible altarpiece had he constructed? Were the claws gripping the murderous baseball?

And so Dan and I became quite emotional, while we struggled to find a way to make the armadillo's appearance acceptable – but that was the point, Dan concluded: there was no way that any or all of this *was* acceptable. What had happened was unacceptable! Yet we still had to live with it.

'It's brilliant, really – it's absolutely original,' Dan kept muttering, until he fell asleep on the other twin bed in my room, where Owen had spent so many nights, and I covered him up and let him sleep. When my grandmother came to kiss me good night, she kissed Dan good night, too. Then, in the weak glow from the night-light, I discovered that by opening the shallow drawer under the top of the night table, I could position the armadillo in such a way that it was possible for me to imagine it was something else. Half in and half out of the drawer, the armadillo resembled a kind of aquatic creature – it was all head and torso; I could imagine that those were some sort of stunted flippers protruding where its claws had been.

Just before I fell asleep, I realized that everything Dan had said about Owen's intentions was correct. How much it has meant to my life that Dan Needham was almost never wrong! I was not as familiar with Wall's *History of Gravesend* as I became when I was eighteen and read the whole thing for myself; but I was familiar with those parts of it that Owen Meany considered 'important.' And just before I fell asleep, I also recognized my armadillo for what it was – in addition to all those things Dan had told me. My armadillo had been amputated to resemble Watahantowet's totem, the tragic and mysterious armless man – for weren't the Indians wise enough to understand that everything had its own soul, its own spirit?

It was Owen Meany who told me that only white men are vain enough to believe that human beings are unique because we have souls. According to Owen, Watahantowet knew better. Watahantowet believed that animals had souls, and that even the much-abused Squamscott River had a soul – Watahantowet knew that the land he sold to my ancestors was absolutely *full* of spirits. The rocks they had to move to plant a field – they were, forever after, restless and displaced spirits. And the trees they cut down to build their homes – they had a different spirit from the spirits that escaped those houses as the smoke from firewood. Watahantowet may have been the last resident of Gravesend, New Hampshire, who really understood what everything *cost*. Here, take my land! There go my arms!

It would take me years to learn everything that Owen Meany was thinking, and I didn't understand him very well that night. Now I know that the armadillo told me what Owen was thinking although Owen himself would not until we were both students at Gravesend Academy; it wasn't until then that I realized Owen had already conveyed his message to me – via the armadillo. Here is what Owen Meany (and the armadillo) said: 'GOD HAS TAKEN YOUR MOTHER. MY HANDS WERE THE INSTRUMENT. GOD HAS TAKEN MY HANDS. I AM GOD'S INSTRUMENT.'

How could it ever have occurred to me that a fellow eleven-year-old was thinking any such thing? That Owen Meany was a Chosen One was the furthest thing from my mind; that

Owen could even consider himself one of God's Appointed would have been a surprise to me. To have seen him up in the air, at Sunday school, you would not have thought he was at work on God's Assignment. And you must remember – forgetting about Owen – that at the age of eleven I did not believe there *were* 'chosen ones,' or that God 'appointed' anyone, or that God gave 'assignments.' As for Owen's belief that he was 'God's instrument,' I didn't know that there was other evidence upon which Owen was basing his conviction that he'd been specially selected to carry out the work of the Lord; but Owen's idea – that God's reasoning was somehow predetermining Owen's every move – came from much more than that one unlucky swing and crack of the bat. As you shall see.

Today – January 30, 1987 – it is snowing in Toronto; in the dog's opinion, Toronto is improved by snow. I enjoy walking the dog when it's snowing, because the dog's enthusiasm is infectious; in the snow, the dog establishes his territorial rights to the St Clair Reservoir as if he were the first dog to relieve himself there – an illusion that is made possible by the fresh snow covering the legion of dog turds for which the St Clair Reservoir is famous.

In the snow, the clock tower of Upper Canada College appears to preside over a preparatory school in a small New England town; when it's not snowing, the cars and buses on the surrounding roads are more numerous, the sounds of traffic are less muted, and the presence of downtown Toronto seems closer. In the snow, the view of the clock tower of Upper Canada College – especially from the distance of Kilbarry Road, or, closer, from the end of Frybrook Road – reminds me of the clock tower of the Main Academy Building in Gravesend; fastidious, sepulchral.

In the snow, there is something almost like New England about where I live on Russell Hill Road; granted, Torontonians do not favor white clapboard houses with dark-green or black shutters, but my grandmother's house, at 80 Front Street, was brick – Torontonians prefer brick and stone. Inexplicably, Torontonians clutter their brick and stone houses with too much trim, or with window trim *and* shutters – and they also carve their shutters with hearts or maple leaves – but the snow conceals these frills; and on some days, like today, when the snow is especially wet and heavy, the snow turns even the brick houses white. Toronto is sober, but not austere; Gravesend is austere, but also pretty; Toronto is not pretty, but in the snow Toronto can look like Gravesend – both pretty and austere.

And from my bedroom window on Russell Hill Road, I can see both Grace Church on-the-Hill and the Bishop Strachan chapel; how fitting that a boy whose childhood was divided by two churches should live out his present life in view of two more! But this suits me now; both churches are Anglican. The cold, gray stones of both Grace Church and The Bishop Strachan School are also improved by snow.

My grandmother liked to say that snow was 'healing' – that it healed everything. A typical Yankee point of view: if it snows a lot, snow must be good for you. In Toronto, it's good for me. And the little children sledding at the St Clair Reservoir: they remind me of Owen, too – because I have fixed Owen at a permanent size, which is the size he was when he was eleven, which was the size of an average five-year-old. But I should be careful not to give too much credit to the snow; there are so many things that remind me of Owen.

I avoid American newspapers and magazines, and American television – and other Americans in Toronto. But Toronto is not far enough away. Just the day before yesterday – January 28, 1987 – the front page of *The Globe and Mail* gave us a full account of President Ronald Reagan's State of the Union Message. Will I ever learn? When I see such things, I know I should simply not read them; I should pick up The Book of Common Prayer, instead. I should not give in to anger; but, God forgive me, I read the State of the Union Message. After almost twenty years in Canada, there are certain American lunatics who still fascinate me.

'There must be no Soviet beachhead in Central America,' President Reagan said. He also insisted that he would not sacrifice his proposed nuclear missiles in space – his beloved Star Wars plan – to a nuclear arms agreement with the Soviet Union. He even said that 'a key element of the U.S.–Soviet agenda' is 'more responsible Soviet conduct around the world' – as if the United States were a bastion of 'responsible conduct around the world'!

I believe that President Reagan can say these things only

because he knows that the American people will never hold him accountable for what he says; it is history that holds you accountable, and I've already expressed my opinion that Americans are not big on history. How many of them even remember their own, recent history? Was twenty years ago so long ago for Americans? Do they remember October 21, 1967? Fifty thousand antiwar demonstrators were in Washington; I was there; that was the 'March on the Pentagon' – remember? And two years later – in October of '69 – there were fifty thousand people in Washington again; they were carrying flashlights, they were asking for peace. There were a hundred thousand asking for peace in Boston Common; there were two hundred fifty thousand in New York. Ronald Reagan had not yet numbed the United States, but he had succeeded in putting California to sleep; he described the Vietnam protests as 'giving aid and comfort to the enemy.' As president, he still didn't know who the enemy was.

I now believe that Owen Meany always knew; he knew everything.

We were seniors at Gravesend Academy in February of 1962; we watched a lot of TV at 80 Front Street. President Kennedy said that U.S. advisers in Vietnam would return fire if fired upon.

'HOPE WE'RE *ADVISING* THE RIGHT GUYS,' Owen Meany said.

That spring, less than a month before Gravesend Academy's graduation exercises, the TV showed us a map of Thailand; five thousand U.S. Marines and fifty jet fighters were being sent there – 'in response to Communist expansion in Laos,' President Kennedy said.

'I HOPE WE KNOW WHAT WE'RE DOING,' said Owen Meany.

In the summer of '63, the summer following our first year at the university, the Buddhists in Vietnam were demonstrating; there were revolts. Owen and I saw our first self-immolation – on television. South Vietnamese government forces, led by Ngo Dinh Diem – the elected president – attacked several Buddhist pagodas; that was in August. In May, Diem's brother – Ngo Dinh Nhu, who ran the secret police force – had broken up a Buddhist celebration by killing eight children and one woman.

'DIEM IS A CATHOLIC,' Owen Meany announced. 'WHAT'S A CATHOLIC DOING AS PRESIDENT OF A COUNTRY OF BUDDHISTS?'

That was the summer that Henry Cabot Lodge became the U.S. ambassador to Vietnam; that was the summer that Lodge received a State Department cable advising him that the United States would 'no longer tolerate' Ngo Dinh Nhu's 'influence' on President Diem's regime. In two months, a military coup toppled Diem's South Vietnamese government; the next day, Diem and his brother, Nhu, were assassinated.

'IT LOOKS LIKE WE'VE BEEN *ADVISING* THE WRONG GUYS,' Owen said.

And the next summer, when we saw on TV the North Vietnamese patrol boats in the Tonkin Gulf – within two days, they attacked two U.S. destroyers – Owen said: 'DO WE THINK THIS IS A MOVIE?'

President Johnson asked Congress to give him the power to 'take all necessary measures to repel an armed attack against the forces of the United States and to prevent further aggression.' The Tonkin Gulf Resolution was approved by the House by a unanimous vote of 416 to 0; it passed the Senate by a vote of 88 to 2. But Owen Meany asked my grandmother's television set a question: 'DOES THAT MEAN THE PRESIDENT CAN DECLARE A WAR WITHOUT DECLARING IT?'

That New Year's Eve – I remember that Hester drank too much; she was throwing up – there were barely more than twenty thousand U.S. military personnel in Vietnam, and only a dozen (or so) had been killed. By the time the Congress put an end to the Tonkin Gulf Resolution – in May of 1970 – there had been more than half a million U.S. military personnel in Vietnam; and more than forty thousand of them were dead.

As early as 1965, Owen Meany detected a problem of strategy.

In March, the U.S. Air Force began Operation Rolling Thunder – to strike targets in North Vietnam; to stop the flow of supplies to the South – and the first American combat troops landed in Vietnam.

'THERE'S NO END TO THIS,' Owen said. 'THERE'S NO GOOD WAY TO END IT.'

On Christmas Day, President Johnson suspended Operation Rolling Thunder; he stopped the bombing. In a month, the bombing began again, and the Senate Foreign Relations Committee opened their televised hearings on the war. That was when my grandmother started paying attention.

In the fall of 1966, Operation Rolling Thunder was said to be 'closing in on Hanoi'; but Owen Meany said, 'I THINK HANOI CAN HANDLE IT.'

Do you remember Operation Tiger Hound? How about Operation Masher/White Wing/Than Phong II? That one produced 2,389 'known enemy casualties.' And then there was Operation Paul Revere/Than Phong 14 – not quite so successful, only 546 'known enemy casualties.' And how about Operation Maeng Ho 6? There were 6,161 'known enemy casualties.'

By New Year's Eve, 1966, a total of 6,644 U.S. military had been killed in action; it was Owen Meany who remembered that was 483 more casualties than the enemy had suffered in Operation Maeng Ho.

'How do you remember such things, Owen?' my grandmother asked him.

From Saigon, General Westmoreland was asking for 'fresh manpower'; Owen remembered that, too. According to the State Department, according to Dean Rusk – remember him? – we were 'winning a war of attrition.'

'THAT'S NOT THE KIND OF WAR WE WIN,' said Owen Meany.

By the end of '67, there were five hundred thousand U.S. military personnel in Vietnam. That was when General Westmoreland said, 'We have reached an important point where the end begins to come into view.'

'*WHAT* END?' Owen Meany asked the general. 'WHAT HAPPENED TO THE "FRESH MANPOWER"? REMEMBER THE "FRESH MANPOWER"?'

I now believe that Owen remembered everything; a part of knowing everything *is* remembering everything.

Do you remember the Tet Offensive? That was in January of '68; 'Tet' is a traditional Vietnamese holiday – the equivalent of our Christmas and New Year's – and it was usual, during the Vietnam War, to observe a cease-fire for the holiday season. But that year the North Vietnamese attacked more than a hundred South Vietnamese towns – more than thirty provincial capitals. That was the year President Johnson announced that he would not seek reelection – remember?

That was the year Robert Kennedy was assassinated; you might recall that. That was the year Richard Nixon was elected president; maybe you remember him. In the following year, in 1969 – the year when Ronald Reagan described the Vietnam protests as 'giving aid and comfort to the enemy' – there were still half a million Americans in Vietnam. I was never one of them.

More than thirty thousand Canadians served in Vietnam, too. And almost as many Americans came to Canada during the Vietnam War; I was one of them – one who stayed. By March of 1971 – when Lt. William Calley was convicted of premeditated murder – I was already a landed immigrant, I'd already applied for Canadian citizenship. It was Christmas, 1972, when President Nixon bombed Hanoi; that was an eleven-day attack, employing more than forty thousand tons of high explosives. As Owen had said: Hanoi could handle it.

What did he ever say that wasn't *right*? I remember what he said about Abbie Hoffman, for example – remember Abbie Hoffman? He was the guy who tried to 'levitate' the Pentagon off its foundations; he was quite a clown. He was the guy who created the Youth International Party, the 'Yippies'; he was very active in antiwar protests, while at the same time he conceived of a meaningful revolution as roughly anything that conveyed irreverence with comedy and vulgarity.

'WHO DOES THIS JERK THINK HE'S *HELPING*?' Owen said.

It was Owen Meany who kept me out of Vietnam – a trick that only Owen could have managed.

'JUST THINK OF THIS AS MY LITTLE GIFT TO YOU' – that was how he put it.

It makes me ashamed to remember that I was angry with him for taking my armadillo's claws. God knows, Owen gave me more than he ever took from me – even when you consider that he took my mother.

3 : THE ANGEL

In her bedroom at 80 Front Street, my mother kept a dressmaker's dummy; it stood at attention next to her bed, like a servant about to awaken her, like a sentry guarding her while she slept – like a lover about to get into bed beside her. My mother was good at sewing; in another life, she could have been a seamstress. Her taste was quite uncomplicated, and she made her own clothes. Her sewing machine, which she also kept in her bedroom, was a far cry from the antique that we children abused in the attic; Mother's machine was a strikingly modern piece of equipment, and it got a lot of use.

For all those years before she married Dan Needham, my mother never had a real job, or pursued a higher education; and although she never lacked money – because my grandmother was generous to her – she was clever at keeping her personal expenses to a minimum. She would bring home some of the loveliest clothes, from Boston, but she would never buy them; she dressed up her dressmaker's dummy in them, and she copied them. Then she'd return the originals to the various Boston stores; she said she always told them the same thing, and they never got angry at her – instead, they felt sorry for her, and took the clothes back without an argument.

'My husband doesn't like it,' she'd tell them.

She would laugh to my grandmother and me about it. 'They must think I'm married to a real tyrant! He doesn't like *anything*!' My grandmother keenly aware that my mother wasn't married at all, would laugh uncomfortably at this, but it seemed such a solitary and innocent piece of mischief that I'm sure Harriet Wheelwright did not object to her daughter having a *little* fun.

And Mother made beautiful clothes: simple, as I've described – most of them were white or black, but they were made of the best material and they fitted her perfectly. The dresses and blouses and skirts she brought home were multicolored, and multipatterned, but my mother would expertly imitate the cut of the clothes in basic black and white. As in many things, my mother could be extremely accomplished without being in the least original or even inventive. The game she acted out upon the perfect body of the dressmaker's dummy must have pleased the frugal, Yankee part of her – the Wheelwright in her.

My mother hated darkness. There could never be enough light to suit her. I saw the dummy as a kind of accomplice to my mother in her war against the night. She would close her curtains only when she was undressing for bed; when she had her nightgown and her robe on, she would open the curtains. When she turned out the lamp on her bedside table, whatever light there was in the night flooded into her room – and there was always some light. There were streetlights on Front Street, Mr Fish left lights on in his house all night, and my grandmother left a light on – it pointlessly illuminated the garage doors. In addition to this neighborhood light, there was starlight, or moonlight, or that unnameable light that comes from the eastern horizon whenever you live near the Atlantic Coast. There was not a night when my mother lay in her bed unable to see the comforting figure of the dressmaker's dummy; it was not only her confederate against the darkness, it was her double.

It was never naked. I don't mean that my mother was so crazy about sewing that there was always a dress-in-progress upon the dummy; whether out of a sense of decency, or a certain playfulness that my mother had not outgrown – from whenever it was that she used to dress up her dolls – the dummy was always dressed. And I don't mean casually; Mother would never allow the dummy to stand around in a slip. I mean that the dummy was always completely dressed – and well dressed, too.

I remember waking up from a nightmare, or waking up and feeling sick, and going down the dark hall from my room to hers – feeling my way to her doorknob. Once in her room, I sensed that I had traveled to another time zone; after the darkness of my room and the black hall, my mother's room glowed – by comparison to the rest of the house, it was always just before dawn in my mother's room. And there would be the dummy, dressed for real life, dressed for the world. Sometimes I would think the dummy was my mother, that she was already out of bed and on her way to my room – possibly she'd heard me coughing, or crying out in my sleep; perhaps she got up early; or maybe she was just coming home, very late. Other times, the dummy would startle me; I would have forgotten all about it, and in the gray half-light of that room I would think it was an assailant – for a figure standing so still beside a sleeping body could as easily be an attacker as a guard.

The point is, it was my mother's body – exactly. 'It can make you look twice,' Dan Needham used to say.

Dan told some stories about the dummy, after he married my mother. When we moved into Dan's dormitory apartment at Gravesend Academy, the dummy – and my mother's sewing machine – became permanent residents of the dining room, which we never once ate in. We ate most of our meals in the school dining hall; and when we did eat at home, we ate in the kitchen.

Dan tried sleeping with the dummy in the bedroom only a few times. 'Tabby, what's wrong?' he asked it the first night, thinking my mother was up. 'Come back to bed,' he said another time. And once he asked the dummy. 'Are you ill?' And my mother, not quite asleep beside him, murmured, 'No. Are *you*?'

Of course, it was Owen Meany who experienced the most poignant encounters with my mother's dummy. Long before Dan Needham's armadillo changed Owen's and my life, a game that Owen enjoyed at 80 Front Street involved dressing and undressing my mother's dummy. My grandmother frowned upon this game – on the basis that we were boys. My mother, in turn, was wary – at first, she feared for her clothes. But she trusted us: we had clean hands, we returned dresses and blouses and skirts to their proper hangers – and her lingerie, properly folded, to its correct drawers. My mother grew so tolerant of our game that she even complimented us – on occasion – for the creation of an outfit she hadn't thought of. And several times, Owen was so excited by our creation that he begged my mother to model the unusual combination herself.

Only Owen Meany could make my mother blush.

'I've had this old blouse and this old skirt for years,' she would say. 'I just never thought of wearing them with this belt! You're a genius, Owen!' she'd tell him.

'BUT EVERYTHING LOOKS GOOD ON YOU,' Owen would tell her, and she'd blush.

If Owen had wanted to be less flattering, he might have remarked that it was easy to dress my mother, or her dummy, because all her clothes were black and white; everything went with everything else.

There was that one red dress, and we could never find a way to make her like it; it was never meant to be a part of her wardrobe, but I believed the Wheelwright in my mother made it impossible for her to give or throw the dress away. She'd found it in an exceptionally posh Boston store; she loved the clingy material, its scooped back, its fitted waist and full skirt, but she hated the color – a scarlet red, a poinsettia red. She'd meant to copy it – in white or in black – like all the others, but she liked the cut of the dress so much that she copied it in white *and* in black. 'White for a tan,' she said, 'and black in the winter.'

When she went to Boston to return the red dress, she said she discovered the store had burned to the ground. For a while, she couldn't remember the store's name; but she asked people in the neighborhood, she wrote to the former address. There was some crisis with insurance and it was months before she finally got to talk with someone, and then it was only a lawyer. 'But I never paid for the dress!' my mother said. 'It was very expensive – I was just trying it out. And I don't want it. I don't want to be billed for it, months later. It was very expensive,' she repeated; but the lawyer said it didn't matter. Everything was burned. Bills of sale were burned. Inventory was burned. Stock was burned. 'The telephone melted,' he said. 'The cash register melted,' he added. 'That dress is the least of their problems. It's *your* dress,' the lawyer said. 'You got lucky,' he told her, in a way that made her feel guilty.

'Good Heavens,' my grandmother said, 'it's so easy to make Wheelwrights feel guilty. Get hold of yourself, Tabitha, and stop complaining. It's a lovely dress – it's a *Christmas* color,' my grandmother decided. 'There are always Christmas parties. It will be perfect.' But I never saw my mother take the dress out of her closet; the only way that dress ever found its way to the dressmaker's dummy – after my mother had copied it – was when Owen dressed the dummy in it. Not even Owen could find a way to make my mother like that red dress.

'It may be a Christmas color,' she said, 'but *I'm* the wrong color – especially at Christmastime – in that dress.' She meant she looked sallow in red when she didn't have a tan, and who in New Hampshire has a tan for Christmas?

'THEN WEAR IT IN THE SUMMER!' Owen suggested.

But it was a show-off thing to wear such a bright red color in the summer; that was making too much of a tan, in my mother's opinion. Dan suggested that my mother donate the red dress to his seedy collection of stage costumes. But my mother thought this was wasteful, and besides; none of the Gravesend Academy boys, and certainly no other woman from our town, had the figure to do that dress justice.

Dan Needham not only took over the dramatic performances of the Gravesend Academy boys, he revitalized the amateur theatrical company of our small town, the formerly lackluster Gravesend Players. Dan talked everyone into The Gravesend Players; he got half the faculty at the academy to bring out the hams in themselves, and he roused the histrionic natures of half the townspeople by inviting them to try out for his productions. He even got my mother to be his leading lady – if only once.

As much as my mother liked to sing, she was extremely shy about acting. She agreed to be in only one play under Dan's direction, and I think she agreed only as an indication of her commitment to their prolonged courtship, and only if Dan was cast opposite her – if he was the leading man – *and* if he was *not* cast as her lover. She didn't want the town imagining all sorts of things about their courtship, she said. After they were married, my mother wouldn't act again; neither would Dan. He was always the director; she was always the prompter. My mother had a good voice for a prompter: quiet but clear. All those singing lessons were good for that, I guess.

Her one role, and it was a starring role, was in *Angel Street*. It was so long ago, I can't remember the names of the characters, or anything about the actual sets for the play. The Gravesend Players used the Town Hall, and sets were never very specially attended to there. What I remember is the movie that was made from *Angel Street*; it was called *Gaslight*, and

I've seen it several times. My mother had the Ingrid Bergman part; she was the wife who was being driven insane by her villainous husband. And Dan was the villain – he was the Charles Boyer character. If you know the story, although Dan and my mother were cast as husband and wife, there is little love evidenced between them onstage; it was the only time or place I ever saw Dan be hateful to my mother.

Dan tells me that there are still people in Gravesend who give him 'evil looks' because of that Charles Boyer role he played; they look at him as if *he* hit that long-ago foul ball – and as if he *meant* to.

And only once in that production – it was actually in dress rehearsal – did my mother wear the red dress. It might have been the evening when she is all dressed up to go to the theater (or somewhere) with her awful husband, but he has hidden the painting and accuses her of hiding it, and he makes *her* believe that she's hidden it, too – and then he banishes her to her room and doesn't let her go out at all. Or maybe it was when they go out to a concert and he finds his watch in her purse – *he* has put it there, but he makes her break down and plead with him to believe her, in front of all those snooty people. Anyway, my mother was supposed to wear the red dress in just one scene, and it was the only scene in the play where she was simply terrible. She couldn't leave the dress alone – she plucked imaginary lint off it; she kept staring at herself, as if the cleavage of the dress, all by itself, had suddenly plunged a foot; she never stopped itching around, as if the material of the dress made her skin crawl.

Owen and I saw every production of *Angel Street*; we saw all of Dan's plays – both the academy plays and the amateur theatricals of The Gravesend Players – but *Angel Street* was one of the few productions that we saw every showing of. To watch my mother onstage, and to watch Dan being awful to her, was such a riveting *lie*. It was not the play that interested us – it was what a lie it was: that Dan was awful to my mother, that he meant her harm. That was fascinating.

Owen and I always knew everyone in all the productions of The Gravesend Players. Mrs Walker, the ogre of our Episcopal Sunday school, played the flirtatious maid in *Angel Street* – the Angela Lansbury character, if you can believe it. Owen and I couldn't. Mrs Walker acting like a tart! Mrs

Walker being vulgar! We kept expecting her to shout: 'Owen Meany, you get *down* from up there! You get back to your seat!' And she wore a French maid's costume, with a very tight skirt and black, patterned stockings, so that every Sunday thereafter, Owen and I would search in vain for her legs – it was such a surprise to see Mrs Walker's legs; and even more of a surprise to discover that she had *pretty* legs!

The good guy role in *Angel Street* – the Joseph Cotten part, I call it – was played by our neighbor Mr Fish. Owen and I knew that he was still in mourning over the untimely death of Sagamore; the horror of the diaper truck disaster on Front Street was still visible in the pained expression with which he followed my mother's every movement onstage. Mr Fish was not exactly Owen's and my idea of a hero; but Dan Needham, with his talent for casting and directing the rankest amateurs, must have been inspired, in the case of Mr Fish, to tap our neighbor's sorrow and anger over Sagamore's encounter with the diaper truck.

Anyway, after the dress rehearsal of *Angel Street*, it was back to the closet with the red dress – except for those many occasions when Owen put it on the dummy. He must have felt especially challenged by my mother's dislike of that dress. It always looked terrific on the dummy.

I tell all this only to demonstrate that Owen was as familiar with that dummy as I was; but he was not familiar with it at night. He was not accustomed to the semidarkness of my mother's room when she was sleeping, when the dummy stood over her – that unmistakable body, in profile, in perfect silhouette. That dummy stood so still, it appeared to be counting my mother's breaths.

One night at 80 Front Street, when Owen lay in the other twin bed in my room, we were a long while falling asleep because – down the hall – Lydia had a cough. Just when we thought she was over a particular fit, or she had died, she would start up again. When Owen woke me up, I had not been asleep for very long; I was in the grips of such a deep and recent sleep that I couldn't make myself move – I felt as if I were lying in an extremely plush coffin and my pallbearers were holding me down, although I was doing my best to rise from the dead.

'I FEEL SICK,' Owen was saying.

'Are you going to throw up?' I asked him, but I couldn't move; I couldn't even open my eyes.

'I DON'T KNOW,' he said. 'I THINK I HAVE A FEVER.'

'Go tell my mother,' I said.

'IT FEELS LIKE A RARE DISEASE,' Owen said.

'Go tell my mother,' I repeated. I listened to him bump into the desk chair. I heard my door open, and close. I could hear his hands brushing against the wall of the hall. I heard him pause with his hand trembling on my mother's doorknob; he seemed to wait there for the longest time.

Then I thought: He's going to be surprised by the dummy. I thought of calling out, 'Don't be startled by the dummy standing there; it looks weird in that funny light.' But I was sunk in my coffin of sleep and my mouth was clamped shut. I waited for him to scream. That's what Owen would do, I was sure; there would be a bloodcurdling wail – '*AAAAAAAHHHHHHH!*' – and the entire household would be awake for hours. Or else, in a fit of bravery, Owen would tackle the dummy and wrestle it to the floor.

But while I was imagining the worst of Owen's encounter with the dummy, I realized he was back in my room, beside my bed, pulling my hair.

'WAKE UP! BUT BE QUIET!' he whispered. 'YOUR MOTHER IS NOT ALONE. SOMEONE STRANGE IS IN HER ROOM. COME SEE! I THINK IT'S AN ANGEL!'

'An angel?' I said.

'SSSSSSHHHHHH!'

Now I was wide awake and eager to see him make a fool of himself, and so I said nothing about the dummy; I held his hand and went with him through the hall to my mother's room. Owen was shivering.

'How do you know it's an angel?' I whispered.

'SSSSSSHHHHHH!'

So we stealthily crept into my mother's room, crawling on our bellies like snipers in search of cover, until the whole picture of her bed – her body in an inverted question mark, and the dummy standing beside her – was visible.

After a while, Owen said, 'IT'S GONE. IT MUST HAVE SEEN ME THE FIRST TIME.'

I pointed innocently at the dummy. 'What's that?' I whispered.

'THAT'S THE DUMMY, YOU IDIOT!' Owen said. 'THE ANGEL WAS ON THE OTHER SIDE OF THE BED.'

I touched his forehead; he was burning up. 'You have a fever, Owen,' I said.

'I SAW AN ANGEL,' he said.

'Is that you, boys?' my mother asked sleepily.

'Owen has a fever,' I said. 'He feels sick.'

'Come here, Owen,' my mother said, sitting up in bed. He went to her and she felt his forehead and told me to get him an aspirin and a glass of water.

'Owen saw an angel,' I said.

'Did you have a nightmare, Owen?' my mother asked him, as he crawled into bed beside her.

Owen's voice was muffled in the pillows. 'NOT EXACTLY,' he said.

When I returned with the water and the aspirin, my mother had fallen asleep with her arm around Owen; with his protrusive ears spread on the pillow, and my mother's arm across his chest, he looked like a butterfly trapped by a cat. He managed to take the aspirin and drink the water without disturbing my mother, and he handed the glass back to me with a stoical expression.

'I'M GOING TO STAY HERE,' he said bravely. 'IN CASE IT COMES BACK.'

He looked so absurd, I couldn't look at him. 'I thought you said it was an angel,' I whispered. 'What harm would an angel do?'

'I DON'T KNOW WHAT KIND OF ANGEL IT WAS,' he whispered, and my mother stirred in her sleep; she tightened her grip around Owen, which must have simultaneously frightened and thrilled him, and I went back to my room alone.

From what nonsense did Owen Meany discern what he would later call a PATTERN? From his feverish imagination? Years later, when he would refer to THAT FATED BASEBALL, I corrected him too impatiently.

'That *accident*, you mean,' I said.

It made him furious when I suggested that *anything* was an 'accident' – especially anything that had happened to him; on the subject of predestination, Owen Meany would accuse Calvin of bad faith. There were *no* accidents; there was a reason for that baseball – just as there was a reason for Owen being small, and a *reason* for his voice. In Owen's opinion, he had INTERRUPTED AN ANGEL, he had DISTURBED

AN ANGEL AT WORK, he had UPSET THE SCHEME OF THINGS.

I realize now that he never thought he saw a guardian angel; he was quite convinced, especially after THAT FATED BASEBALL, that he had interrupted the Angel of Death. Although he did not (at the time) delineate the plot of this Divine Narrative to me, I know that's what he believed: he, Owen Meany, had interrupted the Angel of Death at her holy work; she had reassigned the task – she gave it to *him*. How could these fantasies become so monstrous, and so convincing to him?

My mother was too sleepy to take his temperature, but it's a fact that he had a fever, and that his fever led him to a night in my mother's bed – in her arms. And wouldn't his excitement to find himself there, with her – not to mention his fever – have contributed to his readiness to remain wide-eyed and wide awake, alert for the *next* intruder, be it angel or ghost or hapless family member? I think so.

Several hours later, there came to my mother's room the second fearful apparition. I say 'fearful' because Owen was, at that time, afraid of my grandmother; he must have sensed her distaste for the granite business. I had left the light on in my mother's bathroom and the door to her bathroom open – into the hall – and worse, I had left the cold-water tap running (when I'd fixed Owen a glass of water for his aspirin). My grandmother always claimed she could hear the electric meter counting each kilowatt; as soon as it was dark, she followed my mother through the house, turning off the lights that my mother had turned on. And this night, in addition to her sensing that a light had been left on, Grandmother heard the water running – either the pump in the basement, or the cold-water tap itself. Finding my mother's bathroom in such reckless abandon, Grandmother proceeded to my mother's room – anxious that my mother was ill or else indignant with budget-mindedness and determined to point out my mother's carelessness, even if she had to wake her up.

Grandmother might have just turned out the light, turned off the water, and gone back to bed, *if* she hadn't made the mistake of turning the cold-water tap the wrong way – she turned it much more forcefully *on*, dousing herself in a spray of the coldest possible water; the tap had been left running for hours. Thus was her nightgown soaked; she would have to change it. This must have inspired her to wake my mother; not only had electricity and water been awasting, but here Grandmother was – soaked to the skin in her efforts to put a stop to all this escaping energy. I would guess, therefore, that her manner, upon entering my mother's room, was not calm. And although Owen was prepared for an angel, he might have expected that even the Angel of Death would reappear in a serene fashion.

My grandmother, dripping wet – her usually flowing nightgown plastered to her gaunt, hunched body, her hair arrayed in its nightly curlers, her face thickly creamed the lifeless color of the moon – *burst* into my mother's room. It was days before Owen could tell me what he thought: when you scare off the Angel of Death, the Divine Plan calls for the kind of angels you can't scare away; they even call you by name.

'Tabitha!' my grandmother said.

'*AAAAAAHHHHHH!*'

Owen Meany screamed so terribly that my grandmother could not catch her breath. Beside my mother on the bed, she saw a tiny demon spring bolt upright – propelled by such a sudden and unreal force that my grandmother imagined the little creature was preparing to fly. My mother appeared to levitate beside him. Lydia, who still had both her legs, leaped from her bed and ran straight into her dresser drawers; for days, she would display her bruised nose. Sagamore, who was a short time away from his appointment with the diaper truck, woke up Mr Fish with his barking. Throughout the neighborhood, the lids of trash cans clattered – as cats and raccoons made good their escape from Owen Meany's alarm. A small segment of Gravesend must have rolled over in their beds, imagining that the Angel of Death had clearly come for *someone*.

'Tabitha,' my grandmother said the next day. 'I think it is most strange and improper that you should allow that little devil to sleep in your bed.'

'He had a fever,' my mother said. 'And I was very sleepy.'

'He has something more serious than a fever, all the time,' my grandmother said. 'He acts and sounds as if he's possessed.'

'You find fault with everyone who isn't absolutely perfect,' my mother said.

'Owen thought he saw an angel,' I explained to Grandmother.

'He thought *I* was an angel?' Grandmother asked. 'I told you he was possessed.'

'Owen *is* an angel,' my mother said.

'He is no such thing,' my grandmother said. 'He is a mouse. The Granite Mouse!'

When Mr Fish saw Owen and me on our bicycles, he waved us over to him; he was pretending to mend a loose picket on his fence, but he was really just watching our house – waiting for someone to come down the driveway.

'Hello, boys!' he said. 'That was some hullabaloo last night. I suppose you heard it?' Owen shook his head.

'I heard Sagamore barking,' I said.

'No, no – before that!' Mr Fish said. 'I mean, did you hear what made him bark? Such cries! Such a yell! A real hullabaloo!'

Sometime after she'd managed to catch her breath, Grandmother had cried out, too, and of course Lydia had cried out as well – after she'd collided with her dresser drawers. Owen said later that my grandmother had been WAILING LIKE A BANSHEE, but there had been nothing of a caliber comparable to Owen's scream.

'Owen thought he saw an angel,' I explained to Mr Fish.

'It didn't sound like a very *nice* angel, Owen,' Mr Fish said.

'WELL, ACTUALLY,' Owen admitted, 'I THOUGHT MISSUS WHEELWRIGHT WAS A GHOST.'

'Ah, that explains everything!' Mr Fish said sympathetically. Mr Fish was as afraid of my grandmother as Owen was; at least, regarding all matters concerning the zoning laws and the traffic on Front Street, he was always extremely deferential to her.

What a phrase that is: 'that explains everything!' I know better than to think that *anything* 'explains everything' today.

Later, of course, I would tell Dan Needham the whole story – including Owen's belief regarding his interruption of the Angel of Death and how he was assigned that angel's task.

But one of the things I failed to notice about Owen was how exact he was – how he meant everything *literally*, which is not a usual feature of the language of children. For years he would say, 'I WILL NEVER FORGET YOUR GRANDMOTHER, WAILING LIKE A BANSHEE.' But I paid no attention; I could hardly remember Grandmother making much of a ruckus – what I remembered was Owen's scream. Also, I thought it was just an expression – 'wailing like a banshee' – and I couldn't imagine why Owen remembered my grandmother's commotion with such importance. I must have repeated what Owen said to Dan Needham, because years later Dan asked me, 'Did Owen say your grandmother was a *banshee*?'

'He said she was "wailing like a banshee",' I explained.

Dan got out the dictionary, then; he was clucking his tongue and shaking his head, and laughing to himself, saying, 'That boy! What a boy! Brilliant but preposterous!' And that was the first time I learned, *literally*, what a banshee was – a banshee, in Irish folklore, is a female spirit whose wailing is a sign that a loved one will soon die.

Dan Needham was right, as usual: 'brilliant but preposterous' – that was such an apt description of The Granite Mouse; that was exactly what I thought Owen Meany was, 'brilliant but preposterous.' As time went on – as you shall see – maybe not so preposterous.

It appeared to our town, and to us Wheelwrights ourselves, a strange reversal in my mother's character that she should conduct a four-year courtship with Dan Needham before consenting to marry him. As my Aunt Martha would say, my mother hadn't waited five minutes to have the 'fling' that led to me! But perhaps that was the reason: if her own family, and all of Gravesend, had suspicions regarding my mother's morals – regarding the general ease with which, they might assume, she could be talked into anything – my mother's lengthy engagement to Dan Needham certainly showed them all a thing or two. Because it was obvious, from the start, that Dan and Mother were in love. He was devoted, she dated no one else, they were 'engaged' within a few months – and it was clear to everyone how much I liked Dan. Even my grandmother, who was ever alert for what she feared was her wayward daughter's proclivity to jump into things, was impatient with my mother to set a date for the wedding. Dan Needham's personal charm, not to mention the speed with which he became a favorite in the Gravesend Academy community, had quickly won my grandmother over.

Grandmother was not won over quickly, as a rule – not by anyone. Yet she became infatuated with the magic Dan wrought upon the amateurs at The Gravesend Players, so much so that she accepted a part in Maugham's *The Constant Wife*; she was the regal mother of the deceived wife, and she proved to have the perfect, frivolous touch for drawing-room comedy – she was a model of the kind of sophistication we could all do well without. She even discovered a British accent, with no prodding from Dan, who was no fool and fully realized that a British accent lay never very deeply concealed in the bosom of Harriet Wheelwright – it simply wanted an occasion to bring it out.

'"I hate giving straight answers to a straight question,"' Grandmother, as Mrs Culver, said imperiously – and completely in character. And at another memorable moment, commenting on her son-in-law's affair with her daughter's '"greatest friend,"' she rationalized: '"If John is going to deceive Constance, it's nice it should be somebody we all know."' Well, Grandmother was so marvelous she brought the house down; it was a grand performance, rather wasted – in my opinion – on poor John and Constance, who were drearily played by a somewhat sheepish Mr Fish, our dog-loving neighbor (and a regular choice of Dan's), and by the tyrannical Mrs Walker, whose legs were her sexiest feature – and they were almost completely covered in the long dresses appropriate to this drawing-room comedy. Grandmother, who was rendered coy with false modesty, said simply that she had always had a special understanding of 1927 – and I don't doubt it: she would have been a beautiful young woman then; 'and your mother,' Grandmother told me, 'would have been younger than you.'

So why did Dan and my mother wait four years?

If there were arguments, if they were sorting out some differences of opinion, I never saw or heard them. Having been so improper as to have me, and never explain me, was Mother simply being overly proper the second time around? Was Dan wary of her? He never seemed wary. Was *I* the problem? I used to wonder. But I loved Dan – and he gave me every reason to feel that he loved me. I *know* he loved me; he still does.

'Is it about children, Tabitha?' my grandmother asked one evening at dinner, and Lydia and I sat at attention to hear the answer. 'I mean, does he want them – do you *not* want another? Or is it the other way around? I don't think you should trouble yourself about having or not having children, Tabitha – not if it costs you such a lovely, devoted man.'

'We're just waiting, to be sure,' my mother said.

'Good Heavens, you must be sure, by now,' Grandmother said impatiently. 'Even *I'm* sure, and Johnny's sure. Aren't *you* sure, Lydia?' Grandmother asked.

'Sure, I'm sure,' Lydia said.

'Children are not the issue,' my mother said. 'There is no issue.'

'People have joined the priesthood in less time than it takes you to get married,' Grandmother said to my mother.

As for joining the priesthood, that was a favorite expression of Harriet Wheelwright's; it was always made in connection with some insupportable foolishness, some self-created difficulty, some action as inhuman as it was bizarre. Grandmother meant the Catholic priesthood; yet I know that one of the things that upset her about the possibility of Mother's moving herself and me to the Episcopal Church was that Episcopalians had priests and bishops – and even 'low' Episcopalians were much more like Catholics than like Congregationalists, in her opinion. A good thing: Grandmother never knew much about Anglicans.

In their long courtship, Dan and my mother attended both the Congregational and the Episcopal services, as if they were conducting a four-year theological seminar, in private – and my introduction to the Episcopal Sunday school was also gradual; at my mother's prompting, I attended several classes before Dan and my mother were married, as if Mother already knew where we were headed. What was also gradual was how my mother finally stopped going to Boston for her singing lessons. I never had a hint that Dan was the slightest bothered by this ritual, although I recall my grandmother asking my mother if Dan objected to her spending one night a week in Boston.

'Why should he?' my mother asked.

The answer, which was not forthcoming, was as obvious

to my grandmother as it was to me: that the most likely candidate for the unclaimed position of my father, and my mother's mystery lover, was that 'famous' singing teacher. But neither my grandmother nor I dared to postulate this theory to my mother, and Dan Needham was clearly untroubled by the ongoing singing lessons, and the ongoing one night away; or else Dan possessed some reassuring piece of knowledge that remained a secret from my grandmother and me.

'YOUR FATHER IS NOT THE SINGING TEACHER,' Owen Meany told me matter-of-factly. 'THAT WOULD BE TOO OBVIOUS.'

'This is a real-life story, Owen,' I said. 'It's not a mystery novel.' In real life, I meant, there was nothing written that the missing father couldn't be OBVIOUS – but I didn't really think it was the singing teacher, either. He was only the most likely candidate because he was the *only* candidate my grandmother and I could think of.

'IF IT'S HIM, WHY MAKE IT A SECRET?' Owen asked. 'IF IT'S HIM, WOULDN'T YOUR MOTHER SEE HIM MORE THAN ONCE A WEEK – OR NOT AT ALL?'

Anyway, it was farfetched to think that the singing teacher was the reason my mother and Dan didn't get married for four years. And so I concluded what Owen Meany would call TOO OBVIOUS: that Dan was holding out for more information, concerning *me*, and that my mother wasn't providing it. For wouldn't it be reasonable of Dan to want to know the story of who my father was? And I know that is a story my mother wouldn't have yielded to Dan.

But Owen rebuked me for this idea, too. 'DON'T YOU SEE HOW MUCH DAN LOVES YOUR MOTHER?' he asked me. 'HE LOVES HER AS MUCH AS *WE* DO! HE WOULD NEVER FORCE HER TO TELL HIM *ANYTHING*!'

I believe that now. Owen was right. It was something else: that four-year delay of the obvious.

Dan came from a very high-powered family; they were doctors and lawyers, and they disapproved of Dan for not completing a more serious education. To have started out at Harvard and not gone *on* to law school, not gone *on* to medical school – this was criminal laziness; Dan came from a family very keen about going *on*. They disapproved of him *ending up* as a mere prep-school teacher, and of his indulging his hobby of amateur theatrical performances – they believed these frivolities were unworthy of a grown-up's interest! They disapproved of my mother, too – and that was the end of Dan having any more to do with them. They called her 'the divorcée'; I guess no one in the Needham family had ever been divorced, and so that was the worst thing you could say about a woman – even worse than calling my mother what she really was: an unwed mother. Perhaps an unwed mother sounded merely hapless; whereas a divorcée implied *intent* – a woman who was out to snare their dear underachiever, Dan.

I don't remember much about meeting Dan's family: at the wedding, they chose not to mingle. My grandmother was outraged that there were people who actually dared to condescend to her – to treat her like some provincial fussbudget. I recall that Dan's mother had an acid tongue, and that, when introduced to me, she said, 'So this is *the child*.' And then there followed a period of time in which she scrutinized my face – for any telltale indication of the race of my missing male ancestor, I would guess. But that's all I remember. Dan refused to have anything further to do with them. I cannot think that they played any role at all in the four-year 'engagement.'

And what with all the comparing and contrasting of a theological nature, there was no end of religious approval for matching Dan and my mother; there was, in fact, *double* approval – the Congregationalists and the Episcopalians appeared to be competing for the privilege of having Dan and my mother come worship with them. In my opinion, it should have been no contest; granted, I was happy to have the opportunity to lift Owen up in the air at Sunday school, but that was the beginning and the end to any advantage the Episcopalians had over the Congregationalists.

There were not only those differences I've already mentioned – of an atmospheric and architectural nature, together with those ecclesiastical differences that made the Episcopal service much more Catholic than the Congregational service – CATHOLIC, WITH A BIG C, as Owen would say. But there were also vast differences between the Rev. Lewis Merrill, whom I liked, and the Rev. Dudley Wiggin – the rector of the Episcopal Church – who was a bumpkin of boredom.

To compare these two ministers as dismissively as I did, I confess I was drawing on no small amount of snobbery inherited from Grandmother Wheelwright. The Congregationalists had *pastors* – the Rev. Lewis Merrill was our pastor. If you grow up with that comforting word, it's hard to accept *rectors* – the Episcopal Church had rectors; the Rev. Dudley Wiggin was the rector of Christ Church, Gravesend. I shared my grandmother's distaste for the word *rector* – it sounded too much like *rectum* to be taken seriously.

But it would have been hard to take the Rev. Dudley Wiggin seriously if he'd been a pastor. Whereas the Rev. Mr Merrill had heeded his calling as a young man – he had always been in, and of, the church – the Rev. Mr Wiggin was a former airline pilot; some difficulty with his eyesight had forced his early retirement from the skies, and he had descended to our wary town with a newfound fervor – the zeal of the convert giving him the healthy but frantic appearance of one of those 'elder' citizens who persist in entering vigorous sporting competitions in the over-fifty category. Whereas Pastor Merrill spoke an educated language – he'd been an English major at Princeton; he'd heard Niebuhr and Tillich lecture at Union Theological – *Rector* Wiggin spoke in ex-pilot homilies; he was a pulpit-thumper who had no doubt.

What made Mr Merrill infinitely more attractive was that he was *full* of doubt; he expressed *our* doubt in the most eloquent and sympathetic ways. In his completely lucid and convincing view, the Bible is a book with a troubling plot, but a plot that can be understood: God creates us out of love, but we don't want God, or we don't believe in Him, or we pay very poor attention to Him. Nevertheless, God continues to love us – at least, He continues to try to get our attention. Pastor Merrill made religion seem *reasonable*. And the trick of having faith, he said, was that it was necessary to believe in God *without* any great or even remotely reassuring evidence that we don't inhabit a godless universe.

Although he knew all the best – or, at least, the least boring – stories in the Bible, Mr Merrill was most appealing because he reassured us that doubt was the essence of faith, and not faith's opposite. By comparison, whatever the Rev. Dudley Wiggin had seen to make him believe in God, he had seen absolutely – possibly by flying an airplane too close to the sun. The rector was *not* gifted with language, and he was blind to doubt or worry in any form; perhaps the problem with his 'eyesight' that had forced his early retirement from the airlines was really a euphemism for the blinding power of his total religious conversion – because Mr Wiggin was fearless to an extent that would have made him an unsafe pilot, and to an extent that made him a madman as a preacher.

Even his Bible selections were outlandish; a satirist could not have selected them better. The Rev. Mr Wiggin was especially fond of the word 'firmament'; there was always a firmament in his Bible selections. And he loved all allusions to faith as a *battle* to be savagely fought and won; faith was a war waged against faith's *adversaries*. 'Take the whole armor of God!' he would rave. We were instructed to wear 'the breastplate of righteousness'; our faith was a 'shield' – against 'all the flaming darts of the evil one.' The rector said he wore a 'helmet of salvation.' That's from Ephesians; Mr Wiggin was a big fan of Ephesians. He also whooped it up about Isaiah – especially the part when 'the Lord is sitting upon a throne'; the rector was big on the Lord upon a throne. The Lord is surrounded by seraphim. One of the seraphim flies to Isaiah, who is complaining that he's 'a man of unclean lips.' Not for long; not according to Isaiah. The seraphim touches Isaiah's mouth with 'a burning coal' and Isaiah is as good as new.

That was what we heard from the Rev. Dudley Wiggin: all the unlikeliest miracles.

'I DON'T LIKE THE SERAPHIM,' Owen complained. 'WHAT'S THE POINT OF BEING SCARY?'

But although Owen agreed with me that the rector was a moron who messed up the Bible for tentative believers by assaulting us with the worst of God the Almighty and God the Terrible – and although Owen acknowledged that the Rev. Mr Wiggin's sermons were about as entertaining and convincing as a pilot's voice in the intercom, explaining technical difficulties while the plane plummets toward the earth and the stewardesses are screaming – Owen actually preferred Wiggin to what little he knew of Pastor Merrill. Owen didn't know much about Mr Merrill, I should add; Owen was never a Congregationalist. But Merrill was *such* a popular preacher that parishioners from the other Gravesend churches would frequently skip a service of their own to attend his sermons. Owen did so, on occasion, but Owen was always critical. Even when Gravesend Academy bestowed the intellectual honor upon Pastor Merrill – of inviting him to be a frequent guest preacher in the academy's non-denominational church – Owen was critical.

'BELIEF IS NOT AN INTELLECTUAL MATTER,' he complained. 'IF HE'S GOT SO MUCH DOUBT, HE'S IN THE WRONG BUSINESS.'

But who, besides Owen Meany and Rector Wiggin, had so *little* doubt? Owen was a natural in the belief business, but my appreciation of Mr Merrill and my contempt for Mr Wiggin were based on common sense. I took a particularly Yankee view of them; the Wheelwright in me was all in favor of Lewis Merrill, all opposed to Dudley Wiggin. We Wheelwrights do not scoff at the appearance of things. Things often *are* as they appear. First impressions matter. That clean, well-lit place of worship, which was the Congregational Church – its pristine white clapboards, its tall, clear windows that welcomed the view of branches against the sky – that was a first impression that lasted for me; it was a model of purity and no-nonsense, against which the Episcopal gloom of stone and tapestry and stained glass could pose no serious competition. And Pastor Merrill was also good-looking – in an intense, pale, slightly undernourished way. He had a boyish face – a sudden, winning, embarrassed smile that contradicted a fairly constant look of worry that more usually gave him the expression of an anxious child. An errant lock of hair flopped on his forehead when he looked down upon his sermon, or bent over his Bible – his hair problem was the unruly result of a pronounced widow's peak, which further contributed to his boyishness. And he was always misplacing his glasses, which he didn't seem to need – that is, he could read without them, he could look out upon his congregation without them (at least not appearing to be blind); then, all of a sudden, he would commence a frantic search for them. It was endearing; so was his slight stutter, because it made us nervous for him – afraid for him, should he have his eloquence snatched from him and be struck down with a crippling speech impediment. He was articulate, but he never made speech seem effortless; on the contrary, he exhibited what hard work it was – to make his faith, in tandem with his doubt, clear; to speak well, in spite of his stutter.

And then, to add to Mr Merrill's appeal, we pitied him for

his family. His wife was from California, the sunny part. My grandmother used to speculate that she had been one of those permanently tanned, bouncy blondes – a perfectly wholesome type, but entirely too easily persuaded that good health and boundless energy for good deeds were the natural results of clean living and practical values. No one had told her that health and energy and the Lord's work are harder to come by in bad weather. Mrs Merrill suffered in New Hampshire.

She suffered visibly. Her blondness turned to dry straw; her cheeks and nose turned a raw salmon color, her eyes watered – she caught every flu, every common cold there was; no epidemic missed her. Aghast at the loss of her California color, she tried makeup; but this turned her skin to clay. Even in summer, she couldn't tan; she turned so dead white in the winter, there was nothing for her to do in the sun but burn. She was sick all the time, and this cost her her energy; she grew listless; she developed a matronly spread, and the vague, unfocused look of someone over forty who might be sixty – or would be, tomorrow.

All this happened to Mrs Merrill while her children were still small: they were sickly, too. Although they were successful scholars, they were so often ill and missed so many school days that they had to repeat whole grades. Two of them were older than I was, but not a lot older; one of them was even demoted to my grade – I don't remember which one; I don't even remember which sex. That was another problem that the Merrill children suffered: they were utterly forgettable. If you didn't see the Merrill children for weeks at a time, when you saw them again, they appeared to have been replaced by different children.

The Rev. Lewis Merrill had the appearance of a plain man who, with education and intensity, had risen above his ordinariness; and his rise manifested itself in his gift of speech. But his family labored under a plainness so virulent that the dullness of his wife and children outshone even their proneness to illness, which was remarkable.

It was said that Mrs Merrill had a drinking problem – or, at least, that her modest intake of alcohol was in terrible conflict with her long list of prescription drugs. One of the children once swallowed *all* the drugs in the house and had to have its stomach pumped. And following a kind of pep talk that Mr Merrill gave to the youngest Sunday school class, one of his own children pulled the minister's hair and spit in his face. When the Merrill children were growing up, one of them vandalized a cemetery.

Here was our pastor, clearly bright, clearly grappling with all the most *thoughtful* elements of religious faith, and doubt; yet, clearly, God had cursed his family.

There was simply no comparable sympathy for the Rev. Dudley Wiggin – *Captain* Wiggin, some of his harsher critics called him. He was a hale and hearty type, he had a grin like a gash in his face; his smile was the smirk of a restless survivor. He looked like a former *downed* pilot, a veteran of crash landings, or shoot-outs in the sky – Dan Needham told me that Captain Wiggin had been a bomber pilot in the war, and Dan would know: he was a sergeant himself, in Italy and in Brazil, where he was a cryptographic technician. And even Dan was appalled at the crassness with which Dudley Wiggin directed the Christmas Pageant – and Dan was more tolerant of amateur theatrical performances than the average Gravesend citizen. Mr Wiggin injected a kind of horror-movie element into the Christmas miracle; to the rector, every Bible story was – if properly understood – threatening.

And *his* wife, clearly, had not suffered. A former stewardess, Barbara Wiggin was a brash, backslapping redhead; Mr Wiggin called her 'Barb,' which was how she introduced herself in various charity-inspired phone calls.

'Hi! It's Barb Wiggin! Is your mommy or your daddy home?'

She was very much a *barb*, if not a nail, in Owen's side, because she enjoyed picking him up by his pants – she would grab him by his belt, her fist in his belly, and lift him to her stewardess's face: a frankly handsome, healthy, efficient face. 'Oh, you're a cute-y!' she'd tell Owen. 'Don't you ever dare grow!'

Owen hated her; he always begged Dan to cast her as a prostitute or a child-molester, but The Gravesend Players did not offer many roles of that kind, and Dan admitted to thinking of no other good use for her. Her own children were huge, oafish athletes, irritatingly 'well rounded.' *All* the Wiggins played in touch-football games, which they organized, every Sunday afternoon, on the parish-house lawn. Yet – incredibly! – we moved to the Episcopal Church. It was not for the touch football, which Dan and my mother and

I despised. I could only guess that Dan and my mother had discussed having children of their own, and Dan had wanted his children to be baptized as Episcopalians – although, as I've said, the whole church business didn't appear to matter very much to him. Perhaps my mother took Dan's Episcopalianism more seriously than Dan took it. All that my mother said to me was that it was better if we were all in one church, and that Dan cared more about *his* church than she cared about *hers* – and wasn't it fun for me to be where Owen was? Yes, it was.

Thank Heavens for Hurd's Church; that was the unfortunate name of the nondenominational church at Gravesend Academy – it was named after the academy's founder, that childless Puritan, the Rev. Emery Hurd himself. Without the neutral territory of Hurd's Church, my mother might have started an interdenominational war – because where would she have been married? Grandmother wanted the Rev. Lewis Merrill to perform the ceremony, and the Rev. Dudley Wiggin had every reason to expect that *he* would get to officiate.

Fortunately, there was some middle ground. As a faculty member at Gravesend Academy, Dan Needham had a right to use Hurd's Church – especially for the all-important wedding and the quick-to-follow funeral – and Hurd's Church was a masterpiece of inoffensiveness. No one could remember the denomination of the school minister, a sepulchral old gentleman who favored bow ties and had the habit of pinning his vestment to the floor with an errant stab of his cane; he suffered from gout. His role in Hurd's Church was usually that of a bland master of ceremonies, for he rarely delivered a sermon himself; he introduced one guest preacher after another, each one more flamboyant or controversial than himself. The Rev. 'Pinky' Scammon also taught Religion at Gravesend Academy, where his courses were known to begin and end with apologies for Kierkegaard; but old Pinky Scammon cleverly delegated much of the teaching of his Religion classes to guest preachers, too. He would invariably entice Sunday's minister to stay through the day Monday, and teach his Monday class; the rest of the week, Mr Scammon devoted to discussing with his students what the interesting guest had said.

The gray granite edifice of Hurd's Church, which was so

plain it might have been a Registry of Deeds or a Town Library or a Public Water Works, seemed to have composed itself around old Mr Scammon's gouty limp and his sepulchral features. Hurd's was dark and shabby, but it was comfy – the pews were wide and worn so smooth that they invited instant dozing; the light, which was absorbed by so much stone, was gray but soft; the acoustics, which may have been Hurd's only miracle, were unmuddied and deep. Every preacher sounded better than he was there; every hymn was distinct; each prayer was resonant; the organ had a cathedral tone. If you shut your eyes – and you were inclined to shut your eyes in Hurd's Church – you could imagine you were in Europe.

Generations of Gravesend Academy boys had carved up the racks for the hymnals with the names of their girlfriends and the scores of football games; generations of academy maintenance men had sanded away the more flagrant obscenities, although an occasional 'dork-brain' or 'cunt-face' was freshly etched in the wooden slats that secured the tattered copies of *The Pilgrim Hymnal*. Given the darkness of the place, Hurd's was better suited for a funeral than for a wedding; but my mother had both her wedding and her funeral there.

The wedding service at Hurd's was shared by Pastor Merrill and Rector Wiggin, who managed to avoid any awkwardness – or any open demonstration of the competition between them. Old Pinky Scammon nodded peaceably to what both ministers had to say. Those elements of the celebration that allow the impromptu were the responsibility of Mr Merrill, who was brief and charming – his nervousness was manifest, as usual, only by his slight stutter. Pastor Merrill also got to deliver the 'Dearly beloved' part. ' "We have come together in the presence of God to witness and bless the joining together of this man and this woman in Holy Matrimony," ' he began, and I noticed that Hurd's was packed – there was standing-room only. The academy faculty had turned out in droves, and there were the usual droves of women of my grandmother's generation who turned out whenever there was a public opportunity to observe my grandmother, who was – to women her age – the closest that the Gravesend community came to royalty; and there was something special about her having a 'fallen' daughter who was choosing this moment to haul herself back into the ranks of the respectable. That Tabby Wheelwright has some nerve to wear white, I'm sure some of these old crones from my grandmother's bridge club were thinking. But this sense of the richness of gossip that permeated Gravesend society is, on my part, largely hindsight. At the time, I chiefly thought it was a splendid turnout.

The Ministry of the Word was muttered by Captain Wiggin, who had no understanding of punctuation; he either trampled over it entirely, or he paused and held his breath so long that you were sure someone was pointing a gun at his head. ' "O gracious and everliving God, you have created us male and female in your image: Look mercifully upon this man and this woman who come to you seeking your blessing, and assist them with your grace," ' he gasped.

Then Mr Merrill and Mr Wiggin indulged in a kind of face-off, with each of them demonstrating his particular notion of pertinent passages from the Bible – Mr Merrill's passages being more 'pertinent,' Mr Wiggin's more flowery. It was back to Ephesians for the rector, who intoned that we should pay close attention to 'The Father from whom every family is named'; then he switched to Colossians and that bit about 'Love which binds everything together in harmony'; and, at last, he concluded with Mark – 'They are no longer two but one.'

Pastor Merrill started us off with the Song of Solomon – ' "Many waters cannot quench love," ' he read. Then he hit us with Corinthians ('Love is patient and kind'), and finished us off with John – 'Love one another as I have loved you.' It was Owen Meany who then blew his nose, which drew my attention to his pew, where Owen sat on a precarious stack of hymnals – in order to see over the Eastman family in general, and Uncle Alfred in particular.

There then followed a reception at 80 Front Street. It was a muggy day with a hot, hazy sun, and my grandmother complained that her rose garden was not flattered by the weather; indeed, the roses looked wilted by the heat. It was the kind of day that produces a torpor that can be refreshed by nothing less than a violent thunderstorm; my grandmother complained of the likelihood of a thunderstorm, too. Yet the bar and the buffet tables were set out upon the lawn; the men took off their suit jackets and rolled up their sleeves and loosened their ties and sweated through their shirts – my grandmother particularly disapproved of the men for draping their jackets on the privet hedges, which gave the usually immaculate, dark-green border of the rose garden the appearance of being strewn with litter that had blown in from another part of town. Several of the women fanned themselves; some of them kicked off their high heels and walked barefoot on the lawn.

There had been a brief and abandoned plan to have a dance floor put on the brick terrace, but this plan withered in a disagreement concerning the proper music – and a good thing, too, my grandmother concluded; she meant it was a good thing that there was no dancing in such humid weather.

But it was what a summer wedding should be – sultry, something momentarily pretty, giving way to a heat that is unrestrained. Uncle Alfred showed off for me and my cousins by chugging a beer. A stray beagle, belonging to some new people on Pine Street, made off with several cupcakes from the coffee and dessert table. Mr Meany, standing so stiffly in-waiting at the receiving line that he appeared to have granite in his pockets, blushed when it was his turn to kiss the bride. 'Owen's got the weddin' present,' he said, turning away. 'We got just one present, from the both of us.' Mr Meany and Owen wore the only dark suits at the wedding, and Simon commented to Owen on the inappropriateness of his solemn, Sunday school appearance.

'You look like you're at a funeral, Owen,' Simon said.

Owen was hurt and looked cross.

'I was just kidding,' Simon said.

But Owen was still cross and made a point of rearranging all the wedding presents on the terrace so that his and his father's gift was the centerpiece. The wrapping paper had Christmas trees all over it and the present, which Owen needed both hands to lift, was the size and shape of a brick. I was sure it was granite.

'That's probably Owen's *only* suit, you asshole,' Hester told Simon; they quarreled. It was the first time I'd ever seen Hester in a dress; she looked very pretty. It was a yellow dress; Hester was tan; her black hair was as tangled as a briar patch in the heat, but her reflexes seemed especially primed for the social challenge of an outdoor wedding. When Noah tried to surprise her with a captured toad, Hester got the toad away from him and slapped Simon in the face with it.

'I think you've killed it, Hester,' Noah said, bending over the stunned toad and exhibiting much more concern for it than for his brother's face.

'It's not my fault,' Hester said. 'You started it.'

My grandmother had declared the upstairs bathrooms 'off-limits' to wedding guests, so there got to be quite long lines at the downstairs bathrooms – there were only two. Lydia had hand-painted two shirt cardboards, 'Gentlemen' and 'Ladies'; the 'Ladies' had the much longer of the lines.

When Hester tried to use an upstairs bathroom – she felt that she was 'family,' and therefore not bound by the rules governing the guests – her mother told her that she would wait in line like everyone else. My Aunt Martha – like many Americans – could become quite tyrannical in the defense of democracy. Noah and Simon and Owen and I bragged that we could pee in the bushes, and Hester begged only our slightest cooperation – in order that she could follow us in that pursuit. She asked that one of us stand guard – so that other boys and men, with an urge to pee in the denser sections of the privet hedges, would not surprise her midsquat; and she requested that one of us keep her panties safe for her. Her brothers predictably balked at this and made derisive comments regarding the desirability of holding Hester's panties – under any circumstances. I was, typically, slow to respond. Hester simply stepped out of her underwear and handed her white cotton briefs to Owen Meany.

You would have thought she had handed him a live armadillo; his little face reflected his devout curiosity and his extreme anxiety. But Noah snatched Hester's panties out of Owen's hands and Simon snatched them away from his brother, pulling them over Owen's head – they fit over his head rather easily, with his face peering through the hole for one of Hester's ample thighs. He snatched them off his head, blushing; but when he tried to stuff them into his suit-jacket pocket, he discovered that the side pockets were still sewn shut. Although he'd worn this suit to Sunday school for several years, no one had unsewn the pockets for him; or perhaps he thought they were meant to be closed. He recovered, however, and stuffed the panties into the inside breast pocket of the jacket, where they made quite a lump.

At least he was not wearing the panties on his head when his father walked up to him, and Noah and Simon began to scuff their feet in the rough grass and loose twigs at the foot of the privet hedge; by so doing, they managed to conceal the sound of Hester pissing.

Mr Meany was stirring a glass of champagne with a dill pickle the size of his thick forefinger. He had not drunk a drop of champagne, but he appeared to enjoy using it as a dip for his pickle.

'Are you comin' home with me, Owen?' Mr Meany asked. He had announced, from the moment he arrived at the reception, that he couldn't stay long; my mother and grandmother were most impressed that he'd come at all. He was uncomfortable going out. His simple navy-blue suit was from the same family of cheap material as Owen's – since Owen was often up in the air in his suit, perhaps Mr Meany's suit had been better treated; I could not tell if Mr Meany had unsewn his side pockets. Owen's suit was creased – just above the cuffs of his trousers and at the wrists of his jacket sleeves, indicating that his suit had been let down; but the sleeves and trousers had been 'let down' so little, Owen appeared to be growing at the rate of an underfed tree.

'I WANT TO STAY,' Owen said.

'Tabby won't be bringin' you up the hill on her weddin' day,' Mr Meany told him.

'My father or mother will bring Owen home, sir,' Noah said. My cousins – as rough as they could be with other children – had been brought up to be friendly and polite to adults, and Noah's cheerfulness seemed to surprise Mr Meany. I introduced him to my cousins, but I could tell that Owen wanted to walk his father away from us, immediately – perhaps fearing that Hester would at any moment emerge from the privet hedge and demand her panties back.

Mr Meany had come in his pickup, and several of the guests had blocked it in our driveway, so I went with him and Owen to help identify the cars. We were well across the lawn, and quite far from the hedges, when I saw Hester's bare arm protrude from the dark-green privet. 'Just hand them over!' she was saying, and Noah and Simon began to tease her.

'Hand *what* over?' Simon was saying.

Owen and I wrote down the license-plate numbers of the cars blocking Mr Meany's pickup, and then I presented the list to my grandmother, who enjoyed making announcements in a voice based on Maugham's Mrs Culver from *The Constant Wife*. It took us a while to free Mr Meany from the driveway; Owen was visibly more relaxed after his father had departed.

He was left holding his father's nearly full glass of champagne, which I advised him not to drink; I was sure it tasted heavily of pickle. We went and stared at the wedding presents, until I acknowledged the propitious placement of the present from Owen and his father.

'I MADE IT MYSELF, he said. At first I thought he meant the Christmas wrapping paper, but then I realized that he had made the actual present. 'MY FATHER HELPED ME SELECT THE PROPER STONE,' Owen admitted. Good God, so it *is* granite! I thought.

Owen was upset that the newlyweds would not open their presents until after their honeymoon, but he restrained himself from describing the present to me. I would have many years to see it for myself, he explained. Indeed, I would.

It was a brick-shaped piece of the finest granite – 'MONUMENT QUALITY, AS GOOD AS THEY GET OUT OF BARRE,' Owen would say. Owen had cut it himself, polished it himself; he had designed and chiseled the border himself, and the engraving was all his, too. He had worked on it after school in the monument shop, and on weekends. It looked like a tombstone for a cherished pet – at best, a marker for a stillborn child; but more appropriate for a cat or a hamster. It was meant to lie lengthwise, like a loaf of bread, and it was engraved with the approximate date of my mother's marriage to Dan:

JULY
1952

Whether Owen was unsure of the exact date, or whether it would have meant hours more of engraving – or ruined his concept of the aesthetics of the stone – I don't know. It was too big and heavy for a paperweight. Although Owen later suggested this use for it, he admitted it was more practical as a doorstop. For years – before he gave it to me – Dan Needham dutifully used it as a doorstop and frequently bashed his toes against it. But whatever it would become, it had to be left in the open where Owen would be sure to see it when he visited; he was proud of it, and my mother adored it. Well, my mother adored Owen; if he'd given her a gravestone with the date of death left blank – to be filled in at the appropriate time – she would have loved that, too. As it was, in my opinion – and in Dan's – Owen *did* give her a gravestone. It had been made in a monument shop, with grave-marking tools; it may have had her wedding date on it, but it was a miniature tombstone.

And although there was much mirth in evidence at my mother's wedding, and even my grandmother exhibited an unusual tolerance for the many young and not-so-young adults who were cavorting and jolly with drink, the reception ended in an outburst of bad weather more appropriate for a funeral.

Owen became quite playful regarding his possession of Hester's panties. He was not one to be bold with girls, and only a fool – or Noah or Simon – would be bold with Hester; but Owen managed to surround himself with the crowd, thus making it embarrassing for Hester to take back her panties. 'Give them over, Owen,' she would hiss at him.

'OKAY, SURE, DO YOU WANT THEM?' he would say, reaching for his pocket while standing firmly between Aunt Martha and Uncle Alfred.

'Not *here*!' Hester would say threateningly.

'OH, SO YOU *DON'T* WANT THEM? CAN I KEEP THEM?' he would say.

Hester stalked him through the party; she was only mildly angry, I thought – or she was mildly enjoying herself. It was a flirtation that made me the slightest bit jealous, and it went on so long that Noah and Simon got bored and began to arm themselves with confetti for my mother and Dan's eventual departure.

That came sooner than expected, because they had only begun to cut up the wedding cake when the storm started. It had been growing darker and darker, and the wind now carried some light rain in it; but when the thunder and lightning began, the wind dropped and the rain fell heavily and straight down – in sheets. Guests bolted for the cover of the house; my grandmother quickly tired of telling people to wipe their feet. The caterers struggled with the bar and the tables of food; they had set up a tent that extended over only half the terrace, like an awning, but there was not enough room under it for the wedding presents *and* for all the food and drink; Owen and I helped move the presents inside. My mother and Dan raced upstairs to change their clothes and grab their bags. Uncle Alfred was summoned to fetch the Buick, which he had not vandalized too badly in the usual 'Just Married' fashion. 'Just Married' was written, with chalk, across the tailgate, but the lettering was almost washed away by the time my mother and Dan came downstairs in their traveling clothes, carrying their luggage.

The wedding guests crowded in the many windows that faced the driveway, to see the honeymooners leave; but they had a confused departure. The rain was pelting down as they tried to put the luggage in the car; Uncle Alfred, in the role of their valet, was soaking wet – and since Simon and Noah had hoarded all the confetti for themselves, they were the only throwers. They threw most of it on their father, on Uncle Alfred, because he was so wet that the confetti stuck to him, instantly turning him into a clown.

People were cheering from the windows of 80 Front Street, but my grandmother was frowning. Chaos disturbed her; mayhem was mayhem, even if people were having a good time; bad weather was bad weather, even if no one seemed to mind. And some of her old crones were watching her, too. (How does royalty react to rain at a wedding? It's what that Tabby Wheelwright deserves – her in her white dress.) My Aunt Martha risked the rain to hug and kiss my mother and Dan; Simon and Noah plastered her with confetti, too.

Then, as suddenly as the wind had dropped and the rain had fallen, the rain changed to hail. In New Hampshire, you can't even count on July. Hailstones bounced off the Buick like machine-gun fire, and Dan and my mother jumped into the car; Aunt Martha shrieked and covered her head – she and Uncle Alfred ran to the house. Even Noah and Simon felt the hailstones' sting; they retreated, too. Someone shouted that a hailstone had broken a champagne glass, left on the terrace. The hailstones struck with such force that the people crowded close to the windows stepped back, away from the glass. Then my mother rolled down the car windows; I thought she was waving good-bye but she was calling for me. I held my jacket over my head, but the hailstones were still painful. One of them, the size of a robin's egg, struck the bony knob of my elbow and made me wince.

'Good-bye, darling!' my mother said, pulling my head inside the car window and kissing me. 'Your grandmother knows where we're going, but she won't tell you unless there's an emergency.'

'Have a good time!' I said. When I looked at 80 Front Street, every downstairs window was a portrait – faces looking at me, and at the honeymooners. Well, almost everyone – not Gravesend's two holy men; they weren't watching me, or the newlyweds. At opposite ends of the house, alone in their own little windows, the Rev. Lewis Merrill and the Rev. Dudley Wiggin were watching the sky. Were they taking a religious view of the hailstorm? I wondered. In Rector Wiggin's case, I imagined he was seeing the weather from the point of view of an ex-pilot – that he was simply observing that it would be a shitty day to fly. But Pastor Merrill was searching the heavens for the source of such a violent storm. Was there anything in the Holy Scriptures that tipped him off about the meaning of hailstones? In their zeal to demonstrate their knowledge of appropriate passages from the Bible, neither minister had offered my mother and Dan that most reassuring blessing from Tobit – the one that goes, 'That she and I may grow old together.'

Too bad neither of the ministers thought of that one, but the books of the Apocrypha are usually omitted from Protestant editions of the Bible. There would be no growing old together for Dan Needham and my mother, whose appointment with the ball that Owen hit was only a year away.

I was nearly back inside the house when my mother called me again. 'Where's Owen?' she asked. It took me a while to locate him in the windows, because he was upstairs, in my mother's bedroom; the figure of the woman in the red dress was standing beside him, my mother's double, her dressmaker's dummy. I know now that there were *three* holy men at 80 Front Street that day – three guys with their eyes on the weather. Owen wasn't watching the departing honeymooners, either. Owen was also watching the skies, with one arm around the dummy's waist, sagging on her hip, his troubled face peering upward. I should have known then what angel he was watching for; but it was a busy day, my mother was asking for Owen – I just ran upstairs and brought him to her. He didn't seem to mind the hail; the pellets clattered off the car all around him, but I didn't see one hit him. He stuck his face in the window and my mother kissed him. Then she asked him how he was getting home. 'You're not walking home, or taking your bike, Owen – not in this weather,' she said. 'Do you want a ride?'

'ON YOUR HONEYMOON?' he asked.

'Get in,' she said. 'Dan and I will drop you.'

He looked awfully pleased; that he should get to go on my mother's honeymoon – even for a little bit of the way! He tried to slide into the car, past her, but his trousers were wet and they stuck against my mother's skirt.

'Wait a minute,' she said. 'Let me out. You get in first.' She meant that he was small enough to straddle the drive-shaft hump, in the middle of the seat, between her and Dan, but when she stepped outside the Buick – even for just a second – a hailstone ricocheted off the roof of the car and smacked her right between the eyes.

'*Ow!*' she cried, holding her head.

'I'M SORRY!' Owen said quickly.

'Get in, get in,' Mother said, laughing.

They started to drive away.

It was then Hester realized that Owen had successfully made off with her panties.

She ran out in the driveway and stood with her hands on her hips, staring at the slowly moving car; Dan and my mother, facing forward, stuck their hands out the windows, risking the hailstones, and waved. Owen turned around in the seat between them and faced backward; his grin took up his whole face, and it was very clear, from the flash of white, what he was waving to Hester.

'Hey! You little creep!' Hester called. But the hail was turning back to rain; Hester was instantly soaked as she stood there in the driveway – and her yellow dress clung to her so tenaciously that it was easy to see what she was missing. She bolted for the house.

'Young lady,' my Aunt Martha said to her, 'where on earth are your . . .'

'Merciful Heavens, Hester!' my grandmother said.

But the heavens did not look merciful, not at the moment. And my grandmother's crones, observing Hester, must have been thinking: That may be Martha's girl but she's got more of Tabby's kind of trouble in her.

Simon and Noah were gathering hailstones before they

could melt in the returning rain. I ran outside to join them. They let fly at me with a few of the bigger ones; I gathered my own supply and fired back. I was surprised by the hailstones' coldness – as if they had traveled to earth from another, much icier universe. Squeezing a hailstone the size of a marble in my hand, feeling it melt in my palm, I was also surprised by its hardness; it was as hard as a baseball.

Mr Chickering, our fat and friendly Little League coach and manager – the man who decided, that day, to have Owen bat for me, the man who instructed Owen to 'Swing away!' – Mr Chickering is spending his last days in the Soldiers' Home on Court Street. The wrecked images that his bout with Alzheimer's hurl at him from time to time have left him jumpy and dazed, but curiously alert. Like a man sitting under a tree full of children pelting him with acorns, he seems to expect he'll be hit at any moment, he even appears to be looking forward to it, but he has no notion where the acorns come from (despite what must be the firm feeling of the trunk of the tree against his back). When I visit him – when the acorns fly at him, and hit him just the right way – he perks up instantly. 'You're on deck, Johnny!' he says cheerfully. And once he said, 'Owen's batting for you, Johnny!' But, at other times, he is far away; perhaps he is turning my mother's face to the ground, but taking care to close her eyes first – or else he is pulling down the skirt of her dress, for decency's sake, and pinching her splayed knees together. Once, when he appeared to fail to recognize me – when I could establish no coherent communication with him – he spoke up as I was leaving; it was a sad, reflective voice that said, 'You don't want to see her, Johnny.'

At my mother's funeral, in Hurd's Church, Mr Chickering was visibly moved. I'm certain that his rearranging of my mother's body in its repose had been the only time he had ever touched her; both the memory of that, and of Police Chief Pike's inquiries regarding the 'instrument of death,' the 'murder weapon,' had clearly rattled Mr Chickering, who wept openly at the funeral, as if he were mourning the death of baseball itself. Indeed, not only had Owen and I quit the team – and that infernal game – forever; other members of our Little League team had used the upsetting incident as a means to get out of a tedious obligation that had been much more their parents' notion of something that was 'good for them' than it had ever been their sport of choice. Mr Chickering, who was completely good-hearted, had always told us that when we won, we won as a team, and when we lost, we lost as a team. Now – in his view – we had *killed* as a team; but he wept in his pew as if he bore more than his share of team responsibility.

He had encouraged some of my other teammates and their families to sit with him – among them, the hapless Harry Hoyt, who'd received a base on balls with two outs, who'd made his own, small contribution to Owen Meany coming to the plate. After all, Harry could have been the last out – in which case, my mother would have taken Owen and me home from the game, as usual. But Harry had walked. He sat in Hurd's, quite riveted by Mr Chickering's tears. Harry was almost innocent. We had been so many runs behind, and there were already two outs in our last inning; it made no sense for Harry Hoyt to walk. What possible good could a base on balls have done us? Harry should have been swinging away.

He was an otherwise harmless creature, although he would cause his mother no little grief. His father was dead, his mother was – for years – the receptionist at the Gas Works; she got all the calls about the billing errors, and the leaks. Harry would never be Gravesend Academy material. He dutifully finished Gravesend High School and enlisted in the Navy – the Navy was popular around Gravesend. His mother tried to get Harry out of the service, claiming she was a widow who needed his support; but – in the first place – she had a job, and in the second place, Harry *wanted* to go in the Navy. He was embarrassed by his mother's lack of patriotic zeal; it may have been the only time he argued with anyone, but he won the argument – he got to go to Vietnam, where he was killed by one of the poisonous snakes of that region. It was a Russell's viper and it bit him while he was peeing under a tree; a later revelation was that the tree stood outside a whorehouse, where Harry had been waiting his turn. He was like that; he was a walker – when there was no good reason to walk.

His death made his mother quite political – or at least 'quite political' for Gravesend. She called herself a war resister and she advertised that in her home she would give free counsel on how to evade the draft; it was never very accurately demonstrated that her evening draft-counseling sessions so exhausted her that she became an inadequate receptionist at the Gas Works – yet the Gas Works let her go. Several patriots from the town were apprehended in the act of vandalizing her car and garage; she didn't press charges, but she was gossiped about as a corrupter of the morals of youth. Although she was a plain, even dowdy woman, she was accused of seducing several of her young draft counselees, and she eventually moved away from Gravesend – I think she moved to Portsmouth; that was far enough away. I remember her at my mother's funeral; she didn't sit with her son Harry, where Mr Chickering had gathered the team in adjacent pews. She was never a team player, Mrs Hoyt; but Harry was.

Mrs Hoyt was the first person I remember who said that to criticize a specific American president was *not* anti-American; that to criticize a specific American policy was *not* antipatriotic; and that to disapprove of our involvement in a particular war against the communists was *not* the same as taking the communists' side. But these distinctions were lost on most of the citizens of Gravesend; they are lost on many of my former fellow Americans today.

I don't remember seeing Buzzy Thurston at my mother's funeral. He should have been there. After Harry Hoyt walked, Buzzy Thurston should have been the last out. He hit such an easy grounder – it was as sure an out as I've ever seen – but somehow the shortstop bobbled the ball. Buzzy Thurston reached base on an error. Who was that shortstop? He should have been in Hurd's Church, too.

Possibly Buzzy wasn't there because he was Catholic; Owen suggested this, but there were other Catholics in attendance – Owen was simply expressing his particular prejudice. And I may be doing Buzzy an injustice; maybe he was there – after all, Hurd's was packed; it was as full as it had been for my mother's wedding. All those same crones of my grandmother were there. I know what they came to see. How does royalty react to *this*? How will Harriet Wheelwright respond to Fate with a capital F – to a Freak Accident (with a capital F, too), or to an Act of God (if that's what you believe it was)? All those same crones, as black and hunchbacked as crows gathered around some road kill – they came to the service as if to say: We acknowledge, O God, that Tabby Wheelwright was not allowed to get off scot-free.

Getting off 'scot-free' was a cardinal crime in New Hampshire. And by the birdy alertness visible in the darting eyes of my grandmother's crones, I could tell that – in their view – my mother had not escaped her just reward.

Buzzy Thurston, there or not there, would not get off scot-free, either. I really didn't dislike Buzzy – especially after he spoke up for Owen, when Owen and I got ourselves in hot water with some of Buzzy's Catholic classmates because of a little incident at St Michael's, the parochial school. But Buzzy was judged harshly for his role in reaching base and bringing Owen Meany up to bat (if judgment is what you believe it was). He was not Gravesend Academy material, either; yet he did a postgraduate year at the academy, because he was a fair athlete – your standard outdoor New England variety: a football, hockey, and baseball man. He did not always need to reach base on an error.

He was not outstanding, not at anything, but he was good enough to go to the state university, and he lettered in three sports there. He missed a year of competition with a knee injury, and managed to finagle a fifth year of college – retaining his student draft determent for the extra year. After that, he was 'draft material,' but he rather desperately strove to miss the trip to Vietnam by poisoning himself for his physical. He drank a fifth of bourbon a day for two weeks; he smoked so much marijuana that his hair smelled like a cupboard crammed with oregano; he started a fire in his parents' oven, baking peyote; he was hospitalized with a colon disorder, following an LSD experience wherein he became convinced that his own Hawaiian sports shirt was edible, and he consumed some of it – including the buttons and the contents of the pocket: a book of matches, a package of cigarette papers, and a paper clip.

Given the provincialism of the Gravesend draft board, Buzzy was declared psychologically unfit to serve, which had been his crafty intention. Unfortunately, he had grown to *like* the bourbon, the marijuana, the peyote, and the LSD; in fact, he so worshiped their excesses that he was killed one night on the Maiden Hill Road by the steering column of his Plymouth, when he drove head-on into the abutment of the railroad bridge that was only a few hundred yards downhill from the Meany Granite Quarry. It was Mr Meany who called the police. Owen and I knew that bridge well; it followed an especially sharp turn at the bottom of a steep downhill run – it called for caution, even on our bicycles.

It was the ill-treated Mrs Hoyt who observed that Buzzy Thurston was simply another victim of the Vietnam War; although no one listened to her, she maintained that the war was the cause of the many abuses Buzzy had practiced upon himself – just as surely as the war had axed her Harry. To Mrs Hoyt, these things were symptomatic of the Vietnam years: the excessive use of drugs and alcohol, the suicidally fast driving, and the whorehouses in Southeast Asia, where many American virgins were treated to their first and last sexual experiences – not to mention the Russell's vipers, waiting under the trees!

Mr Chickering *should* have wept – not only for the whimsy with which he'd instructed Owen Meany to 'Swing away!' Had he known everything that would follow, he would have bathed his chubby face in even more tears than he produced that day in Hurd's when he was grieving for and as a *team*.

Naturally, Police Chief Pike sat apart; policemen like to sit by the door. And Chief Pike wasn't weeping. To him, my mother was still a 'case'; for him, the service was an opportunity to look over the suspects – because we were all suspects in Chief Pike's eyes. Among the mourners, Chief Pike suspected the ball-thief lurked.

He was always 'by the door,' Chief Pike. When I dated his daughter, I always thought he would be bursting through a door – or a window – at any moment. It was doubtless a result of my anxiety concerning his sudden entrance that I once tangled my lower lip in his daughter's braces, retreating too quickly from her kiss – certain I had heard the chief's boots creaking in my near vicinity.

That day at Hurd's, you could almost hear those boots creaking by the door, as if he expected the stolen baseball to loose itself from the culprit's pocket and roll across the dark crimson carpeting with incriminating authority. For Chief Pike, the theft of the ball that killed my mother was an offense of a far graver character than a mere misdemeanor; at the very least, it was the work of a felon. That my poor mother had been killed by the ball seemed not to concern Chief Pike; that poor Owen Meany had hit the ball was of slightly more interest to our chief of police – but only because it established a motive for Owen to *possess* the baseball in question. Therefore, it was not upon my mother's closed coffin that our chief of police fixed his stare; nor did Chief Pike pay particular attention to the formerly airborne Captain Wiggin – nor did he show much interest in the slight stutter of the shaken Pastor Merrill. Rather, the intent gaze of our chief of police bore into the back of the head of Owen Meany, who sat precariously upon six or seven copies of *The Pilgrim Hymnal*; Owen tottered on the stack of hymnals, as if the police chief's gaze unbalanced him. He sat as near to our family pews as possible; he sat where he'd sat for my mother's wedding – behind the Eastman family in general, and Uncle Alfred in particular. This time there would be no jokes from Simon about the inappropriateness of Owen's navy-blue Sunday school suit – such a little clone of the suit his father wore. The granitic Mr Meany sat heavily beside Owen.

' "I am the resurrection and the life, saith the Lord," ' said the Rev. Dudley Wiggin. ' "Blessed are the dead who die in the Lord." '

' "O God, whose mercies cannot be numbered," ' said the Rev. Lewis Merrill. ' "Accept our prayers on behalf of thy servant Tabby, and grant her an entrance into the land of light and joy, in the fellowship of thy saints." '

In the dull light of Hurd's Church, only Lydia's wheelchair gleamed – in the aisle beside my grandmother's pew, where Harriet Wheelwright sat alone. Dan and I sat in the pew behind her. The Eastmans sat behind us.

The Rev. Captain Wiggin called upon Corinthians – 'God shall wipe away all tears' – whereupon, Dan began to cry.

The rector, eager as ever to represent belief as a battle, brought up Isaiah – 'He will swallow up death in victory.' Now I heard my Aunt Martha join Dan; but the two of them were no match for Mr Chickering, who had started weeping even before the ministers began their readings of the Old and the New Testament.

Pastor Merrill stuttered his way into Lamentations – 'The Lord is good unto them that wait for him.'

Then we were led through the Twenty-third Psalm, as if there were a soul in Gravesend who didn't know it by heart: 'The Lord is my shepherd; I shall not want' – and so forth. When we got to the part that goes, 'Yea, though I walk through the valley of the shadow of death, I will fear no evil,' that was when I began to hear Owen's voice above all the others.

When the rector said, ' "Give courage to those who are bereaved," ' I was already dreading how loud Owen's voice would be during the final hymn; I knew it was one he liked.

When the pastor said, ' "Help us, we pray, in the midst of things we cannot understand," ' I was already humming the hymn, trying to drown out Owen's voice – in advance.

And when Mr Wiggin and Mr Merrill struggled to say, in unison, ' "Grant us to entrust Tabitha to thy never-failing love," ' I knew it was time; I almost covered my ears.

What else do we sing at an untimely death, what else but that catchy number that is categorized in *The Pilgrim Hymnal* as a favorite hymn of 'ascension and reign' – the popular 'Crown Him with Many Crowns,' a real organ-breaker?

For when else, if not at the death of a loved one, do we most need to hear about the resurrection, about eternal life – about him who has *risen*?

> Crown him with man-y crowns, The Lamb up-on his throne;
> Hark! how the heaven-ly an-them drowns All mu-sic but its own;
> A-wake, my soul, and sing Of him who died for thee,
> And hail him as thy match-less king Through all e-ter-ni-ty.
> Crown him the Lord of love; Be-hold his hands and side,
> Rich wounds, yet vis-i-ble above, In beau-ty glo-ri-fied;
> No an-gel in the sky Can ful-ly bear that sight,
> But down-ward bends his burn-ing eye At mys-ter-ies so bright.

But it was the third verse that especially inspired Owen.

CROWN HIM THE LORD OF LIFE, WHO TRI-UMPHED O'ER THE GRAVE,
AND ROSE VIC-TO-RIOUS IN THE STRIFE FOR THOSE HE CAME TO SAVE;
HIS GLO-RIES NOW WE SING WHO DIED AND ROSE ON HIGH,
WHO DIED, E-TER-NAL LIFE TO BRING, AND LIVES THAT DEATH MAY DIE.

Even later, at the committal, I could hear Owen's awful voice ringing, when Mr Wiggin said, ' "In the midst of life we are in death." ' But it was as if Owen were still humming the tune to 'Crown Him with Many Crowns,' because I seemed to hear nothing else; I think now that is the nature of hymns – they make us want to repeat them, and repeat them; they are a part of any service, and often the only part of a funeral service, that makes us feel everything is acceptable. Certainly, the burial is unacceptable; doubly so, in my mother's case, because – after the reassuring numbness of Hurd's Church – we were standing exposed, outside, on a typical Gravesend summer day, muggy and hot, with the inappropriate sounds of children's voices coming from the nearby high-school athletic fields.

The cemetery, at the end of Linden Street, was within sight of the high school and the junior high school. I would attend the latter for only two years, but that was long enough to hear – many times – the remarks most frequently made by those students who were trapped in the study hall and seated nearest the windows that faced the cemetery: something to the effect that they would be less bored out there, in the graveyard.

'In sure and certain hope of the resurrection to eternal life through our Lord Jesus Christ, we commend to Almighty God our sister Tabitha, and we commit her body to the ground,' Pastor Merrill said. That was when I noticed that Mr Merrill's wife was holding her ears. She was terribly pale, except for the plump backs of her upper arms, which were painful to look at because her sunburn there was so intense; she wore a loose, sleeveless dress, more gray than black – but maybe she didn't have a proper black dress that was sleeveless, and she could not have been expected to force such a sunburn into sleeves. She swayed slightly, squinting her eyes. At first I thought that she held her ears due to some near-blinding pain inside her head; her dry blond hair looked ready to burst into flames, and one of her feet had strayed out of the straps of her sandals. One of her sickly children leaned against her hip. ' "Earth to earth, ashes to ashes, dust to dust," ' said her husband, but Mrs Merrill couldn't have heard him; she not only held her ears, she appeared to be pressing them into her skull.

Hester had noticed. She stared at Mrs Merrill as intently

as I stared at her; all at once Hester's tough face was constricted by pain – or by some sudden, painful memory – and she, too, covered her ears. But the tune to 'Crown Him with Many Crowns' was still in my head; I didn't hear what Mrs Merrill and Hester heard. I thought they were both guilty of extraordinary rudeness toward Pastor Merrill, who was doing his best with the benediction – although he was rushing now, and even the usually unflappable Captain Wiggin was shaking his head, as if to rid *his* ears of water or an unpleasant sound.

' "The Lord bless her and keep her," ' Lewis Merrill said. That was when I looked at Owen. His eyes were shut, his lips were moving; he appeared to be growling, but it was the best he could do at humming – it *was* 'Crown Him with Many Crowns' that I heard; it was *not* my imagination. But Owen held his hands over his ears, too.

Then I saw Simon raise his hands; Noah's hands were already in place – and my Uncle Alfred and my Aunt Martha: they held their ears, too. Even Lydia held her ears in her hands. My grandmother glowered, but she would not raise her hands; she made herself listen, although I could tell it was painful for her to hear it – and that was when *I* heard it: the children on the high-school athletic fields. They were playing baseball. There were the usual shouts, the occasional arguments, the voices coming all at once; and then the quiet, or almost quiet, was punctuated – as baseball games always are – by the crack of the bat. There it went, a pretty solid-sounding hit, and I watched even the rocklike face of Mr Meany wince, his fingers close on Owen's shoulders. And Mr Merrill, stuttering worse than usual, said, ' "The Lord make his face to shine upon her and be gracious unto her, the Lord lift up his countenance upon her and give her peace. *Amen.*" '

He immediately bent down and took some loose dirt in his hand; he was the first to cast earth upon my mother's coffin, where I knew she wore a black dress – the one she'd copied from the red dress, which she'd hated. The white copy, Dan had said, did not look so good on her; I guessed that her death had ill-affected her tan. I'd already been told that the swelling at her temple, and the surrounding discoloration, had made an open coffin inadvisable – not that we Wheelwrights were much for open coffins, under any circumstances; Yankees believe in closed doors.

One by one, the mourners threw dirt on the coffin; then it was awkward to return their hands to their ears – although Hester did, before she thought better of it. The heel of her dirty hand put a smudge on her ear and on the side of her face. Owen would not throw a handful of dirt; I also saw that he would not take his hands from his ears. He would not open his eyes, either, and his father had to walk him out of the cemetery. Twice, I heard him say, 'I'M SORRY!'

I heard a few more cracks of the bat before Dan Needham took me to 80 Front Street. At Grandmother's, there was just 'family.' My Aunt Martha led me up to my old room and we sat on my old bed together. She told me that I could come live with her and Uncle Alfred and Noah and Simon and Hester, 'up north,' where I would always be welcome; she hugged me and kissed me and told me to never forget that there was always that option.

Then my grandmother came to my room: she shooed Aunt Martha away and she sat beside me. She told me that if I didn't mind living with an old woman, I was certainly welcome to have my room back – that it would always be my room, that no one else would ever have any claim to it. She hugged me and kissed me, too; she said that we both had to be sure that we gave a lot of love and attention to Dan.

Dan was next. He sat on my bed, too. He reminded me that he had legally adopted me; that although I was Johnny Wheelwright to everyone in Gravesend, I was as good as a Johnny Needham, to the school, and that meant that I could go to Gravesend Academy – when the time came, and just as my mother had wanted me to – as a legitimate faculty child, just as if I were Dan's actual son. Dan said he thought of me as his son, anyway, and he would never take a job that took him away from Gravesend Academy until I'd had the chance to graduate. He said he'd understand if I found 80 Front Street more comfortable than his dormitory apartment, but that he liked having me live in his apartment, with him, if I wasn't too bored with the confinement of the place. Maybe I'd prefer to spend some nights every week with him, and some nights at 80 Front Street – any nights I wished, in either place.

I said I thought that would be fine, and I asked him to tell Aunt Martha – in a way that wouldn't hurt her feelings – that I really was a Gravesend boy and I didn't want to move 'up north.' Actually, the very thought of living with my cousins exhausted and terrified me, and I was convinced I should be consumed by sinful longing for unnatural acts with Hester if I permitted myself to move in with the Eastmans. (I did *not* tell Dan that he should tell Aunt Martha that.)

When someone you love dies, and you're not expecting it, you don't lose her all at once; you lose her in pieces over a long time – the way the mail stops coming, and her scent fades from the pillows and even from the clothes in her closet and drawers. Gradually, you accumulate the parts of her that are gone. Just when the day comes – when there's a particular missing part that overwhelms you with the feeling that she's gone, forever – there comes another day, and another specifically missing part.

The evening after her funeral, I felt she was gone when it was time for Dan to go home to the dorm. I realized that Dan had choices – he could return to his dormitory apartment, alone, or I could offer to go back with him; or he could stay at 80 Front Street, he could even stay in the other twin bed in my room because I'd already told my grandmother that I didn't want Noah or Simon sleeping there that night. But as soon as I realized what Dan's choices were, I also knew they were – each of them – imperfect in their own way. I realized that the choices available to Dan, regarding where he would sleep, would be imperfect, forever; and that, forever, there would be something unsatisfying about thinking of him alone – and something also incomplete about him being with me.

'Do you want me to come back to the dorm with you?' I asked him.

'Would you like me to stay with you?' he asked me.

But what did it matter?

I watched him walk down Front Street toward the lights of the academy buildings. It was a warm night, with the frequent banging of screen doors and the sounds of rocking chairs on the screened-in porches. The neighborhood kids were playing some game with a flashlight; fortunately, it was too dark for even the most American of kids to be hitting a baseball.

My cousins were uncharacteristically subdued by the tragedy. Noah kept saying 'I can't believe it!' Then he'd put his hand on my shoulder. And Simon rather tactlessly, but innocently, added: 'Who would have thought he could hit a ball *hard* enough?'

My Aunt Martha curled up on the living-room couch with her head in Uncle Alfred's lap; she lay there not moving, like a little girl with an earache. My grandmother sat in her usual thronelike chair in the same room; she and Alfred would occasionally exchange glances and shake their heads. Once Aunt Martha sat up with her hair a mess and pounded her fist on the coffee table. 'It doesn't make any *sense*!' she shouted; then she put her head back down in Uncle Alfred's lap, and cried for a while. To this outburst, my grandmother neither shook nor nodded her head; she looked at the ceiling, ambiguously – either seeking restraint or patience there, or seeking some possible *sense*, which Martha had found to be lacking.

Hester had not changed out of her funeral dress; it was black linen, of a simplicity and good fit that my mother might have favored, and Hester looked especially grown-up in it, although it was badly wrinkled. She kept pinning her hair up on top of her head, because of the heat, but wild strands of it would fall down on her face and neck until, exasperated, she would let it all down again. The fine beads of sweat on her upper lip gave her skin the smoothness and the shine of glass.

'Want to take a walk?' she asked me.

'Sure,' I said.

'Want Noah and me to go with you?' Simon asked.

'No,' Hester said.

Most of the houses on Front Street still had their downstairs lights on; dogs were still outside, and barking; but the kids who'd been playing the flashlight game had been called inside. The heat off the sidewalk still radiated *up* at you; on hot summer nights, in Gravesend, the heat hit your crotch first. Hester took my hand as we walked.

'It's only the second time I've seen you in a dress,' I said.

'I know,' she said.

It was an especially dark night, cloudy and starless; the moon was just an opaque sliver in the fog.

'Just remember,' she said, 'your friend Owen feels worse than you.'

'I know,' I said; but I felt no small surge of jealousy at my admission – and at the knowledge that Hester was thinking about Owen, too.

We left Front Street at the Gravesend Inn; I hesitated before crossing Pine Street, but Hester seemed to know our destination – her hand tugged me along. Once we were on Linden Street, passing the dark high school, it was clear to both of us where we were going. There was a police car in the high-school parking lot – on the lookout for vandals, I suppose, or else to prevent the high-school students from using the parking lot and the athletic fields for illicit purposes at night.

We could hear a motor running; it seemed too deep and throaty a motor to be the squad car, and after we passed the high school, the engine noise grew louder. I didn't believe that a motor was required to run the cemetery, but that's where the sound was coming from. I think now that I must have wanted to see her grave at night, knowing how she hated the darkness; I believe I wanted to reassure myself that some light penetrated even the cemetery at night.

The streetlights on Linden Street shone some distance into the cemetery and clearly illuminated the Meany Granite Company truck, which was parked and idling at the main gate; Hester and I could observe Mr Meany's solemn face behind the steering wheel, his face illuminated by the long drags he took from his cigarette. He was alone in the cab of the truck, but I knew where Owen was.

Mr Meany seemed unsurprised to see me, although Hester made him nervous. Hester made everyone nervous: in good light, in close-up, she looked her age – like a large, overly mature twelve-year-old. But from any distance, with any assistance from the shadows, she looked eighteen – and like a lot of trouble, too.

'Owen had some more to say,' Mr Meany confided to us. 'But he's been at it a while. I'm sure he's about finished.'

I felt another rush of jealousy, to think that Owen's concerns for my mother's first night underground had preceded my own. In the humid air, the diesel exhaust was heavy and foul, but I was sure that Mr Meany could not be prevailed upon to turn the engine off; probably he was keeping the engine running in an effort to hurry up Owen's prayers.

'I want you to know somethin',' Mr Meany said. 'I'm gonna listen to what your mother said. She told me not to interfere if Owen wanted to go to the academy. And I won't,' he said. 'I promised her,' he added.

It would take me years to realize that from the moment Owen hit that ball, Mr Meany wouldn't 'interfere' with *anything* Owen wanted.

'She told me not to worry about the *money*, too,' Mr Meany said. 'I don't know what happens about that – now,' he added.

'Owen will get a full scholarship,' I said.

'I don't know about that,' Mr Meany said. 'I guess so, if he wants one,' he added. 'Your mother was speakin' about his *clothes*,' Mr Meany said. 'All them coats and ties.'

'Don't worry,' I told him.

'Oh, I ain't worryin'!' he said. 'I'm just promisin' you I ain't interferin' – that's the point.'

A light blinked from the cemetery, and Mr Meany saw Hester and me look in its direction.

'He's got a light with him,' Mr Meany said. 'I don't know what's takin' him so long,' he said. 'He's been in there long enough.' He stepped on the accelerator then, as if a little rev would hurry Owen along. But after a while, he said, 'Maybe you better go see what's keepin' him.'

The light in the cemetery was faint and Hester and I walked toward it cautiously, not wanting to tread on other people's flowers or bark our shins on one of the smaller graves. The farther we walked from the Meany Granite Company truck, the more the engine noise receded – but it seemed deeper, too, as if it were the motor at the core of the earth, the one that turned the earth and changed day to night. We could hear snatches of Owen's prayers; I thought he must have brought the flashlight so he could read The Book of Common Prayer – perhaps he was reading every prayer in it.

' "INTO PARADISE MAY THE ANGELS LEAD YOU," ' he read.

Hester and I stopped; she stood behind me and locked her arms around my waist. I could feel her breasts against my shoulder blades, and – because she was a little taller – I could feel her throat against the back of my head; her chin pushed my head down.

' "FATHER OF ALL," ' Owen read. ' "WE PRAY TO YOU FOR THOSE WE LOVE, BUT SEE NO LONGER." ' Hester squeezed me, she kissed my ears. Mr Meany revved the truck, but Owen did not appear to notice; he knelt in front of the first bank of flowers, at the foot of the mound of new earth, in front of my mother's gravestone. He had the prayer book flat upon the ground in front of him, the flashlight pinched between his knees.

'Owen?' I said, but he didn't hear me. 'Owen!' I said more loudly. He looked up, but not at me; I mean, he looked *up* – he'd heard his name called, but he hadn't recognized *my* voice.

'I HEAR YOU!' he shouted angrily. 'WHAT DO YOU WANT? WHAT ARE YOU DOING? WHAT DO YOU WANT OF ME?'

'Owen, it's *me*,' I said; I felt Hester gasp behind me. It had suddenly occurred to her – *Whom* Owen thought he was speaking to.

'It's me, and Hester,' I added, because it occurred to me that the figure of Hester standing behind me, and appearing to loom over me, might also be misunderstood by Owen Meany, who was ever-watchful for that angel he had frightened from my mother's room.

'OH, IT'S YOU,' Owen said; he sounded disappointed. 'HELLO, HESTER. I DIDN'T RECOGNIZE YOU – YOU LOOK SO GROWN UP IN A DRESS. I'M SORRY,' Owen said.

'It's okay, Owen,' I said.

'HOW'S DAN?' he asked.

I told him that Dan was okay, but that he'd gone to his dormitory, alone, for the night; this news made Owen very businesslike.

'I SUPPOSE THE DUMMY'S STILL THERE? IN THE DINING ROOM?' he asked.

'Of course,' I said.

'WELL, THAT'S VERY BAD,' Owen said. 'DAN SHOULDN'T BE ALONE WITH THAT DUMMY. WHAT IF HE JUST SITS AROUND AND STARES AT IT? WHAT IF HE WAKES UP IN THE NIGHT AND HE SEES IT STANDING THERE ON HIS WAY TO THE REFRIGERATOR? WE SHOULD GO GET IT – RIGHT NOW.'

He arranged his flashlight in the flowers, so that the shiny body of the light was completely blanketed by the flowers and the light itself shone upon the mound. Then he stood up and brushed the dirt off the knees of his pants. He closed his prayer book and looked at how the light fell over my mother's grave; he seemed pleased. I was not the only one who knew how my mother had hated the darkness.

We couldn't all fit in the cab of the granite truck, so Owen sat with Hester and me on the dusty floor of the flatbed trailer while Mr Meany drove us to Dan's dorm. The senior students were up; we passed them on the stairwell and in the hall – some of them were in their pajamas, and all of them ogled Hester. I could hear the ice cubes rattling in Dan's glass before he opened the door.

'WE'VE COME FOR THE DUMMY, DAN,' Owen said, immediately taking charge.

'The dummy?' Dan said.

'YOU'RE NOT GOING TO SIT AROUND AND STARE AT IT,' Owen told him. He marched into the dining room where the dressmaker's dummy maintained its sentinel position over my mother's sewing machine; a few dressmaking materials were still spread out on the dining-room table; a drawing of a new pattern was pinned down flat on the table by a pair of shears. The dummy, however, was not newly attired. The dummy wore my mother's hated red dress. Owen had been the last person to dress the dummy; this time, he had tried a wide, black belt – one of Mother's favorites – to try to make the dress more tempting.

He took the belt off and put it on the table – as if Dan might have use for the belt! – and he picked the dummy up by her hips. When they were standing side by side, Owen came up only to the dummy's breasts; when he lifted her, her breasts were above his head – pointing the way.

'YOU DO WHAT YOU WANT, DAN,' Owen told him. 'BUT YOU'RE NOT GOING TO STARE AT THIS DUMMY AND MAKE YOURSELF MORE UNHAPPY.'

'Okay,' Dan said; he took another drink of his whiskey. 'Thank you, Owen,' he added, but Owen was already marching out.

'COME ON,' he said to Hester and me, and we followed him.

We drove out Court Street, and the entire length of Pine Street, with the trees blowing overhead and the granite dust stinging our faces on the flatbed. Owen whacked the truck cab once. 'FASTER!' he shouted to his father, and Mr Meany drove faster.

On Front Street, just as Mr Meany was slowing down, Hester said, 'I could drive like this all night. I could drive to the beach and back. It feels so good. It's the only way to feel cool.'

Owen whacked the truck cab again. 'DRIVE TO THE BEACH!' he said. 'DRIVE TO THE LITTLE BOAR'S HEAD AND BACK!'

We were off. 'FASTER!' Owen shouted once, out on the empty road to Rye. It was a fast eight or ten miles; soon the granite dust was gone from the floor of the flatbed, and the only thing to sting our faces was an occasional insect, pelting by. Hester's hair was wild. The wind rushed around us too forcefully for us to talk. Sweat instantly dried; tears, too. The red dress on my mother's dummy clung and flapped in the wind; Owen sat with his back against the cab of the truck, the dummy outstretched in his lap – as if the two of them were engaged in a half-successful levitation experiment.

At the beach, at Little Boar's Head, we took off our shoes and walked in the surf, while Mr Meany dutifully waited – the engine still idling. Owen carried the dummy the whole time, careful not to go very far into the waves; the red dress never got wet.

'I'LL KEEP THE DUMMY WITH ME,' he said. 'YOUR GRANDMOTHER SHOULDN'T HAVE THIS AROUND TO LOOK AT, EITHER – NOT TO MENTION, YOU,' he added.

'Not to mention, *you*,' Hester said, but Owen ignored this, high-stepping through the surf.

When Mr Meany dropped Hester and me at 80 Front Street, the downstairs lights in the houses along the street were off – except for the lights in Grandmother's house – but a few people were still upstairs, in their beds, reading. On very hot nights, Mr Fish slept in the hammock on his screened-in porch, so Hester and I kept our voices down, saying good night to Owen and his father; Owen told his father to *not* turn around in our driveway. Because the dressmaker's dummy wouldn't fit in the cab – because it couldn't bend – Owen stood on the flatbed with his arms around the hips of the red dress as the truck pulled away. With his free hand, he held fast to one of the loading chains – they were the chains for fastening down the curbstones or the monuments.

If Mr Fish had been in his hammock, and if he had woken up, he would have seen something unforgettable passing under the Front Street lamplights. The dark and massive truck, lumbering into the night, and the woman in the red dress – a headless woman with a stunning figure, but with no arms – held around her hips by a child attached to a chain, or a dwarf.

'I hope you know he's crazy,' said Hester tiredly.

But I looked at Owen's departing image with wonder: he had managed to orchestrate my mourning on the evening of my mother's funeral. And, like my armadillo's claws, he'd taken what he wanted – in this case, my mother's double, her shy dressmaker's dummy in that unloved dress. Later, I thought that Owen must have known the dummy was important; he must have foreseen that even the unwanted dress would have a use – that it had a purpose. But then, that night, I was inclined to agree with Hester; I thought the red dress was merely Owen's idea of a talisman – an amulet, to ward off the evil powers of that 'angel' Owen thought he'd seen. I didn't believe in angels then.

Toronto: February 1, 1987 – the Fourth Sunday After Epiphany. I believe in angels now. I don't necessarily claim that this is an advantage; for example, it was of no particular help to me during last night's Vestry elections – I wasn't even nominated. I've been a parish officer so many times, for so many years, I shouldn't complain; perhaps my fellow parishioners thought they were being kind to me – to give me a year off. Indeed, had I been nominated for warden or deputy warden, I might have declined to accept the nomination. I admit, I'm tired of it; I've done more than my share for Grace Church on-the-Hill. Still, I was surprised I wasn't nominated for a single office; out of politeness – if not out of recognition of my faithfulness and my devotion – I thought I should have been nominated for something.

I shouldn't have let the insult – if it even *is* an insult – distract me from the Sunday service; that was not good. Once I was rector's warden to Canon Campbell – back when Canon Campbell was our rector; when he was alive, I admit I felt a little better-treated. But since Canon Mackie has been rector, I've been deputy rector's warden once – and people's warden, too. And one year I was chairman of sidesmen; I've also been parish council chairman. It's not the fault of Canon Mackie that he'll never replace Canon Campbell in my heart; Canon Mackie is warm and kind – and his loquaciousness doesn't offend me. It is simply that Canon Campbell was special, and those early days were special, too.

I shouldn't brood about such a silly business as the annual installation of parish officers; especially, I shouldn't allow such thoughts to distract me from the choral Eucharist and the sermon. I confess to a certain childishness.

The visiting preacher distracted me, too. Canon Mackie is keen on having guest ministers deliver the sermon – which does spare us the canon's loquacity – but whoever the preacher was today, he was some sort of 'reformed' Anglican, and his thesis seemed to be that everything that first appears to be different is actually the same. I couldn't help thinking what Owen Meany would say about that.

In the Protestant tradition, we turn to the Bible; when we want an answer, that's where we look. But even the Bible distracted me today. For the Fourth Sunday After Epiphany, Canon Mackie chose Matthew – those troublesome Beatitudes; at least, they always troubled Owen and me.

> Blessed are the poor in spirit,
> for theirs is the kingdom of heaven.

It's just so hard to imagine 'the poor in spirit' achieving very much.

> Blessed are those who mourn,
> for they shall be comforted.

I was eleven years old when my mother was killed; I mourn her still. I mourn for more than her, too. I don't feel 'comforted'; not yet.

> Blessed are the meek,
> for they shall inherit the earth.

'BUT THERE'S NO EVIDENCE FOR THAT,' Owen told Mrs Walker in Sunday school.

And on and on:

> Blessed are the pure in heart,
> for they shall see God.

'BUT WILL IT HELP THEM – TO SEE GOD?' Owen Meany asked Mrs Walker.

Did it help Owen – to see God?

'Blessed are you when men revile you and persecute you and utter all kinds of evil against you falsely on my account,' Jesus says. 'Rejoice and be glad, for your reward is great in heaven, for so men persecuted the prophets who were before you.'

That was always something Owen and I found hard to take – *a reward in heaven.*

'GOODNESS AS BRIBERY,' Owen called it – an argument that eluded Mrs Walker.

And then – after the Beatitudes, and the sermon by the stranger – the Nicene Creed felt forced to me. Canon Campbell used to explain everything to me – the part about believing in 'One, Holy, Catholic, and Apostolic Church' bothered me; Canon Campbell helped me see beyond the words, he made me see in what sense 'Catholic,' in what way 'Apostolic.' Canon Mackie says I worry about 'mere words' too much. *Mere words?*

And then there was the business about 'all nations,' and – specifically – 'our Queen'; I'm not an American anymore, but I still have trouble with the part that goes 'grant unto thy servant ELIZABETH our Queen'; and to think that it is possible 'to lead all nations in the way of righteousness' is utterly ridiculous!

And before I received Holy Communion, I balked at the general Confession.

'We acknowledge and confess our manifold sins and wickedness.' Some Sundays, this is so hard to say; Canon Campbell indulged me when I confessed to him that this confession was difficult for me, but Canon Mackie employs the 'mere words' thesis with me until I am seeing him in a most unforgiving light. And when Canon Mackie proceeded with the Holy Eucharist, to the Thanksgiving and Consecration, which he *sang*, I even judged him unfairly for his singing voice, which is not and never will be the equal of Canon Campbell's – God Rest His Soul.

In the entire service, only the psalm struck me as true, and properly shamed me. It was the Thirty-seventh Psalm, and the choir appeared to sing it directly to me:

> Leave off from wrath, and let go displeasure:
> fret not thyself, else shalt thou be moved to do evil.

Yes, it's true: I should 'leave off from wrath, and let go displeasure.' What good is anger? I have been angry before. I have been 'moved to do evil,' too – as you shall see.

4 : THE LITTLE LORD JESUS

The first Christmas following my mother's death was the first Christmas I didn't spend in Sawyer Depot. My grandmother told Aunt Martha and Uncle Alfred that if the family were all together, my mother's absence would be too apparent. If Dan and Grandmother and I were alone in Gravesend, and if the Eastmans were alone in Sawyer Depot, my grandmother argued that we would all miss each other; then, she reasoned, we wouldn't miss my mother so much. Ever since the Christmas of '53, I have felt that the yuletide is a special hell for those families who have suffered any loss or who must admit to any imperfection; the so-called spirit of giving can be as greedy as receiving – Christmas is our time to be aware of what we lack, of who's not home.

Dividing my time between my grandmother's house on 80 Front Street and the abandoned dormitory where Dan had his small apartment also gave me my first impressions of Gravesend Academy at Christmas, when all the boarders had gone home. The bleak brick and stone, the ivy frosted with snow, the dormitories and classroom buildings with their windows all closed – with a penitentiary sameness – gave the campus the aura of a prison enduring a hunger strike; and without the students hurrying on the quadrangle paths, the bare, bone-colored birches stood out in black-and-white against the snow, like charcoal drawings of themselves, or skeletons of the alumni.

The ringing of the chapel bell, and the bell for class hours, was suspended; and so my mother's absence was underlined by the absence of Gravesend's most routine music, the academy chimes I'd taken for granted – until I couldn't hear them. There was only the solemn, hourly bonging of the great clock in the bell tower of Hurd's Church; especially on the most brittle-cold days of December, and against the landscape of old snow – thawed and refrozen to the dull, silver-gray sheen of pewter – the clock-bell of Hurd's Church tolled the time like a death knell.

'Twas *not* the season to be jolly – although dear Dan Needham tried. Dan drank too much, and he filled the empty, echoing dormitory with his strident caroling; his rendition of the Christmas carols was quite painfully a far cry from my mother's singing. And whenever Owen would join Dan for a verse of 'God Rest You Merry, Gentlemen,' or – worse – 'It Came Upon the Midnight Clear,' the old stone stairwells of Dan's dorm resounded with a dirgeful music that was not at all Christmasy but strictly mournful; they were the voices of the ghosts of those Gravesend boys unable to go home for Christmas, singing to their faraway families.

The Gravesend dormitories were named after the long-ago, dead-and-buried faculty and headmasters of the school: Abbot, Amen, Bancroft, Dunbar, Gilman, Gorham, Hooper, Lambert, Perkins, Porter, Quincy, Scott. Dan Needham lived in Waterhouse Hall, so named for some deceased curmudgeon of a classicist, a Latin teacher named Amos Waterhouse, whose rendering of Christmas carols *in Latin* – I was sure – could not have been worse than the gloomy muddle made of them by Dan and Owen Meany.

Grandmother's response to my mother being dead for Christmas was to refuse to participate in the seasonal decoration of 80 Front Street; the wreaths were nailed too low on the doors, and the bottom half of the Christmas tree was overhung with tinsel and ornaments – the result of Lydia applying her heavy-handed touch at wheelchair level.

'We'd all have been better off in Sawyer Depot,' Dan Needham announced, in his cups.

Owen sighed. 'I GUESS I'LL NEVER GET TO GO TO SAWYER DEPOT,' he said morosely.

Where Owen and I went instead was into every room of every boy who'd gone home for Christmas from Waterhouse Hall; Dan Needham had a master key. Almost every afternoon, Dan rehearsed The Gravesend Players for their annual version of *A Christmas Carol*; it was becoming old hat for many of the players, but – to freshen their performances – Dan made them change roles from one Christmas to the next. Hence, Mr Fish, who one year had been Marley's Ghost – and another year, the Ghost of Christmas Past – was now Scrooge himself. After years of using conventionally adorable children who muffed their lines, Dan had begged Owen to be Tiny Tim, but Owen said that everyone would laugh at him – if not on sight, at least when he first spoke – and besides: Mrs Walker was playing Tiny Tim's mother. That, Owen claimed, would give him THE SHIVERS.

It was bad enough, Owen maintained, that he was subject to seasonal ridicule for the role he played in the Christ Church Christmas Pageant. 'JUST YOU WAIT,' he said darkly to me. 'THE WIGGINS ARE *NOT* GOING TO MAKE ME THE STUPID ANGEL AGAIN!'

It would be my first Christmas pageant, since I was usually in Sawyer Depot for the last Sunday before Christmas; but Owen repeatedly complained that he was *always* cast as the Announcing Angel – a role forced upon him by the Rev. Captain Wiggin and his stewardess wife, Barbara, who maintained that there was 'no one cuter' for the part than Owen, whose chore it was to *descend* – in a 'pillar of light' (with the substantial assistance of a cranelike apparatus to which he was attached, with wires, like a puppet). Owen was supposed to *announce* the wondrous new presence that lay in the manger in Bethelehem, all the while flapping his arms (to draw attention to the giant wings glued to his choir robe, and to attempt to quiet the giggles of the congregation).

Every year, a grim group of shepherds huddled at the communion railing and displayed their cowardice to God's Holy Messenger; a motley crew, they tripped on their robes and knocked off each other's turbans and false beards with their staffs and shepherding crooks. Barb Wiggin had difficulty locating them in the 'pillar of light,' while simultaneously illuminating the Descending Angel, Owen Meany.

Reading from Luke, the rector said, ' "And in that region there were shepherds out in the field, keeping watch over their flock by night. And an angel of the Lord appeared to them, and the glory of the Lord shone around them, and they were filled with *fear*." ' Whereupon, Mr Wiggin paused for the full effect of the shepherds cringing at the sight of Owen struggling to get his feet on the floor – Barb Wiggin operated the creaky apparatus that *lowered* Owen, too, placing him dangerously near the lit candles that simulated the campfires around which the shepherds watched their flock.

' "BE NOT AFRAID," ' Owen announced, while still struggling in the air, ' "FOR BEHOLD, I BRING YOU GOOD

NEWS OF A GREAT JOY WHICH WILL COME TO ALL THE PEOPLE; FOR TO YOU IS BORN THIS DAY IN THE CITY OF DAVID A SAVIOR, WHO IS CHRIST THE LORD. AND THIS WILL BE A SIGN FOR YOU: YOU WILL FIND A BABE WRAPPED IN SWADDLING CLOTHES AND LYING IN A MANGER." ' Whereupon, the dazzling, if jerky, 'pillar of light' flashed, like lightning, or perhaps Christ Church suffered an electrical surge, and Owen was raised into darkness – sometimes, *yanked* into darkness; and once, so quickly that one of his wings was torn from his back and fell among the confused shepherds.

The worst of it was that Owen had to remain in the air for the rest of the pageant – there being no method of lowering him *out* of the light. If he was to be concealed in darkness, he had to stay suspended from the wires – above the babe lying in the manger, above the clumsy, nodding donkeys, the stumbling shepherds, and the unbalanced kings staggering under the weight of their crowns.

An additional evil, Owen claimed, was that whoever played Joseph was always smirking – as if Joseph had anything to smirk about. 'WHAT DOES JOSEPH HAVE TO DO WITH ANY OF IT?' Owen asked crossly. 'I SUPPOSE HE HAS TO STAND AROUND THE MANGER, BUT HE SHOULDN'T *SMIRK*!' And always the prettiest girl got to play Mary. 'WHAT DOES *PRETTY* HAVE TO DO WITH IT?' Owen asked. 'WHO SAYS MARY WAS PRETTY?'

And the individual touches that the Wiggins brought to the Christmas Pageant reduced Owen to incoherent fuming – for example, the smaller children disguised as turtledoves. The costumes were so absurd that no one knew what these children were supposed to be; they resembled science-fiction angels, spectacular life-forms from another galaxy, as if the Wiggins had decided that the Holy Nativity had been attended by beings from faraway planets (or should have been so attended). 'NOBODY KNOWS WHAT THE STUPID TURTLEDOVES ARE!' Owen complained.

As for the Christ Child himself, Owen was outraged. The Wiggins insisted that the Baby Jesus not shed a tear, and in this pursuit they were relentless in gathering dozens of babies backstage; they substituted babies so freely that the Christ Child was whisked from the manger at the first unholy croak or gurgle – instantly replaced by a mute baby, or at least a stuporous one. For this chore of supplying a fresh, silent baby to the manger – in an instant – an extended line of ominous-looking grown-ups reached into the shadows beyond the pulpit, behind the purple-and-maroon curtains, under the cross. These large and sure-handed adults, deft at baby-handling, or at least certain not to drop a quickly moving Christ Child, were strangely out of place at the Nativity. Were they kings or shepherds – and why were they so much bigger than the other kings and shepherds, if not exactly larger than life? Their costumes were childish, although some of their beards were real, and they appeared less to relish the spirit of Christmas than they seemed resigned to their task – like a bucket brigade of volunteer firemen.

Backstage, the mothers fretted; the competition for the most properly behaved Christ Child was keen. Every Christmas, in addition to the Baby Jesus, the Wiggins' pageant gave birth to many new members of that most monstrous sorority: stage mothers. I told Owen that perhaps he was better off to be 'above' these proceedings, but Owen hinted that I and other members of our Sunday school class were at least partially responsible for his humiliating elevation – for hadn't *we* been the first to lift Owen into the air? Mrs Walker, Owen suggested, might have given Barb Wiggin the idea of using Owen as the airborne angel.

It's no wonder that Owen was not tickled by Dan's notion of casting him as Tiny Tim. 'WHEN I SAY, "BE NOT AFRAID; FOR BEHOLD, I BRING YOU GOOD NEWS," ALL THE BABIES CRY AND EVERYONE ELSE LAUGHS. WHAT DO YOU THINK THEY'LL DO IF I SAY, "GOD BLESS US, EVERY ONE!"?'

It was his voice, of course; he could have said, 'HERE COMES THE END OF THE WORLD!' People still would have fallen down, laughing. It was torture to Owen that he was without much humor – he was *only* serious – while at the same time he had a chiefly comic effect on the multitude.

No wonder he commenced worrying about the Christmas Pageant as early as the end of November, for in the service bulletin of the Last Sunday After Pentecost there was already an announcement, 'How to Participate in the Christmas Pageant.' The first rehearsal was scheduled after the Annual Parish Meeting and the Vestry elections – almost at the beginning of our Christmas vacation. 'What would you like to be?' the sappy bulletin asked. 'We need kings, angels, shepherds, donkeys, turtledoves, Mary, Joseph, babies, *and more!*'

' "FATHER, FORGIVE THEM; FOR THEY KNOW NOT WHAT THEY DO," ' Owen said.

Grandmother was testy about our playing at 80 Front Street; it's no wonder that Owen and I sought the solitude of Waterhouse Hall. With Dan out of the dorm in the afternoons, Owen and I had the place almost to ourselves. There were four floors of boys' rooms, the communal showers and urinals and crapper stalls on every floor, and one faculty apartment at the end of the hall on each floor, too. Dan's apartment was on the third floor. The second-floor faculty occupant had gone home for Christmas – like one of the boys himself, young Mr Peabody, a fledgling Math instructor, and a bachelor not likely to improve upon his single status, was what my mother had called a 'Nervous Nelly.' He was fastidious and timid and easily teased by the boys on his floor; on the nights he was given dorm duty – for the entire four floors – Waterhouse Hall seethed with revolution. It was during an evening of Mr Peabody's duty that a first-year boy was dangled by his heels from the yawning portal of the fourth-floor laundry chute; his muffled howls echoed through the dorm, and Mr Peabody, opening the laundry portal on the second floor, was shocked to peer two floors up and see the youngster's screaming face looking down at him.

Mr Peabody reacted in a fashion that could have been imitated from Mrs Walker. 'Van Arsdale!' he shouted upward. 'Get out of the laundry chute! Get a grip on yourself, man! Get your feet on the floor!'

He never dreamed, poor Mr Peabody, that Van Arsdale was held fast at both ankles by two brutal linemen from the Gravesend football team; they tortured Van Arsdale daily.

So Mr Peabody had gone home to his parents, which left the second floor free of faculty; and the Physical Education fanatic on the fourth floor – the track-and-field coach, Mr Tubulari – was also away for Christmas. He was also a bachelor, and he had insisted on the fourth floor – for his health; he claimed to relish running upstairs. He had many female visitors; when they wore dresses, or skirts, the boys loved to watch them ascending and descending the stairwell from one of the lower floors. The nights that Waterhouse Hall suffered *his* turn at dorm duty, the boys were very well behaved. Mr Tubulari was fast and silent and thrived on catching boys 'in the act' – in the act of anything: shaving-cream fights, smoking in their rooms, even masturbation. Each floor had a designated common room, a butt room, so-called, for the smokers; but smoking in the dorm rooms was forbidden – as was sex in any form, alcohol in any form, and drugs that had not been prescribed by the school physician. Mr Tubulari even had reservations about aspirin. According to Dan, Mr Tubulari was off competing in some grueling athletic event over Christmas – actually, a pentathlon of the harshest-possible wintertime activities; a 'winterthon,' Mr Tubulari had called it. Dan Needham hated made-up words, and he became quite boisterous on the subject of *what* wintertime events Mr Tubulari was competing in; the fanatic had gone to Alaska, or maybe Minnesota.

Dan would entertain Owen and me by describing Mr Tubulari's pentathlon, his 'winterthon.'

'The first event,' Dan Needham said, 'is something wholesome, like splitting a cord of wood – points off, if you break your ax. Then you have to run ten miles in deep snow, or snowshoe for thirty. Then you chop a hole in the ice, and – carrying your ax – swim a mile under a frozen lake, chopping your way out at the opposite shore. Then you build an igloo – to get warm. Then comes the dogsledding. You have to *mush* a team of dogs – from Anchorage to Chicago. Then you build another igloo – to rest.'

'THAT'S SIX EVENTS,' Owen said. 'A PENTATHLON IS ONLY FIVE.'

'So forget the second igloo,' Dan Needham said.

'I WONDER WHAT MISTER TUBULARI DOES FOR NEW YEAR'S EVE,' Owen said.

'Carrot juice,' Dan said, fixing himself another whiskey. 'Mister Tubulari makes his own carrot juice.'

Anyway, Mr Tubulari was gone. When Dan was out in the afternoons, Owen and I were in total control of the top three floors of Waterhouse Hall. As for the first floor, we had only the Brinker-Smiths to contend with, and they were no match for us – if we were quiet. A young British couple, the Brinker-Smiths had recently launched twins; they were entirely and, for the most part, cheerfully engaged in how to survive life with twins. Mr Brinker-Smith, who was a biologist, also fancied himself an inventor; he invented a double-seater high chair, a double-seater stroller, a double-seater swing – the latter hung in a doorway, where the twins could dangle like monkeys on a vine, in close enough proximity to each other to pull each other's hair. In the double-seater high chair, they could throw food into each other's faces, and so Mr Brinker-Smith improvised a wall between them – too high for them to throw their food over it. Yet the twins would knock at this wall, to assure themselves that the other was really there, and they would smear their food on the wall, almost as a form of finger painting – a preliterate communication among siblings. Mr Brinker-Smith found the twins' methods of thwarting his various inventions 'fascinating'; he was a true scientist – the failures of his experiments were almost as interesting to him as his successes, and his determination to press forward, with more and more twin-inspired inventions, was resolute.

Mrs Brinker-Smith, on the other hand, appeared a trifle tired. She was too pretty a woman to look harried; her exhaustion at the hands of her twins – and with Mr Brinker-Smith's inventions for a better life with them – manifested itself in fits of distraction so pronounced that Owen and Dan and I suspected her of sleepwalking. She literally did not notice us. Her name was Ginger, in reference to her fetching freckles and her strawberry-blond hair; she was an object of lustful fantasies for Gravesend boys, both before and after my time at the academy – given the need of Gravesend boys to indulge in lustful fantasies, I believe that Ginger Brinker-Smith was seen as a sex object even when she was pregnant with her twins. But for Owen and me – during the Christmas of '53 – Mrs Brinker-Smith's appearance was only mildly alluring; she looked as if she slept in her clothes, and I'm sure she did. And her fabled voluptuousness, which I would later possess as firm a memory of as any Gravesend boy, was quite concealed by the great, loose blouses she wore – for such clothes, no doubt, enhanced the speed with which she could snap open her nursing bra. In a European tradition, strangely enlarged by its travel to New Hampshire, she seemed intent on nursing the twins until they were old enough to go to school by themselves.

The Brinker-Smiths were big on nursing, as was evidenced

by Mr Brinker-Smith's demonstrative use of his wife in his biology classes. A well-liked teacher, of liberal methods not universally favored by the stodgier Gravesend faculty, Mr Brinker-Smith enjoyed all opportunities to bring 'life,' as he called it, into the classroom. This included the eye-opening spectacle of Ginger Briker-Smith nursing the twins, an experience – sadly – that was wasted on the biology students of Gravesend, in that it happened before Owen and I were old enough to attend the academy.

Anyway, Owen and I were not fearful of interference from the Brinker-Smiths while we investigated the boys' rooms on the first floor of Waterhouse Hall; in fact, we were disappointed to see so little of the Brinker-Smiths over that Christmas – because we imagined that we might be rewarded with a glimpse of Ginger Brinker-Smith in the act of nursing. We even, occasionally, lingered in the first-floor hall – in the faraway hope that Mr Brinker-Smith might open the door to his apartment, see Owen and me standing there, clearly with nothing educational to do, and therefore invite us forthwith into his apartment so that we could watch his wife nurse the twins. Alas, he did not.

One icy day, Owen and I accompanied Mrs Brinker-Smith to market, taking turns pushing the bundled-up twins in their double-seater – and even carrying the groceries into the Brinker-Smith apartment, after a trip in such inclement weather that it might have qualified as a fifth of Mr Tubulari's winter pentathlon. But did Mrs Brinker-Smith bring forth her breasts and volunteer to nurse the twins in front of us? Alas, she did not.

Thus Owen and I were left to discover what Gravesend prep-school boys kept in their rooms when they went home for Christmas. We took Dan Needham's master key from the hook by the kitchen can opener; we began with the fourth-floor rooms. Owen's excitement with our detective work was intense; he entered every room as if the occupant had *not* gone home for Christmas, but in all likelihood was hiding under the bed, or in the closet – with an ax. And there was no hurrying Owen, not even in the dullest room. He looked in every drawer, examined every article of clothing, sat in every desk chair, lay down on every bed – this was always his last act in each of the rooms: he would lie down on the bed and close his eyes; he would hold his breath. Only when he'd resumed normal breathing did he announce his opinion of the room's occupant – as either happy or unhappy with the academy; as possibly troubled by distant events at home, or in the past. Owen would always admit it – when the room's occupant remained a mystery to him. 'THIS GUY IS A REAL MYSTERY,' Owen would say. 'TWELVE PAIRS OF SOCKS, NO UNDERWEAR, TEN SHIRTS, TWO PAIRS OF PANTS, ONE SPORT JACKET, ONE TIE, TWO LACROSSE STICKS, NO BALL, NO PICTURES OF GIRLS, NO FAMILY PORTRAITS, AND NO SHOES.'

'He's got to be wearing shoes,' I said.

'ONLY ONE PAIR,' Owen said.

'He sent a lot of his clothes to the cleaners, just before vacation,' I said.

'YOU DON'T SEND SHOES TO THE CLEANERS, OR FAMILY PORTRAITS,' Owen said. 'A REAL MYSTERY.'

We learned where to look for the sex magazines, or the dirty pictures: between the mattress and bedspring. Some of these gave Owen THE SHIVERS. In those days, such pictures were disturbingly unclear – or else they were disappointingly wholesome; in the latter category were the swimsuit calendars. The pictures of the more disturbing variety were of the quality of snapshots taken by children from moving cars; the women themselves appeared arrested in motion, rather than posed – as if they'd been in the act of something nasty when they'd been caught by the camera. The acts themselves were unclear – for example, a woman bent over a man for some undetermined purpose, as if she were about to do some violence on an utterly helpless cadaver. And the women's sex parts were often blurred by pubic hair – some of them had astonishingly more pubic hair than either Owen or I thought was possible – and their nipples were blocked from view by the censor's black slashes. At first, we thought the slashes were actual instruments of torture – they struck us as even more menacing than real nudity. The nudity was menacing – to a large extent, because the women weren't pretty; or else their troubled, serious expressions judged their own nakedness severely.

Many of the pictures and magazines were partially destroyed by the effects of the boys' weight grinding them into the metal bedsprings, which were flaked with rust; the bodies of the women themselves were occasionally imprinted with a spiral tattoo, as if the old springs had etched upon the women's flesh a grimy version of lust's own descending spiral.

Naturally, the presence of pornography darkened Owen's opinion of each room's occupant; when he lay on the bed with his eyes closed and, at last, expelled his long-held breath, he would say, 'NOT HAPPY. WHO DRAWS A MOUSTACHE ON HIS MOTHER'S FACE AND THROWS DARTS AT HIS FATHER'S PICTURE? WHO GOES TO BED THINKING ABOUT DOING IT WITH GERMAN SHEPHERDS? AND WHAT'S THE DOG LEASH IN THE CLOSET FOR? AND THE FLEA COLLAR IN THE DESK DRAWER? IT'S NOT LEGAL TO KEEP A PET IN THE DORM, RIGHT?'

'Perhaps his dog was killed over the summer,' I said. 'He kept the leash and the flea collar.'

'SURE,' Owen said. 'AND I SUPPOSE HIS FATHER RAN OVER THE DOG? I SUPPOSE HIS MOTHER *DID IT* WITH THE DOG?'

'They're just things,' I said. 'What can we tell about the guy who lives here, really?'

'NOT HAPPY.' Owen said.

We were a whole afternoon investigating the rooms on just the fourth floor, Owen was so systematic in his methods of search, so deliberate about putting everything back exactly where it had been, as if these Gravesend boys were anything at all like him; as if their rooms were as intentional as the museum Owen had made of his room. His behavior in the rooms was remindful of a holy man's search of a cathedral of antiquity – as if he could divine some ancient and also holy intention there.

He pronounced few boarders happy. These few, in Owen's opinion, were the ones whose dresser mirrors were ringed with family pictures, and with pictures of real girlfriends (they could have been sisters). A keeper of swimsuit calendars could conceivably be happy, or borderline-happy, but the boys who had cut out the pictures of the lingerie and girdle models from the Sears catalog were at least partially unhappy – and there was no saving anyone who harbored pictures of thoroughly naked women. The bushier the women were, the unhappier the boy; the more the women's nipples were struck with the censor's slash, the more miserable the boarder.

'HOW CAN YOU BE HAPPY IF YOU SPEND ALL YOUR TIME THINKING ABOUT *DOING IT*?' Owen asked.

I preferred to think that the rooms we searched were more haphazard and less revealing than Owen imagined – after all, they were supposed to be the monastic cells of transient scholars; they were something between a nest and a hotel room, they were not natural abodes, and what we found there was a random disorder and a depressing sameness. Even the pictures of the sports heroes and movie stars were the same, from room to room; and from boy to boy, there was often a similar scrap of something missed from the life at home: a picture of a car, with the boy proudly at the wheel (Gravesend boarders were not allowed to drive, or even ride in, cars); a picture of a perfectly plain backyard, or even a snapshot of such a deeply private moment – an unrecognizable figure shambling away from the camera, back turned to our view – that the substance of the picture was locked in a personal memory. The effect of these cells, with the terrible sameness of each boy's homesickness, and the choas of travel, was what Owen had meant when he'd told my mother that dormitories were EVIL.

Since her death, Owen had hinted that the strongest force compelling him to attend Gravesend Academy – namely, my mother's insistence – was gone. Those rooms allowed us to imagine what *we* might become – if not exactly boarders (because I would continue to live with Dan, and with Grandmother, and Owen would live at home), we would still harbor such secrets, such barely restrained messiness, such *lusts*, even, as these poor residents of Waterhouse Hall. It was *our* lives in the near future that we were searching for when we searched in those rooms, and therefore it was shrewd of Owen that he made us take our time.

It was in a room on the third floor that Owen discovered the prophylactics; everyone called them 'rubbers,' but in Gravesend, New Hampshire, we called them 'beetleskins.' The origin of that word is not known to me; technically, a 'beetleskin' was a used condom – and, even more specifically, one found in a parking lot or washed up on a beach or floating in the urinal at the drive-in movie. I believe that only those were authentic 'beetleskins': old and very-much-used condoms that popped out at you in public places.

It was in the third-floor room of a senior named Potter – an advisee of Dan's – that Owen found a half-dozen or more prophylactics, in their foil wrappers, not very ably concealed in the sock compartment of the dresser drawers.

'BEETLESKINS!' he cried, dropping them on the floor; we stood back from them. We had never seen unused rubbers in their drugstore packaging before.

'Are you sure?' I asked Owen.

'THEY'RE FRESH BEETLESKINS,' Owen told me. 'THE CATHOLICS FORBID THEM,' he added. 'THE CATHOLICS ARE OPPOSED TO BIRTH CONTROL.'

'Why?' I asked.

'NEVER MIND,' Owen said. 'I'VE NOTHING MORE TO DO WITH THE CATHOLICS.'

'Right,' I said.

We tried to ascertain if Potter would know exactly how many beetleskins he had in his sock drawer – whether he would notice if we opened one of the foil wrappers and examined one of the beetleskins, which naturally, then, we would not put back; we would have to dispose of it. Would Potter miss it? That was the question. Owen determined that an investigation of how organized a boarder Potter was would tell us. Was his underwear all in one drawer, were his T-shirts folded, were his shoes in a straight line on the closet floor, were his jackets and shirts and trousers separated from each other, did his hangers face the same way, did he keep his pens and pencils together, were his paper clips contained, did he have more than one tube of toothpaste that was open, were his razor blades somewhere safe, did he have a necktie rack or hang his ties willy-nilly? And did he keep the beetleskins because he used them – or were they for show?

In Potter's closet, sunk in one of his size-11 hiking boots, was a fifth of Jack Daniel's Old No. 7, Black Label; Owen decided that if Potter risked keeping a bottle of whiskey in his room, the beetleskins were *not* for show. If Potter used them with any frequency, we imagined, he would not miss one.

The examination of the beetleskin was a solemn occasion; it was the nonlubricated kind – I'm not even sure if there *were* lubricated rubbers when Owen and I were eleven – and with some difficulty, and occasional pain, we took turns putting the thing on our tiny penises. This part of our lives in the near future was especially hard for us to imagine; but I realize now that the ritual we enacted in Potter's daring room also had the significance of religious rebellion for Owen

Meany – it was but one more affront to the Catholics whom he had, in his own words, ESCAPED.

It was a pity that Owen could not escape the Rev. Dudley Wiggin's Christmas Pageant. The first rehearsal, in the nave of the church, was held on the Second Sunday of Advent and followed a celebration of the Holy Eucharist. We were delayed discussing our roles because the Women's Association Report preceded us; the women wished to say that the Quiet Day they had scheduled for the beginning of Advent had been very successful – that the meditations, and the following period of quiet, for reflection, had been well received. Mrs Walker, whose own term as a Vestry member was expiring – thus giving her even more energy for her Sunday school tyrannies – complained that attendance at the adult evening Bible study was flagging.

'Well, everyone's so busy at Christmas, you know,' said Barb Wiggin, who was impatient to begin the casting of the pageant – not wanting to keep us potential donkeys and turtledoves waiting. I could sense Owen's irritation with Barb Wiggin, in advance.

Quite blind to his animosity, Barb Wiggin began – as, indeed, the holy event itself had begun – with the Announcing Angel. 'Well, we all know who our Descending Angel is,' she told us.

'NOT ME,' Owen said.

'Why, Owen!' Barb Wiggin said.

'PUT SOMEONE ELSE UP IN THE AIR,' Owen said. 'MAYBE THE SHEPHERDS CAN JUST STARE AT THE "PILLAR OF LIGHT." THE BIBLE SAYS THE ANGEL OF THE LORD APPEARED TO THE SHEPHERDS – NOT TO THE WHOLE CONGREGATION. AND USE SOMEONE WITH A VOICE EVERYONE DOESN'T LAUGH AT,' he said, pausing while everyone laughed.

'But Owen—' Barb Wiggin said.

'No, no, Barbara,' Mr Wiggin said. 'If Owen's tired of being the angel, we should respect his wishes – this is a democracy,' he added unconvincingly. The former stewardess glared at her ex-pilot husband as if he had been speaking, and thinking, in the absence of sufficient oxygen.

'AND ANOTHER THING,' Owen said. 'JOSEPH SHOULD NOT SMIRK.'

'Indeed not!' the rector said heartily. 'I had no idea we'd suffered a smirking Joseph all these years.'

'And who do you think would be a good Joseph, Owen?' Barb Wiggin asked, without the conventional friendliness of the stewardess.

Owen pointed to me; to be singled out so silently, with Owen's customary authority, made the hairs stand up on the back of my neck – in later years, I would think I had been chosen by the Chosen One. But that Second Sunday of Advent, in the nave of Christ Church, I felt angry with Owen – once the hairs on the back of my neck relaxed. For what an uninspiring role it is; to be Joseph – that hapless follower, that stand-in, that guy along for the ride.

'We *usually* pick Mary first,' Barb Wiggin said. 'Then we let Mary pick her Joseph.'

'Oh,' the Rev. Dudley Wiggin said. 'Well, this year we can let Joseph pick *his* Mary! We mustn't be afraid to change!' he added cordially, but his wife ignored him.

'We usually begin with the angel,' Barb Wiggin said. 'We still don't have an angel. Here we are with a Joseph before a Mary, and no angel,' she said. (Stewardesses are orderly people, much comforted by following a familiar routine.)

'Well, who would like to hang in the air this year?' the rector asked. 'Tell them about the view from up there, Owen.'

'SOMETIMES THE CONTRAPTION THAT HOLDS YOU IN THE AIR HAS YOU FACING THE WRONG WAY,' he warned the would-be angels. 'SOMETIMES THE HARNESS CUTS INTO YOUR SKIN.'

'I'm sure we can remedy that, Owen,' the rector said.

'WHEN YOU GO UP OUT OF THE "PILLAR OF LIGHT," IT'S *VERY* DARK UP THERE,' Owen said.

No would-be angel raised his or her hand.

'AND IT'S QUITE A LONG SPEECH THAT YOU HAVE TO MEMORIZE,' Owen added. 'YOU KNOW, "BE NOT AFRAID; FOR BEHOLD, I BRING YOU GOOD NEWS OF A GREAT JOY . . . FOR TO YOU IS BORN . . . IN THE CITY OF DAVID A SAVIOR, WHO IS CHRIST THE LORD" . . .'

'We know, Owen, we know,' Barb Wiggin said.

'IT'S NOT EASY,' Owen said.

'Perhaps we should pick our Mary, and come back to the angel?' the Rev. Mr Wiggin asked.

Barb Wiggin wrung her hands.

But if they thought I was enough of a fool to choose *my* Mary, they had another think coming; what a no-win situation that was – choosing Mary. For what would everyone say about me and the girl I chose? And what would the girls I *didn't* choose think of me?

'MARY BETH BAIRD HAS NEVER BEEN MARY,' Owen said. 'THAT WAY, MARY WOULD BE MARY.'

'*Joseph* chooses Mary!' Barb Wiggin said.

'IT WAS JUST A SUGGESTION,' Owen said.

But how could the role be denied Mary Beth Baird now that it had been offered? Mary Beth Baird was a wholesome lump of a girl, shy and clumsy and plain.

'I've been a turtledove three times,' she mumbled.

'THAT'S ANOTHER THING,' Owen said, 'NOBODY KNOWS WHAT THE TURTLEDOVES *ARE*.'

'Now, now – one thing at a time,' Dudley Wiggin said.

'First, *Joseph* – choose Mary!' Barb Wiggin said.

'Mary Beth Baird would be fine,' I said.

'Well, so Mary is Mary!' Mr Wiggin said. Mary Beth Baird covered her face in her hands. Barb Wiggin also covered her face.

'Now, what's this about the turtledoves, Owen?' the rector asked.

'*Hold* the turtledoves!' Barb Wiggin snapped. 'I want an angel.'

Former kings and shepherds sat in silence; former donkeys did not come forth – and donkeys came in two parts; the hind part of the donkey never got to see the pageant. Even the former hind parts of donkeys did not volunteer to be the angel. Even former turtledoves were not stirred to grab the part.

'The angel is *so* important,' the rector said. 'There's a special apparatus just to raise and lower you, and – for a while – you occupy the "pillar of light" all by yourself. All eyes are on *you*!'

The children of Christ Church did not appear enticed to play the angel by the thought of all eyes being on them. In the rear of the nave, rendered even more insignificant than usual by his proximity to the giant painting of 'The Call of the Twelve,' pudgy Harold Crosby sat diminished by the depiction of Jesus appointing his disciples; all eyes rarely feasted on fat Harold Crosby, who was not grotesque enough to be teased – or even noticed – but who was enough of a slob to be rejected whenever he caused the slightest attention to be drawn to himself. Therefore, Harold Crosby abstained. He sat in the back; he stood at the rear of the line; he spoke only when spoken to; he desired to be left alone, and – for the most part – he was. For several years, he had played a perfect hind part of a donkey; I'm sure it was the only role he wanted. I could see he was nervous about the silence that greeted the Rev. Mr Wiggin's request for an angel; possibly the towering portraits of the disciples in his immediate vicinity made Harold Crosby feel inadequate, or else he feared that – in the absence of volunteers – the rector would select an angel from among the cowardly children, and (God forbid) what if Mr Wiggin chose *him*?

Harold Crosby tipped back in his chair and shut his eyes; it was either a method of concealment borrowed from the ostrich, or else Harold imagined that if he appeared to be asleep, no one would ask him to be more than the hind part of a donkey.

'Someone *has* to be the angel,' Barb Wiggin said menacingly. Then Harold Crosby fell over backward in his chair; he made it worse by attempting to catch his balance – by grabbing the frame of the huge painting of 'The Call of the Twelve'; then he thought better of crushing himself under Christ's disciples and he allowed himself to fall freely. Like most things that happened to Harold Crosby, his fall was more astonishing for its awkwardness than for anything intrinsically spectacular. Regardless, only the rector was insensitive enough to mistake Harold Crosby's clumsiness for volunteering.

'Good for you, Harold!' the rector said. 'There's a brave boy!'

'What?' Harold Crosby said.

'Now we have our angel,' Mr Wiggin said cheerfully. 'What's next?'

'I'm afraid of heights,' said Harold Crosby.

'All the braver of you!' the rector replied. 'There's no time like the present for facing our fears.'

'But the crane,' Barb Wiggin said to her husband. 'The apparatus—' she started to say, but the rector silenced her with an admonishing wave of his hand. Surely you're not going to make the poor boy feel self-conscious about his *weight*, the rector's glance toward his wife implied; surely the wires and the harness are strong enough. Barb Wiggin glowered back at her husband.

'ABOUT THE TURTLEDOVES,' Owen said, and Barb Wiggin shut her eyes; she did not lean back in her chair, but she gripped the seat with both hands.

'Ah, yes, Owen, what was it about the turtledoves?' the Rev. Mr Wiggin asked.

'THEY LOOK LIKE THEY'RE FROM OUTER SPACE,' Owen said. 'NO ONE KNOWS WHAT THEY'RE SUPPOSED TO BE.'

'They're *doves*!' Barb Wiggin said. 'Everyone knows what doves are!'

'THEY'RE *GIANT* DOVES,' Owen said. 'THEY'RE AS BIG AS HALF A DONKEY. WHAT KIND OF BIRD IS THAT? A BIRD FROM MARS? THEY'RE ACTUALLY KIND OF FRIGHTENING.'

'Not everyone can be a king or a shepherd or a donkey, Owen,' the rector said.

'BUT NOBODY'S SMALL ENOUGH TO BE A DOVE,' Owen said. 'AND NOBODY KNOWS WHAT ALL THOSE PAPER STREAMERS ARE SUPPOSED TO BE.'

'They're *feathers*!' Barb Wiggin shouted.

'THE TURTLEDOVES LOOK LIKE *CREATURES*,' Owen said. 'LIKE THEY'VE BEEN ELECTROCUTED.'

'Well, I suppose there were other animals in the manger,' the rector said.

'Are *you* going to make the costumes?' Barb Wiggin asked him.

'Now now,' Mr Wiggin said.

'COWS GO WELL WITH DONKEYS,' Owen suggested.

'Cows?' the rector said. 'Well well.'

'Who's going to make the cow costumes?' Barb Wiggin asked.

'*I* will!' Mary Beth Baird said. She had never volunteered for anything before; clearly her election as the Virgin Mary had energized her – had made her believe she was capable of miracles, or at least cow costumes.

'Good for you, Mary!' the rector said.

But Barb Wiggin and Harold Crosby closed their eyes; Harold did not look well – he seemed to be suppressing vomit, and his face took on the lime-green shade of the grass at the feet of Christ's disciples, who loomed over him.

'THERE'S ONE MORE THING,' said Owen Meany. We gave him our attention. 'THE CHRIST CHILD,' he said, and we children nodded our approval.

'What's wrong with the Christ Child?' Barb Wiggin asked.

'ALL THOSE BABIES,' Owen said. 'JUST TO GET ONE TO LIE IN THE MANGER WITHOUT CRYING – DO WE HAVE TO HAVE ALL THOSE BABIES?'

'But it's like the song says, Owen,' the rector told him. ' "Little Lord Jesus, no crying he makes." '

'OKAY, OKAY,' Owen said. 'BUT ALL THOSE BABIES – YOU CAN HEAR *THEM* CRYING. EVEN OFFSTAGE, YOU CAN HEAR THEM. AND ALL THOSE GROWN-UPS!' he said. 'ALL THOSE BIG MEN PASSING THE BABIES IN AND OUT. THEY'RE SO *BIG* – THEY LOOK RIDICULOUS. THEY MAKE *US* LOOK RIDICULOUS.'

'You know a baby who won't cry, Owen?' Barb Wiggin asked him – and, of course, she knew as soon as she spoke . . . how he had trapped her.

'I KNOW SOMEONE WHO CAN FIT IN THE CRIB,' Owen said. 'SOMEONE SMALL ENOUGH TO *LOOK* LIKE A BABY,' he said. 'SOMEONE OLD ENOUGH NOT TO CRY.'

Mary Beth Baird could not contain herself! '*Owen* can be the Baby Jesus!' she yelled. Owen Meany smiled and shrugged.

'I *CAN* FIT IN THE CRIB,' he said modestly.

Harold Crosby could no longer contain himself, either; he vomited. He vomited often enough for it to pass almost unnoticed, especially now that Owen had our undivided attention.

'And what's more, we can *lift* him!' Mary Beth Baird said excitedly.

'There was never any lifting of the Christ Child before!' Barb Wiggin said.

'Well, I mean, if we *have* to, if we feel like it,' Mary Beth said.

'WELL, IF EVERYONE WANTS ME TO DO IT, I SUPPOSE I COULD,' Owen said.

'Yes!' cried the kings and shepherds.

'Let Owen do it!' said the donkeys and the cows – the former turtledoves.

It was quite a popular decision, but Barb Wiggin looked at Owen as if she were revising her opinion of how 'cute' he was, and the rector observed Owen with a detachment that was wholly out of character for an ex-pilot. The Rev. Mr Wiggin, such a veteran of Christmas pageants, looked at Owen

Meany with profound respect – as if he'd seen the Christ Child come and go, but never before had he encountered a little Lord Jesus who was so perfect for the part.

It was only our second rehearsal of the Christmas Pageant when Owen decided that the crib, in which he could fit – but tightly – was unnecessary and even incorrect. Dudley Wiggin based his entire view of the behavior of the Christ Child on the Christmas carol 'Away in a Manger,' of which there are only two verses.

It was this carol that convinced the Rev. Mr Wiggin that the Baby Jesus mustn't cry.

> The cat-tle are low-ing, the ba-by a-wakes,
> But lit-tle Lord Je-sus, no cry-ing he makes.

If Mr Wiggin put such stock in the second verse of 'Away in a Manger,' Owen argued that we should also be instructed by the very first verse.

> A-way in a man-ger, no crib for his bed,
> The lit-tle Lord Je-sus laid down his sweet head.

'IF IT SAYS THERE WAS NO CRIB, WHY DO WE HAVE A CRIB?' Owen asked. Clearly, he found the crib restraining. ' "THE STARS IN THE SKY LOOKED DOWN WHERE HE LAY, THE LIT-TLE LORD JE-SUS, A-SLEEP *ON THE HAY*," ' Owen sang.

Thus did Owen get his way, again; 'on the hay' was where he would lie, and he proceeded to arrange all the hay within the crèche in such a fashion that his comfort would be assured, and he would be sufficiently elevated and tilted toward the audience – so that no one could possibly miss seeing him.

'THERE'S ANOTHER THING,' Owen advised us. 'YOU NOTICE HOW THE SONG SAYS, "THE CATTLE ARE LOWING"? WELL, IT'S A GOOD THING WE'VE GOT COWS. THE TURTLEDOVES COULDN'T DO MUCH "LOWING." '

If cows were what we had, they were the sort of cows that required as much imagination to identify as the former turtledoves had required. Mary Beth Baird's cow costumes may have been inspired by Mary Beth's elevated status to the role of the Virgin Mary, but the Holy Mother had not offered divine assistance, or even divine workmanship, toward the making of the costumes themselves. Mary Beth appeared to have been confused mightily by *all* the images of Christmas; her cows had not only horns but antlers – veritable *racks*, more suitable to reindeer, which Mary Beth may have been thinking of. Worse, the antlers were soft; that is, they were constructed of a floppy material, and therefore these astonishing 'horns' were always collapsing upon the faces of the cows themselves – obliterating entirely their already impaired vision, and causing more than usual confusion in the crèche: cows stepping on each other, cows colliding with donkeys, cows knocking down kings and shepherds.

'The cows, if that's what they *are*,' Barb Wiggin observed, 'should maintain their positions and *not* move around – not at all. We wouldn't want them to *trample* the Baby Jesus, would we?' A deeply crazed glint in Barb Wiggin's eye made it appear that she thought trampling the Baby Jesus would register in the neighborhood of a divine occurrence, but Owen, who was always anxious about being stepped on – and excessively so, now that he was prone and helpless on the hay – echoed Barb Wiggin's concern for the cows.

'YOU COWS, JUST REMEMBER. YOU'RE SUPPOSED TO BE "LOWING," NOT MILLING AROUND.'

'I don't want the cows "lowing" *or* milling around,' Barb Wiggin said. 'I want to be able to hear the singing, and the reading from the Bible. I want *no* "lowing." '

'LAST YEAR, YOU HAD THE TURTLEDOVES *COOING*,' Owen reminded her.

'Clearly, this isn't last year,' Barb Wiggin said.

'Now now,' the rector said.

'THE SONG SAYS "THE CATTLE ARE LOWING," ' Owen said.

'I suppose you want the donkeys *hee-hawing*!' Barb Wiggin shouted.

'THE SONG SAYS NOTHING ABOUT DONKEYS,' Owen said.

'Perhaps we're being too literal about this song,' Mr Wiggin interjected, but I knew there was no such thing as 'too literal' for Owen Meany, who grasped orthodoxy from wherever it could be found.

Yet Owen relented on the issue of whether or not the cattle should 'low'; he saw there was more to be gained in rearranging the order of music, which he had always found improper. It made no sense, he claimed, to begin with 'We Three Kings of Orient Are' while we watched the Announcing Angel descend in the 'pillar of light'; those were shepherds to whom the angel appeared, not kings. Better to begin with 'O Little Town of Bethlehem' while the angel made good his descent; the angel's announcement would be perfectly balanced if delivered between verses two and three. Then, as the 'pillar of light' leaves the angel – or, rather, as the quickly ascending angel departs the 'pillar of light' – we see the kings. Suddenly, they have joined the astonished shepherds. *Now* hit 'We Three Kings,' and hit it hard!

Harold Crosby, who had not yet attempted a first flight in the apparatus that enhanced his credibility as an angel, wanted to know where 'Ory and R' *were*.

No one understood his question.

' "We Three Kings of Ory and R," ' Harold said. 'Where are "Ory" and "R"?'

' "WE THREE KINGS OF *ORIENT ARE*," ' Owen corrected him. 'DON'T YOU READ?'

All Harold Crosby knew was that he did not *fly*; he would ask any question, create any distraction, procrastinate by any means he could imagine, if he could delay being *launched* by Barb Wiggin.

I – Joseph – had nothing to do, nothing to say, nothing to learn. Mary Beth Baird suggested that, as a helpful husband, I take turns with her in *handling* Owen Meany – if not exactly lifting him out of the hay, because Barb Wiggin was violently opposed to this, then at least, Mary Beth implied, we could fondle Owen, or tickle him, or pat him on the head.

'NO TICKLING,' Owen said.

'No *nothing*!' Barb Wiggin insisted. 'No touching Baby Jesus.'

'But we're his *parents*!' proclaimed Mary Beth, who was being generous to include poor Joseph under this appellation.

'Mary Beth,' Barb Wiggin said, 'if you touch the Baby Jesus, I'm putting you in a cow costume.'

And so it came to pass that the Virgin Mary sulked through our rehearsal – a mother denied the tactile pleasures of her own infant! And Owen, who had built a huge nest for himself – in a mountain of hay – appeared to radiate the truly untouchable quality of a deity to be reckoned with, of a prophet who had no doubt.

Some technical difficulties with the harness spared Harold Crosby his first sensation of angelic elevation; we noticed that Harold's anxiety concerning heights had caused him to forget the lines of his all-important announcement – or else Harold had not properly studied his part, for he couldn't get past 'Be not afraid; for behold, I bring you good news . . .' without flubbing.

The kings and shepherds could not possibly move slowly enough, following the 'pillar of light' in front of the altar toward the arrangement of animals and Mary and Joseph surrounding the commanding presence of the Christ Child enthroned on his mountain of hay; no matter how slowly they moved, they arrived at the touching scene in the stable before the end of the fifth verse of 'We Three Kings of Orient Are.' There they had to wait for the end of the carol, and appear to be surprised by the choir charging immediately into 'Away in a Manger.'

The solution, the Rev. Dudley Wiggin proposed, was to omit the fifth verse of 'We Three Kings,' but Owen denounced this as unorthodox. To conclude with the fourth verse was a far cry from ending with the hallelujahs of the fifth; Owen begged us to pay special attention to the words of the fourth verse – surely we did not wish to arrive in the presence of the Christ Child on such a note.

He sang for us, with emphasis – ' "SOR-ROWING, SIGH-ING, BLEED-ING, DY-ING, SEALED IN A STONE-COLD TOMB." '

'But then there's the refrain!' Barb Wiggin cried. ' "O star of won-der, star of night," ' she sang, but Owen was unmoved.

The rector assured Owen that the church had a long tradition of not singing every verse of each hymn or carol, but somehow Owen made us feel that the tradition of the church – however long – was on less sure footing than the written word. Five verses in print meant we were to sing all five.

' "SORROWING, SIGHING, *BLEEDING, DYING*," ' he repeated. 'SOUNDS VERY CHRISTMASY.'

Mary Beth Baird let everyone know that the matter could

be resolved if she were allowed to shower some affection upon the Christ Child, but it seemed that the only agreements that existed between Barb Wiggin and Owen were that Mary Beth should not be permitted to maul the Baby Jesus, and that the cows not move.

When the crèche was properly formed, which was finally timed upon the conclusion of the *fourth* verse of 'We Three Kings,' the choir then sang 'Away in a Manger' while we shamelessly worshiped and adored Owen Meany.

Perhaps the 'swaddling clothes' should have been reconsidered. Owen had objected to being wrapped in them up to his chin; he wanted to have his arms free – possibly, in order to ward off a stumbling cow or donkey. And so they had swaddled the length of his body, up to his armpits, and then crisscrossed his chest with more 'swaddling,' and even covered his shoulders and neck – Barb Wiggin made a special point of concealing Owen's neck, because she said his Adam's apple looked 'rather grown-up.' It did; it stuck out, especially when he was lying down; but then, Owen's eyes looked 'rather grown-up,' too, in that they bulged, or appeared a trifle haunted in their sockets. His facial features were tiny but sharp, not in the least babylike – certainly not in the 'pillar of light,' which was harsh. There were dark circles under his eyes, his nose was too pointed for a baby's nose, his cheekbones too prominent. Why we didn't just wrap him up in a blanket, I don't know. The 'swaddling clothes' resembled nothing so much as layers upon layers of gauze bandages, so that Owen resembled some terrifying burn victim who'd been shriveled to abnormal size in a fire that had left only his face and arms uncharred – and the 'pillar of light,' and the worshipful postures of all of us, surrounding him, made it appear that Owen was about to undergo some ritual unwrapping in an operating room, and we were his surgeons and nurses.

Upon the conclusion of 'Away in a Manger,' Mr Wiggin read again from Luke: ' "When the angel went away from them into heaven, the shepherds said to one another, 'Let us go over to Bethelehem and see this thing that has happened, which the Lord has made known to us.' And they went with haste, and found Mary and Joseph, and the babe lying in a manger. And when they saw it they made known the saying which had been told them concerning this child; and all who heard it wondered at what the shepherds told them. But Mary kept all these things, pondering them in her heart." '

While the rector read, the kings bowed to the Baby Jesus and presented him with the usual gifts – ornate boxes and tins, and shiny trinkets, difficult to distinguish from the distance of the congregation but somehow regal in appearance. A few of the shepherds offered more humble, rustic presents; one of the shepherds gave the Christ Child a bird's nest.

'WHAT WOULD I DO WITH A BIRD'S NEST?' Owen complained.

'It's for good luck,' the rector said.

'DOES IT SAY SO IN THE BIBLE!' Owen asked.

Someone said that from the audience the bird's nest looked like old, dead grass; someone said it looked like 'dung.'

'Now now,' Dudley Wiggin said.

'It doesn't matter what it *looks* like!' Barb Wiggin said, with considerable pitch in her voice. 'The gifts are *symbolic.*'

Mary Beth Baird foresaw a larger problem. Since the reading from Luke concluded by observing that 'Mary kept all these things, pondering them in her heart' – and surely the 'things' that Mary so kept and pondered were far more matterful than these trivial gifts – shouldn't she *do* something to demonstrate to the audience what a strain on her poor heart it was to do such monumental keeping and pondering?

'What?' Barb Wiggin said.

'WHAT SHE MEANS IS, SHOULDN'T SHE *ACT OUT* HOW A PERSON *PONDERS* SOMETHING,' Owen said. Mary Beth Baird was so pleased that Owen had clarified her concerns that she appeared on the verge of hugging or kissing him, but Barb Wiggin moved quickly between them, leaving the controls of the 'pillar of light' unattended; eerily, the light scanned our little assembly with a will of its own – appearing to settle on the Holy Mother.

There was a respectful silence while we pondered what possible thing Mary Beth Baird *could* do to demonstrate how hard her heart was working; it was clear to most of us that Mary Beth would be satisfied only if she could express her adoration of the Christ Child physically.

'I could kiss him,' Mary Beth said softly. 'I could just bow down and kiss him – on the forehead, I mean.'

'Well, yes, you could try that, Mary Beth,' the rector said cautiously.

'Let's see how it looks,' Barb Wiggin said doubtfully.

'NO,' Owen said. 'NO KISSING.'

'Why not, Owen?' Barb Wiggin asked playfully. She thought an opportunity to tease him was presenting itself, and she was quick to pounce on it.

'THIS IS A VERY HOLY MOMENT,' Owen said slowly.

'Indeed, it is,' the rector said.

'VERY HOLY,' Owen said. 'SACRED,' he added.

'Just on the forehead,' Mary Beth said.

'Let's see how it looks. Let's just try it, Owen,' Barb Wiggin said.

'NO,' Owen said. 'IF MARY IS SUPPOSED TO BE *PONDERING* – "IN HER HEART" – THAT I AM CHRIST THE LORD, THE ACTUAL SON OF GOD . . . A *SAVIOR*, REMEMBER THAT . . . DO YOU THINK SHE'D JUST KISS ME LIKE SOME ORDINARY MOTHER KISSING HER ORDINARY BABY? THIS IS NOT THE ONLY TIME THAT MARY *KEEPS THINGS IN HER HEART*. DON'T YOU REMEMBER WHEN THEY GO TO JERUSALEM FOR PASSOVER AND JESUS GOES TO THE TEMPLE AND TALKS TO THE TEACHERS, AND JOSEPH AND MARY ARE WORRIED ABOUT HIM BECAUSE THEY CAN'T FIND HIM – THEY'RE LOOKING ALL OVER FOR HIM – AND HE TELLS THEM, WHAT ARE YOU WORRIED ABOUT, WHAT ARE YOU LOOKING FOR ME FOR, "DID YOU NOT KNOW THAT I MUST BE IN MY FATHER'S HOUSE?" HE MEANS THE TEMPLE. REMEMBER THAT? WELL, MARY KEEPS THAT IN HER HEART, TOO.'

'But shouldn't I *do* something, Owen?' Mary Beth asked. 'What should I do?'

'YOU KEEP THINGS IN YOUR HEART!' Owen told her.

'She should do nothing?' the Rev. Mr Wiggin asked Owen. The rector, like one of the teachers in the temple, appeared 'amazed.' That is how the teachers in the temple are described – in their response to the Boy Jesus: 'All who heard him were amazed at his understanding and his answers.'

'Do you mean she should do nothing, Owen?' the rector repeated. 'Or that she should do something less, or more, than kissing?'

'MORE,' Owen said. Mary Beth Baird trembled; she

would do anything that he required. 'TRY BOWING,' Owen suggested.

'Bowing?' Barb Wiggin said, with distaste.

Mary Beth Baird dropped to her knees and lowered her head; she was an awkward girl, and this sudden movement caused her to lose her balance. She assumed a three-point position, finally – on her knees, with her forehead resting on the mountain of hay, the top of her head pressing against Owen's hip.

Owen raised his hand over her, to bless her; in a most detached manner, he lightly touched her hair – then his hand hovered above her head, as if he meant to shield her eyes from the intensity of the 'pillar of light.' Perhaps, if only for this gesture, Owen had wanted his arms free.

The shepherds and kings were riveted to this demonstration of what Mary pondered in her heart; the cows did not move. Even the hind parts of the donkeys, who could not see the Holy Mother bowing to the Baby Jesus – or anything at all – appeared to sense that the moment was reverential; they ceased their swaying, and the donkeys' tails hung straight and still. Barb Wiggin had stopped breathing, with her mouth open, and the rector wore the numbed expression of one struck silly with awe. And I, Joseph – I did nothing, I was just the witness. God knows how long Mary Beth Baird would have buried her head in the hay, for no doubt she was ecstatic to have the top of her head in contact with the Christ Child's hip. We might have maintained our positions in this tableau for eternity – we might have made crèche history, a pageant frozen in rehearsal, each of us injected with the very magic we sought to represent: Nativity forever.

But the choirmaster, whose eyesight was failing, assumed he had missed the cue for the final carol, which the choir sang with special gusto.

> Hark! the her-ald an-gels sing, 'Glory to the new-born King;
> Peace on earth, and mer-cy mild, God and sin-ners rec-on-ciled!'
> Joy-ful, all ye na-tions, rise, Join the tri-umph of the skies;
> With the an-gel-ic host pro-claim, 'Christ is born in Beth-le-hem!'
> Hark! the her-ald an-gels sing, 'Glo-ry to the new-born King!'

Mary Beth Baird's head shot up at the first 'Hark!' Her hair was wild and flecked with hay; she jumped to her feet as if the little Prince of Peace had ordered her out of his nest. The donkeys swayed again, the cows – their horns falling about their heads – moved a little, and the kings and shepherds regained their usual lack of composure. The rector, whose appearance suggested that of a former immortal rudely returned to the rules of the earth, found that he could speak again. 'That was perfect, I thought,' he said. 'That was *marvelous*, really.'

'Shouldn't we run through it one more time?' Barb Wiggin asked, while the choir continued to herald the birth of 'the ever-lasting Lord.'

'NO,' said the Prince of Peace. 'I THINK WE'VE GOT IT RIGHT.'

Weekdays in Toronto: 8:00 A.M., Morning Prayer; 5:15 P.M., Evening Prayer; Holy Eucharist every Tuesday, Wednesday, and Friday. I prefer these weekday services to Sunday worship; there are fewer distractions when I have Grace Church on-the-Hill almost to myself – and there are no sermons. Owen never liked sermons – although I think he would have enjoyed delivering a few sermons himself.

The other thing preferable about the weekday services is that no one is there against his will. That's another distraction on Sundays. Who hasn't suffered the experience of having an entire family seated in the pew in front of you, the children at war with each other and sandwiched between the mother and father who are forcing them to go to church? An aura of stale arguments almost visibly clings to the hasty clothing of the children. 'This is the one morning I can sleep in!' the daughter's linty sweater says. 'I get so bored!' says the upturned collar of the son's suit jacket. Indeed, the children imprisoned between their parents moved constantly and restlessly in the pew; they are so crazy with self-pity, they seem ready to scream.

The stern-looking father who occupies the aisle seat has his attention interrupted by fits of vacancy – an expression so perfectly empty accompanies his sternness and his concentration that I think I glimpse an underlying truth to the man's churchgoing: that he is doing it only *for the children*, in the manner that some men with much vacancy of expression are committed to a marriage. When the children are old enough to decide about church for themselves, this man will stay home on Sundays.

The frazzled mother, who is the lesser piece of bread to this family sandwich – and who is holding down that part of the pew from which the most unflattering view of the preacher in the pulpit is possible (directly under the preacher's jowls) – is trying to keep her hand off her daughter's lap. If she smooths out her daughter's skirt only one more time, both of them know that the daughter will start to cry.

The son takes from his suit jacket pocket a tiny, purple truck; the father snatches this away – with considerable bending and crushing of the boy's fingers in the process. 'Just one more obnoxious bit of behavior from you,' the father whispers harshly, 'and you will be grounded – for the rest of the day.'

'The whole rest of the day?' the boy says, incredulous. The apparent impossibility of sustaining *un*obnoxious behavior for even part of the day weighs heavily on the lad, and overwhelms him with a claustrophobia as impenetrable as the claustrophobia of church itself.

The daughter has begun to cry.

'Why is she crying?' the boy asks his father, who doesn't answer. 'Are you having your period?' the boy asks his sister, and the mother leans across the daughter's lap and pinches the son's thighs – a prolonged, twisting sort of pinch. Now he is crying, too. Time to pray! The kneeling pads flop down, the family flops forward. The son manages the old hymnal trick; he slides a hymnal along the pew, placing it where his sister will sit when she's through praying.

'Just one more thing,' the father mutters in his prayers.

But how can you pray, thinking about the daughter's period? She looks old enough to be having her period, and young enough for it to be the first time. Should *you* move the hymnal before she's through praying and sits on it? Should you pick up the hymnal and bash the boy with it? But the father is the one you'd like to hit; and you'd like to pinch the mother's thigh, exactly as she pinched her son. How can you pray?

It is time to be critical of Canon Mackie's cassock; it is the color of pea soup. It is time to be critical of Warden Harding's wart. And Deputy Warden Holt is a racist; he is always complaining that 'the West Indians have taken over

Bathurst Street'; he tells a terrible story about standing in line in the copying-machine store – two young black men are having the entire contents of a pornographic magazine duplicated. For this offense, Deputy Warden Holt wants to have the young man arrested. How can you pray?

The weekday services are almost unattended – quiet, serene. The drumming wing-whir of the slowly moving overhead fan is metronomic, enhancing to the concentration – and from the fourth and fifth rows of pews, you can feel the air moving regularly against your face. In the Canadian climate, the fan is supposed to push the warm, rising air down – back over the chilly congregation. But it is possible to imagine you're in a missionary church, in the tropics.

Some say that Grace Church is overly lighted. The dark-stained, wooden buttresses against the high, vaulted, white-plaster ceiling accentuate how well lit the church is; despite the edifice's predominance of stone and stained glass, there are no corners lost to darkness or to gloom. Critics say the light is too artificial, and too contemporary for such an old building; but surely the overhead fan is contemporary, too – and not propelled by Mother Nature – and no one complains about the fan.

The wooden buttresses are quite elaborate – they are wainscoted, and even the lines of the wainscoting are visible on the buttresses, despite their height; that's how brightly lit the church is. Harold Crosby, or any other Announcing Angel, could never be concealed in these buttresses. Any angel-lowering or angel-raising apparatus would be most visible. The miracle of the Nativity would seem less of a miracle here – indeed, I have never watched a Christmas pageant at Grace Church. I have already seen that miracle; once was enough. The Nativity of '53 is all the Nativity I need.

That Christmas, the evenings were long; dinners with Dan, or with my grandmother, were slow and solemn. My enduring perception of those nights is that Lydia's wheelchair needed to be oiled and that Dan complained, with uncharacteristic bitterness, about what a mess amateurs could make of *A Christmas Carol*. Dan's mood was not improved by the frequent presence of our neighbor – and Dan's most veteran amateur – Mr Fish.

'I'd so looked forward to being Scrooge,' Mr Fish would

say, pretending to stop by 80 Front Street, after dinner, for some other reason – whenever he saw Dan's car in the driveway. Sometimes it was to once again agree with my grandmother about Gravesend's pending leash law; Mr Fish and my grandmother were in favor of leashing dogs. Mr Fish gave no indication that he was even slightly troubled by his hypocrisy on this issue – for surely old Sagamore would roll over in his grave to hear his former master espousing canine restraints of any kind; Sagamore had run free, to the end.

But it was not the leash law Mr Fish really cared about; it was Scrooge – a plum part, ruined (in Mr Fish's view) by amateur ghosts.

'The ghosts are only the beginning of what's wrong,' Dan said. 'By the end of the play, the audience is going to be rooting for Tiny Tim to die – someone might even rush the stage and kill that brat with his crutch.' Dan was still disappointed that he could not entice Owen to play the plucky cripple, but the little Lord Jesus was unmoved by Dan's pleas.

'What wretched ghosts!' Mr Fish whined.

The first ghost, Marley's Ghost, was a terrible ham from the Gravesend Academy English Department; Mr Early embraced every part that Dan gave him as if he were King Lear – madness and tragedy fueled his every action, a wild melancholy spilled from him in disgusting fits and seizures. ' "I am here tonight to warn you," ' Mr Early tells Mr Fish, ' "that you have yet a chance and hope of escaping my fate . . ." ' all the while unwrapping the bandage that dead men wear to keep their lower jaws from dropping on their chests.

' "You were always a good friend to me," ' Mr Fish tells Mr Early, but Mr Early has become entangled in his jaw bandage, the unwinding of which has caused him to forget his lines.

' "You will be haunted by . . . Four Spirits," ' Mr Early says; Mr Fish shuts his eyes.

'Three, not Four!' Dan cries.

'But aren't I the fourth?' Mr Early asks.

'You're the *first*!' Mr Fish tells him.

'But there are three others,' Mr Early says.

'Jesus Christ!' Dan says.

But Marley's Ghost was not as bad as the Ghost of Christmas Past, an irritating young woman who was a member of the

Town Library Board and who wore men's clothes and chain-smoked, aggressively; and *she* was not as bad as the Ghost of Christmas Present, Mr Kenmore, a butcher at our local A&P, who (Mr Fish said) smelled like raw chicken and shut his eyes whenever Mr Fish spoke – Mr Kenmore needed to concentrate with such fervor on his own role that he found Scrooge's presence a distraction. And *none* of them was as bad as the Ghost of Christmas Yet to Come – Mr Morrison, our mailman, who had looked so perfect for the part. He was a tall, thin, lugubrious presence; a sourness radiated from him – dogs not only refrained from biting him, they slunk away from him; they must have known that the taste of him was as toxic as a toad's. He had a gloomy, detached quality that Dan had imagined would be perfect for the grim, final phantom – but when Mr Morrison discovered that he had no lines, that the Ghost of Christmas Yet to Come never speaks, he became contemptuous of the part; he threatened to quit, but then remained in the role with a vengeance, sneering and scoffing at poor Scrooge's questions, and leering at the audience, attempting to seize their attention from Mr Fish (as if to accuse Dan, and Dickens, of idiocy – for denying this most important spirit the power of speech).

No one could remember Mr Morrison ever speaking – as a mailman – and yet, as a harbinger of doom, the poor man clearly felt he had much to say. But the deepest failure was that none of these ghosts was frightening. 'How can I *be* Scrooge if I'm not frightened?' Mr Fish asked Dan.

'You're an actor, you gotta fake it,' Dan said. To my thinking, which was silent, Mrs Walker's legs were again wasted – in the part of Tiny Tim's mother.

Poor Mr Fish. I never knew what he did for a living. He was Sagamore's master, he was the good guy in *Angel Street* – at the end, he took my mother by the arm – he was the unfaithful husband in *The Constant Wife*, he was Scrooge. But what did he *do*? I never knew. I could have asked Dan; I still could. But Mr Fish was the quintessential *neighbor*; he was *all* neighbors – all dog owners, all the friendly faces from familiar backyards, all the hands on your shoulders at your mother's funeral. I don't remember if he had a wife. I don't even remember what he looked like, but he manifested the fussy concentration of a man about to pick up a fallen leaf; he was all rakers of all lawns, all snow-shovelers of all sidewalks. And although he began the Christmas season as an unfrightened Scrooge, I saw Mr Fish when he was frightened, too.

I also saw him when he was young and carefree, which is how he appeared to me before the death of Sagamore. I remember a brilliant September afternoon when the maples on Front Street were starting to turn yellow and red; above the crisp, white clapboards and the slate rooflines of the houses, the redder maples appeared to be drawing blood from the ground. Mr Fish had no children but he enjoyed throwing and kicking a football, and on those blue-sky, fall afternoons, he cajoled Owen and me to play football with him; Owen and I didn't care for the sport – except for those times when we could include Sagamore in the game. Sagamore, like many a Labrador, was a mindless retriever of balls, and it was fun to watch him try to pick up the football in his mouth; he would straddle the ball with his forepaws, pin it to the ground with his chest, but he never quite succeeded in fitting the ball in his mouth. He would coat the ball with slobber, making it exceedingly difficult to pass and catch, and ruining what Mr Fish referred to as the aesthetics of the game. But the game had no aesthetics that were available to Owen Meany and me; I could not master the spiral pass, and Owen's hand was so small that he refused to throw the ball at all – he only kicked it. The ferocity with which Sagamore tried to contain the ball in his mouth and the efforts we made to keep the ball away from him were the most interesting aspects of the sport to Owen and me – but Mr Fish took the perfection of passing and catching quite seriously.

'This will be more fun when you boys get a little older,' he used to say, as the ball rolled under the privet, or wobbled into my grandmother's rose beds, and Owen and I purposely fumbled in front of Sagamore – such was our pleasure in watching the dog lunge and drool, lunge and drool.

Poor Mr Fish. Owen and I dropped so many perfect passes. Owen liked to run with the ball until Sagamore ran him down; and then Owen would kick the ball in no particular or planned direction. It was *dog*ball, not football, that we played on those afternoons, but Mr Fish was ever optimistic that Owen and I would, miraculously – one day – grow up and play pass-and-catch as it was meant to be played.

A few houses down Front Street lived a young couple with

a new baby; Front Street was not much of a street for young couples, and the street had only one new baby. The couple cruised the neighborhood with the air of an entirely novel species – as if they were the first couple in New Hampshire to have given birth. Owen shrieked so loudly when we played football with Mr Fish that the young father or mother from down the street would fretfully appear, popping up over a hedge to ask us if we would keep our voices down '. . . because of the baby.'

His years in The Gravesend Players would exercise Mr Fish's natural ability at rolling his eyes; and after the young parent had returned to guard the precious newborn, Mr Fish would commence rolling his eyes with abandon.

'STUPID BABY,' Owen complained, 'WHO EVER HEARD OF TRYING TO CONTROL THE NOISE OUTDOORS?'

That had just happened – for about the hundredth time – the day Owen managed to punt the football out of the yard . . . out of my grandmother's yard, and beyond Mr Fish's yard, too; the ball floated over the roof of my grandmother's garage and rolled end-over-end down the driveway, toward Front Street, with Owen and me and Sagamore chasing after it. Mr Fish stood sighing, with his hands on his hips; he did not chase after errant passes and kicks – these were imperfections that he sought to eliminate from our game – but on this day he was impressed by the unusual power of Owen Meany's kick (if not the kick's direction).

'That's getting your foot into the ball, Owen!' Mr Fish called. As the ball rolled into Front Street with Sagamore in close pursuit, the baby-rattle tinkle of the odd bell of the diaper truck dinged persistently, even at the moment of the truck's sudden confluence with Sagamore's unlucky head.

Poor Mr Fish; Owen ran to get him, but Mr Fish had heard the squealing tires – and even the dull thud – and he was halfway down the driveway when Owen met him. 'I DON'T THINK YOU WANT TO SEE IT,' Owen said to him. 'WHY DON'T YOU GO SIT DOWN AND LET US TAKE CARE OF THINGS?'

Mr Fish was on his porch when the young parents came up Front Street, to complain again about the noise – or to investigate the delay of the diaper truck, because their baby was the sole reason the truck was there.

The diaper truck driver sat on the running board of the cab.

'Shit,' he said. Up close, the odor of urine radiated from the truck in waves. My grandmother had her kindling delivered in burlap sacks, and my mother helped me empty one; I helped Owen get Sagamore into the sack. The football, still smeared with saliva, had gathered some gravel and a candy-bar wrapper; it lay uninvitingly at the curb.

In late September, in Gravesend, it could feel like August or like November; by the time Owen and I had dragged Sagamore in the sack to Mr Fish's yard, the sun was clouded over, the vividness seemed muted in the maple trees, and the wind that stirred the dead leaves about the lawn had grown cold. Mr Fish told my mother that he would make a 'gift' of Sagamore's body – to my grandmother's roses. He implied that a dead dog was highly prized, among serious gardeners; my grandmother wished to be brought into the discussion, and it was quickly agreed which rose bushes would be temporarily uprooted, and replanted, and Mr Fish began with the spade. The digging was much softer in the rose bed than it would have been in Mr Fish's yard, and the young couple and their baby from down the street were sufficiently moved to attend the burial, along with a scattering of Front Street's other children; even my grandmother asked to be called when the hole was ready, and my mother – although the day had turned much colder – wouldn't even go inside for a coat. She wore dark-gray flannel slacks and a black, V-necked sweater, and stood hugging herself, standing first on one foot, then on the other, while Owen gathered strange items to accompany Sagamore to the underworld. Owen was restrained from putting the football in the burlap sack, because Mr Fish – while digging the grave – maintained that football was still a game that would give us some pleasure, when we were 'a little older.' Owen found a few well-chewed tennis balls, and Sagamore's food dish, and his dog blanket for trips in the car; these he included in the burlap sack, together with a scattering of the brightest maple leaves – and a leftover lamb chop that Lydia had been saving for Sagamore (from last night's supper).

The lights were turned on in some houses when Mr Fish finished digging the grave, and Owen decided that the attendant mourners should hold candles, which Lydia was reluctant to provide; at my mother's urging, Lydia produced the candles, and my grandmother was summoned.

'HE WAS A GOOD DOG,' Owen said, to which there were murmurs of approval.

'I'll never have another one,' said Mr Fish.

'I'll remind you of that,' my grandmother remarked; she must have found it ironic that her rose bushes, having suffered years of Sagamore's blundering, were about to be the beneficiaries of his decomposition.

The candlelit ritual must have looked striking from the Front Street sidewalk; that must be why the Rev. Lewis Merrill and his wife were drawn to our yard. Just as we were faced with a loss for words, the Rev. Mr Merrill – who was already as pale as the winter months – appeared in the rose garden. His wife, red-nosed from the autumn's first good dose of the common cold, was wearing her winter coat, looking prematurely sunk in deepest January. Taking their fragile constitutional, the Merrills had detected the presence of a religious ceremony.

My mother, shivering, seemed quite startled by the Merrills' appearance.

'It makes me cold to look at you, Tabby,' Mr Merrill said, but Mr Merrill glanced nervously from face to face, as if he were counting the living of the neighborhood in order to determine *which* poor soul was at rest in the burlap sack.

'Thank you for coming, Pastor,' said Mr Fish, who was born to be an amateur actor. 'Perhaps you could say a few words appropriate to the passing away of man's best friend?'

But Mr Merrill's countenance was both stricken and uncomprehending. He looked at my mother, and at me; he stared at the burlap sack; he gazed into the hole in the rose bed as it it were his own grave – and no coincidence that a short walk with his wife had ended here.

My grandmother, seeing her pastor so tense and tongue-tied, took his arm and whispered to him, 'It's just a *dog*. Just say a little something, for the children.'

But Mr Merrill began to stutter; the more my mother shivered, the more the Rev. Mr Merrill shivered in response, the more his mouth trembled and he could not utter the simplest rite – he failed to form the first sentence. Mr Fish, who was never a frequenter of any of the town churches, hoisted the burlap sack and dropped Sagamore into the underworld.

It was Owen Meany who found the words: ' "I AM THE

RESURRECTION AND THE LIFE, SAITH THE LORD: HE THAT BELIEVETH IN ME, THOUGH HE WERE DEAD, YET SHALL HE LIVE; AND WHOSOEVER LIVETH AND BELIEVETH IN ME SHALL NEVER DIE."'

It seemed a lot to say – for a dog – and the Rev. Mr Merrill, freed from his stutter, was struck silent.

'". . . SHALL NEVER DIE,"' Owen repeated. The wind, gusting, covered my mother's face with her hair as she reached for Owen's hand.

Over all rituals, over all services – over every rite of passage – Owen Meany would preside.

That Christmas of '53, whether rehearsing the Nativity, or testing Potter's prophylactic on the third floor of Waterhouse Hall, I was only dimly aware of Owen as the conductor of an orchestra of events – and totally unaware that this orchestration would lead to a single sound. Not even in Owen's odd room did I perceive enough, although no one could escape the feeling that – at the very least – an altar-in-progress was under construction there.

It was hard to tell if the Meanys celebrated Christmas. A clump of pine boughs had been crudely gathered and stuck to the front farmhouse door by a huge, ugly staple – the kind fired from a heavy-duty, industrial staple gun. The staple looked strong enough to bind granite to granite, or to hold Christ fast to the cross. But there was no particular arrangement to the pine boughs – it certainly did not resemble a wreath; it was as shapeless a mass as an animal's nest, only hastily begun and abandoned in a panic. Inside the sealed house, there was no tree; there were no Christmas decorations, not even candles in the windows, not even a decrepit Santa leaning against a table lamp.

On the mantel above the constantly smoldering fire – wherein the logs were either chronically wet, or else the coals had been left unstirred for hours – there was a crèche with cheaply painted wooden figures. The cow was three-legged – nearly as precarious as one of Mary Beth Baird's cows; it was propped against a rather menacing chicken that was almost half the cow's size, not unlike the proportions of Barb Wiggin's turtledoves. A gouge through the flesh-toned paint of the Holy Mother's face had rendered her obviously blind and so ghastly to behold that someone in the Meany family had thoughtfully turned her face away from the Christ Child's crib – yes, there *was* a crib. Joseph had lost a hand – perhaps he had hacked it off himself, in a jealous rage, for there was something darkly smoldering in his expression, as if the smoky fire that left the mantel coated with soot had also colored Joseph's mood. One angel's harp was mangled, and from another angel's O-shaped mouth it was easier to imagine the wail of a mourner than the sweetness of singing.

But the crèche's most ominous message was that the little Lord Jesus himself was missing; the crib was empty – that was why the Virgin Mary had turned her mutilated face away; why one angel dashed its harp, and another screamed in anguish; why Joseph had lost a hand, and the cow a leg. The Christ Child was gone – kidnapped, or run away. The very object of worship was absent from the conventional assembly.

There appeared to be more order, more divine management in evidence in Owen's room; still, there was nothing that represented anything as seasonal as Christmas – except the poinsettia-red dress that my mother's dummy wore; but I knew that dress was all the dummy had to wear, year 'round.

The dummy had taken a position at the head of Owen's bed – closer to his bed than my mother had formerly positioned it in relationship to her own bed. From where Owen lay at night, it was instantly clear to me that he could reach out and touch the familiar figure.

'DON'T STARE AT THE DUMMY,' he advised me. 'IT'S NOT GOOD FOR YOU.'

Yet, apparently, it was good for *him* – for there she was, standing over him.

The baseball cards, at one time so very much on display in Owen's room, were not – I was sure – gone; but they were out of sight. There was no baseball in evidence, either – although I was certain that the murderous ball was in the room. The foreclaws of my armadillo were surely there, but they were also not on display. And the Christ Child snatched from the crib . . . I was convinced that the Baby Jesus was somewhere in Owen's room, perhaps in company with Potter's prophylactic, which Owen had taken home with him but which was no more visible than the armadillo's claws, the abducted Prince of Peace, and the so-called instrument of my mother's death.

It was not a room that invited a long visit; our appearances at the Meanys' house were brief, sometimes only for Owen to change his clothes, because – during that Christmas vacation, especially – he stayed overnight with me more than he stayed at home.

Mrs Meany never spoke to me, or took any notice of me at all, when I came to the house; I could not remember the last time Owen had bothered to announce my presence – or, for that matter, his own presence – to his mother. But Mr Meany was usually pleasant; I wouldn't say he was cheerful, or even enthusiastic, and he was not a fellow for small talk, but he offered me his cautious version of humor. 'Why, it's Johnny Wheelwright!' he'd say, as if he were surprised I was there at all, or he hadn't seen me for years. Perhaps this was his unsubtle way of announcing my presence to Mrs Meany, but that lady was unchanged by her husband's greeting; she remained in profile to both the window and to us. For variety, she would at times gaze into the fire, although nothing she saw there ever prompted her to tend to the logs or the coals; possibly she preferred smoke to flames.

And one day, when he must have been feeling especially conversational, Mr Meany said: 'Why, it's Johnny Wheelwright! How goes all that Christmas rehearsin'?'

'Owen's the star of the pageant,' I said. As soon as I spoke, I felt the knuckles of his tiny fist in my back.

'You never said you was the *star*,' Mr Meany said to Owen.

'He's the Baby Jesus!' I said. 'I'm just old Joseph.'

'The Baby Jesus?' said Mr Meany. 'I thought you was an angel, Owen.'

'NOT THIS YEAR,' Owen said. 'COME ON, WE GOTTA GO,' he said to me, pulling the back of my shirt.

'You're the Christ Child?' his father asked him.

'I'M THE ONLY ONE WHO CAN FIT IN THE CRIB,' Owen said.

'Now we're not even using a crib,' I explained. 'Owen's in charge of the whole thing – he's the star *and* the director.' Owen yanked my shirt so hard he untucked it.

'The director,' Mr Meany repeated flatly. That was when I felt cold, as if a draft had pushed itself into the house in an unnatural way – down the warm chimney. But it was no draft; it was Mrs Meany. She had actually moved. She was staring at Owen. There was confusion in her expression, a mix of terror and awe – of shock; but also of a most familiar resentment. By comparison to such a stare, I realized what a relief his mother's profile must be to Owen Meany.

Outside, in the raw wind off the Squamscott, I asked Owen if I had said anything I shouldn't have said.

'I THINK THEY LIKE ME BETTER AS AN ANGEL,' he said.

The snow never seemed to stick on Maiden Hill; it could never get a grip on the huge, upthrust slabs of granite that marked the rims of the quarries. In the pits themselves the snow was dirty, mixed with sand, tracked by birds and squirrels; the sides of the quarries were too steep for dogs. There is always so much sand around a granite quarry; somehow, it works its way to the top of the snow; and around Owen's house there was always so much wind that the sand stung against your face – like the beach in winter.

I watched Owen pull down the earflaps of his red-and-black-checkered hunter's cap; that was when I realized that I'd left my hat on his bed. We were on our way down Maiden Hill; Dan had said he'd meet us with the car, at the boathouse on the Swasey Parkway.

'Just a second,' I told Owen. 'I forgot my hat.' I ran back to the house; I left him kicking at a rock that had been frozen in the ruts of the dirt driveway.

I didn't knock; the clump of pine boughs on the door was blocking the most natural place to knock, anyway. Mr Meany was standing by the mantel, either looking at the crèche or at the fire. 'Just forgot my hat,' I said, when he looked up at me.

I didn't knock on the door of Owen's room, either. At first, I thought the dressmaker's dummy had moved; I thought that somehow it had found a way to bend at the waist and had sat down on Owen's bed. Then I realized that Mrs Meany was sitting on the bed; she was staring quite intently at my mother's figure and she did not interrupt her gaze when I entered the room.

'Just forgot my hat,' I repeated; I couldn't tell if she heard me.

I put on my hat and was leaving the room, closing the door as quietly as I could behind me, when she said, 'I'm sorry about your poor mother.' It was the first time she had ever spoken to me. I peeked back into the room. Mrs Meany hadn't moved; she sat with her head slightly bowed to the dressmaker's dummy, as if she were awaiting some instructions.

It was noon when Owen and I passed under the railroad trestle bridge at the foot of the Maiden Hill Road, a few hundred yards below the Meany Granite Quarry; years later, the abutment of that bridge would be the death of Buzzy Thurston, who had successfully evaded the draft. But that Christmas of '53, when Owen and I walked under the bridge, was the first time our being there coincided with the passing of *The Flying Yankee* – the express train that raced between Portland and Boston, in just two hours. It screamed through Gravesend every day at noon; and although Owen and I had watched it hurtle through town from the Gravesend depot, and although we had put pennies on the tracks for *The Flying Yankee* to flatten, we had never before been directly under the trestle bridge exactly as *The Flying Yankee* was passing over us.

I was still thinking of Mrs Meany's attitude of supplication before my mother's dummy when the trestlework of the bridge began to rattle. A fine grit sifted down between the railroad ties and the trestles and settled upon Owen and me; even the concrete abutments shook, and – shielding our eyes from the loosened sand – we looked up to see the giant, dark underbelly of the train, speeding above us. Through the gaps between the passing cars, flashes of the leaden, winter sky blinked down on us.

'IT'S *THE FLYING YANKEE*!' Owen managed to scream above the clamor. All trains were special to Owen Meany, who had never ridden on a train; but *The Flying Yankee* – its terrifying speed and its refusal to stop in Gravesend – represented to Owen the zenith of travel. Owen (who had never been anywhere) was a considerable romantic on the subject of travel.

'What a coincidence!' I said, when *The Flying Yankee* had gone; I meant that it was a farfetched piece of luck that had landed us under the trestle bridge precisely at noon, but Owen smiled at me with his especially irritating combination of mild pity and mild contempt. Of course, I know now that Owen didn't believe in coincidences. Owen Meany believed that 'coincidence' was a stupid, shallow refuge sought by stupid, shallow people who were unable to accept the fact that their lives were shaped by a terrifying and awesome design – more powerful and unstoppable than *The Flying Yankee.*

The maid who looked after my grandmother, the maid who was Lydia's replacement after Lydia suffered her amputation, was named Ethel, and she was forced to endure the subtle comparisons that both Lydia and my grandmother made of her job-effectiveness. I say 'subtle,' only because my grandmother and Lydia never discussed these comparisons with Ethel directly; but in Ethel's company, Grandmother would say, 'Do you remember, Lydia, how you used to bring up the jams and jellies from those shelves in the secret passageway – where they get so dusty – and line them all up in the kitchen, according to the dates when you'd put them up?'

'Yes, I remember,' Lydia would say.

'That way, I could look them over and say, "Well, we should throw out that one – it doesn't seem to be a favorite around here, and it's two years old." Do you remember?' my grandmother would ask.

'Yes. One year we threw out all the quince,' Lydia said.

'It was just pleasant to know what we had down there in the secret passageway,' my grandmother remarked.

'Don't let *things* get the upper hand on you, I always say,' Lydia said.

And the next morning, of course, poor Ethel – properly, albeit indirectly instructed – would haul out all the jams and jellies and dust them off for my grandmother's inspection.

Ethel was a short, heavyset woman with an ageless, blocky strength; yet her physical power was undermined by a slow mind and a brutal lack of confidence. Her forward motion, even with something as basic as cleaning the house, was characterized by the strong swipes of her stubby arms – but these confident efforts were followed or preceded by the hesitant, off-balance steps of her short, broad feet upon her thick ankles; she was a stumbler. Owen said she was too slow-witted to frighten properly, and therefore we rarely bothered her – even when we discovered opportunities to surprise her, in the dark, in the secret passageway. In this way, too, Ethel was Lydia's inferior, for Lydia had been great fun to terrorize, when she had two legs.

The maid hired to look after Lydia was – as we used to say in Gravesend – 'a whole other ball game.' Her name was

Germaine, and both Lydia and Ethel bullied her; my grandmother purposefully ignored her. Among these contemptuous women, poor Germaine had the disadvantage of being young – and almost pretty, in a shy, mousy way. She possessed the nonspecific clumsiness of someone who makes such a constant effort to be inconspicuous that she is creatively awkward – without meaning to, Germaine hoarded attention to herself; her almost electric nervousness disturbed the atmosphere surrounding her.

Windows, when Germaine was attempting to slip past them, would suddenly shut themselves; doors would open. Precious vases would totter when Germaine approached them; when she reached to steady them, they would shatter. Lydia's wheelchair would malfunction the instant Germaine took tremulous command of it. The light in the refrigerator would burn out the instant Germaine opened the door. And when the garage light was left on all night, it would be discovered – in my grandmother's early-morning investigation – that Germaine had been the last to bed.

'Last one to bed turns out the lights,' Lydia would say, in her litanic fashion.

'I was not only in bed but I was asleep, when Germaine came to bed,' Ethel would announce. 'I know I was asleep because she woke me up.'

'I'm sorry,' Germaine would whisper.

My grandmother would sigh and shake her head, as if several rooms of the great house had been consumed in a fire overnight and there was nothing to salvage – and nothing to say, either.

But I know why my grandmother sought to ignore Germaine. Grandmother, in a fit of Yankee frugality, had given Germaine all my mother's clothes. Germaine was a little too small for the clothes, although they were the nicest clothes Germaine had ever owned and she wore them both happily and reverentially – Germaine never realized that my grandmother resented seeing her in such painfully familiar attire. Perhaps my grandmother never knew how much she would resent seeing those clothes on Germaine when she gave them to her; and Grandmother had too much pride to admit her error. She could only look away. That the clothes didn't fit Germaine was referred to as Germaine's fault.

'You should eat more, Germaine,' Grandmother would say,

not looking at her – and never noticing what Germaine ate; only that my mother's clothes hung limply on her. But Germaine could have gorged herself and never matched my mother's bosom.

'John?' Germaine would whisper, when she would enter the secret passageway. The one overhead bulb at the bottom of those winding stairs never lit that passageway very brightly. 'Owen?' she would ask. 'Are you in here? Don't frighten me.'

And Owen and I would wait until she had turned the L-shaped corner between the tall, dusty shelves at shoulder level – the odd shadows of the jam and jelly jars zigzagging across the cobwebbed ceiling; the higher, more irregular shadows cast by the bigger jars of tomato and sweet-pepper relish, and the brandied plums, were as looming and contorted as volcanic conformations.

' "BE NOT AFRAID," ' Owen would whisper to Germaine in the dark; once, over that Christmas vacation, Germaine burst into tears. 'I'M SORRY!' Owen called after her. 'IT'S JUST *ME*!'

But it was Owen whom Germaine was especially afraid of. She was a girl who believed in the supernatural, in what she was always calling 'signs' – for example, the rather commonplace mutilation and murder of a robin by one of the Front Street cats; to witness the torture was 'a sure sign' you would be involved with an ever greater violence yet to come. Owen himself was taken as a 'sign' by poor Germaine; his diminutive size suggested to her that Owen was small enough to actually enter the body and soul of another person – and cause that person to perform unnatural acts.

It was a dinner table conversation about Owen's voice that revealed to me Germaine's point of view concerning *that* unnatural aspect of him. My grandmother had asked me if Owen or his family had ever taken any pains to inquire if something could be 'done' about Owen's voice – 'I mean medically,' Grandmother said, and Lydia nodded so vigorously that I thought her hair pins might fall onto her dinner plate.

I knew that my mother had once suggested to Owen that her old voice and singing teacher might be able to offer Owen some advice of a corrective kind – or even suggest certain vocal exercises, designed to train Owen to speak more . . . well . . . *normally*. My grandmother and Lydia exchanged their usual glances upon the mere mention of that voice and singing teacher; I explained, further, that Mother had even written out the address and telephone number of this mysterious figure, and she had given the information to Owen. Owen, I was sure, had never contacted the teacher.

'And why not?' Grandmother asked. Why not, *indeed*? Lydia appeared to ask, nodding and nodding. Lydia's *nodding* was the most detectable manifestation of how her senility was in advance of my grandmother's senility – or so my grandmother had observed, privately, to me. Grandmother was extremely – almost clinically – interested in Lydia's senility, because she took Lydia's behavior as a barometer regarding what she could soon expect of herself.

Ethel was clearing the table in her curious combination of aggression and slow motion; she took too many dishes at one time, but she lingered at the table with them for so long that you were sure she was going to put some of them back. I think now that she was just collecting her thoughts concerning where she would take the dishes. Germaine was also clearing – the way a crippled swallow might swoop down for a crumb off your plate at a picnic. Germaine took too little away – one spoon at a time, and often the wrong spoon; or else she took your salad fork before you'd been served your salad. But if her disturbance of your dinner area was slight and fanciful, it was also fraught with Germaine's vast potential for accident. When Ethel approached, you feared a landslide of plates might fall in your lap – but this never happened. When Germaine approached, you guarded your plate and silverware, fearing that something you needed would be snatched from you, and that your water glass would be toppled during the sudden, flighty attack – and this often happened.

It was therefore within this anxious arena – of having the dinner table cleared – that I announced to my grandmother and Lydia why Owen Meany had *not* sought the advice of Mother's voice and singing teacher.

'Owen doesn't think it's right to try to change his voice,' I said.

Ethel, lumbering away from the table under the considerable burden of the two serving platters, the vegetable bowl, and all our dinner plates and silver, held her ground. My grandmother, sensing Germaine's darting presence, held her water glass in one hand, her wine glass in the other. 'Why on earth doesn't he think it's *right*?' she asked, as Germaine pointlessly removed the peppermill and let the salt shaker stay.

'He thinks his voice is for a purpose; that there's a *reason* for his voice being like that,' I said.

'*What* reason?' my grandmother asked.

Ethel had approached the kitchen door, but she seemed to be waiting, shifting her vast armload of dishes, wondering – possibly – if she should take them into the living room, instead. Germaine positioned herself directly behind Lydia's chair, which made Lydia tense.

'Owen thinks his voice comes from God,' I said quietly, as Germaine – reaching for Lydia's unused dessert spoon – dropped the peppermill into Lydia's water glass.

'Merciful Heavens!' Lydia said; this was a pet phrase of my grandmother's, and Grandmother eyed Lydia as if this thievery of her favorite language were another manifestation of Lydia's senility being in advance of her own.

To everyone's astonishment, Germaine spoke. 'I think his voice comes from the Devil,' Germaine said.

'Nonsense!' my grandmother said. 'Nonsense to it coming from God – *or* from the Devil! It comes from *granite*, that's what it comes from. He breathed in all that *dirt* when he was a baby! It made his voice queer and it stunted his growth!'

Lydia, nodding, prevented Germaine from trying to extract the peppermill from her water glass; to be safe, she did it herself. Ethel stumbled into the kitchen door with a great crash; the door swung wide, and Germaine fled the dining room – with absolutely nothing in her hands.

My grandmother sighed deeply; even to Grandmother's sighing, Lydia nodded – a more modest little nod. 'From *God*,' my grandmother repeated contemptuously. And then she said: 'The address and phone number of the voice and singing teacher . . . I don't suppose your little friend would have kept it – not if he didn't intend to use it, I mean?' To this artful question, my grandmother and Lydia exchanged their usual glances; but I considered the question carefully – its many levels of seriousness were apparent to me. I knew this was information that my grandmother had never known – and how it must have interested her! And, of course, I also knew that Owen would *never* have thrown this information away; that he never intended to make use of the information was not the point. Owen rarely threw *anything* away; and something that my mother had given him would not only have been saved – it would have been enshrined!

I am indebted to my grandmother for many things – among them the use of an artful question. 'Why would Owen have kept it?' I asked her innocently.

Again, Grandmother sighed; again, Lydia nodded. 'Why indeed,' Lydia said sadly. It was my grandmother's turn to nod. They were both getting old and frail, I observed, but what I was thinking was *why* I had decided to keep Owen's probable possession of the singing teacher's address and phone number to myself. I didn't *know* why – not then. What I know now is that Owen Meany would have quickly said it was NO COINCIDENCE.

And what would he have said regarding our discovery that we were not alone in the Christmas use we made of the empty rooms in Waterhouse Hall? Would he have termed it NO COINCIDENCE, too, that we (one afternoon) were engaged in our usual investigations of a second-floor room when we heard another master key engage the lock on the door? I was into the closet in a hurry, fearful that the empty coat hangers would not entirely have stopped chiming together by the time the new intruder entered the room. Owen scooted under the bed; he lay on his back with his hands crossed upon his chest, like a soldier in a hasty grave. At first, we thought Dan had caught us – but Dan was rehearsing The Gravesend Players, unless (in despair) he had fired the lot of them and canceled the production. The only other person it could be was Mr Brinker-Smith, the biologist – but he was a first-floor residence; Owen and I were so quiet, we didn't believe our presence could have been detected from the first floor.

'Nap time!' we heard Mr Brinker-Smith say; Mrs Brinker-Smith giggled.

It was instantly apparent to Owen and me that Ginger Brinker-Smith had not brought her husband to this empty room in order to *nurse* him; the twins were not with them – it was 'nap time' for the twins, too. It strikes me now that the Brinker-Smiths were blessed with good-spirited initiative, with an admirable and inventive sense of mischief – for how else could they have maintained one of the pleasures of conjugal relations without disturbing their demanding twins? At the time, of course, it struck Owen and me that the Brinker-

Smiths were dangerously oversexed; that they should make such reckless use of the dormitory beds, including – as we later learned – systematic process through *all* the rooms of Waterhouse Hall . . . well, it was perverse behavior for parents, in Owen's and my view. Day by day, nap by nap, bed by bed, the Brinker-Smiths were working their way to the fourth floor of the dorm. Since Owen and I were working our way to the first floor, it was perhaps inevitable – as Owen would have suggested – and NO COINCIDENCE that we should have encountered the Brinker-Smiths in a second-floor room.

I saw nothing, but heard much, through the closed closet door. (I had never heard Dan with my mother.) As usual, Owen Meany had a closer, more intense perception of this passionate event than I had: the Brinker-Smiths' clothes fell on both sides of Owen; Ginger Brinker-Smith's legendary nursing bra was tossed within inches of Owen's face. He had to turn his face to the side, Owen told me, in order to avoid the sagging bedspring, which began to make violent, chafing contact with Owen's nose. Even with his face sideways, the bedspring would occasionally plunge near enough to the floor to scrape against his cheek.

'IT WAS THE NOISE THAT WAS THE WORST OF IT,' he told me tearfully, after the Brinker-Smiths had returned to their twins. 'I FELT LIKE I WAS UNDERNEATH *THE FLYING YANKEE!*'

That the Brinker-Smiths were engaged in a far more creative and original use of Waterhouse Hall than Owen and I could make of the old dormitory had a radical effect on the rest of our Christmas vacation. Shocked and battered, Owen suggested we return to the tamer investigations of 80 Front Street.

'Hardness! Hardness!' Ginger Brinker-Smith had screamed.

'Wetness! Wetness!' Mr Brinker-Smith had answered her. And bang! bang! bang! beat the bedspring on Owen Meany's head.

'STUPID "HARDNESS," STUPID "WETNESS," ' Owen complained. 'SEX MAKES PEOPLE CRAZY.'

I had only to think of Hester to agree.

And so, because of Owen's and my first contact with the act of love, we were at 80 Front Street – just hanging around – the day our mailman, Mr Morrison, announced his resignation from the role of the Ghost of Christmas Yet to Come.

'Why are you telling *me*?' my grandmother asked. '*I'm* not the director.'

'Dan ain't on my route,' the glum mailman said.

'I don't relay messages of this kind – not even to Dan,' my grandmother told Mr Morrison. 'You should go to the next rehearsal and tell Dan yourself.'

Grandmother kept the storm door ajar, and the bitter December air must have been cold against her legs; it was plenty cold for Owen and me, and we were positioned deeper into the hall, behind my grandmother – and were both wearing wool-flannel trousers. We could feel the chill radiating off Mr Morrison, who held my grandmother's small bundle of mail in his mittened hand; he appeared reluctant to give her the mail, unless she agreed to carry his message to Dan.

'I ain't settin' foot in another of them rehearsals,' Mr Morrison said, shuffling his high-topped boots, shifting his heavy, leather sack.

'If you were resigning from the post office, would you ask someone else to tell the postmaster?' my grandmother asked him.

Mr Morrison considered this; his long face was alternately red and blue from the cold. 'It ain't the part I thought it was,' he said to Grandmother.

'Tell Dan,' Grandmother said. 'I'm sure I don't know the first thing about it.'

'I KNOW ABOUT IT,' said Owen Meany. Grandmother regarded Owen uncertainly; before she allowed him to replace her at the open door, she reached outside and snatched her mail from Mr Morrison's tentative hand.

'What do *you* know about it?' the mailman asked Owen.

'IT'S AN IMPORTANT PART,' Owen said. 'YOU'RE THE LAST OF THE SPIRITS WHO APPEAR TO SCROOGE. YOU'RE THE GHOST OF THE *FUTURE* – YOU'RE THE SCARIEST GHOST OF ALL!'

'I got nothin' to *say*!' Mr Morrison complained. 'It ain't even what they call a speakin' part.'

'A GREAT ACTOR DOESN'T NEED TO *TALK*,' Owen said.

'I wear this big black cloak, with a *hood*!' Mr Morrison protested. 'No one can see my face.'

'There's *some* justice, anyway,' my grandmother said under her breath to me.

'A GREAT ACTOR DOESN'T NEED A *FACE*,' Owen said.

'An actor needs somethin' to *do*!' the mailman shouted.

'YOU SHOW SCROOGE WHAT WILL HAPPEN TO HIM IF HE DOESN'T BELIEVE IN CHRISTMAS!' Owen cried. 'YOU SHOW A MAN HIS OWN *GRAVE*! WHAT CAN BE SCARIER THAN THAT?'

'But all I do is *point*,' Mr Morrison whined. 'Nobody would even know what I was pointin' at if old Scrooge didn't keep givin' speeches to himself – "If there is any person in the town who feels emotion caused by this man's death, show that person to me, Spirit, I beseech you!" *That's* the kind of speech old Scrooge is always makin'!' Mr Morrison shouted. ' "Let me see some tenderness connected with a death," and so on and so forth,' the mailman said bitterly. 'And all I do is *point*! I got *nothin'* to say and all anybody sees of me is one *finger*!' Mr Morrison cried; he pulled his mitten off and pointed a long, bony finger at Owen Meany, who retreated from the mailman's skeletal hand.

'IT'S A GREAT PART FOR A GREAT ACTOR,' Owen said stubbornly. 'YOU HAVE TO BE A *PRESENCE*. THERE'S NOTHING AS SCARY AS THE FUTURE.'

In the hall, behind Owen, an anxious crowd had gathered. Lydia in her wheelchair, Ethel – who was polishing a candlestick – and Germaine, who thought Owen was the Devil . . . they huddled behind my grandmother, who was old enough to take Owen's point of view to heart: nothing *is* as scary as the future, she knew, unless it's someone who *knows* the future.

Owen threw up his hands so abruptly that the women were startled and moved away from him. 'YOU KNOW EVERYTHING *YET TO COME*!' he screamed at the disgruntled mailman. 'IF YOU WALK ONSTAGE AS IF YOU KNOW THE FUTURE – I MEAN, *EVERYTHING*! – YOU'LL SCARE THE SHIT OUT OF EVERYONE.'

Mr Morrison considered this; there was even a glimmer of comprehension in his gaze, as if he saw – albeit momentarily – his own, terrifying potential; but his eyes were quickly fogged over by his breath in the cold air.

'Tell Dan I quit, that's all,' he said. Thereupon, the mailman turned and left – 'most undramatically,' my grandmother would say, later. At the moment, despite her dislike of vulgar language, Grandmother appeared almost charmed by Owen Meany.

'Get away from the open door now, Owen,' she said. 'You've given that fool much more attention than he deserves, and you'll catch your death of cold.'

'I'M CALLING DAN, RIGHT AWAY,' Owen told us matter-of-factly. He went directly to the phone and dialed the number; the women and I wouldn't leave the hall, although I think we were all unconscious of how very much we had become his audience. 'HELLO, DAN?' he said into the phone. 'DAN? THIS IS OWEN!' (As if there could have been any doubt concerning who it was!) 'DAN, THIS IS AN EMERGENCY. YOU'VE LOST THE GHOST OF CHRISTMAS YET TO COME. YES, I MEAN MORRISON – THE COWARDLY MAILMAN!'

'The cowardly mailman!' my grandmother repeated admiringly.

'YES, YES – I KNOW HE WASN'T ANY GOOD,' Owen told Dan, 'BUT YOU DON'T WANT TO BE STUCK WITHOUT A SPIRIT FOR THE FUTURE.'

That was when I saw it coming; the future – or at least one, small part of it. Owen had failed to talk Mr Morrison into the role, but he had convinced himself it was an important part – far more attractive than being Tiny Tim, that mere goody-goody. Furthermore, it was established that the Ghost of Christmas Yet to Come was not a speaking part; Owen would not have to use his *voice* – not as the Christ Child and not as the Ghost of the Future.

'I DON'T WANT YOU TO PANIC, DAN,' Owen said into the phone, 'BECAUSE I THINK I KNOW SOMEONE WHO'D BE PERFECT FOR THE PART – WELL, IF NOT PERFECT, AT LEAST DIFFERENT.'

It was with the word DIFFERENT that my grandmother shivered; it was also the first time she looked at Owen Meany with anything resembling respect.

Once again, I thought, the little Prince of Peace had taken charge. I looked at Germaine, whose lower lip was captured in her teeth; I knew what she was thinking. Lydia, rocking in her wheelchair, appeared to be mesmerized by the one-sided phone conversation; Ethel held the candlestick like a weapon.

'WHAT THE PART REQUIRES IS A CERTAIN *PRESENCE*,' Owen told Dan. 'THE GHOST MUST TRULY APPEAR TO *KNOW* THE FUTURE. IRONICALLY, THE OTHER PART I'M

PLAYING THIS CHRISTMAS – YES, YES, I MEAN THE STUPID PAGEANT – *IRONICALLY*, THIS PREPARES ME FOR THE ROLE. I MEAN, THEY'RE BOTH PARTS THAT FORCE YOU TO TAKE COMMAND OF THINGS, WITHOUT WORDS . . . YES, YES, OF COURSE I MEAN *ME*!' There was a rare pause, while Owen listened to Dan. 'WHO SAYS THE GHOST OF CHRISTMAS YET TO COME HAS TO BE *TALL*?' Owen asked angrily. 'YES, OF COURSE I KNOW HOW TALL MISTER FISH IS. DAN, YOU'RE NOT USING YOUR IMAGINATION.' There was another brief pause, and Owen said: 'THERE'S A SIMPLE TEST. LET ME REHEARSE IT. IF EVERYBODY LAUGHS, I'M OUT. IF EVERYONE IS SCARED, I'M THE ONE. YES, OF COURSE – "INCLUDING MISTER FISH." LAUGH, I'M OUT. SCARED, I'M IN.'

But I didn't need to wait to know the results of *that* test. It was necessary only to look at my grandmother's anxious face, and at the attitudes of the women surrounding her – at the fear of Owen Meany that was registered by Lydia's transfixed expression, by Ethel's whitened knuckles around the candlestick, by Germaine's trembling lip. It wasn't necessary for me to suspend my belief or disbelief in Owen Meany until after his first rehearsal; I already knew what a *presence* he could summon – especially in regard to the future.

That evening, at dinner, we heard from Dan about Owen's triumph – how the cast stood riveted, not even knowing what *dwarf* this was, for Owen was completely hidden in the black cloak and hood; it didn't matter that he never spoke, or that they couldn't see his face. Not even Mr Fish had known who the fearful apparition was.

As Dickens wrote, 'Oh cold, cold, rigid, dreadful Death, set up thine altar here, and dress it with such terrors as thou hast at thy command, for this is thy dominion!'

Owen had a way of gliding across stage; he several times startled Mr Fish, who kept losing his sense of where Owen was. When Owen pointed, it was all of a sudden, a convulsive, twitchy movement – his small, white hand flashing out of the folds of the cloak, which he flapped. He could glide slowly, like a skater running out of momentum; but he could also *skitter* with a bat's repellent quickness.

At Scrooge's grave, Mr Fish said: ' "Before I draw nearer

to that stone to which you point, answer me one question. Are these the shadows of the things that Will be or are they shadows of the things that May be, only?" '

As never before, this question seemed to seize the attention of every amateur among The Gravesend Players; even Mr Fish appeared to be mortally interested in the answer. But the midget Ghost of Christmas Yet to Come was inexorable; the tiny phantom's indifference to the question made Dan Needham shiver.

It was then that Mr Fish approached close enough to the gravestone to read his own name thereon. ' "Ebenezer Scrooge . . . am *I* that man?" ' Mr Fish cried, falling to his knees. It was from the perspective of his knees – when Mr Fish's head was only slightly above Owen Meany's – that Mr Fish received his first full look at the averted face under the hood. Mr Fish did not laugh; he screamed.

He was supposed to say, ' "No, Spirit! Oh, no, no! Spirit, hear me! I am not the man I was!" ' And so on and so forth. But Mr Fish simply screamed. He pulled his hands so fiercely away from Owen's cowl that the hood was yanked off Owen's head, revealing him to the other members of the cast – several of them screamed, too; no one laughed.

'It makes the hair on the back of my neck stand up, just to remember it!' Dan told us, over dinner.

'I'm not surprised,' my grandmother said.

After dinner, Mr Fish made a somewhat subdued appearance.

'Well, at least we've got *one* good ghost,' Mr Fish said. 'It makes my job a lot easier, really,' he rationalized. 'The little fellow is quite effective, quite effective. It will be interesting to see his . . . effect on an audience.'

'We've already seen it,' Dan reminded him.

'Well, yes,' Mr Fish agreed hastily; he looked worried.

'Someone told me that Mr Early's daughter wet her pants,' Dan informed us.

'I'm not surprised,' my grandmother said. Germaine, clearing one teaspoon at a time, appeared ready to wet hers.

'Perhaps you might hold him back a little?' Mr Fish suggested to Dan.

'Hold him back?' Dan asked.

'Well, get him to restrain whatever it is he *does*,' Mr Fish said.

'I'm not at all sure what it *is* he does,' Dan said.

'I'm not either,' Mr Fish said. 'It's just . . . so disturbing.'

'Perhaps, when people are sitting back a few rows – in the audience, I mean – it won't be quite so . . . upsetting,' Dan said.

'Do you think so?' Mr Fish asked.

'Not really,' Dan admitted.

'What if we saw his face – from the beginning?' Mr Fish suggested.

'If you don't pull his hood off, we'll *never* see his face,' Dan pointed out to Mr Fish. 'I think that will be better.'

'Yes, much better,' Mr Fish agreed.

Mr Meany dropped Owen off at 80 Front Street – so he could spend the night. Mr Meany knew that my grandmother resented the racket his truck made in the driveway; that was why we didn't hear him come and go – he let Owen out of the cab on Front Street.

It was quite magical; I mean, the timing: Mr Fish saying good night, opening the door to leave – precisely at the same time as Owen was reaching to ring the doorbell. My grandmother, at that instant, turned on the porch light; Owen blinked into the light. From under his red-and-black-checkered hunter's cap, his small, sharp face stared up at Mr Fish – like the face of a possum caught in a flashlight. A dull, yellowish bruise, the sheen of tarnished silver, marked Owen's cheek – where the Brinker-Smiths' mobile bed had struck him – giving him a cadaver's uneven color. Mr Fish leaped backward, into the hall.

'Speak of the Devil,' Dan said, smiling. Owen smiled back – at us all.

'I GUESS YOU HEARD – I GOT THE PART!' he said to my grandmother and me.

'I'm not surprised, Owen,' my grandmother said. 'Won't you come in?' She actually held the door open for him; she even managed a charming curtsy – inappropriately girlish, but Harriet Wheelwright was gifted with those essentially regal properties that make the inappropriate gesture work . . . those being facetiousness and sarcasm.

Owen Meany did not miss the irony in my grandmother's voice; yet he beamed at her – and he returned her curtsy with a confident bow, and with a little tip of his red-and-black-checkered hunter's cap. Owen had triumphed, and he knew it; my grandmother knew it, too. Even Harriet

Wheelwright – with her *Mayflower* indifference toward the Meanys of this world – even my grandmother knew that there was more to The Granite Mouse than met the eye.

Mr Fish, perhaps to compose himself, was humming the tune to a familiar Christmas carol. Even Dan Needham knew the words. As Owen finished knocking the snow off his boots – as the little Lord Jesus stepped inside our house – Dan half-sang, half-mumbled the refrain we knew so well: '"Hark! the her-ald an-gels sing, "Glo-ry to the new-born King!"'

5 : THE GHOST OF THE FUTURE

Thus did Owen Meany remodel Christmas. Denied his long-sought excursion to Sawyer Depot, he captured the two most major, non-speaking roles in the only dramatic productions offered in Gravesend that holiday season. As the Christ Child and as the Ghost of Christmas Yet to Come, he had established himself as a prophet – disquietingly, it was *our* future he seemed to know something about. Once, he thought, he had seen into my mother's future; he had even become an instrument of her future. I wondered what he thought he knew of Dan's or my grandmother's future – or Hester's, or mine, or his own.

God would tell me who my father was, Owen Meany had assured me; but, so far, God had been silent.

It was Owen who'd been talkative. He'd talked Dan and me out of the dressmaker's dummy; he'd stationed my mother's heartbreaking figure at *his* bedside – to stand watch over *him*, to be *his* angel. Owen had talked himself down from the heavens and into the manger – he'd made me a Joseph, he'd chosen a Mary for me, he'd turned turtledoves to cows. Having revised the Holy Nativity, he had moved on; he was reinterpreting Dickens – for even Dan had to admit that Owen had somehow changed *A Christmas Carol*. The silent Ghost of Christmas Yet to Come had stolen the penultimate scene from Scrooge.

Even *The Gravesend News-Letter* failed to recognize that Scrooge was the main character; that Mr Fish was the principal actor was a fact that entirely eluded *The News-Letter*'s drama critic, who wrote, 'The quintessential Christmas tale, the luster of which has been dulled (at least, for this reviewer) by its annual repetition, has been given a new sparkle.' The critic added, 'The shopworn ghost-story part of the tale has been energized by the brilliant performance of little Owen Meany, who – despite his diminutive size – is a huge presence onstage; the miniature Meany simply dwarfs the other performers. Director Dan Needham should consider casting the Tiny Tim-sized star as Scrooge in next year's *A Christmas Carol*!'

There was not a word about *this* year's Scrooge, and Mr Fish fumed over his neglect. Owen responded crossly to *any* criticism.

'WHY IS IT NECESSARY TO REFER TO ME AS "LITTLE," AS "DIMINUTIVE," AS "MINIATURE"?' Owen raved. 'THEY DON'T MAKE SUCH QUALIFYING REMARKS ABOUT THE OTHER ACTORS!'

'You forgot "Tiny Tim-sized," ' I told him.

'I KNOW, I KNOW,' he said. 'DO THEY SAY, "FORMER DOG-OWNER FISH" IS A SUPERB SCROOGE? DO THEY SAY, "VICIOUS SUNDAY-SCHOOL TYRANT WALKER" MAKES A CHARMING MOTHER FOR TINY TIM?'

'They called you a "star," ' I reminded him. 'They called you "brilliant" – and a "*huge* presence." '

'THEY CALLED ME "LITTLE," THEY CALLED ME "DIMINUTIVE," THEY CALLED ME "MINIATURE"!' Owen cried.

'It's a good thing it wasn't a *speaking* part,' I reminded him.

'VERY FUNNY,' Owen said.

In the case of this particular production, Dan wasn't bothered by the local press; what troubled Dan was what Charles Dickens might have thought of Owen Meany. Dan was sure that Dickens would have disapproved.

'Something's not right,' Dan said. 'Small children burst into tears – they have to be removed from the audience before they get to the happy ending. We've started warning mothers with small children at the door. It's not quite the *family* entertainment it's supposed to be. Kids leave the theater looking like they've seen *Dracula*!'

Dan was relieved to observe, however, that Owen appeared to be coming down with a cold. Owen was susceptible to colds; and now he was overtired all the time – rehearsing the Holy Nativity in the mornings, performing as the Ghost of Christmas Yet to Come at night. Some afternoons Owen was so exhausted that he fell asleep at my grandmother's house; he would drop off to sleep on the rug in the den, lying under the big couch, or on a stack of the couch pillows, where he'd been gunning down my metal soldiers with my toy cannon. I would go to the kitchen to get us some cookies; and when I came back to the den, Owen would be fast asleep. 'He's getting to be like Lydia,' my grandmother observed – because Lydia could not stay awake in the afternoons, either; she would nod off to sleep in her wheelchair, wherever Germaine had left her, sometimes facing into a corner. This was a further indication to my grandmother that Lydia's senility was in advance of her own.

But as Owen began to manifest the early signs of the common cold – a sneeze or a cough now and then, and a runny nose – Dan Needham imagined that his production of *A Christmas Carol* might be the beneficiary of Owen getting sick. Dan didn't want Owen to be ill; it was just a small cough and a sneeze – and maybe even Owen having to blow his nose – that Dan was wishing for. Such a *human* noise from under the dark hood would surely put the audience at ease; Owen sneezing and snorting might even draw a laugh or two. In Dan's opinion, a laugh or two wouldn't hurt.

'It might hurt Owen,' I pointed out. 'I don't think Owen would appreciate any laughter.'

'I don't mean that I want to make the Ghost of the Future a *comic* character,' Dan maintained. 'I would just like to humanize him, a little.' For that was the problem, in Dan's view: Owen did not look human. He was the size of a small child, but his movements were uncannily adult; and his authority onstage was beyond 'adult' – it was supernatural.

'Look at it this way,' Dan said to me. 'A ghost who sneezes, a ghost who coughs – a ghost who has to blow his nose – he's just not quite so scary.'

But what about a Christ Child who sneezes and coughs, and has to blow *his* nose? I thought. If the Wiggins insisted that the Baby Jesus couldn't cry, what would they think of a *sick* Prince of Peace?

Everyone was sick that Christmas: Dan got over bronchitis only to discover he had pinkeye; Lydia had such a violent cough that she would occasionally propel herself backward in her wheelchair. When Mr Early, who was Marley's Ghost, began to hack and sniffle, Dan confided to me that it would be perfect symmetry – for the play – if *all* the ghosts came down with something. Mr Fish, who had by far the most lines, pampered himself so that he wouldn't catch anyone else's cold; thus Scrooge retreated from Marley's Ghost in an even more exaggerated fashion.

Grandmother complained that the weather was too slippery for her to go out; she was not worried about colds, but she dreaded falling on the ice. 'At my age,' she told me, 'it's one fall, one broken hip, and then a long, slow death – from pneumonia.' Lydia coughed and nodded, nodded and coughed, but neither woman would share her elderly wisdom with me . . . concerning *why* a broken hip produced pneumonia; not to mention, 'a long, slow death.'

'But you have to see Owen in *A Christmas Carol*,' I said.

'I see quite enough of Owen,' Grandmother told me.

'Mister Fish is also quite good,' I said.

'I see quite enough of Mister Fish, too,' Grandmother remarked.

The rave review that Owen received from *The Gravesend News-Letter* appeared to drive Mr Fish into a silent depression; when he came to 80 Front Street after dinner, he sighed often and said nothing. As for our morose mailman, Mr Morrison, it is incalculable how much he suffered to hear of Owen's success. He stooped under his leather sack as if he shouldered a burden much more demanding than the excess of Christmas mail. How did it make him feel to deliver all those copies of *The Gravesend News-Letter*, wherein Mr Morrison's former role was described as 'not only pivotal but principal' – and Owen Meany was showered with the kind of praise Mr Morrison might have imagined for himself?

In the first week, Dan told me, Mr Morrison did not come to watch the production. To Dan's surprise, Mr and Mrs Meany had not made an appearance, either.

'Don't they read *The News-Letter*?' Dan asked me.

I could not imagine Mrs Meany reading; the demands on her time were too severe. With all her staring – at walls, into corners, not quite out the window, into the dying fire, at my mother's dummy – when would Mrs Meany have the time to read a newspaper? And Mr Meany was not even one of those men who read about sports. I imagined, too, that the Meanys would never have heard about *A Christmas Carol* from Owen; after all, he hadn't wanted them to know about the pageant.

Perhaps one of the quarrymen would say something about the play to Mr Meany; maybe a stonecutter or the derrickman's wife had seen it, or at least read about it in *The News-Letter*.

'Hear your boy's the star of the theater,' someone might say. But I could hear, too, how Owen would dismiss it.

'I'M JUST HELPING DAN OUT. HE GOT IN A FIX – ONE OF THE GHOSTS QUIT. YOU KNOW MORRISON, THE COWARDLY MAILMAN? WELL, IT WAS A CASE OF STAGE FRIGHT. IT'S A VERY SMALL PART – NOT EVEN A SPEAKING PART. I WOULDN'T RECOMMEND THE PLAY, EITHER – IT'S NOT VERY BELIEVABLE. AND BESIDES, YOU NEVER GET TO SEE MY FACE. I DON'T THINK I'M ONSTAGE FOR MORE THAN FIVE MINUTES . . .'

I was sure that was how Owen would have handled it. I thought he was excessively proud of himself – and that he treated his parents harshly. We all go through a phase – it lasts a lifetime, for some of us – when we're embarrassed by our parents; we don't want them hanging around us because we're afraid they'll do or say something that will make us feel ashamed of them. But Owen seemed to me to suffer this embarrassment more than most; that's why I thought he held his parents at such a great distance from himself. And he was, in my opinion, exceedingly bossy toward his father. At an age when most of our peers were enduring how much their parents bossed them around, Owen was always telling his father what to do.

My sympathy for Owen's embarrassment was slight. After all, I missed my mother; I would have enjoyed her hanging around me. Because Dan wasn't my real father, I had never developed any resentment toward Dan; I always loved having Dan around – my grandmother, although she was a loving grandmother, was aloof.

'Owen,' Dan said one evening. 'Would you like to invite your parents to see the play? Maybe for our last performance – on Christmas Eve?'

'I THINK THEY'RE BUSY ON CHRISTMAS EVE,' Owen said.

'How about one of the earlier evenings, then?' Dan asked. 'Some evening soon – shall I invite them? Any evening would be fine.'

'THEY'RE NOT EXACTLY THEATERGOING TYPES,' Owen said. 'I DON'T MEAN TO INSULT YOU, DAN,

BUT I'M AFRAID MY PARENTS WOULD BE BORED.'

'But surely they'd enjoy seeing *you*, Owen,' Dan said. 'Wouldn't they like your performance?'

'THE ONLY STORIES THEY LIKE ARE TRUE STORIES,' Owen said. 'THEY'RE RATHER REALISTIC, THEY DON'T GET TOO EXCITED ABOUT MADE-UP STORIES. ANYTHING THAT'S SORT OF MAKE-BELIEVE – THAT'S NOT FOR THEM. AND ANYTHING WITH GHOSTS – THAT'S OUT.'

'Ghosts are out?' Dan asked.

'ALL THAT KIND OF STUFF IS OUT – WITH THEM,' Owen said. But – listening to him – I found I had just the opposite impression of his parents. I thought that Owen Meany's mother and father believed *only* in the so-called make-believe; that ghosts were *all* they believed in – that spirits were all they listened to. 'WHAT I MEAN IS, DAN,' Owen said, 'IS THAT I'D RATHER *NOT* INVITE MY PARENTS. IF THEY COME, OKAY; BUT I THINK THEY WON'T.'

'Sure, sure,' Dan said. 'Anything you say, Owen.'

Dan Needham suffered from my mother's affliction: he, too, couldn't keep his hands off Owen Meany. Dan was not a hair-messer, not a patter of butts or shoulders. Dan grabbed your hands and mashed them, sometimes until your knuckles and his cracked together. But Dan's manifestations of physical affection for Owen exceeded, even, his fondness for me; Dan had the good instincts to keep his distance from me – to be *like* a father to me, but not to assert himself too *exactly* in the role. Because of a physical caution that Dan expressed when he touched me, he was less restrained with Owen, whose father never once (at least, not in my presence) touched him. I think Dan Needham knew, too, that Owen was not ever handled at home.

There was a fourth curtain call on Saturday night, and Dan sent Owen out onstage alone. It was apparent that the audience wanted Owen alone; Mr Fish had already been out onstage with Owen, and by himself – it was clearly Owen whom the crowd adored.

The audience rose to greet him, The peak of his death-black hood was a trifle pointy, and too tall for Owen's small head; it had flopped over to one side, giving Owen a gnomish appearance and a slightly cocky, puckish attitude. When he flipped the hood back and showed the audience his beaming face, a young girl in one of the front rows fainted; she was about our age – maybe twelve or thirteen – and she dropped down like a sack of grain.

'It was quite warm where we were sitting,' the girl's mother said, after Dan made sure the girl had recovered.

'STUPID GIRL!' Owen said, backstage. He was his own makeup man. Even though his face remained concealed throughout his performance by the overlarge, floppy hood, he whitened his face with baby powder and blackened the already-dark sockets under his eyes with eyeliner. He wanted even the merest glimpse that the audience might get of him to be properly ghostly; that his cold was worsening enhanced the pallor he desired.

He was coughing pretty regularly by the time Dan drove him home. The last Sunday before Christmas – the day of our pageant – was tomorrow.

'He sounds a little sicker than I had in mind,' Dan told me on our way back to town. 'I may have to play the Ghost of Christmas Yet to Come *myself*. Or maybe – if Owen's too sick – maybe *you* can take the part.'

But I was just a Joseph; I felt that Owen Meany had already chosen me for the only part I could play.

It snowed overnight, not a major storm; then the temperature kept dropping, until it was too cold to snow. A new coat of flat-white, flatter than church-white, lay spread over Gravesend that Sunday morning; the wind, which is the cruelest kind of cold, kicked up wisps and kite tails of the dry powder and made the empty rain gutters at 80 Front Street rattle and moan; the gutters were empty because the new snow was too cold to cling.

The snowplows were in no hurry to be early on Sunday mornings, and the only vehicle that didn't slip and skid as it made its way up Front Street was the heavy truck from the Meany Granite Company. Owen had so many clothes on, he had difficulty bending his knees as he trudged up the driveway – and his arms did not swing close to his sides, but protruded stiffly, like the limbs of a scarecrow. He was so muffled up in a long, dark-green scarf that I couldn't see his face at all – but who could ever mistake Owen Meany for anyone else? It was a scarf my mother had given him – when she'd discovered, one winter, that he didn't own one. Owen called it his LUCKY scarf, and he saved it for important occasions or for when it was especially cold.

The last Sunday before Christmas called for my mother's scarf – on both counts. As Owen and I tramped down Front Street toward Christ Church, the birds took flight at Owen's barking cough; there was a phlegmy rattle in his chest, loud enough for me to hear through his many layers of winter clothes.

'You don't sound very well, Owen,' I pointed out to him.

'IF JESUS HAD TO BE BORN ON A DAY LIKE THIS, I DON'T THINK HE'D HAVE LASTED LONG ENOUGH TO BE CRUCIFIED,' Owen said.

On Front Street's almost-virgin sidewalk, only one set of footprints had broken the snow before us; except for the clumsy peeing of dogs, the sidewalk was an unmarred path of white. The figure who had made the morning's first human tracks in the snow was too bundled up and too far ahead of Owen and me for us to recognize him.

'YOUR GRANDMOTHER ISN'T COMING TO THE PAGEANT?' Owen asked me.

'She's a Congregationalist,' I reminded him.

'BUT IS SHE SO INFLEXIBLE THAT SHE CAN'T SWITCH CHURCHES FOR ONE SUNDAY OF THE YEAR? THE CONGREGATIONALISTS DON'T HAVE A PAGEANT.'

'I know, I know,' I said; but I knew more than that: I knew the Congregationalists didn't even have the conventional morning service on the last Sunday before Christmas – they had Vespers instead. It was a special event, largely for caroling. It wasn't that my grandmother's church service was in conflict with our pageant; it was that Grandmother was not enticed to see Owen play the Christ Child. She had remarked that she found the idea 'repulsive.' Also, she made such a fuss about the weather's potential for breaking her hip that she announced her intention to skip the Vespers at the Congregational Church. By the later afternoon, when the light was gone, it was even easier, she reasoned, to break your hip on the ice in the dark.

The man on the sidewalk ahead of us was Mr Fish, whom we rather quickly caught up to – Mr Fish was making his unreckless way with absurdly great care; he must have feared breaking his hip, too. He was startled by the sight of Owen Meany, wrapped up so tightly in my mother's scarf that only Owen's eyes were showing; but Mr Fish was often startled to see Owen.

'Why aren't you already at the church, getting into your costumes?' he asked us. We pointed out that we would be almost an hour early. Even at the rate Mr Fish was walking, he would be half an hour early; but Owen and I were surprised that Mr Fish was attending the pageant.

'YOU'RE NOT A CHURCHGOER,' Owen said accusingly.

'Why no, I'm not, that's true,' Mr Fish admitted. 'But I wouldn't miss this for the world!'

Owen eyed his costar in *A Christmas Carol* cautiously. Mr Fish seemed both so depressed and impressed by Owen's success that his attendance at the Christ Church Christmas Pageant was suspicious. I suspect that Mr Fish enjoyed depressing himself; also, he was so slavishly devoted to amateur acting that he desperately sought to pick up as many pointers as he could by observing Owen's genius.

'I MAY NOT BE AT MY BEST TODAY,' Owen warned Mr Fish; he then demonstrated his barking cough, dramatically.

'A trouper like you is surely undaunted by a little illness, Owen,' Mr Fish observed. We three trudged through the snow together – Mr Fish coming halfway to meet us, on the matter of pace.

He confided to Owen and me that he was a little nervous about attending church; that he'd never once been forced to go to church when he was a child – his parents had not been religious, either – and that he'd only 'set foot' in churches for weddings and funerals. Mr Fish wasn't even sure how much of Christ's story a Christmas pageant 'covered.'

'NOT THE WHOLE THING,' Owen told him.

'Not the bit on the cross?' Mr Fish asked.

'THEY DIDN'T NAIL HIM TO THE CROSS WHEN HE WAS A *BABY*!' Owen said.

'How about the bit when he does all the healing – and all the lecturing to the disciples?' Mr Fish asked.

'IT DOESN'T GO PAST CHRISTMAS!' Owen said, with exasperation. 'IT'S JUST THE BIRTHDAY SCENE!'

'It's not a speaking part,' I reminded Mr Fish.

'Oh, of course, I forgot about that,' Mr Fish said.

Christ Church was on Elliot Street, at the edge of the Gravesend Academy campus; at the corner of Elliot and Front streets, Dan Needham was waiting for us. Apparently the director intended to pick up a few pointers, too.

'My, my, look who's here!' Dan said to Mr Fish, who blushed.

Owen was cheered to see that Dan was coming.

'IT'S A GOOD THING YOU'RE HERE, DAN,' Owen told him, 'BECAUSE THIS IS MISTER FISH'S FIRST CHRISTMAS PAGEANT, AND HE'S A LITTLE NERVOUS.'

'I'm just not sure when to genuflect, and all that nonsense!' Mr Fish said, chuckling.

'NOT ALL EPISCOPALIANS GENUFLECT,' Owen announced.

'I don't,' I said.

'I DO,' said Owen Meany.

'Sometimes I do and sometimes I don't,' Dan said. 'When I'm in church, I watch the other people – I do what they do.'

Thus did our eclectic foursome arrive at Christ Church.

Despite the cold, the Rev. Dudley Wiggin was standing outdoors on the church steps to greet the early arrivals; he was not wearing a hat, and his scalp glowed a howling red under his thin, gray hair – his ears looked frozen bloodless enough to break off. Barb Wiggin stood in a silver-fur coat beside him, wearing a matching fur hat.

'SHE LOOKS LIKE A STEWARDESS ON THE TRANS-SIBERIAN RAILROAD,' Owen observed.

I got quite a shock to see the Rev. Lewis Merrill and his California wife standing next to the Wiggins; Owen was surprised, too.

'HAVE YOU CHANGED CHURCHES?' Owen asked them.

The long-suffering Merrills appeared not to possess the imaginative capacity to know what Owen meant; it was a question that raised havoc with Mr Merrill's usually slight stutter.

'W-w-w-w-e have *Ves*-p-p-p-pers today!' Mr Merrill told Owen, who didn't understand.

'The Congregationalists have a vesper service today,' I told Owen. 'Instead of the regular morning service,' I added. 'Vespers are in the late afternoon.'

'I KNOW WHAT TIME VESPERS ARE!' Owen answered irritably.

The Rev. Mr Wiggin put his arm around his fellow

clergyman's shoulder, giving the Rev. Mr Merrill such a squeeze that the smaller, paler man looked alarmed. I believe that Episcopalians are generally heartier than Congregationalists.

'Barb and I go to the Vespers, for the caroling – every year,' Rector Wiggin announced. 'And the Merrills come to our pageant!'

'Every year,' Mrs Merrill added neutrally; she looked miserably envious of Owen's face-concealing scarf.

The Rev. Mr Merrill composed himself. I'd not seen him so tongue-tied since Sagamore's spontaneous funeral, and it occurred to me that it might be Owen who so effectively crippled his speech.

'We really go in for the caroling, we celebrate the songs of Christmas – we've always put great emphasis on our *choir*,' Pastor Merrill said. He appeared to single me out for a heartfelt look when he said '*choir*,' as if the mere mention of these trained angels was certain to remind me of my mother's lost voice.

'We go in more for the miracle itself!' said Mr Wiggin joyfully. 'And *this* year,' the rector added, suddenly taking a grip of Owen's shoulder with his steady pilot's hand, '*this* year we've got a little Lord Jesus who's gonna take your breath away!' The Rev. Dudley Wiggin mauled Owen's head in his big paw, managing to push down the visor of Owen's red-and-black-checkered hunter's cap; at the same time, he effectively blinded Owen by scrunching up my mother's LUCKY scarf.

'Yes, sir!' said Rector Wiggin, who now lifted the hunter's cap off Owen's head, so quickly that static electricity caused Owen's silky-thin, babylike hair to stand up and wave in all directions. '*This* year,' Captain Wiggin warned, 'there's not gonna be a dry eye in the house!'

Owen, who appeared to be strangling in his scarf, sneezed.

'Owen, you come with me!' Barb Wiggin said sharply. 'I've got to wrap this poor child in his swaddling clothes – before he catches cold!' she explained to the Merrills; but Mr Merrill and his shivering wife looked in need of being wrapped in swaddling clothes themselves. They seemed aghast at the notion that Owen Meany was cast as the Prince of Peace. The Congregationalists are a lot less miracle-oriented than the Episcopalians, I believe.

In the chilly vestibule of the parish house, Barb Wiggin proceeded to imprison Owen Meany in the swaddling clothes; but however tightly or loosely she bound him in the broad, cotton swathes, Owen complained.

'IT'S TOO TIGHT, I CAN'T BREATHE!' he would say, coughing. Or else he would cry out, 'I FEEL A DRAFT!'

Barb Wiggin worked over him with such a grim, humorless sense of purpose that you would have thought she was embalming him; perhaps that's what she thought of as she swaddled him – to calm herself.

The combination of being so roughly handled by Barb Wiggin and discovering that my grandmother had been free to attend the pageant – but had chosen *not* to attend – was deleterious to Owen's mood; he grew cranky and petulant. He insisted that he be unswaddled, and then reswaddled, in my mother's LUCKY scarf; when this was accomplished, the white cotton swatches could be wrapped over the scarf to conceal it. The point being, he wanted the scarf next to his skin.

'FOR WARMTH AND FOR LUCK,' he said.

'The Baby Jesus doesn't need "luck," Owen,' Barb Wiggin told him.

'ARE YOU TELLING ME CHRIST WAS LUCKY?' Owen asked her. 'I WOULD SAY HE COULD HAVE USED A LITTLE MORE LUCK THAN HE HAD. I WOULD SAY HE RAN OUT OF LUCK, AT THE END.'

'But Owen,' Rector Wiggin said. 'He was crucified, yet he rose from the dead – he was resurrected. Isn't the point that he was saved?'

'HE WAS *USED*,' said Owen Meany, who was in a contrary mood.

The rector appeared to consider whether the time was right for ecclesiastical debate; Barb Wiggin appeared to consider throttling Owen with my mother's scarf. That Christ was lucky or unlucky, that he was saved or used, seemed rather serious points of difference – even in the hurried-up atmosphere of the parish-house vestibule, drafty from the opening and closing of the outside door and at the same time smelling of steam from the wet woolen clothes that dripped melting snow into the heat registers. Yet who was a mere rector of Christ Church to argue with the babe in swaddling clothes about to lie in a manger?

'Wrap him up the way he likes it,' Mr Wiggin instructed his wife; but there was menace in his tone, as if the rector were weighing the possibilities of Owen Meany being the Christ or the Antichrist. With the fury of the strokes with which she unwrapped him, and rewrapped him, Barb Wiggin demonstrated that Owen was no Prince of Peace to *her*.

The cows – the former turtledoves – were staggering around the crowded vestibule, as if made restless by the absence of hay. Mary Beth Baird looked quite lush – like a slightly plump starlet – in her white raiment; but both the Holy Mother effect, and the Holy Virgin effect, were undermined by her long, rakish pigtail. As a typical Joseph, I was attired in a dull brown robe, the biblical equivalent of a three-piece suit. Harold Crosby, delaying his ascension in the often-faulty angel-apparatus, had twice requested a 'last' visit to the men's room. Swaddled as he was, it was a good thing, I thought, that Owen didn't have to pee. He couldn't stand; and even if he'd been propped up on his feet, he couldn't have walked – Barb Wiggin had wrapped his legs too tightly together.

That was the first problem: how to get him to the crèche. So that our creative assembly could gather out of sight of the congregation, a tripartite screen had been placed in front of the rude manger – a gold-brocade cross adorned each purple panel of the triptych. We were supposed to take our places behind this altarpiece – to freeze there, in photographic stillness. And as the Announcing Angel began his harrowing descent to the shepherds, thus distracting the congregation from *us*, the purple screen would be removed. The 'pillar of light,' following the shepherds and kings, would lead the congregation's rapt attention to our assembly in the stable.

Naturally, Mary Beth Baird wanted to carry Owen to the crèche. 'I can do it!' the Virgin Mother proclaimed. 'I've lifted him up before!'

'NO, *JOSEPH* CARRIES THE BABY JESUS!' Owen cried, beseeching me; but Barb Wiggin wished to undertake the task herself. Observing that the Christ Child's nose was running, she deftly wiped it; then she held the handkerchief in place, while instructing him to 'blow.' He blew an inhuman little honk. Mary Beth Baird was provided with a clean handkerchief, in case the Baby Jesus's nose became offensive while he lay in view in the manger; the Virgin Mother was delighted to have been given a *physical* responsibility for Owen.

Before she lifted the little Prince of Peace in her arms, Barb Wiggin bent over him and massaged his cheeks. There was a curious combination of the perfunctory and the erotic in her attentions to Owen Meany. Naturally, I saw something so *stewardesslike* in her performance of these duties – as if she were dispatching with Owen in the manner that she might have changed a diaper; while at the same time there was something salacious in how close she put her face to his, as if she were intent on seducing him. 'You're too pale,' she told him, actually pinching color into Owen's face.

'OW!' he said.

'The Baby Jesus should be apple-cheeked,' she told him. She bent even closer to him and touched the tip of her nose to his nose; quite unexpectedly, she kissed him on the mouth. It was not a tender, affectionate kiss; it was a cruel, teasing kiss that startled Owen – he flushed, he turned the rosy complexion Barb Wiggin had desired; tears sprang to his eyes.

'I know you don't like to be kissed, Owen,' Barb Wiggin told him flirtatiously, 'but that's for good luck – that's all that's for.'

I knew it was the first time Owen had been kissed on the mouth since my mother had kissed him; that Barb Wiggin might have reminded him of my mother, I'm sure, outraged him. He clenched his fists at his sides as Barb Wiggin lifted him, stiffly prone, to her breasts. His legs, too tightly swaddled to bend at the knees, stuck out straight; he appeared to be a successful levitation experiment in the arms of a harlot-magician. Mary Beth Baird, who had once pleaded to be allowed to kiss the Baby Jesus, glared with jealous loathing at Barb Wiggin, who must have been an exceptionally strong stewardess – in her time in the sky. She had no difficulty carrying Owen to his prepared place in the hay. She bore him easily against her breasts with the stern sense of ceremony of a foxy mortician – bearing a child-pharoah into the pyramid's hidden tomb.

'Relax, relax,' she whispered to him; she put her mouth wickedly close to his ear, and he blushed rosier and rosier.

And I, Joseph – forever standing in the wings – saw what the envious Virgin Mary failed to see. I saw it, and I'm sure Barb Wiggin saw it, too – I'm sure it was why she so shamelessly continued to torture him. The Baby Jesus had an erection; its protrusion was visible in spite of the tightly bound layers of his swaddling clothes.

Barb Wiggin laid him in the manger; she smiled knowingly at him, and gave him one more saucy peck, on his rosy cheek – for good luck, no doubt. This was not of the nature of a Christlike lesson for Owen Meany: to learn, as he lay in the manger, that someone you hate can give you a hard-on. Anger and shame flushed Owen's face; Mary Beth Baird, misunderstanding the Baby Jesus' expression, wiped his nose. A cow trod on an angel, who nearly toppled the tripartite, purple screen; the hind part of a donkey was nudged by the teetering triptych. I stared into the darkness of the mock flying buttresses for some reassuring glimpse of the Announcing Angel; but Harold Crosby was invisible – he was hidden, doubtless in fear and trembling, above the 'pillar of light.'

'Blow!' Mary Beth Baird whispered to Owen, who looked ready to explode.

It was the choir that saved him.

There was a metallic clicking, like the teeth of a ratchet, as the mechanism for lowering the angel began its task; this was followed by a brief gasp, the panicked intake of Harold Crosby's breath – as the choir began.

O lit-tle town of Beth-le-hem,
How still we see thee lie!
A-bove thy deep and dream-less sleep
The si-lent stars go by . . .

Only gradually did the Baby Jesus unclench his fists; only slowly did the Christ Child's erection subside. The glint of anger in Owen's eyes was dulled, as if by an inspired drowsiness – a trance of peace blessed the little Prince's expression, which brought tears of adoration to the already moist eyes of the Holy Mother.

'Blow! Why won't you blow?' she whispered plaintively. Mary Beth Baird held the handkerchief to his nose, managing to cover his mouth, too – as if she were administering an anesthetic. With grace, with gentleness, Owen pushed her hand and the handkerchief aside; his smile forgave her everything, even her clumsiness, and the Blessed Virgin tottered a trifle on her knees, as if she were preparing to swoon.

Hidden from the congregation's view, but ominously visible to us, Barb Wiggin seized the controls of the angel-lowering apparatus like a heavy-equipment operator about to attack the terra firma with a backhoe. When Owen caught her eye, she appeared to lose her confidence and her poise; the look he gave her was both challenging and lascivious. A shudder coursed through Barb Wiggin's body; she gave a corresponding jerk of her shoulders, distracting her from her task. Harold Crosby's meant-to-be-stately descent to earth was momentarily suspended.

' "Be not afraid," ' Harold Crosby began, his voice quaking. But I, Joseph – I saw someone who was afraid. Barb Wiggin, frozen at the controls of the 'pillar of light,' arrested in her duties with the angel-lowering apparatus, was afraid of Owen Meany; the Prince of Peace had regained his control. He had made a small but important discovery: a hard-on comes and goes. The 'pillar of light,' which was supposed to follow Harold Crosby's now-interrupted, risky descent, appeared to have a will of its own; it illuminated Owen on the mountain of hay, as if the light had wrested control of itself from Barb Wiggin. The light that was supposed to reveal the angel bathed the manger instead.

From the congregation – as the janitor tiptoed out of sight with the tripartite screen – there arose a single murmur; but the Christ Child quieted them with the slightest movement of his hand. He directed a most unbabylike, sardonic look at Barb Wiggin, who only then regained *her* control; she moved the 'pillar of light' back to the Descending Angel, where it belonged.

' "Be not afraid," ' Harold Crosby repeated; Barb Wiggin, a tad eager at the controls of the angel-lowering apparatus, dropped him suddenly – it was about a ten-foot free fall, before she abruptly halted his descent; his head was jerked and snapped all around, with his mouth open, and he swung back and forth above the frightened shepherds, like a giant gull toying with the wind. ' "Be not afraid"!' Harold cried loudly. There he paused, swinging; he was stalling; he had forgotten the rest of his lines.

Barb Wiggin, trying to prevent the angel from swinging, turned Harold Crosby away from the shepherds and the congregation – so that he continued to swing, but with his back toward everyone, as if he had decided to spurn the world, or retract his message.

'"Be not afraid,"' he mumbled indistinctly.

From the hay in the dark came the cracked falsetto, the ruined voice of an unlikely prompter – but who else would know, by heart, the lines that Harold Crosby had forgotten? Who else but the *former* Announcing Angel?

'"FOR BEHOLD, I BRING YOU GOOD NEWS OF A GREAT JOY WHICH WILL COME TO ALL THE PEOPLE,"' Owen whispered; but Owen Meany couldn't really whisper – his voice had too much sand and gravel in it. Not only Harold Crosby heard the Christ Child's prompting; every member of the congregation heard it, too – the strained, holy voice speaking from the darkened manger, telling the angel what to say. Dutifully, Harold repeated the lines he was given.

Thus, when the 'pillar of light' finally followed the shepherds and kings to their proper place of worship at the crèche, the congregation was also prepared to adore him – whatever *special* Christ this was who not only knew his role but also knew all the other, vital parts of the story.

Mary Beth Baird was overcome. Her face flopped first on the hay, then her cheek bumped the Baby Jesus' hip; then she lunged further into prostration, actually putting her heavy head in Owen's lap. The 'pillar of light' trembled at this shameless, unmotherly behavior. Barb Wiggin's fury, and her keen anticipation of worse to come, suggested the intensity of someone in command of a machine-gun nest; she struggled to hold the light steady.

I was aware that Barb Wiggin had cranked Harold Crosby up so high that he was completely gone from view; up in the dark dust, up in the gloom inspired by the mock flying buttresses, Harold Crosby, who was still probably facing the wrong way, was flapping like a stranded bat – but I couldn't see him. I had only a vague impression of his panic and his helplessness.

'"I love thee, Lord Je-sus, look down from the sky, And stay by my cradle till morn-ing is nigh,"' sang the choir, thus wrapping up 'Away in a Manger.' The Rev Dudley Wiggin was a little slow starting with Luke. Perhaps it had occurred to him that the Virgin Mary was supposed to wait until *after* the reading before 'bowing' to the Baby Jesus; now that Mary Beth's head was already stationed in Owen's lap, the rector might have feared what Mary Beth would think was an appropriate substitute for 'bowing.'

'"When the angel went away from them into heaven,"' the rector began; the congregation, automatically, searched the ceiling for Harold Crosby. In the front pews of faces that I observed, no one sought the disappearing angel with as much fervor as Mr Fish, who was already surprised to hear that Owen Meany *did* have a speaking part.

Owen looked ready to sneeze, or else the weight of Mary Beth's head was restricting his breathing; his nose, unwiped and unblown, had dribbled two shiny rivulets across his upper lip. I could see that he was sweating; it was such a cold day, the old church furnace was throwing out the heat full-tilt – the raised altar area was a lot warmer than the wooden pews, where many of the congregation still wore their outdoor clothes. The heat in the manger was stifling. I pitied the donkeys and the cows; inside their costumes, they had to be perspiring. The 'pillar of light' felt hot enough to ignite the hay where the Baby Jesus lay pinned by the Holy Mother.

We were still listening to the reading from Luke when the first donkey fainted; actually, it was only the hind part of a donkey that fainted, so that the effect of the collapse was quite startling. Many of the congregation were unaware that donkeys came in two parts; the way the donkey crumbled must have been even more alarming to them. It appeared that a donkey's hind legs gave way under him, while the forelegs struggled to remain standing, and the head and neck surged this way and that – for balance. The donkey's ass and hind legs simply dropped to the floor, as if the beast had suffered a selective stroke – or had been shot; its rump was paralyzed. The front half of the donkey made a game effort, but was soon dragged down after its disabled parts. A cow, blinded by its horns – and trying to avoid the falling donkey – butted a shepherd into and over the low communion railing; the shepherd struck the kneeling cushions a glancing blow, and rolled into the center aisle by the first row of pews.

When the second donkey dropped, the Rev. Mr Wiggin read faster.

'"But Mary kept all these things,"' the rector said, '"pondering them in her heart."'

The Virgin Mary lifted her head from the Christ Child's lap, a mystical grin upon her flushed face; she thumped both hands to her heart – as if an arrow, or a lance, had run her through from behind; and her eyes rolled toward her shining forehead as if, even before she could fall, she were giving up the ghost. The Baby Jesus, suddenly anxious about the direction and force of Mother Mary's swoon, reached out his arms to catch her; but Owen was not strong enough to support Mary Beth Baird – chest to chest, she pressed him into the hay, where they appeared to be wrestling.

And I, Joseph – I saw how the little Lord Jesus got his mother off him; he goosed her. It was a fast attack, concealed in a flurry of flying hay; you had to be a Joseph – or Barb Wiggin – to know what happened. What the congregation saw was the Holy Mother roll out of the hay pile and across the floor of the manger, where she collected herself at a safe distance from the unpredictable Prince of Peace; Owen withered Mary Beth with a look as scornful as the look he'd shown Barb Wiggin.

It was the same look he then delivered to the congregation – oblivious to, if not contemptuous of, the gifts the wise men and the shepherds laid at his feet. Like a commanding officer reviewing his troops, the Christ Child surveyed the congregation. The faces I could see – in the frontmost pews – appeared to be tensing for rejection. Mr Fish's face, and Dan's face, too – both of these sophisticates of amateur theater were mouths-agape in admiration, for here was a stage presence that could overcome not only amateurism but the common cold; Owen had overcome error and bad acting *and* deviation from the script.

Then I came to the faces in the congregation that Owen must have seen about the same time I saw them; they bore the most rapt expressions of all. They were Mr and Mrs Meany's faces. Mr Meany's granitic countenance was destroyed by fear, but his attention was riveted; and Mrs Meany's lunatic gawking was characterized by a naked incomprehension. She had her hands clenched together in violent prayer, and her husband held her around her shaking shoulders because she was racked by sobs as disturbing as the animal unhappiness of a retarded child.

Owen sat up so suddenly in the mountain of hay that several front-pew members of the congregation were startled into gasps and cries of alarm. He bent stiffly at the waist, like a tightly wound spring, and he pointed with ferocity at his mother and father; to many members of the congregation, he could have been pointing to anyone – or to them all.

'WHAT DO YOU THINK *YOU'RE* DOING HERE?' the angry Lord Jesus screamed.

Many members of the congregation thought he meant *them*; I could tell what a shock the question was for Mr Fish, but I knew whom Owen was speaking to. I saw Mr and Mrs Meany cringe; they slipped off the pew to the kneeling pad, and Mrs Meany covered her face with both hands.

'YOU SHOULDN'T BE HERE!' Owen shouted at them; but Mr Fish, and surely half the congregation, felt that *they* stood accused. I saw the faces of the Rev. Lewis Merrill and his California wife; it was apparent that they also thought Owen meant *them*.

'IT IS A *SACRILEGE* FOR YOU TO BE HERE!' Owen hollered. At least a dozen members of the congregation guiltily got up from the pews at the rear of the church – to leave. Mr Meany helped his dizzy wife to her feet. She was crossing herself, repeatedly – a helpless, unthinking, *Catholic* gesture; it must have infuriated Owen.

The Meanys conducted an awkward departure; they were big, broad people and their exit out of the crowded pew, their entrance into the aisle – where they stood out, so alone – their every movement was neither easy nor graceful.

'We only wanted to *see* you!' Owen's father told him apologetically.

But Owen Meany pointed to the door at the end of the nave, where several of the faithful had already departed; Owen's parents, like that other couple who were banished from the garden, left Christ Church as they were told. Not even the gusto with which the choir – following frantic signals from the rector – sang 'Hark! The Herald Angels Sing' could spare the congregation the indelible image of how the Meanys had obeyed their only son.

Rector Wiggin, wringing the Bible in both hands, was trying to catch the eye of his wife; but Barb Wiggin was struck as immovable as stone. What the rector wanted was for his wife to darken the 'pillar of light,' which continued to shine on the wrathful Lord Jesus.

'GET ME OUT OF HERE!' the Prince of Peace said to Joseph. And what is Joseph if not a man who does what he's told? I lifted him. Mary Beth Baird wanted to hold a part of him, too; whether his goosing her had deepened her infatuation, or had put her in her place without trampling an iota of her ardor, is uncertain – regardless, she was his slave, at his command. And so together we raised him out of the hay. He was so stiffly wrapped, it was like carrying an unmanageable icon – he simply wouldn't bend, no matter how we held him.

Where to go with him was not instantly clear. The back way, behind the altar area – the unobserved route we'd all taken to the manger – was blocked by Barb Wiggin.

As in other moments of indecision, the Christ Child directed us; he pointed down the centre aisle, in the direction his parents had taken. I doubt that anyone directed the cows and donkeys to follow us; they just needed the air. Our procession gathered the force and numbers of a marching band. The third verse of what was supposed to be the Rev. Mr Wiggin's recessional carol heralded *our* exit.

> Mild he lays his glo-ry by, Born that man no
>   more may die,
> Born to raise the sons of earth, Born to give them
>   sec-ond birth.

All the way down the center aisle, Barb Wiggin kept the 'pillar of light' on us; what possible force could have compelled her to do that? There was nowhere to go but out, into the snow and cold. The cows and the donkeys tore off their heads so that they could get a better look at him; for the most part, these were the younger children – some of them, a very few of them, were actually smaller than Owen. They stared at him, in awe. The wind whipped through his swaddling clothes and his bare arms grew rosy; he hugged them to his birdlike chest. The Meanys, sitting scared in the cab of the granite truck, were waiting for him. The Virgin Mother and I hoisted him into the cab; because of how he was swaddled, he had to be extended full-length across the seat – his legs lay in his father's lap, not quite interfering with Mr Meany's control of the steering wheel, and his head and upper body rested upon his mother, who had reverted to her custom of looking not quite out the window, and not quite at anything at all.

'MY CLOTHES,' the Lord Jesus told me. 'YOU GET THEM AND KEEP THEM FOR ME.'

'Of course,' I said.

'IT'S A GOOD THING I WORE MY LUCKY SCARF,' he told me. 'TAKE ME HOME!' he ordered his parents, and Mr Meany lurched the truck into gear.

A snowplow was turning off Front Street onto Elliot; it was customary in Gravesend to may way for snowplows, but even the snowplow made way for Owen.

Toronto: February 4, 1987 – there was almost no one at the Wednesday morning communion service. Holy Eucharist is better when you don't have to shuffle up the aisle in a herd and stand in line at the communion railing, like an animal awaiting space at the feeding-trough – just like another consumer at a fast-food service. I don't like to take communion with a mob.

I prefer the way the Rev. Mr Foster serves the bread to the mischievous style of Canon Mackie; the canon delights in giving me the tiniest wafer he has in his hand – a veritable crumb! – or else he gives me an inedible hunk of bread, almost too big to fit in my mouth and impossible to swallow without prolonged chewing. The canon likes to tease me. He says, 'Well, I figure that you take communion so often, it's probably bad for your diet – someone's got to look after your diet, John!' And he chuckles about that; or else he says, 'Well, I figure that you take communion so often, you must be starving – someone's got to give you a decent meal!' And he chuckles some more.

The Rev. Mr Foster, our priest associate, at least dispenses the bread with a uniform sense of sacredness; that's all I ask. I have no quarrel with the wine; it is ably served by our honorary assistants, the Rev. Mr Larkin and the Rev. Mrs Keeling – Mrs Katherine Keeling; she's the headmistress at The Bishop Strachan School, and my only qualm with her is when she's pregnant. The Rev. Katherine Keeling is often pregnant, and I don't think she should serve the wine when she's so pregnant that bending forward to put the cup to our lips is a strain; that makes me nervous; also, when she's very pregnant, and you're kneeling at the railing waiting for the wine, it's distracting to see her belly approach you at eye level. Then there's the Rev. Mr Larkin; he sometimes pulls the cup back before the wine has touched your lips – you have to be quick with him; and he's a little careless how he wipes the rim of the cup each time.

Of them all, the Rev. Mrs Keeling is the best to talk to – now that Canon Campbell is gone. I truly like and admire Katherine Keeling. I regretted I couldn't talk to her today, when I really needed to talk to someone; but Mrs Keeling is on temporary leave – she's off having another baby. The Rev. Mr Larkin is as quick to be gone from a conversation as he is quick with the communion cup; and our priest associate, the Rev. Mr Foster – although he burns with missionary zeal – is impatient with the fretting of a middle-aged man like myself, who lives in such comfort in the Forest Hill part of town. The Rev. Mr Foster is all for opening a mission on Jarvis Street – and counseling hookers on the subject of sexually transmitted diseases – and he's up to his neck in volunteer projects for the West Indians on Bathurst Street, the very same people so verbally abused by Deputy Warden Holt; but the Rev. Mr Foster offers scant sympathy for my worries, which, he says, are only in my mind. I love that 'only'!

And that left Canon Mackie to talk to today; Canon Mackie presents a familiar problem. I said, 'Did you read the paper, today's paper – *The Globe and Mail*? It was on the front page.'

'No, I've not had time to read the paper this morning,' Canon Mackie said, 'but let me guess. Was it something about the United States? Something President Reagan said?' He is not exactly condescending, Canon Mackie; he is *in*exactly condescending.

'There was a nuclear test yesterday – the first U.S. explosion of eighty-seven,' I said. 'It was scheduled for tomorrow, but they moved it up – it was a way to fool the protesters. Naturally, there were planned protests – for tomorrow.'

'Naturally,' said Canon Mackie.

'And the Democrats had scheduled a vote – for today – on a resolution to persuade Reagan to cancel the test,' I told the canon. 'The government even lied about the day the test was going to be. A fine use of the taxpayers' money, eh?'

'You're not a taxpayer in the United States – not anymore,' the canon said.

'The Soviets said they wouldn't test any weapons until the U.S. tested first,' I told the canon. 'Don't you see how deliberately provocative this is? How *arrogant*! How unconcerned with *any* arms agreement – of *any* kind! Every American should be forced to live outside the United States for a year or two. Americans should be forced to see how *ridiculous* they appear to the rest of the world! They should listen to someone else's version of themselves – to *anyone else's* version! Every country knows more about America than Americans know about themselves! And Americans know absolutely *nothing* about any other country!'

Canon Mackie observed me mildly. I could see it coming; I talk about one thing, and he bends the subject of our conversation back to *me*.

'I know you were upset about the Vestry elections, John,' he told me. 'No one doubts your devotion to the church, you know.'

Here I am, talking about nuclear war and the usual, self-righteous, American arrogance, and Canon Mackie wants to talk about *me*.

'Surely you know how much this community respects you, John,' the canon told me. 'But don't you see how your . . . *opinions* can be disturbing? It's very *American* – to have opinions as . . . *strong* as your opinions. It's very Canadian to distrust strong opinions.'

'I'm a Canadian,' I said. 'I've been a Canadian for twenty years.'

Canon Mackie is a tall, stooped, bland-faced man, so plainly ugly that his ungainly size is unthreatening – and so plainly decent that even his stubbornness of mind is not generally offensive.

'John, John,' he said to me. 'You're a Canadian citizen, but what are you always talking about? You talk about America more than any American I know! And you're more anti-American than any Canadian I know,' the canon said. 'You're a little . . . well, *one-note* on the subject, wouldn't you say?'

'No, I wouldn't,' I said.

'John, John,' Canon Mackie said. 'Your *anger* – that's not very Canadian, either.' The canon knows how to get to me; through my anger.

'No, and it's not very Christian, either,' I admitted. 'I'm sorry.'

'Don't be sorry!' the canon said cheerfully. 'Try to be a little . . . different!' The man's pauses are almost as irritating as his advice.

'It's the damn Star Wars thing that gets to me,' I tried to tell him. 'The only constraint on the arms race that remains is the nineteen seventy-two Anti-Ballistic Missile Treaty between the United States and the Soviet Union. Now Reagan has given the Soviets an open invitation to test nuclear weapons of their own; and if he proceeds with his missiles-in-space plans, he'll give the Soviets an open invitation to junk the treaty of nineteen seventy-two, as well!'

'You have such a head for history,' the canon said. 'How can you remember the dates?'

'Canon Mackie,' I said.

'John, John,' the canon said, 'I know you're upset; I'm not mocking you. I'm just trying to help you understand – about the Vestry elections—'

'I don't *care* about the Vestry elections!' I said angrily – indicating, of course, how much I cared. 'I'm sorry,' I said.

The canon put his warm, moist hand on my arm.

'To our younger parish officers,' he said, 'you're something of an eccentric. They don't understand those years that brought you here; they wonder *why* – especially, when you defame the United States as vociferously as you do – *why* you aren't more Canadian than you are! Because you're not really a Canadian, you know – and that troubles some of the older members of this parish, too; that troubles even those of us who *do* remember the circumstances that brought you here. If you made the choice to stay in Canada, why do you have so little to do with Canada? Why have you learned so little about us? John: it's something of a joke, you know – how you don't even know your way around Toronto.'

That is Canon Mackie in a nutshell; I worry about a war, and the canon agonizes about how I get lost the second I step out of Forest Hill. I talk about the loss of the most substantive treaty that exists between the Soviet Union and the United States, and the canon teases me about my memory for *dates*!

Yes, I have a good head for dates. How about August 9, 1974? Richard Nixon was finished. How about September 8, 1974? Richard Nixon was pardoned. And then there was April 30, 1975: the U.S. Navy evacuated all remaining personnel from Vietnam; they called this Operation Frequent Wind.

Canon Mackie is skillful with me, I have to admit. He mentions 'dates' and what he calls my 'head for history' to set up a familiar thesis: that I live in the past. Canon Mackie makes me wonder if my devotion to the memory of Canon Campbell is not also an aspect of how much I live in the past;

years ago, when I felt so close to Canon Campbell, I lived less in the past – or else, what we now call the past was then the present; it was the actual time that Canon Campbell and I shared, and we were both caught up in it. If Canon Campbell were alive, if he were still rector of Grace Church, perhaps he would be no more sympathetic to me than Canon Mackie is sympathetic today.

Canon Campbell was alive on January 21, 1977. That was the day President Jimmy Carter issued a pardon to the 'draft-dodgers.' What did I care? I was already a Canadian citizen.

Although Canon Campbell cautioned me about my anger, too, he understood why that 'pardon' made me so angry. I showed Canon Campbell the letter I wrote to Jimmy Carter. 'Dear Mr President,' I wrote. 'Who will pardon the United States?'

Who *can* pardon the United States? How can they be pardoned for Vietnam, for their conduct in Nicaragua, for their steadfast and gross contribution to the proliferation of nuclear arms?

'John, John,' Canon Mackie said. 'Your little speech about Christmas – at the Parish Council meeting? I doubt that even Scrooge would have chosen a Parish Council meeting as the proper occasion for such an announcement.'

'I merely said that I found Christmas depressing,' I said.

' "Merely"!' said Canon Mackie. 'The church counts very heavily on Christmas – for its missions, for its livelihood in this city. And Christmas is the focal point for the children in our church.'

And what would the canon have said if I'd told him that the Christmas of '53 put the finishing touches on Christmas for me? He would have told me, again, that I was living in the past. So I said nothing. I hadn't wanted to talk about Christmas in the first place.

Is it any wonder how Christmas – ever since *that* Christmas – depresses me? The Nativity I witnessed in '53 has replaced the old story. The Christ is born 'miraculously,' to be sure; but even more miraculous are the demands he succeeds in making, even before he can walk! Not only does he demand to be worshiped and adored – by peasants and royalty, by animals and his own parents! – but he also banishes his mother and father from the house of prayer and song itself.

I will never forget the inflamed color of his bare skin in the winter cold, and the hospital white-on-white of his swaddling clothes against the new snow – a vision of the little Lord Jesus as a born victim, born raw, born bandaged, born angry and accusing; and wrapped so tightly that he could not bend at the knees at all and had to lie on his parents' laps as stiffly as someone who, mortally wounded, lies upon a stretcher.

How can you like Christmas after that? Before I became a believer, I could at least enjoy the fantasy.

That Sunday, feeling the wind cut through my Joseph-robe out on Elliot Street, contributed to my belief in – and my dislike of – the miracle. How the congregation straggled out of the nave; how they hated to have their rituals revised without warning. The rector was not on the steps to shake their hands because so many of the congregation had followed *our* triumphant exit, leaving the Rev. Mr Wiggin stranded at the altar with his benediction unsaid – he was supposed to have delivered his benediction from the nave, where the recessional should have led him (and not us).

And what was Barb Wiggin supposed to do with the 'pillar of light,' now that she had craned the light to follow the Lord Jesus and his tribe to the door? Dan Needham told me later that the Rev. Dudley Wiggin made a most unusual gesture for the rector of Christ Church to make from the pulpit; he drew his forefinger across his throat – a signal to his wife to *kill* the light, which (only after we'd departed) she finally did. But to many of the bewildered congregation, who took their cues from the rector – for how else should they know what their next move should be, in this unique celebration? – the gesture of the Rev. Dudley Wiggin slashing his own throat was particularly gripping. Mr Fish, in his inexperience, imitated the gesture as if it were a command – and then looked to Dan for approval. Dan observed that Mr Fish was not alone.

And what were *we* supposed to do? Our gang from the manger, ill-dressed for the weather, huddled uncertainly together after the granite truck turned onto Front Street and out of sight. The revived hind part of one donkey ran to the door of the parish-house vestibule, which he found locked; the cows slipped in the snow. Where could we go but back in the main door? Had someone locked the parish house out of fear that thieves would steal our real clothes? To our knowledge, there was no shortage of clothes like ours in Gravesend, and no robbers. And so we bucked against the grain; we fought against the congregation – they were coming *out* – in order that we might get back *in*. For Barb Wiggin, who wished that every worship service was as smooth as a flight free of bumpy air – and one that departs and arrives on time – the sight of the traffic jam in the nave of the church must have caused further upset. Smaller angels and shepherds darted between the grown-ups' legs; the more stately kings, clutching their toppled crowns – and the clumsier cows, and the donkeys now in halves – made awkward progress against the flow of bulky overcoats. The countenances of many a parishioner reflected shock and insult, as if the Lord Jesus had just spat in their faces – to deem *them* sacrilegious. Among the older members of the congregation – with whom the jocular Captain Wiggin and his brash wife were not an overnight success – there was a stewing anger, apparent in their frowns and scowls, as if the shameful pageant they had just witnessed were the rector's idea of something 'modern.' Whatever it was, they hadn't liked it, and their reluctant acceptance of the ex-pilot would be delayed for a few more years.

I found myself chin-to-chest with the Rev. Lewis Merrill, who was as baffled as the Episcopalian congregation – regarding what he and his wife were supposed to do next. They were nearer the nave of the church than was the rector, who was nowhere to be found, and if the Rev. Mr Merrill continued to press, with the throng, toward the door, he might find himself out on the steps – in a position to shake hands with the departing souls – in advance of the Rev. Mr Wiggin's appearance there. It was surely not Pastor Merrill's responsibility to shake hands with Episcopalians, following their botched pageant. God forbid that any of them might think that *he* was the reason for the pageant being so peculiarly wrecked, or that this was how the Congregationalists interpreted the Nativity.

'Your little friend?' Mr Merrill asked in a whisper. 'Is he always so . . . like that?'

Is he always like *what*? I thought. But in the crush of the crowd, it would have been hard to stand my ground while Mr Merrill stuttered out what he meant.

'Yes,' I said. 'That's Owen, this was pure Owen today. He's unpredictable, but he's always in charge.'

'He's quite . . . miraculous,' the Rev. Mr Merrill said, smiling faintly – clearly glad that the Congregationalists preferred caroling to pageants, and clearly relieved that Owen Meany had moved no farther *down* the Protestant rungs than the Episcopalians. The pastor was probably imagining what sort of damage Owen might accomplish at a Vesper service.

Dan grabbed me in the connecting passage to the parish house; he said he'd wait for me to get my clothes, and Owen's – we could go back to the dorm together, then, or to 80 Front Street. Mr Fish was happy and agitated; if he thought that the Rev. Dudley Wiggin's 'slashing his throat' was a part of the rector's annual performance, he also imagined that everything Owen had done was in the script – and Mr Fish had been quite impressed by the dramatic qualities of the story. 'I *love* the part when he tells the angel what to say – that's brilliant,' Mr Fish said. 'And how he *throws* his mother aside – how he starts right in with the criticism . . . I mean, you get the idea, right away, that this is no ordinary baby. You know, he's the *Lord!* Jesus – from Day One. I mean, he's *born* giving orders, telling *everyone* what to do. I thought you told me he didn't have a speaking part! I had no idea it was so . . . *primitive* a ritual, so violent, so *barbaric*. But it's very moving,' Mr Fish added hastily, lest Dan and I be offended to hear our religion described as 'primitive' and 'barbaric.'

'It's not quite what the . . . author . . . intended,' Dan told Mr Fish. I left Dan explaining the deviations from the expected to the excited amateur actor – I wanted to get dressed, and find Owen's clothes, in a hurry, without encountering either of the Wiggins. But I was a while getting my hands on Owen's clothes. Mary Beth Baird had balled them up with her own in a corner of the vestibule, where she then lay down to weep – on top of them. It was complicated, getting her to relinquish Owen's clothes without striking her; and impossible to interrupt her sobbing. Everything that had upset the little Lord Jesus had been *her* fault, in her opinion; she had not only failed to soothe him – she'd been a bad mother in general. Owen *hated* her, she claimed. How she wished she *understood* him better! Yet, somehow – as she explained to me, through her tears – she was sure she 'understood' him better than anyone else did.

At age eleven, I was too young to glimpse a vision of what

sort of overwrought wife and mother Mary Beth Baird would make; there in the vestibule, I wanted only to hit her – to forcibly take Owen's clothes and leave her in a puddle of tears. The very idea of her *understanding* Owen Meany made me sick! What she really meant was that she wanted to take him home and lie on top of him; her idea of *understanding* him began and ended with her desire to cover his body, to never let him get up.

Because I was slow in leaving the vestibule, Barb Wiggin caught me.

'You can give him this message when you give him his clothes,' she hissed to me, her fingers digging into my shoulder and shaking me. '*Tell* him he's to come see me before he's *allowed* back in this church – *before* the next Sunday school class, *before* he comes to another service. He comes to see me *first*. He's *not allowed* here until he sees me!' she repeated, giving me one last shake for good measure.

I was so upset that I blurted it all out to Dan, who was hanging around the altar area with Mr Fish, who, in turn, was staring at the scattered hay in the manger and at the few gifts abandoned by the Christ Child there, as if some meaning could be discerned from the arrangement of the debris.

I told Dan what Barb Wiggin had said, and how she'd given Owen a hard-on, and how there had been virtual warfare between them – and now, I was sure, Owen would never be 'allowed' to be an Episcopalian again. If seeing her was a prerequisite for Owen to return to Christ Church, then Owen, I knew, would be as shunning of us Episcopalians as he was presently shunning of Catholics. I became quite exercised in relating this scenario to Dan, who sat beside me in a front-row pew and listened sympathetically.

Mr Fish came and told us that the angel was still 'on-high.' He wondered if *this* was a part of the script – to leave Harold Crosby hanging in the rafters long after the manger and the pews had emptied? Harold Crosby, who thought both his God and Barb Wiggin had abandoned him forever, swung like the victim of a vigilante killing among the mock flying buttresses; Dan, an accomplished mechanic of all theatrical equipment, eventually mastered the angel-lowering apparatus and returned the banished angel to terra firma, where Harold collapsed in relief and gratitude. He had thrown up all over himself, and – in attempting to wipe himself with one of his wings – he'd made quite an unsalvageable mess of his costume.

That was when Dan carried out his responsibilities as a stepfather in most concrete, even heroic terms. He carried the sodden Harold Crosby to the parish-house vestibule, where he asked Barb Wiggin if he might have a word with her.

'Can't you see . . .' she asked him, 'that this isn't the best of times?'

'I should not want to bring up the matter – of how you left this boy *hanging* – with the Vestry members,' Dan said to her. He held Harold Crosby with some difficulty – not only because Harold was heavy and wet, but because the stench of vomit, especially in the close air of the vestibule, was overpowering.

'This isn't the best of time to bring up *any*thing with me,' Barb Wiggin cautioned, but Dan Needham was not a man to be bullied by a stewardess.

'Nobody cares what sort of mess-up happens at a children's pageant,' Dan said, 'but this boy was left *hanging* – twenty feet above a concrete floor! A serious accident might have occurred – due to your negligence.' Harold Crosby shut his eyes, as if he feared Barb Wiggin was going to hit him – or strap him back in the angel-raising apparatus.

'I regret—' Barb Wiggin began, but Dan cut her off.

'You will *not* lay down any laws for Owen Meany,' Dan Needham told her. 'You are *not* the rector, you are the rector's *wife*. You had a job – to return this boy, safely, to the floor – and you forgot all about it. *I* will forget all about it, too – and *you* will forget about seeing Owen. Owen is allowed in this church at any time; he doesn't require your permission to be here. If the *rector* would like to speak with Owen, have the rector call *me*.' And here Dan Needham released the slippery Harold Crosby, whose manner of groping for his clothes suggested that the angel apparatus had cut off all circulation to his legs; he wobbled unsteadily about the vestibule – the other children getting out of his way because of his smell. Dan Needham put his hand on the back of my neck; he pushed me gently forward until I was standing directly between Barb Wiggin and him. 'This boy is not your messenger, Missus Wiggin,' Dan said. 'I should not want to bring up *any* of this with the Vestry members,' he repeated.

Stewardesses have, at best, marginal authority; Barb Wiggin

knew when her authority had slipped. She looked awfully ready-to-please, *so* ready-to-please that I was embarrassed for her. She turned her attention, eagerly, to the task of getting Harold Crosby into fresher clothes. She was just in time; Harold's mother entered the vestibule as Dan and I were leaving the parish house. 'My, that looked like fun!' Mrs Crosby said. 'Did you have fun, dear?' she asked him. When Harold nodded, Barb Wiggin spontaneously hugged him against her hip.

Mr Fish had found the rector. The Rev. Dudley Wiggin was occupying himself with the Christmas candles, measuring them to ascertain which were still long enough to be used next year. The Rev. Dudley Wiggin had a pilot's healthy instinct for looking ahead; he did not dwell on the present – especially not on the disasters. He would never call Dan and ask to speak to Owen; Owen would be 'allowed' at Christ Church without any consultation with the rector.

'I like the way Joseph and Mary *carry* the Baby Jesus out of the manger,' Mr Fish was saying.

'Ah, do you? Ah, yes,' the rector said.

'It's a great ending – very dramatic,' Mr Fish pointed out.

'Yes, it *is*, isn't it?' the rector said. 'Perhaps we'll work out a similar ending – next year.'

'Of course, the part requires someone with Owen's *presence*,' Mr Fish said. 'I'll bet you don't get a Christ Child like him every year.'

'No, not like him,' the rector agreed.

'He's a natural,' Mr Fish said.

'Yes, isn't he?' Mr Wiggin said.

'Have you seen *A Christmas Carol*?' Mr Fish asked.

'Not this year,' the rector said.

'What are you doing on Christmas Eve?' Mr Fish asked him.

I knew what I wished I was doing on Christmas Eve: I wished I was in Sawyer Depot, waiting with my mother for Dan to arrive on the midnight train. That's how our Christmas Eves had been, since my mother had gotten together with Dan. Mother and I would enjoy the Eastmans' hospitality, and I would exhaust myself with my violent cousins, and Dan would join us after the Christmas Eve performance of The Gravesend Players. He would be tired when he got off the train from Gravesend, at midnight, but everyone in the

Eastman house – even my grandmother – would be waiting up for him. Uncle Alfred would fix Dan a 'nightcap,' while my mother and Aunt Martha put Noah and Simon and Hester and me to bed.

At a quarter to twelve, Hester and Simon and Noah and I would bundle up and cross the street to the depot; the weather in the north country on a Christmas Eve, at midnight, was not inviting to grown-ups – the grown-ups all approved of letting us kids meet Dan's train. We liked to be early so we could make plenty of snowballs; the train was always on time – in those days. There were few people on it, and almost no one but Dan got off in Sawyer Depot, where we would pelt him with snowballs. As tired as he was, Dan put up a game fight.

Earlier in the evening, my mother and Aunt Martha sang Christmas carols; sometimes my grandmother would join in. We children could remember most of the words to the first verses; it was in the latter verses of the carols that my mother and Aunt Martha put their years in the Congregational Church Choir to the test. My mother won that contest; she knew every word to every verse, so that – as a carol progressed – we heard nothing at all from Grandmother, and less and less from Aunt Martha. In the end, my mother got to sing the last verses by herself.

'What a waste, Tabby!' Aunt Martha would say. 'It's an absolute waste of your memory – knowing all those words to the verses *no one* ever sings!'

'What else do I need my memory for?' my mother asked her sister; the two women would smile at each other – my Aunt Martha coveting that part of my mother's memory that might tell her the story of who my father was. What really irked Martha about my mother's total recall of Christmas carols was that my mother got to sing those last verses *solo*; even Uncle Alfred would stop what he was doing – just to listen to my mother's voice.

I remember – it was at my mother's funeral – when the Rev. Lewis Merrill told my grandmother that he'd lost my mother's voice *twice*. The first time was when Martha got married, because that was when both girls started spending Christmas vacations in Sawyer Depot – my mother would still practice singing carols with the choir, but she was gone to visit her sister by the Sunday of Christmas Vespers. The second time that Pastor Merrill lost my mother's voice was when she moved to Christ Church – when he lost it forever. But I had not lost her voice until Christmas Eve, 1953, when the town I was born in and grew up in felt so unfamiliar to me; Gravesend just never was my Christmas Eve town.

Of course, I was grateful to have something to do. Although I'd seen every production of *A Christmas Carol* – including the dress rehearsal – I was especially glad that the final production was available to take up the time on Christmas Eve; I think both Dan and I wanted our time taken up. After the play, Dan had scheduled a cast party – and I understood why he'd done that: to take up every minute until midnight, and even past midnight, so that he wouldn't be thinking of riding the train to Sawyer Depot (and my mother in the Eastmans' warm house, waiting for him). I could picture the Eastmans having a hard time on Christmas Eve, too; after the first verse, Aunt Martha would be struggling with each carol.

Dan had wanted to have the cast party at 80 Front Street – and I understood that, too: he wanted my grandmother to be just as busy as he was. Of course, Grandmother would have complained bitterly about the party revelers – and about such a 'sundry' guest list, given the diverse personalities and social stations of a typical Dan Needham cast; but Grandmother would, at least, have been occupied. As it was, she refused; Dan had to beg her to get her to see the play.

At first, she gave him every excuse – she couldn't possibly leave Lydia alone, Lydia was sick, there was some congestion in her lungs or bronchial tubes, and it was out of the question that Lydia could go out to a play; furthermore, Grandmother argued, it being Christmas Eve, she had allowed Ethel to visit her next of kin (Ethel would be gone for Christmas Day, and the next day, too), and surely Dan knew how Lydia hated to be left alone with Germaine.

Dan pointed out that he thought Germaine had been hired, specifically, to look after Lydia. Yes, Grandmother nodded, that was certainly true – nevertheless, the girl was dismal, superstitious company, and what Lydia needed on Christmas Eve was *company*. It was, Dan politely reasoned, 'strictly for company's sake' that he wanted my grandmother to see *A Christmas Carol*, and even spend a short time enjoying the festive atmosphere of the cast party. Since my grandmother had refused him the use of 80 Front Street, Dan had decorated the entire third floor of Waterhouse Hall – opening a few of the less-cluttered boys' rooms, and the common room on that floor, for the cast; his own tiny apartment just wouldn't suffice. He'd alerted the Brinker-Smiths that there might be a rumpus two floors above them; they were welcome to join the festivities, or plug up the twins' ears with cotton, as they saw fit.

Grandmother did not see fit to do a damn thing, but she enjoyed Dan's efforts to cajole her out of her veteran, antisocial cantankerousness, and she agreed to attend the play; as for the cast party, she would see how she felt after the performance. And so it fell to me: the task of escorting Grandmother to the closing-night enactment of *A Christmas Carol* in the Gravesend Town Hall. I took many precautions along the way, to protect Grandmother from fracturing her hip – although the sidewalks were safely sanded, there'd been no new snowfall, and the well-oiled wood of the old Town Meeting place was slipperier than any surface Grandmother was likely to encounter outdoors.

The hinges of the ancient folding chairs creaked in unison as I led Harriet Wheelwright to a favored center-aisle seat in the third row, our townspeople's heads turning in the manner that a congregation turns to view a bride – for my grandmother entered the theater as if she were still responding to a curtain call, following her long-ago performance in Maugham's *The Constant Wife*. Harriet Wheelwright had a gift for making a regal entry. There was even some scattered applause, which Grandmother quieted with a well-aimed glower; respect, in the form of awe – preferably, *silent* awe – was something she courted, but hand-clapping was, under the circumstances, vulgar.

It took a full five minutes for her to be comfortably seated – her mink off, but positioned over her shoulders; her scarf loosened, but covering the back of her neck from drafts (which were known to approach from the rear); her hat *on*, despite the fact that no one seated behind her could see over it (graciously, the gentleman so seated moved). At last, I was free to venture backstage, where I had grown used to the aura of spiritual calm surrounding Owen Meany at the makeup mirror.

The trauma of the Christmas Pageant shone in his eyes like a death in the family; his cold had settled deep in his chest, and a fever drove him to alternate states – first he burned, then he sweated, then he shivered. He needed very little eyeliner to deepen the darkness entombing his eyes, and his nightly, excessive applications of baby powder to his face – which was already as white as the face of a china doll – had covered the makeup table with a silt as fine as plaster dust, in which Owen wrote his name with his finger in square, block letters, the style of lettering favored in the Meany Monument Shop.

Owen had offered no explanation regarding the offense he took at his parents' attendance at the Christ Church Nativity. When I suggested that his response to their presence in the congregation had been radical and severe, he dismissed me in a fashion he'd perfected – by forgiving me for what I couldn't be expected to know, and what he would never explain to me: that old UNSPEAKABLE OUTRAGE that the Catholics had perpetrated, and his parents' inability to rise above what amounted to the RELIGIOUS PERSECUTION they had suffered; yet it was my opinion that Owen was persecuting his parents. Why they accepted such persecution was a mystery to me.

From backstage I was uniquely positioned to search the audience for the acquiescent presence of Mr and Mrs Meany; they were not there. My search was rewarded, however, by the discovery of a sanguinary Mr Morrison, the cowardly mailman, his eyes darting daggers in all directions, and wringing his hands – as he might around a throat – in his lap. The look of a man who's come to see What Might Have Been is full of both bloodshed and nostalgia; should Owen succumb to his fever, Mr Morrison looked ready to play the part.

It was a full house; to my surprise, I'd seen many of the audience at earlier performances. The Rev. Lewis Merrill, for example, was back for a second, maybe even a third time! He always came to dress rehearsals, and often to a later performance; he told Dan he enjoyed watching the actors 'settle into' their parts. Being a minister, he must have especially enjoyed *A Christmas Carol*; it was such a heartfelt rendering of a conversion – not just a lesson in Christian charity, but an example of man's humbleness before the spiritual world. Even so, I could not find Rector Wiggin in the audience; I had no expectations of finding Barb, either

– I would guess their exposure to Owen Meany's interpretations of the spiritual world was sufficient to inspire them, until next Christmas.

Lewis Merrill, forever in the company of the sour stamina that radiated from his wife, was also in the company of his troubled children; often rebellious, almost always unruly, uniformly sullen, the Merrill children acted out their displeasure at being dragged to an amateur theatrical. The tallish boy, the notorious cemetery vandal, sprawled his legs into the center aisle, indifferently creating a hazard for the elderly, the infirm, and the unwary. The middle child, a girl – her hair so brutally short, in keeping with her square, shapeless body, that she might have been a boy – brooded loudly over her bubble gum. She had sunk herself so low in her seat that her knees caused considerable discomfort to the back of the neck of the unfortunate citizen who sat in front of her. He was a plump, mild, middle-aged man who taught something in the sciences at Gravesend Academy; and when he turned round in his seat to reprove the girl with a scientific glance, she popped a bubble at him with her gum. The third and youngest child, of undetermined sex, crawled under the seats, disturbing the ankles of several surprised theatergoers and coating itself with a film of grime and ashes – and all manner of muck that the patrons had brought in upon their winter boots.

Through all the unpleasantness created by her children, Mrs Merrill suffered silently. Although they caused her obvious pain, she was unprotesting – since nearly everything caused her pain, she thought it would be unfair to single them out for special distinction. Mr Merrill gazed undistracted toward center stage, apparently transfixed by the crack where the curtain would part; he appeared to believe that by his special scrutiny of this opening, by a supreme act of concentration, he might inspire the curtains to open. Why, then, was he so surprised when they did?

Why was I so surprised by the applause that greeted old Scrooge in his countinghouse? It was the way the play had opened every night; but it wasn't until Christmas Eve that it occurred to me how many of these same townspeople must have been present in those bleacher seats that summer day – applauding, or on the verge of applauding, the force with which Owen Meany struck that ball.

And, yes, there was fat Mr Chickering, whose warm-up jacket had kept me from too close a view of the mortal injury; yes, there was Police Chief Pike. As always, he was stationed by the door, his suspicious eyes roaming the audience as much as they toured the stage, as if Chief Pike suspected that the culprit might have brought the stolen baseball to the play!

' "If I could work my will," ' said Mr Fish indignantly, ' "every idiot who goes about with 'Merry Christmas' on his lips should be boiled with his own pudding, and buried with a stake of holly through his heart." '

I saw Mr Morrison silently move his mouth to every word – in the absence of any lines to learn (as the Ghost of Christmas Yet to Come), he had learned *all* of Scrooge's lines by heart. What had *he* made of the foul ball that so spectacularly spun my mother around? Had he been there to see Mr Chickering pinch her splayed knees together, for modesty's sake?

Just before Owen made contact, my mother had noticed someone in the bleachers; as I remembered it, she was waving to someone just before she was struck. She had not been waving to Mr Morrison, I was sure; his cynical presence didn't inspire a greeting as unselfconscious as a wave – that lugubrious mailman did not invite so much as a nod of recognition.

Yet who was that someone my mother had been waving to, whose was the last face she'd seen, the face she'd singled out in the crowd, the face she'd found there and had closed her eyes upon at the moment of her death? With a shudder, I tried to imagine who it could have been – if *not* my grandmother, if *not* Dan . . .

' "I wear the chain I forged in life," ' Marley's Ghost told Scrooge; with my attention fixed upon the audience, I had known where I was in the play by the clanking of Marley's chains.

' "Mankind was my business," ' Marley told Scrooge. ' "The common welfare was my business; charity, mercy, forbearance, and benevolence were all my business. The dealings of my trade were but a drop of water in the comprehensive ocean of my business!" '

With a shudder, I imagined that it had been *my father* in the bleachers – it had been *my father* she'd waved to the instant she was killed! With no idea how I might hope to recognize him, I began with the front row, left-center; I went through the audience, face by face. From my perspective, backstage, the faces in the audience were almost uniformly still, and the attention upon them was not directed toward me; the faces were, at least in part, strangers to me, and – especially in the back rows – smaller than the faces on baseball cards.

It was a futile search; but it was then and there that I started to remember. From backstage, watching the Christmas Eve faces of my fellow townspeople, I could begin to populate those bleacher seats on that summer day – row by row, I could remember a few of the baseball fans who had been there. Mrs Kenmore, the butcher's wife, and their son Donny, a rheumatic-fever baby who was not allowed to play baseball; they attended every game. They were in attendance at *A Christmas Carol* to watch Mr Kenmore slaughter the part of the Ghost of Christmas Present; but I could see them in their short-sleeved summer garb, with their identically sunburned noses – they always sat down low in the bleachers, because Donny was not agile and Mrs Kenmore feared he would fall through the slats.

And there was Mr Early's daughter, Maureen – reputed to have wet her pants when Owen Meany tried out for the part of the Ghost of Christmas Yet to Come. She was here tonight, and had been present every night, to watch her father's vain attempts to make Marley's Ghost resemble King Lear. She simultaneously worshiped and despised her father, who was a terrible snob and regaled Maureen with both undeserved praise and a staggering list of *his* expectations for her; at the very least, she would one day have her doctorate – and if she were to indulge her fantasy, and become a movie star, she would make her reputation on the silver screen only after numerous triumphs in 'legitimate' theater. Maureen Early was a dreamer who squirmed in her seat – whether she was watching her father overact or watching Owen Meany approach home plate. I remembered that she had been sitting in the top row, squirming beside Caroline O'Day, whose father ran the Chevy dealership. Caroline O'Day was one of those rare parochial-school girls who managed to wear her St Michael's uniform – her pleated flannel skirt and matching burgundy knee socks – as if she were a cocktail waitress in a lounge of questionable repute. With boys,

Caroline O'Day was as aggressive as a Corvette, and Maureen Early enjoyed her company because Mr Early thought the O'Days were vulgar. It had not set well with Mr Early that Caroline's father, Larry O'Day, had secured the part of Bob Crachit; but Mr O'Day was younger and handsomer than Mr Early, and Dan Needham knew that a Chevy salesman's derring-do was far preferable to Mr Early's attempting to turn Bob Crachit into King Lear.

How I remembered them on that summer day – Maureen Early and Caroline O'Day – how they had laughed and squirmed in their seats together when Owen Meany came to bat.

What a power I had discovered! I felt certain I could refill those bleacher seats – one day, I was sure, I could 'see' everyone who'd been there; I could find that special someone my mother had waved to, at the end.

Mr Arthur Dowling had been there; I could see him shade his eyes with one hand, his other hand shading his wife's eyes – he was that sort of servant to her. Arthur Dowling was watching *A Christmas Carol* because his wife, the most officious member of the Town Library Board, was steering her humorless self through the chore of being the Ghost of Christmas Past. Amanda Dowling was a pioneer in challenging sexual stereotypes; she wore men's clothes – fancy dress, for her, meant a coat and tie – and when she smoked, she blew smoke in men's faces, this being at the heart of her opinions regarding how men behaved toward women. Both her husband and Amanda were in favor of creating mayhem with sexual stereotypes, or reversing sexual roles as arduously and as self-consciously as possible – hence, he often wore an apron while shopping; hence, her hair was shorter than his, except on her legs and in her armpits, where she grew it long. There were certain positive words in their vocabulary – 'European,' among them; women who didn't shave their armpits or their legs were more 'European' than American women, to their undoubted advantage.

They were childless – Dan Needham suggested that their sexual roles might be so 'reversed' as to make childbearing difficult – and their attendance at Little League games was marked by a constant disapproval of the sport: that little girls were not allowed to play in the Little League was an example of sexual stereotyping that exercised the Dowlings' humorlessness and fury. Should *they* have a daughter, they warned, *she* would play in the Little League. They were a couple with a theme – sadly, it was their only theme, and a small theme, and they overplayed it, but a young couple with such a burning mission was quite interesting to the generally slow, accepting types who were more typical in Gravesend. Mr Chickering, our fat coach and manager, lived in dread of the day the Dowlings might produce a daughter. Mr Chickering was of the old school – he believed that only boys should play baseball, and that girls should watch them play, or else play softball.

Like many small-town world-changers, the Dowlings were independently wealthy; he, in fact, did nothing – except he was a ceaseless interior decorator of his own well-appointed house and a manicure artist when the subject was his lawn. In his early thirties, Arthur Dowling had developed the habit of puttering to a level of frenzy quite beyond the capacities of the retired, who are conventionally supposed to be the putters. Amanda Dowling didn't work, either, but she was tireless in her pursuit of the board-member life. She was a trustee of *everything*, and the Town Library was not the only board she served; it was simply the board she was most often associated with, because it was a board she served with special vengeance.

Among the methods she preferred for changing the world, banning books was high on her list. Sexual stereotypes did not fall, she liked to say, from the clear blue sky; books were the major influences upon children – and books that had boys being boys, and girls being girls, were among the *worst* offenders! *Tom Sawyer* and *Huckleberry Finn*, for example; they were an education in condescension to women – all by themselves, they *created* sexual stereotypes! *Wuthering Heights*, for example: how that book *taught* a woman to submit to a man made Amanda Dowling 'see red,' as she would say.

As for the Dowlings' participation in The Gravesend Players: they took turns. Their campaign was relentless, but minor; *she* tried out for parts conventionally bestowed upon men; *he* went after the lesser women's roles – preferably nonspeaking. She was more ambitious than he was, befitting a woman determined to reverse sexual stereotypes; she thought that speaking parts for males were perfect for her.

Dan Needham gave them what he could; to deny them

outright would risk the charge they relished to make, and made often – that so-and-so was 'discriminatory.' A patterned absurdity marked each Dowling's role onstage; Amanda was terrible as a man – but she would have been just as terrible as a woman, Dan was quick to point out – and Arthur was simply terrible. The townspeople enjoyed them in the manner that only people from small towns – who know how everyone's apron is tied, and by whom – can enjoy tedious eccentrics. The Dowlings *were* tedious, their eccentricity was flawed and made small by the utter predictability of their highly selective passions; yet they were a fixture of The Gravesend Players that provided constant, if familiar, entertainment. Dan Needham knew better than to tamper with them.

How I astonished myself that Christmas Eve! With diligence, with months – even years – backstage in the Gravesend Town Hall, I knew I could find the face my mother had waved to in the stands. Why not at the baseball games themselves? you might wonder. Why not observe the actual fans in the *actual* bleachers? People tend to take the same seats. But at Dan's theater I had an advantage; I could watch the audience *unseen* – and I would not be drawing attention to myself by putting myself between the field of play and them. Backstage, and all that this implies, is *invisible*. You can see more in faces that can't see you. If I was looking for my father, shouldn't I look for him unobserved?

' "Spirit!" ' said Scrooge to the Ghost of Christmas Past. ' "Remove me from this place." '

And I watched Mr Arthur Dowling watching his wife, who said: ' "I told you these were shadows of the things that had been. That they are what they are," ' Amanda Dowling said, ' "do not blame me!" ' I watched my fellow townspeople snicker – all but Mr Arthur Dowling, who remained seriously impressed by the reversed sexual role he saw before him.

That the Dowlings 'took turns' at The Gravesend Players – that they never took roles in the *same* play – was a great source of mirth to Dan, who enjoyed joking with Mr Fish.

'I wonder if the Dowlings "take turns" *sexually*!' Dan would say.

'It's most unpleasant to imagine,' Mr Fish would say.

What daydreams I accomplished backstage on Christmas Eve! How I fed myself *memories* from the faces of my fellow townspeople! When Mr Fish asked the Ghost of Christmas Present if the poor, wretched children were his, the Spirit told him, ' "They are Man's." ' How proud Mrs Kenmore was of Mr Kenmore, the butcher; how the rheumatic heart of their son Donny jumped for joy to see his father with *words* instead of *meat* at his fingertips! ' "This boy is Ignorance," ' the butcher said. ' "This girl is Want. Beware of them both, and all of their degree, but most of all beware this boy, for on his brow I see that written which is Doom, unless the writing be encased." ' He meant ' "erased" '; but Mr Kenmore was probably thinking of sausages. On the trusting faces of my fellow townspeople there was no more awareness of Mr Kenmore's error than Mr Kenmore himself possessed; of the faces I surveyed, only Harriet Wheelwright – who had seen almost as many versions of *A Christmas Carol* as Dan Needham had directed – winced to hear the butcher butcher his line. My grandmother, a born critic, briefly closed her eyes and sighed.

Such was my interest in the audience, I did not turn to face the stage until Owen Meany made his appearance.

I did not need to see him to know he was there. A hush fell over the audience. The faces of my fellow townspeople – so amused, so curious, so various – were rendered shockingly similar; each face became the model of each other's fear. Even my grandmother – so detached, so superior – drew her fur closer around her shoulders and shivered: an apparent draft had touched the necks of my fellow townspeople; the shiver that passed through my grandmother appeared to pass through them all. Donny Kenmore clutched his rheumatic heart; Maureen Early, determined not to pee in her pants again, shut her eyes. The look of dread upon the face of Mr Arthur Dowling surpassed even his interest in sexual role-reversal – for neither the sex nor the identity of Owen Meany was clear; what was clear was that he *was* a ghost.

' "Ghost of the Future!" ' Mr Fish exclaimed. ' "I fear you more than any specter I have seen." ' To observe the terror upon my fellow townspeople's faces was entirely convincing; it was obvious that they agreed with Mr Fish's assessment of this ghost's fearful qualities. ' "Will you not speak to me?" ' Scrooge pleaded.

Owen coughed. It was not, as Dan had hoped, a 'humanizing'

sound; it was a rattle so deep, and so deeply associated with death, that the audience was startled – people twitched in their seats; Maureen Early, abandoning all hope of containing her urine, opened her eyes wide and stared at the source of such an unearthly bark. That was when I turned to look at him, too – at the instant his baby-powdered hand shot out of the black folds of his cowl, and he pointed. A fever chill sent a spasm down his trembling arm, and his hand responded to the jolt as to electricity. Mr Fish flinched.

' "Lead on!" ' cried Scrooge. ' "Lead on!" ' Gliding across the stage, Owen Meany led him. But the future was never quite clear enough for Scrooge to see it – until, at last, they came to the churchyard. 'A worthy place!' Dickens called it . . . 'overrun by grass and weeds, the growth of vegetation's death, not life; choked up with too much burying, fat with repleted appetite.'

' "Before I draw nearer to that stone to which you point," ' Scrooge began to say. Among the papier-mâché gravestones, where Mr Fish was standing, one stone loomed larger than the others; it was this stone that Owen pointed to – again and again, he pointed and pointed. So that Mr Fish would stop stalling – and get to the part where he reads his own name on that grave – Owen stepped closer to the gravestone himself.

Scrooge began to babble.

' "Men's courses will foreshadow certain ends, to which, if persevered in, they must lead. *But*," ' Mr Fish said to Owen, ' "if the courses be departed from, the ends will change. Say it is thus with what you show me!" '

Owen Meany, not moved to speak, bent over the gravestone; appearing to read the name he saw there to himself, he directly fainted.

'Owen!' Mr Fish said crossly, but Owen was as committed to not answering as the Ghost of the Future. 'Owen?' Mr Fish asked, more sympathetically; the audience appeared to sympathize with Mr Fish's reluctance to touch the slumped, hooded figure.

It would be just like Owen, I thought, to regain consciousness by jumping to his feet and screaming; this was exactly what Owen did – *before* Dan Needham could call for the curtain. Mr Fish fell over what was meant to be his grave, and the sheer terror in Owen's cry was matched by a corresponding terror in the audience. There were screams, there were gasps; I knew that Maureen Early's pants were wet again. Just *what* had the Ghost of the Future actually *seen*?

Mr Fish, a veteran at making the best of a mess, found himself sprawled on the stage in a perfect position to 'read' his own name on the papier-mâché gravestone – which he had half-crushed, in falling over it. ' "Ebenezer Scrooge! Am I that man?" ' he asked Owen, but something was wrong with Owen, who appeared to be more frightened of the papier-mâché gravestone than Scrooge was afraid of it; Owen kept backing away. He retreated across the stage, with Mr Fish imploring him for an answer. Without a word, without so much as pointing again at the gravestone that had the power to frighten even the Ghost of Christmas Yet to Come, Owen Meany retreated offstage.

In the dressing room, he sobbed upon the makeup table, coating his hair with baby powder, the black eyeliner streaking his face. Dan Needham felt his forehead. 'You're burning up, Owen!' Dan said. 'I'm getting you straight home, and straight to bed.'

'What is it? What happened?' I asked Owen, but he shook his head and cried harder.

'He fainted, that's what happened!' Dan said; Owen shook his head.

'Is he all right?' Mr Fish asked from the door; Dan had called for a curtain before Mr Fish's last scene. 'Are you all right, Owen?' Mr Fish asked. 'My God, you looked as if *you'd* seen a ghost!'

'I've seen everything now,' Dan said. 'I've seen Scrooge upstaged, I've seen the Ghost of the Future scare *himself*!'

The Rev. Lewis Merrill came to the crowded dressing room to offer his assistance, although Owen appeared more in need of a doctor than a minister.

'Owen?' Pastor Merrill asked. 'Are you all right?' Owen shook his head. 'What did you see?'

Owen stopped crying and looked up at him. That Pastor Merrill seemed so sure that Owen had *seen* something surprised me. Being a minister, being a man of faith, perhaps he was more familiar with 'visions' than the rest of us; possibly he had the ability to recognize those moments when visions appear to others.

'WHAT DO YOU MEAN?' Owen asked Mr Merrill.

'You *saw* something, didn't you?' Pastor Merrill asked Owen. Owen stared at him. 'Didn't you?' Mr Merrill repeated.

'I SAW MY NAME – ON THE GRAVE,' said Owen Meany.

Dan put his arms around Owen and hugged him. 'Owen, Owen – it's part of the story! You're sick, you have a *fever*! You're too excited. Seeing a name on that grave is just like the *story* – it's make-believe, Owen,' Dan said.

'IT WAS *MY* NAME,' Owen said. 'NOT SCROOGE'S.'

The Rev. Mr Merrill knelt beside him. 'It's a natural thing to see that, Owen,' Mr Merrill told him. 'Your own name on your own grave – it's a vision we *all* have. It's just a bad dream, Owen.'

But Dan Needham regarded Mr Merrill strangely, as if such a vision were quite foreign to Dan's experience; he was not at all sure that seeing one's own name on one's own grave was exactly 'natural.' Mr Fish stared at the Rev. Lewis Merrill as if he expected more 'miracles' on the order of the Nativity he had only recently, and for the first time, experienced.

In the baby powder on the makeup table, the name OWEN MEANY – as he himself had written it – was still visible. I pointed to it. 'Owen,' I said, 'look at what you wrote yourself – just tonight. You see, you were already thinking about it – your name, I mean.'

But Owen Meany only stared at me; he stared me down. Then he stared at Dan until Dan said to Mr Fish, 'Let's get that curtain up, let's get this over with.'

Then Owen stared at the Rev. Mr Merrill until Mr Merrill said, 'I'll take you home right now, Owen. You shouldn't be waiting around for your curtain call with a temperature of the-good-Lord-knows-what.'

I rode with them; the last scene of *A Christmas Carol* was boring to me – after the departure of the Ghost of Christmas Yet to Come, the story turns to syrup.

Owen preferred staring at the darkness out the passenger-side window to the lit road ahead.

'You had a *vision*, Owen,' Pastor Merrill repeated. I thought it was nice of him to be so concerned, and to drive Owen home – considering that Owen had *never* been a Congregationalist. I noticed that Mr Merrill's stutter abandoned him when he was being directly helpful to someone, although Owen responded ungenerously to the pastor's help – he appeared to be sullenly embracing his 'vision,' like the typically doubtless prophet he so often seemed to be, to me. He had 'seen' his own name on his own grave; the *world*, not to mention Pastor Merrill, would have a hard time convincing him otherwise.

Mr Merrill and I sat in the car and watched him hobble over the snow-covered ruts in the driveway; there was an outside light left on for him, and another light was on – in what I knew was Owen's room – but I was shocked to see that, on Christmas Eve, his mother and father had not waited up for him!

'An unusual boy,' said the pastor neutrally, as he drove me home. Without thinking to ask me which of my two 'homes' he should take me to, Mr Merrill drove me to 80 Front Street. I wanted to attend the cast party Dan was throwing in Waterhouse Hall, but Mr Merrill had driven off before I remembered where I wanted to be. Then I thought I might as well go inside and see if my grandmother had come home, or if Dan had persuaded her to kick up her heels – such as she was willing – at the cast party. I knew the instant I opened the door that Grandmother wasn't home – perhaps they were still having curtain calls at the Town Hall; maybe Mr Merrill had been a faster driver than he appeared to be.

I breathed in the still air of the old house; Lydia and Germaine must have been fast asleep, for even someone reading in bed makes a *little* noise – and 80 Front Street was as quiet as a grave. That was when I had the impression that it *was* a grave; the house itself frightened me. I knew I was probably jumpy after Owen's alarming 'vision' – or whatever it was – and I was on the verge of leaving, and of running down Front Street to the Gravesend Academy campus (to Dan's dormitory), when I heard Germaine.

She was difficult to hear because she had hidden herself in the secret passageway, and she was speaking barely above a whisper; but the rest of the house was so very quiet, I could hear her.

'Oh, Jesus, help me!' she was saying. 'Oh, God; oh, dear Christ – oh, good Lord – *help* me!'

So there *were* thieves in Gravesend! I thought. The Vestry members had been wise to lock the parish house. Christmas Eve bandits had pillaged 80 Front Street! Germaine had escaped to the secret passageway, but what had the robbers done to Lydia? Perhaps they had kidnapped her, or stolen her wheelchair and left her helpless.

The books on the bookshelf-door to the secret passageway were tumbled all about – half of them were on the floor, as if Germaine, in her panic, had forgotten the location of the concealed lock and key . . . upon *which* shelf, behind *which* books? She'd made such a mess that the lock and key were now plainly visible to anyone entering the living room – especially since the books strewn upon the floor drew your attention to the bookshelf-door.

'Germaine?' I whispered. 'Have they gone?'

'Have *who* gone?' Germaine whispered back.

'The robbers,' I whispered.

'*What* robbers,' she asked me.

I opened the door to the secret passageway. She was cringing behind the door, near the jams and jellies – as many cobwebs in her hair as adorned the relishes and chutneys and the cans of overused, spongy tennis balls that dated back to the days when my mother saved old tennis balls for Sagamore. Germaine was wearing her ankle-length flannel dressing gown; but she was barefoot – suggesting that the manner of her hiding herself in the secret passageway had not been unlike the way she cleared the table.

'Lydia is dead,' Germaine said. She would not emerge from the cobwebs and shadows, although I held the heavy bookshelf-door wide open for her.

'They killed her!' I said in alarm.

'No one killed her,' Germaine said; a certain mystical detachment flooded her eyes and caused her to slightly revise her statement. 'Death just came for her,' Germaine said, shivering dramatically. She was the sort of girl who personified Death; after all, she thought that Owen Meany's voice was simply the speaking vehicle for the Devil.

'How did she die?' I asked.

'In her bed, when I was reading to her,' Germaine said. 'She'd just corrected me,' Germaine said. Lydia was always correcting Germaine, naturally; Germaine's pronunciation was especially offensive to Lydia, who modeled her own pronunciation exactly upon my grandmother's speech and held Germaine accountable for any failures in imitating my grandmother's reading voice, as well. Grandmother and Lydia often took turns reading to each other – because their eyes, they said, needed rest. So Lydia had died while resting her eyes, informing Germaine of her mispronunciation of this or that. Occasionally, Lydia would interrupt Germaine's reading and ask her to repeat a certain word. Whether correctly or incorrectly pronounced, Lydia would then say, 'I'll bet you don't know what the word means, do you?' So Lydia had died in the act of educating Germaine, a task – in my grandmother's opinion – that had no end.

Germaine had sat with the body as long as she could stand it.

'Things happened to the body,' Germaine explained, venturing cautiously into the living room. She viewed the spilled books with surprise – as if Death had come for them, too; or perhaps Death had been looking for her and had flung the books about in the process.

'What things?' I asked.

'Not nice things,' Germaine said, shaking her head.

I could imagine the old house settling and creaking, groaning against the winter wind; poor Germaine had probably concluded that Death was still around. Possibly Death had expected that coming for Lydia would have been more of a struggle; having found her and taken her so easily, probably Death felt inclined to stay and take a second soul. Why not make a night of it?

We held hands, as if we were siblings taking a great risk together, and went to view Lydia. I was quite shocked to see her, because Germaine had not told me of the efforts she had made to shut Lydia's mouth; Germaine had bound Lydia's jaws together with one of her pink leg-warmers, which she had knotted at the top of Lydia's head. Upon closer inspection, I saw that Germaine had also exercised considerable creativity in her efforts to permanently close Lydia's eyes; upon closing them, she had fastened two unmatched coins – a nickel and a quarter – to Lydia's eyelids, with Scotch tape. She told me that the only matching coins she could find had been dimes, which were too small – and that one eyelid fluttered, or had appeared to flutter, knocking the nickel off; hence the tape. She used the tape on both eyelids, she explained – even though the quarter had stayed in place by itself – because to tape one coin and not the other had not appealed to her sense of symmetry. Years later, I would remember her use of that word and conclude that Lydia and my grandmother had managed to educate Germaine, a little; 'symmetry,' I was sure, was not a word in Germaine's vocabulary *before* she came to live at 80 Front Street. I would remember, too, that although I was only eleven, such words *were* in my vocabulary – largely through Lydia's and my grandmother's efforts to educate *me*. My mother had never paid very particular attention to *words*, and Dan Needham let boys be boys.

When Dan returned to 80 Front Street with my grandmother, Germaine and I were much relieved; we'd been sitting with Lydia's body, reassuring ourselves that Death had come and got what it came for, and gone – that Death had left 80 Front Street in peace, at least for the rest of Christmas Eve. But we could not have gone on sitting with Lydia for very long.

As usual, Dan Needham took charge; he'd brought my grandmother home – from her brief appearance at the cast party – and he allowed the cast party to go on without him. He put Grandmother to bed with a rum toddy; naturally, Owen's outburst in *A Christmas Carol* had upset her – and now she expressed her conviction that Owen had somehow *foreseen* Lydia's death and had confused it with his own. This point of view was immediately convincing to Germaine, who remarked that while she was reading to Lydia, only shortly before Lydia died, *both* of them had thought they'd heard a scream.

Grandmother was insulted that Germaine should actually agree with her about anything and wanted to disassociate herself from Germaine's hocus-pocus; it was nonsense that Lydia and Germaine could have heard Owen screaming all the way from the Gravesend Town Hall, on a windy winter night, with everyone's doors and windows shut. Germaine was superstitious and probably heard screaming, of one kind or another, every night; and Lydia – it was now clearly proven – was suffering from a senility much in advance of my grandmother's. Nonetheless, in Grandmother's view, Owen Meany had certain unlikable 'powers'; that he had 'foreseen' Lydia's death was *not* superstitious nonsense – at least not on the level that Germaine was superstitious.

'Owen *foresaw* absolutely *nothing*,' Dan Needham told the agitated women. 'He must have had a fever of a hundred and four! The only *power* he has is the power of his imagination.'

But against this reasoning, my grandmother and Germaine saw themselves as allies. There was – at the very least –

some ominous connection between Lydia's death and what Owen 'saw'; the powers of 'that boy' went far beyond the powers of the imagination.

'Have another rum toddy, Harriet,' Dan Needham told my grandmother.

'Don't you patronize me, Dan,' my grandmother said. 'And shame on you,' she added, 'for letting a stupid *butcher* get his bloody hands on such a wonderful part. Dismal casting,' she told him.

'I agree, I agree,' Dan said.

It was also agreed that Lydia be allowed to lie in her own room, with the door firmly shut. Germaine would sleep in the other twin bed in my room. Although I much preferred the idea of returning to Waterhouse Hall with Dan, it was pointed out to me that the cast party might 'rage on' into the small hours – a likelihood that I had been looking forward to – and that Germaine, who was 'in a state,' should not be left in a room alone. It would be quite improper for her to share a room with Dan, and unthinkable that my grandmother would sleep in the same room with a maid. After all, I was only eleven.

I had shared that room so many times with Owen; how I wanted to talk to him now! What would he think of my grandmother's suggestion that he had *foreseen* Lydia's death? And would he be relieved to learn that Death didn't have a plan to come for *him*? Would he believe it? I knew he would be deeply disappointed if he missed *seeing* Lydia. And I wanted to tell him about my discovery – while watching the theater audience – that I believed I could, by this means, actually remember the faces in the audience at what Owen called that FATED baseball game. What would Owen Meany say about my sudden inspiration: that it had been my actual *father* whom my mother was waving to, the split second before the ball hit her? In the world of what the Rev. Lewis Merrill called 'visions,' what would Owen make of that one?

But Germaine distracted me. She wanted the night-light left on; she tossed and turned; she lay staring at the ceiling. When I got up to go to the bathroom, she asked me not to be gone long; she didn't want to be left alone – not for a minute.

If she would only fall asleep, I thought, I could telephone Owen. There was only one phone in the Meany house; it was in the kitchen, right outside Owen's bedroom. I could call him at any hour of the night, because he woke up in an instant and his parents slept through the night like boulders – like immovable slabs of granite.

Then I remembered it was Christmas Eve. My mother had once said it was 'just as well' that we went to Sawyer Depot for Christmas, because it prevented Owen from comparing what *he* got for Christmas with what I got.

I got a half-dozen presents from each relative or loved one – from my grandmother, from my aunt and uncle, from my cousins, from Dan; and more than a half-dozen from my mother. I had looked under the Christmas tree this year, in the living room of 80 Front Street, and was touched at Dan's and my grandmother's efforts to match the sheer *number* of presents – for me – that usually lay under the Eastmans' tree in Sawyer Depot. I had already counted them; I had over forty wrapped presents – and, God knows, there was usually something hidden in the basement or in the garage that was too big to wrap.

I never knew what Owen got for Christmas, but it occurred to me that if his parents hadn't even waited up for him – on Christmas Eve! – that Christmas was not especially emphasized in the Meany household. In the past, by the time I came back from Sawyer Depot, half of my lesser toys were broken or lost, and the new things that were truly worth keeping were discovered – by Owen – gradually, over a period of days or weeks.

'WHERE'D YOU GET THAT?'

'For Christmas.'

'OH, YES, I SEE . . .'

Now that I thought of it, I could not remember him ever showing me a single thing he got 'for Christmas.' I wanted to call him, but Germaine kept me in my bed. The more I stayed in my bed, and the more I was aware of her – still awake – the stranger I began to feel. I began to think about Germaine the way I often thought about Hester – and how old would Germaine have been in '53? In her twenties, I suppose. I actually began to wish that she would climb into my bed, and I began to imagine climbing into hers; I don't think she would have prevented me – I think she would have favored an innocent hug and even a not-so-innocent boy in her arms, if only to keep Death away. I began to *scheme* – not at all in the manner of an eleven-year-old, but in the manner of an older, *horny* boy. I began to imagine how much advantage I might take of Germaine, given that she was distraught.

I actually said, 'I believe you, about hearing him scream.' I *lied*! I didn't believe her at all!

'It was *his* voice,' she said instantly. 'Now that I remember it, I know it was.'

I reached out my hand, into the aisle between the twin beds; her hand was there to take mine. I thought about the way Barb Wiggin had kissed Owen; I was rewarded with an erection powerful enough to slightly raise my bed covers; but when I squeezed Germaine's hand especially hard, she made no response – she just held on.

'Go to sleep,' she said. When her hand slipped out of mine, I realized that she had fallen asleep; I stared at her for a long time, but I didn't dare approach her. I was ashamed of how I felt. In the considerably grown-up vocabulary that I had been exposed to through my grandmother and Lydia, I had not been exposed to *lust*; that was not a word I could have learned from them – that was not a feeling I could label. What I was experiencing simply felt *wrong*; it made me feel guilty, that a part of myself was an enemy to the rest of myself, and that was when I thought I understood where the feeling came from; it had to come from my father. It was the part of him that stirred inside me. And for the first time, I began to consider that my father might be evil, or that what of himself he had given to me was what was evil in me.

Henceforward, whenever I was troubled by a way I felt – and especially when I felt *this* way, when I *lusted* – I thought that my father was asserting himself within me. My desire to know who he was took on a new urgency; I did not want to know who he was because I missed him, or because I was looking for someone to love; I had Dan and his love; I had my grandmother – and everything I remembered, and (I'm sure) exaggerated, about my mother. It was not out of love that I wanted to meet my father, but out of the darkest curiosity – to be able to recognize, in myself, what evil I might be capable of.

How I wanted to talk to Owen about *this*!

When Germaine started to snore, I got out of bed and crept downstairs to the kitchen phone to call him.

The sudden light in the kitchen sent a resident mouse into

rapid abandonment of its investigations of the bread box; the light also surprised me, because it turned the myriad Colonial-style windowpanes into fragmented mirror images of myself – there instantly appeared to be many of me, standing outside the house, looking in at me. In one image of my shocked face I thought I recognized the fear and uneasiness peculiar to Mr Morrison; according to Dan, Mr Morrison's response to Owen's fainting spell and fit had been one of shock – the cowardly mailman had fainted. Chief Pike had carried the fallen postal thespian into the bracing night air, where Mr Morrison had revived with a vengeance – wrestling in the snow with Gravesend's determined chief of police, until Mr Morrison yielded to the strong arm of the law.

But I was alone in the kitchen; the small, square, mirror-black panes reflected many versions of my face, but no other face looked in upon me as I dialed the Meanys' number. It rang longer than I expected, and I almost hung up. Remembering Owen's fever, I was afraid he might be more soundly asleep than usual – and that Mr and Mrs Meany would be awakened by my call.

'MERRY CHRISTMAS,' he said, when he finally answered the phone.

I told him everything. He was most sympathetic to the notion that I could 'remember' the audience at the baseball game by observing the audience at Dan's play; he recommended that he watch with me – two pairs of eyes being better than one. As for my 'imagining' that my mother had been waving to my actual father in the last seconds she was alive, Owen Meany believed in trusting such instincts; he said that I must be ON THE RIGHT TRACK, because the idea gave him THE SHIVERS – a sure sign. And as for my desire for Germaine giving me a hard-on, Owen couldn't have been more supportive; if Barb Wiggin could provoke lust in him, there was no shame in Germaine provoking such dreadful feelings in me. Owen had prepared a small sermon on the subject of lust, a feeling he would later describe as A TRUTHFUL PREMONITION THAT DAMNATION IS FOR REAL. As for the unpleasant sensation originating with my father – as for these hated feelings in myself being a first sign of my father's contribution to me – Owen was in complete agreement. Lust, he would later say, was God's way of helping me identify who my father was; in lust had I been conceived, in lust would I discover my father.

It is amazing to me, now, how such wild imaginings and philosophies – inspired by a night charged with frights and calamities – made such perfectly good sense to Owen Meany and me; but good friends are nothing to each other if they are not supportive.

Of course, he agreed with me – how stupid Germaine was, to imagine she'd heard him screaming, all the way from the Gravesend Town Hall!

'I DIDN'T SCREAM *THAT* LOUDLY,' he said indignantly.

It was Grandmother's interpretation of what he had foreseen that provided the only difference of opinion between us. If he had to believe anything, why couldn't he believe Grandmother – that it was Lydia's death that the gravestone foretold; that Owen had simply 'seen' the wrong name?

'NO,' he said. 'IT WAS *MY* NAME. NOT SCROOGE'S – AND NOT LYDIA'S.'

'But that was just your mistake,' I said. 'You were thinking of yourself – you'd even been writing your own name, just moments before. And you had a very high fever. If that gravestone actually *told* you anything, it told you that *someone* was going to die. That someone was Lydia. She's dead, isn't she? And you're *not* dead – are you?'

'IT WAS MY NAME,' he repeated stubbornly.

'Look at it this way: you got it half-right,' I told him. I was trying to sound as if I were an old hand at 'visions,' and at interpreting them. I tried to sound as if I knew more about the matter than Pastor Merrill.

'IT WASN'T *JUST* MY NAME,' Owen said. 'I MEAN, NOT THE WAY I *EVER* WRITE IT – NOT THE WAY I WROTE IT IN THE BABY POWDER. IT WAS MY *REAL* NAME – IT SAID THE WHOLE THING,' he said.

That made me pause; he sounded so unbudging. His 'real' name was Paul – his father's name. His real name was Paul O. Meany, Jr; he'd been baptized a Catholic. Of course, he needed a saint's name, like St Paul; if there *is* a St Owen, I've never heard of him. And because there was already a 'Paul' in the family, I suppose that's why they called him 'Owen'; where that middle name came from, he never said – I never knew.

'The gravestone said, 'Paul O. Meany, *Junior*' – is that right?' I asked him.

'IT SAID THE WHOLE THING,' Owen repeated. He hung up.

He was so crazy, he drove me crazy! I stayed up drinking orange juice and eating cookies; I put some fresh bacon in the mousetrap and turned out the light. Like my mother, I hate darkness; in the dark, it came to me – what he meant by THE WHOLE THING. I turned on the light; I called him back.

'MERRY CHRISTMAS,' he said.

'Was there a *date* on the gravestone?' I asked him. He gave himself away by hesitating.

'NO,' he said.

'What was the date, Owen?' I asked him. He hesitated again.

'THERE WAS NO DATE,' Owen said. I wanted to cry – not because I believed a single thing about his stupid 'vision,' but because it was the first time he had lied to me.

'Merry Christmas,' I said; I hung up.

When I turned the light out a second time, there was more darkness in the darkness.

What was the date? How much time had he given himself?

The only question that I wanted to ask the darkness was the one question Scrooge had also wanted an answer to: '"Are these the shadows of the things that Will be or are they shadows of the things that May be, only?"' But the Ghost of the Future was not answering.

6 : THE VOICE

Above all things that she despised, what my grandmother loathed most was lack of effort; this struck Dan Needham as a peculiar hatred, because Harriet Wheelwright had never worked a day in her life – nor had she ever expected my mother to work; and she never once assigned me a single chore. Nevertheless, in my grandmother's view, it required nearly constant effort to keep track of the world – both our own world and the world outside the sphere of Gravesend – and it required effort and intelligence to make nearly constant comment on one's observations; in these efforts, Grandmother was rigorous and unswerving. It was her belief in the value of effort itself that prevented her from buying a television set.

She was a passionate reader, and she thought that reading was one of the noblest efforts of all; in contrast, she found writing to be a great waste of time – a childish self-indulgence, even messier than finger painting – but she admired reading, which she believed was an unselfish activity that provided information and inspiration. She must have thought it a pity that some poor fools had to waste their lives writing in order for us to have sufficient reading material. Reading also gave one confidence in and familiarity with language, which was a necessary tool for forming those nearly constant comments on what one had observed. Grandmother had her doubts about the radio, although she conceded that the modern world moved at such a pace that keeping up with it defied the written word; listening, after all, required *some* effort, and the language one heard on the radio was not much worse than the language one increasingly stumbled over in newspapers and magazines.

But she drew the line at television. It took no effort to *watch* – it was infinitely more beneficial to the soul, and to the intelligence, to read or to listen – and what she imagined there was to watch on TV appalled her; she had, of course, only read about it. She had protested to the Soldiers' Home, and to the Gravesend Retreat for the Elderly – both of which she served as a trustee – that making television sets available to old people would surely hasten their deaths. She was unmoved by the claim made by both these homes for the aged: that the inmates were often too feeble or inattentive to read, and that the radio put them to sleep. My grandmother visited both homes, and what she observed only confirmed her opinions; what Harriet Wheelwright *always* observed *always* confirmed her opinions: she saw the process of death hastened. She saw very old, infirm people with their mouths agape; although they were, at best, only partially alert, they gave their stuporous attention to images that my grandmother described as 'too surpassing in banality to recall.' It was the first time she had actually seen television sets that were turned on, and she was hooked. My grandmother observed that television was draining what scant life remained in the old people 'clean out of them'; yet she instantly craved a TV of her own!

My mother's death, which was followed in less than a year by Lydia's death, had much to do with Grandmother's decision to have a television installed at 80 Front Street. My mother had been a big fan of the old Victrola; in the evenings, we'd listened to Sinatra singing with the Tommy Dorsey Orchestra – my mother liked to sing along with Sinatra. 'That Frank,' she used to say. 'He's got a voice that's meant for a woman – but no woman was ever that lucky.' I remember a few of her favorites; when I hear them, I'm still tempted to sing along – although I don't have my mother's voice. I don't have Sinatra's voice, either – nor his bullying patriotism. I don't think my mother would have been fond of Sinatra's politics, but she liked what she called his 'early' voice, in particular those songs from Sinatra's first sessions with Tommy Dorsey. Because she liked to sing along with Sinatra, she preferred his voice before the war – when he was more subdued and less of a star, when Tommy Dorsey kept him in balance with the band. Her favorite recordings were from 1940 – 'I'll Be Seeing You,' 'Fools Rush In,' 'I Haven't Time to Be a Millionaire,' 'It's a Lovely Day Tomorrow,' 'All This and Heaven, Too,' 'Where Do You Keep Your Heart?' 'Trade Winds,' 'The Call of the Canyon'; and, most of all, 'Too Romantic.'

I had my own radio, and after Mother died, I listened to it more and more; I thought it would upset my grandmother to play – on the Victrola – those old Sinatra songs. When Lydia was alive, my grandmother seemed content with her reading; either she and Lydia took turns reading to each other, or they forced Germaine to read aloud to them – while they rested their eyes and exercised their acute interest in educating Germaine. But after Lydia died, Germaine refused to read aloud to my grandmother; Germaine was convinced that her reading aloud to Lydia had either killed Lydia or had hastened her death, and Germaine was resolute in not wanting to murder Grandmother in a similar fashion. For a while, my grandmother read aloud to Germaine; but this afforded no opportunity for Grandmother to rest her eyes, and she would often interrupt her reading to make sure that Germaine was paying proper attention. Germaine could not possibly pay attention to the subject – she was so intent on keeping herself alive for the duration of the reading.

You can see that this was a home already vulnerable to invasion by television. Ethel, for example, would never be the companion to my grandmother that Lydia had been. Lydia had been an alert and appreciative audience to my grandmother's nearly constant comments, but Ethel was entirely unresponsive – efficient but uninspired, dutiful but passive. Dan Needham sensed that it was Ethel's lack of spark that made my grandmother feel old; yet whenever Dan suggested to Grandmother that she might replace Ethel with someone livelier, my grandmother defended Ethel with bulldog loyalty. Wheelwrights were snobs but they were fair-minded; Wheelwrights did not fire their servants because they were stodgy and dull. And so Ethel stayed, and my grandmother grew old – old and restless to be entertained; she was vulnerable to invasion by television, too.

Germaine, who was terrified when my grandmother read to her – and too terrified to read aloud to Grandmother at all – had too little to do; she resigned. Wheelwrights accept resignations graciously, although I was sorry to see Germaine go. The desire she had provoked in me – as distasteful as it was to me at the time – was a clue to my father; moreover, the lustful fancies that Germaine provided were, although evil, more entertaining to me than anything I could hear on my radio.

With Lydia gone, and with me spending half my days and nights with Dan, Grandmother didn't need *two* maids; there was no reason to replace Germaine – Ethel would suffice. And with Germaine gone, *I* was vulnerable to invasion by television, too.

'YOUR GRANDMOTHER IS GETTING A *TELEVISION*?' said Owen Meany. The Meanys did not have a television. Dan didn't have one, either; he'd voted against Eisenhower in '52, and he'd promised himself that he wouldn't buy a TV as long as Ike was president. Even the Eastmans didn't have a television. Uncle Alfred wanted one, and Noah and Simon and Hester begged to have one; but TV reception was still rather primitive in the north country, Sawyer Depot received mostly snow, and Aunt Martha refused to build a tower for the necessary antenna – it would be too 'unsightly,' she said, although Uncle Alfred wanted a television so badly that he claimed he would construct an antenna tower capable of interfering with low-flying planes if it could get him adequate reception.

'You're getting a *television*?' Hester said to me on the phone from Sawyer Depot. 'You lucky little prick!' Her jealousy was thrilling to hear.

Owen and I had no idea what would be *on* television. We were used to the Saturday matinees at the decrepit Gravesend movie house, inexplicably called The Idaho – after the faraway western state or the potato of that name, we never knew. The Idaho was partial to Tarzan films, and – increasingly – to biblical epics. Owen and I hated the latter: in his view, they were SACRILEGIOUS; in my opinion, they were boring. Owen was also critical of Tarzan movies.

'ALL THAT STUPID SWINGING ON VINES – AND THE VINES NEVER BREAK. AND EVERY TIME HE GOES SWIMMING, THEY SEND IN THE ALLIGATORS OR THE CROCODILES – ACTUALLY, I THINK IT'S ALWAYS THE SAME ALLIGATOR OR CROCODILE; THE POOR CREATURE IS TRAINED TO WRESTLE WITH TARZAN. IT PROBABLY *LOVES* TARZAN! AND IT'S ALWAYS THE SAME OLD ELEPHANT STAMPEDING – AND THE SAME LION, THE SAME LEOPARD, THE SAME STUPID WARTHOG! AND HOW CAN JANE STAND HIM? HE'S SO STUPID; ALL THESE YEARS HE'S BEEN MARRIED TO JANE, AND HE STILL CAN'T SPEAK ENGLISH. THE STUPID CHIMPANZEE IS SMARTER,' Owen said.

But what really made him cross were the Pygmies; they gave him THE SHIVERS. He wondered if the Pygmies got jobs in other movies; he worried that their blowguns with their poison darts would soon be popular with JUVENILE GANGS.

'Where?' I asked. 'What juvenile gangs?'

'MAYBE THEY'RE IN BOSTON,' he said.

We had no idea what to expect from Grandmother's television.

There may have been Pygmy movies on *The Late Show* in 1954, but Owen and I were not allowed to watch *The Late Show* for several years; my grandmother – for all her love of effort and regulation – imposed no other rules about television upon us. For all I know, there may not have *been* a *Late Show* as long ago as 1954; it doesn't matter. The point is, my grandmother was never a censor; she simply believed that Owen and I should go to bed at a 'decent' hour. She watched television all day, and every evening; at dinner, she would recount the day's inanities to me – or to Owen, to Dan, or even Ethel – and she would offer a hasty preview of the absurdities available for nighttime viewing. On the one hand, she became a slave to television; on the other hand, she expressed her contempt for nearly everything she saw and the energy of her outrage may have added years to her life. She detested TV with such passion and wit that watching television and commenting on it – sometimes, commenting directly *to* it – became her *job*.

There was no manifestation of contemporary culture that did not indicate to my grandmother how steadfast was the nation's decline, how merciless our mental and moral deterioration, how swiftly all-embracing our final decadence. I never saw her read a book again; but she referred to books often – as if they were shrines and cathedrals of learning that television had plundered and then abandoned.

There was much on television that Owen and I were unprepared for; but what we were most unprepared for was my grandmother's active participation in almost everything we saw. On those rare occasions when we watched television without my grandmother, we were disappointed; without Grandmother's running, scathing commentary, there were few programs that could sustain our interest. When we watched TV alone, Owen would always say, 'I CAN JUST HEAR WHAT YOUR GRANDMOTHER WOULD MAKE OF *THIS*.'

Of course, there is no heart – however serious – that finds the death of culture entirely lacking in entertainment; even my grandmother enjoyed one particular television show. To my surprise, Grandmother and Owen were devoted viewers of the *same* show – in my grandmother's case, it was the *only* show for which she felt uncritical love; in Owen's case, it was his favorite among the few shows he at first adored.

The unlikely figure who captured the rarely uncritical hearts of my grandmother and Owen Meany was a shameless crowd pleaser, a musical panderer who chopped up Chopin and Mozart and Debussy into two- and three-minute exaggerated flourishes on a piano he played with diamond-studded hands. He at times played a see-through, glass-topped piano, and he was proud of mentioning the hundreds of thousands of dollars that his pianos cost; one of his diamond rings was piano-shaped, and he never played any piano that was not adorned with an ornate candelabrum. In the childhood of television, he was an idol – largely to women older than my grandmother, and of less than half her education; yet my grandmother and Owen Meany loved him. He'd once appeared as a soloist for the Chicago Symphony, when he was only fourteen, but now – in his wavy-haired thirties – he was a man who was more dedicated to the visual than to the acoustic. He wore floor-length furs and sequined suits; he crammed sixty thousand dollars' worth of chinchilla onto one coat; he had a jacket of twenty-four-karat gold braid; he wore a tuxedo with diamond buttons that spelled out his name.

'LIBERACE!' Owen cried, every time he saw the man; his TV show appeared ten times a week. He was a ridiculous peacock of a man with a honey-coated, feminine voice and dimples so deep that they might have been the handiwork of a ball peen hammer.

'Why don't I slip out and get into something more spectacular?' he would coo; each time, my grandmother and Owen would roar with approval, and Liberace would return to his piano, having changed his sequins for feathers.

Liberace was an androgynous pioneer, I suppose – preparing the society for freaks like Elton John and Boy George – but I could never understand why Owen and Grandmother liked him. It certainly wasn't his music, for he edited Mozart in such a jaunty fashion that you thought he was playing 'Mack the Knife'; now and then he played 'Mack the Knife,' too.

'He loves his mother,' my grandmother would say, in Liberace's defense – and, in truth, it seemed to be true; not only did he *ooh* and *aah* about his mother on TV, but it was reported that he actually lived with the old lady until she died – in 1980!

'HE GAVE HIS BROTHER A JOB,' Owen pointed out, 'AND I DON'T THINK GEORGE IS ESPECIALLY TALENTED.' Indeed, George, the silent brother, played a straight-man's violin until he left the act to become the curator of the Liberace Museum in Las Vegas, where he died – in 1983. But where did Owen get the idea that Liberace *was* ESPECIALLY TALENTED? To me, his principal gift was how unselfconsciously he amused himself – and he was capable of making fun of himself, too. But my grandmother and Owen Meany twittered over him as hysterically as the blue-haired ladies in Liberace's TV audience did – especially when the famous fool skipped into the audience to *dance* with them!

'He actually *likes* old people!' my grandmother said in wonder.

'HE WOULD NEVER HURT ANYONE!' said Owen Meany admiringly.

At the time, I thought he was a fruitcake, but a London columnist who made a similar slur regarding Liberace's sexual preferences lost a libel judgment to him. (That was in 1959; on the witness stand, Liberace testified that he was opposed to homosexuality. I remember how Owen and my grandmother cheered!)

And so, in 1954, my excitement over the new television at 80 Front Street was tempered by the baffling love of my grandmother and Owen Meany for Liberace. I felt quite excluded from their mindless worship of such a kitschy phenomenon – my mother would *never* have sung along with Liberace! – and I expressed my criticism, as always, to Dan.

Dan Needham took a creative, often a positive view of misfortune; many faculty members in even the better secondary schools are failures-in-hiding – lazy men and women whose marginal authority can be exercised *only* over adolescents; but Dan was never one of these. Whether he hoped to retire at Gravesend Academy when he first fell in love and married my mother, I'll never know; but her loss, and his reaction to that injustice, caused him to devote himself to the development of the education of 'the whole boy' in ways that surpassed even the loftily expressed goals in Gravesend's curriculum – where 'the whole boy' was the proposed result of the four-year program of study. Dan became the best of those faculty found at a prep school; he was not only a spirited, good teacher, but he believed that it was a hardship to be young, that it was more difficult to be a teenager than a grown-up – an opinion not widely held among grown-ups, and rarely held among the faculty members at a private school (who more frequently look upon their charges as the privileged louts of the luxury class – spoiled brats in need of discipline). Dan Needham, although he encountered at Gravesend Academy many spoiled brats in need of discipline, simply had more sympathy for people under twenty than he had for people his own age, and older – although he increased his sympathy for the elderly, who (he believed) were suffering a second adolescence and (like the boys at Gravesend) required special care.

'Your grandmother is getting old,' Dan told me. 'She's suffered losses – her husband, your mother. And Lydia – although neither your grandmother nor Lydia knew it – was possibly your grandmother's closest friend. Ethel is no better company than a fire hydrant. If your grandmother loves Liberace, don't fault her for that. Don't be such a snob! If someone makes her happy, don't complain,' Dan said.

But if it was tolerable to be Grandmother's age and adore Liberace, it was intolerable that Owen Meany should also love that simpering, piano-key smile.

'I'm sick of how smart Owen thinks he is,' I said to Dan. 'If he's so smart, how can he like Liberace – at *his* age?'

'Owen *is* smart,' Dan said. 'He's smarter than even he knows. But he is *not* worldly,' Dan added. 'God knows – in his family – what terrible superstitions he's grown up with! His father is an uneducated mystery, and no one knows the measure of his mother's mental problems – she's in such a lunatic state, we can't even guess how insane she is! Maybe Owen likes Liberace because Liberace couldn't exist in Gravesend. Why does he think he'd be so happy in Sawyer Depot?' Dan asked me. 'Because he's never been there.'

I thought Dan was right; but Dan's theories about Owen were always a little too complete. When I told Dan that

Owen remained convinced he had seen the exact date of his own death – and that he refused to tell me what the special day was – Dan too neatly put that problem to rest along with the superstitions Owen's parents had subjected him to; I couldn't help thinking that Owen was more creative, and more responsible, than that.

And if Dan was one of the gifted and tirelessly unselfish faculty members at the academy, his sincere devotion to the goal of 'the whole boy' may have blinded him to the faults of the school – and especially to the many flawed members of the faculty and the administration. Dan believed that Gravesend Academy could *rescue* anyone. All that Owen needed was to survive until he was old enough to enter the academy. Owen's naturally good mind would mature when confronted with the academic challenges; Owen's superstitions would vanish in the company of the academy's more worldly students. Like many dedicated educators, Dan Needham had made education his religion; Owen Meany lacked only the social and intellectual stimulation that a good school could provide. At Gravesend Academy, Dan was sure, the brute-stupid influence of Owen's parents would be washed clean away – as cleanly as the ocean at Little Boar's Head could wash the quarry dust from Owen's body.

My Aunt Martha and Uncle Alfred couldn't wait for Noah and Simon to be old enough to attend Gravesend Academy. The Eastmans, like Dan, believed in the powers of a good private-school education – specifically, in the case of Noah and Simon, in the power to rescue those two daredevils from the standard fates of rural, north country boys: the marriage of driving fast on the back roads, and beer; and the trailer-park girls in the back seats of those cars, those girls who successfully conspired to get pregnant before their high-school graduations. Like many boys who are sent off to private schools, my cousins Noah and Simon had a wildness within them that couldn't be safely contained by their homes or their communities; they had dangerous edges in need of blunting. Everyone suspected that the rigors of a good school would have the desired, dulling effect on Noah and Simon – Gravesend Academy would assault them with a host of new demands, of impossible standards. The sheer volume (if not the value) of the homework would tire them out, and everyone knew that tired boys were safer boys; the numbing routine, the strict attentions paid to the dress code, the regulations regarding only the most occasional and highly chaperoned encounters with the female sex . . . all this would certainly civilize them. Why my Aunt Martha and Uncle Alfred were less concerned with civilizing Hester remains a mystery to me.

That Gravesend Academy did not admit girls, in those days, should not have influenced the Eastmans' decision to send or not to send Hester off to a private school; there were plenty of private schools for girls, and Hester was in as much need of rescuing from the wildness within *her* – and from the rural, north country rituals of *her* sex – as Noah and Simon were in need of saving. But in this interim period of time – when Noah and Simon and Owen and I were *all* waiting to be old enough to attend the academy – Hester began to resent that there were no plans being made for *her* salvation. The idea that she was not in need of rescuing would surely have insulted her; and the notion that my aunt and uncle might have considered her beyond saving would have hurt her in another way.

'EITHER WAY,' said Owen Meany, 'THAT'S WHEN HESTER WENT ON THE WARPATH.'

'What warpath?' Grandmother asked Owen; but Owen and I were careful not to discuss Hester with my grandmother.

A new bond had developed between Owen and Grandmother because of Liberace; they also watched lots of old movies together and encouraged each other's constant comments. It was Grandmother's appreciation of Owen's commentary, which was as ripe with complaint as her own, that enlisted my grandmother's support of Owen as Gravesend Academy 'material.'

'Just what do you mean, you think you "*might not*" go to the academy?' she asked him.

'WELL, I KNOW I'LL GET IN – AND I KNOW I'LL GET A FULL SCHOLARSHIP, TOO,' Owen said.

'Of course you will!' my grandmother said.

'BUT I DON'T HAVE THE RIGHT KIND OF CLOTHES,' Owen said. 'ALL THOSE COATS AND TIES, AND DRESS SHIRTS, AND SHOES.'

'Do you mean, they don't make them in your size?' Grandmother asked him. 'Nonsense! One just has to go shopping in the right places.'

'I MEAN MY PARENTS CAN'T AFFORD THOSE KIND OF CLOTHES,' Owen said.

We were watching an old Alan Ladd movie on *The Early Show*. It was called *Appointment with Danger*, and Owen thought it was ridiculous that all the men in Gary, Indiana, wore suits and hats.

'They used to wear them *here*,' my grandmother said; but, probably, they never wore them at the Meany Granite Quarry.

Jack Webb, before he was the good cop in *Dragnet*, was a bad guy in *Appointment with Danger*; he was, among his other endeavors, attempting to murder a nun. This gave Owen the shivers.

The movie gave my grandmother the shivers, too, because she recalled that she had seen it at The Idaho in 1951 – with my mother.

'The nun will be all right, Owen,' she told him.

'IT'S NOT THE IDEA OF MURDERING HER THAT GIVES ME THE SHIVERS,' Owen explained. 'IT'S THE IDEA OF NUNS – IN GENERAL.'

'I know what you mean,' my grandmother said; she harbored her own misgivings about the Catholics.

'WHAT WOULD IT COST TO HAVE A COUPLE OF SUITS AND A COUPLE OF JACKETS AND A COUPLE OF PAIRS OF DRESS PANTS, AND SHIRTS, AND TIES, AND SHOES – YOU KNOW, THE WORKS?' Owen asked.

'I'm going to take you shopping myself,' Grandmother told him. 'You let me worry about what it will cost. Nobody needs to know what it costs.'

'MAYBE, IN MY SIZE, IT'S NOT SO EXPENSIVE,' Owen said.

And so – even without my mother alive to urge him – Owen Meany agreed that he was Gravesend Academy 'material.' The academy agreed, too. Even without Dan Needham's recommendation, they would have admitted Owen with a full scholarship; he was obviously in need of a scholarship, and he had all A's at Gravesend Junior High School. The problem was – though Dan Needham had legally adopted me, and I therefore had the privileged status of a faculty son – the academy was reluctant to accept me. My junior-high-school performance was so undistinguished that the academy officers advised Dan to have me attend the ninth grade at Gravesend High School; the academy would admit me to *their* ninth-grade class the following year – when, they said, it would be easier for me to make the adjustment because I would be repeating the ninth grade.

I had always known I was a weak student; this was less a blow to my self-esteem than it was painful for me to think of Owen moving ahead of me – we wouldn't be in the same class, we wouldn't graduate together. There was another, more practical consideration; that, in my senior year, I wouldn't have Owen around to help me with my homework. That was a promise Owen had made to my mother: that he would always help me with my homework.

And so, before Grandmother took Owen shopping for his academy clothes, Owen announced his decision to attend the ninth grade at Gravesend High School, too. He would stay with me; he would enter the academy the following year – he could have skipped a grade, yet he volunteered to repeat the ninth grade with me! Dan convinced the admissions officers that although Owen was academically quite advanced, it would also be good for him to repeat a grade, to be a year older as a ninth grader – 'because of his physical immaturity,' Dan argued. When the admissions officers met Owen, of course they agreed with Dan – they didn't know that a year older, in Owen's case, didn't mean that he'd be a year *bigger*.

Dan and my grandmother were quite touched by Owen's loyalty to me; Hester, naturally, denounced Owen's behavior as 'queer'; naturally, I loved him, and I thanked him for his sacrifice – but in my heart I resented his power over me.

'DON'T GIVE IT ANOTHER THOUGHT,' he said. 'WE'RE PALS, AREN'T WE? WHAT ARE FRIENDS FOR? I'LL NEVER LEAVE YOU.'

Toronto: February 5, 1987 – Liberace died yesterday; he was sixty-seven. His fans had been maintaining a candlelit vigil outside his Palm Springs mansion, which was formerly a convent. Wouldn't *that* have given Owen the shivers? Liberace had revised his former opposition to homosexuality. 'If you swing with chickens, that is your perfect right,' he said. Yet he denied the allegations in a 1982 palimony suit that he had paid for the sexual services of a male employee – a former valet and live-in chauffeur. There was a settlement out of court. And Liberace's manager denied that the entertainer was a victim of AIDS; Liberace's recent weight loss was the result, the manager said, of a watermelon-only diet.

What would my grandmother and Owen Meany have said about *that*?

'LIBERACE!' Owen would have cried. 'WHO WOULD HAVE BELIEVED IT POSSIBLE? LIBERACE! KILLED BY WATERMELONS!'

It was Thanksgiving, 1954, before my cousins visited Gravesend and saw Grandmother's TV at 80 Front Street for themselves. Noah had started at the academy that fall, so he'd watched television with Owen and me on occasional weekends; but no judgment on the culture around us could ever be complete without Simon's automatic approval of every conceivable form of entertainment, and Hester's similarly automatic disapproval.

'Neat!' Simon said; he also thought that Liberace was 'neat.'

'It's shit, all of it,' said Hester. 'Until everything's in color, and the color's perfect, TV's not worth watching.' But Hester was impressed by the energy of Grandmother's constant criticism of nearly everything she saw; that was a style Hester sought to imitate – for even 'shit' was worth watching if it afforded one the opportunity to elaborate on what *sort* of shit it was.

Everyone agreed that the movie reruns were more interesting than the actual TV programs; yet in Hester's view, the movies selected were 'too old.' Grandmother liked them old – 'the older the better!' – but she disliked most movie stars. After watching *Captain Blood*, she announced that Errol Flynn was 'no brains, all chest'; Hester thought that Olivia de Havilland was 'cow-eyed.' Owen suggested that pirate movies were all the same.

'STUPID SWORD FIGHTS!' he said. 'AND LOOK AT THE CLOTHES THEY WEAR! IF YOU'RE GOING TO BE FIGHTING WITH SWORDS, IT'S STUPID TO WEAR LOOSE, BAGGY SHIRTS – OF COURSE YOUR SHIRTS ARE GOING TO GET ALL SLASHED TO PIECES!'

Grandmother complained that the choice of movies wasn't even 'seasonal.' What was the point of showing *It Happens Every Spring* in November? No one is thinking about baseball at Thanksgiving, and *It Happens Every Spring* is such a *stupid* baseball movie that I think I could watch it every night and even fail to be reminded of my mother's death. Ray Milland is a college professor who becomes a phenomenal baseball player after discovering a formula that repels wood; how could this remind anyone of anything *real*?

'Honestly, who thinks up these things?' Grandmother asked.

'Peckerheads,' said Hester, who was forever expanding her vocabulary.

If Gravesend Academy had begun the process of saving Noah from himself, we could scarcely tell; it was Simon who seemed subdued, perhaps because he had missed Noah during the fall and was overwhelmed by the instant renewal of their athletic rivalry. Noah was experiencing considerable academic difficulties at the academy, and Dan Needham had several long heart-to-heart talks with Uncle Alfred and Aunt Martha. The Eastmans decided that Noah was intellectually exhausted; the family would spend that Christmas holiday on some recuperative beach in the Caribbean.

'IN THE RELAXING SETTING OF *CAPTAIN BLOOD*!' Owen observed.

Owen was disappointed that the Eastmans were spending Christmas in the Caribbean; another opportunity to go to Sawyer Depot had eluded him.

After Thanksgiving, he was depressed; and – like me – he was thinking about Hester. We went to The Idaho for the usual fare at the Saturday matinee – a double feature: *Treasure of the Golden Condor*, wherein Cornel Wilde is a dashing eighteenth-century Frenchman seeking hidden Mayan riches in Guatemala; and *Drum Beat*, wherein Alan Ladd is a cowboy and Audrey Dalton is an Indian. Between tales of ancient treasure and scalping parties, it was repeatedly clear to Owen and me that we lived in a dull age – that adventure always happened elsewhere, and long ago. Tarzan fit this formula – and so did the dreaded biblical epics. These, in combination with his Christmas pageant experiences, contributed to the newly sullen and withdrawn persona that Owen presented to the world at Christ Church.

That the Wiggins had actually liked *The Robe* made up Owen's mind: whether he ever got to go to Sawyer Depot for Christmas or not, he would never participate in another Nativity. I'm sure his decision did not upset the Wiggins greatly, but Owen was unforgiving on the subject of biblical epics in general and *The Robe* in particular. Although he thought that Jean Simmons was 'PRETTY, LIKE HESTER,' he also thought that Audrey Dalton – in *Drum Beat* – was 'LIKE HESTER IF HESTER HAD BEEN AN INDIAN.' Beyond all three having dark hair, I failed to see any resemblance.

The Robe, to be fair, had hit Owen and me one Saturday afternoon at The Idaho with special force; my mother had been dead less than a year, and Owen and I were not comforted to see Richard Burton and Jean Simmons walk off to their deaths quite so *happily*. Furthermore, they appeared to exit the movie and life itself by walking up into the sky! This was especially offensive. Richard Burton is a Roman tribune who converts to Christianity after crucifying Christ; both Burton and Jean Simmons take turns clutching Christ's *robe* a lot.

'WHAT A BIG FUSS ABOUT A *BLANKET*!' Owen said. 'THAT'S SO CATHOLIC,' he added – 'TO GET VERY RELIGIOUS ABOUT *OBJECTS*.'

This was a theme of Owen's – the Catholics and their adoration of OBJECTS. Yet Owen's habit of collecting objects that *he* made (in his own way) RELIGIOUS was well known: I had only to remember my armadillo's claws. In all of Gravesend, the object that most attracted Owen's contempt was the stone statue of Mary Magdalene, the reformed prostitute who guarded the playground of St Michael's – the parochial school. The life-sized statue stood in a meaningless cement archway – 'meaningless' because the archway led nowhere; it was a gate without a place to be admitted to; it was an entrance without a house. The archway, and Mary Magdalene herself, overlooked the rutted macadam playground of the schoolyard – a surface too broken up to dribble a basketball on; the bent and rusted basket hoops had long ago been stripped of their nets, and the foul lines had been erased or worn away with sand.

It was a forlornly unattended playground on weekends and school holidays; it was used strictly for recesses during school days, when the parochial students loitered there – they were unmoved to play many games. The stern look of Mary Magdalene rebuked them; her former line of work and her harsh reformation shamed them. For although the playground reflected an obdurate disrepair, the statue itself was whitewashed every spring, and even on the dullest, grayest days –

despite being dotted here and there with birdshit and occasional stains of human desecration – Mary Magdalene attracted and reflected more light than any other object or human presence at St Michael's.

Owen looked upon the school as a prison to which he was nearly sent; for had his parents not RENOUNCED the Catholics, St Michael's would have been Owen's school. It had an altogether bleak, reformatory atmosphere; its life was punctuated by the sounds of an adjacent gas station – the bell that announced the arriving and departing vehicles, the accounting of the gas pumps themselves, and the multifarious din from the mechanics laboring in the pits.

But over this unholy, unstudious, unsuitable ground the stone Mary Magdalene stood her guard; under her odd, cement archway, she at times appeared to be tending to an elaborate but crudely homemade barbecue; at other times, she seemed to be a goalie – poised in the goal.

Of course, no Catholic would have fired a ball or a puck or any other missile at her; if the parochial students themselves were tempted, the grim, alert presence of the nuns would have discouraged them. And although the Gravesend Catholic Church was in another part of town, the shabby saltbox where the nuns and some other teachers at St Michael's lived was positioned like a guardhouse at a corner of the playground – in full view of Mary Magdalene. If a passing Protestant felt inclined to show the statue some small gesture of disrespect, the vigilant nuns would exit their guardhouse on the fly – their black habits flapping with the defiant rancorousness of crows.

Owen was afraid of nuns.

'THEY'RE UNNATURAL,' he said; but what, I thought, could be more UNNATURAL than the squeaky falsetto of The Granite Mouse or his commanding presence, which was so out of proportion to his diminutive size?

Every fall, the horse-chestnut trees between Tan Lane and Garfield Street produced many smooth, hard, dark-brown missiles; it was inevitable that Owen and I should pass by the statue of Mary Magdalene with our pockets full of chestnuts. Despite his fear of nuns, Owen could not resist the target that the holy goalie presented; I was a better shot, but Owen threw his chestnuts more fervently. We left scarcely any marks on Mary Magdalene's ground-length robe, on her bland, snowy face, or on her open hands – outstretched in apparent supplication. Yet the nuns, in a fury that only religious persecution can account for, would attack us; their pursuit was erratic, their shrieks like the cries of bats surprised by sunlight – Owen and I had no trouble outrunning them.

'PENGUINS!' Owen would cry as he ran; everyone called nuns 'penguins.' We'd run up Cass Street to the railroad tracks and follow the tracks out of town. Before we reached Maiden Hill, or the quarries, we would pass the Fort Rock Farm and throw what remained of our chestnuts at the black angus cattle grazing there; despite their threatening size and their blue lips and tongues, the black angus wouldn't chase us as enthusiastically as the penguins, who always gave up their pursuit before Cass Street.

And every spring, the swamp between Tan Lane and Garfield Street produced a pondful of tadpoles and toads. Who hasn't already told you that boys of a certain age are cruel? We filled a tennis-ball can with tadpoles and – under the cover of darkness – poured them over the feet of Mary Magdalene. The tadpoles – those that didn't turn quickly into toads – would dry up and die there. We even slaughtered toads and indelicately placed their mutilated bodies in the holy goalie's upturned palms, staining her with amphibian gore. God forgive us! We were such delinquents only in these few years of adolescence before Gravesend Academy could save us from ourselves.

In the spring of '57, Owen was especially destructive to the helpless swamplife of Gravesend, and to Mary Magdalene; just before Easter, we'd been to The Idaho, where we suffered through Cecil B. DeMille's *The Ten Commandments* – the life of Moses, represented by Charlton Heston undergoing various costume changes and radical hairstyles.

'IT'S ANOTHER MALE-NIPPLE MOVIE,' Owen said; and, indeed, in addition to Charlton Heston's nipples, there is evidence of Yul Brynner and John Derek and even Edward G. Robinson having nipples, too.

That The Idaho should show *The Ten Commandments* so close to Easter was another example of what my grandmother called the poor 'seasonal' taste of nearly everyone in the entertainment business: that we should see the Exodus of the Chosen People on the eve of our Lord's Passion and

Resurrection was outrageous – 'ALL THAT OLD-TESTAMENT HARSHNESS WHEN WE SHOULD BE THINKING ABOUT JESUS!' as Owen put it. The parting of the Red Sea especially offended him.

'YOU CAN'T TAKE A MIRACLE AND JUST SHOW IT!' he said indignantly. 'YOU CAN'T PROVE A MIRACLE – YOU JUST HAVE TO BELIEVE IT! IF THE RED SEA ACTUALLY PARTED, IT DIDN'T LOOK LIKE THAT,' he said. 'IT DIDN'T LOOK LIKE ANYTHING – IT'S NOT A PICTURE ANYONE CAN EVEN IMAGINE!'

But there wasn't logic to his anger. If *The Ten Commandments* made him cross, why take it out on Mary Magdalene and a bunch of toads and tadpoles?

In these years before we attended Gravesend Academy, Owen and I were educated – primarily – by what we saw at The Idaho and on my grandmother's television. Who hasn't been 'educated' in this slovenly fashion? Who can blame Owen for his reaction to *The Ten Commandments*? Almost any reaction would be preferable to *believing* it! But if a movie as stupid as *The Ten Commandments* could make Owen Meany murder toads by throwing them at Mary Magdalene, a performance as compelling as Bette Davis's in *Dark Victory* could convince Owen that he, too, had a brain tumor.

At first, Bette Davis is dying and doesn't know it. Her doctor and her best friend won't tell her.

'THEY SHOULD TELL HER IMMEDIATELY!' Owen said anxiously. The doctor was played by George Brent.

'He could never do anything right, anyway,' Grandmother observed.

Humphrey Bogart is a stableman who speaks with an Irish accent. It was the Christmas of '56 and we were watching a movie made in 1939; it was the first time Grandmother had permitted us to watch *The Late Show* – at least, I *think* it was *The Late Show*. After a certain evening hour – or whenever it was that my grandmother began to feel tired – she *called* everything *The Late Show*. She felt sorry for us because the Eastmans were spending another Christmas in the Caribbean; Sawyer Depot was a pleasure slipping into the past, for me – for Owen, it was becoming mere wishful thinking.

'You'd think that Humphrey Bogart could learn a better Irish accent than that,' my grandmother complained.

Dan Needham said that he wouldn't give George Brent a part in a production of The Gravesend Players; Owen added that Mr Fish would have been a more convincing doctor to Bette Davis, but Grandmother argued that 'Mr Fish would have his hands full as Bette Davis's husband' – her doctor eventually gets to be her husband, too.

'*Anyone* would have his hands full as Bette Davis's husband,' Dan observed.

Owen thought it was cruel that Bette Davis had to find out she was dying all by herself; but *Dark Victory* is one of those movies that presumes to be instructive on the subject of how to die. We see Bette Davis accepting her fate gracefully; she moves to Vermont with George Brent and takes up gardening – cheerfully living with the fact that one day, suddenly, darkness will come.

'THIS IS VERY SAD!' Owen cried 'HOW CAN SHE NOT THINK ABOUT IT?'

Ronald Reagan is a vapid young drunk.

'She should have married *him*,' Grandmother said. 'She's dying and he's already dead.'

Owen said that the symptoms of Bette Davis's terminal tumor were familiar to him.

'Owen, you *don't* have a brain tumor,' Dan Needham told him.

'Bette Davis doesn't have one, either!' Grandmother said. 'But I think Ronald Reagan has one.'

'Maybe George Brent, too,' Dan said.

'YOU KNOW THE PART ABOUT THE DIMMING VISION?' Owen asked. 'WELL, SOMETIMES MY VISION DIMS – JUST LIKE BETTE DAVIS'S!'

'You should have your eyes examined, Owen,' Grandmother said.

'You *don't* have a brain tumor!' Dan Needham repeated.

'I HAVE *SOMETHING*,' said Owen Meany.

In addition to watching television, Owen and I spent many nights backstage with The Gravesend Players, but we rarely watched the performances; we watched the audiences – we repopulated those bleacher seats at that Little League game in the summer of '53; gradually, the stands were filling. We had no doubts about the exact placement of the Kenmores or the Dowlings; Owen disputed my notion that Maureen Early and Caroline O'Day were in the top row – he SAW them nearer the bottom. And we couldn't agree about the Brinker-Smiths.

'THE BRITISH NEVER WATCH BASEBALL!' Owen said.

But I always had an eye for Ginger Brinker-Smith's fabled voluptuousness; I argued that she had been there, that I 'saw' her.

'YOU WOULDN'T HAVE LOOKED TWICE IF SHE *HAD* BEEN THERE – NOT THAT SUMMER,' Owen insisted. 'YOU WERE TOO YOUNG, AND BESIDES – SHE'D JUST HAD THE TWINS, SHE WAS A MESS!'

I suggested that Owen was prejudiced against the Brinker-Smiths ever since their strenuous lovemaking had battered him under their bed; but, for the most part, we agreed about who had been at the game, and where they had been sitting. Morrison the mailman, we had no doubt, had never watched a game; and poor Mrs Merrill – despite how fondly the baseball season must have reminded her of the perpetual weather of her native California – was never a fan, either. We were not sure about the Rev. Mr Merrill; we decided against his being there on the grounds that we had rarely seen him anywhere without his wife. We were sure the Wiggins had *not* been there; they were often in attendance, but they displayed such a boorish enthusiasm for every pitch that if they'd been at that game, we would have noticed them. Since it had been a time when Barb Wiggin still thought of Owen as 'cute,' she would have rushed to console him for his unfortunate contact with the fated ball – and Rector Wiggin would have bungled some rites over my mother's prostrate form, or pounded my shaking shoulders with manly camaraderie.

As Owen put it, 'IF THE WIGGINS HAD BEEN THERE, THEY WOULD HAVE MADE A SPECTACLE OF THEMSELVES – WE WOULD NEVER HAVE FORGOTTEN IT!'

Despite how exciting is *any* search for a missing parent – however mindless the method – Owen and I had to admit that, so far, we'd discovered a rather sparse and uninteresting lot of baseball fans. It never occurred to us to question whether the town's ardent Little League followers were also steady patrons of The Gravesend Players.

'THERE'S ONE THING YOU MUST NEVER FORGET,' Owen told me. 'SHE WAS A GOOD MOTHER. IF SHE THOUGHT THE GUY COULD BE A GOOD FATHER TO YOU, YOU'D ALREADY KNOW HIM.'

'You sound so sure,' I said.

'I'M JUST WARNING YOU,' he said. 'IT'S EXCITING TO LOOK FOR YOUR FATHER, BUT DON'T EXPECT TO BE THRILLED WHEN YOU FIND HIM. I HOPE YOU KNOW WE'RE NOT LOOKING FOR ANOTHER *DAN*!'

I didn't know; I thought Owen presumed too much. It *was* exciting to look for my father – that much I knew.

THE LUST CONNECTION, as Owen called it, also contributed to our ongoing enthusiasm for THE FATHER HUNT – as Owen called our overall enterprise.

'EVERY TIME YOU GET A BONER, TRY TO THINK IF YOU REMIND YOURSELF OF ANYONE YOU KNOW' – that was Owen's interesting advice on the matter of my lust being my most traceable connection to my missing father.

As for lust, I had hoped to see more of Hester – now that Noah *and* Simon were attending Gravesend Academy. But, in fact, I saw her less. Noah's academic difficulties had caused him to repeat a year; Simon's first year had been smoother, probably because it thrilled Simon to have Noah demoted to *his* grade in school. Both boys, by the Christmas of '57, were juniors at Gravesend – and so thoroughly involved in what Owen and I presumed to be the more sophisticated activities of private-school life that I saw only slightly more of them than I saw of Hester. It was rare that Noah and Simon were so bored at the academy that they visited 80 Front Street – not even on weekends, which they increasingly spent with their doubtless more exotic classmates. Owen and I assumed that – in Noah's and Simon's eyes – we were too immature for them.

Clearly, we were too immature for Hester, who – in response to Noah being forced to repeat a grade – had managed to have herself promoted. She encountered few academic difficulties at Sawyer Depot High School, where – Owen and I imagined – she was terrorizing faculty and students alike. She had probably gone to some effort to skip a grade, motivated – as she always was – to get the better of her brothers. Nonetheless, all three of my cousins were scheduled to graduate with the Class of '59 – when Owen and I would be completing our first and lowly ninth-grade year at the academy; *we* would graduate with the class of '62. It was humiliating to me; I'd hoped that, one day, I would feel more equal to my exciting cousins, but I felt I was less equal to them than I'd ever been. Hester, in particular, seemed beyond my reach.

'WELL, SHE *IS* YOUR COUSIN – SHE *SHOULD* BE BEYOND YOUR REACH,' Owen said. 'ALSO, SHE'S DANGEROUS – YOU'RE PROBABLY LUCKY SHE'S BEYOND YOUR REACH. HOWEVER,' Owen added, 'IF YOU'RE REALLY CRAZY ABOUT HER, I THINK IT WILL WORK OUT – HESTER WOULD DO *ANYTHING* TO DRIVE HER PARENTS NUTS, SHE'D EVEN MARRY YOU!'

'*Marry* me!' I cried; the thought of *marrying* Hester gave me the shivers.

'WELL, THAT WOULD DRIVE HER PARENTS AROUND THE BEND,' Owen said. 'WOULDN'T IT?'

It would have; and Owen was right: Hester was obsessed with driving her parents – and her brothers – crazy. To drive them to madness was the penalty she exacted for all of them treating her 'like a girl'; according to Hester, Sawyer Depot was 'boys' heaven' – my Aunt Martha was a 'fink of womanhood'; she bowed to Uncle Alfred's notion that the *boys* needed a private-school education, that the *boys* needed to 'expand their horizons.' Hester would expand her own horizons in directions conceived to educate her parents regarding the errors of their ways. As for Owen's idea that Hester would go to the extreme of marrying her own cousin, if that could provide Aunt Martha and Uncle Alfred with an educational wallop . . . it was inconceivable to me!

'I don't think that Hester even *likes* me,' I told Owen; he shrugged.

'THE POINT IS,' said Owen Meany, 'HESTER WOULDN'T NECESSARILY MARRY YOU BECAUSE SHE *LIKED* YOU.'

Meanwhile, we couldn't even manage to get ourselves invited to Sawyer Depot for Christmas. After their holidays in the Caribbean, the Eastmans had decided to stay at home for the Yuletide of '57; Owen and I got our hopes up, but – alas! – they were quickly dashed; we were not invited to Sawyer Depot. The reason the Eastmans weren't going to the Caribbean was that Hester had been corresponding with a black boatman who had proposed a rendezvous in the British Virgin Islands; Hester had involved herself with this particular black boatman the previous Christmas, in Tortola – when she'd been only fifteen! Naturally, *how* she had 'involved herself' was not made explicitly clear to Owen and me; we had to rely on those parts of the story that my Aunt Martha had reported to Dan – substantially more of the story than she had reported to my grandmother, who was of the opinion that a sailor had made a 'pass' at poor Hester, an exercise in crudeness that had made Hester *want* to stay home. In fact, Hester was threatening to escape to Tortola. She was also not speaking to Noah and Simon, who had shown the black boatman's letters to Uncle Alfred and Aunt Martha, and who had fiercely disappointed Hester by not introducing her to a single one of their Gravesend Academy friends.

Dan Needham described the situation in the form of a headline: 'Teenage Traumas Run Wild in Sawyer Depot!' Dan suggested to Owen and me that we were better off to not involve ourselves with Hester. How true! But how we *wanted* to be involved in the thrilling, real-life sleaziness that we suspected Hester was in the thick of. We were in a phase, through television and the movies, of living only vicariously. Even faintly sordid silliness excited us if it put us in contact with love.

The closest that Owen Meany and I could get to love was a front-row seat at The Idaho. That Christmas of '57, Owen and I were fifteen; we told each other that we had fallen in love with Audrey Hepburn, the shy bookstore clerk in *Funny Face*; but we *wanted* Hester. What we were left with was a sense of how little, in the area of love, we must be worth; we felt more foolish than Fred Astaire, dancing with his own raincoat. And how worried we were that the sophisticated world of Gravesend Academy would esteem us even less than we esteemed ourselves.

Toronto: April 12, 1987 – a rainy Palm Sunday. It is not a warm spring rain – not a 'seasonal' rain, as my grandmother liked to say. It is a raw cold rain, a suitable day for the Passion of Our Lord Jesus Christ. At Grace Church on-the-Hill, the children and the acolytes stood huddled in the narthex; holding their palm fronds, they resembled tourists who'd landed in the tropics on an unseasonably cold day. The organist chose Brahms for the processional – '*O Welt ich muss dich lassen*'; 'O world I must leave you.'

Owen hated Palm Sunday: the treachery of Judas, the cowardice of Peter, the weakness of Pilate.

'IT'S BAD ENOUGH THAT THEY CRUCIFIED HIM,' Owen said, 'BUT THEY MADE FUN OF HIM, TOO!'

Canon Mackie read heavily from Matthew: how they mocked Jesus, how they spit on him, how he cried, 'My God, my God, why hast thou forsaken me?'

I find that Holy Week is draining; no matter how many times I have lived through his crucifixion, my anxiety about his resurrection is undiminished – I am terrified that, this year, it won't happen; that, that year, it didn't. Anyone can be sentimental about the Nativity; any fool can feel like a Christian at Christmas. But Easter is the main event; if you don't believe in the resurrection, you're not a believer.

'IF YOU DON'T BELIEVE IN EASTER,' Owen Meany said, 'DON'T KID YOURSELF – DON'T CALL YOURSELF A CHRISTIAN.'

For the Palm Sunday recessional, the organist chose the usual 'Alleluias.' In a chilling drizzle, I crossed Russell Hill Road and went in the service entrance of The Bishop Strachan School; I passed through the kitchen, where the working women and the boarders whose turn it was to help with the Sunday meal all spoke to me. The headmistress, the Rev. Mrs Katherine Keeling, sat in her usual head-of-table position among the housemothers. About forty boarders – the poor girls who had no local friends to ask them home for the weekend, and the girls who were happy to stay at school – sat around the other tables. It is always a surprise to see the girls *not* in their uniforms; I know it's a great relief to them to wear their uniforms day in, day out – because they don't have to worry about what to wear. But they are so lazy about *how* they wear their uniforms – they don't have much experience in dressing themselves – that when they have a choice, when they're allowed to wear their own clothes, they appear wholly less sophisticated, less worldly, than they appear in their uniforms.

In the twenty years that I have been a teacher at The Bishop Strachan School, the girls' uniforms haven't changed very significantly; I've grown rather fond of them. If I were a girl, of any age, I would wear a middie, a loosely tied necktie, a blazer (with my school crest), knee socks – which the Canadians used to call 'knee highs' – and a pleated skirt; when they kneel, it used to be the rule that the skirt should just touch the floor.

But for Sunday boarders' lunch, the girls wear their own clothes; some of them are so badly dressed, I fail to recognize them – they make fun of me for that, naturally. Some of them dress like boys – others, like their mothers or like the floozies they see in movies or on TV. As I am, routinely, the only man in the dining room for Sunday boarders' lunch, perhaps they dress for me.

I've not seen my friend – and, technically, my boss – Katherine Keeling since she delivered her last baby. She has a large family – she's had so many children, I've lost count – but she makes an effort to sit at the housemothers' table on Sundays; and she chatters amiably to the weekend girls. I think Katherine is terrific; but she is too thin. And she always is embarrassed when I catch her not eating, although she should get over the surprise; I'm a more consistent fixture at the housemothers' table for Sunday boarders' lunch than she is – I don't take time off to have babies! But there she was on Palm Sunday, with mashed potatoes and stuffing and turkey heaped upon her plate.

'Turkey rather dry, is it?' I asked; the ladies, routinely, laughed – Katherine, typically, blushed. When she's wearing her clerical collar, she looks slightly more underweight than she actually is. She's my closest friend in Toronto, now that Canon Campbell is gone; and even though she's my boss, I've been at Bishop Strachan longer than she has.

Old Teddybear Kilgour, as we called him, was principal when I was hired. Canon Campbell introduced us. Canon Campbell had been the chaplain at Bishop Strachan before they made him rector of Grace Church on-the-Hill; I couldn't have had anyone recommend me for a job at Bishop Strachan who was more 'connected' to the school than Canon Campbell – not even old Teddybear Kilgour himself. I still tease Katherine about those days. What if she'd been headmistress when I applied for a job? Would *she* have hired me? A young man from the States in those Vietnam years, a not unattractive young man, and without a wife; Bishop Strachan has never had many male teachers, and in my twenty years of teaching these young girls, I have occasionally been the *only* male teacher at the school.

Canon Campbell and old Teddybear Kilgour don't count; they were not male in the threatening sense – they were not potentially dangerous to young girls. Although the canon taught Scripture and History, in addition to his duties as chaplain, he was an elderly man; and he and old Teddybear Kilgour were 'married up to their ears,' as Katherine Keeling likes to say.

Old Teddybear did ask me if I was 'attracted to young girls'; but I must have impressed him that I would take my faculty responsibilities seriously, and that I would concern myself with those young girls' *minds* and not their bodies.

'And *have* you?' Katherine Keeling likes to ask me. How the housemothers titter at the question – like Liberace's live audiences of long ago!

Katherine is a much more jubilant soul than my grandmother, but she has a certain twinkling sarcasm – and the proper elocution, the good diction – that reminds me of Grandmother. They would have liked each other; Owen would have liked the Rev. Mrs Keeling, too.

I've misled you if I've conveyed an atmosphere of loneliness at Sunday boarders' lunch. Perhaps the boarders feel acutely lonely then, but I feel fine. Rituals are comforting; rituals combat loneliness.

On Palm Sunday, there was much talk about the weather. The week before, it had been so cold that everyone commented on the annual error of the birds. Every spring – at least, in Canada – some birds fly north too soon. Thousands are caught in the cold; they return south in a reverse migration. Most common were tales of woe concerning robins and starlings. Katherine had seen some killdeer flying south – I had a common-snipe story that impressed them all. We'd all read *The Globe and Mail* that week: we'd loved the story about the turkey vultures who 'iced up' and couldn't fly; they were mistaken for hawks and taken to a humane society for thawing-out – there were nine of them and they threw up all over their handlers. The humane society could not have been expected to know that turkey vultures vomit when attacked. Who would guess that turkey vultures are so smart?

I've also misled you if I've conveyed an atmosphere of trivia at Sunday boarders' lunch; these lunches are important to me. After the Palm Sunday lunch, Katherine and I walked over to Grace Church and signed up for the All Night Vigil on the notice board in the narthex. Every Maundy Thursday, the Vigil of Prayer and Quiet is kept from nine o'clock that evening until nine o'clock in the morning of Good Friday. Katherine and I always choose the hours no one else wants; we take the Vigil from three to five o'clock in the morning, when Katherine's husband and children are asleep and don't need her.

This year she cautioned me: 'I may be a little late – if the two-o'clock feeding is much later than two o'clock!' She laughs, and her endearingly stick-thin neck looks especially vulnerable in her clerical collar. I see many parents of the Bishop Strachan girls – they are so smartly dressed, they drive Jaguars, they never have time to talk. I know that they dismiss the Rev. Mrs Katherine Keeling as a typical headmistress type – Katherine is not the sort of woman they would look at twice. But she is wise and kind and witty and articulate; and she does not bullshit herself about what Easter means.

'EASTER MEANS WHAT IT SAYS,' said Owen Meany.

At Christ Church on Easter Sunday, Rector Wiggin always said: 'Alleluia. Christ is risen.'

And we, the People – we said: 'The Lord is risen indeed. Alleluia.'

Toronto: April 19, 1987 – a humid, summery Easter Sunday. It does not matter what prelude begins the service; I will always hear Handel's *Messiah* – and my mother's not-quite-trained soprano singing, 'I know that my Redeemer liveth.'

This morning, in Grace Church on-the-Hill, I sat very still, waiting for that passage in John; I knew what was coming. In the old King James version, it was called a 'sepulchre'; in the Revised Standard version, it is just a 'tomb.' Either way, I know the story by heart.

'Now on the first day of the week Mary Magdalene came to the tomb early, while it was still dark, and saw that the stone had been taken away from the tomb. So she ran, and went to Simon Peter and the other disciple, the one whom Jesus loved, and said to them, "They have taken the Lord out of the tomb, and we do not know where they have laid him." '

I remember what Owen used to say about that passage; every Easter, he would lean against me in the pew and whisper into my ear. 'THIS IS THE PART THAT ALWAYS GIVES ME *THE SHIVERS*.'

After the service today, my fellow Torontonians and I stood

in the sun on the church steps – and we lingered on the sidewalk along Lonsdale Road; the sun was so welcome, and so hot. We were childishly delighted by the heat, as if we'd spent years in an atmosphere as cold as the tomb where Mary Magdalene found Jesus missing. Leaning against me, and whispering into my ear – in a manner remindful of Owen Meany – Katherine Keeling said: 'Those birds that flew north, and then south – today they're flying north again.'

'Alleluia,' I said. I was thinking of Owen when I added, 'He is risen.'

'Alleluia,' said the Rev. Mrs Keeling.

That the television was always 'on' at 80 Front Street ceased to tempt Owen and me. We could hear Grandmother, talking either to herself or to Ethel – or directly commenting *to* the TV – and we heard the rise and fall of the studio-made laughter. It was a big house; for four years, Owen and I had the impression that there was always a forbidding gathering of grown-ups, chattering away in a distant room. My grandmother sounded as if she were the haranguing leader of a compliant mob, as if it were her special responsibility to berate her audience and to amuse them, almost simultaneously – for they rewarded her humor with their punctual laughter, as if they were highly entertained that the tone of voice she used on them was uniformly abusive.

Thus Owen Meany and I learned what crap television was, without ever thinking that we hadn't come to this opinion by ourselves; had my grandmother allowed us only two hours of TV a day, or not permitted us more than one hour on a 'school night,' we probably would have become as slavishly devoted to television as the rest of our generation. Owen started out loving only a few things he saw on television, but he saw everything – as much of everything as he could stand.

After four years of television, though, he watched nothing but Liberace and the old movies. I did, or tried to do, everything Owen did. For example: in the summer of '58 when we were both sixteen, Owen got his driver's license before I got mine – not only because he was a month older, but because he already knew how to drive. He'd taught himself with his father's various trucks – he'd been driving on those steep, loopy roads that ran around the quarries that pockmarked most of Maiden Hill.

He took his driver's test on the day of his sixteenth birthday, using his father's tomato-red pickup truck; in those days, there was no driver education course in New Hampshire, and you took your test with a local policeman in the passenger seat – the policeman told you where to turn, when to stop or back up or park. The policeman, in Owen's case, was Chief Ben Pike himself; Chief Pike expressed concern regarding whether or not Owen could reach the pedals – or see over the steering wheel. But Owen had anticipated this: he was mechanically inclined, and he'd raised the seat of the pickup so high that Chief Pike hit his head on the roof; Owen had slid the seat so far forward that Chief Pike had considerable difficulty cramming his knees under the dashboard – in fact, Chief Pike was so physically uncomfortable in the cab of the pickup that he cut Owen's test fairly short.

'HE DIDN'T EVEN MAKE ME PARALLEL-PARK!' Owen said; he was disappointed that he was denied the opportunity to show off his parallel-parking abilities – Owen Meany could slip that tomato-red pickup into a parking space that would have been challenging for a Volkswagen Beetle. In retrospect, I'm surprised that Chief Pike didn't search the interior of the pickup for that 'instrument of death' he was always looking for.

Dan Needham taught me to drive; it was the summer Dan directed *Julius Caesar* in the Gravesend Academy summer school, and he would take me for lessons every morning before rehearsals. Dan would drive me out the Swasey Parkway and up Maiden Hill. I practiced on the back roads around the quarries – the roads on which Owen Meany learned to drive were good enough for me; and Dan judged it safer for me off the public highways, although the Meany Granite Company vehicles flew around those roads with reckless abandon.

The quarrymen were fearless drivers and they trucked the granite and their machinery at full throttle; but, in the summer, the trucks raised so much dust that Dan and I had warning when one was coming – I always had time to pull over, while Dan recited his favorite Shakespeare from *Julius Caesar*.

> Cowards die many times before their deaths;
> The valiant never taste of death but once.

Whereupon, Dan would grip the dashboard and tremble while a dynamite truck hurtled past us.

> Of all the wonders that I yet have heard,
> It seems to me the most strange that men should fear;
> Seeing that death, a necessary end,
> Will come when it will come.

Owen, too, was fond of that passage. When we saw Dan's production of *Julius Caesar*, later that summer, I had passed my driver's test; yet, in the evenings, when Owen and I would drive down to the boardwalk and the casino at Hampton Beach together, we took the tomato-red pickup and Owen always drove. I paid for the gas. Those summer nights of 1958 were the first nights I remember feeling 'grown up'; we'd drive half an hour from Gravesend for the fleeting privilege of inching along a crowded, gaudy strip of beachfront, looking at girls who rarely looked at us. Sometimes, they looked at the truck. We could drive along this strip only two or three times before a cop would motion us over to the side of the street, examine Owen's driver's license – in disbelief – and then suggest that we find a place to park the truck and resume our looking at girls on foot, on either the boardwalk or on the sidewalk that threaded the arcades.

Walking with Owen Meany at Hampton Beach was ill-advised; he was so strikingly small, he was teased and roughed up by the delinquent young men who tilted the pinball machines and swaggered in the heated vicinity of the girls in their cotton-candy-colored clothes. And the girls, who rarely returned our glances when we were secure in the Meany Granite Company pickup, took very long (and giggling) looks at Owen when we were on foot. When he was walking, Owen didn't dare look at the girls.

Therefore, when a cop would, inevitably, advise us to park the truck and pursue our interests 'on foot,' Owen and I would drive back to Gravesend. Or we would drive to a popular daytime beach – Little Boar's Head, which was beautifully empty at night. We'd sit on the sea wall, and feel the cool air off the ocean, and watch the phosphorescence sparkle in the surf. Or we would drive to Rye Harbor and sit on the breakwater, and watch the small boats slapping on the ruffled, pondlike surface; the breakwater itself had been built with the slag – the broken slabs – from the Meany Granite Quarry.

'THEREFORE, I HAVE A RIGHT TO SIT HERE,' Owen always said; no one, of course, ever challenged our being there.

Even though the girls ignored us that summer, that was when I noticed that Owen was attractive to women – not only to my mother.

It is difficult to say how he was attractive, or why; but even when he was sixteen, even when he was especially shy or awkward, he looked like someone who had *earned* what grasp of the world he had. I might have been particularly conscious of this aspect of him because he had truly earned so much more than *I* had. It was not just that he was a better student, or a better driver, or so philosophically sure of himself; here was someone I had grown up with, and had grown used to teasing – I had picked him up over my head and passed him back and forth, I had derided his smallness as surely as the other children had – and yet, suddenly, by the time he was sixteen, he appeared *in command*. He was more in command of himself than the rest of us, he was more in command of *us* than the rest of us – and with women, even with those girls who giggled when they looked at him, you sensed how compelled they were to *touch* him.

And by the end of the summer of '58, he had something astonishing for a sixteen-year-old – in those days before all this ardent and cosmetic weightlifting, he had *muscles*! To be sure, he was tiny, but he was fiercely strong, and his sinewy strength was as visible as the strength of a whippet; although he was frighteningly lean, there was already something very adult about his muscular development – and why not? After all, he'd spent the summer working with granite. I hadn't even been working.

In June, he'd started as a stonecutter; he spent most of the working day in the monument shop, cutting with the grain, WITH THE RIFT, as he called it – using the wedge and feathers. By the middle of the month, his father had taught him how to saw against the grain; the sawyers cut up the bigger slabs, and they finished the gravestones with what was called a diamond wheel – a circular blade, impregnated with diamonds. By July, he was working in the quarries – he was often the signalman, but his father apprenticed him to the other quarrymen: the channel bar drillers, the derrickman, the dynamiters. It seemed to me that he spent most of the month of August in a single, remote pit – one hundred and seventy-five feet deep, a football field in diameter. He and the other men were lowered to work in a grout bucket – 'grout' is waste, the rubble of broken rock that is raised from the pit all day long. At the end of the day, they bring up the men in the bucket.

Granite is a dense, heavy stone; it weighs close to two hundred pounds per cubic foot. Ironically – even though they worked with the diamond wheel – most of the sawyers had all their fingers; but none of the quarrymen had all their fingers; only Mr Meany had all his.

'I'LL KEEP ALL MINE, TOO,' Owen said. 'YOU'VE GOT TO BE MORE THAN QUICK. YOU'VE GOT TO FEEL WHEN THE ROCK'S GOING TO MOVE BEFORE IT MOVES – YOU'VE GOT TO MOVE BEFORE THE ROCK MOVES.'

Just the slightest fuzz grew on his upper lip; nowhere else did his face show traces of a beard, and the faint mustache was so downy and such a pale-gray color that I first mistook it for pulverized granite, the familiar rock dust that clung to him. Yet his face – his nose, the sockets for his eyes, his cheekbones, and the contours of his jaw – had the gaunt definition that one sees in the faces of sixteen-year-olds only when they are starving.

By September, he was smoking a pack of Camels a day. In the yellow glow of the dashboard lights, when we went out driving in the pickup at night, I would catch a glimpse of his profile with the cigarette dangling from his lips; his face had a permanent adult quality.

Those mothers' breasts he'd once unfavorably compared to my mother's breasts were beneath his interest now, although Barb Wiggin's were still TOO BIG, Mrs Webster's were still TOO LOW, and Mrs Merrill's only VERY FUNNY. While Ginger Brinker-Smith, as a younger mother, had claimed our attention, we now (for the most part) coolly assessed our peers. THE TWO CAROLINES – Caroline Perkins and Caroline O'Day – appealed to us, although the breasts of Caroline O'Day were devalued, in Owen's view, by her Catholicism. Maureen Early's bosom was judged to be PERKY; Hannah Abbot's breasts were SMALL BUT SHAPELY; Irene Babson, who had given Owen the shivers as long ago as when my mother's bosom was under review, was now so out of control as to be SIMPLY SCARY. Deborah Perry, Lucy Dearborn, Betsy Bickford, Sarah Tilton, Polly Farnum – to their names, and to the contours of their young breasts, Owen Meany would inhale a Camel deeply. The summer wind rushed through the rolled-down window of the pickup; when he exhaled, slowly, through his nostrils, the cigarette smoke was swept away from his face – dramatically exposing him as if he were a man miraculously emerging from a fire.

'IT'S TOO SOON TO TELL – WITH MOST SIXTEEN-YEAR-OLDS,' Owen said, sounding already worldly enough for any conversation he might encounter at Gravesend Academy – although we both knew that the problem with the sixteen-year-old girls who interested us was that they dated *eighteen*-year-olds. 'BY THE TIME WE'RE EIGHTEEN, WE'LL GET THEM BACK,' Owen said. 'AND WE'LL GET ALL THE SIXTEEN-YEAR-OLDS, TOO – THE ONES WE WANT,' he added, inhaling again and squinting into the oncoming headlights.

By the fall of '58, when we entered Gravesend Academy, Owen seemed very sophisticated to me; the wardrobe my grandmother had acquired for him was more stylish than anything you could buy in New Hampshire. My clothes all came from Gravesend, but Grandmother took Owen shopping in Boston; it was his first time on a train, and – since they were both smokers – they rode in the smoking coach together and shared their nearly constant (and critical) comments on the attire of their fellow passengers on the Boston & Maine, and on the comparative courtesy (or lack thereof) of the conductors. Grandmother outfitted Owen almost entirely at Filene's and Jordan Marsh, one of which had a Small Gentlemen's Department, which the other called A Small Man's Special Needs. Jordan Marsh and Filene's were pretty flashy labels by New Hampshire standards – 'THIS IS NOT BARGAIN-BASEMENT STUFF!' Owen said proudly. For our first day of classes, Owen showed up looking like a small Harvard lawyer.

He was not intimidated by the bigger boys because he had always been smaller; and he was not intimidated by the older boys because he was smarter. He saw immediately a crucial difference between Gravesend, the town, and Gravesend, the academy: the town paper, *The Gravesend News-Letter*, reported all the news that was decent and believed that all things decent were important; the school newspaper, which was called *The Grave*, reported every indecency that could escape the censorship of the paper's faculty adviser and believed that all things decent were boring.

Gravesend Academy embraced a cynical tone of voice, savored a criticism of everything that anyone took seriously; the students hallowed, above everyone else, that boy who saw himself as born to break the rules, as destined to change the laws. And to the students of Gravesend who thus chafed against their bonds, the only accepted tone was caustic – was biting, mordant, bitter, scathing *sarcasm*, the juicy vocabulary of which Owen Meany had already learned from my grandmother. He had mastered sarcasm in much the same way he had become a smoker; he was a pack-a-day man in a month. In his first fall term at Gravesend, the other boys nicknamed him 'Sarcasm Master.' In the lingo of those times, everyone was a *something* 'master'; Dan Needham tells me that this is one of those examples of student language that endures – at Gravesend Academy, the term is still in use. I have never heard it at Bishop Strachan.

But Owen Meany was Sarcasm Master in the way that big Buster York was Barf Master, that Skipper Hilton was Zit Master, that Morris West was Nose Master, that Duffy Swain (who was prematurely bald) was Hair Master, that George Fogg (the hockey player) was Ice Master, that Horace Brigham (a lady's man) was Snatch Master. No one found a name for me.

Among the editors of *The Grave*, in which Owen published the first essay he was assigned in English class, Owen was known as 'The Voice.' His essay was a satire on the source of food in the school dining hall – 'MYSTERY MEAT,' Owen titled the essay and the unrecognizable, gray steaks we were served weekly; the essay, which was published as an editorial, described the slaughter and refrigeration of an unidentified, possibly prehistoric beast that was dragged to the underground kitchen of the school in chains, 'IN THE DEAD OF NIGHT.'

The editorial and the subsequent weekly essays that Owen published in *The Grave* were ascribed not to Owen Meany by name, but to 'The Voice'; and the text was printed in uniform upper-case letters. 'I'M ALWAYS GOING TO BE PUBLISHED IN CAPITALS,' Owen explained to Dan and me, 'BECAUSE IT WILL INSTANTLY GRAB THE READER'S ATTENTION, ESPECIALLY AFTER "THE VOICE" GETS TO BE A KIND OF INSTITUTION.'

By the Christmas of 1958, in our first year at the academy, that is what Owen Meany had become: The Voice – A KIND OF INSTITUTION. Even the Search Committee – appointed to find a new headmaster – was interested in what The Voice had to say. Applicants for the position were given a subscription to *The Grave*; the snide, sneering precocity of the student body was well represented in its pages – and best represented by the capitals that commanded one's gaze to Owen Meany. There were some old curmudgeons on the faculty – and some young fuddy-duddies, too – who objected to Owen's style; and I don't mean that they objected only to his outrageous capitalization. Dan Needham told me that there'd been more than one heated debate in faculty meeting concerning the 'marginal taste' of Owen's blanket criticism of the school; granted, it was well within a long-established tradition for Gravesend students to complain about the academy, but Owen's sarcasm suggested, to some, a total and threatening irreverence. Dan defended Owen; but The Voice was a proven irritant to many of the more insecure members of the Gravesend community – including those faraway but important subscribers to *The Grave*: 'concerned' parents and alumni.

The subject of 'concerned' parents and alumni yielded an especially lively and controversial column for The Voice.

'WHAT ARE THEY "CONCERNED" ABOUT?' Owen pondered. 'ARE THEY "CONCERNED" WITH OUR EDUCATION – THAT IT BE BOTH "CLASSICAL" AND "TIMELY" – OR ARE THEY "CONCERNED" THAT WE MIGHT POSSIBLY LEARN MORE THAN THEY HAVE LEARNED. THAT WE MIGHT INFORM OURSELVES SUFFICIENTLY TO CHALLENGE A FEW OF THEIR MORE HARDENED AND IDIOTIC OPINIONS? ARE THEY "CONCERNED" ABOUT THE QUALITY AND VIGOROUSNESS OF OUR EDUCATION; OR ARE THEY MORE SUPERFICIALLY "CONCERNED" THAT WE MIGHT FAIL TO GET INTO THE UNIVERSITY OR COLLEGE OF *THEIR* CHOICE?'

Then there was the column that challenged the coat-and-tie dress code, arguing that it was 'INCONSISTENT TO DRESS US LIKE GROWN-UPS AND TREAT US LIKE CHILDREN.' And there was the column about required church-attendance, arguing that 'IT RUINS THE PROPER ATMOSPHERE FOR PRAYER AND WORSHIP TO HAVE THE CHURCH – *ANY* CHURCH – FULL OF RESTLESS ADOLESCENTS WHO WOULD RATHER BE SLEEPING LATE OR INDULGING IN SEXUAL FANTASIES OR PLAYING SQUASH. FURTHERMORE, REQUIRING ATTENDANCE AT CHURCH – *FORCING* YOUNG PEOPLE TO PARTICIPATE IN THE RITUALS OF A BELIEF THEY DON'T SHARE – SERVES MERELY TO PREJUDICE THOSE SAME YOUNG PEOPLE AGAINST *ALL* RELIGIONS, AND AGAINST SINCERELY RELIGIOUS BELIEVERS. I BELIEVE THAT IT IS *NOT* THE PURPOSE OF A LIBERAL EDUCATION TO BROADEN AND EXPAND OUR PREJUDICES.'

And on and on. You should have heard him on the subject of required athletics: 'BORN OF A BROWN-SHIRT MENTALITY, A CONCEPT EMBRACED BY THE HITLER YOUTH!' And on the regulation that boarders were not allowed to enjoy more than three weekends off-campus in a single term: 'ARE WE SO SIMPLE, IN THE ADMINISTRATION'S VIEW, THAT WE ARE CHARACTERIZED AS CONTENT TO SPEND OUR WEEKENDS AS ATHLETIC HEROES OR FANS OF SPECTATOR SPORTS; IS IT NOT POSSIBLE THAT SOME OF US MIGHT FIND MORE STIMULATION AT HOME OR AT THE HOME OF A FRIEND – OR (EVEN) AT A *GIRLS'* SCHOOL? AND I *DON'T* MEAN AT ONE OF THOSE OVERORGANIZED AND CHARMLESSLY CHAPERONED *DANCES*!'

The Voice was *our* voice; he championed our causes; he made us proud of ourselves in an atmosphere that belittled and intimidated us. But his was also a voice that could criticize us. When a boy was thrown out of school for killing cats – he was ritualistically lynching cats that were pets of faculty families – we were quick to say how 'sick' he was; it was Owen who reminded us that *all* boys (himself included) were touched by that same sickness. 'WHO ARE WE TO BE RIGHTEOUS?' he asked us. 'I HAVE MURDERED TADPOLES AND TOADS – I'VE BEEN A MASS-

MURDERER OF INNOCENT WILDLIFE!' He described his mutilations in a self-condemnatory, regretful tone; although he also confessed his slight vandalism of the sainted Mary Magdalene, I was amused to see that he offered no apologies to the nuns of St Michael's – it was the tadpoles and toads he was sorry about. 'WHAT BOY HASN'T KILLED LIVE THINGS? OF COURSE, IT'S "SICK" TO BE A HANGMAN OF POOR CATS – BUT HOW IS IT *WORSE* THAN WHAT MOST OF US HAVE DONE? I HOPE WE'VE OUTGROWN IT, BUT DOES THAT MEAN WE FORGET THAT WE WERE LIKE THAT? DO THE FACULTY REMEMBER BEING BOYS? HOW CAN THEY PRESUME TO TEACH US ABOUT OURSELVES IF THEY DON'T REMEMBER BEING LIKE US? IF THIS IS A PLACE WHERE WE THINK THE TEACHING IS SO GREAT, WHY NOT *TEACH* THE KID THAT KILLING CATS IS "SICK" – WHY THROW HIM OUT?'

It would grow to be a theme of Owen's: 'WHY THROW HIM OUT?' he would ask, repeatedly. When he agreed that someone *should* have been thrown out, he said so. Drinking was punishable by dismissal, but Owen argued that getting other students drunk should be a more punishable offense than solitary drinking; also, that most forms of drinking were 'NOT AS DESTRUCTIVE AS THE ALMOST-ROUTINE HARASSMENT OF STUDENTS WHO ARE NOT "COOL" BY STUDENTS WHO THINK IT IS "COOL" TO BE HARSHLY ABUSIVE – BOTH VERBALLY ABUSIVE AND PHYSICALLY INTIMIDATING. CRUEL AND DELIBERATE MOCKERY IS WORSE THAN DRINKING; STUDENTS WHO BAIT AND MERCILESSLY TEASE THEIR FELLOW STUDENTS ARE GUILTY OF WHAT *SHOULD* BE A MORE "PUNISHABLE OFFENSE" THAN GETTING DRUNK – ESPECIALLY IN THOSE INSTANCES WHEN YOUR DRUNKENNESS HURTS NO ONE BUT YOURSELF.'

It was well known that The Voice didn't drink; he was 'black-coffee Meany,' and 'pack-a-day Meany'; he believed in his own alertness – he was sharp, he wanted to stay sharp. His column on 'THE PERILS OF DRINK AND DRUGS' must have appealed even to his critics; if he was not afraid of the faculty, he was also not afraid of his peers. It was still only our first, our ninth-grade year, when Owen invited Hester to the Senior Dance – in Noah and Simon's graduating year, Owen Meany dared to invite their dreaded sister to their senior-class dance!

'She'll just use you to meet other guys,' Noah warned him.

'She'll fuck our whole class and leave you looking at the chandelier,' Simon told Owen.

I was furious with him. I wished I'd had the nerve to ask Hester to be *my* date; but how do you 'date' your first cousin?

Noah and Simon and I commiserated; as much as Owen had captured our admiration, he had risked embarrassing himself – and all of us – by being the instrument of Hester's debut at Gravesend Academy.

'Hester the Molester,' Simon repeated and repeated.

'She's just a Sawyer Depot kind of girl,' Noah said condescendingly.

But Hester knew much more about Gravesend Academy than any of us knew she knew; on that balmy, spring weekend in 1959, Hester arrived *prepared*. After all, Owen had sent her every issue of *The Grave*; if she had once regarded Owen with distaste – she had called him queer and crazy, and a creep – Hester was no fool. She could tell when a star had risen. And Hester was committed to irreverence; it should have been no surprise to Noah and Simon and me that The Voice had won her heart.

Whatever had been her actual experience with the black boatman from Tortola, the encounter had lent to Hester's recklessly blooming young womanhood a measure of restraint that women gain from only the most tragic entanglements with love; in addition to her dark and primitive beauty, and a substantial loss of weight that drew one's attention to her full, imposing bosom and to the hardness of the bones in her somber face, Hester now held herself back just enough to make her dangerousness both more subtle and more absolute. Her wariness matured her; she had always known how to dress – I think it ran in the family. In Hester's case, she wore simple, expensive clothes – but more casually than the designer had intended, and the fit was never quite right; her body belonged in the jungle, covered only essentially, possibly with fur or grass. For the Senior Dance, she wore a short black dress with spaghetti straps as thin as string; the dress had a full skirt, a fitted waist, and a deeply plunging neckline that exposed a broad expanse of Hester's throat and chest – a fetching background for the necklace of rose-gray pearls my Aunt Martha had given her for her seventeenth birthday. She wore no stockings and danced barefoot; around one ankle was a black rawhide thong, from which a turquoise bauble dangled – touching the top of her foot. Its value could have been only sentimental; Noah implied that the Tortola boatman had given it to her. At the Senior Dance, the faculty chaperones – and their wives – never took their eyes off her. We were all enthralled. When Owen Meany danced with Hester, the sharp bridge of his nose fit perfectly in her cleavage; no one even 'cut in.'

There we were, in our rented tuxedos, boys more afraid of pimples than of war; but Owen's tux was not rented – my grandmother had bought it for him – and in its tailoring, in its lack of shine, in its touch of satin on its slim lapels, it eloquently spoke to the matter that was so obvious to us all: how The Voice expressed what we were unable to say.

Like all dances at the academy, this one ended under extreme supervision; no one could leave the dance early; and when one left, and had escorted one's date to the visitor's dorm, one returned to one's own dorm and 'checked in' precisely fifteen minutes after having 'checked out' of the dance. But Hester was staying at 80 Front Street.

I was too mortified to spend that weekend at my grandmother's – with Hester as Owen's date – and so I returned to Dan's dorm with the other boys who marched to the school's rules. Owen, who had the day boy's standing permission to drive himself to and from the academy, drove Hester back to 80 Front Street. Once in the cab of the tomato-red pickup, Hester and Owen were freed from the regulations of the Dance Committee; they lit up, the smoke from their cigarettes concealed the assumed complacency of their expressions, and each of them lolled an arm out a rolled-down window as Owen turned up the volume of the radio and drove artfully away. With his cigarette, with Hester beside him – in his tux, in the high cab of that tomato-red pickup – Owen Meany looked almost *tall*.

Other boys claimed that they 'did it' in the bushes – between leaving the dance and arriving at their dorms. Other boys displayed kissing techniques in lobbies, risked 'copping a feel' in coat rooms, defied the chaperones' quick censure of anything as vulgar as sticking a tongue in a girl's ear. But beyond the indisputable fact of his nose embedded in Hester's cleavage, Owen and Hester did not resort to either common or gross forms of public affection. And how he later rebuked our childishness by refusing to talk about her; if he 'did it' with her, The Voice was not bragging about it. He took Hester back to 80 Front Street and they watched *The Late Show* together; he drove himself back to the quarry – 'IT WAS RATHER LATE,' he admitted.

'What was the movie?' I asked.

'WHAT MOVIE?'

'On *The Late Show*!'

'OH, I FORGET . . .'

'Hester must have fucked his brains out,' Simon said morosely; Noah hit him. 'Since when does Owen "forget" a movie?' Simon cried; but Noah hit him again. 'Owen even remembers *The Robe*!' Simon said; Noah hit him in the mouth, and Simon started swinging. 'It doesn't *matter*!' Simon yelled. 'Hester fucks *everybody*!'

Noah had his brother by the throat. 'We don't *know* that,' he said to Simon.

'We *think* it!' Simon cried.

'It's okay to think it,' Noah told his brother; he rubbed his forearm back and forth across Simon's nose, which began to bleed. 'But if we don't know it, we don't *say* it.'

'Hester fucked Owen's brains out!' Simon screamed; Noah drove the point of his elbow into the hollow between Simon's eyes.

'We don't *know* that,' he repeated; but I had grown accustomed to their savage fights – they no longer frightened me. Their brutality seemed plain and safe alongside my conflicted feelings for Hester, my crushing envy of Owen.

Once again, The Voice put us in our places. 'IT IS HARD TO KNOW, IN THE WAKE OF THE DISTURBING DANCE-WEEKEND, WHETHER OUR ESTEEMED PEERS OR OUR ESTEEMED FACULTY CHAPERONES SHOULD BE MORE ASHAMED OF THEMSELVES. IT IS PUERILE FOR YOUNG MEN TO DISCUSS WHAT DEGREE OF ADVANTAGE THEY TOOK OF THEIR DATES; IT IS DISRESPECTFUL OF WOMEN – ALL THIS CHEAP BRAGGING – AND IT GIVES MEN A BAD REPUTATION. WHY SHOULD WOMEN TRUST US? BUT IT IS HARD TO SAY WHETHER THIS BOORISH BEHAVIOR IS WORSE OR BETTER THAN

THE GESTAPO TACTICS OF OUR PURITAN CHAPERONES. THE DEAN'S OFFICE TELLS ME THAT TWO SENIORS HAVE RECEIVED NOTICE OF DISCIPLINARY PROBATION – FOR THE REMAINDER OF THE TERM! – FOR THEIR ALLEGED "OVERT INDISCRETIONS"; I BELIEVE THE TWO INCIDENTS FALL UNDER THE PUNISHABLE OFFENSE OF "MORALLY REPREHENSIBLE CONDUCT WITH GIRLS."

'AT THE RISK OF SOUNDING *PRURIENT*, I SHALL REVEAL THE SHOCKING NATURE OF THESE TWO SINS AGAINST THE SCHOOL AND WOMANKIND. ONE! A BOY WAS FOUND "FONDLING" HIS DATE IN THE TROPHY ROOM OF THE GYM: AS THE COUPLE WAS FULLY DRESSED – AND STANDING – AT THE TIME, IT SEEMS UNLIKELY THAT A PREGNANCY COULD HAVE RESULTED FROM THEIR EXCHANGE; AND ALTHOUGH THE GYM IS NOTORIOUS FOR IT, I'M SURE THEY HADN'T EVEN EXPOSED THEMSELVES SUFFICIENTLY TO RISK AN ATHLETE'S FOOT INFECTION. TWO! A BOY WAS SEEN LEAVING THE BUTT ROOM IN BANCROFT HALL WITH HIS TONGUE IN HIS DATE'S EAR – AN ODD AND OSTENTATIOUS MANNER IN WHICH TO EXIT A SMOKING LOUNGE, I WILL AGREE, BUT THIS DEGREE OF PHYSICAL CONTACT IS ALSO NOT KNOWN TO RESULT IN A PREGNANCY. TO MY KNOWLEDGE, IT IS EVEN DIFFICULT TO COMMUNICATE THE COMMON COLD BY THIS METHOD.'

After that one, it became customary for the applicants – for the position of headmaster – to request to meet him when they were interviewed. The Search Committee had a student subcommittee available to interview each candidate; but when the candidates asked to meet The Voice, Owen insisted that he be given A PRIVATE AUDIENCE. The issue of Owen being granted this privilege was the subject of a special faculty meeting where tempers flared; Dan said there was a movement to replace the faculty adviser to *The Grave* – there were those who said that the 'pregnancy humor' in Owen's column about the Senior Dance should not have escaped the adviser's censorship. But the faculty adviser to *The Grave* was an Owen Meany supporter; Mr Early – that deeply flawed thespian who brought to every role he was given in The

Gravesend Players an overblown and befuddled sense of Learlike doom – cried that he would defend the 'unsullied genius' of The Voice, if necessary, 'to the death.' That would not be necessary, Dan Needham was sure; but that Owen was supported by such a boob as Mr Early was conceivably worse than no defense at all.

Several applicants for the headmaster position admitted that their interviews with The Voice had been 'daunting'; I'm sure that they were unprepared for his size, and when they heard him speak, I'm sure they got the shivers and were troubled by the absurdity of *that* voice communicating strictly in upper-case letters. One of the favored candidates withdrew his application; although there was no direct evidence that Owen had contributed to the candidate's retreat, the man admitted there was a certain quality of 'accepted cynicism' among the students that had 'depressed' him. The man added that these students demonstrated an 'attitude of superiority' – and 'such a degree of freedom of speech as to make their liberal education *too* liberal.'

'Nonsense!' Dan Needham had cried in the faculty meeting. 'Owen Meany isn't cynical! If this guy *was* referring to Owen, he was referring to him incorrectly. Good riddance!'

But not all the faculty felt that way. The Search Committee would need another year to satisfy their search; the present headmaster cheerfully agreed – for the good of the school – to stall his retirement. He was all 'for the good of the school,' the old headmaster; and it was *his* support of Owen Meany that – for a while – kept Owen's enemies from his throat.

'He's a delightful little fella!' the headmaster said. 'I wouldn't miss reading The Voice – not for all the world!'

His name was Archibald Thorndike, and he'd been headmaster forever; he'd married the daughter of the headmaster before him, and he was about as 'old school' as a headmaster could get. Although the newer, more progressive-minded faculty complained about Archie Thorndike's reluctance to change a single course requirement – not to mention his views of 'the whole boy' – the headmaster had no enemies. Old 'Thorny,' as he was called – and he encouraged even the boys to address him as 'Thorny' – was so headmasterly in every pleasing, comfortable, superficial way that no one could feel unfriendly toward him. He was a tall, broad-shouldered, white-haired man with a face as serviceable as an oar; in fact, he was an oarsman, and an outdoorsman – a man who preferred soft, unironed trousers, maybe khakis or corduroys, and a tweed jacket with the elbow patches in need of a thread here or there. He went hatless in our New Hampshire winters, and was such a supporter of our teams – in the rawest weather – that he wore a scar from an errant hockey puck as proudly as a merit badge; the puck had struck him above the eye while he'd tended the goal during the annual Alumni-Varsity game. Thorny was an honorary member of several of Gravesend's graduating classes. He played every alumni game in the goal.

'Ice hockey's not a sissy sport!' he liked to say. In another vein, in defense of Owen Meany, he maintained: 'It is the well educated who will improve society – and they will improve it, at first, by criticizing it, and we are giving them the tools to criticize it. Naturally, as students, the brighter of them will begin their improvements upon society by criticizing *us*.' To Owen, old Archie Thorndike would sing a slightly different song: 'It is your responsibility to find fault with me, it is mine to hear you out. But don't expect me to change. *I'm* not going to change; I'm going to *retire*! Get the *new* headmaster to make the changes; that's when *I* made changes – when I was new.'

'WHAT CHANGES DID YOU MAKE?' Owen Meany asked.

'That's another reason I'm retiring!' old Thorny told Owen amiably. 'My memory's shot!'

Owen thought that Archibald Thorndike was a blithering, glad-handing fool; but everyone, even The Voice, thought that old Thorny was a nice guy. 'NICE GUYS ARE THE TOUGHEST TO GET RID OF,' Owen wrote for *The Grave*; but even Mr Early was smart enough to censor *that*.

Then it was summer; The Voice went back to work in the quarries – I don't think he said much down in the pits – and I had my first job. I was a guide for the Gravesend Academy Admissions Office; I showed the school to prospective students and their parents – it was boring, but it certainly wasn't hard. I had a ring of master keys, which amounted to the greatest responsibility anyone had given me, and I had freedom of choice regarding which typical classroom I would show, and which 'typical' dormitory room. I chose rooms at random in Waterhouse Hall, in the vague hope that I might surprise Mr and Mrs Brinker-Smith at their game of musical beds; but the twins were older now, and maybe the Brinker-Smiths didn't 'do it' with their former gusto.

In the evenings, at Hampton Beach, Owen looked tired to me; I reported to the Admissions Office for my first guided tour at ten, but Owen was stepping into the grout bucket by seven every morning. His fingernails were cracked; his hands were cut and swollen; his arms were tanned and thin and hard. He didn't talk about Hester. The summer of '59 was the first summer that we met with any success in picking up girls; or, rather, Owen met with this success, and he introduced the girls he met to me. We didn't 'do it' that summer; at least, *I* didn't, and – to my knowledge – Owen never had a date alone.

'IT'S A DOUBLE DATE OR IT'S NOTHING,' he'd tell one surprised girl after another. 'ASK YOUR FRIEND OR FORGET IT.'

And we were no longer afraid to cruise the pinball arcades around the casino on foot; delinquent thugs would still pick on Owen, but he quickly established a reputation as an untouchable.

'YOU WANT TO BEAT ME UP?' he'd say to some punk. 'YOU WANT TO GO TO JAIL? YOU'RE SO UGLY – YOU THINK I'LL HAVE TROUBLE REMEMBERING YOUR FACE?' Then he'd point to me. 'YOU SEE HIM? ARE YOU SUCH AN ASSHOLE YOU DON'T KNOW WHAT A *WITNESS* IS? GO AHEAD – BEAT ME UP!' Only one guy did – or tried. It was like watching a dog go after a raccoon; the dog does all the work, but the raccoon gets the better of it. Owen just covered up; he grabbed for hands and feet, he went for the fingers first, but he was content to tear off a shoe and go for the toes. He took a pounding but he wrapped himself into a ball; he left no extremities showing. He broke the guy's pinky – he bent it so sharply that after the fight the guy's little finger pointed straight up off the back of his hand. He tore one of the guy's shoes off and bit his toes; there was a lot of blood, but the guy was wearing a sock – I couldn't see the actual damage, only that he had trouble walking. The guy was pulled off Owen by a cotton-candy vendor – he was arrested shortly thereafter for screaming obscenities, and we heard he was sent to reform school because he turned out to be driving a stolen car. We never saw him on the beachfront again, and the word about Owen – on the strip, around the casino, and along the boardwalk – was that he was dangerous to pick a fight with; the rumor was that he'd bitten off someone's ear. Another summer, I heard that he'd blinded a guy with a Popsicle stick. That these reports weren't exactly true did not matter at Hampton Beach. He was 'that little dude in the red pickup,' he was 'the quarry-worker – he carries some kind of tool on him.' He was 'a mean little fucker – watch out for him.'

We were seventeen; we had a sullen summer. In the fall, Noah and Simon started college out on the West Coast; they went to one of those California universities that no one on the East Coast can ever remember the name of. And the Eastmans continued their folly of considering Hester as less of an investment; they sent her to the University of New Hampshire, where – as a resident – she merited in-state tuition. 'They want to keep me in their own backyard,' was how Hester put it.

'THEY PUT HER IN *OUR* BACKYARD,' was how Owen put it; the state university was only a twenty-minute drive from Gravesend. That it was a better university than the tanning club that Noah and Simon attended in California was not an argument that impressed Hester; the *boys* got to travel, the *boys* got the more agreeable climate – *she* got to stay home. To New Hampshire natives, the state university – notwithstanding how basically solid an education it offered – was not exotic; to Gravesend Academy students, with their elitist eyes on the Ivy League schools, it was 'a cow college,' wholly beyond redemption. But in the fall of '59, when Owen and I began our tenth-grade year at the academy, Owen was regarded as especially gifted – by our peers – because he was dating a college girl; that Hester was a cow-college girl did not tarnish Owen's reputation. He was Ladies' Man Meany, he was Older-Woman Master; and he was still and would always be The Voice. He demanded attention; and he got it.

Toronto: May 9, 1987 – Gary Hart, a former U.S. senator from Colorado, quit his campaign for the presidency after some Washington reporters caught him shacked up for the weekend with a Miami model; although both the model and the candidate claimed that nothing 'immoral' occurred – and Mrs Hart said that she supported her husband, or maybe it was that she 'understood' him – Mr Hart decided that such intense scrutiny of his personal life created an 'intolerable situation' for him and his family. He'll be back; want to bet? In the United States, no one like him disappears for long; remember Nixon?

What *do* Americans know about morality? They don't want their presidents to have penises but they don't mind if their presidents covertly arrange to support the Nicaraguan rebel forces after Congress has restricted such aid; they don't want their presidents to deceive their wives but they don't mind if their presidents deceive Congress – lie to the people and violate the *people's* constitution! What Mr Hart should have said was that nothing *unusually* immoral had occurred, or that what happened was only *typically* immoral; or that he was testing his abilities to deceive the American people by deceiving his wife first – and that he hoped the people would see by this example that he was immoral *enough* to be good presidential material! I can just hear what The Voice would have said about all this.

A sunny day; my fellow Canadians in Winston Churchill Park have their bellies turned toward the sun. All the girls at Bishop Strachan are tugging up their middies and hiking up their pleated skirts; they are pushing their knee socks down around their ankles; the whole world wants a tan. But Owen hated the spring; the warm weather made him think that school was almost over, and Owen loved school. When school was over, Owen Meany went back to the quarries.

When school began again – when we started the fall term of 1959 – I realized that The Voice had not been idle for the summer; Owen came back to school with a stack of columns ready for *The Grave*. He charged the Search Committee to find a new headmaster who was dedicated to serving the faculty and the students – 'NOT A SERVANT OF THE ALUMNI AND THE TRUSTEES.' Although he made fun of Thorny – particularly, of old Archie Thorndike's notion of 'the whole boy' – Owen praised our departing headmaster for being 'AN EDUCATIOR FIRST, A FUND-RAISER SECOND,' Owen cautioned the Search Committee to 'BEWARE OF THE BOARD OF TRUSTEES – THEY'LL PICK A HEADMASTER WHO CARES MORE ABOUT FUND DRIVES THAN THE CURRICULUM OR THE FACULTY WHO TEACH IT. AND

DON'T LISTEN TO THE ALUMNI!' warned The Voice; Owen had a low opinion of the alumni. 'THEY CAN'T EVEN BE TRUSTED TO REMEMBER WHAT IT WAS REALLY LIKE TO BE HERE; THEY'RE ALWAYS TALKING ABOUT WHAT THE SCHOOL *DID* FOR THEM – OR HOW THE SCHOOL *MADE* SOMETHING OUT OF THEM, AS IF THEY WERE UNFORMED CLAY WHEN THEY CAME HERE. AS FOR HOW HARSH THE SCHOOL COULD BE, AS FOR HOW MISERABLE THEY WERE WHEN THEY WERE STUDENTS – THE ALUMNI HAVE CONVENIENTLY FORGOTTEN.'

Someone in faculty meeting called Owen 'that little turd'; Dan Needham argued that Owen truly adored the school, but that a Gravesend education did not and should not teach respect for uncritical love, for blind devotion. It became harder to defend Owen when he started the petition against fish on Fridays.

'WE HAVE A NONDENOMINATIONAL CHURCH,' he stated. 'WHY DO WE HAVE A CATHOLIC DINING HALL? IF CATHOLICS WANT TO EAT FISH ON FRIDAY, WHY MUST THE REST OF US JOIN THEM? MOST KIDS HATE FISH! SERVE FISH BUT SERVE SOMETHING ELSE, TOO – COLD CUTS, OR EVEN PEANUT-BUTTER-AND-JELLY SANDWICHES. WE ARE FREE TO LISTEN TO THE GUEST PREACHER AT HURD'S CHURCH, OR WE CAN ATTEND ANY OF THE TOWN CHURCHES OF OUR CHOICE; JEWS AREN'T FORCED TO TAKE COMMUNION, UNITARIANS AREN'T DRAGGED TO MASS – OR TO CONFESSION – BAPTISTS AREN'T ROUNDED UP ON SATURDAYS AND HERDED OFF TO SYNAGOGUE (OR TO THEIR OWN, UNWILLING CIRCUMCISIONS). YET NON-CATHOLICS MUST EAT FISH; ON FRIDAYS, IT'S EAT FISH OR GO HUNGRY. I THOUGHT THIS WAS A DEMOCRACY. ARE WE ALL FORCED TO SUBSCRIBE TO THE CATHOLIC VIEW OF BIRTH CONTROL? WHY ARE WE FORCED TO EAT CATHOLIC FOOD?'

He set up a chair and desk in the school post office to collect signatures for his petition – naturally, everyone signed it. 'EVEN THE CATHOLICS SIGNED IT!' announced The Voice. Dan Needham said that the food service manager put on quite a show in faculty meeting.

'Next thing you know, *that little turd* will want a salad bar!

He'll want an alternative to *every* menu – not just fish on Fridays!'

In his first column, The Voice had attacked MYSTERY MEAT; now it was fish. 'THIS UNJUST IMPOSITION ENCOURAGES RELIGIOUS PERSECUTION,' said The Voice; Owen saw signs of anti-Catholicism springing up everywhere. 'THERE'S SOME BAD TALK GOING AROUND,' he reported. 'THE CLIMATE OF THE SCHOOL IS BECOMING DISCRIMINATORY. I HEAR THE OFFENSIVE SLUR, "MACKEREL-SNAPPER" – AND YOU NEVER USED TO HEAR THAT KIND OF TALK AROUND HERE.' Frankly, *I* never heard anyone use the term 'mackerel-snapper' – except Owen!

And we couldn't pass St Michael's – not to mention the sainted statue of Mary Magdalene – without his saying, 'I WONDER WHAT THE PENGUINS ARE UP TO? DO YOU THINK THEY'RE ALL LESBIANS?'

It was the first Friday following Thanksgiving vacation when they served cold cuts and peanut-butter-and-jelly sandwiches with the standard fish dish; you could also get a bowl of tomato soup, and potato salad. He had won. He got a standing ovation in the dining hall. As a scholarship boy, he had a job – he was a waiter at a faculty table; the serving tray was half his size and he stood at attention beside it, as if it were a shield, while the students applauded him and the faculty smiled a trifle stiffly.

Old Thorny called him into his office. 'You know, I like you, little fella,' he told Owen. 'You're a go-getter! But let me give you some advice. Your friends don't watch you as closely as your enemies – and you've got enemies. You've made more enemies in less than two years than I've made in more than twenty! Be careful you don't give your enemies a way to get you.'

Thorny wanted Owen to cox the varsity crew; Owen was the perfect size for a coxswain, and – after all – he'd grown up on the Squamscott. But Owen said that the racing shells had always offended his father – 'IT'S A MATTER OF BLOOD BEING THICKER THAN SCHOOL,' he told the headmaster; furthermore, the river was polluted. In those days, the town didn't have a proper sewage system; the textile mill, my late grandfather's former shoe factory, and many private homes simply dumped their waste into the Squamscott. Owen said he had often seen 'beetleskins' floating in the river; beetleskins still gave him the shivers.

Besides, in the fall he liked soccer; of course, he wasn't on the varsity or the junior varsity – but he had fun playing soccer, even on the lowest club-level. He was fast and scrappy – although, from all his smoking, he was easily winded. And in the spring – the other season for crew – Owen liked to play tennis; he wasn't very good, he was just a beginner, but my grandmother bought him a good racquet and Owen appreciated the orderliness of the game. The straight white lines, the proper tension in the net at its exactly correct height, the precise scoring. In the winter – God knows why! – he liked basketball; perversely, perhaps, because it was a tall boy's game. He played only in pickup games, to be sure – he could never have played on any of the teams – but he played with enthusiasm; he was quite a leaper, he had a jump shot that elevated him almost to eye-level with the other players, and he became obsessed with an impossible frill of the game ('impossible' for him): the slam-dunk. We didn't call it a 'slam-dunk' then; we called it 'stuffing' the ball, and there wasn't very much of it – most kids weren't tall enough. Of course, Owen could never leap high enough to be above the basket; to stuff the ball *down* into the basket was a nonsense idea he had – it was his absurd goal.

He would devise an approach to the basket; dribbling at good speed, he would time his leap to coincide with a teammate's readiness to *lift* him higher – he would jump into a teammate's waiting arms, and the teammate would (occasionally) *boost* Owen above the basket's rim. I was the only one who was willing to practice the timing with him; it was such a ridiculous thing for him to want to do – for someone his size to set himself the challenge of soaring and reaching so high . . . it was just silliness, and I tired of the mindless, repetitive choreography.

'Why are we doing this?' I'd ask him. 'It would never work in a game. It's probably not even legal. I can't *lift* you up to the basket, I'm sure that's not allowed.'

But Owen reminded me that I had once enjoyed *lifting* him up – at Sunday school. Now that it mattered to him, to get the timing of his leap adjusted to my lifting him even higher, why couldn't I simply indulge him without criticizing him?

'I TOLERATED YOU LIFTING ME UP – ALL THOSE YEARS WHEN I ASKED YOU NOT TO!' he said.

' "All those years," ' I repeated. 'It was only a few Sunday school classes, it was only for a *couple* of years – and we didn't do it every time.'

But it was important to him now – this crazy lifting him up – and so we did it. It became a very well-rehearsed stunt with us; 'Slam-Dunk Meany,' some of the boys on the basketball team began to call him – Slam-Dunk Master, after he'd perfected the move. Even the basketball coach was appreciative. 'I may use you in a game, Owen,' the coach said, joking with him.

'IT'S NOT FOR A GAME,' said Owen Meany, who had his own reasons for everything.

That Christmas vacation of '59, we were in the Gravesend gym for hours every day; we were alone, and undisturbed – all the boarders had gone home – and we were full of contempt for the Eastmans, who appeared to be making a point of not inviting us to Sawyer Depot. Noah and Simon had brought a friend home from California; Hester was 'in and out'; and some old friend of my Aunt Martha, from her university days, 'might' be visiting. The real reason we were not invited, Owen and I were sure, was that Aunt Martha wanted to discourage the relationship between Owen and Hester. Hester had told Owen that her mother referred to him as 'the boy who hit that ball,' and as 'that strange little friend of John's' – and 'that boy my mother is dressing up like a little doll.' But Hester thought so ill of her mother, and she was such a troublemaker, she might have made up all that and told Owen – chiefly so that Owen would dislike Aunt Martha, too. Owen didn't seem to care.

I had been granted an extension to make up two late term papers over the vacation – so it wasn't much of a vacation, anyway; Owen helped me with the history paper and he wrote the English paper for me. 'I PURPOSELY DIDN'T SPELL EVERYTHING CORRECTLY. I MADE A FEW GRAMMATICAL ERRORS – OF THE KIND YOU USUALLY MAKE,' he told me. 'I REPEATED MYSELF OCCASIONALLY, AND THERE'S NO MENTION OF THE MIDDLE OF THE BOOK – AS IF YOU SKIPPED THAT PART. THAT'S THE PART YOU SKIPPED, RIGHT?'

It was a problem: how my in-class writing, my quizzes and

examinations, were not at all as good as the work Owen helped me with. But we studied for all announced tests together, and I was – gradually – improving as a student. Because of my weak spelling I was enrolled in an extra, remedial course, which was marginally insulting, and – also because of my spelling, and my often erratic performance when I was called upon in the classroom – I was asked to see the school psychiatrist once a week. Gravesend Academy was used to good students; when someone struggled, academically – even when one simply couldn't spell properly! – it was assumed to be a matter for a shrink.

The Voice had something to say about that, too. 'IT SEEMS TO ME THAT PEOPLE WHO DON'T LEARN AS EASILY AS OTHERS SUFFER FROM A KIND OF LEARNING DISABILITY – THERE IS SOMETHING THAT INTERFERES WITH THE WAY THEY PERCEIVE NUMBERS AND LETTERS, THERE IS SOMETHING DIFFERENT ABOUT THE WAY THEY COMPREHEND UNFAMILIAR MATERIAL – BUT I FAIL TO SEE HOW THIS DISABILITY IS IMPROVED BY PSYCHIATRIC CONSULTATION. WHAT SEEMS TO BE LACKING IS A TECHNICAL ABILITY THAT THOSE OF US CALLED "GOOD STUDENTS" ARE BORN WITH. SOMEONE SHOULD CONCRETELY STUDY THESE SKILLS AND TEACH THEM. WHAT DOES A SHRINK HAVE TO DO WITH THE PROCESS?'

These were the days before we'd heard about dyslexia and other 'learning disabilities'; students like me were simply thought to be stupid, or slow. It was Owen who isolated my problem. 'YOU'RE MAINLY SLOW,' he said. 'YOU'RE ALMOST AS SMART AS I AM, BUT YOU NEED TWICE THE TIME.' The school psychiatrist – a retired Swiss gentleman who returned, every summer, to Zürich – was convinced that my difficulties as a student were the result of my best friend's 'murder' of my mother, and the 'tensions and conflicts' that he saw as the 'inevitable result' of my dividing my life between my grandmother and my stepfather.

'At times, you must hate him – yes?' Dr Dolder mused.

'Hate who?' I asked. 'My stepfather? No – I *love* Dan!'

'Your best friend – at times, you hate *him*. Yes?' Dr Dolder asked.

'No!' I said. 'I *love* Owen – it was an *accident*.'

'Yes, I know,' Dr Dolder said. 'But nonetheless . . . your grandmother, perhaps, she is a most difficult reminder – yes?'
'A "reminder"?' I said. 'I *love* my grandmother!'
'Yes, I know,' Dr Dolder said. 'But this baseball business – it's most difficult, I imagine . . .'
'Yes!' I said. 'I hate baseball.'
'Yes, for sure,' Dr Dolder said. 'I've never seen a game, so it's hard for me to imagine exactly . . . perhaps we should take in a game together?'
'No,' I said. 'I don't play baseball, I don't even watch it!'
'Yes, I see,' Dr Dolder said. 'You hate it *that* much – I see!'
'I can't spell,' I said. 'I'm a slow reader, I get tired – I have to keep my finger on the particular sentence, or I'll lose my place . . .'
'It must be rather *hard* – a baseball,' Dr Dolder said. 'Yes?'
'Yes, it's very hard,' I said; I sighed.
'Yes, I see,' Dr Dolder said. 'Are you tired now? Are you getting tired?'
'It's the *spelling*,' I told him. 'The spelling and the reading.'
There were photographs on the wall of his office in the Hubbard Infirmary – they were old black-and-white photographs of the clockfaces on the church spires in Zürich; and photographs of the water birds in the Limmat, and of the people feeding the birds from those funny, arched footbridges. Many of the people wore hats; you could almost hear those cathedral clocks sounding the hour.
Dr Dolder had a quizzical expression on his long, goat-shaped face; his silver-white Vandyke beard was neatly trimmed, but the doctor often tugged its point.
'A baseball,' he said thoughtfully. 'Next time, you will bring a baseball – yes?'
'Yes, of course,' I said.
'And this little baseball-hitter – The Voice, yes? – I would very much like to talk to him, too,' said Dr Dolder.
'I'll ask Owen if he's free,' I said.
'NOT A CHANCE,' said Owen Meany, when I asked him. 'THERE'S NOTHING THE MATTER WITH MY SPELLING!'

Toronto: May 11, 1987 – I regret that I had the right change to get *The Globe and Mail* out of the street-corner box; I had three dimes in my pocket, and a sentence in a front-page article proved irresistible. 'It was unclear how Mr Reagan intended to have his Administration maintain support for the contras while remaining within the law.'

Since when did Mr Reagan care about 'remaining within the law'? I wish the president would spend a weekend with a Miami model; he could do a lot less harm that way. Think how relieved the Nicaraguans would be, if only for a weekend! We ought to find a model for the president to spend *every* weekend with! If we could tire the old geezer out, he wouldn't be capable of more damaging mischief. Oh, what a nation of moralists the Americans are! With what fervor do they relish bringing their sexual misconduct to light! A pity that they do not bring their moral outrage to bear on their president's arrogance above the law; a pity that they do not unleash their moral zest on an administration that runs guns to terrorists. But, of course, boudoir morality takes less imagination, and can be indulged in without the effort of keeping up with world affairs – or even bothering to know 'the whole story' behind the sexual adventure.

It's sunny again in Toronto today; the fruit trees are blossoming – especially the pears and apples and crab apples. There's a chance of showers. Owen liked the rain. In the summer, in the bottom of a quarry, it could be brutally hot, and the dust was always a factor; the rain cooled the rock slabs, the rain held the dust down. 'ALL QUARRYMEN LIKE RAIN,' said Owen Meany.

I told my Grade 12 English class that they should reread what Hardy called the first 'phase' of *Tess of the d'Urbervilles*, the part called 'The Maiden'; although I had drawn their attention to Hardy's fondness for foreshadowing, the class was especially sleepyheaded at spotting these devices. How could they have read over the death of the horse so carelessly? 'Nobody blamed Tess as she blamed herself,' Hardy writes; he even says, 'Her face was dry and pale, as though she regarded herself in the light of a murderess.' And what did the class make of Tess's physical appearance? 'It was a luxuriance of aspect, a fullness of growth, which made her appear more of a woman than she really was.' They made nothing of it.

'Don't some of you look like that – to yourselves?' I asked the class. 'What do you think about when you see one of yourselves who looks like that?'

Silence.

And what did they think happened at the end of the first 'phase' – was Tess seduced, or was she raped? 'She was sleeping soundly,' Hardy writes. Does he mean that d'Urberville 'did it' to her when she was asleep?

Silence.

Before they trouble themselves to read the second 'phase' of *Tess*, called 'Maiden No More,' I suggested that they trouble themselves to *re*read 'The Maiden' – or, perhaps, read it for the first time, as the case may be!

'Pay attention,' I warned them. 'When Tess says, "Did it never strike your mind that what every woman says some women may feel?" – pay attention! Pay attention to *where* Tess's child is buried – "in that shabby corner of God's allotment where he lets the nettles grow, and where all unbaptized infants, notorious drunkards, suicides, and others of the conjecturally damned are laid." Ask yourself what Hardy thinks of "God's allotment" – and what does he think of bad luck, of coincidence, of so-called circumstances beyond our control? And does he imagine that being a *virtuous* character exposes you to greater or fewer liabilities as you roam the world?'

'Sir?' said Leslie Ann Grew. That was very old-fashioned of her; it's been years since anyone called me 'Sir' at Bishop Strachan – unless it was a new kid. Leslie Ann Grew has been here for years. 'If it's another nice day tomorrow,' said Leslie Ann, 'can we have class *outside*?'

'No,' I said; but I'm so slow – I feel so dull. I know what The Voice would have told her.

'ONLY IF IT RAINS,' Owen would have said. 'IF IT POURS, THEN WE CAN HAVE CLASS OUTSIDE.'

At the start of the winter term of our tenth-grade year at Gravesend Academy, the school's gouty minister – the Rev. Mr Scammon, the officiant of the academy's non-denominational faith and the lackluster teacher of our Religion and Scripture classes – cracked his head on the icy steps of Hurd's Church and failed to regain consciousness. Owen was of the opinion that the Rev. Mr Scammon never *was* fully conscious. For weeks after his demise, his vestments and his cane hung from the coat tree in the vestry office – as if old Mr Scammon had journeyed no farther from this world than to the adjacent toilet. The Rev. Lewis Merrill was hired as his temporary replacement in our Religion and Scripture classes, and a Search Committee was formed to find a new school minister.

Owen and I had suffered through Religion One together in our ninth-grade year: old Mr Scammon's sweeping, Caesar-to-Eisenhower approach to the major religions of the world. We had been suffering Scammon's Scripture course – and his Religion Two – when the icy steps of Hurd's Church rose to meet him. The Rev. Mr Merrill brought his familiar stutter and his almost-as-familiar doubts to both courses. In Scripture, he set us to work in our Bibles – to find plentiful examples of Isaiah 5:20: 'Woe unto them that call evil good and good evil.' In Religion Two – a heavy-reading course in 'religion and literature' – we were instructed to divine Tolstoy's meaning: 'There was no solution,' Tolstoy writes in *Anna Karenina*, 'but the universal solution that life gives to all questions, even the most complex and insoluble. That answer is: one must live in the needs of the day – that is forget oneself.'

In both classes, Pastor Merrill preached his doubt-is-the-essence-of-and-not-the-opposite-of-faith philosophy; it was a point of view that interested Owen more than it had once interested him. The apparent secret was 'belief without miracles'; a faith that needed a miracle was not a faith at all. Don't ask for proof – that was Mr Merrill's routine message.

'BUT EVERYONE NEEDS A *LITTLE* PROOF,' said Owen Meany.

'Faith itself is a miracle, Owen', said Pastor Merrill. 'The first miracle that I believe in is my own faith itself.'

Owen looked doubtful, but he didn't speak. Our Religion Two class – and our Scripture class, too – was an atheistic mob; except for Owen Meany, we were such a negative, anti-everything bunch of morons that we thought Jack Kerouac and Allen Ginsberg were more interesting writers than Tolstoy. And so the Rev. Lewis Merrill, with his stutter and his well-worn case of doubt, had his hands full with us. He made us read Greene's *The Power and the Glory* – Owen wrote his term paper on 'THE WHISKEY PRIEST: A SEEDY SAINT.' We also read Joyce's *Portrait of the Artist as a Young Man* and Lagerkvist's *Barabbas* and Dostoevski's *The Brothers Karamazov* – Owen wrote *my* term paper on 'SIN AND SMERDYAKOV: A LETHAL COMBINATION.' Poor Pastor

Merrill! My old Congregationalist minister was suddenly cast in the role of Christianity's defender – and even Owen argued with the terms of Mr Merrill's defense. The class loved Sartre and Camus – the concept of 'the unyielding evidence of a life without consolation' was thrilling to us teenagers. The Rev. Mr Merrill countered humbly with Kierkegaard: 'What no person has a right to is to delude others into the belief that faith is something of no great significance, or that it is an easy matter, whereas it is the greatest and most difficult of all things.'

Owen, who'd had his doubts about Pastor Merrill, found himself in the role of the minister's defender. 'JUST BECAUSE A BUNCH OF ATHEISTS ARE BETTER WRITERS THAN THE GUYS WHO WROTE THE BIBLE DOESN'T NECESSARILY MAKE THEM *RIGHT*!' he said crossly. 'LOOK AT THOSE WEIRDO TV MIRACLE-WORKERS – THEY'RE TRYING TO GET PEOPLE TO BELIEVE IN MAGIC! BUT THE *REAL* MIRACLES AREN'T ANYTHING YOU CAN SEE – THEY'RE THINGS YOU HAVE TO BELIEVE WITHOUT SEEING. IF SOME PREACHER'S AN ASSHOLE, THAT'S NOT PROOF THAT GOD DOESN'T EXIST!'

'Yes, but let's not say "asshole" in class, Owen,' Pastor Merrill said.

And in our Scripture class, Owen said, 'IT'S TRUE THAT THE DISCIPLES ARE STUPID – THEY NEVER UNDERSTAND WHAT JESUS MEANS, THEY'RE A BUNCH OF BUNGLERS, THEY DON'T BELIEVE IN GOD AS MUCH AS THEY *WANT* TO BELIEVE, AND THEY EVEN BETRAY JESUS. THE POINT IS, GOD DOESN'T LOVE US BECAUSE WE'RE SMART OR BECAUSE WE'RE GOOD. WE'RE STUPID AND WE'RE BAD AND GOD LOVES US ANYWAY – JESUS ALREADY TOLD THE DUMB-SHIT DISCIPLES WHAT WAS GOING TO HAPPEN. "THE SON OF MAN WILL BE DELIVERED INTO THE HANDS OF MEN, AND THEY WILL KILL HIM . . ." REMEMBER? THAT WAS IN *MARK* – RIGHT?'

'Yes, but let's not say "dumb-shit disciples" in class, Owen,' Mr Merrill said; but although he struggled to defend God's Holy Word, Lewis Merrill – for the first time, in my memory – appeared to be enjoying himself. To have his faith assailed perked him up; he was livelier and less meek.

'I DON'T THINK THE CONGREGATIONALISTS EVER TALK TO HIM,' Owen suggested. 'I THINK HE'S LONELY FOR CONVERSATION; EVEN IF ALL HE GETS IS AN ARGUMENT, AT LEAST WE'RE TALKING TO HIM.'

'I see no evidence that his *wife* ever talks to him,' Dan Needham observed. And the monosyllabic utterances of Pastor Merrill's surly children were not of the engaging tones that invited conversation.

'WHY DOES THE SCHOOL WASTE ITS TIME WITH *TWO* SEARCH COMMITTEES?' asked The Voice in *The Grave*. 'FIND A HEADMASTER – WE *NEED* A HEADMASTER – BUT WE DON'T NEED A SCHOOL MINISTER. WITH NO DISRESPECT FOR THE DEAD, THE REV. LEWIS MERRILL IS A MORE-THAN-ADEQUATE REPLACEMENT FOR THE LATE MR SCAMMON: FRANKLY, MR MERRILL IS AN IMPROVEMENT IN THE CLASSROOM. AND THE SCHOOL THINKS WELL ENOUGH OF HIS POWERS IN THE PULPIT TO HAVE ALREADY INVITED HIM TO BE THE GUEST PREACHER AT HURD'S CHURCH – ON SEVERAL OCCASIONS. THE REV. MR MERRILL WOULD BE A GOOD SCHOOL MINISTER. WE SHOULD FIND OUT WHAT THE CONGREGATIONALISTS ARE PAYING HIM AND OFFER HIM MORE.'

And so they hired him away from the Congregationalists; once more, The Voice did not go unheard.

Toronto: May 12, 1987 – a sunny, cool day, a good day to mow a lawn. The smell of freshly cut grass all along Russell Hill Road reflects how widespread is my neighbors' interest in lawnmowing. Mrs Brocklebank – whose daughter, Heather, is in my Grade 12 English class – took a slightly different approach to her lawn; I found her ripping her dandelions out by their roots.

'You'd better do the same thing,' she said to me. 'Pull them out, don't mow them under. If you chop them up with the mower, you'll just make more of them.'

'Like starfish,' I said; I should have known better – it's never a good idea to introduce Mrs Brocklebank to a new subject, not unless you have time to kill. If I'd assigned 'The Maiden' to Mrs Brocklebank, she would have gotten everything right – the first time.

'What do you know about starfish?' she asked.

'I grew up on the seacoast,' I reminded her. It is occasionally necessary for me to tell Torontonians of the presence of the Atlantic and Pacific oceans; they tend to think of the Great Lakes as the waters of the world.

'So what about starfish?' Mrs Brocklebank asked.

'You cut them up, they grow more starfish,' I said.

'Is that in a book?' asked Mrs Brocklebank. I assured her that it was. I even have a book that describes the life of the starfish, although Owen and I knew not to chop them up long before we read about them; every kid in Gravesend learned all about starfish at the beach at Little Boar's Head. I remember my mother telling Owen and me not to cut them up; starfish are very destructive, and their powers of reproduction are not encouraged in New Hampshire.

Mrs Brocklebank is persistent regarding new information; she goes after everything as aggressively as she attacks her dandelions. 'I'd like to see that book,' she announced.

And so I began again with what has become a fairly routine labor: discouraging Mrs Brocklebank from reading another book – I work as hard at discouraging her, and with as little success, as I sometimes labor to *encourage* those BSS girls to read their assignments.

'It's not a very good book,' I said. 'It's written by an amateur; it's published by a vanity press.'

'So what's wrong with an amateur writing a book?' Mrs Brocklebank wanted to know. She is probably writing one of her own, it occurs to me now. 'So what's wrong with a "vanity press"?' she asked.

The book that tells the truth about the starfish is called *The Life of the Tidepool* by Archibald Thorndike. Old Thorny was an amateur naturalist *and* an amateur diarist, and after he retired from Gravesend Academy, he spent two years scrutinizing a tidepool in Rye Harbor; at his own expense, he published a book about it and sold autographed copies of the book every Alumni Day. He parked his station wagon by the tennis courts and sold his books off the tailgate, chatting with all the alumni who wanted to talk to him; since he was a very popular headmaster – and since he was replaced by a particularly *un*popular headmaster – almost all the alumni wanted to talk to old Thorny. I suppose he sold a lot of copies of *The Life of the Tidepool*; he might even have made money. Maybe he wasn't such an amateur, after all. He knew how to handle The Voice – by not handling him. And The Voice would prove to be the undoing of the *new* headmaster, in the end.

In the end, I yielded to Mrs Brocklebank's frenzy to educate herself; I said I'd lend her my copy of *The Life of the Tidepool*.

'Be sure to remind Heather to reread the first "phase" of *Tess*,' I told Mrs Brocklebank.

'Heather's not reading her assignments?' Mrs Brocklebank asked in alarm.

'It's spring,' I reminded her. '*All* the girls aren't reading their assignments. Heather's doing just fine.' Indeed, Heather Brocklebank is one of my better students; she has inherited her mother's ardor – while, at the same time, her imagination ranges far beyond dandelions.

In a flash, I think of giving my Grade 12 English class a sneak quiz; if they gave the first 'phase' of *Tess* such a sloppy reading, I'll bet they skipped the Introduction altogether – and I had assigned the Introduction, too; I don't always do that, but there's an Introduction by Robert B. Heilman that's especially helpful to first readers of Hardy. I know a really nasty quiz question! I think – looking at Mrs Brocklebank, clutching her murdered dandelions.

'What was Thomas Hardy's earlier title for *Tess*?'

Ha! It's nothing they could ever guess; if they'd read the Introduction, they'd know it was *Too Late Beloved* – they'd at least remember the 'too late' part. *Then* I remembered that Hardy had written a story – before *Tess* – called 'The Romantic Adventures of a Milkmaid'; I wondered if I could throw in that title, to confuse them. *Then* I remembered that Mrs Brocklebank was standing on the sidewalk with her handful of dandelions, waiting for me to fetch her *The Life of the Tidepool*. And last of all I remembered that Owen Meany and I first read *Tess of the d'Urbervilles* in our tenth-grade year at Gravesend Academy; we were in Mr Early's English class – it was the winter term of 1960 – and I was struggling with Thomas Hardy to the point of tears. Mr Early was a fool to try *Tess* on tenth graders. At Bishop Strachan, I have long argued with my colleagues that we should teach Hardy in Grade 13 – even Grade 12 is too soon! Even *The Brothers Karamazov* is easier than *Tess*!

'I can't read this!' I remember saying to Owen. He tried to help me; he helped me with everything else, but *Tess* was simply too difficult. 'I can't read about milking cows!' I screamed.

'IT'S NOT ABOUT MILKING COWS,' Owen said crossly.

'I don't care what it's about; I hate it,' I said.

'THAT'S A TRULY INTELLIGENT ATTITUDE,' Owen said. 'IF YOU CAN'T READ IT, DO YOU WANT ME TO READ IT ALOUD TO YOU?'

I am so ashamed of myself to remember this: that he would do *even that* for me – that he would read *Tess of the d'Urbervilles* aloud to me! At the time, the thought of hearing that whole novel in his voice was staggering.

'I can't read it and I can't listen to it, either,' I said.

'FINE,' Owen said. 'THEN YOU TELL ME WHAT YOU WANT ME TO DO. I CAN TELL YOU THE WHOLE STORY, I CAN WRITE YOUR TERM PAPER – AND IF THERE'S AN EXAM, YOU'LL JUST HAVE TO BULLSHIT AS WELL AS YOU CAN: IF I TELL YOU THE WHOLE STORY, MAYBE YOU'LL ACTUALLY REMEMBER SOME OF IT. THE POINT IS, I CAN DO YOUR HOMEWORK FOR YOU – IT'S NOT HARD FOR ME AND I DON'T MIND DOING IT – OR I CAN TEACH YOU HOW TO DO YOUR OWN HOMEWORK. THAT WOULD BE A LITTLE HARDER – FOR BOTH OF US – BUT IT MIGHT TURN OUT TO BE USEFUL FOR YOU TO BE ABLE TO DO YOUR OWN WORK. I MEAN, WHAT ARE YOU GOING TO DO – AFTER I'M GONE?'

'What do you mean, after you're *gone*?' I asked him.

'LOOK AT IT ANOTHER WAY,' he said patiently. 'ARE YOU GOING TO GET A JOB? AFTER YOU'RE THROUGH WITH SCHOOL, I MEAN – ARE YOU GOING TO WORK? ARE YOU GOING TO A UNIVERSITY? ARE WE GOING TO GO TO THE *SAME* UNIVERSITY? AM I GOING TO DO YOUR HOMEWORK THERE, TOO? WHAT ARE YOU GOING TO MAJOR IN?'

'What are *you* going to major in?' I asked him; my feelings were hurt – but I knew what he was driving at, and he was right.

'GEOLOGY,' he said. 'I'M IN THE GRANITE BUSINESS.'

'That's crazy!' I said. 'It's not *your* business. You can study anything you want, you don't have to study *rocks*!'

'ROCKS ARE INTERESTING,' Owen said stubbornly. 'GEOLOGY IS THE HISTORY OF THE EARTH.'

'I can't read *Tess of the d'Urbervilles*!' I cried. 'It's too hard!'

'YOU MEAN IT'S HARD TO MAKE YOURSELF READ IT, YOU MEAN IT'S HARD TO MAKE YOURSELF PAY ATTENTION,' he said. 'BUT IT'S NOT *TESS OF THE D'URBERVILLES* THAT'S HARD. THOMAS HARDY MAY BORE YOU BUT HE'S VERY EASY TO UNDERSTAND – HE'S OBVIOUS, HE TELLS YOU EVERYTHING YOU HAVE TO KNOW.'

'He tells me *more* than I *want* to know!' I cried.

'YOUR BOREDOM IS YOUR PROBLEM,' said Owen Meany. 'IT'S YOUR LACK OF IMAGINATION THAT BORES YOU. HARDY HAS THE WORLD FIGURED OUT. TESS IS DOOMED. FATE HAS IT IN FOR HER. SHE'S A VICTIM; IF YOU'RE A VICTIM, THE WORLD WILL USE YOU. WHY SHOULD SOMEONE WHO'S GOT SUCH A WORKED-OUT WAY OF SEEING THE WORLD BORE YOU? WHY SHOULDN'T YOU BE INTERESTED IN SOMEONE WHO'S WORKED OUT A WAY TO SEE THE WORLD? THAT'S WHAT MAKES WRITERS INTERESTING! MAYBE YOU SHOULD BE AN ENGLISH MAJOR. AT LEAST, YOU GET TO READ STUFF THAT'S WRITTEN BY PEOPLE WHO CAN *WRITE*! YOU DON'T HAVE TO *DO* ANYTHING TO BE AN ENGLISH MAJOR, YOU DON'T NEED ANY SPECIAL TALENT, YOU JUST HAVE TO PAY ATTENTION TO WHAT SOMEONE WANTS YOU TO SEE – TO WHAT MAKES SOMEONE ANGRIEST, OR THE MOST EXCITED IN SOME OTHER WAY. IT'S SO *EASY*; I THINK THAT'S WHY THERE ARE SO MANY ENGLISH MAJORS.'

'It's not easy for me!' I cried. 'I *hate* reading this book!'

'DO YOU HATE TO READ MOST BOOKS?' Owen asked me.

'Yes!' I said.

'DO YOU SEE THAT THE PROBLEM IS NOT *TESS*?' he asked me.

'Yes,' I admitted.

'NOW WE'RE GETTING SOMEWHERE,' said Owen Meany – my friend, my teacher.

Standing on the sidewalk with Mrs Brocklebank, I felt the tears start to come.

'Do you have allergies?' Mrs Brocklebank asked me; I shook my head. I feel so ashamed of myself that – even for a moment – I could consider zapping my Grade 12 girls with a nasty quiz on *Tess of the d'Urbervilles.* Remembering how I suffered as a student, remembering how much I needed Owen's help, how could I even think of being a *sneaky* teacher?

'I think you *do* have an allergy,' Mrs Brocklebank concluded from my tears. 'Lots of people have allergies and don't even know; I've read about that.'

'It must be the dandelions,' I said; and Mrs Brocklebank glared at the pestilential weeds with a fresh hatred.

Every spring there are dandelions; they always remind me of the spring term of 1960 – the burgeoning of that old decade that once seemed so new to Owen Meany and me. That was the spring when the Search Committee found a new headmaster. That was the decade that would defeat us.

Randolph White had been the headmaster of a small private day school in Lake Forest, Illinois; I'm told that is a super-rich and exclusively WASP community that does its utmost to pretend it is not a suburb of Chicago – but that may be unfair; I've never been there. Several Gravesend students came from there, and they unanimously groaned to hear the announcement of Randolph White's appointment as headmaster at the academy; apparently, the idea that anyone from Lake Forest had followed them to New Hampshire depressed them.

At the time, Owen and I knew a kid from Bloomfield Hills, Michigan, and he told us that Bloomfield Hills was to Detroit what Lake Forest was to Chicago, and that – in his view – Bloomfield Hills 'sucked'; he offered a story about Bloomfield Hills as an example of what he meant – it was a story about a black family that moved there, and they were forced to sell and move out because their neighbors kept burning crosses on their lawn. This shocked Owen and me; in New Hampshire, we thought such things happened only in the South – but a black kid from Atlanta informed us that we knew 'shit' about the problem; they burned crosses all over the country, the black kid said, and we weren't exactly 'overwhelmed by a sea of black faces' at Gravesend Academy, were we? No, Owen and I agreed; we were not.

Then another kid from Michigan said that Grosse Pointe was more to Detroit what Lake Forest was to Chicago – that

Bloomfield Hills wasn't a proper analogy – and some other kid argued that Shaker Heights was more to Cleveland what Lake Forest was to Chicago . . . and so forth. Owen and I were not very knowledgeable of the geography of the country's rich and exclusive; when a Jewish kid from Highland Park, Illinois, told us that there were 'no Jews allowed' in Lake Forest, Owen and I began to wonder what ominous *kind* of small private day school in Lake Forest our new headmaster had come from.

Owen had another reason to be suspicious of Randolph White. Of all the candidates whom the Search Committee dragged through the school in our tenth-grade year, only Randolph White had not accepted the invitation for A PRIVATE AUDIENCE with The Voice. Owen had met Mr White outside Archie Thorndike's office; Thorny introduced the candidate to The Voice and told them he would, as usual, vacate his office in order for them to be alone for Owen's interview.

'What's this?' Randolph White asked. 'I thought I already had the student interview.'

'Well,' old Thorny said, 'Owen, you know, is The Voice – you know our school newspaper, *The Grave*?'

'I know who he *is*,' Mr White said; he had still not shaken Owen's outstretched hand. 'Why didn't he interview me when the other students interviewed me?'

'That was the student subcommittee,' Archie Thorndike explained. 'Owen has requested "a private audience" . . .'

'Request denied, Owen,' said Randolph White, finally shaking Owen's small hand. 'I want to have plenty of time to talk with the department heads,' Mr White explained; Owen rubbed his fingers, which were still throbbing from the candidate's handshake.

Old Thorny tried to salvage the disaster. 'Owen is *almost* a department head,' he said cheerfully.

'Student opinion isn't a department, is it?' Mr White asked Owen, who was speechless. White was a compact, trimly built man who played an aggressive, relentless game of squash – daily. His wife called him 'Randy'; he called her 'Sam' – from Samantha. She came from a 'meat money' family in the Chicago area; his was a 'meat family' background, too – although there was said to be more money in the meat she came from. One of the less-than-kind Chicago newspapers described their wedding as a 'meat marriage.' Owen remembered from the candidate's dossier that White had been credited with 'revolutionizing packaging and distribution of meat products'; he'd left meat for education rather recently – when his own children (in his opinion) were in need of a better school; he'd started one up, from scratch, and the school had been quite a success in Lake Forest. Now White's children were in college and White was looking for a 'bigger challenge in the education business.' In Lake Forest, he'd had no 'tradition' to work with; White said he liked the idea of 'being a change-maker within a great tradition.'

Randy White dressed like a businessman; he looked exceedingly sharp alongside old Archie Thorndike's more rumpled and wrinkled appearance. White wore a steel-gray, pin-striped suit with a crisp white shirt; he liked a thin, gold collar pin that pulled the unusually narrow points of his collar a little too closely together – the pin also thrust the perfectly tight knot of his necktie a little too far forward. He put his hand on top of Owen Meany's head and rumpled Owen's hair; before the famous Nativity of '53, Barb Wiggin used to do that to Owen.

'I'll talk to Owen *after* I get the job!' White said to old Thorny. He smiled at his own joke. 'I know what Owen wants, anyway,' White said; he winked at Owen. ' "An educator first, a fund-raiser second" – isn't that it?' Owen nodded, but he couldn't speak. 'Well, I'll tell you what a headmaster is, Owen – he's a *decision-maker*. He's *both* an educator *and* a fund-raiser, but – first and foremost – he makes decisions.' Then Randy White looked at his watch; he steered old Thorny back into the headmaster's office. 'Remember, I've got that plane to catch,' White said. 'Let's get those department heads together.' And just before old Archie Thorndike closed his office door, Owen heard what White said; in Owen's view, he was *supposed* to hear what White said. 'I hope that kid hasn't stopped *growing*,' said Randy White. Then the door to the headmaster's office was closed; The Voice was left speechless; the candidate had not heard a word from Owen Meany.

Of course, the Ghost of the Future saw it coming; sometimes I think Owen saw everything that was coming. I remember how he predicted that the school would pick Randolph White. For *The Grave*, The Voice titled his column 'WHITEWASH.'

He began: 'THE TRUSTEES LIKE BUSINESSMEN – THE TRUSTEES *ARE* BUSINESSMEN! THE FACULTY ARE A BUNCH OF TYPICAL TEACHERS – INDECISIVE, WISHY-WASHY, THEY'RE ALWAYS SAYING "ON THE OTHER HAND." NOW ALONG COMES THIS GUY WHO SAYS HIS SPECIALTY IS MAKING DECISIONS. ONCE HE STARTS *MAKING* THOSE DECISIONS, HE'LL DRIVE EVERYONE CRAZY – WAIT UNTIL EVERYONE SEES WHAT BRILLIANT DECISIONS THE GUY COMES UP WITH! BUT RIGHT NOW, EVERYONE THINKS SOMEONE WHO MAKES DECISIONS IS JUST WHAT WE NEED. RIGHT NOW, EVERYONE'S A SUCKER FOR A DECISION-MAKER,' Owen wrote. 'WHAT GRAVESEND *NEEDS* IS A HEADMASTER WITH A STRONG EDUCATIONAL BACKGROUND; MR WHITE'S BACKGROUND IS *MEAT*.' There was more, and it was worse. Owen suggested that someone check into the admissions policy at the small private day school in Lake Forest; were there any Jews or blacks in Mr White's school? Mr Early, in his capacity as faculty advisor to *The Grave*, killed the column; the part about the faculty being 'TYPICAL TEACHERS – INDECISIVE, WISHY-WASHY' . . . that was what forced Mr Early's hand. Dan Needham agreed that the column should have been killed.

'You can't *imply* that someone is a racist or an anti-Semite, Owen,' Dan told him. 'You have to have proof.'

Owen sulked about such a stern rejection from *The Grave*; but he took Dan's advice seriously. He talked to the Gravesend students who came from Lake Forest, Illinois; he encouraged them to write to their mothers and fathers and urge *them* to inquire about the admissions policy at Mr White's school. The parents could pretend they were considering the school for their children; they could even ask directly if their children were going to be rubbing shoulders with blacks or Jews. The result – the unhappily second- and third-hand information – was typically unclear; the parents were told that the school had 'no specific admissions policy'; they were also told that the school had no blacks or Jews.

Dan Needham had his own story about meeting Randy White; that was after White was offered the job. It was a beautiful spring day – the forsythia and the lilacs were in blossom – and Dan Needham was walking in the main quadrangle with Randy White and his wife, Sam; it was Sam's first visit to the school, and she was interested in the theater. Almost immediately upon the Whites' arrival, Mr White made his decision to accept the headmastership. Dan said the school had never looked prettier. The grass was trim and a spring-green color, but it had not been mowed so recently that it looked shorn; the ivy was glossy against the red-brick buildings, and the arborvitae and the privet hedges that outlined the quadrangle paths stood in uniform, dark-green contrast to the few, bright-yellow dandelions. Dan let the new headmaster maul the fingers of his right hand; Dan looked into the pretty-blonde blandness of Sam's vacant, detached smile.

'Look at those dandelions, dear,' said Randolph White.

'They should be ripped out by their roots,' Mrs White said decisively.

'They should, they should – and they *will* be!' said the new headmaster.

Dan confessed to Owen and me that the Whites had given him the shivers.

'YOU THINK THEY GIVE YOU THE SHIVERS NOW,' Owen said. 'JUST WAIT UNTIL HE STARTS MAKING *DECISIONS*!'

Toronto: May 13, 1987 – another gorgeous day, sunny and cool; Mrs Brocklebank and others of my neighbors who were attacking their dandelions, yesterday, are having a go at their lawns today. It smells as fresh as a farm along Russell Hill Road and Lonsdale Road. I read *The Globe and Mail* again, but I was good; I didn't bring it to school with me, and I resolved that I would *not* discuss the sales of U.S. arms to Iran and the diversion of the profits to the Nicaraguan rebels – *or* the gift from the sultan of Brunei that was supposed to help support the rebels but was instead transferred to the *wrong* account in a Swiss bank. A ten-million-dollar 'mistake'! *The Globe and Mail* said: 'Brunei was only one foreign country approached during the Reagan Administration's attempt to find financial support for the contras after Congress forbade any money's being spent on their behalf by the U.S. Government.' But in my Grade 13 English class, the ever-clever Claire Clooney read that sentence aloud to the class and then asked me if I didn't think it was 'the awkwardest sentence alive.'

I have encouraged the girls to find clumsy sentences in newspapers and magazines, and to bring them into class for our hearty ridicule – and that bit about 'any money's being spent' is enough to turn an English teacher's eyeballs a blank shade of pencil-gray – but I knew that Claire Clooney was trying to get me started; I resisted the bait.

It is that time in the spring term when the minds of the Grade 13 girls are elsewhere, and I reminded them that – yesterday – we had not traveled sufficiently far in our perusal of Chapter Three of *The Great Gatsby*; that the class had bogged down in a mire of interpretations regarding the 'quality of eternal reassurance' in Gatsby's smile; and that we'd wasted more valuable time trying to grasp the meaning of Jordan Baker exhibiting 'an urban distaste for the concrete.' Claire Clooney, I might add, has such a *general* 'distaste for the concrete' that she confused Daisy Buchanan with Myrtle Wilson. I suggested that mistaking a wife for a mistress was of more dire substance than a slip of the tongue. I suspect that Claire Clooney is too clever for an error of this magnitude; that, yesterday, she had not read past Chapter One; and that, today – by her ploy of distracting me with the news – she was not finished with Chapter Four.

'Here's another one,' Mr Wheelwright,' Claire Clooney said, continuing her merciless attack on *The Globe and Mail*. 'This is the *second*-awkwardest sentence alive,' she said. 'Get this: "Mr Reagan denied yesterday that he had solicited third-country aid for the rebels, as Mr McFarlane had said on Monday." That's some dangling clunker there, isn't it?' Claire Clooney asked me. 'I like that, "as Mr McFarlane had said" – it's just like tacked on to the sentence!' she cried.

'Is it "*like* tacked on" or is it tacked on?' I asked her. She smiled; the other girls tittered. They were not going to get me to blow a forty-minute class on Ronald Reagan. But I had to keep my hands under the desk – my *fists* under the desk, I should say. The White House, that whole criminal mob, those arrogant goons who see themselves as *justified* to operate above the law – they disgrace democracy by claiming that what they do they do *for* democracy! They should be in jail. They should be in *Hollywood*!

I know that some of the girls have told their parents that I deliver 'ranting lectures' to them about the United States; some parents have complained to the headmistress, and

Katherine has cautioned me to keep my politics out of the classroom – 'or at least say something about *Canada*; BSS girls are *Canadians*, for the most part, you know.'

'I don't know anything about Canada,' I say.

'I *know* you don't!' the Rev. Mrs Keeling says, laughing; she is always friendly, even when she's teasing me, but the substance of her remark hurts me – if only because it is the same, critical message that Canon Mackie delivers to me, without cease. In short: You've been with us for twenty years; when are you going to take an interest in *us*?

In my Grade 13 English class, Frances Noyes said: '*I* think he's lying.' She meant President Reagan, of course.

'They should impeach him. Why can't they impeach him?' said Debby LaRocca. 'If he's lying, they should impeach him. If he's not lying – if all these other clowns are running his administration for him – then he's too stupid to be president. Either way, they should impeach him. In Canada, they'd call for a vote of confidence and he'd be gone!'

Sandra Darcy said, 'Yeah.'

'What do you think, Mr Wheelwright?' Adrienne Hewlett asked me sweetly.

'I think that some of you have not read to the end of Chapter Four,' I said. 'What does it mean that Gatsby was "delivered suddenly from the womb of his purposeless splendor" – what does that mean?' I asked them.

At least Ruby Newell had done her homework. 'It means that Gatsby bought the house so that Daisy would be just across the bay – that all the parties he throws . . . in a way, he throws them for her. It means that he's not just crazy – that he's made all the money, and he's spending all the money, just for *her*! To catch her eye, you know?' Ruby said.

'I like the part about the guy who fixed the World Series!' Debby LaRocca cried.

'Meyer Wolfshears!' said Claire Clooney.

'*-shiem*,' I said softly. 'Meyer Wolfsheim.'

'Yeah!' Sandra Darcy said.

'I like the way he says "Oggsford" instead of Oxford,' Debby LaRocca said.

'Like he thinks Gatsby's an "Oggsford man," ' said Frances Noyes.

'I think the guy who's telling the story is a snob,' said Adrienne Hewlett.

'Nick,' I said softly. 'Nick Carraway.'

'Yeah,' Sandra Darcy said. 'But he's *supposed* to be a snob – that's part of it.'

'And when he says he's so honest, that he's "one of the few honest people" he's ever known, I think we're not supposed to trust him – not completely, I mean,' Claire Clooney said. 'I know he's the one telling the story, but he's a part of them – he's judging them, but he's one of them.'

'They're trashy people, all of them,' Sandra Darcy said.

' "Trashy"?' I asked.

'They're very *careless* people,' Ruby Newell said correctly.

'Yes,' I said. 'They certainly are.' Very smart, these BSS girls. They know what's going on in *The Great Gatsby*, and they know what should be done to Ronald Reagan's rotten administration, too! But I contained myself very well in class today. I restricted my observations to *The Great Gatsby*. I bade the class to look with special care in the following chapters at Gatsby's notion that he can 'repeat the past,' at Gatsby's observation of Daisy – that 'her voice is full of money' – and at the frequency of how often Gatsby appears in moonlight (once, at the end of Chapter Seven, 'watching over nothing'). I asked them to consider the *coincidence* of Nick's thirtieth birthday; the meaning of the sentence 'Before me stretched the portentous, menacing road of a new decade' might give our class as much trouble as the meaning of 'an urban distaste for the concrete.'

'And remember what Ruby said!' I told them. 'They're very "careless" people.' Ruby Newell smiled; 'careless' is how Fitzgerald himself described those characters; Ruby knew that I knew she had already read to the end of the book.

'They were careless people,' the book says '. . . they smashed up things and creatures and then retreated back into their money or their vast carelessness, or whatever it was that kept them together, and let other people clean up the mess they had made . . .'

The Reagan administration is full of such 'careless people'; their kind of carelessness is immoral. And President Reagan calls himself a Christian! How does he dare? The kind of people claiming to be in communication with God today . . . they are enough to drive a *real* Christian crazy! And how about these evangelical types, performing miracles for money? Oh, there's big bucks in interpreting the gospel for idiots –

or in having idiots interpret the gospel for you – and some of these evangelists are even hypocritical enough to indulge in sexual activity that would embarrass former Senator Hart. Perhaps poor Gary Hart missed his true calling, or are they all the same – these presidential candidates and evangelicals who are caught with their pants down? Mr Reagan has been caught with his pants down, too – but the American people reserve their moral condemnation for sexual misconduct. Remember when the country was killing itself in Vietnam, and the folks at home were outraged at the length and cleanliness of the protesters' *hair*?

In the staff room, Evelyn Barber, one of my colleagues in the English Department, asked me what I thought of the contra-aid article in *The Globe and Mail*. I said I thought that the Reagan administration exhibited 'an urban distaste for the concrete.' That got quite a few laughs from my colleagues, who were expecting a diatribe from me; on the one hand, they complain about my 'predictable politics,' but they are just like the students – they enjoy getting me riled up. I have spent twenty years teaching teenagers; I don't know if I've been a maturing influence on any of them, but they have turned me and my colleagues into teenagers. We teenagers are much maligned; for example, *we* would not keep Mr Reagan in office.

In the staff room, my colleagues were yapping about the school elections; the elections were yesterday, when I noticed an impatient thrill in morning chapel – before the balloting for head girl. The girls sang 'Sons of God' with even more pep than usual; how I love to hear them sing that hymn! There are verses only the voices of young girls can convincingly sing.

> Brothers, sisters, we are one,
> and our life has just begun;
> in the Spirit we are young,
> we can live for ever!

It was Owen Meany who taught me that any good book is always in motion – from the general to the specific, from the particular to the whole, and back again. Good reading – and good writing about reading – moves the same way. It was Owen, using *Tess of the d'Urbervilles* as an example, who showed me how to write a term paper, describing the incidents that determine Tess's fate by relating them to that portentous sentence that concludes Chapter Thirty-six – 'new growths insensibly bud upward to fill each vacated place; unforeseen accidents hinder intentions, and old plans are forgotten.' It was a triumph for me: by writing my first successful term paper about a book I'd read, I also learned to read. Most mechanically, Owen helped my reading by another means: he determined that my eyes wandered to both the left and to the right of where I was in a sentence, and that – instead of following the elusive next word with my finger – I should highlight a spot on the page by reading through a hole cut in a piece of paper. It was a small rectangle, a window to read through; I moved the window over the page – it was a window that opened no higher than two or three lines. I read more quickly and more comfortably than I ever had read with my finger; to this day, I read through such a window.

As for my spelling, Owen was more helpful than Dr Dolder. It was Owen who encouraged me to learn how to type; a typewriter doesn't cure the problem, but I often can recognize that a typewritten word *looks* wrong – in longhand, I was (and am) a disaster. And Owen made me read the poems of Robert Frost aloud to him – 'IN *MY* VOICE, THEY DON'T SOUND SO GOOD.' And so I memorized 'Nothing Gold Can Stay' and 'Fire and Ice' and 'Stopping by Woods on a Snowy Evening'; Owen memorized 'Birches,' but that one was too long for me.

That summer of 1960, when we swam in the abandoned quarry lake, we no longer tied a rope around ourselves or swam one-at-a-time – Mr Meany had either lost interest in the rule, or in enforcing it; or he had acknowledged that Owen and I were no longer children. That was the summer we were eighteen. When we swam in the quarry, it didn't seem dangerous; nothing seemed dangerous. That was the summer we registered for the draft, too; it was no big deal. When we were sixteen, we got our driver's licenses; when we were eighteen, we registered for the draft. At the time, it seemed no more perilous than buying an ice-cream cone at Hampton Beach.

On Sunday – when it was not a good beach day – Owen

and I played basketball in the Gravesend Academy gym; the summer-school kids had an outdoor sports program, and they were so stir-crazy on weekends that they went to the beach even when it rained. We had the basketball court to ourselves, and it was cool in the gym. There was an old janitor who worked the weekends and who knew us from the regular school-year; he got us the best basketballs and clean towels out of the stock room, and sometimes he even let us swim in the indoor pool – I think he was a trifle retarded. He must have been damaged in some fashion because he actually enjoyed watching Owen and me practice our idiotic stunt with the basketball – the leaping, lift-him-up, slam-dunk shot.

'LET'S PRACTICE THE SHOT,' Owen would say; that was all we ever called it – 'the shot.' We'd go over it again and again. He would grasp the ball in both hands and leap into my arms (but he never took his eyes from the rim of the basket); sometimes he would twist in the air and slam the ball into the hoop backward – sometimes he would dunk it with one hand. I would turn in time to see the ball in the net and Owen Meany descending – his hands still higher than the rim of the basket but his head already below the net, his feet kicking the air. He always landed gracefully.

Sometimes we could entice the old janitor to time us with the official scorer's clock. 'SET IT TO EIGHT SECONDS,' Owen would instruct him. Over the summer, we twice managed 'the shot' in under five seconds. 'SET IT TO FOUR,' Owen would say, and we'd keep practicing; under four seconds was tough. When I'd get bored, Owen would quote me a little Robert Frost. ' "ONE COULD DO WORSE THAN BE A SWINGER OF BIRCHES." '

In our wallets, in our pockets, the draft cards weighed nothing at all; we never looked at them. It wasn't until the fall term of 1960 – with Headmaster White at the helm – that Gravesend Academy students found an interesting use for draft cards. Naturally, it was Owen Meany who made the discovery. He was in the office of *The Grave*, experimenting with a brand-new photocopier; he found that he could copy his draft card – then he found a way to make a blank draft card, one without a name and without a date of birth. The drinking age in New Hampshire was twenty-one; although Owen Meany didn't drink, he knew there were a lot of students at Gravesend Academy who liked to drink themselves silly – and none of them was twenty-one.

He charged twenty-one dollars a card. 'THAT'S THE MAGIC NUMBER,' he said. 'JUST MAKE UP YOUR OWN BIRTHDAY. DON'T TELL ANYONE WHERE YOU GOT THIS. IF YOU GET CAUGHT, I DON'T KNOW YOU.'

It was the first time he'd broken the law – unless you count the business with the tadpoles and toads, and Mary Magdalene in her goal.

Toronto: May 14, 1987 – another sunny morning, but rain developing.

President Reagan is now taking the tack that he's proud of every effort he's made for the contras, whom he calls 'the moral equivalent of our founding fathers.' The president confirmed that he had 'discussed' the matter of aid with King Fahd of Saudi Arabia; he's changed his story from only two days ago. *The Globe and Mail* pointed out that 'the king had brought up the subject'; does it *matter* who brought it up? 'My diary shows I never brought it up,' the president said. 'I expressed pleasure that he was doing that.' I never thought the president could do anything that would make me feel at all close to him; but Mr Reagan keeps a diary, too!

Owen kept a diary.

The first entry was as follows: 'THIS DIARY WAS GIVEN TO ME FOR CHRISTMAS, 1960, BY MY BENEFACTOR, MRS HARRIET WHEELWRIGHT; IT IS MY INTENTION TO MAKE MRS WHEELWRIGHT PROUD OF ME.'

I don't believe that Dan Needham and I thought of my grandmother as Owen's BENEFACTOR, although – quite literally – that is what she'd become; but that Christmas of 1960, Dan and I – and Grandmother – had reason to be especially proud of Owen Meany. He'd had a busy fall.

Randy White, our new headmaster, had also been busy; he'd been making decisions, left and right, and The Voice had not allowed a single headmasterly move to pass unchallenged. The first decision had actually been *Mrs* White's; she'd not liked the Thorndikes' old home – it was, traditionally, the headmaster's house, it had already housed three headmasters (two of them had died there; old Thorny, when he retired, had moved to his former summer home in Rye, where he planned to live year 'round). But the traditional house was not up to the Lake Forest standards that the Whites were used to; it was a well-kept, colonial house on Pine Street, but it was 'too old' for the Whites – and 'too dark,' she said, and 'too far from the main campus,' he said; and a 'poor place to entertain,' they both agreed. Apparently, Sam White liked to 'entertain.'

'WHOM ARE THEY GOING TO ENTERTAIN?' asked The Voice, who was critical of what he called 'THE WHITES' SOCIAL PRIORITIES.' Indeed, it was an expensive decision, too; a new house was built for the headmaster – so central in its location that its ongoing construction was a campus eyesore throughout Owen's and my eleventh-grade year. There had been some problems with the architect – or else Mrs White had changed her mind about a few of the interior particulars – after the construction was in progress; hence the delay. It was a rather plain saltbox – 'NOT IN KEEPING WITH THE OLDER FACULTY HOUSES,' as Owen pointed out; also, its positioning interrupted a broad, beautiful expanse of lawn between the old library and the Main Academy Building.

'There's going to be a *new* library one day soon, anyway,' the headmaster said; he was working up an expanded building proposal that included a new library, two new dormitories, a new dining hall, and – 'down the road' – a new gym with coeducational facilities. 'Coeducation,' the headmaster said, 'is a part of the future of any progressive school.'

The Voice said: 'IT IS IRONIC AND SELF-SERVING THAT THE SO-CALLED "EXPANDING BUILDING PROPOSAL" SHOULD BEGIN WITH A NEW HOUSE FOR THE HEADMASTER. IS HE GOING TO "ENTERTAIN" ENOUGH HIGH-INCOME ALUMNI IN THAT HOUSE TO GET THE SO-CALLED "CAPITAL FUND DRIVE" OFF THE GROUND? IS THIS THE HOUSE THAT PAYS FOR EVERYTHING – FROM THE GYM ON DOWN?'

When the headmaster's house was finally ready for occupancy, the Rev. Mr Merrill and his family were moved out of a rather crowded dormitory apartment and into the former headmaster's house on Pine Street. It was, impractically, at some distance from Hurd's Church; but the Rev. Lewis Merrill, as a newcomer to the school, must have been grateful to have been given such a nice, old home. As soon as Randy White had done Mr Merrill this favor, the headmaster made another decision. Morning chapel, which was daily, had always been held in Hurd's Church; it was not really a religious service, except for the ritual of singing an opening and closing hymn – and concluding the morning remarks or announcements with a prayer. The school minister did not usually officiate morning chapel; the most frequent officiant was the headmaster himself. Sometimes a faculty member gave us a mini-lecture in his field, or one of the students delivered an impassioned plea for a new club. Occasionally, something exciting happened: I remember a fencing demonstration; another time, one of the alumni – who was a famous magician – gave us a magic show, and one of the rabbits escaped in Hurd's Church and was never found.

What Mr White decided was that Hurd's Church was too gloomy a place for us to start our mornings; he moved our daily assembly to the theater in the Main Academy Building – The Great Hall, it was called. Although the morning light was more evident there and the room had a high-ceilinged loftiness to it, it was, at the same time, austere – the towering portraits of former headmasters and faculty frowned grimly down upon us in their deep-black academic regalia. The faculty who chose to attend morning chapel (they were not required to be there, as we were) now sat on the elevated stage and looked down upon us, too. When the stage was set for a school play, the curtain was drawn and there was little room for the faculty on the narrow front of the stage. That was the first thing that Owen criticized about the decision: in Hurd's Church, the faculty had sat in pews with the students – the faculty felt encouraged to attend. But in The Great Hall, when one of Dan's plays was set on the stage, there was room for so few chairs that faculty attendance was discouraged. In addition, Owen felt that 'THE ELEVATION OF THE STAGE AND THE BRIGHTNESS OF THE MORNING LIGHT PROVIDE THE HEADMASTER WITH SUCH AN EXAGGERATED PLATFORM FROM WHICH TO SPEAK; AND OFTEN, THERE'S A KIND OF SPOTLIGHT, PROVIDED BY THE SUN, THAT GIVES US ALL THE FEELING THAT WE'RE IN THE PRESENCE OF AN EXALTED PERSONAGE. I WONDER IF THIS IS THE INTENDED EFFECT,' wrote The Voice.

I confess, I rather liked the change, which was popular with most students. The Great Hall was on the second floor of the Main Academy Building; it could be approached from two directions – up two wide and sweeping marble staircases, through two high and wide double doors. There was no lining up to enter or leave; and many of us were already in the building for our first morning class. In the winter, especially, it was a tramp to Hurd's Church, which was set off from all the classroom buildings. But Owen insisted that the headmaster was GRANDSTANDING – and that Randy White had skillfully manipulated the Rev. Mr Merrill into a position where the minister would have felt ungrateful if he complained; after all, he had a good house to live in. If taking morning chapel from Hurd's Church was a move away from the Rev. Mr Merrill's territory – and if the minister resented the change – we did not hear a word of protest from the quiet Congregationalist about it; only The Voice complained.

But Randy White was just warming up; his next decision was to abolish the Latin requirement – a requirement that everyone (except the members of the Latin Department) had moaned about for years. The old logic that Latin helped one's understanding of *all* languages was not a song that was often sung outside the Latin Department. There were six members in the Latin Department and three of them within a year or two of retirement. White anticipated that enrollment in Latin would drop to half of what it was (three years of the language had been a graduation requirement); in a year or two, there would be the correctly reduced number of teachers in the department to teach Latin, and new faculty could be hired in the more popular Romance languages – French and Spanish. There were cheers in morning meeting when White announced the change – in quite a short time, we had begun to call 'morning chapel' by another name; *White* called it 'morning meeting,' and the new name stuck.

It was the *way* he had scrapped the Latin that was wrong, Owen pointed out.

'IT IS SHREWD OF THE NEW HEADMASTER TO MAKE SUCH A POPULAR DECISION – AND WHAT COULD BE MORE POPULAR WITH STUDENTS THAN ABOLISHING A REQUIREMENT? *LATIN*, ESPECIALLY! BUT THIS SHOULD HAVE BEEN ACCOMPLISHED BY A VOTE – IN FACULTY MEETING. I'M SURE THAT IF THE HEADMASTER HAD PROPOSED THE CHANGE, THE FACULTY

WOULD HAVE ENDORSED IT. THE HEADMASTER HAS A CERTAIN SINGULAR POWER: BUT WAS IT NECESSARY FOR HIM TO DEMONSTRATE HIS POWER SO WHIMSICALLY? HE COULD HAVE ACHIEVED THIS GOAL MORE DEMOCRATICALLY; WAS IT NECESSARY TO SHOW THE FACULTY THAT HE DIDN'T *NEED* THEIR APPROVAL? AND WAS IT ACTUALLY *LEGAL*, UNDER OUR CHARTER OR OUR CONSTITUTION, FOR THE HEADMASTER TO CHANGE A GRADUATION REQUIREMENT ALL BY HIMSELF?'

That occasioned the first instance of the headmaster using the platform of morning meeting to answer The Voice. We were, after all, a captive audience. 'Gentlemen,' Mr White began. 'I do not have the advantage of what amounts to a weekly editorial column in *The Grave*, but I should like to use my brief time – between hymns, and before our prayer – to enlighten you on the subject of our dear old school's charter, and its constitution. In neither document is the faculty empowered with *any* authority over the school's chosen headmaster, who is designated as the principal, meaning the principal faculty member; in neither the charter nor the constitution are the decision-making powers of the headmaster or principal inhibited in *any* way. Let Us Pray . . .'

Mr White's next decision was to replace our school attorney – a local lawyer – with an attorney-friend from Lake Forest, the former head of a law firm that had successfully fought off a food-poisoning suit against one of the big Chicago meat companies; tainted meat had made a lot of people sick, but the Lake Forest attorney steered the blame away from the meat company, and the packager, and rested the fault upon a company of refrigeration trucks. On the advice of this attorney, Randy White changed the dismissal policy at Gravesend Academy.

In the past, a so-called Executive Committee listened to the case of any boy who faced dismissal; that committee made its recommendation to the faculty, and the whole faculty voted for the boy to stay or go. The Lake Forest attorney suggested that the school was vulnerable to a lawsuit in the case of a dismissal; that the whole faculty was 'acting as a jury without the in-depth understanding of the case that was afforded to the Executive Committee.' The attorney advised that the Executive Committee make the entire decision regarding the boy's dismissal and the faculty not be involved. This was approved by Headmaster White, and the change was announced – in the manner of dropping the Latin requirement – in morning meeting.

'FOR THE SAKE OF AVOIDING A HYPOTHETICAL LAWSUIT,' wrote Owen Meany, 'THE HEADMASTER HAS CHANGED A DEMOCRACY TO AN OLIGARCHY – HE HAS TAKEN THE FUTURE OF A BOY IN TROUBLE OUT OF THE HANDS OF MANY AND PLACED THE FATE OF THAT BOY INTO THE HANDS OF A FEW. AND LET US EXAMINE THESE FEW. THE EXECUTIVE COMMITTEE IS COMPOSED OF THE HEADMASTER, THE DEAN OF STUDENTS, THE DIRECTOR OF SCHOLARSHIPS, AND FOUR MEMBERS OF THE FACULTY – ONLY TWO OF WHOM ARE ELECTED BY THE WHOLE FACULTY; THE OTHER TWO ARE APPOINTED BY THE HEADMASTER. I SUGGEST THAT THIS IS A STACKED DECK! WHO KNOWS *ANY* BOY BEST? HIS DORM ADVISER, HIS CURRENT TEACHERS AND COACHES. IN THE PAST, IN FACULTY MEETING, THESE WERE THE PEOPLE WHO SPOKE UP IN A BOY'S DEFENSE – OR THEY WERE THE PEOPLE WHO KNEW BEST THAT THE BOY DID NOT DESERVE DEFENDING. I SUGGEST THAT ANY BOY WHO IS DISMISSED BY THIS EXECUTIVE COMMITTEE *SHOULD* SUE THE SCHOOL. WHAT BETTER GROUNDS ARE THERE FOR A LAWSUIT IN THE CASE OF A DISMISSAL THAN THESE: THE PEOPLE IN A POSITION TO KNOW BEST THE VALUE OF YOUR CONTRIBUTION TO THE SCHOOL ARE NOT IN A POSITION TO EVEN *SPEAK* IN YOUR DEFENSE – NOT TO MENTION, *VOTE*?

'I WARN YOU: ANYONE WHO GETS SENT UP BEFORE THIS EXECUTIVE COMMITTEE IS ALREADY A GONER! THE HEADMASTER AND HIS TWO APPOINTEES VOTE AGAINST YOU; THE TWO *ELECTED* FACULTY MEMBERS OF THE COMMITTEE VOTE FOR YOU. NOW YOU'RE BEHIND, 3–2. AND WHAT DO THE DEAN OF STUDENTS AND THE DIRECTOR OF SCHOLARSHIPS DO? THEY DON'T KNOW YOU FROM THE CLASSROOM, OR FROM THE GYM, OR FROM THE DORM: THEY'RE *ADMINISTRATORS* – LIKE THE HEADMASTER. *MAYBE* THE DIRECTOR OF SCHOLARSHIPS LOOKS KINDLY ON YOU IF YOU'RE A SCHOLARSHIP BOY; THAT WAY, YOU

LOSE 4 – 3 INSTEAD OF 5 – 2. EITHER WAY, YOU LOSE.

'LOOK UP "OLIGARCHY" IN THE DICTIONARY IF YOU DON'T KNOW WHAT I MEAN: "A FORM OF GOVERNMENT IN WHICH THE POWER IS VESTED IN A FEW PERSONS OR IN A DOMINANT CLASS OR CLIQUE; GOVERNMENT BY THE FEW." '

But there were other issues of 'government' that captured everyone's attention at the time; even Owen was distracted from the decision-making capacities of the new headmaster. Everyone was talking about Kennedy or Nixon; and it was Owen who initiated a mock election among the Gravesend Academy students – he organized it, he set up the balloting in the school post office, he seated himself behind a big table and checked off every student's name. He caught a few kids voting twice, he sent 'runners' to bother kids in the dorm who had not yet voted. For two days, he spent all his time between classes behind that big table; he wouldn't let anyone else be the checker. The ballots themselves were secured in a locked box that was kept in the director of scholarships' office – whenever it was out of Owen's sight. There he sat at the table, with a campaign button as big as a baseball on the lapel of his sport jacket:

All the Way
with J F K

He wanted a Catholic!

'THERE'S NO MONKEY BUSINESS ABOUT THIS ELECTION,' he told the voters. 'IF YOU'RE ENOUGH OF AN ASSHOLE TO VOTE FOR NIXON, YOUR DUMB VOTE WILL BE COUNTED – JUST LIKE ANYBODY ELSE!'

Kennedy won, in a landslide, but The Voice predicted that the *real* vote – in November – would be much closer; yet Owen believed that Kennedy would, and should, triumph. 'THIS IS AN ELECTION THAT YOUNG PEOPLE CAN FEEL A PART OF,' announced The Voice; indeed, although Owen and I were too young to vote, we felt very much a part of all that youthful 'vigor' that Kennedy represented. 'WOULDN'T IT BE NICE TO HAVE A PRESIDENT WHOM PEOPLE UNDER THIRTY WON'T *LAUGH* AT? WHY VOTE FOR EISENHOWER'S FIVE O'CLOCK SHADOW WHEN YOU CAN HAVE JACK KENNEDY?'

Once again, the headmaster saw fit to challenge the 'editorial nature' of The Voice in morning meeting. 'I'm a Republican,' Randy White told us. 'So that you don't think that *The Grave* represents Republicans with even marginal objectivity, allow me to take a minute of your time – while, perhaps, the euphoria of John Kennedy's landslide election *here* is still high but (I hope) subsiding. I'm not surprised that so youthful a candidate has charmed many of you with his "*vigah*," but – fortunately – the fate of the country is not decided by young men who are not old enough to vote. Mr Nixon's experience may not seem so glamorous to you; but a presidential election is not a sailing race, or a beauty contest between the candidates' wives.

'I'm an *Illinois* Republican,' the headmaster said. 'Illinois is the Land of Lincoln, as you boys know.'

'ILLINOIS IS THE LAND OF ADLAI STEVENSON,' Owen Meany wrote. 'AS FAR AS I KNOW, ADLAI STEVENSON IS A MORE *RECENT* RESIDENT OF ILLINOIS THAN ABRAHAM LINCOLN – AS FAR AS I KNOW, ADLAI STEVENSON IS A DEMOCRAT AND HE'S STILL ALIVE.'

And this little difference of opinion, as far as *I* know, was what prompted Randy White to make another decision. He replaced Mr Early as the faculty adviser to *The Grave*; Mr White made himself the faculty adviser – and so The Voice was presented with a more adversarial censor than Owen had ever faced in Mr Early.

'You'd better be careful, Owen,' Dan Needham advised.

'You better watch your ass, man,' I told him.

It was a very cold evening after Christmas when he pulled the tomato-red pickup into the parking lot behind St Michael's – the parochial school. His headlights shone across the playground, which had been flooded by an earlier, unseasonable rain that had now frozen to the black, reflecting sheen of a pond. 'TOO BAD WE DON'T HAVE OUR SKATES,' Owen said. At the far end of the smooth sheet of ice, the truck's headlights caused the statue of Mary Magdalene to glow in her goal. 'TOO BAD WE DON'T HAVE OUR HOCKEY STICKS, AND A PUCK,' Owen said. A light went on – and then another light – in the saltbox where the nuns lived; then the porch light was turned on, too, and two of the nuns came out on the porch and stared at our headlights. 'EVER SEE PENGUINS ON ICE?' Owen said.

'Better not do anything,' I advised him, and he turned the truck around in the parking lot and drove to 80 Front Street. There was a 'creature feature' on *The Late Show*; Owen and I were now of the opinion that the only good movies were the really bad ones.

He never showed me what he wrote in his diary – not then. But after that Christmas he often carried it with him, and I knew it was important to him because he kept it by his bed, on his night table, right next to his copies of Robert Frost's poems and under the guardianship of my mother's dress-maker's dummy. When he spent the night with me, at Dan's or at 80 Front Street, he always wrote in the diary before he allowed me to turn out the light.

The night I remember him writing most furiously was the night following President Kennedy's inauguration; that was in January of 1961, and I kept begging him to turn the light out, but he went on, just writing and writing, and I finally fell asleep with the light on – I don't know when he stopped. We'd watched the inauguration on television at 80 Front Street; Dan and my grandmother watched with us, and although my grandmother complained that Jack Kennedy was 'too young and too handsome' – that he looked 'like a movie star' and that 'he should wear a hat' – Kennedy was the first Democrat that Harriet Wheelwright had *ever* voted for, and she liked him. Dan and Owen and I were crazy about him.

It was a bright, cold, and windy day in Washington – and in Gravesend – and Owen was worried about the weather. 'IT'S TOO BAD IT COULDN'T BE A NICER DAY,' Owen said.

'He should learn to wear a hat – it won't *kill* him,' my grandmother complained. 'In this weather, he'll catch his death.'

When our old friend Robert Frost tried to read his inaugural poem, Owen became more upset; maybe it was the wind, maybe Frost's eyes were tearing in the cold, or else it was the glare from the sun, or simply that the old man's eyesight was failing – whatever, he looked very feeble and he couldn't read his poem properly.

'The land was ours before we were the land's,' Frost began. It was 'The Gift Outright,' and Owen knew it by heart.

'SOMEONE HELP HIM!' Owen cried, when Frost began

to struggle. Someone tried to help him – maybe it was the president himself, or Mrs Kennedy; I don't remember.

It was not much help, in any case, and Frost went on struggling with the poem. Owen tried to prompt him, but Robert Frost could not hear The Voice – not all the way from Gravesend. Owen recited from memory; his memory of the poem was better than Frost's.

> SOMETHING WE WERE WITHHOLDING MADE US WEAK
> UNTIL WE FOUND OUT THAT IT WAS OURSELVES
> WE WERE WITHHOLDING FROM OUR LAND OF LIVING,
> AND FORTHWITH FOUND SALVATION IN SURRENDER.

It was the same voice that had prompted the Announcing Angel, who'd forgotten *his* lines eight years ago; it was the Christ Child speaking from the manger again.

'JESUS, WHY CAN'T ANYONE *HELP* HIM?' Owen cried.

It was the president's speech that really affected us; it left Owen Meany speechless and had him writing in his diary into the small hours of the night. Some years later – after everything – I would get to read what he had written; at the time, I knew only how excited he was – how he felt that Kennedy had changed everything for him.

'NO MORE SARCASM MASTER,' he wrote in his diary. 'NO MORE CYNICAL, NEGATIVE, SMART-ASS, ADOLESCENT BULLSHIT! THERE IS A WAY TO BE OF *SERVICE* TO ONE'S COUNTRY WITHOUT BEING A FOOL; THERE IS A WAY TO BE *OF USE* WITHOUT BEING USED – WITHOUT BEING A SERVANT OF OLD MEN, AND THEIR OLD IDEAS.' There was more, much more. He thought that Kennedy was religious, and – incredibly – he didn't mind that Kennedy was a Catholic. 'I BELIEVE HE'S A KIND OF SAVIOR,' Owen wrote in his diary. 'I DON'T CARE IF HE'S A MACKEREL-SNAPPER – HE'S GOT SOMETHING WE NEED.'

In Scripture class, Owen asked the Rev. Mr Merrill if he didn't agree that Jack Kennedy was 'THE VERY THING ISAIAH HAD IN MIND – YOU KNOW, "THE PEOPLE

WHO WALKED IN DARKNESS HAVE SEEN A GREAT LIGHT; THOSE WHO DWELT IN A LAND OF DEEP DARKNESS, ON THEM HAS LIGHT SHINED." YOU REMEMBER THAT?'

'Well, Owen,' Mr Merrill said cautiously, 'I'm sure Isaiah would have *liked* John Kennedy; I don't know, however, if Kennedy was "the very thing Isaiah had in mind," as you say.'

' "FOR TO US A CHILD IS BORN," ' Owen recited, ' "TO US A SON IS GIVEN; AND THE GOVERNMENT WILL BE UPON HIS SHOULDER" – REMEMBER THAT?'

I remember; and I remember how long it was after Kennedy's inauguration that Owen Meany would *still* recite to me from Kennedy's speech: ' "ASK NOT WHAT YOUR COUNTRY CAN DO FOR YOU – ASK WHAT YOU CAN DO FOR YOUR COUNTRY." '

Remember that?

7 : THE DREAM

Owen and I were nineteen-year-old seniors at Gravesend Academy – at least a year older than the other members of our class – when Owen told me, point-blank, what he had expressed to me, symbolically, when he was eleven and had mutilated my armadillo.

'GOD HAS TAKEN YOUR MOTHER,' he said to me, when I was complaining about practicing the shot; I thought he would never slam-dunk the ball in under four seconds, and I was bored with all our trying. 'MY HANDS WERE THE INSTRUMENT,' he said. 'GOD HAS TAKEN MY HANDS. I AM GOD'S INSTRUMENT.'

That he *might* have thought such a thing when he was eleven – when the astonishing results of that foul ball were such a shock to us both, and when whatever UNSPEAKABLE OUTRAGE his parents had suffered had plunged his religious upbringing into confusion and rebellion – I could understand him thinking *anything* then. But *not* when we were nineteen! I was so surprised by the matter-of-fact way he simply announced his insane belief – 'GOD HAS TAKEN MY HANDS' – that when he jumped into *my* hands, I dropped him. The basketball rolled out of bounds. Owen didn't look much like GOD'S INSTRUMENT in his fallen position – holding his knee, which he'd twisted in his fall, and writhing around on the gym floor under the basket.

'If you're God's instrument, Owen,' I said, 'how come you need *my* help to stuff a basketball?'

It was Christmas vacation, 1961, and we were alone in the gym – except for our old friend (and our only audience) the retarded janitor, who operated the official scorer's clock whenever Owen was in the mood to get serious about timing the shot. I wish I could remember his name; he was often the only janitor on duty during school holidays and summer weekends, and there was a universal understanding that he was retarded or 'brain damaged' – and Owen had heard that the janitor had suffered 'shell shock' in the war. We didn't even know *which* war – we didn't know what 'shell shock' even *was*.

Owen sat on the basketball court, rubbing his knee.

'I SUPPOSE YOU HEARD THAT FAITH CAN MOVE MOUNTAINS,' he said. 'THE TROUBLE WITH YOU IS, YOU DON'T HAVE ANY FAITH.'

'The trouble with you is, you're crazy,' I told him; but I retrieved the basketball. 'It's simply irresponsible,' I said – 'for someone your age, and of your education, to go around thinking he's God's instrument!'

'I FORGOT I WAS TALKING TO MISTER RESPONSIBILITY,' he said.

He'd started calling me Mr Responsibility in the fall of '61, when we were engaged in that senior-year agony commonly called college-entrance applications and interviews; because I'd applied to only the state university, Owen said I'd taken zero responsibility for my own self-improvement. Naturally, he'd applied to Harvard and Yale; as for the state university, the University of New Hampshire had offered him a so-called Honor Society Scholarship – and Owen hadn't even applied for admission there. The New Hampshire Honor Society gave a special scholarship each year to someone they selected as the state's best high-school or prep-school student. You had to be a bona fide resident of the state, and the prize scholarship was usually awarded to a public-school kid who was at the top of his or her graduating class; but Owen was at the top of our Gravesend Academy graduating class, the first time a New Hampshire resident had achieved such distinction – 'Competing Against the Nation's Best, Gravesend Native Wins!' was the headline in *The Gravesend News-Letter*: the story appeared in many of New Hampshire's papers. The University of New Hampshire never imagined that Owen would accept the scholarship; indeed, the Honor Society Scholarship was offered every year to New Hampshire's 'best' – with the tragic understanding that the recipient would probably go to Harvard or Yale, or to some other 'better' school. It was obvious to me that Owen would be accepted – *and* offered full scholarships – at Harvard and Yale; Hester was the only reason he might accept the scholarship to the University of New Hampshire – and what would be the point of that? Owen would begin his university career in the fall of '62 and Hester would graduate in the spring of '63.

'YOU MIGHT AT LEAST *TRY* TO GET INTO A BETTER UNIVERSITY,' Owen told me.

I was *not* asking him to give up Harvard or Yale to keep me company at the University of New Hampshire. I thought it was unfair of him to expect me to go through the motions of applying to Harvard and Yale – just to experience the rejections. Although Owen had substantially improved my abilities as a student, he could do little to improve my mediocre college-board scores; I simply wasn't Harvard or Yale material. I had become a good student in English and History courses; I was a slow but thorough reader, and I could write a readable, well-organized paper; but Owen was still holding my hand through the Math and Science courses, and I still plodded my dim way through foreign languages – as a student, I would never be what Owen was: a natural. Yet he was cross with me for accepting that I could do no better than the University of New Hampshire; in truth, I *liked* the University of New Hampshire. Durham, the town, was no more threatening than Gravesend; and it was near enough to Gravesend so that I could continue to see a lot of Dan and Grandmother – I could even continue to live with them.

'I'M SURE I'LL END UP IN DURHAM, TOO,' Owen said – with just the smallest touch of self-pity in his voice; but it infuriated me. 'I DON'T SEE HOW I CAN LET YOU FEND FOR YOURSELF,' he added.

'I'm perfectly capable of *fending* for myself,' I said. 'And I'll come visit you at Harvard or Yale.'

'NO, WE'LL BOTH MAKE OTHER FRIENDS, WE'LL DRIFT APART – THAT'S THE WAY IT HAPPENS,' he said philosophically. 'AND YOU'RE NO LETTER-WRITER – YOU DON'T EVEN KEEP A DIARY,' he added.

'If you lower your standards and come to the University of New Hampshire for *my* sake, I'll kill you,' I told him.

'THERE ARE ALSO MY PARENTS TO CONSIDER,' he said. 'IF I WERE IN SCHOOL AT DURHAM, I COULD STILL LIVE AT HOME – AND LOOK AFTER THEM.'

'What do you need to look after them for?' I asked him. It appeared to me that he spent as little time with his parents as possible!

'AND THERE'S ALSO HESTER TO CONSIDER,' he added.

'Let me get one thing straight,' I said to him. 'You and Hester – it seems to be the most on-again, off-again thing. Are you even *sleeping* with her – have you *ever* slept with her?'

'FOR SOMEONE YOUR AGE, AND OF YOUR EDUCATION, YOU'RE AWFULLY *CRUDE*,' Owen said.

When he got up off the basketball court, he was limping. I passed him the basketball; he passed it back. The idiot janitor reset the scorer's clock: the numbers were brightly lit and huge.

00:04

That's what the clock said. I was so sick of it!

I held the ball; he held out his hands.

'READY?' Owen said. On that word, the janitor started the clock. I passed Owen the ball; he jumped into my hands; I lifted him; he reached higher and higher, and – pivoting in the air – stuffed the stupid basketball through the hoop. He was so precise, he never touched the rim. He was midair, returning to earth – his hands still above his head but empty, his eyes on the scorer's clock at midcourt – when he shouted, 'TIME!' The janitor stopped the clock.

That was when I would turn to look; usually, our time had expired.

00:00

But this time, when I looked, there was one second left on the clock.

00:01

He had sunk the shot in under four seconds!

'YOU SEE WHAT A LITTLE FAITH CAN DO?' said Owen Meany. The brain-damaged janitor was applauding. 'SET THE CLOCK TO *THREE* SECONDS!' Owen told him.

'Jesus Christ!' I said.

'IF WE CAN DO IT IN UNDER FOUR SECONDS, WE CAN DO IT IN UNDER THREE,' he said. 'IT JUST TAKES A LITTLE MORE FAITH.'

'It takes more *practice*,' I told him irritably.
'FAITH TAKES PRACTICE,' said Owen Meany.

Nineteen sixty-one was the first year of our friendship that was marred by unfriendly criticism and quarreling. Our most basic dispute began in the fall when we returned to the academy for our senior year, and one of the privileges extended to seniors at Gravesend was responsible for an argument that left Owen and me feeling especially uneasy. As seniors, we were permitted to take the train to Boston on either Wednesday or Saturday afternoon; we had no classes on those afternoons; and if we told the Dean's Office where we were going, we were allowed to return to Gravesend on the Boston & Maine – as late as 10:00 P.M. on the same day. As day boys, Owen and I didn't really have to be back to school until the Thursday morning meeting – or the Sunday service at Hurd's Church, if we chose to go to Boston on a Saturday.

Even on a Saturday, Dan and my grandmother frowned upon the idea of our spending most of the night in the 'dreaded' city; there was a so-called milk train that left Boston at two o'clock in the morning – it stopped at *every* town between Boston and Gravesend, and it didn't get us home until 6:30 A.M. (about the time the school dining hall opened for breakfast) – but Dan and my grandmother said that Owen and I should live this 'wildly' on only the most special occasions. Mr and Mrs Meany didn't make any rules for Owen, at all; Owen was content to abide by the rules Dan and Grandmother made for me.

But he was *not* content to spend his time in the dreaded city in the manner that most Gravesend seniors spent their time. Many Gravesend graduates attended Harvard. A typical outing for a Gravesend senior began with a subway ride to Harvard Square; there – with the use of a fake draft card, or with the assistance of an older Gravesend graduate (now attending Harvard) – *booze* was purchased in abundance and consumed with abandon. Sometimes – albeit, rarely – *girls* were met. Fortified by the former (and *never* in the company of the latter), our senior class then rode the subway back to Boston, where – once again, falsifying our age – we gained admission to the striptease performances that were much admired by our age group at an establishment known as Old Freddy's.

I saw nothing that was morally offensive in this rite of passage. At nineteen, I was a virgin. Caroline O'Day had not permitted the advance of even so much as my hand – at least not more than an inch or so above the hem of her pleated skirt or her matching burgundy knee socks. And although Owen had told me that it was only Caroline's Catholicism that prevented me access to her favors – 'ESPECIALLY IN HER SAINT MICHAEL'S UNIFORM!' – I had been no more successful with Police Chief Ben Pike's daughter, Lorna, who was not Catholic, and not wearing a uniform of any kind when I snagged my lip on her braces. Apparently, it was either my blood or my pain – or both – that disgusted her with me. At nineteen, to experience lust – even in its shabbiest forms at Old Freddy's – was at least to experience *something*; and if Owen and I had at first imagined what love was at The Idaho, I saw nothing wrong in lusting at a burlesque show. Owen, I imagined, was *not* a virgin; how *could* he have remained a virgin with Hester? So I found it sheer hypocrisy for him to label Old Freddy's DISGUSTING and DEGRADING.

At nineteen, I drank infrequently – and entirely for the maturing thrill of becoming drunk. But Owen Meany didn't drink; he disapproved of losing control. Furthermore, he had interpreted Kennedy's inaugural charge – to *do* something for his country – in a typically single-minded and literal fashion. He would falsify no more draft cards; he would produce no more fake identification to assist the illegal drinking and burlesque-show attendance of his peers – and he was loudly self-righteous about his decision, too. Fake draft cards were WRONG, he had decided.

Therefore, we walked soberly around Harvard Square – a part of Cambridge that is not necessarily enhanced by sobriety. Soberly, we looked up our former Gravesend schoolmates – and, *soberly*, I imagined the Harvard community (and how it might be morally altered) with Owen Meany in residence. One of our former schoolmates even *told* us that Harvard was a depressing experience – when sober. But Owen insisted that our journeys to the dreaded city be conducted as joyless research; and so they were.

To maintain sobriety and to attend the striptease performances at Old Freddy's was a form of unusual torture; the women at Old Freddy's were only watchable to the blind drunk. Since Owen had made fake draft cards for himself and me before his lofty, Kennedy-inspired resolution not to break the law, we used the cards to be admitted to Old Freddy's.

'THIS IS DISGUSTING!' Owen said.

We watched a heavy-breasted woman in her forties remove her panties with her teeth; she then spat them into the eager audience.

'THIS IS DEGRADING!' Owen said.

We watched another unfortunate pick up a tangerine from the dirty floor of the stage; she lifted the tangerine almost to knee level by picking it up from the floor with the labia of her vulva – but she could raise it no higher. She lost her grip on the tangerine, and it rolled off the stage and into the crowd – where two or three of our schoolmates fought over it. *Of course* it was DISGUSTING and DEGRADING – we were *sober*!

'LET'S FIND A NICE PART OF TOWN,' Owen said.

'And do *what*?' I asked him.

'LOOK AT IT,' Owen said.

It occurs to me now that most of the seniors at Gravesend Academy had grown up looking at the nice parts of towns; but quite apart from stronger motives, Owen Meany was interested in what that was like.

That was how we ended up on Newbury Street – one Wednesday afternoon in the fall of '61. I know now that it was NO ACCIDENT that we ended up there.

There were some art galleries on Newbury Street – and some very posh stores selling pricey antiques, and some very fancy clothing stores. There was a movie theater around the corner, on Exeter Street, where they were showing a foreign film – not the kind of thing that was regularly shown in the vicinity of Old Freddy's; at The Exeter, they were showing movies you had to *read*, the kind with subtitles.

'Jesus!' I said. 'What are we going to do *here*?'

'YOU'RE SO UNOBSERVANT,' Owen said.

He was looking at a mannequin in a storefront window – a disturbingly faceless mannequin, severely modern for the period in that she was bald. The mannequin wore a hip-length, silky blouse; the blouse was fire-engine red and it was cut along the sexy lines of a camisole. The mannequin wore nothing else; Owen stared at her.

'This is really great,' I said to him. 'We come two hours on the train – we're going to ride two more hours to get *back*

– and here you are, staring at another dressmaker's *dummy*! If that's all you want to do, you don't even have to leave your own *bedroom*!'

'NOTICE ANYTHING FAMILIAR?' he asked me.

The name of the store, 'Jerrold's,' was painted in vivid-red letters across the window – in a flourishing, handwritten style.

Jerrold's

'Jerrold's,' I said. 'So what's "familiar"?'

He put his little hand in his pocket and brought out the label he had removed from my mother's old red dress; it was the dummy's red dress, really, because my mother had hated it. It was FAMILIAR – what the label said.

Everything I could see in the store's interior was the same vivid shade of fire-engine poinsettia *red*.

'She said the store burned down, didn't she?' I asked Owen.

'SHE ALSO SAID SHE COULDN'T REMEMBER THE STORE'S NAME, THAT SHE HAD TO ASK PEOPLE IN THE NEIGHBORHOOD,' Owen said. 'BUT THE NAME WAS ON THE LABEL – IT WAS ALWAYS ON THE BACK OF THE DRESS.'

With a shudder, I thought again about my Aunt Martha's assertion that my mother was a little simple; no one had ever said she was a liar.

'She said there was a lawyer who told her she could

keep the dress,' I said. 'She said that *everything* burned, didn't she?'

'BILLS OF SALE WERE BURNED, INVENTORY WAS BURNED, STOCK WAS BURNED – THAT'S WHAT SHE *SAID*,' Owen said.

'The telephone melted – remember that part?' I asked him.

'THE CASH REGISTER MELTED – REMEMBER *THAT*?' he asked me.

'Maybe they rebuilt the place – after the fire,' I said. 'Maybe there was another store – maybe there's a *chain* of stores.'

He didn't say anything; we both knew it was unlikely that the public's interest in the color red would support a *chain* of stores like Jerrold's.

'How'd you know the store was here?' I asked Owen.

'I SAW AN ADVERTISEMENT IN THE SUNDAY *BOSTON HERALD*,' he said. 'I WAS LOOKING FOR THE FUNNIES AND I RECOGNIZED THE HANDWRITING – IT WAS THE SAME STYLE AS THE LABEL.'

Leave it to Owen to recognize the handwriting; he had probably studied the label in my mother's red dress for so many years that he could have written 'Jerrold's' in the exact same style himself!

'WHAT ARE WE WAITING FOR?' Owen asked me. 'WHY DON'T WE GO INSIDE AND ASK THEM IF THEY EVER HAD A FIRE?'

Inside the place, we were confronted by a spareness as eccentric as the glaring color of every article of clothing in sight; if Jerrold's could be said to have a theme, it appeared to be – stated, and overstated – that there was only one of everything: one bra, one nightgown, one half-slip, one little cocktail dress, one long evening dress, one long skirt, one short skirt, the one blouse on the one mannequin we had seen in the window, and one counter of four-sided glass that contained a single pair of red leather gloves, a pair of red high heels, a garnet necklace (with a matching pair of earrings), and one very thin belt (also red, and probably alligator or lizard). The walls were white, the hoods of the indirect lights were black, and the one man behind the one counter was about the age my mother would have been if she'd been alive.

The man regarded Owen and me disdainfully: he saw two teenage boys, not dressed for Newbury Street, possibly (if so, pathetically) shopping for a mother or for a girlfriend; I doubt that we could have afforded even the cheapest version of the color red available in Jerrold's.

'DID YOU EVER HAVE A FIRE?' Owen asked the man.

Now the man looked less sure about us; he thought we were too young to be selling insurance, but Owen's question – not to mention Owen's *voice* – had disarmed him.

'It would have been a fire in the forties,' I said.

'OR THE EARLY FIFTIES,' said Owen Meany.

'Perhaps you haven't been here – at this location – for that long?' I asked the man.

'ARE YOU JERROLD?' Owen asked the man; like a miniature policeman, Owen Meany pushed the wrinkled label from my mother's dress across the glass-topped counter.

'That's our label,' the man said, fingering the evidence cautiously. 'We've been here since before the war – but I don't think we've ever had a fire. What *sorta* fire do you mean?' he asked Owen – because, naturally, Owen appeared to be in charge.

'ARE *YOU* JERROLD?' Owen repeated.

'That's my father – *Giordano*,' the man said. 'He was Giovanni Giordano, but they fucked around with his name when he got off the boat.'

This was an immigration story, and *not* the story Owen and I were interested in, so I asked the man, politely: 'Is your father alive?'

'Hey, Poppa!' the man shouted. 'You alive?'

A white door, fitted so flush to the white wall that Owen and I had not noticed it was there, opened. An old man with a tailor's measuring tape around his neck, and a tailor's many pins adorning the lapels of his vest, came into the storeroom.

'Of course I'm alive!' he said. 'You waitin' for some miracle? You in a hurry for your inheritance?' He had a mostly-Boston, somewhat-Italian accent.

'Poppa, these young men want to talk to "Jerrold" about some fire,' the son said; he spoke laconically and with a more virulent Boston accent than his father's.

'*What* fire?' Mr Giordano asked us.

'We were told that your store burned down – sometime in the forties, or the fifties,' I said.

'This is big news to me!' said Mr Giordano.

'My mother must have made a mistake,' I explained. I showed the old label to Mr Giordano. 'She bought a dress in your store – sometime in the forties, or the fifties.' I didn't know what else to say. 'It was a red dress,' I added.

'No kiddin',' said the son.

I said: 'I wish I had a picture of her – perhaps I could come back, with a photograph. You might remember something about her if I showed you a picture,' I said.

'Does she want the dress *altered*?' the old man asked me. 'I didn't mind makin' alterations – but she's got to come into the store herself. I don't do alterations from *pictures!*'

'SHE'S DEAD,' said Owen Meany. His tiny hand went into his pocket again. He brought out a neatly folded envelope; in the envelope was the picture my mother had given him – it was a wedding picture, very pretty of her and not bad of Dan. My mother had included the photo with a thank-you note to Owen and his father for their unusual wedding present. 'I JUST HAPPEN TO HAVE BROUGHT A PICTURE,' Owen said, handing the sacred object to Mr Giordano.

'Frank Sinatra!' the old man cried; his son took the picture from him.

'That don't look like Frank Sinatra to me,' the son said.

'No! No!' the old man cried; he grabbed the photo back. 'She loved those Sinatra songs – she sang 'em real good, too. We used to talk about "Frankie Boy" – your mother said he shoulda been a *woman*, he had such a pretty voice,' Mr Giordano said.

'DO YOU KNOW WHY SHE BOUGHT THE DRESS?' Owen asked.

'Sure, I know!' the old man told us. 'It was the dress she always *sang* in! "I need somethin' to *sing* in!" – that's what she said when she walked in here. "I need somethin' *not like me!*" – that's what she said. I'll never forget her. But I didn't know who she *was* – not when she come in here, not *then!*' Mr Giordano said.

'Who the fuck *was* she?' the son asked. I shuddered to hear him ask; it had just occurred to me that I didn't know who my mother was, either.

'She was "The Lady in Red" – don't you remember her?' Mr Giordano asked his son. 'She was still singin' in that place when you got home from the war. What *was* that place?'

The son grabbed the photo back.

'It's *her*!' he cried.

' "The Lady in Red"!' the Giordanos cried together.

I was trembling. My mother was a singer – in some *joint*! She was someone called 'The Lady in Red'! She'd had a *career* – in *nightlife*! I looked at Owen; he appeared strangely at ease – he was almost calm, and he was smiling. 'ISN'T THIS MORE INTERESTING THAN OLD FREDDY'S?' Owen asked me.

What the Giordanos told us was that my mother had been a female vocalist at a supper club on Beacon Street – 'a perfectly proper sorta place!' the old man assured us. There was a black pianist – he played an old-fashioned piano, which (the Giordanos explained) meant that he played the old tunes, and quietly, 'so's you could hear the singer!'

It was not a place where single men or women went; it was not a bar; it was a supper club, and a supper club, the Giordanos assured us, was a restaurant with live entertainment – 'somethin' relaxed enough to digest to!' About ten o'clock, the singer and pianist served up music more suitable for dancing than for dinner-table conversation – and there was dancing, then, until midnight; men with their wives, or at least with 'serious' dates. It was 'no place to take a floozy – or to find one.' And most nights there was 'a sorta famous female vocalist, someone you woulda heard of'; although Owen Meany and I had never heard of *anyone* the Giordanos mentioned. 'The Lady in Red' sang only one night a week; the Giordanos had forgotten *which* night, but Owen and I could provide that information. It would have been Wednesday – always Wednesday. Supposedly, the singing teacher my mother was studying with was so famous that he had time for her only on Thursday mornings – and so early that she had to spend the previous night in the 'dreaded' city.

Why she never sang under her own name – why she was always 'The Lady in Red' – the Giordanos didn't know. Nor could they recall the name of the supper club; they just knew it wasn't there anymore. It had always had the look of a private home; now it had, in fact, become one – 'somewheres on Beacon Street,' that was all they could remember. It was either a private home or doctors' offices. As for the owner of the club, he was a Jewish fellow from Miami. The Giordanos had heard that the man had gone back to Miami. 'I guess they still have supper clubs down there,' old Mr Giordano said. He was sad and shocked to hear that my mother was dead;

'The Lady in Red' had become quite popular among the local patrons of the club – 'not famous, not like some of them others, but a kinda regular feature of the place.'

The Giordanos remembered that she had come, and that she had gone away – for a while – and then she'd come back. Later, she had gone away for good; but people didn't believe it and they would say, for years, that she was coming back again. When she'd been away – 'for a while' – that was when she'd been having *me*, of course.

The Giordanos could almost remember the name of the black pianist; 'he was there as long as the place was there,' they said. But the closest they could come to the man's name was 'Buster.'

'Big Black Buster!' Mr Giordano said.

'I don't think *he* was from Miami,' the son said.

'CLEARLY,' said Owen Meany, when we were once more out on Newbury Street, ' "BIG BLACK BUSTER" IS *NOT* YOUR FATHER!'

I wanted to ask Owen if he still had the name and address – and even the phone number – of my mother's singing and voice teacher; I knew Mother had given the particulars to Owen, and I doubted that Owen would have discarded *anything* she gave him.

But I didn't have to ask. Once more, his tiny hand shot into his pocket. 'THE ADDRESS IS IN THE NEIGHBORHOOD,' he told me. 'I MADE AN APPOINTMENT, TO HAVE MY VOICE "ANALYZED"; WHEN THE GUY HEARD MY VOICE – OVER THE PHONE – HE SAID HE'D GIVE ME AN APPOINTMENT WHENEVER I WANTED ONE.'

Thus had Owen Meany come to Boston, the dreaded city; he had come prepared.

There were some elegant town houses along the most densely tree-lined part of Commonwealth Avenue where Graham McSwiney, the voice and singing teacher, lived; but Mr McSwiney had a small and cluttered walk-up apartment in one of the less-restored old houses that had been divided and subdivided almost as many times as the collective rent of the various tenants had been withheld, or paid late. Since we were early for Owen's appointment, we sat in a corridor outside Mr McSwiney's apartment door, on which was posted (by a thumbtack) a hand-lettered sign.

Don't! ! ! Knock Or Ring Bell
If You Hear Singing! ! ! !

'Singing' was not quite what we heard, but some sort of exercise was in progress behind Mr McSwiney's closed door, and so Owen and I didn't knock or ring the bell; we sat on a comfortable but odd piece of furniture – not a couch, but what appeared to be a seat removed from a public bus – and listened to the singing or voice lesson we were forbidden to disturb.

A man's powerful, resonant voice said: '*Me-me-me-me-me-me-me-me!*'

A woman's absolutely thrilling voice repeated: '*Me-me-me-me-me-me-me-me!*'

Then the man said: '*No-no-no-no-no-no-no-no!*'

And the woman answered: '*No-no-no-no-no-no-no-no!*'

And then the man sang just a line from a song – it was a song from *My Fair Lady*, the one that goes, 'All I want is a room somewhere . . .'

And the woman sang: 'Far away from the cold night air . . .'

And together they sang: 'With one enormous chair . . .'

And the woman took it by herself: 'Oh, wouldn't it be lov-er-ly!'

'*Me-me-me-me-me-me-me-me!*' said the man again; now, a piano was involved – just one key.

Their voices, even in this silly exercise, were the most wonderful voices Owen Meany and I had heard; even when she sang '*No-no-no-no-no-no-no-no!*' the woman's voice was much more beautiful than my mother's.

I was glad that Owen and I had to wait, because it gave me time to be grateful for at least this part of our discovery: that Mr McSwiney really *was* a voice and singing teacher, and that he seemed to have a perfectly wonderful voice – and that he had a pupil with an even *better* voice than my mother's . . . this at least meant that *something* I thought I knew about my mother was true. The shock of our discovery in Jerrold's needed time to sink in.

It did not strike me that my mother's lie about the red dress was a devastating sort of untruth; even that she had been an actual singer – an actual performer! – didn't strike me as such an awful thing for her to have hidden from me, or even from Dan (if she'd kept Dan in the dark, too). What struck me was my memory of how *easily* and *gracefully* she had told that little lie about the store burning down, how she had fretted so *convincingly* about the red dress. Quite probably, it occurred to me, she had been a better liar than a singer. And if she'd lied about the dress – and had never told anyone in her life in Gravesend about 'The Lady in Red' – what *else* had she lied about?

In addition to not knowing who my father was, what *else* didn't I know?

Owen Meany, who thought much more quickly than I did, put it very simply; he whispered, so that he wouldn't disturb Mr McSwiney's lesson. 'NOW YOU DON'T KNOW WHO YOUR *MOTHER* IS, *EITHER*,' Owen said.

Following the exit of a small, flamboyantly dressed woman from Mr McSwiney's apartment, Owen and I were admitted to the teacher's untidy hovel; the disappointingly small size of the departing singer's bosom was a contradiction to the power we had heard in her voice – but we were impressed by the air of professional disorder that greeted us in Graham McSwiney's studio. There was no door on the cubicle bathroom, in which the bathtub appeared to be hastily, even comically placed; it was detached from the plumbing and full of the elbow joints of pipes and their fittings – a plumbing project was clearly in progress there; and progressing at no great pace.

There was no wall (or the wall had been taken down) between the cubicle kitchen and the living room, and there were no doors on the kitchen cabinets, which revealed little besides coffee cups and mugs – suggesting that Mr McSwiney either restricted himself to an all-caffeine diet or that he took his meals elsewhere. And there was no bed in the living room – the only real room in the tiny, crowded apartment – suggesting that the couch, which was covered with sheet music, concealed a foldaway bed. But the placement of the sheet music had the look of meticulous specificity, and the sheer volume of it argued that the couch was never sat upon – not to mention, unfolded – and this evidence suggested that Mr McSwiney slept elsewhere, too.

Everywhere, there were mementos – playbills from opera houses and concert halls: newspaper clippings of people singing; and framed citations and medals hung on ribbons, suggesting golden-throat awards of an almost athletic order of recognition. Everywhere, too, were framed, poster-sized drawings of the chest and throat, as clinical in detail as the drawings in *Gray's Anatomy*, and as simplistic in their arrangement around the apartment as the educational diagrams in certain doctors' offices. Beneath these anatomical drawings were the kind of optimistic slogans that gung-ho coaches hang in gyms:

Begin With The *Breastbone*!
Keep Upper Chest Filled With Air *All The Time*!
The Diaphragm Is A *One-Way* Muscle – It Can *Only* Inhale!
Practice Your Breathing *Separately* From Your Singing!
Never Lift Your Shoulders!
Never Hold Your Breath!

One whole wall was devoted to instructive commands regarding vowels; over the doorway of the bathroom was the single exclamation: Gently! Dominating the apartment, from the center stage of the living room – big and black and perfectly polished, and conceivably worth twice the annual rent on Mr McSwiney's place of business – was the piano.

Mr McSwiney was completely bald. Wild, white tufts of hair sprang from his ears – as if to protect him from the volume of his own huge voice. He was hearty-looking, in his sixties (or even in his seventies), a short, muscular man whose chest descended to his belt – or whose round, hard belly consumed his chest and rested under his chin, like a beer-drinker's boulder.

'So! Which one of you's got *the voice*?' Mr McSwiney asked us.

'I HAVE,' said Owen Meany.

'You certainly have!' cried Mr McSwiney, who paid little attention to me, even when Owen took special pains to introduce me by putting unmistakable emphasis on my last name, which we thought might be familiar to the singing and voice teacher.

'THIS IS MY FRIEND, JOHN *WHEELWRIGHT*,' Owen said, but Mr McSwiney couldn't wait to have a look at Owen's Adam's apple; the name 'Wheelwright' appeared to ring no bells for him.

'It's all the same thing, whatever you call it,' Mr McSwiney said. 'An Adam's apple, a larynx, a voice box – it's the most important part of the vocal apparatus,' he explained, sitting Owen in what he called 'the singer's seat,' which was a plain, straight-backed chair directly in front of the piano. Mr McSwiney put his thumb and index finger on either side of Owen's Adam's apple. 'Swallow!' he instructed. Owen swallowed. When I held my own Adam's apple and swallowed, I could feel my Adam's apple jump higher up my neck; but Owen's Adam's apple hardly moved.

'Yawn!' said Mr McSwiney. When I yawned, my Adam's apple moved *down* my neck, but Owen Meany's Adam's apple stayed almost exactly where it was.

'Scream!' said Mr McSwiney.

'AAAAAHHHHHH!' said Owen Meany; again, his Adam's apple hardly moved.

'Amazing!' said Mr McSwiney. 'You've got a permanently fixed larynx,' he told Owen. 'I've rarely seen such a thing,' he said. 'Your voice box is never in repose – your Adam's apple sits up there in the position of a *permanent scream*. I could try giving you some exercises, but you might want to see a throat doctor; you might have to have surgery.'

'I DON'T WANT TO HAVE SURGERY, I DON'T NEED ANY EXERCISES,' said Owen Meany. 'IF GOD GAVE ME THIS VOICE, HE HAD A *REASON*,' Owen said.

'How come his voice doesn't *change*?' I asked Mr McSwiney, who seemed on the verge of a satirical remark – regarding God's role in the position of Owen's voice box. 'I thought *every* boy's voice changed – at puberty,' I said.

'If his voice hasn't changed already, it's probably never going to change,' Mr McSwiney said. 'Vocal cords don't make words – they just vibrate. Vocal cords aren't really "cords" – they're just *lips*. It's the opening between those lips that's called the "glottis." It's nothing but the act of breathing on the *closed* lips that makes a sound. When a male voice changes, it's just a *part* of puberty – it's called a "secondary sexual development." But I don't think *your* voice is going to change,' Mr McSwiney told Owen. 'If it was going to change, it would have.'

'THAT DOESN'T EXPLAIN WHY IT ALREADY *HASN'T*,' said Owen Meany.

'I can't explain that,' Mr McSwiney admitted. 'I can give you some exercises,' he repeated, 'or I can recommend a doctor.'

'I DON'T *EXPECT* MY VOICE TO CHANGE,' said Owen Meany.

I could see that Mr McSwiney was learning how exasperating Owen's belief in God's plans could be.

'Why'd you come to see me, kid?' Mr McSwiney asked him.

'BECAUSE YOU KNOW HIS MOTHER,' Owen said, pointing to me. Graham McSwiney assessed me, as if he feared I might represent an elderly paternity suit.

'Tabitha Wheelwright,' I said. 'She was called Tabby. She was from New Hampshire, and she studied with you in the forties and the fifties – from before I was born until I was eight or nine.'

'OR TEN,' said Owen Meany; into his pocket went his hand, again – he handed Mr McSwiney the photograph.

' "The Lady in Red"!' Mr McSwiney said. 'I'm sorry, I forgot her name,' he told me.

'But you remember her?' I asked.

'Oh sure, I remember her,' he said. 'She was pretty, and very pleasant – and I got her that silly job. It wasn't much of a gig, but she had fun doing it; she had this idea that someone might "discover" her if she kept singing there – but I told her no one ever got *discovered* in Boston. And certainly not in that *supper club*!'

Mr McSwiney explained that the club often called him and raided his students for local talent; as the Giordanos had told us, the club hired more established female vocalists for gigs that lasted for a month or more – but on Wednesdays, the club rested their stars; that's when they called upon 'local talent.' In my mother's case, she had gained a small, neighborhood reputation and the club had made a habit of her. She'd not wanted to use her name – a form of shyness, or provincialism, that Mr McSwiney found as silly as her idea that anyone might 'discover' her.

'But she was charming,' he said. 'As a singer, she was all "head" – she had no "chest" – and she was lazy. She liked to perform simple, popular songs; she wasn't very ambitious. And she wouldn't practice.'

He explained the two sets of muscles involved in a 'head voice' and in a 'chest voice'; although this was not what interested Owen and me about my mother, we were polite and allowed Mr McSwiney to elaborate on his *teacher's* opinion of her. Most women sing with the larynx in a high position, or with only what Mr McSwiney called a 'head voice'; they experience a lack of power from the E above middle C, downward – and when they try to hit their high notes *loudly*, they hit them shrilly. The development of a 'chest voice' in women is very important. For men, it is the 'head voice' that needs the development. For both, they must be willing to devote *hours*.

My mother, a once-a-week singer, was what Mr McSwiney called 'the vocal equivalent of a weekend tennis player.' She had a *pretty* voice – as I've described it – but Mr McSwiney's assessment of her voice was consistent with my memory of her; she did not have a *strong* voice, she was not ever as *powerful* as Mr McSwiney's previous pupil had sounded to Owen and me through a closed door.

'Who thought of the *name* "The Lady in Red"?' I asked the old teacher – in an effort to steer him back to what interested us.

'She found a red dress in a store,' Mr McSwiney said. 'She told me she wanted to be "wholly out of character – but only once a week"!' He laughed. 'I never went to hear her perform,' he said 'It was just a supper club,' he explained. 'Really, *no one* who sang there was very good. Some of the better ones would work with me, so I heard them *here* – but I never set foot in the place. I knew Meyerson on the telephone; I don't remember that I actually met him. I think Meyerson called her "The Lady in Red." '

'Meyerson?' I asked.

'He owned the club, he was a nice old guy – from Miami, I think. He was honest, and unpretentious. The singers I sent to him all liked him – they said he treated them respectfully,' Mr McSwiney said.

'DO YOU REMEMBER THE NAME OF THE CLUB?' Owen asked him.

It had been called The Orange Grove; my mother had joked to Mr McSwiney about the door, which she said was dotted everywhere with potted orange trees and tanks full of tropical fish – and husbands and wives celebrating their anniversaries. Yet she had imagined she might be 'discovered' there!

'DID SHE HAVE A BOYFRIEND?' Owen asked Mr McSwiney, who shrugged.

'She wasn't interested in *me* – that's all I know!' he said. He smiled at me fondly. 'I know, because I made a pass at her,' he explained. 'She handled it very nicely and I never tried it again,' he said.

'There was a pianist, a black pianist – at The Orange Grove,' I said.

'You bet there was, but he was all over – he played all over town, for years, before he ended up there. And after he left there, he played all over town again,' Mr McSwiney said. 'Big Black Buster Freebody!' he said, and laughed.

'Freebody,' I said.

'It was as made-up a name as "The Lady in Red,"' said Mr McSwiney. 'And he wouldn't have been your mother's boyfriend, either – Buster was as queer as a cat fart.'

Graham McSwiney also told us that Meyerson had gone back to Miami; but Mr McSwiney added that Meyerson was *old* – even in the forties and fifties, he'd been old; he was so old that he'd have to be dead now, 'or at least lying down on a shuffleboard court.' As for Buster Freebody, Mr McSwiney couldn't remember where the big black man had played after The Orange Grove had seen its days. 'I used to run into him in so many places,' Mr McSwiney said. 'I was as used to seeing Buster as a light fixture.' Buster Freebody had played what Mr McSwiney called a 'real soft' piano; singers liked him because they could be heard over him.

'She had some trouble – your mother,' Mr McSwiney remembered. 'She went away – for a while – and then she came back again. And then she went away for good.'

'*HE* WAS THE TROUBLE,' said Owen Meany, pointing to me.

'Are you looking for your father?' the singing teacher asked me. 'Is that it?'

'Yes,' I said.

'Don't bother, kid,' said Mr McSwiney. 'If he was looking for you, he would have found you.'

'GOD WILL TELL HIM WHO HIS FATHER IS,' Owen said; Graham McSwiney shrugged.

'I'm not God,' Mr McSwiney said. 'This God you know,' he told Owen – 'this God must be pretty busy.'

I gave him my phone number in Gravesend – in case he ever remembered the last place he'd heard Buster Freebody play the piano. Buster Freebody, Mr McSwiney warned me, was old enough to be 'lying down on a shuffleboard court,' too. Mr McSwiney asked Owen Meany for *his* phone number – in case he ever heard a theory regarding why Owen's voice hadn't already changed.

'IT DOESN'T MATTER,' Owen said, but he gave Mr McSwiney his number.

'Your mother was a nice woman, a good person – a *respectable* woman,' Mr McSwiney told me.

'Thank you,' I said.

'The Orange Grove was a *stupid* place,' he told me, 'but it wasn't a *dive* – nothing cheap would have happened to her there,' he said.

'Thank you,' I said again.

'All she ever sang was Sinatra stuff – it used to bore me to tears,' Mr McSwiney admitted.

'I THINK WE CAN ASSUME THAT *SOMEBODY* LIKED TO LISTEN TO IT,' said Owen Meany.

Toronto: May 30, 1987 – I should know better than to read even as much as a headline in *The New York Times*; although, as I've often pointed out to my students at Bishop Strachan, this newspaper's use of the semicolon is exemplary.

Reagan Declares
Firmness on Gulf;
Plans Are Unclear

Isn't that a classic? I don't mean the semicolon; I mean, isn't that just what the world needs? Unclear firmness! That is typical American policy: don't be clear, but be firm!

In November, 1961 – after Owen Meany and I learned that his voice box was never in repose, and that my mother had enjoyed (or suffered) a more secret life than we knew – Gen. Maxwell Taylor reported to President Kennedy that U.S. military, economic, and political support could secure a victory for the South Vietnamese *without* the United States taking over the war. (Privately, the general recommended sending eight thousand U.S. combat troops to Vietnam.)

That New Year's Eve, which Owen and Hester and I celebrated at 80 Front Street – in the desultory manner that describes the partying habits of the late teen years (Hester was twenty), and in a relatively quiet manner (because Grandmother had gone to bed) – there were only 3,205 U.S.

military personnel in Vietnam.

Hester would usher in the New Year more emphatically than Owen or I could manage; she greeted the New Year on her knees – in the snow, in the rose garden, where Grandmother would not hear her retching up her rum and Coke (a concoction she had learned to fancy in the budding days of her romance in Tortola). I was less enthusiastic about the watershed changing of the year; I fell asleep watching Charlton Heston's agonies in *Ben-Hur* – somewhere between the chariot race and the leper colony, I nodded off. Owen watched the whole movie; during the commercials, he turned his detached attention to the window that overlooked the rose garden, where Hester's pale figure could be discerned in the ghostly glow of the moonlight against the snow. It is a wonder to me that the changing of the year had so little effect on Owen Meany – when I consider that he thought he 'knew,' at the time, exactly how many years he had left. Yet he appeared content to watch *Ben-Hur*, and Hester throwing up; maybe that's what faith is – exactly that contentment, even facing the future.

By our next New Year's Eve together, in 1962, there would be 11,300 U.S. military personnel in Vietnam. And once again, on the morning of New Year's Day, my grandmother would notice the frozen splatter of Hester's vomit in the snow – defacing that usually pristine area surrounding the birdbath in the center of the rose garden.

'Merciful Heavens!' Grandmother would say. 'What's all that *mess* around the birdbath?'

And just as he'd said the year before, Owen Meany said, 'DIDN'T YOU HEAR THE BIRDS LAST NIGHT, MISSUS WHEELWRIGHT? I'D BETTER HAVE A LOOK AT WHAT ETHEL'S PUTTING IN YOUR BIRD FEEDERS.'

Owen would have respected a book I read only two years ago: *Vietnam War Almanac*, by Col. Harry G. Summers, Jr. Colonel Summers is a combat infantry veteran of Korea and Vietnam; he doesn't beat around the bush, as we used to say in Gravesend. Here is the first sentence of his very fine book: 'One of the great tragedies of the Vietnam war is that although American armed forces defeated the North Vietnamese and Viet Cong in every major battle, the United States still suffered the greatest defeat in its history.' Imagine that! On the first page of his book, Colonel Summers tells a story about

President Franklin D. Roosevelt at the Yalta Conference in 1945, when the Allied powers were trying to decide the composition of the postwar world. President Roosevelt wanted to give Indo-China to China's leader, General Chiang Kai-shek, but the general knew a little Vietnamese history and tradition; Chiang Kai-shek understood that the Vietnamese were *not* Chinese, and that they would never allow themselves to be comfortably absorbed by the Chinese people. To Roosevelt's generous offer – to give him Indo-China – Chiang replied: 'We don't want it.' Colonel Summers points out that it took the United States thirty years – and a war that cost them nearly fifty thousand American lives – to find out what Chiang Kai-shek explained to President Roosevelt in 1945. Imagine *that*!

Is it any surprise that President Reagan is promising 'firmness' in the Persian Gulf, and that his 'plans are unclear'?

Soon the school year will be over; soon the BSS girls will be gone. It is hot and humid in the summer in Toronto, but I like to watch the sprinklers wetting down the grass on the St Clair Reservoir; they keep Winston Churchill Park as green as a jungle – all summer long. And the Rev. Katherine Keeling's family owns an island in Georgian Bay; Katherine always invites me to visit her – I usually go there at least once every summer – and so I get my annual fix of swimming in fresh water and fooling around with someone else's kids. Lots of wet life vests, lots of leaky canoes, and the smell of pine needles and wood preservative – a little of that lasts a long time for a fussy old bachelor like me.

And in the summers I go to Gravesend and visit with Dan, too. It would hurt Dan's feelings if I didn't come to see a theatrical performance of his Gravesend summer-school students; he understands why I decline to see the performances of The Gravesend Players. Mr Fish is quite old, but still acting; many of the town's older amateurs are still acting for Dan, but I'd just as soon not see them anymore. And I don't care for the view of the audience that, for a period of time, more than twenty years ago, intrigued Owen Meany and me.

'IS HE OUT THERE TONIGHT?' Owen would whisper to me. 'DO YOU SEE HIM?'

In 1961, Owen and I searched the audience for that special face in the bleacher seats – maybe a familiar face; and maybe not. We were looking for the man who responded – or did not respond – to my mother's wave. It was a face, we were sure, that would have registered *some* expression – upon witnessing the results of Owen Meany making contact with that ball. It was a face, we suspected, that my mother would have seen in many audiences before – not just at Little League games, but staring out at her from the potted orange trees and the tanks full of tropical fish at The Orange Grove. We were looking for a face that 'The Lady in Red' would have *sung* to . . . at least once, if not many times.

'Do *you* see him?' I would ask Owen Meany.

'NOT TONIGHT,' Owen would say. 'EITHER HE'S NOT HERE, OR HE'S NOT THINKING ABOUT YOUR MOTHER,' he said one night.

'What do you mean?' I asked him.

'SUPPOSE DAN DIRECTED A PLAY ABOUT *MIAMI*?' said Owen Meany. 'SUPPOSE THE GRAVESEND PLAYERS PUT ON A PLAY ABOUT A SUPPER CLUB IN MIAMI, AND IT WAS CALLED THE ORANGE GROVE, AND THERE WAS A SINGER CALLED "THE LADY IN RED," AND SHE SANG ONLY THE OLD SINATRA SONGS.'

'But there *is* no play like that,' I said.

'JUST *SUPPOSE*!' Owen said. 'USE YOUR *IMAGINATION*. GOD CAN TELL YOU WHO YOUR FATHER IS, BUT YOU HAVE TO *BELIEVE* IT – YOU'VE GOT TO GIVE GOD A LITTLE *HELP*! JUST *SUPPOSE* THERE WAS SUCH A PLAY!'

'Okay,' I said. 'I'm supposing.'

'AND WE CALLED THE PLAY EITHER *THE ORANGE GROVE* OR *THE LADY IN RED* – DON'T YOU SUPPOSE THAT YOUR FATHER WOULD COME TO SEE *THAT* PLAY? AND DON'T YOU SUPPOSE WE COULD RECOGNIZE HIM *THEN*?' asked Owen Meany.

'I suppose so,' I said.

The problem was, Owen and I didn't dare tell Dan about The Orange Grove and 'The Lady in Red'; we weren't sure that Dan didn't already *know*. I thought it would hurt Dan to know that he wasn't *enough* of a father to me – for wouldn't he interpret my curiosity regarding my biological father as an indication that he (Dan) was less adequate in his adoptive role?

And if Dan *didn't* know about The Orange Grove and 'The

Lady in Red,' wouldn't *that* hurt him, too? It made my mother's past – before Dan – appear more romantic than *I* ever thought it had been. Why would Dan Needham want to dwell on my mother's romantic past?

Owen suggested that there was a way to get The Gravesend Players to perform a play about a female vocalist in a Miami supper club without involving Dan in our discovery.

'I COULD WRITE THE PLAY,' said Owen Meany. 'I COULD SUBMIT IT TO DAN AS THE FIRST *ORIGINAL* PRODUCTION OF THE GRAVESEND PLAYERS. I COULD TELL IN ONE SECOND IF DAN ALREADY KNEW THE STORY.'

'But *you* don't know the story,' I pointed out to Owen. 'You don't have a story, you just have a *setting* – and a very sketchy cast of characters.'

'IT CAN'T BE VERY HARD TO MAKE UP A GOOD STORY,' said Owen Meany. 'CLEARLY, YOUR MOTHER HAD A TALENT FOR IT – AND SHE WASN'T EVEN A WRITER.'

'I suppose you're a writer,' I said; Owen shrugged.

'IT CAN'T BE VERY HARD,' Owen repeated.

But I said I didn't want him to try it and take a chance of hurting Dan; if Dan already knew the story – even if he knew only the 'setting' – he *would* be hurt, I said.

'I DON'T THINK IT'S DAN YOU'RE WORRIED ABOUT,' said Owen Meany.

'What do you mean, Owen?' I asked him; he shrugged – sometimes I think that Owen Meany *invented* shrugging.

'I THINK YOU'RE AFRAID TO FIND OUT WHO YOUR FATHER IS,' he said.

'Fuck you, Owen,' I said; he shrugged again.

'LOOK AT IT THIS WAY,' said Owen Meany. 'YOU'VE BEEN GIVEN A CLUE. NO EFFORT FROM YOU WAS REQUIRED. *GOD* HAS GIVEN YOU A CLUE. NOW YOU HAVE A CHOICE: EITHER YOU USE GOD'S GIFT OR YOU WASTE IT. I THINK A LITTLE EFFORT FROM YOU IS REQUIRED.'

'I think you care more about who my father is than *I* do,' I told him; he nodded. It was the day of New Year's Eve, December 31, 1961, about two o'clock in the afternoon, and we were sitting in the grubby living room of Hester's apartment in Durham, New Hampshire; it was a living room we routinely shared with Hester's roommates – two university girls who were almost Hester's equal in slovenliness, but sadly no match for Hester in sex appeal. The girls were not there; they had gone to their parents' homes for Christmas vacation. Hester was not there, either; Owen and I would never have discussed my mother's secret life in Hester's presence. Although it was only two o'clock in the afternoon, Hester had already consumed several rum and Cokes; she was sound asleep in her bedroom – as oblivious to Owen's and my discussion as my mother was.

'LET'S DRIVE TO THE GYM AND PRACTICE THE SHOT,' said Owen Meany.

'I don't feel like it,' I said.

'TOMORROW IS NEW YEAR'S DAY,' Owen reminded me. 'THE GYM WILL BE CLOSED TOMORROW.'

From Hester's bedroom – even though the door was closed – we could hear her breathing; Hester's breathing, when she'd been drinking, was something between a snore and a moan.

'Why does she drink so much?' I asked Owen.

'HESTER'S AHEAD OF HER TIME,' he said.

'What's that mean?' I asked him. 'Do we have a generation of *drunks* to look forward to?'

'WE HAVE A GENERATION OF PEOPLE WHO ARE *ANGRY* TO LOOK FORWARD TO,' Owen said. 'AND MAYBE *TWO* GENERATIONS OF PEOPLE WHO DON'T GIVE A SHIT,' he added.

'How do *you* know?' I asked him.

'I DON'T KNOW HOW I KNOW,' said Owen Meany. 'I JUST KNOW THAT I KNOW,' he said.

Toronto: June 9, 1987 – after a weekend of wonderful weather here, sunny and clear-skyed and as cool as it is in the fall, I broke down and bought *The New York Times*; thank God, no one I know saw me. One of the Brocklebank daughters got married on the weekend in the Bishop Strachan chapel; the BSS girls tend to do that – they come back to the old school to tie the knot, even the ones who were miserable when they were students here. Sometimes, I'm invited to the weddings – Mrs Brocklebank invited me to this one – but this particular daughter had managed to escape ever being a student of mine, and I felt that Mrs Brocklebank invited me only because I ran into her while she was fiercely trimming her hedge. No one sent me a formal invitation. I like to stand on a *little* ceremony; I felt it wasn't my place to attend. And besides: the Brocklebank daughter was marrying an American. I think it's because I ran into a carload of Americans on Russell Hill Road that I broke down and bought *The New York Times*.

The Americans were lost; they couldn't find The Bishop Strachan School or the chapel – they had a New York license plate and no understanding of how to pronounce Strachan.

'Where's Bishop *Stray*-chen?' a woman asked me.

'Bishop *Strawn*,' I corrected her.

'What?' she said. 'I can't understand him,' she told her husband, the driver. 'I think he's speaking French.'

'I was speaking English,' I informed the idiot woman. 'They speak French in Montreal. You're in Toronto. We speak English here.'

'Do you know where Bishop *Stray*-chen is?' her husband shouted.

'It's Bishop *Strawn*!' I shouted back.

'No, *Stray*-chen!' shouted the wife.

One of the kids in the back seat spoke up.

'I think he's telling you how to *pronounce* it,' the kid told his parents.

'I don't want to know how to pronounce it,' his father said, 'I just want to know where it *is*.'

'Do you know where it is?' the woman asked me.

'No,' I said. 'I've never heard of it.'

'He's never heard of it!' the wife repeated. She took a letter out of her purse, and opened it. 'Do you know where Lonsdale Road is?' she asked me.

'Somewhere around here,' I said. 'I think I've heard of that.'

They drove off – in the direction of St Clair, and the reservoir; they went the wrong way, of course. Their plans were certainly unclear, but they exhibited an exemplary American firmness.

And so I must have been feeling a little homesick; I get that way from time to time. And what a day it was to buy *The New York Times*! I don't suppose there's ever a *good* day to buy it. But what a story I read!

Nancy Reagan Says Hearings
Have Not Affected President

Oh, boy. Mrs Reagan said that the congressional hearings on the Iran-contra deals had not affected the president. Mrs Reagan was in Sweden to observe a drug-abuse program in a high school in a Stockholm suburb; I guess she's one of those many American adults of a certain advanced age who believe that the root of all evil lies in the area of young people's self-abuse. Someone should tell Mrs Reagan that young people – not even young people on drugs – are *not* the ones responsible for the major problems besetting the world!

The wives of American presidents have always been active in eradicating their pet peeves; Mrs Reagan is all upset about drug abuse. I think it was Mrs Johnson who wanted to rid the nation of junk cars; those cars that no longer could be driven anywhere, but simply sat – rusting into the landscape . . . they made her absolutely passionate about their removal. And there was another president's wife; or maybe it was a vice-president's wife, who thought it was a *disgrace* how the nation, as a whole, paid so little attention to 'art'; I forget what it was that she wanted to do about it.

But it doesn't surprise me that the president is 'not affected' by the congressional hearings; he hasn't been too 'affected' by what the Congress tells him he can and can't do, either. I doubt that these hearings are going to 'affect' him very greatly.

Who *cares* if he 'knew' – exactly, or inexactly – that money raised by secret arms sales to Iran was being diverted to the support of the Nicaraguan rebels? I don't think most Americans care.

Americans got bored with hearing about Vietnam before they got out of Vietnam; Americans got bored with hearing about Watergate, and what Nixon did or didn't do – even before the evidence was all in. Americans are already bored with Nicaragua; by the time these congressional hearings on the Iran-contra affair are over, Americans won't know (or care) *what* they think – except that they'll be sick and tired of it. After a while, they'll be tired of the Persian Gulf, too. They're already sick to death of Iran.

This syndrome is as familiar to me as Hester throwing up on New Year's Eve. It was New Year's Eve, 1963; Hester was vomiting in the rose garden, and Owen and I were watching TV. There were 16,300 U.S. military personnel in Vietnam.

On New Year's Eve in '64, a total of 23,300 Americans were there; Hester was barfing her brains out again. I think the January thaw was early that year; I think that was the year Hester was puking in the rain, but maybe the early thaw was New Year's Eve in 1965, when there were 184,300 U.S. military personnel in Vietnam. Hester just threw up; she was nonstop. She was violently opposed to the Vietnam War; she was *radically* opposed to it. Hester was so ferociously antiwar that Owen Meany used to say that he knew of only one good way to get all those Americans out of Vietnam.

'WE SHOULD SEND HESTER INSTEAD,' he used to say. 'HESTER SHOULD *DRINK* HER WAY THROUGH NORTH VIETNAM,' Owen would say. 'WE SHOULD SEND HESTER TO HANOI,' he told me. 'HESTER, I'VE GOT A GOOD IDEA,' Owen said to her. 'WHY DON'T YOU GO THROW UP ON HANOI INSTEAD?'

On New Year's Eve, 1966, there were 385,300 U.S. military personnel in Vietnam; 6,644 had been killed in action. Hester and Owen and I weren't together for New Year's Eve that year. I watched the television at 80 Front Street by myself. Somewhere, I was sure, Hester was throwing up; but I didn't know where. In '67, there were 485,600 Americans in Vietnam; 16,021 had been killed there. I watched television at 80 Front Street, alone again. I'd had a little too much to drink myself; I was trying to remember when Grandmother had purchased a color television set, but I couldn't. I'd had enough to drink so that *I* was sick in the rose garden; it was cold enough to make me hope, for Hester's sake, that she was throwing up in a warmer climate.

Owen *was* in a warmer climate.

I don't remember where I was or what I did for New Year's Eve in 1968. There were 536,100 U.S. military personnel in Vietnam; that was still about 10,000 short of what our peak number would be. Only 30,610 Americans had been killed in action, about 16,000 short of the number of Americans who would die there. Wherever I was for New Year's Eve, 1968, I'm sure I was drunk and throwing up; wherever Hester was, I'm sure she was drunk and throwing up, too.

As I've said, Owen didn't show me what he wrote in his diary; it was much later – after everything, after almost everything – when I saw what he'd written there. There is one particular entry I wish I could have read *when* he wrote it; it is a very early entry, not far from his excited optimism following Kennedy's inauguration, not all that far from his thanking my grandmother for the gift of the diary and his announced intention to make her proud of him This entry strikes me as important; it is dated January 1, 1962, and it reads as follows:

> I KNOW THREE THINGS. I KNOW THAT MY VOICE DOESN'T CHANGE, AND I KNOW WHEN I'M GOING TO DIE. I WISH I KNEW *WHY* MY VOICE NEVER CHANGES, I WISH I KNEW *HOW* I WAS GOING TO DIE; BUT GOD HAS ALLOWED ME TO KNOW MORE THAN MOST PEOPLE KNOW – SO I'M NOT COMPLAINING. THE THIRD THING I KNOW IS THAT I AM GOD'S INSTRUMENT; I HAVE FAITH THAT GOD WILL LET ME KNOW WHAT I'M SUPPOSED TO DO, AND WHEN I'M SUPPOSED TO DO IT. HAPPY NEW YEAR!

That was the January of our senior year at Gravesend Academy; if I had understood then that this was his fatalistic acceptance of what he 'knew,' I could have better understood why he behaved as he did – when the world appeared to turn against him, and he hardly raised a hand in his own defense.

We were hanging around the editorial offices of *The Grave* – that year The Voice was also editor-in-chief – when a totally unlikable senior named Larry Lish told Owen and me that President Kennedy was 'diddling' Marilyn Monroe.

Larry Lish – Herbert Lawrence Lish, Jr (his father was the movie producer Herb Lish) – was arguably Gravesend's most cynical and decadent student. In his junior year, he'd gotten a town girl pregnant, and his mother – only recently divorced from his father – had so skillfully and swiftly arranged for the girl's abortion that not even Owen and I knew who the girl was; Larry Lish had spoiled a lot of girls' good times. His mother was said to be ready to fly his girlfriends to Sweden at the drop of a hat; it was rumored that she accompanied the girls, too – just to make sure they went through with it. And after these return trips from Sweden, the girls never wanted to see Larry again. He was a charming sociopath, the kind of creep who makes a good first impression on those poor, sad people who are dazzled by top-drawer accents and custom-made dress shirts.

He was witty – even Owen was impressed by Lish's editorial cleverness for *The Grave* – and he was cordially loathed by students and faculty alike; I say 'cordially,' in the case of the students, because no one would have refused an invitation to one of his father's or his mother's parties. In the case of the faculty, they exercised a 'cordial' hatred of Lish because his father was so famous that many faculty members were afraid of him – and Lish's mother, the divorcée, was a beauty and a whorish flirt. I'm sure that some of the faculty lived for the glimpse they might get of her on Parents' Day; many of the students felt that way about Larry Lish's mother, too.

Owen and I had never been invited to one of Mr or Mrs Lish's parties; New Hampshire natives are not regularly within striking distance of New York City – not to mention Beverly Hills. Herb Lish lived in Beverly Hills; those were Hollywood parties, and Larry Lish's Gravesend acquaintances who were fortunate enough to come from the Los Angeles area claimed to have met actual 'starlets' at those lavish affairs.

Mrs Lish's Fifth Avenue parties were no less provocative; the seduction and intimidation of young people was an activity both Lishes enjoyed. And the New York girls – although they weren't always aspiring actresses – were reputed to 'do it' with even less resistance than the marginal protestations offered by the California variety.

Mr and Mrs Lish, following their divorce, were in competition for young Larry's doubtful affection; they had chosen a route to his heart that was strewn with excessive partying and expensive sex. Larry divided his vacations between New York City and Beverly Hills. On both coasts, the segment of society that Mr and Mrs Lish 'knew' was comprised of the kind of people who struck many Gravesend Academy seniors as the most fascinating people *alive*; Owen and I, however, had never *heard* of most of these people. But we had certainly heard of President John F. Kennedy; and we had certainly seen every movie that starred Marilyn Monroe.

'You know what my mother told me over the vacation?' Larry Lish asked Owen and me.

'Let me guess,' I said. 'She's going to buy you an airplane.'

'AND WHEN YOUR FATHER HEARD ABOUT IT,' said Owen Meany, 'HE SAID HE'D BUY YOU A VILLA IN FRANCE – ON THE RIVIERA!'

'Not this year,' Larry Lish said slyly. 'My mother told me that JFK was diddling Marilyn Monroe – and countless others,' he added.

'THAT IS A TRULY TASTELESS LIE!' said Owen Meany.

'It's the truth,' Larry Lish said, smirking.

'SOMEONE WHO SPREADS THAT KIND OF RUMOR OUGHT TO BE IN *JAIL!*' Owen said.

'Can you see my mother in jail?' Lish asked. 'This is no *rumor*. The truth is, the prez makes Ladies' Man Meany look like a *virgin* – the prez gets any woman he wants.'

'HOW DOES YOUR MOTHER KNOW THIS?' Owen asked Lish.

'She knows *all* the Kennedys,' Lish said, after a moderately tense silence. 'And my dad knows Marilyn Monroe,' he said.

'I SUPPOSE THEY "DO IT" IN THE WHITE HOUSE?' Owen asked.

'I know they've done it in New York,' Lish said. 'I don't know where *else* they've done it – all I know is, they've been doing it for *years*. And when the prez isn't interested in her anymore, I hear that *Bobby's* going to get her.'

'YOU'RE DISGUSTING!' said Owen Meany.

'The *world's* disgusting!' Larry Lish said cheerfully. 'Do you think I'm lying?'

'YES, I DO,' Owen said.

'My mother's going to pick me up and take me skiing – next weekend,' Lish said. 'You can ask her yourself.'

Owen shrugged.

'Do you think *she's* lying?' Lish asked; Owen shrugged again. He hated Lish – *and* Lish's mother; or, at least, he hated the kind of woman he imagined Larry Lish's mother was. But Owen Meany wouldn't have called anyone's mother a liar.

'Let me tell you, Sarcasm Master,' Larry Lish said. 'My mother's a gossip, and she's a bitch, but she's *not* a liar; she doesn't have enough imagination to make anything up!'

It was one of the more painful things about our peers at Gravesend Academy; it hurt Owen and me to hear how many of our schoolmates commonly put their parents down. They took their parents' money, and they abused their parents' summer houses and weekend retreats – when their parents weren't even aware that the kids had their own keys! And they frequently spoke of their parents as if they thought their parents were trash – or, at least, ignorant beyond saving.

'DOES *JACKIE* KNOW ABOUT MARILYN MONROE?' Owen asked Larry Lish.

'You can ask my mother,' Lish said.

The prospect of conversation with Larry Lish's mother was not relaxing to Owen Meany. He brooded all week. He avoided the editorial offices of *The Grave*, a hangout in which Owen was regularly king. Owen, after all, had been *inspired* by JFK; although the subject of the president's personal (or sexual) morality would not have dampened everyone's enthusiasm for his political ideals and his political goals, Owen Meany was not 'everyone' – nor was he sophisticated enough to separate public and private morality. I doubt that Owen ever would have become 'sophisticated' enough to make that separation – not even today, when it seems that the only people who are adamant in their claim that public and private morality are *in*separable are those creep-evangelists who profess to 'know' that God prefers capitalists to communists, and nuclear power to long hair.

Where would Owen fit in today? He was shocked that JFK – a married man! – could have been 'diddling' Marilyn Monroe; not to mention 'countless others.' But Owen would never have claimed that he 'knew' what God wanted; he always hated the sermon part of the service – of *any* service. He hated anyone who claimed to 'know' God's opinion of current events.

Today, the fact that President Kennedy enjoyed carnal knowledge of Marilyn Monroe and 'countless others' – even *during* his presidency – seems only moderately improper, and even stylish, in comparison to the willful secrecy and deception, and the unlawful policies, so broadly practiced by the entire Reagan administration. The idea of President Reagan getting laid, at all – by *anyone*! – comes only as welcome and comic relief alongside all his *other* mischief!

But 1962 was not today; and Owen Meany's expectations for the Kennedy administration were ripe with the hopefulness and optimism of a nineteen-year-old who desired to *serve* his country – to be of *use*. In the previous spring, the Bay of Pigs invasion of Cuba had upset Owen; but although that was a disturbing error, it was not adultery.

'IF KENNEDY CAN *RATIONALIZE* ADULTERY, WHAT *ELSE* CAN HE RATIONALIZE?' Owen asked me. Then he got angry and said: 'I'M FORGETTING HE'S A MACKEREL-

SNAPPER! IF CATHOLICS CAN CONFESS ANYTHING, THEY CAN FORGIVE THEMSELVES ANYTHING, TOO! CATHOLICS CAN'T EVEN GET DIVORCED; MAYBE THAT'S THE PROBLEM. IT'S *SICK* NOT TO LET PEOPLE GET DIVORCED!'

'Look at it this way,' I told him. 'You're president of the United States; you're very good-looking. Countless women want to sleep with you – countless and beautiful women will do anything you ask. They'll even come to the linen-service entrance of the White House after midnight!'

'THE LINEN-SERVICE ENTRANCE?' said Owen Meany.

'You know what I mean,' I said. 'If you could fuck absolutely any woman you wanted to fuck, *would* you – or wouldn't you?'

'I CAN'T BELIEVE THAT YOUR UPBRINGING AND YOUR EDUCATION HAVE BEEN *WASTED* ON YOU,' he said. 'WHY STUDY HISTORY OR LITERATURE – NOT TO MENTION RELIGIOUS KNOWLEDGE AND SCRIPTURE AND ETHICS? WHY *NOT* DO ANYTHING – IF THE ONLY REASON NOT TO IS NOT TO GET CAUGHT?' he asked. 'DO YOU CALL THAT MORALITY? DO YOU CALL THAT *RESPONSIBLE*? THE PRESIDENT IS ELECTED TO UPHOLD THE CONSTITUTION; TO PUT THAT MORE BROADLY, HE'S CHOSEN TO UPHOLD THE *LAW* – HE'S NOT GIVEN A LICENSE TO OPERATE *ABOVE* THE LAW, HE'S SUPPOSED TO BE OUR *EXAMPLE*!'

Remember that? Remember *then*?

I remember what Owen said about 'Project 100,000,' too – remember that? That was a draft program outlined by the secretary of defense, Robert McNamara, in 1966. Of the first 240,000 taken into the military between 1966 and 1968, 40 percent read below sixth-grade level, 41 percent were black, 75 percent came from low-income families, 80 percent had dropped out of high school. 'The poor of America have not had the opportunity to earn their fair share of this nation's abundance,' Secretary McNamara said, 'but they can be given an opportunity to serve in their country's defense.'

That made Owen Meany hopping mad.

'DOES HE THINK HE'S DOING "THE POOR OF AMERICA" SOME *FAVOR*?' Owen cried. 'WHAT HE'S *SAYING* IS, YOU DON'T HAVE TO BE WHITE – OR A GOOD READER – TO *DIE*! THAT'S *SOME* "OPPORTUNITY"!

I'LL BET "THE POOR OF AMERICA" ARE REALLY GOING TO BE *GRATEFUL* FOR THIS!'

Toronto: July 11, 1987 – it's been so hot, I wish Katherine would invite me up to her family's island in Georgian Bay; but she has such a large family, I'm sure she's suffered her share of houseguests. I have fallen into a bad habit here: I buy *The New York Times* almost every day. I don't exactly know why I want or need to know anything *more*.

According to *The New York Times*, a new poll has revealed that most Americans believe that President Reagan is lying; what they should be asked is, *Do they care?*

I wrote Katherine and asked her when she was going to invite me to Georgian Bay. 'When are you going to rescue me from my own bad habits?' I asked her. I wonder if you can buy *The New York Times* in Pointe au Baril Station; I hope not.

Larry's mother, Mitzy Lish, had honey-colored, slightly sticky-looking hair – it was coiffed in a bouffant style – and her complexion was much improved by a suntan; in the winter months, when she'd not just returned from her annual pilgrimage to Round Hill, Jamaica, her skin turned a shade sallow. Because her complexion was further wrecked by blotchiness in the extreme cold, and because her excessive smoking had ill-influenced her circulation, a weekend of winter skiing in New England – even to forward the cause of her competition for her son's affection – did not favor either Mrs Lish's appearance or her disposition. Yet it was impossible not to see her as an attractive 'older' woman; she was not quite up to President Kennedy's standards, but Mitzy Lish was a beauty by any standard Owen and I had to compare her to.

Hester's early-blooming eroticism, for example, had not been improved by her carelessness or by alcohol; even though Mrs Lish smoked up a storm, and her amber hair was dyed (because she was graying at her roots), Mrs Lish looked sexier than Hester.

She wore too much gold and silver for New Hampshire; in New York, I'm sure, she was certainly in vogue – but her clothes and her jewelry, and her bouffant, were more suited to the kind of hotels and cities where 'evening' or formal clothes are standard. In Gravesend, she stood out; and it is hard to imagine that there was a small skiers' lodge in New Hampshire, or in Vermont, that ever could have pleased her. She had ambitions beyond the simple luxury of a private bath; she was a woman who needed room service – who wanted her first cigarette and her coffee and her *New York Times* before she got out of bed. And then she would need sufficient light and a proper makeup mirror, in front of which she would require a decent amount of time; she would be snappish if *ever* she was rushed.

Her days in New York, before lunch, consisted *only* of cigarettes and coffee and *The New York Times* – and the patient, loving task of making herself up. She was an impatient woman, but never when applying her makeup. Lunch with a fellow gossip, then: or, these days, following her divorce, with her lawyer or a potential lover. In the afternoon, she'd have her hair done or she'd do a little shopping; at the very least, she'd buy a few new magazines or see a movie. She might meet someone for a drink, later. She possessed all the up-to-date information that often passes for intelligence among people who make a daily and extensive habit of *The New York Times* – and the available, softer gossip – and she had *oodles* of time to consume all this contemporary news. She had never worked.

She took quite a lot of time for her evening bath, too, and then there was the evening makeup to apply; it irritated her to make any dinner plans that required her presence before eight o'clock – but it irritated her *more* to have *no* dinner plans. She didn't cook – not even eggs. She was too lazy to make real coffee; the instant stuff went well enough with her cigarettes and her newspaper. She would have been an early supporter of those sugar-free, diet soft drinks – because she was obsessed with losing weight (and opposed to exercise).

She blamed her troublesome complexion on her ex-husband, who had been stressful to live with; and their divorce had cut her out of California – where she preferred to spend the winter months, where it was better for her skin. She swore her pores were actually *larger* in New York. But she maintained the Fifth Avenue apartment with a vengeance; and included in her alimony was the expense of her annual pilgrimage to Round Hill, Jamaica – always at a time in the winter when her complexion had become intolerable to her –

and a summer rental in the Hamptons (because not even Fifth Avenue was any fun in July and August). A woman of her sophistication – and used to the standard of living she'd grown accustomed to, as Herb Lish's wife and the mother of his only child – simply needed the sun and the salt air.

She would be a popular divorcée for quite a number of years; she would appear in no hurry to remarry – in fact, she'd turn down a few proposals. But, one year, she would either anticipate that her looks were going, or she would notice that her looks had gone; it would take her more and more time in front of the makeup mirror – simply to salvage what used to be there. Then she would change; she would become quite aggressive on the subject of her second marriage; she realized it was time. Pity whatever boyfriend was with her at this time; he would be blamed for leading her on – and worse, for never allowing her to develop a proper career. There was no honorable course left to him but to marry the woman he had made so dependent on him – whoever he was. She would say he was the reason she'd never stopped smoking, too; by not marrying her, he had made her too nervous to stop smoking. And her oily complexion, formerly the responsibility of her ex-husband, was now the present boyfriend's fault, too; if she was sallow, she was sallow because of *him*.

He was also the cause of her announced depression. Were he to leave her – were he to *abandon* her, to *not* marry her – he could at the very least assume the financial burden of maintaining her psychiatrist. Without *his* aggravation, after all, she would never have *needed* a psychiatrist.

How – you may ask – do I, or did I, 'know' so much about my classmate's unfortunate mother, Mitzy Lish? I told you that Gravesend Academy students were – many of them – very sophisticated; and none of them was more 'sophisticated' than Larry Lish. Larry told everyone everything he knew about his mother; imagine that! Larry thought his mother was a joke.

But in January of 1962, Owen Meany and I were terrified of Mrs Lish. She wore a fur coat that was responsible for the death of countless small mammals, she wore sunglasses that completely concealed her opinion of Owen and me – although we were sure, somehow, that Mrs Lish thought we were rusticated to a degree that defied our eventual education;

we were sure that Mrs Lish would rather suffer the agonies of giving up smoking than suffer such boredom as an evening of *our* company.

'HELLO, MISSUS LISH,' said Owen Meany. 'IT'S NICE TO SEE YOU AGAIN.'

'Hello!' I said. 'How are you?'

She was the kind of woman who drank nothing but vodka-tonics, because she cared about her breath; because of her smoking, she was extremely self-conscious about her breath. Nowadays, she'd be the kind of woman who'd carry one of those breath-freshening atomizers in her purse – gassing herself with the atomizer, all day long, just in case someone might be moved to spontaneously kiss her.

'Go on, *tell* him,' Larry Lish said to his mother.

'My son says you doubt that the president fools around,' Mrs Lish said to Owen. When she said 'fools around,' she opened her fur – her perfume rushed out at us, and we breathed her in. 'Well, let me tell you,' said Mitzy Lish, 'he fools around – plenty.'

'WITH MARILYN MONROE?' Owen asked Mrs Lish.

'With her – and with countless others,' Mrs Lish said; she wore a little too much lipstick – even for 1962 – and when she smiled at Owen Meany, we could see a smear of lipstick on one of her big, upper-front teeth.

'DOES JACKIE KNOW?' Owen asked Mrs Lish.

'She must be used to it,' Mrs Lish said; she appeared to relish Owen's distress. 'What do you think of *that*?' she asked Owen; Mitzy Lish was the kind of woman who bullied young men, too.

'I THINK IT'S *WRONG*,' said Owen Meany.

'Is he for real?' Mrs Lish asked her son. Remember that? Remember when people used to ask if you were 'for real'?

'Isn't he a *classic*?' Larry Lish asked his mother.

'This is the editor-in-chief of your school newspaper?' Mrs Lish asked her son; he was laughing.

'That's right,' Larry Lish said; his mother really cracked him up.

'This is the valedictorian of your *class*?' Mitzy Lish asked Larry.

'Yes!' Larry said; he couldn't stop laughing. Owen was so serious about being the valedictorian of our class that he was already writing his commencement speech – and it was only

January. In many schools, they don't even know who the class valedictorian *is* until the spring term; but Owen Meany's grade-point average was perfect – no other student was even close.

'Let me ask you something,' Mrs Lish said to Owen. 'If Marilyn Monroe wanted to sleep with *you*, would you *let* her?' I thought that Larry Lish was going to fall down – he was laughing so hard. Owen looked fairly calm. He offered Mrs Lish a cigarette, but she preferred her own brand; he lit her cigarette for her, and then he lit one for himself. He appeared to be thinking over the question very carefully.

'Well? Come on,' Mrs Lish said seductively. 'We're talking *Marilyn Monroe* – we're talking the most perfect piece of ass you can *imagine*! Or don't you like Marilyn Monroe?' She took off her sunglasses; she had very pretty eyes, and she knew it. 'Would you or wouldn't you?' she asked Owen Meany. She winked at him; and then, with the painted nail of her long index finger, she touched him on the tip of his nose.

'NOT IF I WERE THE *PRESIDENT*,' Owen said. 'AND CERTAINLY NOT IF I WERE *MARRIED*!'

Mrs Lish laughed; it was something between a hyena and the sounds Hester made in her sleep when she'd been drinking.

'This is the *future*?' Mitzy Lish asked. 'This is the head of the class of the country's most prestigious fucking school – and *this* is what we can expect of our future *leaders*?'

No, Mrs Lish – I can answer you now. This was *not* what we could expect of our future leaders. This was not where our future would lead us; our future would lead us elsewhere – and to leaders who bear little resemblance to Owen Meany.

But, at the time, I was not bold enough to answer her. Owen, however, was no one anyone could bully – Owen Meany accepted what he thought was his fate, but he would not tolerate being treated *lightly*.

'OF COURSE, *I'M NOT THE PRESIDENT*,' *Owen said shyly*. '*AND I'M NOT MARRIED, EITHER. I DON'T EVEN KNOW* MARILYN MONROE, OF COURSE,' he said. 'AND SHE PROBABLY WOULDN'T *EVER* WANT TO SLEEP WITH ME. BUT – YOU KNOW WHAT?' he asked Mrs Lish, who was – with her son – overcome with laughter. 'IF *YOU* WANTED TO SLEEP WITH ME – I MEAN *NOW*, WHEN I'M NOT THE PRESIDENT, AND I'M NOT MARRIED –

WHAT THE HELL,' Owen said to Mitzy Lish, 'I SUPPOSE I'D *TRY* IT.'

Have you ever seen dogs choke on their food? Dogs *inhale* their food – they're quite dramatic chokers. I never saw anyone stop laughing as quickly as Mrs Lish and her son – they stopped cold.

'What did you say to me?' Mrs Lish asked Owen.

'WELL? COME ON,' said Owen Meany. 'WOULD YOU OR WOULDN'T YOU?' He didn't wait for an answer; he shrugged. We were standing in the dry, dusty stink of cigarettes that was the commonplace air in the editorial offices of *The Grave*, and Owen simply walked over to the coat tree and removed his red-and-black-checkered hunter's cap and his jacket of the same well-worn material; then he walked out in the cold, which so ill-affected Mrs Lish's troublesome complexion. Larry Lish was such a coward, he never said a word to Owen – nor did he jump on Owen's back and pound Owen's head into the nearest snowbank. Either Larry was a coward or he knew that his mother's 'honor' was not worth such a robust defense; in my opinion, Mitzy Lish was not worth a defense of any kind.

But our headmaster, Randy White, was a chivalrous man – he was a gallant of the old school, when it came to defending the weaker sex. Naturally, he was outraged to hear of Owen's insulting remarks to Mrs Lish; naturally, he was grateful for the Lishes' support of the Capital Fund Drive, too. 'Naturally,' Randy White assured Mrs Lish, he would 'do something' about the indignity she had suffered.

When Owen and I were summoned to the headmaster's office, we did not know everything that Mitzy Lish had said about the 'incident' – that was how Randy White referred to it.

'I intend to get to the bottom of this disgraceful *incident*,' the headmaster told Owen and me. 'Did you or did you not *proposition* Missus Lish in the editorial offices of *The Grave*?' Randy White asked Owen.

'IT WAS A JOKE,' said Owen Meany. 'SHE WAS LAUGHING AT ME, ALL THE TIME – SHE MADE IT CLEAR THAT SHE THOUGHT I WAS A JOKE,' he said, 'AND SO I SAID SOMETHING THAT I THOUGHT WAS *APPROPRIATE*.'

'How could you *ever* think it was "appropriate" to proposition a fellow student's *mother*?' Randy White asked him. 'On school property!' the headmaster added.

Owen and I found out, later, that the business about the proposition occurring 'on school property' had especially incensed Mrs Lish; she'd told the headmaster that this was surely 'grounds for dismissal.' It was Larry Lish who told us that; he didn't like us, but Larry was a trifle ashamed that his mother was so intent on having Owen Meany thrown out of school.

'How could you think it "appropriate" to proposition a fellow student's *mother*?' Randy White repeated to Owen.

'I MEANT THAT MY REMARKS WERE "APPROPRIATE" TO *HER* BEHAVIOR,' Owen said.

'She was rude to him,' I pointed out to the headmaster.

'SHE MADE FUN OF ME BEING THE CLASS VALEDICTORIAN,' said Owen Meany.

'She laughed out loud at Owen,' I said to Randy White. 'She laughed in his face – she *bullied* him,' I added.

'SHE WAS *SEXY* WITH ME!' Owen said.

At the time, neither Owen nor I were capable of putting into words the correct description of the kind of sexual bully Mrs Lish was; maybe even Randy White would have understood our animosity toward a woman who lorded her sexual sophistication over us so cruelly – over Owen, in particular. She had flirted with him, she had taunted him, she had humiliated him – or she had *tried* to. What right did she have to be insulted by *his* rudeness to her, in return?

But I couldn't articulate this when I was nineteen and fidgeting in the headmaster's office.

'You asked another student's mother if she would sleep with you – in the presence of her own son!' said Randy White.

'YOU DON'T UNDERSTAND THE *CONTEXT*,' said Owen Meany.

'Tell me the "context,"' said Randy White.

Owen looked stricken.

'MISSUS LISH REVEALED TO US SOME PARTICULARLY DAMNING AND UNPLEASANT GOSSIP,' Owen said. 'SHE SEEMED PLEASED AT HOW THE NATURE OF THE GOSSIP UPSET ME.'

'That's true, sir,' I said.

'What was the gossip?' asked Randy White. Owen was silent.

'Owen – in your own defense, for God's sake!' I said.

'SHUT UP!' he told me.

'Tell me what she said to you, Owen,' the headmaster said.

'IT WAS VERY UGLY,' said Owen Meany, who actually thought he was protecting the president of the United States! Owen Meany was protecting the reputation of his commander-in-chief!

'Tell him, Owen!' I said.

'IT IS CONFIDENTIAL INFORMATION,' Owen said. 'YOU'LL JUST HAVE TO BELIEVE ME – SHE WAS *UGLY*. SHE DESERVED A JOKE – AT HER OWN EXPENSE,' Owen said.

'Missus Lish says that you crudely propositioned her in front of her son – I repeat, "crudely," ' said Randy White. 'She says you were insulting, you were lewd, you were obscene – and you were anti-Semitic,' the headmaster said.

'IS MISSUS LISH *JEWISH*?' Owen asked me. 'I DIDN'T EVEN *KNOW* SHE WAS JEWISH!'

'She says you were anti-Semitic,' the headmaster said.

'BECAUSE I *PROPOSITIONED* HER?' Owen asked.

'Then you admit that you "propositioned" her?' Randy White asked him. 'Suppose she'd said "Yes"?'

Owen Meany shrugged. 'I DON'T KNOW,' he said thoughtfully. 'I SUPPOSE I *WOULD* HAVE – WOULDN'T *YOU*?' he asked me. I nodded. 'I KNOW *YOU* WOULDN'T!' Owen said to the headmaster – 'BECAUSE YOU'RE *MARRIED*,' he added. 'THAT WAS SORT OF THE POINT I WAS MAKING – WHEN SHE BEGAN TO MAKE FUN OF ME,' he told Randy White. 'SHE ASKED ME IF I'D "DO IT" WITH MARILYN MONROE,' Owen explained, 'AND I SAID, "NOT IF I WERE MARRIED," AND SHE STARTED LAUGHING AT ME.'

'Marilyn Monroe?' the headmaster asked. 'How did Marilyn Monroe get involved in this?'

But Owen would say no more. Later, he told me, 'THINK OF THE *SCANDAL*! THINK OF SUCH A RUMOR LEAKING TO THE *NEWSPAPERS*!'

Did he think that the downfall of President Kennedy might come from an editorial in *The Grave*?

'Do you want to get kicked out of school for protecting the president?' I asked him.

'HE'S MORE IMPORTANT THAN I AM,' said Owen Meany. Nowadays, I'm not sure that Owen was right about that; he was right about most things – but I'm inclined to think that Owen Meany was as worthy of protection as JFK.

Look at what *assholes* are trying to protect the president these days!

But Owen Meany could not be persuaded to protect himself; he told Dan Needham that the nature of Mrs Lish's incitement constituted 'A THREAT TO NATIONAL SECURITY'; not even to save himself from Randy White's wrath would Owen Meany repeat what a slanderous rumor he had heard.

In faculty meeting, the headmaster argued that this kind of disrespect to adults – to school parents! – could not be tolerated. Mr Early argued that there was no school rule against propositioning *mothers*; Owen, Mr Early argued, had not broken a rule.

The headmaster attempted to have the matter turned over to the Executive Committee; but Dan Needham knew that Owen's chances of survival would be poor among *that* group of (largely) the headmaster's henchmen – at least, they comprised the majority in any vote, as The Voice had pointed out. It was not a matter for the Executive Committee, Dan argued; Owen had not committed an offense in any category that the school considered 'grounds for dismissal.'

Not so! said the headmaster. What about 'reprehensible conduct with girls'? Several faculty members hastened to point out that Mitzy Lish was 'no girl.' The headmaster then read a telegram that had been sent to him from Mrs Lish's ex-husband, Herb. The Hollywood producer said that he hoped the insult suffered by his ex-wife – and the embarrassment caused his son – would not go unpunished.

'So put Owen on disciplinary probation,' Dan Needham said. 'That's punishment; that's more than enough.'

But Randy White said there was a more serious charge against Owen than the mere propositioning of someone's mother; did the faculty not consider anti-Semitism 'serious'? Could a school of such a broadly based ethnic population tolerate this kind of 'discrimination'?

But Mrs Lish had never substantiated the charge that Owen had been anti-Semitic. Even Larry Lish, when questioned, couldn't remember anything in Owen's remarks that could be construed as anti-Semitic; Larry, in fact, admitted that his mother had a habit of labeling *everyone* who treated her with less than complete reverence as an anti-Semite – as if, in

Mrs Lish's view, the only *possible* reason to dislike her was that she was Jewish. Owen, Dan Needham pointed out, hadn't even *known* that the Lishes were Jewish.

'How could he not *know*?' Headmaster White cried.

Dan suggested that the headmaster's remark was more anti-Semitic than any remark attributed to Owen Meany.

And so he was spared; he was put on disciplinary probation – for the remainder of the winter term – with the warning, understood by all, that *any* offense of *any* kind would be considered 'grounds for dismissal'; in such a case, he would be judged by the Executive Committee and none of his friends on the faculty could save him.

The headmaster proposed – in addition to Owen's probation – that he be removed from his position as editor-in-chief of *The Grave*, or that The Voice should be silenced until the end of the winter term; or both. But this was not approved by the faculty.

In truth, Mrs Lish's charge of anti-Semiticism had backfired with a number of the faculty, who were quite belligerently anti-Semitic themselves. As for Randy White: Dan and Owen and I suspected that the headmaster was about as anti-Semitic as anyone we knew.

And so the incident rested with Owen Meany receiving the punishment of disciplinary probation for the duration of the winter term; aside from the jeopardy this put him in – in regard to any other trouble he might get into – disciplinary probation was no great imposition, especially for a day boy. Basically, he lost the senior privilege to go to Boston on Wednesday and Saturday afternoons; if he'd been a boarder, he would have lost the right to spend any weekend away from school, but since he was a day boy, he spent every weekend at home – or with me – anyway.

Yet Owen was not grateful for the leniency shown to him by the school; he was outraged that he had been punished at all. His hostility, in turn, was not appreciated by the faculty – including many of his supporters. They wanted to be congratulated for their generosity, and for standing up to the headmaster; instead, Owen cut them dead on the quadrangle paths. He greeted no one; he wouldn't even look up. He wouldn't speak – not even in class! – unless spoken to; and when forced to speak, his responses were uncharacteristically brief. As for his duties as editor-in-chief of *The Grave*, he simply stopped contributing the column that had given The Voice his name and his fame.

'What's happened to The Voice, Owen?' Mr Early asked him.

'THE VOICE HAS LEARNED TO KEEP HIS MOUTH SHUT,' Owen said.

'Owen,' Dan Needham said, 'don't piss off your friends.'

'THE VOICE HAS BEEN CENSORED,' said Owen Meany. 'JUST TELL THE FACULTY AND THE HEADMASTER THAT THE VOICE IS BUSY – *REVISING* HIS VALEDICTORY! I GUESS NO ONE CAN THROW ME OUT OF SCHOOL FOR WHAT I SAY AT *COMMENCEMENT*!'

Thus did Owen Meany respond to his punishment, by *threatening* the headmaster and the faculty with The Voice – only momentarily silenced, we all knew; but full of rage, we all were sure.

It was that numbskull from Zürich, Dr Dolder, who proposed to the faculty that Owen Meany should be required to talk with *him*.

'Such hostility!' Dr Dolder said. 'He has a talent for speaking out – yes? And now he is withholding his talent from us, he is denying himself the pleasure of speaking his mind – why? Without expression, his hostility will only increase – no?' Dr Dolder said. 'Better I should give him the opportunity to *vent* his hostility – on *me*!' the doctor said. 'After all, we would not want a repeated incident with *another* older woman. Maybe this time, it's a faculty *wife* – yes?' he said.

And so they told Owen Meany that he had to see the school psychiatrist.

' "FATHER, FORGIVE THEM; FOR THEY KNOW NOT WHAT THEY DO," ' he said.

Toronto: July 14, 1987 – still waiting for my invitation to Georgian Bay; it can't come soon enough. *The New York Times* appears to have reduced the Iran-contra affair to the single issue of whether or not President Reagan 'knew' that profits from the secret arms sales to Iran were being diverted to support the Nicaraguan contras. Jesus Christ! Isn't it enough to 'know' that the president wanted and intended to continue his support of the contras after Congress told him what was *enough*?

It makes me sick to hear the lectures delivered to Lt Col

Oliver North. What are they lecturing *him* for? The colonel wants to support the contras – 'for the love of God and for the love of country'; he's already testified that he'd do anything his commander-in-chief wanted him to do. And now we get to listen to the senators and the representatives who are running for office again; they tell the colonel all he doesn't know about the U.S. Constitution; they point out to him that patriotism is not necessarily defined as blind devotion to a president's particular agenda – and that to dispute a presidential policy is not necessarily anti-American. They might add that God is not a *proven* right-winger! Why are they pontificating the obvious to Colonel North? Why don't they have the balls to say this to their blessed commander-in-chief?

If Hester has been paying attention to any of this, I'll bet she's throwing up; I'll bet she's barfing her brains out. She would remember, of course, those charmless bumper stickers from the Vietnam era – those cunning American flags, and the red, white, and blue lettering of the name of our beloved nation. I'll bet Colonel North remembers them.

America!

said the bumper stickers.

Love It or
Leave It!

That made a lot of sense, didn't it? Remember that?

And now we have to hear a civics lecture – the country's elected officials are instructing a lieutenant colonel in the Marine Corps on the subject that love of country and love of God (and hatred of communism) can conceivably be represented, in a democracy, by differing points of view. The colonel shows no signs of being converted; why are these pillars of self-righteousness wasting their breath on *him*? I doubt that President Reagan could be converted to democracy, either.

I know what my grandmother used to say, whenever she saw or read anything that was just a lot of *bullshit*. Owen picked up the phrase from her; he was quite lethal in its application, our senior year at Gravesend. Whenever anyone said anything that was a lot of *bullshit* to him, Owen Meany used to say, 'YOU KNOW WHAT THAT IS? THAT'S *MADE FOR TELEVISION* – THAT'S WHAT THAT IS.' And that's what Owen would have said about the Iran-contra hearings – concerning what President Reagan did or didn't 'know.'

'MADE FOR TELEVISION,' he would have said.

That's how he referred to his sessions with Dr Dolder; the school made him see Dr Dolder twice a week, and when I asked him to describe his dialogue with the Swiss idiot, Owen said, 'MADE FOR TELEVISION.' He wouldn't tell me much else about the sessions, but he liked to mock some of the questions Dr Dolder had asked him by exaggerating the doctor's accent.

'ZO! YOU ARE ATTRACTED TO ZE OLDER *VIMMEN* – VY IS DAT?'

I wondered if he answered by saying he'd always been fond of my mother – maybe, he'd even been in love with her. That would have caused Dr Dolder great excitement, I'm sure.

'ZO! ZE *VOOMIN* YOU KILT MIT ZE BASEBALL – SHE MADE YOU VANT TO PROP-O-SI-TION PEOPLE'S *MUDDERS*, YES?'

'Come on,' I said to Owen. 'He's not *that* stupid!'

'ZO! *VITCH* FACULTY VIFE HAF YOU GOT YOUR EYES ON?'

'Come on!' I said. 'What kind of stuff does he ask you, *really*?'

'ZO! YOU BELIEF IN *GOT* – DAT'S FERRY IN-TER-EST-INK!'

Owen would never tell me what really went on in those sessions. I knew Dr Dolder was a moron; but I also knew that even a moron would have discovered some disturbing things about Owen Meany. For example, Dr Dolder – dolt though he was – would have heard at least a little of the GOD'S INSTRUMENT theme; even Dr Dolder would have uncovered Owen's perplexing and troubling anti-Catholicism. And Owen's particular brand of fatalism would have been challenging for a *good* psychiatrist; I'm sure Dr Dolder was scared to death about it. And would Owen have gone so far as to tell Dr Dolder about Scrooge's grave? Would Owen have suggested that he KNEW how much time he had left on our earth?

'What do you tell him?' I asked Owen.

'THE TRUTH,' said Owen Meany. 'I ANSWER EVERY

QUESTION HE ASKS TRUTHFULLY, AND WITHOUT HUMOR,' he added.

'My God!' I said. 'You could really get yourself in trouble!'

'VERY FUNNY,' he said.

'But, Owen,' I said. 'You tell him *everything* you think about, and everything you *believe*? *Not* everything you believe, right?' I asked.

'EVERYTHING,' said Owen Meany. 'EVERYTHING HE ASKS.'

'Jesus Christ!' I said. 'And what has *he* got to say? What's he told you?'

'HE TOLD ME TO TALK WITH PASTOR MERRILL – SO I HAVE TO SEE *HIM* TWICE A WEEK, TOO,' Owen said. 'AND WITH EACH OF THEM, I SIT THERE AND TALK ABOUT WHAT I TALKED ABOUT TO THE *OTHER* ONE. I GUESS THEY'RE FINDING OUT A LOT ABOUT EACH OTHER.'

'I see,' I said; but I didn't.

Owen had taken *all* the Rev. Lewis Merrill's courses at the academy; he had consumed all the Religion and Scripture courses so voraciously that there weren't any left for him in his senior year, and Mr Merrill had permitted him to pursue some independent study in the field. Owen was particularly interested in the miracle of the resurrection; he was interested in miracles in general, and life after death in particular, and he was writing an interminable term paper that related these subjects to that old theme from Isaiah 5:20, which he loved. 'Woe unto them that call evil good and good evil.' Owen's opinion of Pastor Merrill had improved considerably from those earlier years when the issue of the minister's doubt had bothered Owen's dogmatic side; Mr Merrill had to be aware – awkwardly so – of the role The Voice had played in securing his appointment as school minister. When they sat together in Pastor Merrill's vestry office, I couldn't imagine them – not either of them – as being quite at ease; yet there appeared to be much respect between them.

Owen did not have a relaxing effect on anyone, and no one I knew was ever *less* relaxed than the Rev. Lewis Merrill; and so I imagined that Hurd's Church would be creaking excessively during their interviews – or whatever they called them. They would both be fidgeting away in the vestry office, Mr Merrill opening and closing the old desk drawers, and sliding that old chair on the casters from one end of the desk to the other – while Owen Meany cracked his knuckles, crossed and uncrossed his little legs, and shrugged and sighed and reached out his hands to the Rev. Mr Merrill's desk, if only to pick up a paperweight or a prayer book and put it down again.

'What do you talk about with Mister Merrill?' I asked him.

'I TALK ABOUT DOCTOR DOLDER WITH PASTOR MERRILL, AND I TALK ABOUT PASTOR MERRILL WITH DOCTOR DOLDER,' Owen said.

'No, but I know you *like* Pastor Merrill – I mean, sort of. Don't you?' I asked him.

'WE TALK ABOUT LIFE AFTER DEATH,' said Owen Meany.

'I see,' I said; but I didn't. I didn't realize the degree to which Owen Meany never got tired of talking about that.

Toronto: July 21, 1987 – it is a scorcher in town today. I was getting my hair cut in my usual place, near the corner of Bathurst and St Clair, and the girl-barber (something I'll *never* get used to!) asked me the usual: 'How short?'

'As short as Oliver North's,' I said.

'Who?' she said. O Canada! But I'm sure there are young girls cutting hair in the United States who don't know who Colonel North is, either; and in a few years, almost no one will remember him. How many people remember Melvin Laird? How many people remember Gen. Creighton Abrams or Gen. William Westmoreland – not to mention, which one replaced the other? And who replaced Gen. Maxwell Taylor? Who replaced Gen. Curtis LeMay? And whom did Ellsworth Bunker replace? Remember that? Of course you don't!

There was a terrible din of construction going on outside the barbershop at the corner of Bathurst and St Clair, but I was sure that my girl-barber had heard me.

'Oliver North,' I repeated. 'Lieutenant Colonel Oliver North, United States Marine Corps,' I said.

'I guess you want it really short,' she said.

'Yes, please,' I said; I've simply got to stop reading *The New York Times*! There's nothing in the news that's worth remembering. Why, then, do I have such a hard time forgetting it?

No one had a memory like Owen Meany. By the end of the

winter term of '62, I'll bet he never once confused what he'd said to Dr Dolder with what he'd said to the Rev. Lewis Merrill – but I'll bet *they* were confused! By the end of the winter term, I'll bet they thought that either he *should* have been thrown out of school or he should have been made the new headmaster. By the end of *every* winter term at Gravesend Academy, the New Hampshire weather had driven *everyone* half crazy.

Who doesn't get tired of getting up in the dark? And in Owen's case, he had to get up earlier than most; because of his scholarship job, as a faculty waiter, he had to arrive in the dining-hall kitchen at least one hour before breakfast – on those mornings he waited on tables. The waiters had to set the tables – and eat their own breakfasts, in the kitchen – before the other students and the faculty arrived; then they had to clear the tables between the official end of breakfast and the beginning of morning meeting – as the new headmaster had so successfully called what used to be our morning chapel.

That Saturday morning in February, the tomato-red pickup was dead and he'd had to jump-start the Meany Granite Company trailer-truck and get it rolling down Maiden Hill before it would start – it was so cold. He did not like to have dining-hall duty, as it was called, on the weekend; and there was the added problem of him being a day boy and having to drive himself that extra distance to school. I guess he was cross when he got there; and there was another car parked in the circular driveway by the Main Academy Building, where he always parked. The trailer-truck was so big that the presence of only one other car in the circular driveway would force him to park the truck out on Front Street – and in the winter months, there was a ban regarding parking on Front Street, a snow-removal restriction that the town imposed, and Owen was hopping mad about that, too. The car that kept Owen from parking his truck in the circular driveway adjacent to the Main Academy Building was Dr Dolder's Volkswagen Beetle.

In keeping with the lovable and exasperating tidiness of his countrymen, Dr Dolder was exact and predictable about his little VW. His bachelor apartment was in Quincy Hall – a dormitory on the far side of the Gravesend campus; it seemed to be 'the far side' from *everywhere*, but it was as far from the Main Academy Building as you could get and still be on the Gravesend campus. Dr Dolder parked his VW by the Main Academy Building only when he'd been drinking.

He was a frequent dinner guest of Randy and Sam White's; he parked by the Main Academy Building when he ate with the Whites – and when he drank too much, he left his car there and walked home. The campus was not so large that he couldn't (or shouldn't) have walked *both* ways – to dinner and back – but Dr Dolder was one of those Europeans who had fallen in love with a most American peculiarity: how Americans will walk *nowhere* if they can drive there. In Zürich, I'm sure, Dr Dolder walked everywhere; but he drove his little VW across the Gravesend campus, as if he were touring the New England states.

Whenever Dr Dolder's VW was parked in the circular driveway by the Main Academy Building, *everyone* knew that the doctor was simply exercising his especially Swiss prudence; he was *not* a drunk, and the few small roads he might have traveled on to drive himself from dinner at the Whites' to Quincy Hall would not have given him much opportunity to maim many of the sober and innocent residents of Gravesend. There's a good chance he would never have encountered *anyone*; but Dr Dolder loved his Beetle, and he was a cautious man.

Once – in the fresh snow upon his Volkswagen's windshield – a first-year German student had written with his finger: *Herr Doktor Dolder hat zu viel betrunken!* I could usually tell – when I saw Owen, either at breakfast or at morning meeting – if Dr Dolder had had too much to drink the night before; if it was winter, and if Owen was surly-looking, I knew he'd faced an early-morning parking problem. I knew when the pickup had failed to start – and there was no room for him to park the trailer-truck – just by *looking* at him.

'What's up?' I would ask him.

'THAT TIGHT-ASS TIPSY SWISS *DINK*!' Owen Meany would say.

'I see,' I would say.

And this particular February morning, I can imagine how the Swiss psychiatrist's Beetle would have affected him.

I guess Owen must have been sitting in the frigid cab of the truck – you could drive that big hauler for an hour before you'd even *notice* that the heater was on – and I'll bet he was smoking, and probably talking to himself, too, when he looked into the path of his headlights and saw about three quarters of the basketball team walking his way. In the cold air, their breathing must have made him think that they were smoking, too – although he knew all of them, and knew they didn't smoke; he entertained them at least two or three times a week by his devotion to practicing the shot.

He told me later that there were about eight or ten basketball players – not quite the whole team. All of them lived in the same dorm – it was one of the traditional jock dorms on the campus; and because the basketball team was playing at some faraway school, they were on their way to the dining hall for an early breakfast with the waiters who had dining-hall duty. They were big, happy guys with goofy strides, and they didn't mind being out of bed before it was light – they were going to miss their Saturday morning classes, and they saw the whole day as an adventure. Owen Meany was not quite in such a cheerful mood; he rolled down the window of the big truck's frosty cab and called them over.

They were friendly, and – as always – extremely glad to see him, and they jumped onto the flatbed of the trailer and roughhoused with each other, pushing each other off the flatbed, and so forth.

'YOU GUYS LOOK VERY *STRONG* TODAY,' said Owen Meany, and they hooted in agreement. In the path of the truck's headlights, the innocent shape of Dr Dolder's Volkswagen Beetle stood encased in ice and dusted very lightly with last night's snow. 'I'LL BET YOU GUYS AREN'T STRONG ENOUGH TO PICK UP THAT VOLKSWAGEN,' said Owen Meany. But, of course, they were strong enough; they were not only strong enough to lift Dr Dolder's Beetle – they were strong enough to carry it out of town.

The captain of the basketball team was an agreeable giant; when Owen practiced the shot with this guy, the captain lifted Owen with one hand.

'No problem,' the captain said to Owen. 'Where do you want it?'

Owen swore to me that it wasn't until that moment that he got THE IDEA.

It's clear to me that Owen never overcame his irritation with Randy White for moving morning chapel from Hurd's Church to the Main Academy Building and calling it morning meeting, that he still thought of that as the headmaster's GRANDSTANDING. The sets for Dan's winter-term play had already been dismantled; the stage of The Great Hall, as it was called, was bare. And that broad, sweeping, marble stairway that led up to The Great Hall's triumphant double doors . . . all of that, Owen was sure, was big enough to permit the easy entrance of Dr Dolder's Volkswagen. And wouldn't *that* be something: to have that perky little automobile parked on center stage – a kind of cheerful, harmless message to greet the headmaster and the entire student body; a little something to make them smile, as the dog days of March bore down upon us and the long-awaited break for spring vacation could not come soon enough to save us all.

'CARRY IT INTO THE MAIN ACADEMY BUILDING,' Owen Meany told the captain of the basketball team. 'TAKE IT UPSTAIRS TO THE GREAT HALL AND CARRY IT UP ON THE STAGE,' said The Voice. 'PUT IT RIGHT IN THE MIDDLE OF THE STAGE, FACING FORWARD – RIGHT NEXT TO THE HEADMASTER'S PODIUM. BUT BE CAREFUL YOU DON'T SCRATCH IT – AND FOR GOD'S SAKE DON'T *DROP* IT! DON'T PUT A MARK ON *ANYTHING*,' he cautioned the basketball players. 'DON'T DO THE SLIGHTEST DAMAGE – NOT TO THE CAR AND NOT TO THE STAIRS, NOT TO THE DOORS OF THE GREAT HALL, NOT TO THE STAGE,' he said. 'MAKE IT LOOK LIKE IT *FLEW* UP THERE,' he told them. 'MAKE IT LOOK LIKE AN *ANGEL* DROVE IT ONSTAGE,' said Owen Meany.

When the basketball players carried off Dr Dolder's Volkswagen, Owen thought very carefully about using the available parking space; he decided it was wiser to drive all the way over to Waterhouse Hall and park next to Dan's car, instead. Not even Dan saw him park the truck there; and if anyone had seen him running across the campus, as it was growing light, that would not have seemed strange – he was just a faculty waiter with dining-hall duty, hurrying so that he wouldn't be late.

He ate his breakfast in the dining-hall kitchen with the other waiters and with an extraordinarily hungry and jolly bunch of basketball players. Owen was setting the head faculty table when the captain of the basketball team said good-bye to him.

'There wasn't the slightest damage – not to anything,' the captain assured him.

'HAVE A GOOD GAME!' said Owen Meany.

It was one of the janitors in the Main Academy Building who discovered the Beetle onstage – when he was raising the blinds on the high windows that welcomed so much morning light into The Great Hall. Naturally, the janitor called the headmaster. From the kitchen window of his obtrusive house, directly across from the Main Academy Building, Headmaster White could see the small rectangle of bare ground where Dr Dolder's Volkswagen had spent the night.

According to Dan Needham, the headmaster called him while he was getting out of the shower; most of the faculty made breakfast for themselves at home, or they skipped breakfast rather than eat in the school dining hall. The headmaster told Dan that he was rounding up all able-bodied faculty for the purpose of removing Dr Dolder's Volkswagen from the stage of The Great Hall – *before* morning meeting. The students, the headmaster told Dan, were *not* going to have 'the last laugh.' Dan said he didn't feel particularly able-bodied himself, but he'd certainly try to help out. When he hung up the phone, he was laughing to himself – until he looked out the window of Waterhouse Hall and saw the Meany Granite Company trailer-truck parked next to his own car. Dan suddenly thought that THE IDEA of putting Dr Dolder's Volkswagen on the stage of The Great Hall had Owen Meany's name written all over it.

That was exactly what the headmaster said, when he and about a dozen, *not*-very-able-bodied faculty members, along with a few hefty faculty wives, were struggling with Dr Dolder's Beetle.

'This has Owen Meany's name written all over it!' the headmaster said.

'I don't think Owen could lift a Volkswagen,' Dan Needham ventured cautiously.

'I mean, *the idea*!' the headmaster said.

As Dan describes it, the faculty were ill-trained for lifting anything; even the athletic types were neither as strong nor as flexible as young basketball players – and they should have considered something basic to their task: it is much easier to carry something heavy and awkward *up*stairs than it is to lug it *down*.

Mr Tubulari, the track-and-field coach, was overzealous in his descent of the stairs from the stage; he fell off and landed on the hard, wooden bench in the front row of assembled seats – a hymnal fortunately cushioned the blow to his head, or he might have been knocked senseless. Dan Needham described Mr Tubulari as 'already senseless, before his fall,' but the track-and-field coach severely sprained his ankle in the mishap and had to be carried to the Hubbard Infirmary. That left even fewer less-than-able-bodied faculty – and some beefy wives – to deal with the unfortunate wreck of Dr Dolder's Volkswagen, which now stood on its rear end, which is a Beetle's heavy end, where its engine is. The little car, standing so oddly upright, appeared to be saluting or applauding the weary faculty who had so ungracefully dropped it offstage.

'It's a good thing Dr Dolder isn't here,' Dan observed.

Because the headmaster was so riled up, no one wished to point out the obvious: that they would have been better off to let the students have 'the last laugh' – then the faculty could have ordered a strong, healthy bunch of students to carry the car safely offstage. If the *students* wrecked the car in the course of its removal from the Main Academy Building, then the *students* would have been responsible. As it was, things went from bad to worse, as they often will when amateurs are involved in an activity that they perform in bad temper – and in a hurry.

The students would be arriving for morning meeting in another ten or fifteen minutes; a smashed Volkswagen sitting on its rear end in the front of The Great Hall might very well produce a louder and longer laugh than a natty, well-cared for car facing them, undamaged, onstage. But there was brief discussion, if any, of this; the headmaster, bright-red in the face with the strain of lifting the solid little German marvel of the highways, urged the faculty to put their muscles into the chore and spare him their comments.

But there had been ice, and a little snow, on the VW; this was melted now. The car was wet and slippery; puddles of water were underfoot. One of the faculty wives – one especially prolific with progeny, and one whose maternal girth was more substantial than well coordinated – slipped *under* the Volkswagen as it was being returned to its wheels; although she was not hurt, she was wedged quite securely under the stubborn automobile. Volkswagens were pioneers in sealing the bottoms of their cars, and the poor faculty wife discovered that there was no gap beneath the car that would allow her to wriggle free.

This presented – with less than ten minutes before morning meeting – a new humiliation for the headmaster: Dr Dolder's damaged Volkswagen, leaking its engine and transmission oil upon the prostrate body of a *trapped* faculty wife; she was not an especially *popular* faculty wife among the students, either.

'Jesus Fucking Christ!' said Randy White.

Some of the 'early nerds' were already arriving. 'Early nerds' were students who were so eager for the school day to begin that they got to morning meeting long before the time they were required to be there. I don't know what they are called today; but I'm sure that such students are never called anything *nice*.

Some of these 'early nerds' were quite startled to be shouted at by the headmaster, telling them to 'come back at the proper time!' Meanwhile, in tilting the VW to its side – enough to allow the safe deliverance of the rotund faculty wife – the inexperienced car handlers tilted the Beetle too far; it fell flat on the driver's side (there went that window and that sideview mirror; the debris, together with the taillight glass from the VW's inexpert fall from the stage, was hastily swept under the front-row wooden bench where the injured Mr Tubulari had fallen).

Someone suggested getting Dr Dolder; if the doctor unlocked the car, the stalwart vehicle could be rolled, if not driven, to the head of the broad and sweeping marble stairway. Perhaps it would be easier to navigate the staircase with someone inside, behind the wheel?

'Nobody's calling Dolder!' the headmaster cried. Someone pointed out that – since the window was broken – it was, in any case, an unnecessary step. Also, someone else pointed out, the Volkswagen could not be driven, or rolled, on its *side*; better to solve *that* problem. But according to Dan, the untrained faculty were unaware of their own strength; in attempting to right the car upon its wheels, they heaved too hard and tossed it from the driver's side to the passenger side – flattening the front-row wooden bench (and there went the passenger-side window, and the *other* sideview mirror).

'Perhaps we should cancel morning meeting?' Dan Needham cautiously suggested. But the headmaster – to everyone's astonishment – actually righted the Volkswagen, upon its wheels, by *himself*! I guess his adrenal glands were pumping! Randy White then seized his lower back with both hands and dropped, cursing, to his knees.

'Don't touch me!' the headmaster cried. 'I'm fine!' he said, grimacing – and coming unsteadily to his feet. He sharply kicked the rear fender of Dr Dolder's car. Then he reached through the hole where the driver's-side window had been and unlocked the door. He sat behind the wheel – with apparent jolts of extreme discomfort assailing him from the region of his lower back – and commanded the faculty to push him.

'Where?' Dan Needham asked the headmaster.

'Down the Jesus Fucking Christ *stairs*!' Headmaster White cried. And so they pushed him; there was little point in trying to *reason* with him, Dan Needham later explained.

The bell for morning meeting was already ringing when Randy White began his bumpy descent of the broad and sweeping marble stairway; several students – *normal* students, in addition to the 'early nerds' – were milling around in the foyer of the Main Academy Building, at the foot of the staircase.

Who can really piece together all the details of such a case – I mean, who can ever get straight what happened *exactly*? It was an emotional moment for the headmaster. And there is no overestimating the pain in his lower back; he had *lifted* the car all by himself – whether his back muscles went into spasms *while* he was attempting to steer the VW downstairs, or whether he suffered the spasms *after* his spectacular accident . . . well, this is academic, isn't it?

Suffice it to say that the students in the foyer fled from the wildly approaching little vehicle. No doubt, the melted snow and ice were on the Beetle's tires, too – and marble, as everyone knows, is slippery. This way and that way, the dynamic little car hopped down the staircase; great slabs of marble appeared to leap off the polished handrails of the stairway – the result of the Volkswagen's gouging out hunks of marble as it skidded from side to side.

There's an old New Hampshire phrase that is meant to express extreme fragility – and damage: 'Like a robin's egg rollin' down the spout of a rain gutter!'

Thus did the headmaster descend the marble staircase from

The Great Hall to the foyer of the Main Academy Building – except that he didn't quite arrive at his destination. The car flipped and landed on its roof, and jammed itself sideways – and upside down – in the middle of the stairway. The doors could not be opened – nor could the headmaster be removed from the wreckage; such spasms assailed his lower back that he could not contort himself into the necessary posture to make an exit from the car through the space where the windshield had been. Randy White, sitting upside down and holding fast to the steering wheel, cried out that there was a 'conspiracy of students and faculty' who were – clearly – 'against' him. He said numerous, unprintable things about Dr Dolder's 'fussy-fucking drinking habits,' about *all* German-manufactured cars, about what 'wimps and pussys' were masquerading as 'able-bodied' among the faculty – *and* their wives! – and he shouted and *screamed* that his back was 'killing' him, until his wife, Sam, could be brought to the scene, where she knelt on the chipped marble stairs and gave her upside-down husband what comfort she could. Professionals were summoned to extricate him from the destroyed Volkswagen; later – long after morning meeting was over – they finally rescued the headmaster by removing the driver's-side door of Dr Dolder's poor car with a torch.

The headmaster was confined to the Hubbard Infirmary for the remainder of the day; the nurses, and the school doctor, wanted to keep him – for observation – overnight, but the headmaster threatened to fire all of them if he was not released.

Over and over again, Randy White was heard to shout or cry out or mutter to his wife: 'This has Owen Meany's name written all over it!'

It was an interesting morning meeting, that morning. We were more than twice as long being seated, because only one staircase ascending to The Great Hall was available for our passage – and then there was the problem of the front-row bench being smashed; the boys who regularly sat there had to find places for themselves on the floor, or onstage. There were crushed beads of glass, and chipped paint, and puddles of engine and transmission oil everywhere – and except for the opening and closing hymn, which drowned out the cries of the trapped headmaster, we were forced to listen to the ongoing drama on the stairway. I'm afraid this distracted us from the Rev. Mr Merrill's prayer, and from Mr Early's annual pep talk to the seniors. We should not allow our anxieties about our pending college admission (or our rejection) to keep us from having a good spring holiday, Mr Early advised us.

'Goddamn Jesus Fucking *Christ* – keep that blowtorch away from my *face*!' we all heard the headmaster cry.

And at the end of morning meeting, the headmaster's wife, Sam, shouted at those students who attempted to descend the blocked staircase by climbing over the ruined Volkswagen – in which the headmaster was *still* imprisoned.

'Where are your *manners*?' Mrs White shouted.

It was after morning meeting before I had a chance to speak to Owen Meany.

'I don't suppose *you* had anything to do with all of that?' I asked him.

'FAITH AND PRAYER,' he said. 'FAITH AND PRAYER – THEY *WORK*, THEY REALLY DO.'

Toronto: July 23, 1987 – Katherine invited me to her island; no more stupid newspapers; I'm going to Georgian Bay! Another stinking-hot day.

Meanwhile – on the front page of *The Globe and Mail* (it must be a slow day) – there's a story about Sweden's Supreme Court making 'legal history'; the Supreme Court is hearing an appeal in a custody case involving a dead cat. What a world! MADE FOR TELEVISION!

I haven't been to church in more than a month; too many newspapers. Newspapers are a bad habit, the reading equivalent of junk food. What happens to me is that I seize upon an issue in the news – the issue is the moral/philosophical, political/intellectual equivalent of a cheeseburger with *everything* on it; but for the duration of my interest in it, all my other interests are consumed by it, and whatever appetites and capacities I may have had for detachment and reflection are suddenly subordinate to this *cheeseburger* in my life! I offer this as self-criticism; but what it means to be 'political' is that you welcome these obsessions with cheeseburgers – at great cost to the rest of your life.

I remember the independent study that Owen Meany was conducting with the Rev. Lewis Merrill in the winter term of 1962. I wonder if those cheeseburgers in the Reagan administration are familiar with Isaiah 5:20. As The Voice would say: 'WOE UNTO THEM THAT CALL EVIL GOOD AND GOOD EVIL.'

After me, Pastor Merrill was the first to ask Owen if he'd had anything to do with the 'accident' to Dr Dolder's Volkswagen; the unfortunate little car would spend our entire spring vacation in the body shop.

'DO I UNDERSTAND CORRECTLY THAT THE SUBJECT OF OUR CONVERSATION IS CONFIDENTIAL?' Owen asked Pastor Merrill. 'YOU KNOW WHAT I MEAN – LIKE YOU'RE THE PRIEST AND I'M THE CONFESSOR; AND, SHORT OF MURDER, YOU WON'T REPEAT WHAT I TELL YOU?' Owen Meany asked him.

'You understand correctly, Owen,' the Rev. Mr Merrill said.

'IT WAS MY IDEA!' Owen said. 'BUT I DIDN'T LIFT A FINGER. I DIDN'T EVEN SET FOOT IN THE BUILDING – NOT EVEN TO WATCH THEM DO IT!'

'Who did it?' Mr Merrill asked.

'MOST OF THE BASKETBALL TEAM,' said Owen Meany. 'THEY JUST HAPPENED ALONG.'

'It was completely spur-of-the-moment?' asked Mr Merrill.

'OUT OF THE BLUE – IT HAPPENED IN A FLASH. YOU KNOW, LIKE THE BURNING BUSH,' Owen said.

'Well, not quite like *that*, I think,' said the Rev. Mr Merrill, who assured Owen that he only wanted to know the particulars so that he could make every effort to steer the headmaster *away* from Owen, who was Randy White's prime suspect. 'It helps,' said Pastor Merrill, 'if I can tell the headmaster that I know, for a fact, that you didn't *touch* Doctor Dolder's car, or set foot in the building – as you say.'

'DON'T RAT ON THE BASKETBALL TEAM, EITHER,' Owen said.

'Of course not!' said Mr Merrill, who added that he didn't think Owen should be as candid with Dr Dolder – should the doctor inquire if Owen knew anything about the 'accident.' As much as it was understood that the subject of conversation between a psychiatrist and his patient was also 'confidential,' Owen should understand the degree to which the fastidious Swiss gentleman had cared for his car.

'I KNOW WHAT YOU MEAN,' said Owen Meany.

Dan Needham, who said to Owen that he didn't want to hear a word about what Owen did or didn't know about

Dr Dolder's car, told us that the headmaster was screaming to the faculty about 'disrespect for personal property' and 'vandalism'; both categories of crimes fell under the rubric of 'punishable by dismissal.'

'IT WAS THE HEADMASTER AND THE FACULTY WHO TRASHED THE VOLKSWAGEN,' Owen pointed out. 'THERE WASN'T ANYTHING THE MATTER WITH THAT CAR UNTIL THE HEADMASTER AND THOSE OAFS GOT THEIR HANDS ON IT.'

'As one of "those oafs," I don't want to know *how* you know that, Owen,' Dan told him. 'I want you to be very careful what you say – to anybody!'

There were only a few days left before the end of the winter term, which would also mark the end of Owen Meany's 'disciplinary probation.' Once the spring term started, Owen could afford a few, small lapses in his adherence to school rules; he wasn't much of a rule-breaker, anyway.

Dr Dolder, naturally, saw what had happened to his car as a crowning example of the 'hostility' he often felt from the students. Dr Dolder was extremely sensitive to both real and imagined hostility because not a single student at Gravesend Academy was known to seek the psychiatrist's advice willingly; Dr Dolder's *only* patients were either required (by the school) or forced (by their parents) to see him.

In their first session together following the destruction of his VW, Dr Dolder began with Owen by saying to him, 'I know you hate me – yes? But *why* do you hate me?'

'I HATE HAVING TO TALK WITH YOU,' Owen admitted, 'BUT I DON'T HATE *YOU* – *NOBODY* HATES YOU, DOCTOR DOLDER!'

'And what did he say when you said *that*?' I asked Owen Meany.

'HE WAS QUIET FOR A LONG TIME – I THINK HE WAS CRYING,' Owen said.

'Jesus!' I said.

'I THINK THAT THE ACADEMY IS AT A LOW POINT IN ITS HISTORY,' Owen observed. That was so typical of him; that in the midst of a precarious situation, he would suggest – as a subject for criticism – something far removed from himself!

But there was no hard evidence against him; not even the zeal of the headmaster could put the blame for the demolished

Beetle on Owen Meany. Then, as soon as that scare was behind him, there was a worse problem. Larry Lish was 'busted' while trying to buy beer at a local grocery store; the manager of the store had confiscated Lish's fake identification – the phony draft card that falsified his age – and called the police. Lish admitted that the draft card had been created from a blank card in the editorial offices of *The Grave* – his illegal identification had been invented on the photocopier. According to Lish, 'countless' Gravesend Academy students had acquired fake draft cards in this fashion.

'And whose idea was that?' the headmaster asked him.

'Not mine,' said Larry Lish. 'I *bought* my card – like everyone else.'

I can only imagine that the headmaster was trembling with excitement; this interrogation took place in the Police Department offices of Gravesend's own chief of police – our old 'murder weapon' and 'instrument of death' man, Chief Ben Pike! Chief Pike had already informed Larry Lish that falsifying a draft card carried 'criminal charges.'

'Who was selling and making these fake draft cards, Larry?' Randy White asked.

Larry Lish would make his mother proud of him – I have no doubt about that.

'Owen Meany,' said Larry Lish.

And so the spring vacation of 1962 did not come quite soon enough. The headmaster made a deal with Police Chief Pike: no 'criminal charges' would be brought against anyone at the academy if the headmaster could turn over to Chief Pike all the fake draft cards at the school. That was pretty easy. The headmaster told every boy at morning meeting to leave his wallet on the stage before he left The Great Hall; boys without their wallets would return immediately to their dormitory rooms and hand them over to an attendant faculty member. Every boy's wallet would be returned to him in his post-office box.

There were no morning classes; the faculty was too busy looking through each boy's wallet and removing his fake draft card.

In the emergency faculty meeting that Randy White called, Dan Needham said: 'What you're doing isn't even *legal*! Every parent of every boy at this school should *sue* you!'

But the headmaster argued that he was sparing the school

the disgrace of having 'criminal charges' brought against Gravesend students. The academy's reputation as a good school would not suffer by this action of confiscation as much as that reputation would suffer from 'criminal charges.' And as for the *criminal* who had actually manufactured and sold these false identification cards – 'for a profit!' – naturally, the headmaster said, *that* student's fate would be decided by the Executive Committee.

And so they crucified him – it happened that quickly. It didn't matter that he told them he had given up his illegal enterprise; it didn't matter to them that he said he had been inspired to correct his behavior by JFK's inaugural speech – or that he knew the fake draft cards were being used to illegally purchase alcohol, and that he didn't approve of drinking; it didn't matter to them that he didn't even drink! Larry Lish, and everyone in possession of a fake draft card, was put on disciplinary probation – for the duration of the spring term. But the Executive Committee crucified Owen Meany – they axed him; they gave him the boot; they threw him out.

Dan tried to block Owen's dismissal by calling for a special vote among the faculty; but the headmaster said that the Executive Committee decision was final – 'vote or no vote.' Mr Early telephoned each member of the Board of Trustees; but there were only two days remaining in the winter term – the trustees could not possibly be assembled before the spring vacation, and they would not overrule an Executive Committee decision without a proper meeting.

The decision to throw Owen Meany out of school was so unpopular that the former headmaster, old Archibald Thorndike, emerged from his retirement to express his disapproval; old Archie told one of the students who wrote for *The Grave* – and a reporter from the town paper, *The Gravesend News-Letter* – that 'Owen Meany is one of the best citizens the academy has ever produced; I expect great things from that little fella,' the former headmaster said. Old Thorny also disapproved of what he called 'the *Gestapo* methods of seizing the students' billfolds,' and he questioned Randy White's tactics on the grounds that they 'did little to teach respect for personal property.'

'That old fart,' Dan Needham said. 'I know he means well, but no one listened to him when he was headmaster; no one's going to listen to him now.' In Dan's opinion, it was self-serving to credit the academy with 'producing' students; least of all, Dan said, could the academy claim to have 'produced' Owen Meany. And regarding the merits of teaching 'respect for personal property,' that was an old-fashioned idea; and the word 'billfolds,' in Dan's opinion, was outdated – although Dan agreed with old Archibald Thorndike that Randy White's tactics were pure '*Gestapo*.'

All this talk did nothing for Owen. The Rev. Lewis Merrill called Dan and me and asked us if we knew where Owen was – Pastor Merrill had been trying to reach him. But whenever anyone called the Meanys' house, either the line was busy – probably the receiver was off the hook – or else Mr Meany answered the phone and said that he thought Owen was 'in Durham.' That meant he was with Hester; but when I called her, she wouldn't admit he was there.

'Have you got some good news for him?' she asked me. 'Is that fucking creep school going to let him graduate?'

'No,' I said. 'I don't have any good news.'

'Then just leave him alone,' she suggested.

Later, I heard Dan on the telephone, talking to the headmaster.

'You're the worst thing that ever happened to this school,' Dan told Randy White. 'If you survive this disaster, *I* won't be staying here – and I won't leave alone. You've permitted yourself a fatal and childish indulgence, you've done something one of the *boys* might do, you've engaged in a kind of *combat* with a student – you've been *competing* with one of the kids. You're such a kid yourself, you let Owen Meany get to you. Because a *kid* took a dislike to you, you decided to *pay him back* – that's just the way a *kid* thinks! You're not grown-up enough to run a school.

'And this was a *scholarship* boy!' Dan Needham yelled in the telephone. 'This is a boy who's going to go to college on a scholarship, too – or else he won't go. If Owen Meany doesn't get the best deal possible, from the best college around – you're responsible for that, too!'

Then I think the headmaster hung up on him; at least, it appeared to me that Dan Needham had much more to say, but he suddenly stopped talking and, slowly, he returned the receiver to its cradle. 'Shit,' he said.

Later that night, my grandmother called Dan and me to say that *she* had heard from Owen.

'MISSUS WHEELWRIGHT?' Owen had said to her, over the phone.

'Where are you, Owen?' she asked him.

'IT DOESN'T MATTER,' he told her. 'I JUST WANTED TO SAY I WAS SORRY THAT I LET YOU DOWN. I DON'T WANT YOU TO THINK I'M NOT GRATEFUL FOR THE OPPORTUNITY YOU GAVE ME – TO GO TO A GOOD SCHOOL.'

'It doesn't sound like such a good school to me – not anymore, Owen,' my grandmother told him. 'And you didn't let me down.'

'I PROMISE TO MAKE YOU PROUD OF ME,' Owen told her.

'I *am* proud of you, Owen!' she told him.

'I'M GOING TO MAKE YOU PROUDER!' Owen said; then – almost as an afterthought – he said, 'PLEASE TELL DAN AND JOHN TO BE SURE TO GO TO CHAPEL IN THE MORNING.'

That was just like him, to call it 'chapel' after everyone else had been converted to calling it morning meeting.

'Whatever he's going to do, we should try to stop him,' Dan told me. 'He shouldn't do anything that might make it worse – he's got to concentrate on getting into college and getting a scholarship. I'm sure that Gravesend High School will *give* him a diploma – but he shouldn't do anything crazy.'

Naturally, we still couldn't locate him. Mr Meany said he was 'in Durham'; Hester said she didn't know where he was – she thought he was doing some job for his father because he had been driving the big truck, not the pickup, and he was carrying a lot of equipment on the flatbed.

'What sort of equipment?' I asked her.

'How would I know?' she said. 'It was just a lot of heavy-looking *stuff*.'

'Jesus Christ!' said Dan. 'He's probably going to dynamite the headmaster's house!'

We drove all around the town and the campus, but there was no sign of him or the big truck. We drove in and out of town a couple of times – and up Maiden Hill, to the quarries, just to see if the hauler was safely back at home; it wasn't. We drove around all night.

'Think!' Dan instructed me. 'What will he do?'

'I don't know,' I said. We were coming back into town, passing the gas station next to St Michael's School. The predawn light had a flattering effect on the shabby, parochial playground; the early light bathed the ruts in the ruptured macadam and made the surface of the playground appear as smooth as the surface of a lake unruffled by any wind. The house where the nuns lived was completely dark, and then the sun rose – a pink sliver of light lay flat upon the playground; and the newly white-washed stone archway that sheltered the statue of the sainted Mary Magdalene reflected the pink light brightly back to me. The only problem was, the holy goalie was not in her goal.

'Stop the car,' I said to Dan. He stopped; he turned around. We drove into the parking lot behind St Michael's, and Dan inched the car out onto the rutted surface of the playground; he drove right up to the empty stone archway.

Owen had done a very neat job. At the time, I wasn't sure of the equipment he would have used – maybe those funny little chisels and spreaders, the things he called wedges and feathers; but the tap-tap-tap of metal on stone would have awakened the ever-vigilant nuns. Maybe he used one of those special granite saws; the blade is diamond-studded; I'm sure it would have done a faultless job of taking Mary Magdalene clean off her feet – actually, he'd taken her feet clean off her pedestal. It's even possible that he used a touch of dyanmite – artfully placed, of course. I wouldn't put it past him to have devised a way to *blast* the sainted Mary Magdalene off her pedestal – I'm sure he could have muffled the explosion so skillfully that the nuns would have slept right through it. Later, when I asked him how he did it, he would give me his usual answer.

'FAITH AND PRAYER. FAITH AND PRAYER – THEY *WORK*, THEY REALLY DO.'

'That statue's got to weigh three or four hundred pounds!' Dan Needham said.

Surely the heavy equipment that Hester had seen would have included some kind of hydraulic hoist or crane, although that wouldn't have helped him get Mary Magdalene up the long staircase in the Main Academy Building – or up on the stage of The Great Hall. He would have had to use a hand dolly for that; and it wouldn't have been easy.

'I'VE MOVED HEAVIER GRAVESTONES,' he would say, later; but I don't imagine he was in the habit of moving gravestones *upstairs*.

When Dan and I got to the Main Academy Building and climbed to The Great Hall, the janitor was already sitting on one of the front-row benches, just staring up at the saintly figure; it was as if the janitor thought that Mary Magdalene would speak to him, if he would be patient enough – even though Dan and I immediately noticed that Mary was not her usual self.

'It's *him* who did it – that little fella they threw out, don't you suppose?' the janitor asked Dan, who was speechless.

We sat beside the janitor on the front-row bench in the early light. As always, with Owen Meany, there was the necessary consideration of the *symbols* involved. He had removed Mary Magdalene's arms, above the elbows, so that her gesture of beseeching the assembled audience would seem all the more an act of supplication – and all the more helpless. Dan and I both knew that Owen suffered an obsession with armlessness – this was Watahantowet's familiar totem, this was what Owen had done to my armadillo. My mother's dressmaker's dummy was armless, too.

But neither Dan nor I was prepared for Mary Magdalene being *headless* – for her head was cleanly sawed or chiseled or blasted off. Because my mother's dummy was also headless, I thought that Mary Magdalene bore her a stony three- or four-hundred-pound resemblance; my mother had the better figure, but Mary Magdalene was taller. She was also taller than the headmaster, even without her head; compared to Randy White, the decapitated Mary Magdalene was a little bigger than life-sized – her shoulders and the stump of her neck stood taller above the podium onstage than the headmaster would. And Owen had placed the holy goalie on no pedestal. He had bolted her to the stage floor. And he had strapped her with those same steel bands the quarrymen used to hold the granite slabs on the flatbed; he had bound her to the podium and fastened her to the floor, making quite certain that she would not be as easily removed from the stage as Dr Dolder's Volkswagen.

'I suppose,' Dan said to the janitor, 'that those metal bands are pretty securely attached.'

'Yup!' the janitor said.

'I suppose those bolts go right *through* the podium, and right *through* the stage,' Dan said, 'and I'll bet he put those nuts on pretty *tight*.'

'Nope!' the janitor said. 'He *welded* everything together.'
'That's pretty tight,' said Dan Needham.
'Yup!' the janitor said.
I had forgotten: Owen had learned welding – Mr Meany had wanted at least one of his quarrymen to be a welder, and Owen, who was such a natural at learning, had been the one to learn.
'Have you told the headmaster?' Dan asked the janitor.
'Nope!' the janitor said. 'I ain't goin' to, either,' he said – 'not *this* time.'
'I suppose it wouldn't do any good for him to know, anyway,' Dan said.
'That's what I thought!' the janitor said.
Dan and I went to the school dining hall, where we were unfamiliar faces at breakfast; but we were very hungry, after driving around all night – and besides, I wanted to pass the word: 'Tell everyone to get to morning meeting a little early,' I told my friends. I heard Dan passing the word to some of his friends on the faculty: 'If you go to only one more morning meeting for the rest of your life, I think this should be the one.'
Dan and I left the dining hall together. There wasn't time to return to Waterhouse Hall and take a shower before morning meeting, although we badly needed one. We were both anxious for Owen, and agitated – not knowing how his presentation of the mutilated Mary Magdalene might make his dismissal from the academy appear more justified than it was; we were worried how his desecration of the statue of a saint might give those colleges and universities that were sure to accept him a certain *reluctance*.
'Not to mention what the Catholic Church – I mean, Saint Michael's – is going to do to him,' Dan said. 'I better have a talk with the head guy over there – Father What's-His-Name.'
'Do you know him?' I asked Dan.
'No, not really,' Dan said; 'but I think he's a friendly sort of fellow – Father O'Somebody, I think. I wish I could remember his name – O'Malley, O'Leary, O'Rourke, O'*Somebody*,' he said.
'I'll bet Pastor Merrill knows him,' I said. And that was why Dan and I walked to Hurd's Church before morning meeting; sometimes the Rev. Lewis Merrill said his prayers there before walking to the Main Academy Building; sometimes

he was up early, just biding his time in the vestry office. Dan and I saw the trailer-truck from the Meany Granite Company parked behind the vestry. Owen was sitting in the vestry office – in Mr Merrill's usual chair, behind Mr Merrill's desk, tipping back in the creaky old chair and rolling the chair around on its squeaky casters. There was no sign of Pastor Merrill.

'I HAVE AN EARLY APPOINTMENT,' Owen explained to Dan and me. 'PASTOR MERRILL'S A LITTLE LATE.'

He looked all right – a little tired, a little nervous, or just restless. He couldn't sit still in the chair, and he fiddled with the desk drawers, pulling them open and closing them – not appearing to pay any attention to what was inside the drawers, but just opening and closing them because they were there.

'You've had a busy night, Owen,' Dan told him.

'PRETTY BUSY,' said Owen Meany.

'How *are* you?' I asked him.

'I'M FINE,' he said. 'I BROKE THE LAW, I GOT CAUGHT, I'M GOING TO PAY – THAT'S HOW IT IS,' he said.

'You got screwed!' I said.

'A LITTLE BIT,' he nodded – then he shrugged. 'IT'S NOT AS IF I'M ENTIRELY *INNOCENT*,' he added.

'The important thing for you to think about is getting into college,' Dan told him. 'The important thing is that you get in, and that you get a scholarship.'

'THERE ARE MORE IMPORTANT THINGS,' said Owen Meany. He opened, in rapid succession, the three drawers on the right-hand side of the Rev. Mr Merrill's desk; then he closed them, just as rapidly. That was when Pastor Merrill walked into the vestry office.

'What are you doing?' Mr Merrill asked Owen.

'NOTHING,' said Owen Meany. 'WAITING FOR YOU.'

'I mean, at my desk – you're sitting at my desk,' Mr Merrill said. Owen looked surprised.

'I GOT HERE EARLY,' he explained. 'I WAS JUST SITTING IN YOUR CHAIR – I WASN'T *DOING* ANYTHING.' He got up and walked to the front of Pastor Merrill's desk, where he sat down in his usual chair – at least, I guess it was his 'usual' chair; it reminded me of 'the singer's seat' in Graham McSwiney's funny studio. I was disappointed that I hadn't heard from Mr McSwiney; I guessed that he had no news about Big Black Buster Freebody.

'I'm sorry if I snapped at you, Owen,' Pastor Merrill said. 'I know how upset you must be.'

'I'M FINE,' Owen said.

'I was glad you called me,' Mr Merrill told Owen.

Owen shrugged. I had not seen him *sneer* before, but it seemed to me that he almost sneered at the Rev. Mr Merrill.

'Oh, well!' Mr Merrill said, sitting down in his creaky desk chair. 'Well, I'm *very* sorry, Owen – for everything,' he said. He had a way of entering a room – a classroom, The Great Hall, Hurd's Church, or even his own vestry office – as if he were offering an apology to *everyone*. At the same time, he was struggling so sincerely that you didn't want to stop or interrupt him. You liked him and just wished that he could *relax*; yet he made you feel guilty for being irritated with him, because of how hard *and* unsuccessfully he was trying to put you at ease.

Dan said: 'I came here to ask you if you knew the name of the head guy at Saint Michael's – it's the *same* guy, for the church and for the school, isn't it?'

'That's right,' Pastor Merrill said. 'It's Father Findley.'

'I guess I don't know him,' Dan said. 'I thought it was a Father O'Somebody.'

'No, it's not an O'Anybody,' said Mr Merrill. 'It's Father Findley.'

The Rev. Mr Merrill did not yet know *why* Dan wanted to know who the Catholic 'head guy' was. Owen, of course, knew what Dan was up to.

'YOU DON'T HAVE TO DO ANYTHING FOR ME, DAN,' Owen said.

'I can try to keep you out of *jail*,' Dan said. 'I *want* you to get into college – and to have a scholarship. But, at the very least, I can try to keep you from getting charged with theft and vandalism,' Dan said.

'What did you do, Owen?' the Rev. Mr Merrill asked him.

Owen bowed his head; for a moment, I thought he was going to cry – but then he shrugged off this moment, too. He looked directly into the Rev. Lewis Merrill's eyes.

'I WANT YOU TO SAY A PRAYER FOR ME,' said Owen Meany.

'A p-p-p-prayer – for *you*?' the Rev. Mr Merrill stuttered.

'JUST A LITTLE SOMETHING – IF IT'S NOT TOO

MUCH TO ASK,' Owen said. 'IT'S YOUR *BUSINESS*, ISN'T IT?'

The Rev. Mr Merrill considered this. 'Yes,' he said cautiously. 'At morning meeting?' he asked.

'TODAY – IN FRONT OF EVERYBODY,' said Owen Meany.

'Yes, all right,' the Rev. Lewis Merrill said; but he looked as if he might panic.

Dan took my arm and steered me toward the door of the vestry office.

'We'll leave you alone, if you want to talk,' Dan said to Mr Merrill and Owen.

'Was there anything else you wanted?' Mr Merrill asked Dan.

'No, just Father Findley – his name,' Dan said.

'And was that all you wanted to see me about – the prayer?' Mr Merrill asked Owen, who appeared to consider the question very carefully – or else he was waiting for Dan and me to leave.

We were outside the vestry office, in the dark corridor where two rows of wooden pegs – for coats – extended for the entire length of two walls; off in the darkness, several lost or left-behind overcoats hung there, like old churchgoers who had loitered so long that they had fallen asleep, slumped against the walls. And there were a few pairs of galoshes in the corridor; but they were not directly beneath the abandoned overcoats, so that the churchgoers in the darkness appeared to have been separated from their feet. On the wooden peg nearest the door to the vestry office was the Rev. Mr Merrill's double-breasted and oddly youthful Navy pea jacket – and, on the peg next to it, his seaman's watch cap. Dan and I, passing these, heard Pastor Merrill say: 'Owen? Is it the dream? Have you had that dream again?'

'YES,' said Owen Meany, who began to cry – he started to sob, like a child. I had not heard him sound like that since the Thanksgiving vacation when he'd peed in his pants – when he'd peed on Hester.

'Owen? Owen, listen to me,' Mr Merrill said. 'Owen? It's *just a dream* – do you hear me? It's just a dream.'

'NO!' said Owen Meany.

Then Dan and I were outside in the February cold and gray; the old footprints in the rutted slush were frozen – fossils of the many souls who had traveled to and from Hurd's

Church. It was still early morning; although Dan and I had seen the sun rise, the sun had been absorbed by the low, uniformly ice-gray sky.

'*What* dream?' Dan Needham asked me.

'I don't know,' I said.

Owen hadn't told me about the dream; not yet. He would tell me – and I would tell him what the Rev. Mr Merrill had told him: that it was 'just a dream.'

I have learned that the consequences of our past actions are always interesting; I have learned to view the present with a forward-looking eye. But not then; at that moment, Dan and I were not imagining very much beyond Randy White's reaction to the headless, armless Mary Magdalene – whose steely embrace of the podium on the stage of The Great Hall would force the headmaster to address the school from a new and more naked position.

Directly opposite the Main Academy Building, the headmaster was getting into his camelhair overcoat; his wife, Sam, was brushing the nap of that pretty coat for him, and kissing her husband good-bye for the day. It would be a bad day for the headmaster – a FATED day, Owen Meany might have called it – but I'm sure Randy White didn't have his eyes on the future that morning. He thought he was finished with Owen Meany. He didn't know that, in the end, Owen Meany would defeat him; he didn't know about the vote of 'no confidence' the faculty would give him – or the decision of the Board of Trustees to not renew his appointment as headmaster. He couldn't have imagined what a travesty Owen Meany's absence would make of the commencement exercises that year – how such a timid, rather plain, and much-ignored student, who was the *replacement* valedictorian of our class, would find the courage to offer as a valedictory only these words: 'I am *not* the head of this class. The head of this class is Owen Meany; he is The Voice of our class – and the only voice we want to listen to.' Then that good, frightened boy would sit down – to tumultuous pandemonium: our classmates raising their voices for The Voice, bedsheets and more artful banners displaying his name in capital letters (of course), and the chanting that drowned out the headmaster's attempts to bring us to order.

'*Owen Meany! Owen Meany! Owen Meany!*' cried the Class of '62.

But that February morning when the headmaster was outfitting himself in his camelhair coat, he couldn't have known that Owen Meany would be his undoing. How frustrated and powerless Randy White would appear at our commencement, when he threatened to withhold our diplomas if we didn't stop our uproar; he must have known then that he had lost . . . because Dan Needham and Mr Early, and a solid one third or one half of the faculty stood up to applaud our riotous support of Owen; and we were joined by several informed members of the Board of Trustees as well, not to mention all those parents who had written angry letters to the headmaster regarding that illiberal business of confiscating our wallets. I wish Owen could have been there to see the headmaster then; but, of couse, Owen wasn't there – he wasn't graduating.

And he was not at morning meeting on that February day, just before spring vacation; but the surrogate he had left onstage was grotesquely capable of holding our attention. It was a packed house – so many of the faculty had turned out for the occasion. And Mary Magdalene was there to greet us: armless, but reaching out to us; headless, but eloquent – with the clean-cut stump of her neck, which was slashed to her Adam's apple, expressing so dramatically that she had much to say to us. We sat in a hush in The Great Hall, waiting for the headmaster.

What a horrible man Randy White was! There is a tradition among 'good' schools: when you throw out a senior – only months before he's scheduled to graduate – you make as little trouble for that student's college admission as you have to. Yes, you tell the colleges what they need to know; but you have already done *your* damage – you've fired the kid, you don't try to keep him out of college, too! But not Randy White; the headmaster would do his damnedest to put an end to Owen Meany's university life before it began!

Owen was accepted at Harvard; he was accepted at Yale – and he was offered full scholarships by both. But in addition to what Owen's record said: that he was expelled from Gravesend Academy for printing fake draft cards, and selling them to other students . . . in addition to that, the headmaster told Harvard and Yale (*and* the University of New Hampshire) much more. He said that Owen Meany was 'so virulently antireligious' that he had 'desecrated the statue of a saint at

Roman Catholic school'; that he had launched a 'deeply anti-Catholic campaign' on the Gravesend campus, under the demand of not wanting a fish-only menu in the school dining hall on Fridays: and that there was 'charges against him for being anti-Semitic, too.'

As for the New Hampshire Honor Society, they withdrew their offer of an Honor Society Scholarship; a student of Owen Meany's academic achievements was welcome to attend the University of New Hampshire, but the Honor Society – 'in the light of this distressing and distasteful information' – could not favor him with a scholarship; if he attended the University of New Hampshire, he would do so at his own expense.

Harvard and Yale were more forgiving; but they were also more complicated. Yale wanted to interview him again; they quickly saw the anti-Semitic 'charges' for what they were – a lie – but Owen was undoubtedly too frank about his feelings for (or, rather, against) the Catholic Church. Yale wanted to delay his acceptance for a year. In that time, their admissions director suggested Owen should 'find some meaningful employment'; and his employer should write to Yale periodically and report on Owen's 'character and commitment.' Dan Needham told Owen that this was reasonable, fair-minded, and not uncommon behavior – on the part of a university as good as Yale. Owen didn't disagree with Dan; he simply refused to do it.

'IT'S LIKE BEING ON PAROLE,' he said.

Harvard was also fair-minded and reasonable – and slightly more demanding and creative than Yale. Harvard said they wanted to delay his acceptance, too; but they were more specific about the kind of 'meaningful employment' they wanted him to take. They wanted him to work for the Catholic Church – in some capacity; he would volunteer his time for Catholic Relief Services, he could be a kind of social worker for one of the Catholic charities, or he could even work for the very same parochial school whose statue of Mary Magdalene he had ruined. Father Findley, at St Michael's, turned out to be a nice man; not only did he not press charges against Owen Meany – after talking to Dan Needham, Father Findley agreed to help Owen's cause (regarding his college admission) in any way he could.

Even some parochial students had spoken up for Owen.

Buzzy Thurston – who hit that easy ground ball, the one that should have been the last out, the one that should have kept Owen Meany from ever coming to bat – even Buzzy Thurston spoke up for Owen, saying that Owen had had 'a tough time'; Owen 'had his reasons' for being upset, Buzzy said. Headmaster White and Chief Ben Pike were all for 'throwing the book' at Owen Meany for the theft and mutilation of Mary Magdalene. But St Michael's School, and Father Findley, were very forgiving.

Dan said that Father Findley 'knew the family' and was most sympathetic when he realized who Owen's parents were – he'd had dealings with the Meanys; and although he wouldn't go into any detail regarding what those 'dealings' had been, Father Findley said he would do anything he could to help Owen. 'I certainly won't lift a finger to *hurt* him!' Father Findley said.

Dan Needham told Owen that Harvard had a good idea. 'Lots of Catholics do lots of good things, Owen,' Dan said. 'Why not see what some of the good things are?'

For a while, I thought Owen was going to accept the Harvard proposal – 'THE CATHOLIC DEAL,' he called it. He even went to see Father Findley; but it seemed to confuse him – how genuinely concerned for Owen's welfare Father Findley was. Maybe Owen *liked* Father Findley; that might have confused him, too.

In the end, he would turn THE CATHOLIC DEAL down.

'MY PARENTS WOULD NEVER UNDERSTAND IT,' he said. 'BESIDES, I WANT TO GO TO THE UNIVERSITY OF NEW HAMPSHIRE – I WANT TO STICK WITH YOU, I WANT TO GO WHERE YOU GO,' he told me.

'But they're not offering you a scholarship,' I reminded him.

'DON'T WORRY ABOUT THAT,' he said. He wouldn't tell me, at first, how he'd already got a 'scholarship' there.

He went to the U.S. Army recruiting offices in Gravesend; it was arranged 'in the family,' as we used to say in New Hampshire. They already knew who he was – he was the best of his class at Gravesend Academy, even if he ended up just barely getting his diploma from Gravesend High School. He was admitted to the University of New Hampshire – they also knew that; they had *read* about it in *The Gravesend News-Letter*. What's more, he was a kind of local hero; even though he had been absent, he had disrupted the academy's commencement exercises. As for making and selling the fake draft cards, the U.S. Army recruiters knew what that was about: that was about drinking – no disrespect for the draft had been intended, they certainly knew that. And what red-blooded American young man didn't indulge in a little vandalism, from time to time?

And that was how Owen Meany got his 'scholarship' to the University of New Hampshire; he signed up for the Reserve Officers Training Corps – ROTC, we called it '*rot*-see'; remember that? You went to college at the expense of the U.S. Army, and while you were in college, you took a few courses that the U.S. Army offered – Military History and Small Unit Tactics; stuff like that, not terribly taxing. The summer following your junior year, you would be required to take a little Basic Training – the standard, six-week course. And upon your graduation you would receive your commission; you would graduate a second lieutenant in the United States Army – and you would owe your country four years of active duty, plus two years in the Army Reserve.

'WHAT COULD POSSIBLY BE THE MATTER WITH THAT?' Owen Meany asked Dan and me. When he announced his plans to us, it was only 1962; a total of 11,300 U.S. military personnel were in Vietnam, but not a single one of them was in combat.

Even so, Dan Needham was uncomfortable with Owen's decision. 'I liked the Harvard deal better, Owen,' Dan said.

'THIS WAY, I DON'T HAVE TO WAIT A YEAR,' he said. 'AND I GET TO BE WITH YOU – ISN'T THAT GREAT?' he asked me.

'Yeah, that's great,' I said. 'I'm just a little surprised, that's all,' I told him.

I was *more* than 'a little surprised' – that the U.S. Army had *accepted* him was astonishing to me!

'Isn't there a height requirement?' Dan Needham whispered to me.

'I thought there was a weight requirement, too,' I said.

'IF YOU'RE THINKING ABOUT THE HEIGHT AND WEIGHT REQUIREMENTS,' Owen said, 'IT'S FIVE FEET – EVEN – AND ONE HUNDRED POUNDS.'

'Are you five feet tall, Owen?' Dan asked him.

'Since when do you weigh a hundred pounds?' I said.

'I'VE BEEN EATING A LOT OF BANANAS, AND ICE

CREAM,' said Owen Meany, 'AND WHEN THEY MEASURED ME, I TOOK A DEEP BREATH AND STOOD ON MY TOES!'

Well, it was only proper to congratulate him; he was quite pleased with arranging his college 'scholarship' in his own way. And, at the time, it appeared that he had defeated Randy White completely. Back then, neither Dan nor I knew about his 'dream'; I think we might have been a little worried about his involvement with the U.S. Army if we'd had that dream described to us.

And that February morning, when the Rev. Lewis Merrill entered The Great Hall and stared with such horror at the decapitated and amputated Mary Magdalene, Dan Needham and I weren't thinking very far into the future; we were worried only that the Rev. Mr Merrill might be too terrified to deliver his prayer – that the condition of Mary Magdalene might seize hold of his normally slight stutter and render him incomprehensible. He stood at the foot of the stage, staring up at her – for a long moment, he even forgot to remove his Navy pea jacket and his seaman's watch cap; and since Congregationalists don't always wear the clerical collar, the Rev. Lewis Merrill looked less like our school minister than like a drunken sailor who had finally staggered up against the incentive for his own religious conversion.

The Rev. Mr Merrill was standing there, thus stricken, when the headmaster arrived in The Great Hall. If Randy White was surprised to see so many faculty faces at morning meeting, it did not alter his usual aggressive stride; he took the stairs up to the stage at his usual two-at-a-time pace. And the headmaster did not flinch – or even appear the slightest surprised – to see someone already standing at the podium. The Rev. Lewis Merrill often announced the opening hymn; Pastor Merrill often followed the opening hymn with *his* prayer. Then the headmaster would make his remarks – he also told us the page number for the closing hymn; and that would be that.

It took the headmaster a few seconds to recognize Mr Merrill, who was standing at the foot of the stage in his pea jacket and wearing his watch cap and gawking at the figure who beseeched us from the podium. Our headmaster was a man who was used to taking charge – he was used to making decisions, our Randy White. When he saw the monstrosity at the podium, he did the first and most headmasterly thing that came into his mind; he strode up to the saint and seized her around her modest robes – he grabbed her around her waist and attempted to lift her. I don't think he took any notice of the steel bands girdling her hips, or the four-inch bolts that penetrated her feet and were welded to their respective nuts under the stage. I suppose his back was still a trifle sore from his impressive effort with Dr Dolder's Volkswagen; but the headmaster didn't pay any attention to his back, either. He simply seized Mary Magdalene around her middle; he gave a grunt – and nothing happened. Mary Magdalene, and all that she represented, was not as easy to throw around as a Volkswagen.

'I suppose you think this is *funny*!' the headmaster said to the assembled school; but nobody was laughing. 'Well, *I'll* tell you what this is,' said Randy White. 'This is a *crime*,' he said. 'This is vandalism, this is theft – and desecration! This is willful abuse of personal, even *sacred* property.'

One of the students yelled. 'What's the hymn?'

'What did you say?' Randy White said.

'Tell us the number of the hymn!' someone shouted.

'What's the *hymn*?' said a few more students – in unison.

I had not seen the Rev. Mr Merrill climb – I suppose, shakily – to the stage; when I noticed him, he was standing beside the martyred Mary Magdalene. 'The hymn is on page three-eighty-eight,' Pastor Merrill said clearly. The headmaster spoke sharply to him, but we couldn't hear what the headmaster said – there was too much creaking of benches and bumping of hymnals as we rose to sing. I don't know what influenced Mr Merrill's choice of the hymn. If Owen had told me about his dream, I might have found the hymn especially ominous; but as it was, it was simply familiar – a frequent choice, probably because it was victorious in tone, and squarely in that category of 'pilgrimage and conflict,' which is often so inspiring to young men.

The Son of God goes forth to war,
  A king-ly crown to gain;
His blood-red ban-ner streams a-far;
  Who follows in his train?
Who best can drink his cup of woe,
  Tri-um-phant o-ver pain,
Who pa-tient bears his cross be-low,
  He fol-lows in his train.

It was a hymn that Owen liked, and we belted it out; we sang much more heartily – much more defiantly – than usual. The headmaster had nowhere to stand; he occupied the center stage – but with nothing to stand *behind*, he looked exposed and unsure of himself. As we roared out the hymn, the Rev. Lewis Merrill appeared to gain in confidence – and even in stature. Although he didn't look exactly comfortable beside the headless Mary Magdalene, he stood so close to her that the podium light shone on him, too. When he finished the hymn, the Rev. Mr Merrill said: 'Let us pray. Let us pray for Owen Meany,' he said.

It was very quiet in The Great Hall, and although our heads were bowed, our eyes were on the headmaster. We waited for Mr Merrill to begin. Perhaps he was *trying* to begin, I thought; then I realized that – awkward as ever – he had meant for *us* to pray for Owen. What he'd meant was that we were to offer our silent prayers for Owen Meany; and as the silence went on, and on, it became clear that the Rev. Lewis Merrill had no intention of hurrying us. He was not a brave man, I thought; but he was trying to be brave. On and on, we prayed and prayed; and if I had known about Owen's dream, I would have prayed much harder.

Suddenly, the headmaster said, 'That's enough.'

'I'm s-s-s-sorry,' Mr Merrill stuttered, 'but *I'll* say when it's "enough." '

I think that was when the headmaster realized he had lost; he realized then that he was finished. Because, what could he do? Was he going to tell us to stop praying? We kept our heads bowed; and we kept praying. Even as awkward as he was, the Rev. Mr Merrill had made it clear to us that there was no end to praying for Owen Meany.

After a while, Randy White left the stage; he had the good sense, if not the decency, to leave quietly – we could hear his careful footsteps on the marble staircase, and the morning ice was still so brittle that we could even hear him crunching his way on the path outside the Main Academy Building. When we could no longer hear his footsteps in our silent prayers for Owen Meany, Pastor Merrill said, 'Amen.'

Oh God, how often I have wished that I could relive that moment; I didn't know how to pray very well then – I didn't even believe in prayer. If I were given the opportunity to pray for Owen Meany now, I could do a better job of it;

knowing what I know now, I might be able to pray hard enough.

It would have helped me, of course, if I could have seen his diary; but he wasn't offering it – he was keeping his diary to himself. So often in its pages he had written his name – his *full* name – in the big block letters he called MONUMENT STYLE or GRAVESEND LETTERING; so many times he had transcribed, in his diary, his name exactly the way he had seen it on Scrooge's grave. And I mean, *before* all the ROTC business – even before he was thrown out of school and knew that the U.S. Army would be his ticket through college. I mean, *before he knew* he was signing up – even then he had written his name in that way you see names inscribed on graves.

1LT PAUL O. MEANY, JR.

That's how he wrote it; that was what the Ghost of the Future had seen on Scrooge's grave; that and the date – the date was written in the diary, too. He wrote the date in the diary many, many times, but he never told me what it was. Maybe I could have helped him, if I'd known that date. Owen believed he knew when he was going to die; he also believed he knew his *rank* – he would die a first lieutenant.

And after the dream, he believed he knew more. The certainty of his convictions was always a little scary, and his diary entry about the dream is no exception.

> YESTERDAY I WAS KICKED OUT OF SCHOOL. LAST NIGHT I HAD A DREAM. NOW I KNOW FOUR THINGS. I KNOW THAT MY VOICE DOESN'T CHANGE – BUT I STILL DON'T KNOW WHY. I KNOW THAT I AM GOD'S INSTRUMENT. I KNOW WHEN I'M GOING TO DIE – AND NOW A DREAM HAS SHOWN ME *HOW* I'M GOING TO DIE. I'M GOING TO BE A *HERO!* I TRUST THAT GOD WILL HELP ME, BECAUSE WHAT I'M SUPPOSED TO DO LOOKS VERY HARD.

8 : THE FINGER

Until the summer of 1962, I felt that I couldn't wait to grow up and be treated with the kind of respect I imagined adults were routinely offered and adamantly thought they deserved – I couldn't wait to wallow in the freedom and the privileges I imagined grown-ups enjoyed. Until that summer, my long apprenticeship to maturity struck me as arduous and humiliating; Randy White had confiscated my fake draft card, and I wasn't yet old enough to buy beer – I wasn't independent enough to merit my own place to live. I wasn't earning enough to afford my own car, and I wasn't *something* enough to persuade a woman to bestow her sexual favors upon me. Not one woman had I ever persuaded! Until the summer of '62, I thought that childhood and adolescence were a purgatory without apparent end; I thought that youth, in a word, 'sucked.' But Owen Meany, who believed he knew when and how he was going to die, was in no hurry to grow up. And as to my calling the period of our youth a 'purgatory,' Owen said simply, 'THERE *IS* NO PURGATORY – THAT'S A CATHOLIC INVENTION. THERE'S LIFE ON EARTH, THERE'S HEAVEN – AND THERE'S HELL.'

'I think life on earth *is* hell,' I said.

'I HOPE YOU HAVE A NICE SUMMER,' Owen said.

It was the first summer we spent apart. I suppose I should be grateful for that summer, because it afforded me my first glimpse of what my life without Owen would be like – you might say, it prepared me. By the end of the summer of 1962, Owen Meany had made me afraid of what the next phase was going to be. I didn't want to grow up anymore: what I wanted was for Owen and me to go on being kids for the rest of our lives – sometimes Canon Mackie tells me, rather ungenerously, that I have succeeded. Canon Campbell, God Rest His Soul, used to tell me that being a kid for the rest of my life was a perfectly honorable aspiration.

I spent that summer of '62 in Sawyer Depot, working for my Uncle Alfred. After what had happened to Owen, I didn't want to work for the Gravesend Academy Admissions Office and give guided tours of the school – not anymore. The Eastman Lumber Company offered me a good job. It was tiring, outdoor work; but I got to spend my time with Noah and Simon – and there were parties on Loveless Lake almost every night, and swimming and waterskiing on Loveless Lake nearly every day, after work, and every weekend. Uncle Alfred and Aunt Martha welcomed me into the family; they gave me Hester's room for the summer. Hester was keeping her school-year apartment in Durham, working as a waitress in one of those sandy, lobster-house restaurants . . . I think it was in Kittery or Portsmouth. After she got off work, she and Owen would cruise 'the strip' at Hampton Beach in the tomato-red pickup. Hester's school-year roommates were elsewhere for the summer, and Hester and Owen spent every night in her Durham apartment, alone. They were 'living together as man and wife' – that was the disapproving and frosty way Aunt Martha put it, when she discussed it at all, which was rarely.

Despite the fact that Owen and Hester were living together as man and wife, Noah and Simon and I could never be sure if they were actually 'doing it.' Simon was sure that Hester could not live without doing it, Noah somehow felt that Owen and Hester *had* done it – but that, for some special reason, they had stopped. I had the strangest feeling that *anything* between them was possible: that they did it and had always done it with abandon; that they had never done it, but that they might be doing something even worse – or better – and that the *real* bond between them (whether they 'did it' or not) was even more passionate and far sadder than sex. I felt cut off from Owen – I was working with wood and smelling a cool, northern air that was scented with trees; he was working with granite and feeling the sun beat down on the unshaded quarry, inhaling the rock dust and smelling the dynamite.

Chain saws were relatively new then; the Eastman Company used them for their logging operations, but very selectively – they were heavy and cumbersome, not nearly so light and powerful as they are today. In those days, we brought the logs out of the woods by horse and crawler tractor, and the timber was often cut by crosscut saws and axes. We loaded the logs onto the trucks by hand, using peaveys or cant dogs; nowadays, Noah and Simon have shown me, they use self-loading trucks, grapple skidders, and chippers. Even the sawmill has changed; there's no more sawdust! But in '62, we debarked the logs at the mill and sawed them into various grades and sizes of lumber, and all that bark and sawdust was wasted; nowadays, Noah and Simon refer to that stuff as 'wood-fired waste' or even 'energy' – they use it to make their own electricity!

'How's *that* for progress?' Simon is always saying.

Now we're the grown-ups we were in such a hurry to become; now we can drink all the beer we want, with no one asking us for proof of our age. Noah and Simon have their own houses – their own wives and children – and they do an admirable job of looking after old Uncle Alfred and my Aunt Martha, who is still a lovely woman, although she's quite gray; she looks much the way Grandmother looked to me in the summer of '62.

Uncle Alfred's had two bypass operations, but he's doing fine. The Eastman Company has provided him and my Aunt Martha with a good and long life. My aunt manifests only the most occasional vestige of her old interest in who my actual father is or was; last Christmas, in Sawyer Depot, she managed to get me alone for a second and she said, 'Do you *still* not know? You can tell me. I'll bet you know! How could you *not* have found out something – in all this time?'

I put my finger to my lips, as if I were going to tell her something that I didn't want Uncle Alfred or Dan or Noah or Simon to hear. Aunt Martha grew very attentive – her eyes sparkling, her smile widening with mischief and conspiracy.

'Dan Needham is the best father a boy could have,' I whispered to her.

'I know – Dan is wonderful,' Aunt Martha said impatiently; this was not what she wanted to hear.

And what do Noah and Simon and I *still* talk about – after all these years? We talk about what Owen 'knew' or thought he knew; and we talk about Hester. We'll talk about Hester in our graves!

'Hester the Molester!' Simon says.

'Who would have thought any of it *possible*?' Noah asks.

And every Christmas, Uncle Alfred or Aunt Martha will say: 'I believe that Hester will be home for Christmas *next* year – that's what she says.'

And Noah and Simon will say: 'That's what she *always* says.'

I suppose that Hester is my aunt and uncle's only unhappiness. Even in the summer of '62, I felt this was true. They treated her differently from the way they treated Noah and Simon, and she made them pay for it; how angry they made her! She took her anger away from Sawyer Depot and everywhere she went she found other things and people to fuel her colossal anger.

I don't think Owen was angry, not exactly. But they shared a sense of some unfairness; there was an atmosphere of injustice that enveloped them both. Owen felt that God had assigned him a role that he was powerless to change; Owen's sense of his own destiny – his belief that he was on a mission – robbed him of his capacity for *fun*. In the summer of '62, he was only twenty; but from the moment he was told that Jack Kennedy was 'diddling' Marilyn Monroe, he stopped doing anything for pleasure. Hester was just plain pissed off; she just didn't give a shit. They were such a depressing couple!

But in the summer of '62, I thought my Aunt Martha and Uncle Afred were a *perfect* couple; and yet they depressed me because of how happy they were. In their happiness they reminded me of the brief time my mother and Dan Needham had been together – and how happy they'd been, too.

Meanwhile, that summer, I couldn't manage to have a successful date. Noah and Simon did everything they could for me. They introduced me to every girl on Loveless Lake. It was a summer of wet bathing suits drying from the radio aerial of Noah's car – and the closest I came to sex was the view I had of the crotches of various girls' bathing suits, snapping in the wind that whipped past Noah's car. It was a convertible, a black-and-white '57 Chevy, the kind of car that had fins. Noah would let me take it to the drive-in, if and when I managed to get a date.

'How was the movie?' Noah would always ask me – when I brought the car home, always much too early.

'He looks like he saw every minute of it,' Simon would say – and I had. I saw every minute of every movie I took every girl to. And more's the shame: Noah and Simon created countless opportunities for me to be alone with various dates at the Eastman boathouse. At night, that boathouse had the reputation of a cheap motel; but all I ever managed was a long game of darts, or sometimes my date and I would sit on the dock, withholding any comment on the spectacle of the hard and distant stars until (finally) Noah or Simon would arrive to rescue us from our awkward torment.

I started feeling afraid – for no reason I could understand.

Georgian Bay: July 25, 1987 – it's a shame you can buy *The Globe and Mail* and *The Toronto Star* in Pointe au Baril Station; but, thank God, they don't carry *The New York Times*! The island in Georgian Bay that has been in Katherine Keeling's family since 1933 – when Katherine's grandfather reputedly won it in a poker game – is about a fifteen-minute boat ride from Pointe au Baril Station; the island is in the vicinity of Burnt Island and Hearts Content Island and Peesay Point. I think it's called Gibson Island or Ormsby Island - there are both Gibsons and Ormsbys in Katherine's family; I believe that Gibson was Katherine's maiden name, but I forget.

Anyway, there are a bunch of notched cedarwood cottages on the island, which is not served by electric power but is comfortably and efficiently supplied with propane gas – the refrigerators, the hot-water heater, the stoves, and the lamps are all run on propane; the tanks of gas are delivered to the island by boat. The island has its own septic system, which is a subject often discussed by the hordes of Keelings and Gibsons and Ormsbys who empty themselves into it – and who are fearful of the system's eventful rebellion.

I would not have wanted to visit the Keelings – or the Gibsons, or the Ormsbys – on their island *before* the septic system was installed; but that period of unlighted encounters with spiders in outhouses, and various late-night frights in the privy-world, is another favorite topic of discussion among the families who share the island each summer. I have heard, many times, the story of Uncle Bulwer Ormsby who was attacked by an owl in the privy – which had no door, 'the better to air it out!' the Keelings and the Gibsons and the Ormsbys all claimed. Uncle Bulwer was pecked on top of his head during a fortunate hiatus in what should have been a most private action, and he was so fearful of the attacking owl that he fled the privy with his pants down at his ankles, and did even greater injury to himself – greater than the *owl's* injury – by running headfirst into a pine tree.

And every year that I've visited the island, there are the

familiar disputes regarding what *kind* of owl it was - or even if it *was* an owl. Katherine's husband, Charlie Keeling, says it was probably a horsefly or a moth. Others say it was surely a screech owl – for they are known to be fierce in the defense of their nests, even to the extent of attacking humans. Others say that a screech owl's range does not extend to Georgian Bay, and that it was surely a merlin – a pigeon hawk; they are *very* aggressive and are often mistaken for the smaller owls at night.

The company of Katherine's large and friendly family is comforting to me. The conversations tend toward legendary occurrences on the island – many of which include acts of bravery or cowardice from the old outhouse or privy period of their lives. Disputed encounters with nature are also popular; my days here are most enjoyably spent in identifying species of bird and mammal and fish and reptile and, unfortunately, insect – almost none of which is well known to me.

Was that an otter or a mink or a muskrat? Was that a loon or a duck or a scoter? Does it sting or bite, or is it poisonous? These distinctions are punctuated by more direct questions to the children. Did you flush, turn off the gas, close the screen door, leave the water running (the pump is run by a gasoline engine) – and did you hang up your bathing suit and towel where they will dry? It is remindful to me of my Loveless Lake days – without the agony of dating; and Loveless Lake is a dinky pond compared to Georgian Bay. Even in the summer of '62, Loveless Lake was overrun by motorboats – and in those days, many summer cottages flushed their toilets directly into the lake. The so-called great outdoors is so much greater and so much nicer in Canada than it ever was – in my time – in New Hampshire. But pine pitch on your fingers is the same everywhere; and the kids with their hair damp all day, and their wet bathing suits, and someone always with a skinned knee, or a splinter, and the sound of bare feet on a dock . . . and the quarreling, all the quarreling. I love it; for a short time, it is very soothing. I can almost imagine that I have had a life very different from the life I have had.

One can learn much through the thin walls of summer houses. For example, I once heard Charlie Keeling tell Katherine that I was a 'nonpracticing homosexual.'

'What does *that* mean?' Katherine asked him.

I held my breath, I strained to hear Charlie's answer – for years I've wanted to know what it *means* to be a 'nonpracticing homosexual.'

'You know what I mean, Katherine,' Charlie said.

'You mean he doesn't do it,' Katherine said.

'I believe he doesn't,' Charlie said.

'But when he thinks about doing it, he thinks about doing it with men?' Katherine asked.

'I believe he doesn't think about it, at all,' Charlie answered.

'Then in what way is he "homosexual," Charlie?' Katherine asked.

Charlie sighed; in summer houses, one can even hear the sighs.

'He's not unattractive,' Charlie said. 'He doesn't have a girlfriend. Has he *ever* had a girlfriend?'

'I fail to see how this makes him *gay*,' Katherine said. 'He doesn't seem gay, not to me.'

'I didn't say he was *gay*,' Charlie said. 'A nonpracticing homosexual doesn't always *know* what he is.'

So that's what it means to be a 'nonpracticing homosexual,' I thought: it means I don't know *what* I am!

Every day there is a discussion of what we will eat – and who will take the boat, or one of the boats, to the station to fetch the food and the vitals. The shopping list is profoundly basic.

gasoline
batteries
Band-Aids
corn (if any)
insect repellent
hamburg and buns (lots)
eggs
milk
flour
butter
beer (lots)
fruit (if any)
bacon
tomatoes
clothespins (for Prue)

lemons
live bait

I let the younger children show me how they have learned to drive the boat. I let Charlie Keeling take me fishing; I really enjoy fishing for smallmouth bass – one day a year. I lend a hand to whatever the most pressing project on the island is: the Ormsbys need to rebuild their deck; the Gibsons are replacing shingles on the boathouse roof.

Every day, I volunteer to be the one to go to the station; shopping for a large family is a treat for me – for such a short time. I take a kid or two with me – for the pleasure of driving the boat would be wasted on me. And I always share my room with one of the Keeling children – or, rather, the child is required to share *his* room with me. I fall asleep listening to the astonishing complexity of a child breathing in his sleep – of a loon crying out on the dark water, of the waves lapping the rocks onshore. And in the morning, long before the child stirs, I hear the gulls and I think about the tomato-red pickup cruising the coastal road between Hampton Beach and Rye Harbor; I hear the raucous, embattled crows, whose shrill disputations and harangues remind me that I have awakened in the *real* world – in the world I know – after all.

For a moment, until the crows commence their harsh bickering, I can imagine that here, on Georgian Bay, I have found what was once called The New World – all over again, I have stumbled ashore on the undamaged land that Watahantowet sold to my ancestor. For in Georgian Bay it is possible to imagine North America as it was – before the United States began the murderous deceptions and the unthinking carelessness that have all but *spoiled* it!

Then I hear the crows. They bring me back to the world with their sounds of mayhem. I try not to think about Owen. I try to talk with Charlie Keeling about otters.

'They have a long, flattened tail – the tail lies horizontally on the water,' Charlie told me.

'I see,' I said. We were sitting on the rocks, on that part of the shoreline where one of the children said he'd seen a muskrat.

'It was an otter,' Charlie told the child.

'You didn't see it, Dad,' another of the children said.

So Charlie and I decided to wait the creature out. A lot of

freshwater clamshells marked the entrance to the animal's cave in the rocks onshore.

'An otter is a lot faster in the water than a muskrat,' Charlie told me.

'I see,' I said. We sat for an hour or two, and Charlie told me how the water level of Georgian Bay – and of all the Lake Huron – was changing; every year, it changes. He said he was worried that the acid rain – from the United States – was starting to kill the lake, beginning, as it always does (he said), with the bottom of the food chain.

'I see,' I said.

'The weeds have changed, the algae have changed, you can't catch the pike you used to – and *one* otter hasn't killed all these clams!' he said, indicating the shells.

'I see,' I said.

Then, when Charlie was peeing – in 'the bush,' as Canadians say – an animal about the size of a small beagle, with a flattened sort of head and dark-brown fur, swam out from the shore.

'Charlie!' I called. The animal dove; it did not come up again. One of the childen was instantly beside me.

'What was it?' the child asked..

'I don't know,' I said.

'Did it have a flattened tail?' Charlie called from the bush.

'It had a flattened sort of *head*,' I said.

'That's a muskrat,' one of the children said.

'You didn't see it,' said his sister.

'What kind of *tail* did it have?' Charlie called.

'I didn't see its tail,' I admitted.

'It was *that* fast, huh?' Charlie asked me – emerging from the bush, zipping up his fly.

'It was pretty fast, I guess,' I said.

'It was an otter,' he said.

(I am tempted to say it was a 'nonpracticing homosexual,' but I don't).

'See the duck?' a little girl asked me.

'That was no duck, you fool,' her brother said.

'You didn't see it – it dove!' the girls said.

'It was a female *something*,' someone else said.

'Oh, what do *you* know?' another child said.

'I didn't see anything,' I said.

'Look over there – just keep looking,' Charlie Keeling said

to me. 'It has to come up for air,' he explained. 'It's probably a pintail or a mallard or a blue-winged teal – if it's a female,' he said.

The pines smell wonderful, and the lichen on the rocks smell wonderful, and even the smell of fresh water is wonderful – or is it, really, the smell of some organic *rot* that is carrying on, just under the surface of all that water? I don't know what makes a lake smell that way, but it's wonderful. I could ask the Keeling family to tell me *why* the lake smells that way, but I prefer the silence – just the breeze that's almost constant in the pines, the lap of the waves, and the gulls' cries, and the shrieks of the terns.

'That's a *Caspian* tern,' one of the Keeling boys said to me. 'See the long red bill, see the black feet?'

'I see,' I said. But I wasn't paying attention to the tern; I was remembering the letter I wrote to Owen Meany in the summer of 1962. Dan Needham had told me that he had seen Owen one Sunday in the Gravesend Academy gym. Dan said that Owen had the basketball, but he wasn't shooting; he was standing at the foul line, just looking up at the basket – he wasn't even dribbling the ball, and he wouldn't take a shot. Dan said it was the strangest thing.

'He was just *standing* there,' Dan said. 'I must have watched him for five minutes, and he didn't move a muscle – he just held the ball and stared at the basket. He's so small, you know, the basket must look like it's a mile away.'

'He was probably thinking about the shot,' I told Dan.

'Well, I didn't bother him,' Dan said. 'Whatever he was thinking about, he was concentrating so hard he didn't see me – I didn't even say hello. I don't think he would have heard me, anyway,' Dan said.

Hearing about him made me even miss practicing that stupid *shot;* and so I wrote to him, just casually – since when would a twenty-year-old actually come out and *say* he missed his best friend?

'Dear Owen,' I wrote him. 'What are you up to? It's kind of boring here. I like the work in the woods best – I mean, the logging. Except there are deer flies. The work at the sawmill, and in the lumberyards, is much hotter – but there are no deer flies. Uncle Alfred insists that Loveless Lake is "potable" – he says we have swallowed so much of it, we would be dead if it weren't. But Noah says there's much more piss and shit in it than there is in the ocean. I miss the beach – how's the beach this summer? Maybe next summer your father would give me a job in the quarries?'

He wrote back; he didn't bother to begin with the usual 'Dear John' – The Voice had his own style, nothing fancy, strictly capitals.

'ARE YOU CRAZY?' Owen wrote me. 'YOU WANT TO WORK IN THE QUARRIES? YOU THINK IT'S HOT IN A LUMBERYARD? MY FATHER DOESN'T DO A LOT OF HIRING – AND I'M SURE HE WON'T PAY YOU AS MUCH AS YOUR UNCLE ALFRED. IT SOUNDS TO ME LIKE YOU HAVEN'T MET THE RIGHT GIRL UP THERE.'

'So how's Hester?' I asked him, when I wrote him back. 'Be sure to tell her that I love her room – that'll piss her off! I don't suppose she's been helping you practice the shot – if you lose your touch, that'll be too bad. You were so close to doing it in under three seconds.'

He wrote back immediately: 'UNDER THREE SECONDS IS DEFINITELY POSSIBLE. I HAVEN'T BEEN PRACTICING BUT THINKING ABOUT IT IS ALMOST AS GOOD. MY FATHER WILL HIRE YOU NEXT SUMMER – IT WON'T BE TOO BAD IF YOU START OUT SLOWLY, MAYBE IN THE MONUMENT SHOP. BY THE WAY, THE BEACH HAS BEEN GREAT – LOTS OF GOOD-LOOKING GIRLS AROUND, AND CAROLINE O'DAY HAS BEEN ASKING ABOUT YOU. YOU OUGHT TO SEE HOW SHE LOOKS WHEN SHE'S NOT WEARING HER ST MICHAEL'S UNIFORM. SAW DAN ON HIS BICYCLE – HE SHOULD LOSE A LITTLE WEIGHT. AND HESTER AND I SPENT AN EVENING WITH YOUR GRANDMOTHER; WE WATCHED THE IDIOT BOX, OF COURSE, AND YOU SHOULD HAVE HEARD YOUR GRANDMOTHER ON THE SUBJECT OF THE GENEVA CONFERENCE – SHE SAID SHE'D BELIEVE IN THE "NEUTRALITY" OF LAOS WHEN THE SOVIETS DECIDED TO RELOCATE . . . ON THE MOON! SHE SAID SHE'D BELIEVE IN THE GENEVA ACCORDS WHEN THERE WAS NOTHING BUT PARROTS AND MONKEYS MOVING ALONG THE HO CHI MINH TRAIL! I WON'T REPEAT WHAT HESTER SAID ABOUT YOU USING HER ROOM – IT'S THE SAME THING SHE SAYS ABOUT HER MOTHER AND FATHER AND NOAH AND SIMON AND ALL THE GIRLS ON LOVE-

LESS LAKE, SO PERHAPS YOU'RE FAMILIAR WITH THE EXPRESSION.'

I wrote a letter to Caroline O'Day; she never answered me. It was August, 1962. I remember one very hot day – humid, with a hazy sky; a thunderstorm was threatening, but it never came. It was very much like the day of my mother's wedding, before the storm; it was what Owen Meany and I called typical Gravesend weather.

Noah and Simon and I were logging; the deer flies were driving us crazy, and there were mosquitoes, too. Simon was the easiest to drive crazy; of the three of us, the deer flies and mosquitoes liked Simon the best. Logging is most dangerous if you're impatient; saws and axes, peavys and cant dogs – these tools belong in patient hands. Simon got a little sloppy and reckless with his cant dog – he chased after a deer fly with the hook end and speared himself in the calf. It was a deep gash, about three or four inches long – not serious; but he would require some stitches to close the wound, and a tetanus shot.

Noah and I were elated; even Simon, who had a high tolerance for pain, was pretty pleased – the injury meant we could all get out of the woods. We drove the Jeep out the logging road to Noah's Chevy; we took the Chevy out on the highway, through Sawyer Depot and Conway, to the emergency entrance of the North Conway Hospital.

There'd been an automobile accident somewhere near the Maine border, so Simon rated a low priority in the emergency room; that was fine with all of us, because the longer it took for Simon to get his tetanus shot and his stitches, the longer we would be away from the deer flies and the mosquitoes and the heat. Simon even pretended not to know if he was allergic to anything; Aunt Martha and Uncle Alfred had to be called, and that took more time. Noah started flirting with one of the nurses; with any luck, Noah knew, we could fart around the whole rest of the day, and never go back to work.

One of the less-mangled victims of the auto accident sat in the waiting room with us. He was someone Noah and Simon knew vaguely – a type not uncommon in the north country, one of these ski bums who don't seem to know what to do with themselves when there isn't any snow. This was a guy who'd been drinking a bottle of beer when one car hit another; he'd been the driver of one of the cars, he said, and the bottle neck had broken in his mouth on impact – he had lacerations on the roof of his mouth, and his gums were slashed, and the broken neck of the bottle had pierced his cheek. He proudly showed us the lacerations inside his mouth, and the hole in his cheek – all the while mopping up his mouth and face with a blood-soaked wad of gauze, which he periodically wrung out in a blood-soaked towel. He was precisely the sort of north country lunatic who gave Hester great disdain for Sawyer Depot, and led her to maintain her residence in the college community of Durham year 'round.

'Did you hear about Marilyn Monroe?' the ski bum asked us.

We were prepared for a dirty joke – an absolutely filthy joke. The ski bum's smile was a bleeding gash in his face; his smile was the repulsive equal to his gaping wound in his cheek. He was lascivious, depraved – our much-appreciated holiday in the emergency room had taken a nasty turn. We tried to ignore him.

'Did you hear about Marilyn Monroe?' he asked us again. Suddenly, it didn't sound like a joke. Maybe it's about the Kennedys! I thought.

'No. What about her?' I said.

'She's dead,' the ski bum said. He took such a sadistic pleasure in his announcement, his smile appeared to pump the blood out of his mouth and the hole in his cheek; I thought that he was as pleased by the shock value of what he had to say as he was thrilled by the spectacle of wringing his own blood from the sodden gauze pad into the sodden towel. Forever after, I would see his bleeding face whenever I imagined how Larry Lish and his mother must have responded to this news; how eagerly, how greedily they must have spread the word! 'Have you heard? You mean, you haven't heard!' he rapture of so much amateur conjecturing and surmising would flush their faces as irrepressibly as blood!

'How?' I asked the ski bum.

'An overdose,' he said; he sounded disappointed – as if he'd been hoping for something bloodier. 'Maybe it was an accident, maybe it was suicide,' he said.

Maybe it was the Kennedys, I thought. It made me feel afraid; at first, that summer, it was something vague that had made me feel afraid. Now something concrete made me feel afraid – but my fear itself was still vague: what could Marilyn Monroe's death ever have to do with *me*?

'IT HAS TO DO WITH *ALL* OF US,' said Owen Meany, when I called him that night. 'SHE WAS JUST LIKE OUR WHOLE COUNTRY – NOT QUITE YOUNG ANYMORE, BUT NOT OLD EITHER; A LITTLE BREATHLESS, VERY BEAUTIFUL, MAYBE A LITTLE STUPID, MAYBE A LOT SMARTER THAN SHE SEEMED, AND SHE WAS LOOKING FOR SOMETHING – I THINK SHE WANTED TO BE GOOD. LOOK AT THE MEN IN HER LIFE – JOE DIMAGGIO, ARTHUR MILLER, MAYBE THE KENNEDYS. LOOK AT HOW GOOD THEY *SEEM*! LOOK AT HOW *DESIRABLE* SHE WAS! THAT'S WHAT SHE WAS: SHE WAS DESIRABLE. SHE WAS FUNNY AND SEXY – AND SHE WAS VULNERABLE, TOO. SHE WAS NEVER QUITE HAPPY, SHE WAS ALWAYS A LITTLE OVERWEIGHT. SHE WAS JUST LIKE OUR WHOLE COUNTRY,' he repeated; he was on a roll. I could hear Hester playing her guitar in the background, as if she were trying to improvise a folk song from everything he said. 'AND THOSE MEN,' he said. 'THOSE FAMOUS, POWERFUL MEN – DID THEY REALLY LOVE HER? DID THEY TAKE CARE OF HER? IF SHE WAS EVER WITH THE KENNEDYS, THEY COULDN'T HAVE LOVED HER – THEY WERE JUST USING HER, THEY WERE JUST BEING CARELESS AND TREATING THEMSELVES TO A THRILL. THAT'S WHAT POWERFUL MEN DO TO THIS COUNTRY – IT'S A BEAUTIFUL, SEXY, BREATHLESS COUNTRY, AND POWERFUL MEN USE IT TO TREAT THEMSELVES TO A THRILL! THEY SAY THEY LOVE IT BUT THEY DON'T MEAN IT. THEY SAY THINGS TO MAKE THEMSELVES APPEAR GOOD – THEY MAKE THEMSELVES APPEAR *MORAL*. THAT'S WHAT I THOUGHT KENNEDY WAS: A MORALIST. BUT HE WAS JUST GIVING US A SNOW JOB, HE WAS JUST BEING A GOOD SEDUCER. I THOUGHT HE WAS A *SAVIOR*. I THOUGHT HE WANTED TO USE HIS POWER TO DO GOOD. BUT PEOPLE WILL SAY AND DO ANY-THING JUST TO GET POWER; THEN THEY'LL USE THE POWER JUST TO GET A THRILL. MARILYN MONROE WAS ALWAYS LOOKING FOR THE BEST MAN – MAYBE SHE WANTED THE MAN WITH THE *MOST* INTEGRITY, MAYBE SHE WANTED THE MAN WITH THE MOST ABILITY TO DO GOOD. AND SHE WAS SEDUCED, OVER AND OVER AGAIN – SHE GOT FOOLED, SHE WAS

TRICKED, SHE GOT USED, SHE WAS USED *UP*. JUST LIKE THE COUNTRY. THE COUNTRY WANTS A SAVIOR. THE COUNTRY IS A SUCKER FOR POWERFUL MEN WHO *LOOK* GOOD. WE THINK THEY'RE *MORALISTS* AND THEN THEY JUST USE US. THAT'S WHAT'S GOING TO HAPPEN TO YOU AND ME,' said Owen Meany. 'WE'RE GOING TO BE USED.'

Georgian Bay: July 26, 1987 – *The Toronto Star* says that President Reagan actually led the first efforts to conceal essential details of his secret arms-for-hostages program and keep it alive after it became public.' *The Toronto Star* added that 'the President subsequently made misleading statements about the arms sales' – on four separate occasions!

Owen used to say that the most disturbing thing about the antiwar movement – against the Vietnam War – was that he suspected self-interest motivated many of the protesters; he thought that if the issue of many of the protesters being drafted was removed from the issue of the war, there would be very little protest at all.

Look at the United States today. Are they drafting young Americans to fight in Nicaragua? No; not yet. Are *masses* of young Americans outraged at the Reagan administration's shoddy and deceitful behavior? Ho hum; not hardly.

I know what Owen Meany would say about that; I know what he *did* say – and it still applies.

'THE ONLY WAY YOU CAN GET AMERICANS TO *NOTICE* ANYTHING IS TO TAX THEM OR DRAFT THEM OR KILL THEM.' Owen said. He said that once – when Hester proposed abolishing the draft. 'IF YOU ABOLISH THE DRAFT,' said Owen Meany, 'MOST AMERICANS WILL SIMPLY STOP CARING ABOUT WHAT WE'RE DOING IN OTHER PARTS OF THE WORLD.'

I saw a mink run under the boathouse today; it had such a slender body, it was only slightly larger than a weasel – with a weasel's undulating movement. It had such a thick, glossy coat of fur, I was instantly reminded of Larry Lish's mother. Where is she now? I wondered.

I know where Larry Lish is; he's a well-known journalist in New York – 'an investigative reporter' is what he's called. I've read a few of his pieces; they're not bad – he was always clever – and I notice that he's acquired a necessary quality in his voice ('necessary,' I think, if a journalist is going to make a name for himself, and gain an audience, and so forth). Larry Lish has become particularly self-righteous, and the quality in his voice that I call 'necessary' is a tone of moral indignation. Larry Lish has become a *moralist* – imagine that!

I wonder what his mother has become. If she got the right guy to marry her – before it was too late – maybe Mitzy Lish has become a moralist, too!

In the fall of '62 when Owen Meany and I began our life as freshmen at the University of New Hampshire, we enjoyed certain advantages that set us apart from our lowly, less-experienced peers. We were not subject to dormitory rules because we lived at home – we were commuters from Gravesend and were permitted to park our own means of transportation on campus, which other freshmen were not allowed to do. I divided my at-home time between Dan and my grandmother; this had an added advantage, in that when there was a late-night university party in Durham, I could tell Dan I was staying with my grandmother and tell Grandmother I was staying with Dan – and *never* come home! Owen was not required to be home at any special time; considering that he spent every night of the summer at Hester's apartment, I was surprised that he was going through the motions of living at home at all. Hester's roommates were back, however; if Owen stayed at Hester's, there was no question regarding the bed in which he spent the night – whether he and Hester 'did it' or not, they were at least familiar with the intimate proximity that Hester's queen-size mattress forced upon them. But once our classes began, Owen didn't sleep at Hester's apartment more than once or twice a week.

Our other advantages over our fellow freshmen were several. We had suffered the academic rigors of Gravesend Academy; the course work at the University of New Hampshire was very easy in comparison. I benefited greatly from this, because – as Owen had taught me – I chiefly needed to give myself more time to do the work assigned. So much *less* work was assigned than what I had learned to expect from the academy that – for once – I had ample time. I got good grades, almost easily; and for the first time – although this took two or three years – I began to think of myself as 'smart.' But the relatively undemanding expectations of the university had quite a different effect on Owen Meany.

He could do everything he was asked without half trying, and this made him lazy. He quickly fell into a habit of getting no better grades than he needed to satisfy his ROTC 'scholarship'; to my surprise, his best grades were always in the ROTC courses – in so-called Military Science. We took many of the same classes; in English and History, I actually got better grades than Owen – The Voice had become indifferent about his writing!

'I AM DEVELOPING A MINIMALIST'S STYLE,' he told our English teacher, who'd complained that Owen never expanded a single point in any of his papers; he never employed more than one example for each point he made. 'FIRST YOU TELL ME I CAN'T WRITE USING ONLY CAPITAL LETTERS, NOW YOU WANT ME TO "ELABORATE" – TO BE MORE "EXPANSIVE." IS THAT CONSISTENT?' he asked our English teacher. 'MAYBE YOU WANT ME TO CHANGE MY PERSONALITY, TOO?'

If, at Gravesend Academy, The Voice had persuaded the majority of the faculty that his eccentricities and peculiarities were not only his individual rights but were inseparable from his generally acknowledged brilliance, the more diverse but also more specialized faculty at the University of New Hampshire were not interested in 'the whole boy,' not at all; they were not even a community, the university faculty, and they shared no general opinion that Owen Meany was brilliant, they expressed no general concern that his individual rights needed protection, and they had no tolerance for eccentricities and peculiarities. The classes they taught were for no student's special development; their interests were the subject themselves – their passions were for the politics of the university, or of their own departments within it – and their overall view of us students was that we should conform ourselves to *their* methods of *their* disciplines of study.

Owen Meany, who had been so conspicuous – all my life – was easily overlooked at the University of New Hampshire. He was in none of his classes as distinguished as the tomato-red pickup, which was so readily distinguishable among the many economy-model cars that most parents bought for most students who had their own cars – my grandmother had bought me a Volkswagen Beetle; in the campus parking lots, there were so many VWs of the same year and navy-blue color that I could identify mine only by its license plate or by the familiarity of whatever I had left on the back seat.

And although Owen and I first counted Hester's friendship as an advantage, her friendship was another means by which Owen Meany became lost in Durham; Hester had a lot of friends among the seniors in what was our first year. These seniors were the people Owen and I hung out with; we didn't have to make friends among the freshmen – and when Hester and her friends graduated, Owen and I didn't have any friends.

As for whatever had made me feel afraid in the summer of '62 – whatever that fear was, it was replaced by a kind of solitariness, a feeling of being oddly set apart, but without loneliness; the loneliness would come later. And as for fear, you would have thought the Cuban Missile Crisis – that October – would have sufficed; you would have thought that would have scared the shit out of us, as people in New Hampshire are *always* untruthfully claiming. But Owen said to Hester and me, and to a bunch of hangers-on in Hester's apartment, 'DON'T BE AFRAID. THIS IS NO BIG DEAL, THIS IS JUST A BIT OF NUCLEAR *BLUFFING* – NOTHING HAPPENS AS A RESULT OF THIS. BELIEVE ME. I KNOW.'

What he meant was that he believed he 'knew' what would happen to *him*; that it wasn't missiles that would get him – neither the Soviets' nor ours – and that, whatever 'it' was, it didn't happen in October, 1962.

'How do *you* know nothing's going to happen?' someone asked him. It was the guy who hung around Hester's apartment as if he were waiting for Owen Meany to drop dead. He kept encouraging Hester to read The Alexandria Quartet – especially *Justine* and *Clea*, which this guy claimed he had read four or five times. Hester wasn't much of a reader, and I had read only *Justine*. Owen Meany had read the whole quartet and had told Hester and me not to bother with the last three novels.

'IT'S JUST MORE OF THE SAME, AND NOT SO WELL DONE,' Owen said. 'ONE BOOK ABOUT HAVING SEX IN A FOREIGN ATMOSPHERE IS ENOUGH.'

'What do *you* know about "sex in a foreign atmosphere"?' the quartet-lover had asked Owen. Owen had not answered the guy. He surely knew the guy was a rival for Hester's affections; he also knew that rivals are best unmanned by being ignored.

'Hey!' the guy shouted at Owen. 'I'm talking to *you*. What makes you think you know there's not going to be a war?'

'OH, THERE'S GOING TO BE A WAR, ALL RIGHT,' said Owen Meany. 'BUT NOT NOW – NOT OVER CUBA. EITHER KHRUSHCHEV WILL PULL THE MISSILES OUT OF CUBA OR KENNEDY WILL OFFER HIM SOMETHING TO HELP HIM SAVE FACE.'

'This little man knows everything,' the guy said.

'Don't you call him "little," ' Hester said. 'He's got the biggest penis *ever*. If there's a bigger one, I don't want to know about it,' Hester said.

'THERE'S NO NEED TO BE CRUDE,' said Owen Meany.

That was the last we ever saw of the guy who wanted Hester to read The Alexandria Quartet. I will confess that in the showers in the Gravesend Academy gym – after practicing the shot – I *had* noticed that Owen's doink was especially large; at least, it was disproportionately large. Compared to the rest of him, it was *huge*!

My cousin Simon, whose doink was rather small – perhaps owing to Hester's childhood violence upon it – once claimed that small doinks grew much, much bigger when they were erect; big doinks, Simon said, never grew much when they got hard. I confess: I don't know – I have no doink theory as adamant or hopeful as Simon's. The only time I saw Owen Meany with an erection, he was wrapped in swaddling clothes – he was only an eleven-year-old Baby Jesus; and although his hard-on was highly inappropriate, it didn't strike me as astonishing.

As for the shot, Owen and I were guilty of lack of practice; by the end of our freshman year, by the summer of 1963 – when we were twenty-one, the legal drinking age at last! – we had trouble sinking the shot in under *five* seconds. We had to work at it all summer – just to get back to where we had been, just to break four seconds again. It was the summer the Buddhists in Vietnam were demonstrating – they were setting themselves on fire. It was the summer when Owen said, 'WHAT'S A CATHOLIC DOING AS PRESIDENT OF A COUNTRY OF BUDDHISTS?' It was the summer when President Diem was not long for this world; President John F. Kennedy was not long for this world, either. And it was the first summer I went to work for Meany Granite.

It was my illusion that I worked for Mr Meany; it was his illusion, too. It had been amply demonstrated to me – who bossed whom, in that family. I should have known, from the start, that Owen was in charge.

'MY FATHER WANTS TO START YOU OUT IN THE MONUMENT SHOP,' he told me. 'YOU BEGIN WITH AN UNDERSTANDING OF THE FINISHED PRODUCT – IN THIS BUSINESS, IT'S EASIER TO BEGIN WITH THE FINE-TUNING. IT'S GETTING THE STUFF OUT OF THE GROUND THAT CAN BE TRICKY. I HOPE YOU DON'T THINK I'M CONDESCENDING, BUT WORKING WITH GRANITE IS A LOT LIKE WRITING A TERM PAPER – IT'S THE FIRST DRAFT THAT CAN KILL YOU. ONCE YOU GET THE GOOD STUFF INTO THE SHOP, THE FINE WORK IS EASY: CUTTING THE STONE, EDGING THE LETTERS – YOU'VE JUST GOT TO BE FUSSY. IT'S ALL SMOOTHING AND POLISHING – YOU'VE GOT TO GO SLOWLY.

'DON'T BE IN A HURRY TO WORK IN THE QUARRIES. AT THE MONUMENT-END, AT LEAST THE SIZE AND WEIGHT OF THE STONE ARE MANAGEABLE – YOU'RE WORKING WITH SMALLER TOOLS AND A SMALLER PRODUCT. AND IN THE SHOP, EVERY DAY IS DIFFERENT; YOU NEVER KNOW HOW BUSY YOU'LL BE – MOST PEOPLE DON'T DIE ON SCHEDULE, MOST FAMILIES DON'T ORDER GRAVESTONES IN ADVANCE.'

I don't doubt that he was genuinely concerned for my safety, and I know he knew everything about granite; it was wise to develop a feeling for the stone – on a smaller, more refined scale – before one encountered the intimidating size and weight of it in the quarry. All the quarrymen – the signalman, the derrickman, the channel bar drillers, and the dynamiters – and even the sawyers who had to handle the rock before it was cut down to monument size . . . *all* the men who worked at the quarries were afforded a less generous margin for error than those of us who worked in the monument shop. Even so, I thought there was more than caution motivating Owen to *keep* me working in the monument shop for the entire summer of '63. For one thing, I wanted muscles; and the physical work in the monument shop was a lot less strenuous than being a logger for my Uncle Alfred. For another thing,

I envied Owen his tan – he worked in the quarries, unless it was raining; on rainy days, he worked in the shop with me. And we called him in from the quarries whenever there was a customer placing an order for a gravestone; Owen insisted that he be the one to handle that – and when the order was not placed by a funeral home, when the customer was a family member or a close friend of the deceased, we were all grateful that Owen wanted to handle it.

He was very good at that part of it – very respectful of grief, very tactful (while at the same time he managed to be *very* specific). I don't mean that this was simply a matter of spelling the name correctly and double-checking the date of birth, and the date of death; I mean that the personality of the deceased was discussed, in depth – Owen sought nothing less than a PROPER monument, a COMPATIBLE monument. The aesthetics of the deceased were taken into consideration; the size, shape, and color of the stone were only the rough drafts of the business; Owen wanted to know the tastes of those mourners who would be viewing the gravestone more than once. I never saw a customer who was displeased with the final product; unfortunately – for the enterprises of Meany Granite – I never saw very *many* customers, either.

'DON'T BE VAIN,' Owen told me, when I complained about the length of my apprenticeship in the monument shop. 'IF YOU'RE STANDING IN THE BOTTOM OF A QUARRY, THINKING ABOUT WHAT KIND OF TAN YOU'RE GETTING – OR YOUR STUPID MUSCLES – YOU'RE GOING TO END UP UNDER TEN TONS OF GRANITE. BESIDES, MY FATHER THINKS YOU'RE DOING A GREAT JOB WITH THE GRAVESTONES.'

But I don't think Mr Meany ever noticed the work I was doing with the monuments; it was August before I even saw Mr Meany in the shop, and he looked surprised to see me – but he always said the same thing, whenever and wherever he saw me. 'Why, it's Johnny Wheelwright!' he'd always say.

And when it wasn't raining – or when Owen wasn't talking directly to a customer – the only other time that Owen was in the shop was when there was an especially difficult piece of stonecutting assigned, a particularly complicated gravestone, a demanding shape, lots of tight curves and sharp angles, and so forth. And the typical Gravesend families were plain and dour in the face of death; we had few calls for elaborate coping, even fewer for archways with dosserets, and not one for angels sliding down barber poles. That was too bad, because to see Owen at work with the diamond wheel was to witness state-of-the-art monument-making. There was no one as precise with the diamond wheel as Owen Meany.

A diamond wheel is similar to a radial-arm saw, a wood saw familiar to me from my uncle's mill; a diamond wheel is a table saw but the blade is not part of the table – the blade, which is a diamond-impregnated wheel, is lowered *to* the table in a gantry. The wheel blade is about two feet in diameter and studded (or 'tipped') with diamond segments – these are pieces of diamond, only a half inch long, only a quarter inch wide. When the blade is lowered onto the granite, it cuts through the stone at a preset angle into a waiting block of wood. It is a very sharp blade, it makes a very exact and smooth cut; it is perfect for making the precise, polished edges on the tops and sides of gravestones – like a scalpel, it makes no mistakes, or only the user's mistakes. By comparison to other saws in the granite business, it is so fine and delicate a tool that it isn't even called a saw – it is always called 'the diamond wheel.' It passes through granite with so little resistance that its sound is far less snarly than many wood saws of the power type; a diamond wheel makes a single, high-pitched scream – very plaintive. Owen Meany said: 'A DIAMOND WHEEL MAKES A GRAVESTONE SOUND AS IF THE STONE ITSELF IS MOURNING.'

Think of how much time he spent in that creepy monument shop on Water Street, the unfinished lettering of the names of the dead surrounding him – is it any wonder that he SAW his own name and the date of his death on Scrooge's grave? No; it's a wonder he didn't SEE such horrors every day! And when he put on those crazy-looking safety goggles and lowered the diamond wheel into cutting position, the terribly consistent scream of that blade must have reminded him of the 'permanent scream,' which was his own unchanging voice – to use Mr McSwiney's term for it. After my summer in the monument shop, I could appreciate what might have appealed to Owen Meany about the quiet of churches, the peace of prayer, the easy cadence of hymns and litanies – and even the simplistic, athletic ritual of practicing the shot.

As for the rest of the summer of 1963 – when the Buddhists in Vietnam were torching themselves, and time was running out on the Kennedys – Hester was working as a lobster-house waitress again.

'So much for a B.A. in Music,' she said.

At least I could appreciate what Owen Meany meant, when he said of Randy White: 'I'D LIKE TO GET HIM UNDER THE DIAMOND WHEEL – ALL I'D NEED IS JUST A FEW SECONDS. I'D LIKE TO PUT HIS *DOINK* UNDER THE DIAMOND WHEEL,' Owen said.

As for *doinks* – as for mine, in particular – I had another slow summer. The Catholic Church had reason to be proud of the insurmountable virtue of Caroline O'Day, with or without her St Michael's uniform – and of the virtue of countless others, any church could be proud; they were all virtuous with me. I felt someone's bare breast, briefly – only once, and it was an accident – one warm night when we went swimming off the beach at Little Boar's Head and the phosphorescence, in my opinion, was especially seductive. The girl was a musical friend of Hester's, and in the tomato-red pickup, on the ride back to Durham, Hester volunteered to be the one to sit on my lap, because my date was so displeased by my awkward, amateurish advances.

'Here, you sit in the middle, *I'll* sit on him,' Hester told her friend. 'I've felt his silly hard-on before, and it doesn't bother me.'

'THERE'S NO NEED TO BE CRUDE,' said Owen Meany.

And so I rode from Little Boar's Head to Durham with Hester on my lap – once again, humiliated by my hard-on. I thought that just a few seconds under the diamond wheel would certainly suffice for *me;* and if someone were to put my doink under the wheel, I considered that it would be no great loss.

I was twenty-one and I was still a Joseph; I was a Joseph then, and I'm just a Joseph now.

Georgian Bay: July 27, 1987 – why can't I just enjoy all the nature up here? I coaxed one of the Keeling kids to take me in one of the boats to Pointe au Baril Station. Miraculously, no one on the island needed anything from the station: not an egg, not a scrap of meat, or a bar of soap; not even any live bait. I was the only one who needed anything; I 'needed' a newspaper, I'm ashamed to say. Needing to know the news – it's such a weakness, it's worse than many other addictions, it's an especially debilitating illness.

The Toronto Star said the White House was so frustrated by both Congress and the Pentagon that a small, special-forces group within the military was established; and that actual, active-duty American troops fired rockets and machine guns at Nicaraguan soldiers – all this was unknown to the Congress or the Pentagon. Why aren't Americans as disgusted by themselves – as fed up with themselves – as everyone else is? All their lip service to democracy, all their blatantly undemocratic behavior! I've got to stop reading about this whole silly business! All these headlines can turn your mind to mush – headlines that within a year will seem most unmemorable; and if memorable, merely quaint. I live in Canada, I have a Canadian passport – why should I waste my time caring what the Americans are doing, especially when they don't care themselves?

I'm going to try to interest myself in something more cosmic – in something more universal, although I suppose that a total lack of integrity in government is 'universal,' isn't it?

There was another story in *The Toronto Star*, more appropriate to the paradisiacal view of the universe one can enjoy from Georgian Bay. It was a story about black holes: scientists say that black holes could engulf two whole galaxies! The story was about the potential 'collapse of the star system' – what could be more important than *that*?

Listen to this: 'Black holes are concentrations of matter so dense they have collapsed upon themselves. Nothing, not even light, can escape their intense gravitational pull.' Imagine that! Not even *light* – my God! I announced this news to the Keeling family; but one of the middle children – a sort of science-prize student – responded to me rather rudely.

'Yeah,' he said, 'but all the black holes are about two million light-years away from Earth.'

And I thought: That is about as far away from Earth as Owen Meany is; that is about as far away from Earth as I would like to be.

And where is JFK today? How far away is he?

On November 22, 1963, Owen Meany and I were in my room at 80 Front Street, studying for a Geology exam. I was angry with Owen for manipulating me into taking Geology, the true nature of which was concealed – at the University of New Hampshire – in the curriculum catalog under the hippie-inspired title of Earth Science. Owen had misled me into thinking that the course would be an easy means of satisfying a part of our science requirement - he knew all about rocks, he assured me, and the rest of the course would concern itself with fossils. 'IT'LL BE NEAT TO KNOW ALL ABOUT THE DINOSAURS!' Owen had said; he seduced me. We spent less than a week with the dinosaurs – and far less time with fossils than we spent learning the horrible names of the ages of the earth. And it turned out that Owen Meany didn't know a metamorphic schist from an igneous intrusion – unless the latter was granite.

On November 22, 1963, I had just confused the Paleocene epoch with the Pleistocene, and I was further confused by the difference between an epoch and an era.

'The Cenozoic is an *era*, right?' I asked him.

'WHO CARES?' said Owen Meany. 'YOU CAN FORGET THAT PART. AND YOU CAN FORGET ABOUT ANYTHING AS BROAD AS THE TERTIARY OR THE QUATERNARY – THAT'S TOO BROAD, TOO. WHAT YOU'VE GOT TO KNOW IS MORE SPECIFIC, YOU'VE GOT TO KNOW WHAT CHARACTERIZED AN EPOCH – FOR EXAMPLE, WHICH EPOCH IS *CHARACTERIZED* BY THE TRIUMPH OF BIRDS AND PLACENTAL MAMMALS?'

'Jesus, how'd I ever let you talk me into this?' I said.

'PAY ATTENTION,' said Owen Meany. 'THERE ARE WAYS TO REMEMBER EVERYTHING. THE WAY TO REMEMBER *PLEISTOCENE* IS TO REMEMBER THAT THIS EPOCH WAS CHARACTERIZED BY THE APPEARANCE OF MAN AND WIDESPREAD GLACIAL ICE – REMEMBER THE *ICE*, IT RHYMES WITH *PLEIS* IN PLEISTOCENE.'

'Jesus Christ!' I said.

'I'M JUST TRYING TO HELP YOU REMEMBER,' Owen said. 'IF YOU'RE CONFUSING THE BLOSSOMING OF BIRDS AND PLACENTAL MAMMALS WITH THE FIRST APPEARANCE OF *MAN*, YOU'RE ABOUT SIXTY MILLION YEARS OFF – YOU'RE MAKING A PRETTY BIG MISTAKE!'

'The biggest mistake I made was to take Geology!' I said. Suddenly, Ethel was in my room; we hadn't heard her knock or open the door – I don't remember ever seeing Ethel in my room before (or since).

'Your grandmother wishes to see you in the TV room,' Ethel said.

'IS SOMETHING WRONG WITH THE TV?' Owen asked her.

'Something is wrong with the president,' Ethel said.

When we found out what was wrong with Kennedy – when we saw him shot, and, later, when we learned he was dead – Owen Meany said, 'IF WE FIRST APPEAR IN THE PLEISTOCENE, I THINK THIS IS WHEN WE *DISAPPEAR* – I GUESS A MILLION YEARS OF MAN IS ENOUGH.'

What we witnessed with the death of Kennedy was the triumph of television; what we saw with his assassination, and with his funeral, was the beginnning of television's dominance of our culture – for television is at its most solemnly self-serving and at its mesmerizing best when it is depicting the untimely deaths of the chosen and the golden. It is as witness to the butchery of heroes in their prime – and of all holy-seeming innocents – that television achieves its deplorable greatness. The blood on Mrs Kennedy's clothes and her wrecked face under her veil; the fatherless children; LBJ taking the oath of office; and brother Bobby – looking so very much the next in line.

'IF BOBBY WAS NEXT IN LINE FOR MARILYN MONROE, WHAT ELSE IS HE NEXT IN LINE FOR?' said Owen Meany.

Not even five years later, when Bobby Kennedy was assassinated, Hester would say, 'Television gives good disaster.' I suppose this was nothing but a more vernacular version of my grandmother's observation of the effect of TV on old people: that watching it would hasten their deaths. If watching television doesn't hasten death, it surely manages to make death very inviting; for television so shamelessly sentimentalizes and romanticizes death that it makes the living feel they have missed something – just by staying alive.

At 80 Front Street, that November of '63, my grandmother and Owen Meany and I watched the president be killed for hours; for *days* we watched him be killed and re-killed, again and again.

'I GET THE POINT,' said Owen Meany. 'IF SOME MANIAC MURDERS YOU, YOU'RE AN INSTANT HERO – EVEN IF ALL YOU WERE DOING IS RIDING IN A MOTORCADE!'

'I wish some maniac would murder *me*,' my grandmother said.

'MISSUS WHEELWRIGHT! WHAT DO YOU MEAN?' Owen said.

'I mean, why can't some maniac murder someone *old* - like me?' Grandmother said. 'I'd rather be murdered by a maniac than have to leave my home – and that's what *will* happen to me,' she said. 'Maybe Dan, maybe Martha – maybe *you*,' she said accusingly to me. 'One of you, or all of you – either way, you're going to force me to leave this house. You're going to put me in a place with a bunch of old people who are *crazy*,' Grandmother said. 'And I'd rather be murdered by a maniac instead – that's all I mean. One day, Ethel won't be able to manage – one day, it will take a *hundred* Ethels just to clean up the mess I make!' my grandmother said. 'One day, not even *you* will want to watch television with me,' she said to Owen. 'One day,' she said to me, 'you'll come to visit me and I won't even know who you are. Why doesn't someone train the maniacs to murder *old* people and leave the young people alone? What a *waste*!' she cried. A lot of people were saying this about the death of President Kennedy – with a slightly different meaning, of course. 'I'm going to be an incontinent idiot,' my grandmother said; she looked directly at Owen Meany. 'Wouldn't *you* rather be murdered by a maniac?' she asked him.

'IF IT WOULD DO ANY *GOOD* – YES, I WOULD,' said Owen Meany.

'I think we've been watching too much television,' I said.

'There's no remedy for that,' my grandmother said.

But after the murder of President Kennedy, it seemed to me that there was 'no remedy' for Owen Meany, either; he succumbed to a state of mind that he would not discuss with me – he went into a visible decline in communication. I would often see the tomato-red pickup parked behind the vestry of Hurd's Church; Owen had kept in touch with the Rev. Lewis Merrill, whose silent and extended prayer for Owen had gained him much respect among the faculty and students at Gravesend. Pastor Merrill had always been 'liked'; but before his prayer he had lacked respect. I'm sure that Owen, too, was grateful for Mr Merrill's gesture – even if the gesture had been a struggle, and not of the minister's own initiative. But after JFK's death, Owen appeared to see more of the Rev. Mr Merrill; and Owen wouldn't tell me what they talked about. Maybe they talked about Marilyn Monroe and the Kennedys. They talked about 'the dream,' I suppose; but I had not yet been successful in coaxing that dream out of Owen Meany.

'What's this I hear about a *dream* you keep having?' I asked him once.

'I DON'T KNOW WHAT YOU'VE HEARD,' he said.

And shortly before that New Year's Eve, I asked Hester if *she* knew anything about any dream. Hester had had a few drinks; she was getting into her throwing-up mood, but she was rarely caught off-guard. She eyed me suspiciously.

'What do *you* know about it?' she asked me.

'I just know that he has a dream – and that it bothers him,' I added.

'I know that it bothers *me*,' she said. 'It wakes *me* up – when he has it. And I don't like to look at him when he's having it, or after it's over. Don't ask *me* what it's about!' she said. 'I can tell you one thing: you don't want to know.'

And occasionally I saw the tomato-red pickup parked at St Michael's – not at the school, but by the curb at the rectory for St Michael's *Catholic Church*! I figured he was talking to Father Findley; maybe because Kennedy had been a Catholic, maybe because some kind of ongoing dialogue with Father Findley had actually been required of Owen – in lieu of his being obliged to compensate the Catholic Church for the damage done to Mary Magdalene.

'How's it going with Father Findley?' I asked him once.

'I BELIEVE HE MEANS WELL,' Owen said cautiously. 'BUT THERE'S A FUNDAMENTAL LEAP OF FAITH THAT ALL HIS TRAINING – ALL THAT CATHOLIC BACKGROUND – SIMPLY CANNOT ALLOW HIM TO MAKE. I DON'T THINK HE'LL EVER UNDERSTAND THE *MAGNITUDE* . . . THE UNSPEAKABLE OUTRAGE . . .' Then he stopped talking.

'Yes?' I said. 'You were saying . . . "the unspeakable outrage" . . . was that to your parents, do you mean?'

'FATHER FINDLEY SIMPLY CANNOT GRASP HOW THEY HAVE BEEN MADE TO SUFFER,' said Owen Meany.

'Oh,' I said. 'I see.' I was joking, of course! But either my humor eluded him, or else Owen Meany had no intention of making himself any clearer on this point.

'But you *like* Father Findley?' I asked. 'I mean, sort of . . . "he means well," you say. You enjoy talking to him – I guess.'

'IT TURNS OUT IT'S IMPOSSIBLE TO RESTORE MARY MAGDALENE EXACTLY AS SHE WAS – I MEAN, THE STATUE,' he said. 'MY FATHER KNOWS A COMPANY THAT MAKES SAINTS, AND OTHER HOLY FIGURES – I MEAN, GRANITE, YOU KNOW,' he said. 'BUT THEIR PRICES ARE RIDICULOUS. FATHER FINDLEY'S BEEN VERY PATIENT. I'M GETTING HIM GOOD GRANITE - AND SOMEONE WHO SCULPTS THESE SAINTS A LITTLE CHEAPER, AND MAKES THEM A LITTLE MORE PERSONALLY . . . YOU KNOW, NOT ALWAYS EXACTLY THE SAME GESTURE OF SUPPLICATION, SO THAT THEY DON'T ALWAYS LOOK LIKE BEGGARS. I'VE TOLD FATHER FINDLEY THAT I CAN MAKE HIM A MUCH BETTER PEDESTAL THAN THE ONE HE'S GOT, AND I'VE BEEN TRYING TO CONVINCE HIM TO GET RID OF THAT STUPID ARCHWAY – IF SHE DOESN'T LOOK LIKE A GOALIE IN A GOAL, MAYBE KIDS WON'T ALWAYS BE TAKING SHOTS AT HER. YOU KNOW WHAT I MEAN.'

'It's been almost two years!' I said. 'I didn't know you were *still* involved in replacing Mary Magdalene – I didn't know you were ever *this* involved,' I added.

'WELL, SOMEONE'S GOT TO TAKE CHARGE,' he said. 'FATHER FINDLEY DID ME A FAVOR – I DON'T LIKE TO SEE THESE GRANITE GUYS TAKING ADVANTAGE OF HIM. SOMEONE NEEDS A SAINT OR A HOLY FIGURE IN A HURRY, AND WHAT DO THEY DO? THEY MAKE YOU PAY FOR IT, OR THEY MAKE YOU WAIT FOREVER – THEY FIGURE THEY'VE GOT YOU BY THE BALLS. AND WHO CAN AFFORD *MARBLE*? I'M JUST TRYING TO RETURN A FAVOR.'

And was he asking Father Findley about the dream? I wondered. It bothered me that he was seeing someone I didn't even know – and maybe talking to this person about things he wouldn't discuss with me. I suppose that bothered me about Hester, too – and even the Rev. Lewis Merrill began to irritate me. I didn't run into him very often – although he was a regular in attendance at the rehearsals and performances of The Gravesend Players – but whenever I did run into him, he looked at me as if he knew something special about me (as if Owen had been talking about *me* to him, as if *I* were in Owen's damn dream, or so I imagined).

In my opinion, 1964 was not a very exciting year. General Greene replaced General Shoup; Owen told me lots of military news – as a good ROTC student, he prided himself on knowing these things. President Johnson ordered the withdrawal of American dependents from South Vietnam.

'THIS ISN'T GENERALLY AN OPTIMISTIC SIGN,' said Owen Meany. If the majority of his professors at the University of New Hampshire found Owen less than brilliant, his professors of Military Science were completely charmed. It was the year when Admiral Sharp replaced Admiral Felt, when General Westmoreland replaced General Harkins, when General Wheeler replaced General Taylor, when General Johnson replaced General Wheeler – when General Taylor replaced Henry Cabot Lodge as U.S. ambassador to Vietnam.

'LOTS OF STUFF IS IN THE WORKS,' said Owen Meany. It was the year of the Tonkin Gulf Resolution, which prompted Owen to ask 'DOES THAT MEAN THE PRESIDENT CAN DECLARE A WAR WITHOUT DECLARING IT?' It was the year when Owen's grade-point average fell below mine; but in Military Science, his grades were perfect.

Even the summer of '64 was uninspired – except for the completion of the replacement Mary Magdalene, which was firmly set upon Owen Meany's formidable pedestal in the St Michael's schoolyard, more than two years after the attack upon her predecessor.

'YOU'RE SO UNOBSERVANT,' Owen told me. 'THE GOALIE'S BEEN OUT OF THE GOAL FOR TWO YEARS, AND YOU HAVEN'T EVEN NOTICED!'

What I noticed straightaway was that he'd talked Father Findley into removing the goal. The whitewashed stone archway was gone; so was the notion of whitewash. The new Mary Magdalene was granite-gray, gravestone-gray, a color Owen Meany called NATURAL. Her face, like her color was slightly downcast, almost apologetic; and her arms were not outstretched in obvious supplication – rather, she clasped her hands together at her slight breast, her hands just barely emerging from the sleeves of her robe, which shapelessly draped her body to her small, bare, plain-gray feet. She seemed altogether too demure for a former prostitute –

and too withholding of any gesture for a saint. Yet she radiated a certain compliance; she looked as easy to get along with as my mother.

And the pedestal upon which Owen had stood her – in contrast to Mary's own rough finish (granite is never as smooth as marble) – was highly polished, exquisitely beveled; Owen had cut some very fine edges with the diamond wheel, creating the impression that Mary Magdalene either stood upon or was rising from her grave.

'WHAT DO YOU THINK?' Owen asked Hester and me. 'FATHER FINDLEY WAS VERY PLEASED.'

'It's sick – it's all sick,' said Hester. 'It's just death and more death – that's all it is with you, Owen.'

'HESTER'S SO SENSITIVE,' Owen said.

'I like it better than the *other* one,' I ventured cautiously.

'THERE'S NO COMPARISON!' said Owen Meany.

'I like the pedestal,' I said. 'It's almost as if she's . . . well, you know . . . stepping out of her own grave.'

Owen nodded vigorously. 'YOU HAVE A GOOD EYE,' he said. 'THAT'S EXACTLY THE EFFECT I WANTED. THAT'S WHAT IT MEANS TO BE A SAINT, ISN'T IT? A SAINT SHOULD BE AN EMBLEM OF IMMORTALITY!'

'What a lot of *shit*!" said Hester. It was an uninspired year for Hester, too; here she was, a college graduate, still living in her squalid apartment in her old college town, still waitressing in the lobster-house restaurant in Kittery or Portsmouth. I had never eaten there, but Owen said it was nice enough – on the harbor, a little overquaint with the seafood theme (lobster pots and buoys and anchors and mooring ropes were prevalent in the decor). The problem was, Hester hated lobster – she called them 'insects of the sea,' and she washed her hair every night with lemon juice because she thought her hair smelled fishy.

I think that her late hours (she waitressed only at night) were in part responsible for Owen Meany's decline as a student; he was loyal about picking her up – and it seemed to me that she worked most nights. Hester had her own driver's license and her own car – actually, it was Noah's old '57 Chevy – but she hated to drive; that Uncle Alfred and Aunt Martha had given her a hand-me-down might have had something to do with it. In Owen's view, the '57 Chevy was in better shape than his tomato-red pickup; but Hester knew it had been secondhand when the Eastmans gave it to Noah, who had passed it to Simon, who'd had a minor accident with it before he'd handed it down to Hester.

But by picking up Hester after work, Owen Meany rarely got back to Hester's apartment before one o'clock in the morning; Hester was so keyed up after waitressing that she wasn't ready to go to bed before two – first, she had to wash her hair, which further woke her up; and then she needed to complain. Often someone had insulted her; sometimes it had been a customer who'd tried to pick her up – and failing that, had left her a rotten tip. And the other waitresses were 'woefully unaware,' Hester said; what they were unaware *of*, she wouldn't say – but they often insulted Hester, too. And if Owen Meany *didn't* spend the night in her apartment – if he drove home to Gravesend – he sometimes didn't get to bed before *three*.

Hester slept all morning; but Owen had morning classes – or, in the summer, he was at work very early in the quarries. Sometimes he looked like a tired, old man to me – a tired, old, *married* man. I tried to nag him into taking more of an interest in his studies; but, increasingly, he spoke of school as something to get out of.

'WHEN I GET OUT OF HERE,' he said, 'I'VE GOT MY ACTIVE DUTY TO SERVE, AND I DON'T WANT TO SERVE IT AT A *DESK* – WHO WANTS TO BE IN THE ARMY FOR THE *PAPERWORK*?'

'Who wants to be in the Army *at all*?' I asked him. 'You ought to sit at a *desk* a little more often than you do – the way you're going to college, you might as well be in the Army already. I don't understand you – with your natural ability, you ought to be sailing through this place with the highest honors.'

'IT DID ME A LOT OF GOOD TO SAIL THROUGH GRAVESEND ACADEMY WITH THE HIGHEST HONORS, DIDN'T IT?' he said.

'Maybe if you weren't a stupid Geology major, you could be a little more enthusiastic about your courses,' I told him.

'GEOLOGY IS EASY FOR ME,' Owen said. 'AT LEAST, I ALREADY KNOW SOMETHING ABOUT ROCKS.'

'You didn't used to do things just because they were *easy*,' I said.

He shrugged. Remember when people 'dropped out' –

remember that? Owen Meany was the first person I ever saw 'drop out.' Hester, of course, was *born* 'dropped out'; maybe Owen got the idea from Hester, but I think he was more original than that. He was original, and stubborn.

I was stubborn, too; twenty-two-year-olds are stubborn. Owen tried to keep me working in the monument shop the whole summer of '64. I said that one whole summer in the monument shop was enough – either he would let me work in the quarries or I would quit.

'IT'S FOR YOUR OWN GOOD,' he said. 'IT'S THE BEST WORK IN THE BUSINESS – AND THE EASIEST.'

'So maybe I don't want what's "easiest," ' I said. 'So maybe you should let *me* decide what's "best." '

'GO AHEAD AND QUIT,' he said.

'Fine,' I said. 'I guess I should speak to your father.'

'MY FATHER DIDN'T HIRE YOU,' said Owen Meany.

Naturally, I didn't quit; but I matched his stubbornness sufficiently – I hinted that I was losing my interest in practicing the shot. In the summer of '64, Owen Meany resembled a dropout – in many ways – but his fervor for practicing the shot had reappeared. We compromised: I apprenticed myself to the diamond wheel until August; and that August – when the USS *Maddox* and the USS *Turner Joy* were attacked in the Tonkin Gulf – Owen set me to work as a signalman in the quarries. When it rained, he let me work with the sawyers, and by the end of the summer he apprenticed me to the channel-bar drillers.

'NEXT SUMMER, I'LL LET YOU TRY THE DERRICK,' he said. 'NEXT AUGUST, I'LL GIVE YOU A LITTLE DYNAMITE LESSON – WHEN I GET BACK FROM BASIC TRAINING.'

Just before we began our junior year at the University of New Hampshire – just before the students returned to Gravesend Academy, and to all the nation's other schools and universities – Owen Meany slamdunked the basketball in the Gravesend Academy gym in under three seconds.

I suggested that the retarded janitor might have started the official scorer's clock a little late; but Owen insisted that we had sunk the shot in record time – he said that the clock had been accurate, that our success was official.

'I COULD FEEL THE DIFFERENCE – IN THE AIR,'

he said excitedly. 'EVERYTHING WAS JUST A LITTLE QUICKER, A LITTLE MORE SPONTANEOUS.'

'Now I suppose you'll tell me that under *two* seconds is possible,' I said.

He was dribbling the ball – crazily, in a frenzy, like a speeded-up film of one of the Harlem Globetrotters. I didn't think he'd heard me.

'I suppose you think that under *two* seconds is possible!' I shouted.

He stopped dribbling. 'DON'T BE RIDICULOUS,' he said. 'THREE SECONDS IS FAST ENOUGH.'

I was surprised. 'I thought the idea was to see how fast we can get. We can always get faster,' I said.

'THE IDEA IS TO BE FAST ENOUGH,' he said. 'THE TRICK IS, CAN WE DO IT IN UNDER THREE SECONDS *EVERY TIME*? THAT'S THE IDEA.'

So we kept practicing. When there were students in the Gravesend Academy gym, we went to the playground at St Michael's. We had no one to time us – we had nothing resembling the official scorer's clock in the gym, and Hester was unwilling to participate in our practices; she was no substitute for the retarded janitor. And the rusty hoop of the basket was a little crooked, and the net long gone – and the macadam of the playground was so broken up, we couldn't even dribble the ball; but we could still practice. Owen said he could FEEL when we were dunking the shot in under three seconds. And although there was no retarded janitor to cheer us on, the nuns in the saltbox at the far end of the playground often noticed us; sometimes, they even waved, and Owen Meany would wave back – although he said that nuns still gave him the shivers. And always Mary Magdalene watched over us: we could feel her silent encouragement. When it snowed. Owen would brush her off. It snowed early that fall – long before Thanksgiving. I remember practicing the shot with my ski hat and my gloves on; but Owen Meany would always do it bare-handed. And in the afternoons, when it grew dark early, the lights in the nuns' house would be lit before we finished practicing. Mary Magdalene would turn a darker shade of gray; she would almost disappear in the shadows.

Once, when it was almost too dark to see the basket, I caught just a glimpse of her – standing at the edge of total darkness. I imagined that she resembled the angel that Owen thought he had seen at my mother's bed. I said this to him, and he looked at Mary Magdalene; blowing on his cold, bare hands, he looked at her very intently.

'NO, THERE'S NOT REALLY ANY RESEMBLANCE,' he said. 'THAT ANGEL WAS VERY *BUSY* – SHE WAS MOVING, ALWAYS MOVING. ESPECIALLY, HER HANDS – SHE KEPT REACHING OUT WITH HER HANDS.'

It was the first I'd heard that the angel had been moving – about what a busy angel he thought he'd seen.

'You never said it was *moving*,' I said.

'IT WAS MOVING, ALL RIGHT,' said Owen Meany. 'THAT'S WHY I NEVER HAD ANY DOUBT. IT COULDN'T HAVE BEEN THE DUMMY BECAUSE IT WAS MOVING,' he said. 'AND IN ALL THESE YEARS THAT I'VE HAD THE DUMMY, THE DUMMY HAS NEVER MOVED.'

Since when, I wondered, did Owen Meany *ever* have ANY DOUBT? And how often had he stared at my mother's dressmaker's dummy? He *expected* it to move, I thought.

When it was so dark at the St Michael's playground that we couldn't see the basket, we couldn't see Mary Magdalene, either. What Owen liked best was to practice the shot until we lost Mary Magdalene in the darkness. Then he would stand under the basket with me and say, 'CAN YOU SEE HER?'

'Not anymore,' I'd say.

'YOU CAN'T SEE HER, BUT YOU KNOW SHE'S STILL THERE – RIGHT?' he would say.

'Of *course* she's still there!' I'd say.

'YOU'RE SURE?' he'd ask me.

'Of *course* I'm sure!' I'd say.

'BUT YOU CAN'T *SEE* HER,' he'd say – very teasingly. 'HOW DO YOU KNOW SHE'S STILL THERE IF YOU CAN'T ACTUALLY SEE HER?'

'Because I *know* she's still there – because I know she couldn't have gone anywhere – because I just *know*!' I would say.

And one cold, late-fall day – it was November or even early December; Johnson had defeated Goldwater for the presidency; Khrushchev had been replaced by Brezhnev and Kosygin; five Americans had been killed in a Viet Cong attack on the air base at Bien Hoa – I was especially exasperated by this game he played about not seeing Mary Magdalene but still knowing she was there.

'YOU HAVE NO DOUBT SHE'S THERE?' he nagged at me.

'Of *course* I have no doubt!' I said.

'BUT YOU CAN'T SEE HER – YOU COULD BE WRONG,' he said.

'No, I'm *not* wrong – she's there, I *know* she's there!' I yelled at him.

'YOU ABSOLUTELY KNOW SHE'S THERE – EVEN THOUGH YOU CAN'T SEE HER?' he asked me.

'*Yes!*' I screamed.

'WELL, NOW YOU KNOW HOW I FEEL ABOUT GOD,' said Owen Meany. 'I CAN'T SEE HIM – BUT I ABSOLUTELY KNOW HE IS THERE!'

Georgian Bay: July 29, 1987 – Katherine told me today that I should make an effort not to read *any* newspapers. She saw how *The Globe and Mail* ruined my day – and it is so gorgeous, so peaceful on this island, on all this water; it's such a shame *not* to relax here, *not* to take the opportunity to think more tranquilly, more reflectively. Katherine wants only the best for me; I know she's right – I should give up the news, just give it up. You can't understand anything by reading the news, anyway.

If someone ever presumed to teach Charles Dickens or Thomas Hardy or Robertson Davies to my Bishop Strachan students with the same, shallow, superficial understanding that I'm sure *I* possess of world affairs – or, even, American wrongdoing – I would be outraged. I am a good enough English teacher to know that my grasp of American misadventures – even in Vietnam, not to mention Nicaragua – *is* shallow and superficial. Whoever acquired any real or substantive intelligence from reading *newspapers*? I'm sure I have no in-depth comprehension of American villainy; yet I can't leave the news alone! You'd think I might profit from my experience with ice cream. If I have ice cream in my freezer, I'll eat it – I'll eat *all* of it, all at once. Therefore, I've learned not to buy ice cream. Newspapers are even worse for me than ice cream; headlines, and the big issues that generate the headlines, are pure fat.

The island library, to be kind, is full of field guides – to everything I never knew enough about; I mean, *real* things, not 'issues.' I could study pine needles, or bird identification – there are even categories for studying the latter: in-flight movement, perching silhouettes, feeding and mating cries. It's fascinating – I suppose. And with all this water around, I could certainly take more than *one* day to go fishing with Charlie; I know it disappoints him that I'm not more interested in fishing. And Katherine has pointed out to me that it's been a long time since she and I have talked about our respective beliefs – the shared and private articles of our faith. I used to talk about this for *hours* with her – and with Canon Campbell, before her. Now I'm ashamed to tell Katherine how many Sunday services I've skipped.

Katherine's right. I'm going to try to give up the news. *The Globe and Mail* said today that the Nicaraguan contras have executed prisoners; the contras are being investigated for '22 major cases of human-rights abuse' – and these same filthy contras are the 'moral equivalent of our founding fathers,' President Reagan says! Meanwhile, the spiritual leader of Iran, the ayatollah, urged all Moslems to 'crush America's teeth in its mouth'; this sounds like just the guy the Americans should sell arms to – right? The United States simply isn't making sense.

I agree with Katherine. Time to fish; time to observe the flatness of that small, aquatic mammal's tail – is it an otter or is it a muskrat? Time to find out. And out there, where the water of the bay turns blue-green and then to the color of a bruise, is that a loon or a coot I see diving there? Time to see; time to forget about the rest. And it's 'high time' – as Canon Mackie is always saying – for me to try to *be* a Canadian!

When I first came to Canada, I thought it was going to be easy to be a Canadian; like so many stupid Americans, I pictured Canada as simply some northern, colder, possibly more provincial region of the United States – I imagined it would be like moving to Maine, or Minnesota. It was a surprise to discover that Toronto wasn't as snowy and cold as New Hampshire – and not nearly as provincial, either. It was more of a surprise to discover how different Canadians were – they were so polite! Naturally, I started out apologizing. 'I'm not really a draft dodger,' I would say; but most Canadians didn't care *what* I was. 'I'm not here to evade the draft,' I would explain. 'I would certainly classify myself as antiwar,' I said in those days. 'I'm comfortable with the term "war resister," ' I told everyone, 'but I don't *need* to dodge or evade the draft – that's not why I'm here.'

But most Canadians didn't care *why* I'd come; they didn't ask any questions. It was 1968, probably the midpoint of Vietnam 'resisters' coming to Canada; most Canadians were sympathetic – they thought the war in Vietnam was stupid and wrong, too. In 1968, you needed fifty points to become a landed immigrant; landed immigrants could apply for Canadian citizenship, for which they'd be eligible in five years. Earning my fifty 'points' was easy for me; I had a B.A. *cum laude*, and a Master's degree in English – with Owen Meany's help, I'd written my Master's thesis on Thomas Hardy. I'd also had two years' teaching experience; while I was in graduate school at the University of New Hampshire, I taught part-time at Gravesend Academy – Expository Writing for ninth graders. Dan Needham and Mr Early had recommended me for the job.

In 1968, one out of every nine Canadians was an immigrant; and the Vietnam 'resisters' were better-educated and more employable than most immigrants in Canada. That year the so-called Union of American Exiles was organized; compared to Hester – and her SDS friends, those so-called Students for a Democratic Society – a few guys I knew in the Union of American Exiles were a pretty tame lot. I was used to *rioters*; Hester was big on riots then. That was the year she was arrested in Chicago.

Hester had her nose broken while rioting at the site of the Democratic Party's national convention. She said a policeman mashed her face against the sliding side door of a van; but Hester would have been disappointed to return from Chicago with all her bones intact. The Americans I ran into in Toronto – even the AMEX organizers, even the deserters – were a whole lot more reasonable than Hester and many other Americans I had known 'at home.'

There was a general misunderstanding about the so-called deserters; the deserters I knew were politically mild. I never met one who'd actually been in Vietnam; I never met one who was even scheduled to go. They were just guys who'd been drafted and had hated the service; some of them had even enlisted. Only a few of them told me that they'd deserted because it had shamed them to maintain *any* association with that insupportable war; as for a couple of the ones who told me that – I had the feeling that their stories weren't true, that they were only saying they'd deserted because the war was 'insupportable'; they'd learned that this was politically acceptable to say.

And there was another, general misunderstanding at that time: contrary to popular belief, coming to Canada was *not* a very shrewd way to beat the draft; there were better and easier ways to 'beat' it – I'll tell you about one, later. But coming to Canada – either as a draft dodger *or* as a deserter, or even for my own, more complicated reasons – was a very forceful political statement. Remember that? Remember when what you did was a kind of 'statement'? I remember one of the AMEX guys telling me that 'resistance as exile was the ultimate judgment.' How I agreed with him! How self-important it seemed: to be making 'the ultimate judgment.'

The truth is, I never had to suffer. When I first came to Toronto in '68, I met a few confused and troubled young Americans; I was a little older than most of them – and they certainly seemed no more confused or troubled than many of the Americans I had known at home. Unlike Buzzy Thurston, for example, they had not driven their cars head-on into a bridge abutment in an effort to beat the draft. Unlike Harry Hoyt, they had not been bitten to death by a Russell's viper while waiting for their turn with a Vietnamese whore.

And to my surprise, the Canadians I met actually *liked* me. And with my graduate degree – and even my junior teaching experience at such a prestigious school as Gravesend Academy – I was instantly respectable and almost immediately employed. The distinction I hastened to make, to almost every Canadian I met, was probably a waste of time; that I *wasn't* there as a draft dodger or a deserter didn't really matter very much to the Canadians. It mattered to the Americans I met, and I didn't like how they responded: that I was in Canada by choice, that I was *not* a fugitive, and that I didn't *have* to be in Toronto – in my view, this made my commitment more serious; but in their view I was less desperate and, therefore, *less* serious. It's true: we Wheelwrights have rarely suffered. And unlike most of those other Americans, I also had the church; don't underestimate the church – its healing power, and the comforting way it can set you apart.

My first week in Toronto, I had an interview at Upper

Canada College; the whole school made me feel that I'd never left Gravesend Academy! They didn't have an opening in their English Department, but they assured me that my *vitae* was 'most laudable' and that I'd have no trouble finding a job. They were so helpful, they sent me the short distance down Lonsdale Road to Grave Church on-the-Hill; Canon Campbell, they said, was especially interested in helping Americans.

Indeed he was. When the canon asked me what my church was, I said, 'I guess I'm an Episcopalian.'

'You *guess*?' he said.

I explained that I'd not attended an actual service in the Episcopal Church since the famous Nativity of '53; thinking of Hurd's Church and Pastor Merrill's rather lapsed Congregationalism, I said, 'I guess I'm sort of nondenominational.'

'Well, we'll fix *that*!' Canon Campbell said. He gave me my first *Anglican* prayer book, my first *Canadian* prayer book; it is The Book of Common Prayer that I still use. It was as simple as that: joining a church, becoming an Anglican. I wouldn't call any of it suffering.

And so the first Canadians I knew were churchgoers – an almost universally helpful lot, and much less confused and troubled than the few Americans I'd met in Toronto (and *most* Americans I had known at home). These Grace Church on-the-Hill Anglicans were conservative; 'conservative' – about certain matters of propriety, especially – is perfectly all right with us Wheelrights. About such matters, New Englanders have more in common with Canadians than we have with *New Yorkers*! For example, I quickly learned to prefer the positions stated by the Toronto Anti-Draft Programme to those more abrasive stances of the Union of American Exiles. The Toronto Anti-Draft Programme favored 'assimilation into mainstream Canadian life'; they considered the Union of American Exiles 'too political' – by which they meant, too activist, too militantly anti-United States. Possibly, the Union of American Exiles was contaminated by their open dealings with deserters. The object of the Toronto Anti-Draft Programme was to get Americans 'assimilated' *quickly*; they reasoned that we Americans should begin the process of our assimilation by *dropping* the subject of the United States.

At the beginning, this seemed so reasonable – and so easy – to me.

Within a year of my arrival, even the Union of American

Exiles showed signs of 'assimilation.' The acronym AMEX changed in meaning from American Exile to American Expatriate. Doesn't that sound more agreeable to the aim of 'assimilation into mainstream Canadian life'? I thought so.

When some of those Grace Church on-the-Hill Anglicans asked me what I *thought* of Prime Minister Pearson's 'old point of view' – that the deserters (as opposed to the war resisters) were in a category of U.S. citizens to be discouraged from coming to Canada – I actually said I agreed! Even though – as I've admitted – I'd never met a *harsh* deserter, not one. The ones I met were 'in a category of citizens' that *any* country could have used and even appreciated. And when it was aired in the Twenty-eighth Parliament – in 1969 – that U.S. deserters were being turned back at the border because they were 'persons who were likely to become public charges,' I never actually *said* – to any of my Canadian friends – that I suspected these deserters were no more likely to become 'public charges' than *I* was likely to become such a charge. By then, Canon Campbell had introduced me to old Teddybear Kilgore, who had hired me to teach at Bishop Strachan. We Wheelwrights have always benefited from our connections.

Owen Meany didn't have any connections. It was never easy for him to fit in. I think I know what he would have said to that bullshit that was printed in *The Toronto Star*; at the time, I thought that bullshit was so right-on-target that I cut it out of the newspaper and taped it to my refrigerator door – December 17, 1970. It was in response to the AMEX published statement of the 'first five priorities' for American expatriates (the fifth being 'to try to fit into Canadian life'). To quote *The Toronto Daily Star*: 'Unless the young Americans for whom AMEX speaks revise their priorities and put Number Five first, they risk arousing a growing hostility and suspicion among Canadians.' I never doubted that this was true. But I know what Owen Meany would have said about that. 'THAT SOUNDS LIKE SOMETHING AN *AMERICAN* WOULD SAY!' Owen Meany would have said. 'THE "FIRST PRIORITY" IN EVERY YOUNG AMERICAN'S LIFE IS TO TRY TO FIT INTO *AMERICAN* LIFE. DOESN'T THE STUPID *TORONTO DAILY STAR* KNOW WHO THESE YOUNG AMERICANS IN CANADA *ARE*? THESE ARE AMERICANS WHO LEFT THEIR COUNTRY BECAUSE

THEY *COULDN'T* AND DIDN'T *WANT* TO "FIT IN." NOW THEY'RE SUPPOSED TO MAKE IT THEIR "FIRST PRIORITY" TO "FIT IN" *HERE*? BOY – THAT MAKES A LOT OF SENSE; THAT'S REALLY BRILLIANT. THAT'S WORTH ONE OF THOSE STUPID JOURNALISM *AWARDS*!'

But I didn't complain; I didn't bitch about anything – not then. I thought I'd heard Hester 'bitch' enough for a lifetime. Remember the War Measures Act? I didn't say a word; I agreed with everything. So what if civil liberties were suspended for six months? So what that there could be searches without warrants? So what if people could be detained without counsel for up to ninety days? All the action was happening in Montreal. If Hester had been in Toronto then, not even Hester would have been arrested! I just kept quiet; I was cultivating my Canadian friendships, and most of my friends thought that Trudeau could do no wrong, that he was a prince. Even my dear old friend Canon Campbell made a rather empty remark to me – but I would never challenge him. Canon Campbell said: 'Trudeau is *our* Kennedy, you know.' I was glad that Canon Campbell didn't say 'Trudeau is *our* Kennedy' to Owen Meany; I think I know what Owen would have said.

'OH, YOU MEAN TRUDEAU DIDDLED MARILYN MONROE?' Owen Meany would have said.

But I didn't come to Canada to be a smart-ass American; and Canon Campbell told me that most smart-ass Canadians tend to move to the United States. I didn't *want* to be one of those people who are critical of everything. In the seventies, there were a lot of complaining Americans in Toronto; some of them complained about Canada, too – Canada sold the United States over five hundred million dollars' worth of ammunition and other war supplies, these complainers said.

'Is that Canadian or U.S. dollars?' I would ask. I was very cool; I wasn't going to jump into anything. In short, I was doing my best to *be* a Canadian; I wasn't ranting my head off about the goddamn U.S. *this* or the motherfucking U.S. *that*! And when I was told that, by 1970, Canada – 'per capita' – was earning more money as an international arms exporter than any other nation in the *world*, I said, 'Really? That's very interesting!'

Someone said to me that most war resisters who returned to the United States couldn't take the Canadian *climate*; and what did I think of the seriousness of the war resistance if 'these people' could be deterred from their commitment by a little cold weather?

I said it was colder in New Hampshire.

And did I know why not so many black Americans had come to Canada? someone asked me. And the ones who come don't stay, someone else said. It's because the ghetto where they come from treats them nicer, said someone else. I didn't say a word.

I was more of an Anglican than I *ever* was either a Congregationalist or an Episcopalian – or even a non-denominational, Hurd's Church *whatever*-I-was. I was a participant at Grace Church on-the-Hill in a way that I had *never* been a participant before; and I was getting to be a good teacher, too. I was still young then; I was only twenty-six. And I didn't have a girlfriend when I started teaching all those BSS girls – and I never once looked at one of them in that way; not once, not even at the ones who had their schoolgirl crushes on me. Oh, there were quite a few years when those girls had their crushes on me – not anymore; not now, of course. But I still remember those pretty girls; some of them even asked me to attend their weddings!

In those early years, when Canon Campbell was such a friend and an inspiration to me – when I carried my Book of Common Prayer, and my *Manual for Draft-Age Immigrants to Canada*, everywhere I went! – I was a veritable card-carrying Canadian.

Whenever I'd run into one of that AMEX crowd – and I didn't run into them often, not in Forest Hill – I wouldn't even *talk* about the United States, or Vietnam. I must have believed that my anger and my loneliness would simply go away – if I simply let them go.

There were rallies; of course, there were protests. But I didn't attend; I didn't even hang out in Yorkville – that's how out of it I was! When 'The Riverboat' was gone, I didn't mourn – or even sing old folk songs to myself. I'd heard enough of Hester singing folk songs. I cut my hair short then; I cut it short today. I've never had a beard. All those hippies, all those days of protest songs and 'sexual freedom'; remember that? Owen Meany had sacrificed much more, he had suffered much more – I was not even remotely interested in other people's sacrifices or in what they imagined was their heroic suffering.

They say there's no zeal like the zeal of the convert – and that's the kind of Anglican I was. They say there's no citizen as patriotic as the new immigrant – and there was no one who tried any harder to be 'assimilated' than I tried. They say there's no teacher with such a desire for his subject as the novice possesses – and I taught those BSS girls to read and write their little *middies* off!

In 1967, there were 40,227 deserters from the U.S. armed forces; in 1970, there were 89,088 – that year, only 3,712 Americans were prosecuted for Selective Service violations. I wonder how many more were burning or had already burned their draft cards. What did I care? Burning your draft card, coming to Canada, getting your nose busted by a cop in Chicago – I never thought these gestures were heroic, not compared to Owen Meany's commitment. And by 1970, more than forty thousand Americans had died in Vietnam; I don't imagine that a single one of them would have thought that draft-card burning or coming to Canada was especially 'heroic' – nor would they have thought that getting arrested for rioting in Chicago was such a big fucking deal.

And as for Gordon Lightfoot and Neil Young, as for Joni Mitchell and Ian and Sylvia – I'd already heard Bob Dylan and Joan Baez, and Hester. I'd even heard Hester sing 'Four Strong Winds.' She was always quite good with the guitar, she had her mother's pretty voice – although Aunt Martha's voice was not as pretty as my mother's – which was *merely* pretty, not strong enough, not developed. Hester could have stood about five years of lessons from Graham McSwiney, but she didn't believe in being taught to sing. Singing was something 'inside' her, she claimed.

'YOU MAKE IT SOUND LIKE A DISEASE,' Owen told her; but he was her number-one supporter. When she was struggling to write her own songs, I know that Owen gave her some ideas; later she told me that he'd even written some songs for her. And in those days she looked like a folk singer – which is to say any old way she wanted, or like everyone else: a little dirty, a little worldly, a lot knocked-about. She looked hard-traveled, she looked as if she slept on a rug (with lots of men), she *looked* as if her hair smelled of lobster.

I remember her singing 'Four Strong Winds' – I remember this very vividly.

I think I'll go out to Alberta,
Weather's good there in the fall;
I got some friends that I can go to workin' for.

'WHERE'S ALBERTA?' Owen Meany had asked her.

'In Canada, you asshole,' Hester had said.

'THERE'S NO NEED TO BE CRUDE,' Owen had told her. 'IT'S A PRETTY SONG. IT MUST BE SAD TO GO TO CANADA.'

It was 1966. He was about to become a second lieutenant in the U.S. Army.

'You think it's "sad" to go to *Canada*?' Hester screamed at him. 'Where they're going to send you is a lot *sadder*.'

'I DON'T WANT TO DIE WHERE IT'S COLD,' said Owen Meany.

What he meant was, he believed he knew that he would die where it was *warm* - very warm.

On Christmas Eve, 1964, two American servicemen were killed in Saigon when Viet Cong terrorists bombed the U.S. billets; one week later, on New Year's Eve, Hester threw up – perhaps she upchucked with special verve, because Owen Meany was prompted to take the power of Hester's puking as a sign.

'IT LOOKS LIKE IT'S GOING TO BE A BAD YEAR,' Owen observed, while we watched Hester's spasms in the rose garden.

Indeed, it was the year the war began in earnest; at least, it was the year when the average unobservant American began to notice that we had a problem in Vietnam. In February, the U.S. Air Force conducted Operation Flaming Dart – a 'tactical air reprisal.'

'What does that mean?' I asked Owen, who was doing so well in his studies of Military Science.

'THAT MEANS WE'RE BOMBING THE SHIT OUT OF TARGETS IN NORTH VIETNAM,' he said.

In March, the U.S. Air Force began Operation Rolling Thunder – 'to interdict the flow of supplies to the south.'

'What does *that* mean?' I asked Owen.

'THAT MEANS WE'RE BOMBING THE SHIT OUT OF TARGETS IN NORTH VIETNAM,' said Owen Meany.

That was the month when the first American combat troops

landed in Vietnam; in April, President Johnson authorized the use of U.S. ground troops – 'for offensive operations in South Vietnam.'

'THAT MEANS, "SEARCH AND DESTROY, SEARCH AND DESTROY," ' Owen said.

In May, the U.S. Navy began Operation Market Time – 'to detect and intercept surface traffic in South Vietnam coastal waters.' Harry Hoyt was there; Harry was very happy in the Navy, his mother said.

'But what are they *doing* there?' I asked Owen.

'THEY'RE SEIZING AND DESTROYING ENEMY CRAFT,' said Owen Meany. It was out of conversations he had been having with one of his professors of Military Science that he was prompted to observe: 'THERE'S NO END TO THIS. WHAT WE'RE DEALING WITH IS GUERRILLA WARFARE. ARE WE PREPARED TO OBLITERATE THE WHOLE COUNTRY? YOU CAN CALL IT "SEARCH AND DESTROY" OR "SEIZE AND DESTROY" – EITHER WAY, IT'S DESTROY AND DESTROY. THERE'S NO GOOD WAY TO END IT.'

I could not get over the idea of Harry Hoyt 'seizing and destroying enemy craft'; he was such an idiot! He didn't even know how to play Little League baseball! I simply couldn't forgive him for the base on balls that led to Buzzy Thurston's easy grounder . . . that led to Owen Meany coming to the plate. If Harry had only struck out or hit the ball, everything might have turned out differently. But he was a walker.

'How could Harry Hoyt possibly be involved in 'seizing and destroying' *anything*?' I asked Owen. 'Harry isn't smart enough to *recognize* an "enemy craft" if one sailed right over his head!'

'HAS IT OCCURRED TO YOU THAT VIETNAM IS *FULL* OF HARRY HOYTS?' Owen asked.

The professor of Military Science who had impressed Owen, and given him a sense of catastrophe about the tactical and strategic management of the war, was some crusty and critical old colonel of infantry – a physical-fitness nut who thought Owen was too small for the combat branches of the Army. I believe that Owen excelled in his Military Science courses in an effort to persuade this old thug that he could more than compensate for his size; Owen spent much after-class time chatting up the old buzzard – it was Owen's intention to be *the* honor graduate, the number-one graduate from his ROTC unit. With a number-one rating, Owen was sure, he would be assigned a 'combat arms designator' – Infantry, Armor, or Artillery.

'I don't understand why you *want* a combat branch,' I said to him.

'IF THERE'S A WAR AND I'M IN THE ARMY, I WANT TO BE *IN* THE WAR,' he said. 'I DON'T WANT TO SPEND THE WAR AT A *DESK*. LOOK AT IT THIS WAY: WE AGREE THAT HARRY HOYT IS AN IDIOT. WHO'S GOING TO KEEP THE HARRY HOYTS FROM GETTING THEIR HEADS BLOWN OFF?'

'Oh, so you want to be a *hero*!' I told him. 'If you were any smarter than Harry Hoyt, you'd be smart enough to spend the war at a *desk*!'

I began to think more highly of the colonel who thought Owen was too small for a combat branch. His name was Eiger, and I tried to talk to him once; in my view, I was doing Owen a favor.

'Colonel Eiger, sir,' I said to him. Despite the liver spots on the backs of his hands and the roll of sun-wrecked skin that only slightly overlapped his tight, brown collar, he looked capable of about seventy-five fast push-ups on command. 'I know that you know Owen Meany, sir,' I said to him; he didn't speak – he waited for me to continue, chewing his gum so conservatively that you weren't sure he had any gum in his mouth at all; he might have been engaged in some highly disciplined pattern of exercises for his tongue. 'I want you to know that I agree with you, sir,' I said. 'I don't think Owen Meany is suitable for combat.' The colonel – although this was barely detectable – stopped chewing. 'It's not just his size,' I ventured. 'I am his *best* friend, and even I have to question his stability – his emotional stability,' I said.

'Thank you. That will be all,' the colonel said.

'Thank you, sir,' I said.

It was May, 1965; I watched Owen closely – to see if he'd received any further discouragement from Colonel Eiger. Something must have happened – the colonel must have said something to him – because that was the spring when Owen Meany stopped smoking; he just gave it up, cold. He took up running! In two weeks, he was running five miles a day; he said his goal – by the end of the month – was to average six minutes per mile. And he took up beer.

'Why the beer?' I asked him.

'WHOEVER HEARD OF SOMEONE IN THE ARMY *NOT* DRINKING BEER?' he asked me.

It sounded like something Colonel Eiger would have said to him; probably the colonel thought it was a further indication that Owen was a wimp – that he didn't drink.

And so, by the time he left for Basic Training, he was in pretty good shape – all that running, even with the beer, was a favorable exchange for a pack a day. He admitted that he didn't like the running; but he'd developed a taste for beer. He never drank very much of it – I never saw him get drunk, not before Basic Training – but Hester remarked that the beer vastly improved his disposition.

'Nothing would make Owen exactly *mellow*,' she said, 'but believe me: the beer helps.'

I felt funny working for Meany Granite when Owen wasn't there.

'I'M ONLY GONE FOR SIX WEEKS,' he pointed out. 'AND BESIDES: I FEEL BETTER KNOWING YOU'RE IN CHARGE OF THE MONUMENT SHOP. IF SOMEONE DIES, YOU'VE GOT THE PROPER MANNERS TO HANDLE THE ORDER FOR THE GRAVESTONE. I TRUST YOU TO HAVE THE RIGHT TOUCH.'

'Good luck!' I said to him.

'DON'T EXPECT ME TO HAVE TIME TO WRITE – IT'S GOING TO BE PRETTY INTENSE,' he said. 'BASICALLY, I'VE GOT TO EXCEL IN THREE AREAS – ACADEMICS, LEADERSHIP, PHYSICAL FITNESS. FRANKLY, IN THE LATTER CATEGORY, I'M WORRIED ABOUT THE OBSTACLE COURSE – I HEAR THERE'S A WALL, ABOUT TWELVE FEET. THAT MIGHT BE A LITTLE HIGH FOR ME.'

Hester was singing; she refused to participate in a conversation about Basic Training; she said that if she heard Owen recite his preferred COMBAT BRANCHES one more time, she would throw up. I'll never forget what Hester was singing; it's a *Canadian* song, and – over the years – I've heard this song a hundred times. I guess it will always give me the shivers.

If you were even just barely alive in the sixties, I'm sure

you've heard the song that Hester sang, the song I remember so vividly.

> Four strong winds that blow lonely,
> Seven seas that run high,
> All those things that don't change come what may.
> But our good times are all gone,
> And I'm bound for movin' on,
> I'll look for you if I'm ever back this way.

They sent him to Fort Knox, or maybe it was Fort Bragg; I forget – once I asked Hester if she remembered which place it was where Owen was sent for Basic Training.

'All I know is, he shouldn't have gone – he should have gone to *Canada*,' Hester said.

How often I have thought that! There are times when I catch myself looking for him – even expecting to see him. Once, in Winston Churchill Park, when there were children roughhousing – at least, moving quickly – I saw someone about his size, standing slightly to the side of whatever activity was consuming the others, looking a trifle tentative but very alert, certainly eager to *try* what the others were doing, but restraining himself, or else picking the exactly perfect moment to take charge.

But Owen didn't come to Canada; he went to Fort Knox or Fort Bragg, where he failed the obstacle course. He was the best academically; he had the highest marks in leadership – whatever *that* is, and however the U.S. Army determines what it is. But he had been right about the wall; it was a little high for him – he simply couldn't get over it. He 'failed to negotiate the wall' – that was how the Army put it. And since class rank in ROTC is composed of excellence in Academics, in Leadership, and in Physical Fitness, Owen Meany – just that simply – failed to get a number-one ranking; his choice of a 'combat arms designator' was, therefore, *not* assured.

'But you're such a good *jumper*!' I told him. 'Couldn't you just *jump* it – couldn't you grab hold of the top of the wall and haul yourself over it?'

'I COULDN'T *REACH* THE TOP OF THE WALL!' he said. 'I *AM* A GOOD JUMPER, BUT I'M FUCKING FIVE FEET TALL! IT'S NOT LIKE PRACTICING THE SHOT, YOU

KNOW – I'M NOT ALLOWED TO HAVE ANYONE *BOOST* ME UP!'

'I'm sorry,' I said. 'You've still got your whole senior year. Can't you work on Colonel Eiger? I'll bet you can convince him to give you what you want.'

'I'VE GOT A NUMBER-TWO RANKING – DON'T YOU UNDERSTAND? IT'S BY THE BOOK. COLONEL EIGER *LIKES* ME – HE JUST DOESN'T THINK I'M *FIT*!' He was so distracted by his failure, I didn't press him about giving me a dynamite lesson. I felt guilty for ever speaking to Colonel Eiger – Owen was so upset. But, at the same time, I didn't want him to get a combat-branch assignment.

In the fall of '65, when we returned to Durham for our senior year, there were already protests against U.S. policy in Vietnam; that October, there were protests in thirty or forty American cities – I think Hester attended about half of them. Typical of me, I felt unsure: I thought the protesters made more sense than anyone who remotely subscribed to 'U.S. policy'; but I also thought that Hester and most of her friends were losers and jerks. Hester was already beginning to call herself a 'socialist.'

'OH, EXCUSE ME, I THOUGHT YOU WERE A *WAITRESS*!' Owen Meany said. 'ARE YOU SHARING ALL YOUR TIPS WITH THE OTHER WAITRESSES?'

'Fuck you, Owen,' Hester said. 'I could call myself a *Republican*, and I'd still make more sense than *you*!'

I had to agree. At the very least, it was inconsistent of Owen Meany to want a combat-branch assignment; with the keen eye he had always had for spotting *bullshit*, why would he *want* to go to Vietnam? And the war, and the protests – they were just beginning; anyone could see that.

On Christmas Day, President Johnson suspended Operation Rolling Thunder – no more bombing of North Vietnam, 'to induce negotiations for peace.' Was anyone fooled by that?

'MADE FOR TELEVISION!' said Owen Meany. So why did he want to go there? Did he want to be a hero so badly that he would have gone *anywhere*?

That fall he was told he was Adjutant General's Corps 'material'; that was not what he wanted to hear – the Adjutant General's Corps was not a combat branch. He was appealing the decision; mistakes of this kind – regarding one's orders – were almost common, he claimed.

'I THINK COLONEL EIGER IS IN MY CORNER,' Owen said. 'AS FAR AS I'M CONCERNED, I'M STILL WAITING TO HEAR ABOUT A COMBAT BRANCH.'

By New Year's Eve, 1965 – when Hester was making her usual statement in the rose garden at 80 Front Street – only 636 U.S. military personnel had been killed in action; it was just the beginning. I guess that figure did not include the death of Harry Hoyt; 'in action' was not exactly how poor Harry was killed. It had been just like another base on balls for Harry Hoyt, I thought – snake-bit while waiting his turn with a whore, snake-bit while peeing under a tree.

'JUST LIKE DRAWING A WALK,' said Owen Meany. 'POOR HARRY.'

'His poor mother,' my grandmother said; she was moved to expand upon her thesis on dying. 'I would rather be murdered by a maniac than bitten by a snake,' she said.

And so, in Gravesend, our first vision of death in Vietnam was not of that standard Viet Cong soldier in his sandals and black pajamas, with something that looked like a lampshade for a hat – and with the Soviet AK-47 assault rifle, using a 7.62mm bullet, fired either single-shot or on full automatic. Rather, we turned to my grandmother's *Wharton Encyclopedia of Venomous Snakes* – which had already provided Owen and me with several nightmares, when we were children – and there we found our vision of the enemy in Southest Asia: Russell's viper. Oh, it was so tempting to reduce the United States' misadventure in Vietnam to an enemy one could *see*!

Harry Hoyt's mother made up her mind that *we* were our enemy. Less than a month after the New Year – after we had resumed our bombing of North Vietnam and Operation Rolling Thunder was back on target – Mrs Hoyt created her disturbance in the office of the Gravesend local draft board, choosing to use their bulletin board to advertise that she would give free draft-counseling advice in her home – sessions in how to evade the draft. She managed to advertise herself all around the university, in Durham, too – Hester told me that Mrs Hoyt drew more of a crowd from the university community than she was able to summon among the locals in Gravesend. The university students were closer to being drafted than those Gravesend High School students who could manage to be accepted by even the lowliest college or university.

In 1966, two million Americans had so-called student deferments that protected them from the draft. In a year, this would be modified – to exclude graduate students; but those graduate students in their second year, or further along in their studies, would keep their exemptions. I would fall perfectly into the crack. When draft deferments for graduate students got the ax, I would be in my *first* year of graduate school; my draft deferment would get the ax, too. I would be summoned for a preinduction physical at my local Gravesend draft board, where I had every reason to expect I would be found fully acceptable for induction – what was called 1-A – fit to serve, and standing at the head of the line.

That was the kind of thing that Mrs Hoyt was attempting to prepare us for – as early as February, 1966, she started warning the young people who would listen to her; she made contact with all of Harry's contemporaries in Gravesend.

'Johnny Wheelwright, you listen to me!' she said; she got me on the telephone at 80 Front Street, and I was afraid of her. Even my grandmother thought that Mrs Hoyt should be conducting herself 'in a manner more suitable to mourning'; but Mrs Hoyt was as mad as a hornet. She'd give Owen a lecture at the monument shop when she was picking out a stone for Harry!

'I don't want a cross,' she told Owen. 'A lot of good God ever did him!'

'YES, MA'AM,' said Owen Meany.

'And I don't want one of those things that look like a stepping-stone – that's just like the military, to give you a grave that people can *walk* on!' Mrs Hoyt said.

'I UNDERSTAND,' Owen told her.

Then she lit into him about his ROTC 'obligation,' about how he should do everything he could to end up with a 'desk job' – if he knew what was good for him.

'And I don't mean a desk job in *Saigon*!' she told him. 'Don't you dare be a participant in that *genocide*!' she told him. 'Do you want to set fire to small Asian women and children?' she asked him.

'NO, MA'AM!' said Owen Meany.

To me, she said: 'They're not going to let you be a graduate student in English. What do they care about *English*? They barely speak it!'

'Yes, ma'am,' I said.

'You can't hide in graduate school – believe me, it won't work,' said Mrs Hoyt. 'And unless you've got something wrong with you – I mean, physically – you're going to die in a rice paddy. Is there anything wrong with you?' she asked me.

'Not that I know of, ma'am,' I said.

'Well, you ought to think of something,' Mrs Hoyt told me. 'I know someone who does psychiatric counseling; he can coach you – he can make you seem crazy. But that's risky, and you've got to start now – you need time to develop a history, if you're going to convince anybody you're insane. It's no good just getting drunk and smearing dog shit in your hair the night before your physical – if you don't develop a mental *history*, it won't work to try to fake it.'

That, however, is what Buzzy Thurston tried – and it worked. It worked a little too well. He didn't develop a 'history' that was one day longer than two weeks; but even in that short time, he managed to force enough alcohol and drugs into his body to convince his body that it *liked* this form of abuse. To Mrs Hoyt, Buzzy would be as much a victim of the war as her Harry; Buzzy would kill himself trying to stay out of Vietnam.

'Have you thought about the Peace Corps?' Mrs Hoyt asked me. She said she'd counseled one young man – also an English major – to apply to the Peace Corps. He'd been accepted as an English teacher in Tanzania. It was a pity, she admitted, that the Red Chinese had sent about four hundred 'advisers' to Tanzania in the summer of '65; the Peace Corps, naturally, had withdrawn in a hurry. 'Just think about it,' Mrs Hoyt said to me. 'Even *Tanzania* is a better idea than Vietnam!'

I told her I'd think about it; but I thought I had so much time! Imagine this: you're a university senior, you're a virgin – do you believe it when someone tells you that you have to make up your mind between Vietnam and Tanzania?

'You better believe it,' Hester told me.

That was the year – 1966, in February – when the Senate Foreign Relations Committee began televised hearings on the war.

'I think you better talk to Mrs Hoyt,' my grandmother told me. 'I don't want any grandson of mine to have anything to do with this mess.'

'Listen to me, John,' Dan Needham said. 'This is *not* the time to do what Owen Meany does. This time Owen is making a mistake.'

I told Dan that I was afraid I might be responsible for sabotaging Owen's desire for a 'combat arms designator'; I confessed that I'd told Colonel Eiger that Owen's 'emotional stability' was questionable, and that I'd agreed with the colonel that Owen was not suitable for a combat branch. I told Dan I felt guilty that I'd said these things 'behind Owen's back.'

'How can you feel "guilty" for trying to save his life?' Dan asked me.

Hester said the same thing, when I confessed to her that I had betrayed Owen to Colonel Eiger.

'How can you say you "betrayed" him? If you love him, how could you want what he wants? He's crazy!' Hester cried. 'If the Army insists that he's not "fit" for combat, I could even learn to love the fucking Army!'

But *everyone* was beginning to seem 'crazy' to me. My grandmother just muttered away at the television – all day and all night. She was beginning to forget things and people – if she hadn't seen them on TV – and more appalling, she remembered everything she'd seen on television with a mindless, automatic accuracy. Even Dan Needham seemed crazy to me; for how many years could *anyone* maintain enthusiasm for amateur theatricals, in general – and for the question of which role in *A Christmas Carol* best suited Mr Fish, in particular? And although I did not sympathize with the Gravesend Gas Works for firing Mrs Hoyt as their receptionist, I thought Mrs Hoyt was crazy, too. And those town 'patriots' who were apprehended in the act of vandalizing Mrs Hoyt's car and garage were even crazier than she was. And Rector Wiggin, and his wife, Barbara . . . they had *always* been crazy; now they were claiming that God 'supported' the U.S. troops in Vietnam – their implication being that *not* to support the presence of those troops was both anti-American and ugodly. Although the Rev. Lewis Merrill was – with Dan Needham – the principal spokesman for what amounted to the antiwar movement within Gravesend Academy, even Mr Merrill looked crazy to me; for all his talk about peace, he wasn't making any progress with Owen Meany.

Of course, Owen was the craziest; I suppose it was always

a toss-up between Owen and Hester, but regarding the subject of Owen wanting and actively seeking a combat-branch assignment, there was no doubt in my mind that Owen was the craziest.

'Why do you *want* to be a hero?' I asked him.

'YOU DON'T UNDERSTAND,' he said.

'No, I don't,' I admitted. It was the spring of our senior year, 1966; I'd already been accepted into the graduate school at the University of New Hampshire – for the next year, at least, I wouldn't be going anywhere; I had my 2-S deferment and was hanging on to it. Owen had already filled out his Officer Assignment Preference Statement – his DREAM SHEET, he called it. On his Personnel Action Form, he'd noted that he was 'volunteering for oversea service.' On both forms, he'd specified that he wanted to go to Vietnam: Infantry, Armor, or Artillery – in that order. He was *not* optimistic; with his number-two ranking in his ROTC unit, the Army was under no obligation to honor his choice. He admitted that no one had been very encouraging regarding his appeal to change his assignment from the Adjutant General's Corps to a combat branch – not even Colonel Eiger had encouraged him.

'THE ARMY OFFERS YOU THE ILLUSION OF CHOICE – THE SAME CHOICE AS EVERYONE ELSE,' Owen said. While he was hoping to be reassigned, he would toss around all the bullshit phrases favored by the Department of the Army Headquarters: RANGER TRAINING, AIRBORNE TRAINING, SPECIAL FORCES TRAINING – one day when he said he wished he'd gone to JUMP SCHOOL, or to JUNGLE SCHOOL, Hester threw up.

'Why do you *want* to go – at all?' I screamed at him.

'I KNOW THAT I *DO* GO,' he said. 'IT'S NOT NECESSARILY A MATTER OF *WANTING* TO.'

'Let me make sure I get this right,' I said to him. 'You "know" that you go *where*?'

'TO VIETNAM,' he said.

'I see,' I said.

'No, you don't "see,"' Hester said. 'Ask him *how* he "knows" that he goes to Vietnam,' she said.

'How do you *know*, Owen?' I asked him; I thought I knew how he knew – it was the *dream*, and it gave me the shivers.

Owen and I were sitting in the wooden, straight-backed chairs in Hester's roach-infested kitchen. Hester was making a tomato sauce; she was not an exciting cook, and the kitchen retained the acidic, oniony odor of many of her previous tomato sauces. She wilted an onion in cheap olive oil in a cast-iron skillet; then she poured in a can of tomatoes. She added water – and basil, oregano, salt, red pepper, and sometimes a leftover bone from a pork chop or a lamb chop or a steak. She would reduce this mess to a volume that was less than the original can of tomatoes, and the consistency of paste. This glop she would dump over pasta, which had been boiled until it was much too soft. Occasionally, she would surprise us with a salad – the dressing for which was composed of too much vinegar and the same cheap olive oil she had employed in her assault of the onion.

Sometimes, after dinner, we would listen to music on the living-room couch – or else Hester would sing something to Owen and me. But the couch was at present uninviting, the result of Hester taking pity on one of Durham's stray dogs; the mutt had demonstrated its gratitude by bestowing upon Hester's living-room couch an infestation of fleas. This was the life that Hester and I thought Owen valued too little.

'I DON'T *WANT* TO BE A HERO,' said Owen Meany. 'IT'S NOT THAT I *WANT* TO BE – IT'S THAT I *AM* A HERO. I KNOW THAT'S WHAT I'M *SUPPOSED* TO BE.'

'*How* do you know?' I asked him.

'IT'S NOT THAT I *WANT* TO GO TO VIETNAM – IT'S WHERE I *HAVE* TO GO. IT'S WHERE I'M A HERO. I'VE GOT TO BE THERE,' he said.

'Tell him how you "know" this, you asshole!' Hester screamed at him.

'THE WAY YOU KNOW SOME THINGS – YOUR OBLIGATIONS, YOUR DESTINY OR YOUR FATE,' he said. 'THE WAY YOU KNOW WHAT GOD WANTS YOU TO DO.'

'God wants you to go to Vietnam?' I asked him.

Hester ran out of the kitchen and shut herself in the bathroom; she started running the water in the bathtub. 'I'm not listening to this shit, Owen – not one more time, I told you!' she cried.

When Owen got up from the kitchen table to turn the flame down under the tomato sauce, we could hear Hester being sick in the bathroom.

'It's this dream, isn't it?' I asked him. He stirred the tomato sauce as if he knew what he was doing. 'Does Pastor Merrill tell you that God wants you to go to Vietnam?' I asked him. 'Does Father Findley tell you that?'

'THEY SAY IT'S JUST A DREAM,' said Owen Meany.

'That's what *I* say – I don't even know what it is, but I say it's just a dream,' I said.

'BUT YOU HAVE NO FAITH,' he said. 'THAT'S YOUR PROBLEM.'

In the bathroom, Hester was sounding like New Year's Eve; the tomato sauce just simmered.

Owen Meany could manifest a certain calmness that I had never quite liked; when he got like that when we were practicing the shot, I didn't want to touch him – when I passed him the ball, I felt uneasy; and when I had to put my hands on him, when I actually lifted him up, I always felt I was handling a creature that was not exactly human, or not quite real. I wouldn't have been surprised if he had twisted in the air, in my hands, and bitten me; or if – after I'd lifted him – he'd just kept on flying.

'It's only a dream,' I repeated.

'IT'S NOT *YOUR* DREAM,' said Owen Meany.

'Don't be coy, don't play around with me,' I told him.

'I'M NOT PLAYING AROUND,' he said. 'WOULD I REQUEST A COMBAT ASSIGNMENT IF I WERE PLAYING AROUND?'

I began again. 'In this dream, you're a hero?' I asked him.

'I SAVE THE CHILDREN,' said Owen Meany. 'I SAVE LOTS OF CHILDREN.'

'Children?' I said.

'IN THE DREAM,' he said – 'THEY'RE NOT SOLDIERS, THEY'RE CHILDREN.'

'Vietnamese children?' I asked.

'THAT'S HOW I KNOW WHERE I AM – THEY'RE DEFINITELY VIETNAMESE CHILDREN, AND I SAVE THEM. I WOULDN'T GO TO ALL THIS TROUBLE IF I WAS SUPPOSED TO SAVE *SOLDIERS*!' he added.

'Owen, this is so childish,' I said. 'You can't believe that everything that pops into your head *means* something! You can't have a dream and believe that you "know" what you're *supposed* to do!'

'THAT ISN'T EXACTLY WHAT FAITH IS,' he said, turning his attention to the tomato sauce. 'I DON'T BELIEVE EVERYTHING THAT *POPS* INTO MY HEAD – FAITH

IS A LITTLE MORE SELECTIVE THAN THAT.'

Some dreams, I suppose, are MORE SELECTIVE, too. Under the big pot of water for the pasta, Owen turned the flame on – as if the sounds of Hester's dry heaves in the bathroom were an indication to him that her appetite would be returning soon. Then he went into Hester's bedroom and fetched his diary. He didn't show it to me; he simply found the part he was looking for, and he began to read to me. I didn't know I was hearing an edited version. The word 'dream' was never mentioned in his writing, as if it were not a dream he was describing but rather something he had seen with much more certainty and authority than anything appearing to him in his sleep – as if he were describing an order of events he had absolutely witnessed. Yet he remained removed from what he saw, like someone watching through a window, and the tone of the writing was not at all as urgent as the tone so often employed by The Voice; rather, the certainty and authority that I heard reminded me of the plain, less-than-enthusiastic report of a documentary, which is the tone of voice of those undoubting parts of the Bible.

'I NEVER HEAR THE EXPLOSION. WHAT I HEAR IS THE AFTERMATH OF AN EXPLOSION. THERE IS A RINGING IN MY EARS, AND THOSE HIGH-PITCHED POPPING AND TICKING SOUNDS THAT A HOT ENGINE MAKES AFTER YOU SHUT IT OFF; AND PIECES OF THE SKY ARE FALLING, AND BITS OF WHITE – MAYBE PAPER, MAYBE PLASTER – ARE FLOATING DOWN LIKE SNOW. THERE ARE SILVERY SPARKLES IN THE AIR, TOO – MAYBE IT'S SHATTERED GLASS. THERE'S SMOKE, AND THE STINK OF BURNING; THERE'S NO FLAME, BUT EVERYTHING IS SMOLDERING.

'WE'RE ALL LYING ON THE FLOOR. I KNOW THE CHILDREN ARE ALL RIGHT BECAUSE – ONE BY ONE – THEY PICK THEMSELVES UP OFF THE FLOOR. IT MUST HAVE BEEN A LOUD EXPLOSION BECAUSE SOME OF THE CHILDREN ARE STILL HOLDING THEIR EARS; SOME OF THEIR EARS ARE BLEEDING. THE CHILDREN DON'T SPEAK ENGLISH, BUT THEIR VOICES ARE THE FIRST HUMAN SOUNDS TO FOLLOW THE EXPLOSION. THE YOUNGER ONES ARE CRYING; BUT THE OLDER ONES ARE DOING THEIR BEST TO BE COMFORTING – THEY'RE CHATTERING AWAY,

THEY'RE REALLY BABBLING, BUT THIS IS REASSURING.

'THE WAY THEY LOOK AT ME, I KNOW TWO THINGS. I KNOW THAT I SAVED THEM – I DON'T KNOW HOW. AND I KNOW THAT THEY'RE AFRAID FOR ME. BUT I DON'T *SEE* ME – I CAN'T TELL WHAT'S WRONG WITH ME. THE CHILDREN'S FACES TELL ME SOMETHING IS WRONG.

'SUDDENLY, THE NUNS ARE THERE; *PENGUINS* ARE PEERING DOWN AT ME – ONE OF THEM BENDS OVER ME. I CAN'T HEAR WHAT I SAY TO HER, BUT SHE APPEARS TO UNDERSTAND ME – MAYBE SHE SPEAKS ENGLISH. IT'S NOT UNTIL SHE TAKES ME IN HER ARMS THAT I SEE ALL THE BLOOD – HER WIMPLE IS BLOOD-STAINED. WHILE I'M LOOKING AT THE NUN, HER WIMPLE CONTINUES TO BE SPLASHED WITH BLOOD – THE BLOOD SPATTERS HER FACE, TOO, BUT SHE'S NOT AFRAID. THE FACES OF THE CHILDREN – LOOKING DOWN AT ME – ARE FULL OF FEAR; BUT THE NUN WHO HOLDS ME IN HER ARMS IS VERY PEACEFUL.

'OF COURSE, IT'S *MY* BLOOD – SHE'S COVERED WITH MY BLOOD – BUT SHE'S VERY CALM. WHEN I SEE SHE'S ABOUT TO MAKE THE SIGN OF THE CROSS OVER ME, I REACH OUT TO TRY TO STOP HER. BUT I CAN'T STOP HER – IT'S AS IF I DON'T HAVE ANY ARMS. THE NUN JUST SMILES AT ME. AFTER SHE'S MADE THE SIGN OF THE CROSS OVER ME, I LEAVE ALL OF THEM – I JUST LEAVE. THEY ARE STILL EXACTLY WHERE THEY WERE, LOOKING DOWN AT ME; BUT I'M NOT REALLY THERE. *I'M* LOOKING DOWN AT ME, TOO. I LOOK LIKE I DID WHEN I WAS THE BABY JESUS – YOU REMEMBER THOSE STUPID SWADDLING CLOTHES? THAT'S HOW I LOOK WHEN I LEAVE ME.

'BUT NOW ALL THE PEOPLE ARE GROWING SMALLER – NOT JUST ME, BUT THE NUNS AND THE CHILDREN, TOO. I'M QUITE FAR ABOVE THEM, BUT THEY NEVER LOOK UP; THEY KEEP LOOKING DOWN AT WHAT *USED* TO BE ME. AND SOON I'M ABOVE EVERYTHING; THE PALM TREES ARE VERY STRAIGHT AND TALL, BUT SOON I'M HIGH ABOVE THE PALM TREES, TOO. THE SKY AND THE PALM TREES ARE SO BEAUTIFUL, BUT IT'S VERY HOT – THE AIR IS HOTTER THAN ANY

PLACE I'VE EVER BEEN. I KNOW I'M NOT IN NEW HAMPSHIRE.'

I didn't say anything; he put his diary back in Hester's bedroom, he stirred the tomato sauce, he looked under the lid of the water pot to see if the water was near to boiling. Then he went and knocked on the bathroom door; it was quiet in there.

'I'll be out in a minute,' Hester said.

Owen returned to the kitchen and sat down at the table with me.

'It's just a dream, Owen,' I said to him. He folded his hands and regarded me patiently. I remembered that time he untied the safety rope when we'd been swimming in the old quarry. I remembered how angry he was – when we hadn't immediately jumped in the water to save him.

'YOU LET ME DROWN!' he'd said. 'YOU DIDN'T DO ANYTHING! YOU JUST WATCHED ME DROWN! I'M ALREADY DEAD!' he'd told us. 'REMEMBER THAT: YOU LET ME DIE.'

'Owen,' I said. 'Given your sensitive feelings for Catholics, why *wouldn't* you dream that a nun was your own special Angel of Death?'

He looked down at his hands folded on top of the table; we could hear Hester's bath emptying.

'It's just a dream,' I repeated; he shrugged. There was in his attitude toward me that same mild pity and mild contempt I had seen before – when *The Flying Yankee* had passed over the Maiden Hill trestle bridge, precisely as Owen and I had passed under it, and I'd called this a 'coincidence.'

Hester came out of the bathroom wrapped in a pale-yellow towel, carrying her clothes. She went into the bedroom without looking at us; she shut the door, and we could hear her shaking the chest of drawers, the coat hangers protesting her roughness in the closet.

'Owen,' I said. 'You're very original, but the dream is a stereotype – the dream is stupid. You're going in the Army, there's a war in Vietnam – do you think you'd have a dream about saving *American* children? And, naturally, there would be palm trees – what would you expect? Igloos?'

Hester came out of the bedroom in fresh clothes; she was roughly toweling her hair dry. Her clothes were almost an exact exchange for what she'd worn before – she wore a different pair of blue jeans and a different, ill-fitting turtleneck jersey; the extent to which Hester ever changed her clothes was a change from black to navy blue, or vice versa.

'Owen,' I said. 'You *can't* believe that God wants you to go to Vietnam for the purpose of making yourself available to rescue these characters in a *dream*!'

He neither nodded nor shrugged; he sat very still looking at his hands folded on top of the table.

'That's exactly what he believes – you've hit the nail on the head,' Hester said. She gripped the damp, pale-yellow towel and rolled it tightly into what we used to call a 'rat's tail.' She snapped the towel very close to Owen Meany's face, but Owen didn't move. 'That's it, isn't it? You asshole!' she yelled at him. She snapped the towel again – then she unrolled it and ran at him, wrapping the towel around his head. 'You think *God* wants you to go to Vietnam – don't you?' she screamed at him.

She wrestled him out of his chair – she held his head in the towel in a headlock and she lay on her side across his chest, pinning him to the kitchen floor, while she began to pound him in the face with the fist of her free hand. He kicked his feet, he tried to grab for her hair; but Hester must have outweighed Owen Meany by at least thirty pounds, and she appeared to be hitting him as hard as she could. When I saw the blood seep through the pale-yellow towel, I grabbed Hester around her waist and tried to pull her off him.

It wasn't easy; I had to get my hands on her throat and threaten to strangle her before she stopped hitting him and tried to hit me. She was very strong, and she was hysterical; she tried to demonstrate her headlock on me, but Owen got the towel off his head and tackled Hester at her ankles. Then it was his turn to attempt to get her off me. Owen's nose was bleeding and his lower lip, which was split and puffy, was bleeding, too; but together we managed to take control of her. Owen sat on the backs of her legs, and I kneeled between her shoulder blades and pulled her arms down flush to her sides; this still left her free to thrash her head all around – she tried to bite me, and when she couldn't, she began to bang her face on the kitchen floor until *her* nose was bleeding.

'You don't love me, Owen!' Hester screamed. 'If you loved me, you wouldn't go – not for all the goddamn children in the *world*! You wouldn't go if you loved me!'

Owen and I stayed on top of her until she started to cry, and she stopped banging her face on the floor.

'YOU BETTER GO,' Owen said to me.

'No, *you* better go, Owen,' Hester said to him. 'You better get the fuck out of here!'

And so he took his diary from Hester's bedroom, and we left together. It was a warm spring night. I followed the tomato-red pickup to the coast; I knew where he was going. I was sure that he wanted to sit on the breakwater at Rye Harbor. The breakwater was made of the slag – the broken slabs – from the Meany Granite Quarry; Owen always felt he had a right to sit there. From the breakwater, you got a pretty view of the tiny harbor; in the spring, not that many boats were in the water – it didn't quite feel like summer, which was the time of year when we usually sat there.

But this summer would be different, anyway. Because I was teaching ninth-grade Expository Writing at Gravesend Academy in the fall, I wasn't going to work this summer. Even a part-time job at Gravesend Academy would more than compensate for my graduate-school expenses; even a part-time job – for the whole school year – was worth more than another summer working for Meany Granite.

Besides: my grandmother had given me a little money, and Owen would be in the Army. He had treated himself to thirty days between his graduation and the beginning of his active duty as a second lieutenant. We'd talked about taking a trip together. Except for his Basic Training – at Fort Knox or Fort Bragg – Owen had never been out of New England; I'd never been out of New England, either.

'Both of you should go to *Canada*,' Hester had told us. 'And you should *stay* there!'

The salt water rushed in and out of the breakwater; pools of water were trapped in the rocks below the high-tide mark. Owen stuck his face in one of these tide pools; his nose had stopped bleeding, but his lip was split quite deeply – it continued to bleed – and there was a sizable swelling above one of his eyebrows. He had two black eyes, one very much blacker than the other and so puffy that the eye was closed to a slit.

'YOU THINK VIETNAM IS DANGEROUS,' he said. 'YOU OUGHT TO TRY LIVING WITH *HESTER*!'

But he was so exasperating! How could *anyone* live with

Owen Meany and, knowing what he thought he knew, *not* be moved to beat the shit out of him?

We sat on the breakwater until it grew dark and the mosquitoes began to bother us.

'Are you hungry?' I asked him.

He pointed to his lower lip, which was still bleeding, 'I DON'T THINK I CAN EAT ANYTHING,' he said, 'BUT I'LL GO WITH YOU.'

We went to one of those clam-shack restaurants on 'the strip.' I ate a lot of fried clams and Owen sipped a beer – through a straw. The waitress knew us – she was a University of New Hampshire girl.

'You better get some stitches in that lip before it falls off,' she told Owen.

We drove – Owen in the tomato-red pickup, and I followed him in my Volkswagen – to the emergency room of the Gravesend Hospital. It was a slow night – not the summer, and not a weekend – so we didn't have to wait long. There was a hassle concerning how he intended to pay for his treatment.

'SUPPOSE I CAN'T PAY?' he asked. 'DOES THAT MEAN YOU DON'T TREAT ME?'

I was surprised that he had no health insurance; apparently, there was no policy for coverage in his family and he hadn't even paid the small premium asked of students at the university for group benefits. Finally, I said that the hospital could send the bill to my grandmother; everyone knew who Harriet Wheelwright was – even the emergency-room receptionist – and, after a phone call to Grandmother, this method of payment was accepted.

'WHAT A COUNTRY!' said Owen Meany, while a nervous-looking young doctor – who was not an American – put four stitches in his lower lip. 'AT LEAST WHEN I GET IN THE ARMY, I'LL HAVE SOME HEALTH INSURANCE!'

Owen said he was ashamed to take money from my grandmother – 'SHE'S ALREADY GIVEN ME MORE THAN I DESERVED!' But when we arrived at 80 Front Street, a different problem presented itself.

'Merciful Heavens, Owen!' my grandmother said. 'You've been in a *fight*!'

'I JUST FELL DOWNSTAIRS,' he said.

'Don't you lie to me, Owen Meany!' Grandmother said.

'I WAS ATTACKED BY JUVENILE DELINQUENTS AT HAMPTON BEACH,' Owen said.

'Don't you lie to me!' Grandmother repeated.

I could see that Owen was struggling to ascertain the effect upon my grandmother of telling her that her granddaughter had beaten the shit out of him; Hester – except for her vomiting – was always relatively subdued around Grandmother.

Owen pointed to me. '*HE* DID IT,' Owen said.

'Merciful Heavens!' my grandmother said. 'You should be ashamed of yourself!' she said to me.

'I didn't mean to,' I said. 'We weren't having a *real* fight – we were just roughhousing.'

'IT WAS DARK,' said Owen Meany. 'HE COULDN'T SEE ME VERY CLEARLY.'

'You should still be ashamed of yourself!' my grandmother said to me.

'Yes,' I said.

This little misunderstanding seemed to cheer up Owen. My grandmother commenced to wait on him, hand and foot – and Ethel was summoned and directed to concoct something nourishing for him in the blender: a fresh pineapple, a banana, some ice cream, some brewer's yeast. 'Something the poor boy can drink through a straw!' my grandmother said.

'YOU CAN LEAVE OUT THE BREWER'S YEAST,' said Owen Meany.

After my grandmother went to bed, we sat up watching *The Late Show* and he teased me about my new reputation – as a bully. The movie on *The Late Show* was at least twenty years old – Betty Grable in *Moon over Miami*. The music, and the setting, made me think of the place called The Orange Grove and my mother performing as 'The Lady in Red.' I would probably never know any more about that, I thought.

'You remember the play you were going to write?' I asked Owen. 'About the supper club – about "The Lady in Red"?'

'SURE, I REMEMBER. YOU DIDN'T WANT ME TO DO IT,' he said.

'I thought you might have done it, anyway,' I said.

'I STARTED IT – A COUPLE OF TIMES,' he said. 'IT WAS HARDER THAN I THOUGHT – TO MAKE UP A STORY.'

Carole Landis was in *Moon over Miami*, and Don Ameche;

remember them? It's a story about husband-hunting in Florida. Just the glow of the television lit Owen's face when he said, 'YOU'VE GOT TO LEARN TO FOLLOW THINGS THROUGH – IF YOU CARE ABOUT SOMETHING, YOU'VE GOT TO SEE IT ALL THE WAY TO THE END, YOU'VE GOT TO TRY TO FINISH IT. I'LL BET YOU NEVER EVEN LOOKED IN A BOSTON TELEPHONE DIRECTORY – FOR A BUSTER FREEBODY,' he said.

'It's a made-up name,' I said.

'IT'S THE ONLY NAME WE KNOW,' Owen said.

'No, I didn't look it up,' I said.

'YOU SEE?' he said. 'THERE ACTUALLY ARE A FEW FREEBODYS – BUT NO "BUSTER," ' he said.

'Maybe "Buster" is just a nickname,' I said – with more interest now.

'NONE OF THE FREEBODYS I SPOKE WITH HAD EVER HEARD OF A "BUSTER," ' said Owen Meany. 'AND THE OLD PEOPLE'S HOMES WON'T RELEASE A LIST OF NAMES – DO YOU KNOW WHY?' he asked me.

'Why?' I asked him.

'BECAUSE CRIMINALS COULD USE THE NAMES TO FIND OUT WHO'S NO LONGER LIVING AT HOME. IF THE SAME NAME IS STILL IN THE PHONE BOOK – AND IF THE HOUSE OR THE APARTMENT HASN'T BEEN REOCCUPIED – THEN THE CRIMINALS HAVE FOUND AN EASY PLACE TO ROB: NOBODY HOME. THAT'S WHY THE OLD PEOPLE'S HOMES DON'T GIVE OUT ANY NAMES,' he said. 'INTERESTING, HUH? IF IT'S TRUE,' he added.

'You've been busy,' I said; he shrugged.

'AND THE LISTINGS IN THE YELLOW PAGES – THOSE PLACES THAT OFFER "LIVE MUSIC," ' he said. 'NOT ONE OF THOSE PLACES IN ALL OF BOSTON HAS EVER HEARD OF A BIG BLACK BUSTER FREEBODY! IT WAS SO LONG AGO, BUSTER FREEBODY MUST BE DEAD.'

'I'd hate to see your phone bill,' I told him.

'I USED HESTER'S PHONE,' he said.

'I'm surprised she didn't beat the shit out of you for *that*,' I said.

'SHE *DID*,' Owen said; he turned his face away from the glowing light of the TV. 'I WOULDN'T TELL HER WHAT

THE PHONE CALLS WERE ABOUT, AND SHE THOUGHT I HAD ANOTHER GIRLFRIEND.'

'Why *don't* you have another girlfriend?' I asked him; he shrugged again.

'SHE DOESN'T BEAT ME UP ALL THE TIME,' Owen said.

What could I say? I didn't even have a girlfriend.

'We ought to think about our *trip*,' I said to him. 'We've got thirty days coming up – where do you want to go?'

'SOMEWHERE *WARM*,' said Owen Meany.

'It's warm everywhere – in June,' I reminded him.

'I'D LIKE TO GO WHERE THERE ARE PALM TREES,' Owen said.

We watched *Moon over Miami* for a while, in silence.

'We could drive to Florida,' I said.

'NOT IN THE PICKUP,' he said. 'THE PICKUP WOULDN'T MAKE IT TO FLORIDA.'

'We could take my Volkswagen,' I said. 'We could drive to California in the Beetle – no problem.'

'BUT WHERE WOULD WE SLEEP?' Owen asked me. 'I CAN'T AFFORD MOTELS.'

'Grandmother would lend us the money,' I said.

'I'VE TAKEN ENOUGH MONEY FROM YOUR GRANDMOTHER,' he said.

'Well, *I* could lend you the money,' I said.

'IT'S THE SAME MONEY,' said Owen Meany.

'We could take a tent – and sleeping bags,' I said. 'We could camp out.'

'I'VE THOUGHT OF THAT,' he said. 'IF WE CARRY A LOT OF CAMPING STUFF, WE'D BE BETTER OFF IN THE PICKUP – BUT THE PICKUP WOULD DIE ON US, ON A TRIP OF THAT DISTANCE.'

Was there anything Owen Meany hadn't thought of before I'd thought of it? I wondered.

'WE DON'T *HAVE* TO GO WHERE THERE ARE PALM TREES – IT WAS JUST AN IDEA,' Owen said.

We weren't in the mood for *Moon over Miami*; a story about husband-hunting requires a special mood. Owen went out to the pickup and got his flashlight; then we walked up Front Street to Linden Street – past the Gravesend High School to the cemetery. The night was still warm, and not especially dark. As graves go, my mother's grave looked pretty nice.

Grandmother had planted a border of crocuses and daffodils and tulips, so that even in the spring there was color; and Grandmother's touch with roses was evident by the well-pruned rose bush that took very firm grasp of the trellis that stood like a comfortable headboard directly behind my mother's grave. Owen played the flashlight over the beveled edges of the gravestone; I'd seen better work with the diamond wheel – Owen's work was much, much better. But I never supposed that Owen had been old enough to fashion my mother's stone.

'MY FATHER WAS NEVER AN EXPERT WITH THE DIAMOND WHEEL,' Owen observed.

Dan Needham had recently placed a fresh bouquet of spring flowers in front of the gravestone, but Owen and I could still manage to see the lettering of my mother's name – and the appropriate dates.

'If she were alive, she'd be forty-three!' I said. 'Imagine that.'

'SHE'D STILL BE BEAUTIFUL!' said Owen Meany.

When we were walking back along Linden Street, I was thinking that we could take a trip 'Down East,' as people in New Hampshire say – by which they mean, along the coast of Maine, all the way to Nova Scotia.

'Could the pickup make it to Nova Scotia?' I asked Owen. 'Suppose we just took it easy, and drive along the coast of Maine – not in any hurry, not caring about when we arrived in Nova Scotia, not even caring if we *ever* arrived there – do you think the pickup could handle that?'

'I'VE BEEN THINKING ABOUT THAT,' he said. 'YES, I THINK WE COULD DO THAT – IF WE DIDN'T TRY TO DRIVE TOO MANY MILES IN ONE DAY. WITH THE PICK-UP WE COULD CERTAINLY CARRY ALL THE CAMPING GEAR WE'D EVER NEED – WE COULD EVEN PITCH THE TENT IN THE BACK OF THE PICKUP, IF WE EVER HAD A PROBLEM FINDING DRY OR LEVEL GROUND . . .'

'That would be fun!' I said. 'I've never been to Nova Scotia – I've never been very far into Maine.'

On Front Street, we stopped to pet someone's cat.

'I'VE ALSO BEEN THINKING ABOUT SAWYER DEPOT,' said Owen Meany.

'What about it?' I asked him.

'I'VE NEVER BEEN THERE, YOU KNOW,' he said.

'It's not really very interesting in Sawyer Depot,' I said

cautiously. I didn't think my Aunt Martha and Uncle Alfred would welcome Owen Meany into their home with open arms; and considering what had just happened with Hester, I wondered what attraction Sawyer Depot still had for Owen.

'I'D JUST LIKE TO SEE IT,' he said. 'I'VE HEARD SO MUCH ABOUT IT. EVEN IF THE EASTMANS WOULDN'T WANT ME IN THE HOUSE, PERHAPS YOU COULD SHOW ME LOVELESS LAKE – AND THE BOATHOUSE, AND MAYBE THE MOUNTAIN WHERE ALL OF YOU WENT SKIING. AND FIREWATER!' he said.

'Firewater's been dead for years!' I told him.

'OH,' he said.

My grandmother's driveway looked like a parking lot. There was Grandmother's old Cadillac, and my Volkswagen Beetle, and the dusty tomato-red pickup; and parked at the rear of the line was Hester's hand-me-down '57 Chevy.

She must have been out looking for Owen; and when she'd seen the pickup in Grandmother's driveway, she must have gone into 80 Front Street to find him. We found her asleep on the couch; the only light that flashed over her was the ghastly, bone-colored glow from the TV, which she had turned to another channel – apparently, Hester hadn't been in the mood for *Moon over Miami*, either. She had fallen asleep watching *Duchess of Idaho*.

'HESTER HATES ESTHER WILLIAMS, UNLESS ESTHER IS UNDERWATER,' said Owen Meany. He went and sat beside Hester on the couch; he touched her hair, then her cheek. I switched the channel; there was never just one *Late Show* – not anymore. *Moon over Miami* was over; something called *The Late, Late Show* had begun in its place – John Wayne, in *Operation Pacific*.

'HESTER HATES JOHN WAYNE,' Owen said, and Hester woke up.

John Wayne was in a submarine in World War Two; he was battling the Japanese.

'I'm not watching a war movie,' Hester said; she turned on the lamp on the end table next to the couch – she examined the stitches in Owen's lip closely. 'How many?' she asked him.

'FOUR,' he told her.

She kissed him very softly on his upper lip and on the tip of his nose, and on the corners of his mouth – being very careful not to kiss the stitches. 'I'm sorry! I love you!' she whispered to him.

'I'M OKAY,' said Owen Meany.

I flicked through the channels until I found something interesting – *Sherlock Holmes in Terror by Night*, with Basil Rathbone.

'I can't remember if I've seen this one,' Hester said.

'I know I've seen it, but I can't remember it,' I said.

'IT'S THE ONE WITH THE JEWEL ON THE TRAIN – IT'S A PRETTY GOOD ONE,' said Owen Meany. He curled up next to Hester on the couch; he laid his head against her bosom, and she cradled him in her arms. In a few minutes, he was fast asleep.

'Better turn the volume down,' Hester whispered to me. When I looked at her – to see if I'd lowered the volume enough – she was crying.

'I think I'll go to bed,' I told her quietly. 'I've seen Sherlock Holmes a hundred times.'

'We'll stay a while,' Hester said. 'Good night.'

'He wants to go to Sawyer Depot,' I told her.

'I know,' she said.

I lay in bed awake a long time. When I heard their voices in the driveway, I got up and went into my mother's empty bedroom; from the window there, I could see them. The curtains were never drawn in my mother's bedroom, in memory of how she had hated the darkness.

It was almost dawn, and Hester and Owen were discussing how they would drive back to Durham.

'I'll follow you,' Hester said.

'NO, I'LL FOLLOW YOU,' he told her.

Then I graduated from the University of New Hampshire – a B.A. in English, *cum laude*. Owen just plain graduated – Second Lieutenant Paul O. Meany, Jr, with B.S. in Geology. He was *not* reassigned to a combat branch; he was ordered to report to Fort Benjamin Harrison in Indiana, where he would undertake an eight- to ten-week course in Basic Administration for the Adjutant General's Corps. After that, the Army wanted him to report to a communications command in Arizona. Although the Army might later send him anywhere in the country – or even to Saigon – they were assigning him to a *desk job*.

'SECOND LIEUTENANTS ARE SUPPOSED TO BE

PLATOON LEADERS!' said Owen Meany. Naturally, Hester and I had to conceal how pleased we were. Even in Vietnam, the Adjutant General's Corps was not a branch with a high rate of casualties. We knew he wouldn't give up; every few months he would fill out another Personnel Action Form, requesting a new assignment – and he claimed that Colonel Eiger had provided him with the name and telephone number of someone in the Pentagon, a certain major who allegedly supervised the personnel files and assignments of the junior officers. Hester and I knew better than to ever underestimate Owen's powers of manipulation.

But, for the moment, we thought he was safe; and the U.S. Army, I believed, was not as easy to manipulate as a children's Christmas pageant.

'What exactly does the Adjutant General's Corps *do*?' I asked him cautiously. But he wouldn't discuss it.

'THIS IS JUST AN *INTERIM* ASSIGNMENT,' said Owen Meany.

Dan and I had to laugh; it was funny to think of him suffering through a Basic Administration course in Indiana when what he had imagined for himself was jumping out of a helicopter and hacking his way through a jungle with his machete and his M-16. Owen was angry, but he wasn't depressed; he was irritable, but he was determined.

Then one evening I was walking through the Gravesend Academy campus and I saw the tomato-red pickup parked in the circular driveway from which poor Dr Dolder's Volkswagen Beetle had been elevated to its moment in history. The headlights of the pickup were shining across the vast lawn in front of the Main Academy Building; the lawn was full of chairs. Rows upon rows of chairs, and the benches from The Great Hall, were spread out across the lawn – I would estimate that there was seating for five hundred people. It was that time of the year when Gravesend Academy hoped it wouldn't rain; the chairs and benches were assembled for the annual commencement. If it rained – to everyone's sorrow – there was no place large enough to hold the commencement, except the gym; not even The Great Hall would hold the crowd.

Commencement had been outdoors the year I graduated – the year Owen *should* have graduated, the year he should have been our class valedictorian.

Hester was sitting by herself in the cab of the pickup; she motioned to me to get in and sit beside her.

'Where is he?' I asked her. She pointed into the path of the pickup truck's headlights. Beyond the rows upon rows of chairs and benches was a makeshift stage, draped with the Gravesend Academy banner and dotted with chairs for the dignitaries and the speakers; at the center of this stage was the podium, and at the podium was Owen Meany. He was looking out over the hundreds of empty seats – he appeared to be a little blinded by the pickup truck's headlights, but he needed the light in order to see his valedictory speech, which he was reading.

'He doesn't want anyone to hear it – he just wants to *say* it,' Hester said.

When he joined Hester and me in the cab of the pickup, I said to him: 'I would have liked to hear that. Won't you read it to us?'

'IT'S OVER,' said Owen Meany. 'IT'S JUST SOME OLD HISTORY.'

And so we departed for the north country – for Sawyer Depot, and Loveless Lake. We took the pickup; we did not take Hester. I'm not sure if she wanted to come. She had made the effort to speak to her parents; Uncle Alfred and Aunt Martha were always happy to see me, and they were polite – if not exactly warm – to Owen Meany. We spent the first night of our trip in the Eastmans' house in Sawyer Depot. I slept in Noah's bed; Noah was in the Peace Corps – I believe he was teaching Forestry, or 'Forest Management,' to Nigerians. Uncle Alfred referred to what Noah was doing as a 'ticket' – Africa, or the Peace Corps, was Noah's 'ticket out of Vietnam,' Uncle Alfred said.

That summer, Simon was running the sawmill; over the years, Simon had injured his knees so often – skiing – that Simon's knees were *his* ticket out of Vietnam. Simon had a 4-F deferment; he was judged physically unfit for service. 'Unless the country is invaded by aliens,' Simon said, 'good old Uncle Sam won't take me!'

Owen referred to his course in Basic Administration for the Adjutant General's Corps as TEMPORARY. Arizona would also be TEMPORARY, Owen said. Uncle Alfred was very respectful of Owen's desire to go to Vietnam, but Aunt Martha – over our elegant dinner – questioned the war's 'morality.'

'YES, I QUESTION THAT, TOO,' said Owen Meany. 'BUT I FEEL ONE HAS TO SEE SOMETHING FIRSTHAND TO BE SURE. I'M CERTAINLY INCLINED TO AGREE WITH KENNEDY'S ASSESSMENT OF THE VIETNAMESE PROBLEM – WAY BACK IN NINETEEN SIXTY-THREE. YOU MAY RECALL THAT THE PRESIDENT SAID: "WE CAN HELP THEM, WE CAN GIVE THEM EQUIPMENT, WE CAN SEND OUR MEN OUT THERE AS ADVISERS, BUT THEY HAVE TO WIN IT, THE PEOPLE OF VIETNAM." I THINK THAT POINT IS STILL VALID – AND IT'S CLEAR TO ALL OF US THAT THE "PEOPLE OF VIETNAM" ARE *NOT* WINNING THE WAR. WE APPEAR TO BE TRYING TO WIN IT FOR THEM.

'BUT LET'S SUPPOSE, FOR A MOMENT, THAT WE BELIEVE IN THE STATED OBJECTIVES OF THE JOHNSON ADMINISTRATION'S VIETNAM POLICY – AND THAT WE SUPPORT THIS POLICY. WE AGREE TO RESIST COMMUNIST AGGRESSION IN SOUTH VIETNAM – WHETHER IT COMES FROM THE NORTH VIETNAMESE OR THE VIET CONG. WE SUPPORT THE IDEA OF SELF-DETERMINATION FOR SOUTH VIETNAM – AND WE WANT PEACE IN SOUTHEAST ASIA. IF THESE *ARE* OUR OBJECTIVES – IF WE AGREE THAT THIS IS WHAT WE WANT – WHY ARE WE ESCALATING THE WAR?

'THERE DOESN'T APPEAR TO BE A GOVERNMENT IN SAIGON THAT CAN DO VERY WELL WITHOUT US. DO THE SOUTH VIETNAMESE PEOPLE EVEN *LIKE* THE MILITARY JUNTA OF MARSHAL KY? NATURALLY, HANOI AND THE VIET CONG WILL NOT NEGOTIATE FOR A PEACEFUL SETTLEMENT IF THEY THINK THEY CAN WIN THE WAR! THERE'S EVERY REASON FOR THE UNITED STATES TO KEEP ENOUGH OF OUR GROUND FORCES IN SOUTH VIETNAM TO PERSUADE HANOI AND THE VIET CONG THAT THEY COULD NEVER ACHIEVE A MILITARY VICTORY. BUT WHAT DOES IT ACCOMPLISH FOR US TO BOMB THE NORTH?

'SUPPOSING THAT WE MEAN WHAT WE SAY – THAT WE WANT SOUTH VIETNAM TO BE FREE TO GOVERN ITSELF – WE *SHOULD* BE PROTECTING SOUTH VIETNAM FROM ATTACK. BUT IT APPEARS THAT *WE* ARE ATTACKING THE WHOLE COUNTRY – FROM THE AIR!

IF WE BOMB THE WHOLE COUNTRY TO BITS – TO *PROTECT* IT FROM COMMUNISM – WHAT KIND OF *PROTECTION* IS THAT?

'I THINK THAT'S THE PROBLEM,' said Owen Meany, 'BUT I'D LIKE TO SEE THE SITUATION FOR MYSELF.'

My Uncle Alfred was speechless. My Aunt Martha said: 'Yes, I see!' Both of them were impressed. I realized that a part of the reason why Owen had wanted to come to Sawyer Depot was to give himself an opportunity to impress Hester's parents. I'd heard Owen's Vietnam thesis before; it was not very original – I think it was borrowed from something Arthur Schlesinger, Jr, had written or said – but Owen's delivery was impressive. I thought it was sad that Hester made so little effort to impress Uncle Alfred and Aunt Martha, and that she was so unimpressed by them.

At bedtime, I could hear Owen babbling away to Aunt Martha – she had put him in Hester's room. Owen was inquiring about the specific teddy bears and dolls and figurines.

'AND HOW OLD WAS SHE WHEN SHE LIKED *THIS* ONE?' he would ask Aunt Martha. 'AND I SUPPOSE THAT THIS ONE DATES BACK TO THE FIREWATER ERA,' he would say.

Before I went to bed, Simon said to me appreciatively: 'Owen's just as weird as ever! Isn't he *great*?'

I fell asleep remembering how Owen had first appeared to my cousins – that day in the attic at 80 Front Street when we were contending over the sewing machine and Owen stood in the sun from the skylight that blazed through his ears. I remembered how he had appeared to all of us: like a descending angel – a tiny but fiery god, sent to adjudicate the errors of our ways.

In the morning, Owen suggested that we move on to Loveless Lake. Simon advised us to use the boathouse as a base camp. When he got off work at the sawmill, Simon said, he would come take us waterskiing; we could sleep in the boathouse at night. There were a couple of comfortable couches that unfolded to make beds, and the boathouse had new screens on the windows. There were some kerosene lamps; there was an outhouse nearby, and a hand pump drew the lake water into a sink by the bar; there was a propane-gas stove, and some kettles for boiling water – for drinking. In those days, we were allowed to bathe (with soap!) in the lake.

Owen and I agreed that it was cozier than camping in our tent; also, for me it was relaxing to get away from Uncle Alfred and Aunt Martha – and the effort that Owen made to impress them. At the lake, we were left alone; Simon appeared only at the end of the day to take us waterskiiing – he had a steady girlfriend, so we rarely saw him at night. We cooked hamburgers on a charcoal grill on the boatslip; we caught sunfish and perch off the dock – and smallmouth bass when we went out in the canoe. At night, Owen and I sat on the dock until the mosquitoes bothered us. Then we went into the boathouse and turned on the kerosene lamps and talked for a while, or read our books.

I was trying to read *Parade's End*; I was just beginning it. Graduate students have serious reading ambitions, but they don't finish a lot of books they start; I wouldn't finish *Parade's End* until I was in my forties – when I tried it again. Owen was reading a Department of the Army field manual called *Survival, Evasion, and Escape.*

'I'LL READ YOU SOME OF MINE IF YOU READ ME SOME OF YOURS,' Owen said.

'Okay,' I said.

' "SURVIVAL IS LARGELY A MATTER OF MENTAL OUTLOOK," ' he read.

'Sounds reasonable,' I said.

'BUT LISTEN TO THIS,' he said. 'THIS IS ABOUT HOW TO GET ALONG WITH THE NATIVES.' I couldn't help but imagine that the only 'natives' Owen was going to have to get along with were the residents of Indiana and Arizona. ' "RESPECT PERSONAL PROPERTY, ESPECIALLY THEIR WOMEN," ' he read.

'It doesn't say that!' I said.

'LISTEN TO THIS!' he said. ' "AVOID PHYSICAL CONTACT WITHOUT SEEMING TO DO SO." '

We both thought that was a scream – although I didn't tell him that I was laughing, in part, because I was thinking about the 'natives' of Indiana and Arizona.

'WANT TO HEAR HOW TO TAKE CARE OF YOUR FEET?' Owen asked me.

'Not really,' I said.

'HOW ABOUT "PRECAUTION AGAINST MOSQUITO BITES"?' he asked. ' "SMEAR MUD ON YOUR FACE,

ESPECIALLY BEFORE GOING TO BED,"' he read. We laughed hysterically for a while.

'HERE'S A PART ABOUT FOOD AND WATER,' he said. '"DO NOT DRINK URINE."'

'This sounds like a field manual for *children*!' I said.

'THAT'S WHO MOST OF THE PEOPLE IN THE ARMY *ARE*,' said Owen Meany.

'What a world!' I said.

'HERE'S SOME GOOD ADVICE ABOUT ESCAPING FROM A MOVING TRAIN,' Owen said. '"BEFORE JUMPING, MAKE SURE YOUR EXIT WILL BE MADE FROM THE APPROPRIATE SIDE, OR YOU MAY JUMP INTO THE PATH OF AN ONCOMING TRAIN."'

'No shit!' I cried.

'LISTEN TO THIS,' he said. '"*STRYCHNINE* PLANTS GROW WILD THROUGHOUT THE TROPICS. THE LUSCIOUS-LOOKING WHITE OR YELLOW FRUIT IS ABUNDANT IN SOUTHEAST ASIA. THE FRUIT HAS AN EXCEEDINGLY BITTER PULP, AND THE SEEDS CONTAIN A POWERFUL POISON."'

I restrained myself from saying that I doubted any strychnine grew in Indiana or Arizona.

'HERE'S ANOTHER ENTRY IN THE "NO KIDDING!" CATEGORY,' Owen said. 'THEY'RE TALKING ABOUT "EVASION TECHNIQUES WHEN THERE IS LITTLE DISTINCTION BETWEEN FRIENDLY AND HOSTILE TERRITORY" – GET THIS: "IT IS DIFFICULT TO DISTINGUISH THE INSURGENT FROM THE FRIENDLY POPULACE."'

I couldn't help myself; I said: 'I hope you don't run into that problem in Indiana or Arizona.'

'LET'S HEAR SOMETHING FROM *YOUR* BOOK,' he said, closing his field manual.

I tried to explain about Mrs Satterthwaite's daughter – that she was a woman who'd left her husband and child to run off with another man, and now she wanted her husband to take her back, although she hated him and intended to make him miserable. A friend of the family – a priest – is confiding to Mrs Satterthwaite his opinion of how her daughter will, one day, respond to an infidelity of her husband's, which the priest believes is only to be expected. The priest believes that the daughter will 'tear the house down'; that 'the world will echo with her wrongs.'

Here is the scene I read to Owen Meany:

' "Do you mean to say," Mrs Satterthwaite said, "that Sylvia would do anything vulgar?"

' "Doesn't every woman who's had a man to torture for years when she loses him?" the priest asked. "The more she's made an occupation of torturing him the less right she thinks she has to lose him." '

'WHAT A WORLD!' said Owen Meany.

There were more motorboats than loons on Loveless Lake; even at night, we heard more noise from engines than we heard from wildlife. We decided to drive north, through Dixville Notch, to Lake Francis; that was 'real wilderness,' Simon had told us. Indeed, the camping on Lake Francis, which is one of New Hampshire's northernmost lakes, was spectacular; but Owen Meany and I were not campers. On Lake Francis, the cries of the loons were so mournful that they frightened us; and the utter blackness of that empty lakeshore at night was terrifying. There was so much noise at night – insect, bird, and animal hoopla – that we couldn't sleep. One morning, we saw a moose.

'LET'S GO HOME, BEFORE WE SEE A BEAR,' said Owen Meany. 'BESIDES,' he said, 'I SHOULD SPEND A LITTLE TIME WITH HESTER.'

But when we left Lake Francis, he turned the pickup north – toward Quebec.

'WE'RE VERY CLOSE TO CANADA,' he said. 'I WANT TO SEE IT.'

At that particular border, there's little to see – just forests, for miles, and a thin road so beaten by the winter that it is bruised to the color of pencil lead and pockmarked with frost heaves. The border outpost – the customs house – was a cabin; the gate across the road was as flimsy and innocent-looking as the gate guarding a railroad crossing – in fact, it was raised. The Canadian customs officers at the border didn't pay any attention to us – although we parked the pickup truck about a hundred yards from the border, facing back toward the United States; then we lowered the tailgate of the truck and sat on it for a while, facing Canada. We sat there for half an hour before one of the Canadian customs officers walked a short distance in our direction and stood there, staring back at us.

No traffic passed us in either direction, and the dark fir

trees that towered on either side of the border indicated no special respect for national boundaries.

'I'M SURE IT'S A NICE COUNTRY TO LIVE IN,' said Owen Meany, and we drove home to Gravesend.

We had a modest going-away party for him at 80 Front Street; Hester and Grandmother were a trifle teary, but the overall tone of our celebration was jolly. Dan Needham – our historian – delivered a lengthy and unresolved meditation on whether Fort Benjamin Harrison was named after William Henry Harrison's father or grandson; Dan offered a similarly unresolved speculation on the origins of 'Hoosier,' which we all knew was a nickname for a native of Indiana – but no one knew what else, if anything, a 'Hoosier' was. Then we made Owen Meany stand in the dark inside the secret passageway, while Mr Fish recited, too loudly, the passage that Owen had always admired from Shakespeare's *Julius Caesar*.

' "Cowards die many times before their deaths; the valiant never taste of death but once," ' Mr Fish intoned.

'I KNOW! I KNOW! OPEN THE DOOR!' cried Owen Meany.

' "Of all the wonders that I have yet heard," ' said Mr Fish, ' "it seems to me the most strange that men should fear; seeing that death, a necessary end, will come when it will come." '

'OKAY! OKAY! I'M *NOT* AFRAID – BUT THERE ARE COBWEBS IN HERE! OPEN THE DOOR!' Owen cried.

Perhaps the darkness inspired him to insist that Hester and I follow him up to the attic. He wanted us to stand in the closet of Grandfather's clothes with him; but this time we were not playing the armadillo game – we had no flashlight – and we were not in danger of having Hester grab our doinks. Owen just wanted us all to stand there for a moment, in the dark.

'Why are we doing this?' Hester asked.

'SSSHHH! FORM A CIRCLE, HOLD HANDS!' he commanded. We did as we were told; Hester's hand was much bigger than Owen's

'Now what?' Hester asked.

'SSSHHH!' Owen said. We breathed in the mothballs; the old clothes stirred against themselves – the mechanisms of the old umbrellas were so rusty that the umbrellas, I was sure, could never be opened again; and the brims of the old hats were so dry that they would crack if anyone attempted to give shape to them. 'DON'T BE AFRAID,' said Owen Meany. That was all he had to say to us before he left for Indiana.

Several weeks went by before Hester and I heard from him; I guess they kept him pretty busy at Fort Benjamin Harrison. I would see Hester sometimes at night, along 'the strip' at Hampton Beach; usually, some guy was with her – rarely the same guy, and never anyone she bothered to introduce me to.

'Have you heard anything from him?' I would ask her.

'Nothing yet,' she'd say. 'Have you?'

When we heard from him, we heard together; his first letters weren't very special – he sounded more bored than overwhelmed. Hester and I probably put more effort into *talking* about those first letters than Owen had put into writing them.

There was a major who'd taken a liking to him; Owen said that his writing and editorial work for *The Grave* had provided him with a better background for what the Army seemed to want of him than anything he'd learned in ROTC, or in Basic Training. Hester and I agreed that Owen sounded despondent. He said simply: 'A GREAT DEAL HAS TO BE WRITTEN EVERY DAY.'

The second month he'd been away, or thereabouts, his letters were perkier. He was more optimistic about his orders; he'd heard some good things about Fort Huachuca, Arizona. All the talk at Fort Benjamin Harrison told him that Fort Huachuca was a fortunate place to be; he'd be working in the Adjutant's Office of the Strategic Communications Command – he'd been told that the major general who was in charge was 'flexible' on the subject of reassignments; the major general had been known to assist his junior officers with their requests for transfers.

When I started graduate school in the fall of '66, I was still looking for an apartment in Durham – or even in Newmarket, between Durham and Gravesend. I was looking halfheartedly, but – at twenty-four – I knew I had to admit to myself that what Owen had told me was true: that I was too old to be living with my stepfather or my grandmother.

'Why don't you move in with me?' Hester said. 'You'd have your own bedroom,' she added – unnecessarily.

When her two precious roommates had graduated, Hester had replaced only one of them; after all, Owen was there much of the time – Hester having only one roommate made it less awkward for Owen. When the one roommate had left to get married, Hester hadn't replaced her. My first anxiety about sharing an apartment with Hester was that Owen might disapprove.

'It was Owen's idea,' Hester told me. 'Didn't he write *you* about it?'

That letter came along, after he'd settled into Fort Huachuca.

'IF HESTER STILL DOESN'T HAVE A ROOMMATE, WHY DON'T YOU MOVE IN WITH HER?' he wrote. 'THAT WAY, I COULD CALL YOU BOTH – COLLECT! – AT THE SAME NUMBER.

'YOU SHOULD SEE FORT HUACHUCA! SEVENTY-THREE THOUSAND ACRES! PRAIRIE GRASSLAND, ELEVATION ABOUT FIVE THOUSAND FEET – EVERYTHING IS YELLOW AND TAN, EXCEPT THE MOUNTAINS IN THE DISTANCE ARE BLUE AND PURPLE AND EVEN PINK. THERE'S A FISHING LAKE JUST BEHIND THE OFFICERS' CLUB! THERE ARE ALMOST TWENTY THOUSAND PERSONNEL HERE, BUT THE FORT IS SO SPREAD OUT, YOU'D NEVER KNOW THEY WERE HERE – IT'S SIX MILES FROM THE WEST ENTRANCE OF THE FORT TO THE AIRFIELD, AND ANOTHER MILE TO THE HEADQUARTERS BARRACKS, AND YOU CAN GO EAST ANOTHER SIX MILES FROM THERE. I'M GOING TO START PLAYING TENNIS – I CAN TAKE FLYING LESSONS, IF I WANT TO! AND MEXICO IS ONLY TWENTY MILES AWAY! THE PRAIRIE IS NOT LIKE THE DESERT – BUT THERE ARE JOSHUA TREES AND PRICKLY PEAR, AND THERE ARE WILD PIGS CALLED *JAVELINA*, AND COYOTE. YOU KNOW WHAT COYOTES LIKE TO EAT *BEST*? HOUSE CATS!

'FORT HUACHUCA HAS THE LARGEST HORSE POPULATION OF ANY ARMY POST. THE HORSES AND THE TURN-OF-THE-CENTURY ARCHITECTURE OF THE OLD HOUSES, AND THE WOODEN BARRACKS, AND THE PARADE GROUNDS – WHICH ARE LEFT OVER FROM THE INDIAN WARS – MAKE EVERYTHING FEEL LIKE THE PAST. AND ALTHOUGH EVERYTHING IS HUGE, IT IS ALSO ISOLATED; THAT FEELS LIKE THE PAST, TOO.

'WHEN IT RAINS, YOU CAN SMELL THE CREOSOTE BUSHES. MOSTLY, IT'S SUNNY AND WARM – NOT TERRIBLY HOT; THE AIR IS DRIER THAN ANY PLACE I'VE EVER BEEN. BUT – *DON'T WORRY* – THERE ARE NO PALM TREES!'

And so I moved in with Hester. I quickly realized that I had done her a disservice – to think of her as slovenly. It was only herself she treated carelessly; she kept the shared rooms of the apartment fairly neat, and she even picked up my clothes and books – when I left them in the kitchen or in the living room. Even the roaches in the kitchen were not there out of any dirtiness that could be ascribed to Hester; and although she appeared to know a lot of guys, not one of them ever returned to the apartment and spent the night with her. She often came home quite late, but she always came home. I did not ask her if she was being 'faithful' to Owen Meany; I wanted to give her the benefit of the doubt – and besides: who could even guess what *Owen* was doing?

From his letters, we gathered he was doing a lot of *typing;* he was playing tennis, which Hester and I found unlikely – and he had actually taken a couple of flying lessons, which we found unbelievable. He complained that his room in the Bachelor Officers' Quarters – a dormitory-type room, with a private bath – was stifling. But he complained, for a while, of almost nothing else.

He confessed he was 'BUTTERING UP THE COMMANDER' – a certain Major General LaHoad. 'WE CALL HIM LATOAD,' Owen wrote, 'BUT HE'S A GOOD GUY. I COULD DO A LOT WORSE THAN END UP AS HIS AIDE-DE-CAMP – THAT'S THE ANGLE I'M SHOOTING. FORGIVE THE EXPRESSION – I'VE BEEN SHOOTING SOME POOL IN THE COMPANY DAY ROOM.

'TYPICAL ARMY: WHEN I ARRIVE AND REPORT TO THE STRATEGIC COMMUNICATIONS COMMAND, THEY TELL ME THERE'S BEEN A MISTAKE – THEY WANT ME IN THE PERSONNEL SECTION, INSTEAD. THEY CALL IT "PERSONNEL AND COMMUNITY ACTION" AT THE POST. I SIGN DISCHARGE PAPERS, I ATTEND THE OCS AND WARRANT OFFICER BOARDS – HAVE BEEN "RECORDER" FOR THE LATTER. SCARIEST THING I DO IS PLAY NIGHT WATCHMAN: I CARRY A FLASHLIGHT AND A MILITARY-POLICE

RADIO. IT TAKES TWO HOURS TO CHECK ALL THE LOCKS YOU THINK MIGHT BE JIMMIED AROUND THE FORT: THE SHOPS AND THE CLUBS AND THE STORAGE SHEDS, THE MOTOR POOL AND THE COMMISSARY AND THE AMMO DUMP. MEANWHILE, I KNOW THE EMERGENCY PROCEDURES IN THE STAFF DUTY OFFICER'S NOTEBOOK BY HEART – "UPON WARNING OF A NUCLEAR ATTACK YOU SHOULD NOTIFY . . ." AND SO FORTH.

'IDEALLY, MAJOR GENERAL LAHOAD WILL CHOOSE ME TO BE THE BARTENDER AT HIS PARTIES – AT THE LAST PARTY, I BROUGHT DRINKS TO HIS FLUFF OF A WIFE *ALL NIGHT;* STILL COULDN'T FILL HER UP, BUT SHE LIKED THE ATTENTION. SHE THINKS I'M "CUTE" – YOU KNOW THE TYPE. I FIGURE IF I COULD BE LATOAD'S AIDE-DE-CAMP – IF I COULD SWING IT – THE MAJOR GENERAL WOULD LOOK KINDLY UPON MY REQUEST FOR TRANSFER. THINK WHAT A BLOW IT WOULD BE TO THE PERSONNEL SECTION – HOW THEY WOULD MISS ME! TODAY I SIGNED A CHAPLAIN OUT ON LEAVE, AND I HELPED A HYSTERICAL MOTHER LOCATE HER SON IN THE SIGNAL GROUP – APPARENTLY, THE BAD BOY HADN'T WRITTEN HOME.

'SPEAKING OF HOME, I'M TAKING TEN DAYS' LEAVE FOR CHRISTMAS!'

And so Hester and I waited to see him. That October, President Johnson visited the U.S. troops in Vietnam; but we heard no further word from Owen Meany – concerning what progress or success he had encountered with his efforts to be reassigned. All Owen said was: 'MAJOR GENERAL LAHOAD IS THE KEY. I SCRATCH HIS BACK . . . YOU KNOW THE REST.'

It was December before he mentioned that he'd sent another Personnel Action Form to Washington, asking for transfer to Vietnam; those forms, as many times as he would submit them, were routed through his chain of command – including Major General LaHoad. By December, the major general had Owen working as a casualty assistance officer in the Personnel Section. Apparently, Owen had made a favorable impression upon some grieving Arizona family who had connections at the Pentagon; through the chain of command, the major general had received a special letter of commendation

– the Casualty Branch at the post had reason to be proud: a Second Leiutenant Paul O. Meany, Jr, had been of great comfort to the parents of a 2LT infantry type who'd been killed in Vietnam. Owen had been especially moving when he'd read the award citation for the Silver Star medal to the next of kin. Major General LaHoad had congratulated Owen personally.

At Fort Huachuca, the Casualty Branch was composed of Second Lieutenant Paul O. Meany, Jr, and a staff sergeant in his thirties – 'A DISGRUNTLED CAREER MAN,' according to Owen; but the staff sergeant had an Italian wife whose homemade pasta was 'SUCH AN IMPROVEMENT ON HESTER'S THAT IT MAKES THE STAFF SERGEANT OCCASIONALLY WORTH LISTENING TO.' In the Casualty Branch, the second lieutenant and the staff sergeant were assisted by 'A TWENTY-THREE-YEAR-OLD SPEC5 AND A TWENTY-TWO-YEAR-OLD SPEC4.'

'He might as well be talking about *insects* – for all I know!' Hester said. 'What the fuck is a "Spec Four" and a "Spec Five" – and how does he expect us to know what he's talking about?'

I wrote back to him. 'What exactly does a casualty assistance officer *do*?' I asked.

On the walls of the Casualty Branch Office at Fort Huachuca, Owen said there were maps of Arizona and Vietnam – and a roster of Arizona men who were prisoners of war or missing in action, along with the names of their next of kin. When the body of an Arizona man arrived from Vietnam, you went to California to escort the body home – the body, Owen explained, had to be escorted by a man of the same rank or higher; thus a private's body might be brought home by a sergeant, and a second lieutenant would escort the body of another second lieutenant or (let's say) of a warrant officer.

'Hester!' I said. 'He's delivering *bodies*! He's the one who brings the casualties home!'

'That's his line of work, all right,' Hester said. 'At least he's familiar with the territory.'

My 'line of work,' it seemed to me, was reading; my ambitions extended no further than to my choice of reading material. I *loved* being a graduate student; I loved my first teaching job, too – yet I felt I was so undaring. The very thought of bringing bodies home to their next of kin gave me the shivers.

In his diary, he wrote: 'THE OFFICE FOR THE CASUALTY BRANCH IS IN THE PART OF THE POST THAT WAS BUILT JUST AFTER BLACK JACK PERSHING'S EXPEDITION AGAINST PANCHO VILLA – OUR BUILDING IS OLD AND STUCCOED AND THE MINT-GREEN PAINT ON THE CEILING IS PEELING. WE HAVE A WALL POSTER DEPICTING ALL THE MEDALS THE ARMY OFFERS. WITH A GREASE PENCIL, ON TWO PLASTIC-COVERED CHARTS, WE WRITE THE NAMES OF THE WEEK'S CASUALTIES, ALONGSIDE THE ARIZONA PRISONERS OF WAR. WHAT THE ARMY CALLS ME IS A "CASUALTY ASSISTANCE OFFICER"; WHAT I AM IS A BODY ESCORT.'

'Jesus! Tell me all about it!' I said – when he was home on leave for Christmas.

'SO HOW DO YOU LIKE BEING A GRADUATE STUDENT?' he asked me. 'SO WHAT'S HE LIKE FOR A ROOMMATE?' he asked Hester. He was tan and fit-looking; maybe it was all the tennis. His uniform had only one medal on it.

'THEY GIVE IT TO EVERYONE!' said Owen Meany. On his left sleeve was a patch indicating his post, and on each shoulder epaulet was a brass bar signifying that he was a second lieutenant; on each collar was the brass U.S. insignia and the red-and-blue-striped silver shield of his branch: the Adjutant General's Corps. The MEANY name tag was the only other hardware on his uniform – there were no marksmanship badges, or anything else.

'NO OVERSEAS PATCH – I'M NOT MUCH TO LOOK AT,' he said shyly; Hester and I couldn't take our eyes off him.

'Are they really in plastic bags – the bodies?' Hester asked him.

'Do you have to check the contents of the bags?' I asked him.

'Are there sometimes just parts of a head and loose fingers and toes?' Hester asked him.

'I suppose this might change how you feel – about going over there?' I said to him.

'Do the parents *freak*?' Hester asked. 'And the wives – do you have to talk to the *wives*?'

He looked so awfully composed – he made us feel as if we'd never left school; of course, we hadn't.

'IT'S A WAY TO GO TO CALIFORNIA,' Owen said evenly. 'I FLY TO TUCSON. I FLY TO OAKLAND – IT'S THE ARMY BASE IN OAKLAND WHERE YOU GET YOUR BODY INSTRUCTIONS.'

'What are "body instructions," for Christ's sake?' Hester said; but Owen ignored her.

'SOMETIMES I FLY BACK FROM SAN FRANCISCO,' he said. 'EITHER WAY, I GO CHECK THE CONTAINER IN THE BAGGAGE AREA – ABOUT TWO HOURS BEFORE WE TAKE OFF.'

'You check the plastic bag?' I asked him.

'IT'S A PLYWOOD CONTAINER,' he said. 'THERE'S NO BAG. THE BODY IS EMBALMED. IT'S IN A CASKET. IN CALIFORNIA, I JUST CHECK THE PLYWOOD CONTAINER.'

'For what?' I said.

'FOR LEAKS,' he said. Hester looked as if she might throw up. 'AND THERE'S INFORMATION STAPLED TO THE CONTAINER – I JUST MATCH THAT UP WITH THE K.I.A. SHEET.'

' "K.I.A." – what's that?' I said.

'KILLED IN ACTION,' he said.

'Yes, of course,' I said.

'BACK IN ARIZONA, IN THE FUNERAL HOME – THAT'S WHEN I CHECK THE BODY,' he said.

'I don't want to hear any more,' Hester said.

'OKAY,' he said; he shrugged.

When we got away from Hester – we went to the Gravesend Academy gym to practice the shot, of course – I kept asking him about the bodies.

'USUALLY, YOU DISCUSS WITH THE MORTICIAN WHETHER OR NOT THE BODY IS SUITABLE FOR VIEWING – WHETHER OR NOT THE FAMILY SHOULD SEE IT,' he said. 'SOMETIMES THE FAMILY WANTS TO BE CLOSE TO YOU – THEY FEEL YOU'RE ONE OF THEM. OTHER TIMES, YOU GET THE FEELING YOU SHOULD KEEP OUT OF THEIR WAY – YOU HAVE TO PLAY THIS PART BY EAR. AND THEN THERE'S THE FOLDING OF THE FLAG – YOU GIVE THE FLAG TO THE MOTHER, USUALLY; OR TO THE WIFE, IF THERE'S A WIFE. THAT'S WHEN YOU GIVE YOUR LITTLE SPEECH.'

'What do you say?' I asked him.

He was dribbling the basketball, his head nodding almost

imperceptibly to the rhythm of the ball bouncing on the floor, his eyes always on the rim of the basket. ' "IT IS MY PRIVILEGE TO PRESENT TO YOU OUR COUNTRY'S FLAG IN GRATEFUL APPRECIATION FOR THE SERVICE RENDERED TO THIS NATION BY YOUR SON" – NATURALLY, YOU SAY "BY YOUR HUSBAND," IF YOU'RE GIVING THE FLAG TO A WIFE,' he added.

'Naturally,' I said; he passed me the ball.

'READY?' he said. He was already moving toward me – already timing his leap and, in his mind's eye, seeing the shot fall – when I passed the ball back to him.

Those were brief days and nights; we tried to remember which government spokesman had said that Operation Rolling Thunder was 'closing in on Hanoi.' That was what had prompted Owen to say: 'I THINK HANOI CAN HANDLE IT.'

According to the State Department – according to Dean Rusk – we were 'winning a war of attrition.' That was what prompted Owen to say: 'THAT'S NOT THE KIND OF WAR WE WIN.'

He had revised a few of his earlier views of our Vietnam policy. Some veterans of the war, whom he'd met at Fort Huachuca, had convinced him that Marshal Ky had *once* been popular, but now the Viet Cong was gaining the support of South Vietnamese peasants – because our troops had pulled out of the populated areas and were wasting their time chasing the North Vietnamese through the jungles and the mountains. Owen wanted to learn why our troops didn't pull back into the populated areas and wait for the North Vietnamese and the Viet Cong to come to *them*. If we were 'protecting' South Vietnam, why didn't we stay *with* the people and protect them?

On the other hand, it was confusing because many of the Vietnam veterans Owen had met were of the opinion that we should be fighting more 'all-out,' that we should bomb North Vietnam even *more*, mine the harbors, and make an amphibious landing north of the DMZ to cut the supply lines for the North Vietnamese Army – in short, fight to win. There was no way really to know what we should do if one didn't go over there and see it, Owen said, but he believed that trying to win a conventional war against North Vietnam was stupid. We should stay in South Vietnam and protect the South Vietnamese from North Vietnamese aggression, and from the Viet Cong – until such time as the South Vietnamese developed an army and, more important, a government that was strong and popular enough to make South Vietnam capable of protecting itself.

'Then the South Vietnamese will be able to attack North Vietnam all by themselves – is that what you mean?' Hester asked him. 'You make about as much sense as LBJ,' she said. Hester wouldn't say 'President Johnson.'

As for President Johnson, Owen said: 'THERE HAS NEVER BEEN A WORSE PRESIDENT – THERE *COULDN'T* BE A WORSE ONE, UNLESS THEY ELECT MCNAMARA.'

Hester talked about the 'Peace Movement.'

'*WHAT* "PEACE MOVEMENT" '? – OR DO YOU MEAN THE *DON'T-GET-DRAFTED* MOVEMENT? THAT'S THE ONLY "MOVEMENT" I SEE,' said Owen Meany.

We talked like the war itself, going nowhere. I moved out of the apartment, so that he could have some nights alone with Hester – I don't know if either of them appreciated it. I spent a few pleasant evenings with Dan and Grandmother.

I had convinced Grandmother to take the train, with me, to Sawyer Depot for Christmas; Grandmother had decided, previously, that she no longer took trains. It was arranged that Dan would take the Christmas Eve train from Gravesend, following the closing performance of *A Christmas Carol*. And Aunt Martha and Uncle Alfred had prevailed upon Hester to bring Owen to Sawyer Depot for Christmas – that was how significantly Owen had managed to impress them. Hester kept threatening to back out of these lavish reunion plans; I believe it was only for Owen's sake that she was agreeing to go home at all – especially for Christmas.

Then all these plans fell through. No one had noticed how severely the train service had been deteriorating; it turned out that it wasn't possible to take a train from Gravesend to Sawyer Depot – and on Christmas Eve, the stationmaster told Dan, it was impossible to take a train *anywhere*! And so we once more reverted to our isolated Christmases. On the day of Christmas Eve, Owen and I were practicing the shot in the Gravesend Academy gym and he told me he was simply spending a quiet Christmas with his parents; I was spending the day with Grandmother and Dan. Hester, according to Owen, had – on the spur of the moment – accepted an invitation to SOMEWHERE SUNNY.

'YOU OUGHT TO THINK ABOUT JOINING THE "PEACE MOVEMENT," OLD BOY,' he told me. I guess he had picked up the OLD BOY at Fort Huachuca. 'AS I UNDERSTAND IT, IT'S A GOOD WAY TO GET LAID. YOU JUST MAKE YOURSELF LOOK A LITTLE DISTRACTED – LOOKING ANGRY ALSO HELPS – AND YOU KEEP SAYING YOU'RE "AGAINST THE WAR." OF COURSE, I DON'T ACTUALLY KNOW ANYONE WHO'S *FOR* IT – BUT JUST KEEP SAYING YOU'RE "AGAINST THE WAR," AND LOOK AS IF THE WHOLE THING CAUSES YOU A LOT OF PERSONAL ANGUISH. NEXT THING YOU KNOW, YOU'LL GET LAID – YOU CAN COUNT ON IT!'

We just kept sinking the shot; it still takes my breath away to remember how good we were at it. I mean – *zip!* – he would pass me the ball. 'READY?' he would ask, and – *zip!* - I would pass it back to him and get ready to lift him. It was automatic; almost as soon as I passed him the ball, he was there – in my arms, and soaring. He didn't bother to yell 'TIME' - not anymore. We didn't bother to time ourselves; we were consistently under three seconds – we had no doubt about that – and sometimes I think we were faster.

'How many bodies a week are there?' I asked him.

'IN ARIZONA? I WOULD GUESS THAT WE AVERAGE TWO – AT THE MOST, THREE – CASUALTIES A WEEK. SOME WEEKS THERE AREN'T ANY, OR ONLY ONE. AND I WOULD ESTIMATE THAT ONLY HALF OF *OUR* CASUALTIES HAVE ANYTHING TO DO WITH VIETNAM – THERE ARE A LOT OF CAR ACCIDENTS. YOU KNOW, AND SOME SUICIDES.'

'What percentage of the bodies is not – how did you put it? – "suitable for viewing"?' I asked him.

'FORGET ABOUT THE BODIES,' Owen said. 'THEY'RE NOT YOUR PROBLEM – *YOUR* PROBLEM IS YOU'RE RUNNING OUT OF TIME. WHAT ARE YOU GOING TO DO WHEN YOU LOSE YOUR STUDENT DEFERMENT? DO YOU HAVE A PLAN? DO YOU EVEN KNOW WHAT YOU *WANT* TO DO – PROVIDED THERE'S A WAY TO DO IT? I DON'T SEE YOU BEING HAPPY IN THE ARMY. I *KNOW* YOU DON'T WANT TO GO TO VIETNAM. BUT I DON'T SEE YOU IN THE PEACE CORPS, EITHER. ARE YOU PREPARED TO GO TO CANADA? YOU DON'T LOOK PREPARED – NOT TO ME. YOU DON'T EVEN LOOK LIKE

MUCH OF A PROTESTER. YOU'RE PROBABLY THE ONE PERSON I KNOW WHO COULD JOIN WHAT HESTER CALLS THE "PEACE MOVEMENT" AND MANAGE *NOT* TO GET LAID. I DON'T SEE YOU HANGING OUT WITH THOSE ASSHOLES – I DON'T SEE YOU HANGING OUT WITH *ANYBODY*. WHAT I'M TELLING YOU IS, IF YOU WANT TO DO THINGS YOUR OWN WAY, YOU'RE GOING TO HAVE TO MAKE A *DECISION* – YOU'RE GOING TO HAVE TO FIND A LITTLE COURAGE.'

'I want to go on being a student,' I told him. 'I want to be a teacher. I'm just a *reader*,' I said.

'DON'T SOUND SO ASHAMED,' he said. 'READING IS A GIFT.'

'I learned it from you,' I told him.

'IT DOESN'T MATTER WHERE YOU LEARNED IT – IT'S A GIFT. IF YOU CARE ABOUT SOMETHING, YOU HAVE TO PROTECT IT – IF YOU'RE LUCKY ENOUGH TO FIND A WAY OF LIFE YOU LOVE, YOU HAVE TO FIND THE COURAGE TO *LIVE* IT.'

'What do *I* need courage for?' I asked him.

'YOU *WILL* NEED IT,' he told me. 'WHEN YOU'RE NOTIFIED TO REPORT FOR YOUR PREINDUCTION PHYSICAL, YOU'RE GOING TO NEED SOME COURAGE THEN. AFTER YOUR PHYSICAL – WHEN THEY PRONOUNCE YOU "FULLY ACCEPTABLE FOR INDUCTION" – IT WILL BE A LITTLE LATE TO MAKE A *DECISION* THEN. ONCE THEY CLASSIFY YOU ONE-A, A LOT OF GOOD A LITTLE COURAGE WILL DO YOU. BETTER THINK ABOUT IT, OLD BOY,' said Owen Meany.

He reported back to Fort Huachuca before New Year's Eve; Hester stayed away, wherever she was, and I spent New Year's Eve alone – Grandmother said she was too old to stay up to welcome in the New Year. I didn't drink too much, but I drank a little. Hester's damage to the rose garden was surely of the stature of a tradition; her absence, and Owen's, seemed ominous to me.

There were more than 385,000 Americans in Vietnam, and almost 7,000 Americans had been killed there; it seemed only proper to drink something for them.

When Hester returned from SOMEWHERE SUNNY, I refrained from commenting on her lack of a tan. There were more protests, more demonstrations; she didn't ask me to accompany her when she went off to them. Yet no one was allowed to spend the night with her in our apartment: when we talked about Owen, we talked about how much we loved him.

'Between how much you love him and whatever it is that you think of me, I sometimes wonder if you'll *ever* get laid,' Hester told me.

'I could always join the "Peace Movement," ' I told her. 'You know, I could simply make myself look a little distracted – looking angry also helps – and I could keep saying I am "against the war." Personal anguish – that's the key! I could convey a lot of personal anguish in regard to my anger "against the war" – next thing you know, I'll get laid!' Hester didn't even crack a smile.

'I've heard that one,' she said.

I wrote Owen that I had selected Thomas Hardy as the subject for my Master's thesis; I doubt he was surprised. I also told him that I had given much thought to his advice to me: that I should gather the courage to make a decision about what to do when faced with the loss of my draft deferment. I was trying to determine what sort of decision I might make – I couldn't imagine a very satisfying solution; and I was puzzled about what sort of COURAGE he'd imagined would be required of me. Short of my deciding to go to Vietnam, the other available decisions didn't strike me as requiring a great deal in the way of courage.

'You're always telling me I don't have any faith,' I wrote to Owen. 'Well – don't you see? – that's a part of what makes me so indecisive. I wait to see what will happen next – because I don't believe that anything I might decide to do would *matter*. You know Hardy's poem 'Hap' – I know you do. You remember . . . "How arrives it joy lies slaine,/And why unblooms the best hope ever sown?/ – Crass Casualty obstructs the sun and rain,/And dicing Time for gladness casts a moan . . ./These purblind Doomsters had as readily strown/ Blisses about my pilgrimage as pain." I know you know what that means: you believe in God but I believe in "Crass Casualty" – in *chance*, in *luck*. That's what I mean. You see? What *good* does it do to make whatever decision you're talking about? What good does courage do – when what happens next is up for grabs?'

Owen Meany wrote to me: 'DON'T BE SO CYNICAL – NOT EVERYTHING IS "UP FOR GRABS." YOU THINK

THAT ANYTHING YOU DECIDE TO DO DOESN'T *MATTER*? LET ME TELL YOU ABOUT THE BODIES. SAY YOU'RE LUCKY – SAY YOU NEVER GO TO VIETNAM, SAY YOU NEVER HAD A WORSE JOB THAN *MY* JOB. YOU HAVE TO TELL THEM HOW TO LOAD THE BODY ON THE AIRPLANE, AND HOW TO UNLOAD IT – YOU HAVE TO BE SURE THEY KEEP THE HEAD HELD HIGHER THAN THE FEET. IT'S PRETTY AWFUL IF ANY FLUID ESCAPES THROUGH THE ORIFICES – PROVIDED THERE ARE ANY ORIFICES.

'THEN THERE'S THE LOCAL MORTICIAN. PROBABLY HE NEVER KNEW THE DECEASED. EVEN SUPPOSING THAT THERE'S A WHOLE BODY – EVEN SUPPOSING THAT THE BODY ISN'T BURNED, AND THAT IT HAS A WHOLE NOSE, AND SO FORTH – NEITHER OF YOU KNOWS WHAT THE BODY *USED TO* LOOK LIKE. THE MORTUARY SECTIONS BACK AT THE COMMAND POSTS IN VIETNAM ARE NOT KNOWN FOR THEIR ATTENTION TO VERISIMILITUDE. IS THAT FAMILY GOING TO BELIEVE IT'S EVEN *HIM*? BUT IF YOU TELL THE FAMILY THAT THE BODY *ISN'T* "SUITABLE FOR VIEWING," HOW MUCH WORSE IS IT GOING TO BE FOR THEM? – JUST IMAGINING WHAT A HORRIBLE *THING* IS UNDER THE LID OF THAT CASKET. SO IF YOU SAY, "NO, YOU SHOULDN'T VIEW THE BODY," YOU FEEL YOU SHOULD ALSO SAY, "LISTEN, IT ISN'T REALLY *THAT* BAD." AND IF YOU LET THEM LOOK, YOU DON'T WANT TO BE THERE. SO IT'S A TOUGH DECISION. YOU'VE GOT A TOUGH DECISION, TOO – BUT IT'S NOT *THAT* TOUGH, AND YOU BETTER MAKE IT SOON.'

In the spring of 1967, when I received the notice from the local Gravesend draft board to report for my preinduction physical, I *still* wasn't sure what Owen Meany meant. 'You better call him,' Hester said to me; we kept reading the notice, over and over. 'You better find out what he means – in a hurry,' she said.

'DON'T BE AFRAID,' he told me. *DON'T* REPORT FOR YOUR PHYSICAL – DON'T DO *ANYTHING*,' he said. 'YOU'VE GOT A LITTLE TIME. I'M TAKING A LEAVE. I'LL BE THERE AS SOON AS I CAN MAKE IT. ALL YOU'VE GOT TO KNOW IS WHAT YOU *WANT*. DO YOU WANT TO GO TO VIETNAM?'

'No,' I said.

'DO YOU WANT TO SPEND THE REST OF YOUR LIFE IN CANADA – THINKING ABOUT WHAT YOUR COUNTRY *DID* TO YOU?' he asked me.

'Now that you put it that way – no,' I told him.

'FINE. I'LL BE RIGHT THERE – DON'T BE AFRAID. THIS TAKES JUST A LITTLE COURAGE,' said Owen Meany.

'*What* takes "just a little courage"?' Hester asked me.

It was a Sunday in May when he called me from the monument shop; U.S. planes had just bombed a power plant in Hanoi, and Hester had only recently returned from a huge antiwar protest rally in New York.

'What are you doing at the monument shop?' I asked him; he said he'd been helping his father, who had fallen behind on a few crucial orders. Why didn't I meet him there?

'Why don't we meet somewhere nicer – for a beer?' I asked him.

'I'VE GOT PLENTY OF BEER HERE,' he said.

It was odd to meet him in the monument shop on a Sunday. He was alone in that terrible place. He wore a surprisingly clean apron – and the safety goggles, loosely, around his neck. There was an unfamiliar smell in the shop – he had already opened a beer for me, and he was drinking one himself; maybe the beer was the unfamiliar smell.

'DON'T BE AFRAID,' Owen said.

'I'm not really afraid,' I said. 'I just don't know what to do.'

'I KNOW, I KNOW,' he said; he put his hand on my shoulder.

Something was different about the diamond wheel.

'Is that a new saw?' I asked him.

'JUST THE BLADE IS NEW,' he said. 'JUST THE DIAMOND WHEEL ITSELF.'

I had never seen it gleam so; the diamond segments truly sparkled.

'IT'S NOT JUST NEW – I *BOILED* IT,' he said. 'AND THEN I WIPED IT WITH ALCOHOL.' *That* was the unfamiliar smell! I thought – alcohol. The block of wood on the saw table looked new – the cutting block, we called it; it didn't have a nick in it. 'I SOAKED THE WOOD IN ALCOHOL AFTER I BOILED IT, TOO,' Owen said.

I've always been pretty slow; I'm the perfect reader! It

wasn't until I caught the whiff of a hospital in the monument shop that I realized what he meant by JUST A LITTLE COURAGE. Behind the diamond wheel was a workbench for the lettering and edging tools: it was upon this bench that Owen had laid out the sterile bandages, and the makings for a tourniquet.

'NATURALLY, THIS IS YOUR DECISION,' he told me.

'Naturally,' I said.

'THE ARMY REGULATION IN QUESTION STATES THAT A PERSON WOULD NOT BE PHYSICALLY QUALIFIED TO SERVE IN THE CASE OF THE ABSENCE OF THE FIRST JOINT OF EITHER THUMB, OR THE ABSENCE OF THE FIRST *TWO* JOINTS ON EITHER THE INDEX, MIDDLE, OR RING FINGER. I KNOW TWO JOINTS WILL BE TOUGH,' said Owen Meany, 'BUT YOU DON'T WANT TO BE WITHOUT A THUMB.'

'No, I don't,' I said.

'YOU UNDERSTAND THAT THE MIDDLE OR RING FINGER IS A LITTLE HARDER FOR *ME*: I SHOULD SAY IT'S HARDER FOR THE DIAMOND WHEEL TO BE AS *PRECISE* AS I WOULD LIKE TO BE – IN THE CASE OF EITHER A MIDDLE OR A RING FINGER. I WANT TO PROMISE YOU THERE'LL BE NO MISTAKE. THAT'S AN EASIER PROMISE FOR ME TO MAKE IF IT'S AN INDEX FINGER,' he said.

'I understand you,' I said.

'THE ARMY REGULATION DOESN'T STATE THAT BEING RIGHT-HANDED OR LEFT-HANDED MATTERS – BUT YOU'RE RIGHT-HANDED, AREN'T YOU?' he asked me.

'Yes,' I said.

'THEN I THINK IT OUGHT TO BE THE RIGHT INDEX FINGER – JUST TO BE SAFE, he said. 'I MEAN, OFFICIALLY, WE'RE TALKING ABOUT YOUR TRIGGER FINGER.'

I froze. He walked to the table under the diamond wheel and demonstrated how I should put my hand on the block of wood – but he didn't touch the wood; if he'd touched it, that would have spoiled his opinion that it was sterile. He made a fist, pinning his other fingers under his thumb, and he spread his index finger flat on its side. 'LIKE THIS,' he said. 'IT'S THE KNUCKLE OF YOUR MIDDLE FINGER YOU'VE GOT TO KEEP OUT OF MY WAY.' I couldn't speak, or move, and Owen Meany looked at me. 'BETTER HAVE ANOTHER BEER,' he said. 'YOU CAN BE A READER WITH ALL YOUR OTHER FINGERS – YOU CAN TURN THE PAGES WITH ANY OLD FINGER,' he said. He could see I didn't have the nerve for it.

'IT'S LIKE ANYTHING ELSE – IT'S LIKE LOOKING FOR YOUR FATHER. IT TAKES GUTS. AND FAITH,' he added. 'FAITH WOULD HELP. BUT, IN YOUR CASE, YOU SHOULD CONCENTRATE ON THE GUTS. YOU KNOW, I'VE BEEN THINKING ABOUT YOUR FATHER – YOU REMEMBER THE SO-CALLED LUST CONNECTION? WHOEVER HE WAS, YOUR FATHER MUST HAVE HAD THAT PROBLEM – IT'S SOMETHING YOU DON'T LIKE IN YOURSELF. WELL, WHOEVER HE WAS – I'M TELLING YOU – HE WAS PROBABLY AFRAID. THAT'S SOMETHING YOU DON'T LIKE IN YOURSELF, TOO. WHOEVER YOUR MOTHER WAS, I'LL BET SHE WAS NEVER AFRAID,' said Owen Meany. I not only couldn't speak, or move; I couldn't swallow. 'IF YOU'RE NOT GOING TO HAVE ANOTHER BEER,' he said, 'AT LEAST TRY TO FINISH THAT ONE!'

I finished it. He pointed to the sink.

'BETTER WASH YOUR HAND – SCRUB IT GOOD,' he said. 'AND THEN RUB ON THE ALCOHOL.'

I did as I was told.

'YOU'RE GOING TO BE FINE,' he said. 'I'LL HAVE YOU AT THE HOSPITAL IN FIVE MINUTES – UNDER TEN MINUTES, TOPS! WHAT'S YOUR BLOOD TYPE?' he asked me; I shook my head – I didn't know my blood type. Owen laughed. 'I KNOW WHAT IT IS – YOU DON'T REMEMBER *ANYTHING*! YOU'RE THE SAME TYPE AS ME! IF YOU NEED ANY, YOU CAN HAVE SOME OF MINE.' I couldn't move away from the sink.

'I WASN'T GOING TO TELL YOU THIS – I DIDN'T WANT TO WORRY YOU – BUT YOU'RE IN THE DREAM. I DON'T UNDERSTAND HOW YOU *COULD* BE IN IT, BUT YOU ARE – EVERY TIME, YOU'RE IN IT,' he said.

'In *your* dream?' I asked him.

'I KNOW YOU THINK IT'S "JUST A DREAM" – I KNOW, I KNOW – BUT IT BOTHERS ME THAT YOU'RE IN IT. I FIGURE,' said Owen Meany, 'THAT IF YOU DON'T GO TO VIETNAM, YOU *CAN'T* BE IN THAT DREAM.'

'You're absolutely crazy, Owen,' I told him; he shrugged – then he smiled at me.

'IT'S YOUR DECISION,' he told me.

I got myself from the sink to the saw table; the diamond wheel was so bright, I couldn't look at it. I put my finger on the block of wood. Owen started the saw.

'DON'T LOOK AT THE BLADE, AND DON'T LOOK AT YOUR FINGER,' he told me. 'LOOK RIGHT AT ME.' I shut my eyes when he put the safety goggles in place. 'DON'T SHUT YOUR EYES – THAT MIGHT MAKE YOU DIZZY,' he said. 'KEEP LOOKING AT ME. THE ONLY THING YOU SHOULD BE AFRAID OF IS *MOVING* – JUST DON'T MOVE,' he said. 'BY THE TIME YOU FEEL ANYTHING, IT WILL BE OVER.'

'I can't do it,' I said.

'DON'T BE AFRAID,' Owen told me. 'YOU CAN DO ANYTHING YOU WANT TO DO – IF YOU BELIEVE YOU CAN DO IT.'

The lenses of the safety goggles were very clean; his eyes were very clear.

'I LOVE YOU,' Owen told me. 'NOTHING BAD IS GOING TO HAPPEN TO YOU – TRUST ME,' he said. As he lowered the diamond wheel in the gantry, I tried to put the sound of it out of my mind. Before I felt anything, I saw the blood spatter the lenses of the safety goggles, through which his eyes never blinked – he was such an expert with that thing. 'JUST THINK OF THIS AS MY LITTLE GIFT TO YOU,' said Owen Meany.

9 : THE SHOT

Whenever I hear someone generalizing favorably about 'the sixties,' I feel like Hester, I feel like throwing up. I remember those ardent simpletons who said – and this was *after* the massacre of those 2,800 civilians in Hué, in '68 – that the Viet Cong and the North Vietnamese were our moral superiors. I remember a contemporary of mine asking me – with a killing lack of humor – if I didn't sometimes think that our whole generation took itself too seriously; and didn't I sometimes wonder if it was only the marijuana that made us more aware?

'MORE AWARE OF *WHAT*?' Owen Meany would have asked.

I remember the aggressiveness of the so-called flower children – yes, righteousness in the cause of peace, or in any other cause, *is* aggressive. And the mystical muddiness of so much of the thinking – I remember that, too; and talking to plants. And, with the exception of Owen Meany and the Beatles, I remember that there was precious little irony.

That's why Hester failed as a singer and as a songwriter – a deadly absence of irony. Perhaps this is also why she's so successful now: with the direction her music traveled, from folk to rock, and with the visual aid of those appalling rock videos – those lazy-minded, sleazy associations of 'images' that pass for narrative on all the rock-video television channels around the world – irony is no longer necessary. Only the name that Hester took for herself reflects the irony with which she was once so familiar – in her relationship with Owen Meany. As a folksinger, she was Hester Eastman – an earnest nobody, a flop. But as an aging hard-rock star, a fading queen of the grittiest and randiest sort of rock 'n' roll, she is *Hester the Molester*!

'Who would have believed it?' Simon says. ' "Hester the Molester" is a fucking household word. The bitch should pay me a commission - it was *my* name for her!'

That I am the first cousin of Hester the Molester distinguishes me among my Bishop Strachan students, who are otherwise inclined to view me as fussy and curmudgeonly – a cranky, short-haired type in his corduroys and tweeds, eccentric only in his political tempers and in his nasty habit of tamping the bowl of his pipe with the stump of his amputated index finger. And why not? My finger is a perfect fit; we handicapped people must learn to make the best of our mutilations and disfigurements.

When Hester has a concert in Toronto, my students who number themselves among her adoring fans always approach *me* for tickets; they know I'm good for a dozen or so. And that I attend Hester's occasional concerts here in the company of such attractive young girls allows me to infiltrate the crowd of raving-maniac rowdies unnoticed; that I come to her concerts as the escort of these young girls also makes me almost 'cool' in Hester's eyes.

'There's hope for you yet,' my cousin invariably says to me, while my students are crowding into her messy, backstage dressing room – naturally, speechless with awe at the sight of Hester in her typically lewd dishevelment.

'They're my *students*,' I reminded Hester.

'Don't let that stop you,' Hester tells me. And to one or more of my students, Hester always says: 'If you're worried about "safe sex," you ought to try it with *him*—' and she then lays her heavy paw upon my shoulder. 'He's a virgin, you know,' she tells my students. 'There's no one safer!'

And they titter and giggle at her joke – they think it *is* a joke. It's precisely the outrageous sort of joke that they would expect from Hester the Molester. I can tell: they don't even consider that Hester's claim – that I'm a virgin – might be *true*!

Hester knows it's true. I don't know why she finds my position offensive. After so many humiliating years of trying to lose my virginity, which no one but myself appeared even slightly interested in – hardly anyone has wanted to take it from me – I decided that, in the long run, my virginity was valuable only if I kept it. I don't think I'm a 'nonpracticing homosexual,' whatever that means. What has happened to me has simply *neutered* me. I just don't feel like 'practicing.'

Hester, in her own fashion, has remained a kind of virgin,

too. Owen Meany was the love of her life; after him, she never allowed herself to become so seriously involved.

She says: 'I like a young boy, every so often. In keeping with the times, you know, I'm in favor of "safe sex"; therefore, I prefer a virgin. And those young boys don't dare lie to me! And they're easy to say good-bye to – in fact, they're even kinda grateful. What could be better?' my cousin asks me. I have to smile back at her wicked smile.

Hester the Molester! I have all her albums, but I don't have a record player; I have all her tapes, too, but I don't own a tape deck – not even the kind that fits in a car. I don't even own a car. My students can be relied upon to keep me informed about Hester's new rock videos.

'Mister Wheelwright! Have you seen "Drivin' with No Hands"?' I shudder at the idea. Eventually, I see them all – you can't escape the damn things; Hester's rock videos are notorious. The Rev Katherine Keeling herself is addicted! She claims it's because her children watch them, and Katherine wants to keep up with whatever new atrocity is on her children's minds.

Hester's videos are truly ugly. Her voice has gotten louder, if not better; her accompanying music is full of electric bass and other vibrations that lower her nasal tones to the vocal equivalent of an abused woman crying for help from the bottom of an iron barrel. And the *visual* accompaniment is a mystifying blend of contemporary, carnal encounters with unidentified young boys intercut with black-and-white, documentary footage from the Vietnam War. Napalm victims, mothers cradling their murdered children, helicopters landing and taking off and crashing in the midst of perilous ground fire, emergency surgeries in the field, countless GI's with their heads in their hands – and Hester herself, entering and leaving different but similar hotel rooms, wherein a sheepish young boy is always just putting on or just taking off his clothes.

The age group of that young boy – especially, young *girls*! – thinks that Hester the Molester is both profound and humane.

'It's not like it's just her music, or her voice, you know – it's her whole *statement*,' one of my students told me; I felt so sick to my stomach that I couldn't speak.

'It's not even her lyrics – it's her whole, you know, like

commentary,' said another student. And these are *smart* girls – these are educated young women from sophisticated families!

I don't deny that Hester was damaged by what happened to Owen Meany; I'm sure she thinks she was damaged even more than I was damaged – and I wouldn't argue the point with her. We were both damaged by what happened to Owen; who cares about *more*? But what an irony it is that Hester the Molester has converted her damage into millions of dollars and fame – that out of Owen's suffering, and her own, Hester has made a mindless muddle of sex and protest, which young girls who have *never* suffered feel they can 'relate to.'

What would Owen Meany have said about that? I can only imagine how Owen would have critiqued one of Hester the Molester's rock videos:

'HESTER, ONE WOULD NEVER SUSPECT – FROM THIS MINDLESS MESS – THAT YOU WERE A MUSIC MAJOR, AND A SOCIALIST. ONE WOULD TEND TO CONCLUDE – UPON THE EVIDENCE OF THIS DISJOINTED *WALLOWING* – THAT YOU WERE BORN TONE-DEAF, AND THAT YOU ARE DRAWING, ALMOST EXCLUSIVELY, UPON YOUR EXPERIENCES AS A *WAITRESS*!'

And what would Owen Meany have made of the crucifixes? Hester the Molester likes crucifixes, or else she likes to mock them – all kinds, all sizes; around her neck and in her ears. Occasionally, she even wears one in her nose; her right nostril is pierced.

'Are you Catholic?' an interviewer asked her once.

'Are you kidding?' Hester said.

The English major in me must point out that Hester has an ear for titles, if not for music.

'Drivin' with No Hands'; 'Gone to Arizona'; 'No Church, No Country, No More'; 'Just Another Dead Hero'; 'I Don't Believe in No Soul'; 'You Won't See Me at His Funeral'; 'Life After You'; 'Why the Boys Want Me'; 'Your Voice Convinces Me'; 'There's No Forgettin' Nineteen Sixty-eight.'

I've got to admit, Hester's titles were catchy; and she has as much of a right as I have to interpret the silence that Owen Meany left behind. I should be careful not to generalize 'the silence'; in my case, Owen didn't leave me in absolute peace and quiet. Twice, in fact, Owen has let me hear from him –

I mean, in both cases, that he let me hear from him *after* he was gone.

Most recently – only this August – I heard from him in a manner typical of Owen; which is to say, in a manner open to interpretation and dispute.

I was staying up late at 80 Front Street, and I confess that my senses were impaired; Dan Needham and I were enjoying our usual vacation – we were drinking too much. We were recalling the measures we took, years ago, to allow Grandmother to go on living at 80 Front Street as long as possible; we were remembering the incidents that finally led us to commit Grandmother to the Gravesend Retreat for the Elderly. We hated to do it, but she left us no choice; she drove Ethel crazy – we couldn't find a maid, or a nurse, whom Grandmother couldn't drive crazy. After Owen Meany was gone, everyone was too dull-witted to keep Harriet Wheelwright company.

For years, her groceries had been delivered by the Poggio brothers – Dominic Poggio, and the dead one, whose name I no longer remember. Then the Poggios stopped making all home deliveries. Out of fondness for my grandmother – who was his oldest-living customer, and his only customer who always paid her bills on time – Dominic Poggio generously offered to continue to make deliveries to 80 Front Street.

Was Grandmother appreciative of Dominic's generosity? She was not only *un*appreciative; she could not remember that the Poggios didn't deliver to anyone else – that they were doing her a special favor. People had always done special favors for Harriet Wheelwright; Grandmother took such treatment for granted. And she was not only unappreciative; she was complaining. She telephoned Dominic Poggio almost daily, and she upbraided him that his delivery service was going to the dogs. In the first place, she reproached him, the delivery boys were 'total strangers.' They were nothing of the kind; they were Dominic Poggio's grandchildren – my grandmother simply forgot who they were, and that she had seen them delivering her groceries for years. Furthermore, my grandmother complained, these 'total strangers' were guilty of *startling* her – she had no fondness for surprises, she reminded poor Dominic.

Couldn't the Poggios telephone her before they made their frightening deliveries? Grandmother asked. That way she would at least be forewarned that the total strangers were coming.

Dominic agreed. He was a sweet man who cherished my grandmother; also, probably, he had wrongly predicted that she would die any day now – and he would, he'd imagined, be rid of this nuisance.

But Grandmother lived on and on. When the Poggios called her and told her that the delivery boys were on their way, my grandmother thanked them politely, hung up the telephone, and promptly forgot that anyone was coming – or that she'd been forewarned. When the boys would 'startle' her, she would telephone Dominic in a rage and say: 'If you're going to send *total strangers* to this house, you might at least have the courtesy to *warn* me when they're coming!'

'Yes, Missus Wheelwright!' Dominic always said. Then he would call Dan to complain; he even called me a few times – in Toronto!

'I'm getting worried about your grandmother, John,' Dominic would say.

By this time, Grandmother had lost all her hair. She owned a chest of drawers that was full of wigs, and she abused Ethel – and several of Ethel's replacements – by complaining that her wigs were badly treated by the chest of drawers, in addition to being inexpertly attached to her old bald head by Ethel and the others. Grandmother developed such contempt for Ethel – and for Ethel's inept replacements – that she plotted with considerable cunning to undermine what she regarded as the already woefully inadequate abilities of her serving women. They were no match for her. Grandmother *hid* her wigs so that these luckless ladies could not find them: then she would abuse these fools for misplacing her vital headpieces.

'Do you actually expect me to wander the world as if I were an addlepated bald woman escaped from the circus?' she would say.

'Missus Wheelwright – where did you put your wigs?' the women would ask her.

'Are you actually accusing me of *intentionally* desiring to look like the lunatic victim of a nuclear disaster?' my grandmother would ask them. 'I would rather be murdered by a maniac than be *bald*!'

More wigs were bought; most – but by no means all – of

her old wigs were found. When Grandmother especially disliked a wig, she would retire it in the rose garden by submerging it in the birdbath.

And when the Poggios continued to send total strangers to her door – intent on startling her – Harriet Weelwright responded by startling them in return. She would dart to open the door for them – sprinting ahead of Ethel or Ethel's replacements – and she would greet the terrified delivery boys by snatching her wig off her head and shrieking at them while she was bald.

Poor Dominic Poggio's grandchildren! How they fought among themselves *not* to be the boy who delivered the groceries to 80 Front Street.

It was shortly after the fourth or fifth such incident when Dan telephoned me – in Toronto – and said: 'It's about your grandmother. You *know* how much I love her. But I think it's time.'

Even this August, the memory of those days made Dan Needham and me laugh. It was late at night, and we'd been drinking – as usual.

'Do you know what?' Dan said. 'There are *still* all those damn jams and jellies and some simply awful things that she had *preserved* – they're still on those shelves, in the secret passageway!'

'Not really!' I said.

'Yes, really! See for yourself,' he said. Dan tried to get out of his chair – to investigate the mysteries of the secret passageway with me – but he lost his balance in the great effort he made to rise to his feet, and he settled back into his chair apologetically. 'See for yourself!' he repeated, burping.

I had some difficulty opening the concealed door; I don't think that door had been opened for years. I knocked a few books off the shelves on the door while I was fumbling with the lock and key. I was reminded that Germaine had once been no less clumsy – when Lydia had died, and Germaine had chosen the secret passageway as the place to hide from Death itself.

Then the door swung open. The secret passageway was dark; yet I could discern the scurrying of spiders. The cobwebs were dense. I remembered when I'd trapped Owen in the secret passageway and he'd cried out that something wet was licking him – he didn't think it was a cobweb, he thought it was SOMETHING WITH A TONGUE. I also remembered the time we'd shut him in there during his going-away party, when Mr Fish had recited those lines from *Julius Caesar* – just outside the closed door. 'Cowards die many times before their deaths; the valiant never taste of death but once' – and so forth. And I remembered how Owen and I had scared Germaine in there – and poor Lydia, before Germaine.

There were a lot of old memories lurking in the cobwebs in the secret passageway; I groped for the light switch, and couldn't find it. I didn't want to touch those dark objects on the shelves without seeing what they were.

Then Dan Needham shut the door on me.

'Cut it out, Dan!' I cried. I could hear him laughing. I reached out into the blackness. My hand found one of the shelves; I felt along the shelf, passing through cobwebs, in the direction of the door. I thought the light switch was near the door. That was when I put my hand on something *awful*. It felt springy, alive – I imagined a nest of newly born rats! – and I stepped backward and screamed.

What my hand had found was one of Grandmother's hidden wigs; but I didn't know that. I stepped too far back, to the edge of the top step of the long stairs; I felt myself losing my balance and starting to fall. In less than a second, I imagined how Dan would discover my body on the dirt floor at the foot of the stairs – when a small, strong hand (or something like a small, strong hand) *guided* my own hand to the light switch; a small, strong hand, or something like it, *pulled* me forward from where I teetered on the top step of the stairs. And his voice – it was unmistakably Owen's voice – said 'DON'T BE AFRAID, NOTHING BAD IS GOING TO HAPPEN TO YOU.'

I screamed again.

When Dan Needham opened the door, it was his turn to scream. 'Your *hair*!' he cried. When I looked in a mirror, I thought it was the cobwebs – my scalp appeared to have been dusted with flour. But when I brushed my hair, I saw that the roots had turned white. That was this August: my hair has grown in all-white since then. At my age, my hair was already turning gray; even my students think that my white hair is distinguished – an improvement.

The morning after Owen Meany 'spoke' to me, Dan Needham said: 'Of course, we were both drunk – *you*, especially.'

'*Me*, "especially"!' I said.

'That's right,' Dan said. 'Look: I have never mocked your belief – have I? I will never make fun of your religious faith – you know that. But you can't expect *me* to believe that Owen Meany's *actual hand* kept you from falling down those cellar stairs; you can't expect me to be convinced that Owen Meany's *actual voice* "spoke" to you in the secret passageway.'

'Dan,' I said, 'I understand you. I'm not a proselytizer, I'm no evangelist. Have I ever tried to make you a believer? If I wanted to *preach*, I'd be a minister, I'd have a congregation – wouldn't I?'

'Look: I understand you,' Dan said; but he couldn't stop staring at the snow-white roots of my hair.

A little later, Dan said: 'You actually felt *pulled* – you felt an actual tug, as if from an actual hand?'

'I admit I was drunk' I said.

And a little later, Dan said: 'It was *his* voice – you're sure it wasn't something I said that you heard? It was *his* voice?'

I replied rather testily: 'How many voices have you heard, Dan, that could ever be mistaken for *his* voice?'

'Well, we were both drunk – weren't we? That's my point,' Dan Needham said.

I remember the summer of 1967, when my finger was healing – how that summer slipped away. That was the summer Owen Meany was promoted; his uniform would look a little different when Hester and I saw him again – he would be a first lieutenant. The bars on his shoulder epaulets would turn from brass to silver. He would also help me begin my Master's thesis on Thomas Hardy. I had much trouble beginning anything – and, according to Owen, even more trouble seeing something through.

'YOU MUST JUST PLUNGE IN,' Owen wrote to me. 'THINK OF HARDY AS A MAN WHO WAS ALMOST RELIGIOUS, AS A MAN WHO CAME SO CLOSE TO BELIEVING IN GOD THAT WHEN HE REJECTED GOD, HIS REJECTION MADE HIM FEROCIOUSLY BITTER. THE KIND OF FATE HARDY BELIEVES IN IS ALMOST LIKE BELIEVING IN GOD – AT LEAST IN THAT TERRIBLE, JUDGMENTAL GOD OF THE OLD TESTAMENT. HARDY HATES INSTITUTIONS: THE CHURCH – MORE THAN FAITH OR BELIEF – AND CERTAINLY MARRIAGE (THE INSTITUTION OF IT), AND THE

INSTITUTION OF EDUCATION. PEOPLE ARE HELPLESS TO FATE, VICTIMS OF TIME – THEIR OWN EMOTIONS UNDO THEM, AND SOCIAL INSTITUTIONS OF ALL KINDS FAIL THEM.

'DON'T YOU SEE HOW A BELIEF IN SUCH A BITTER UNIVERSE IS NOT UNLIKE RELIGIOUS FAITH? LIKE FAITH, WHAT HARDY BELIEVED WAS NAKED, PLAIN, VULNERABLE. BELIEF IN GOD, OR A BELIEF THAT – EVENTUALLY – *EVERYTHING* HAS TRAGIC CONSEQUENCES . . . EITHER WAY, YOU DON'T LEAVE YOURSELF ANY ROOM FOR PHILOSOPHICAL DETACHMENT. EITHER WAY, YOU'RE NOT BEING VERY CLEVER. NEVER THINK OF HARDY AS *CLEVER*; NEVER CONFUSE FAITH, OR BELIEF – OF ANY KIND – WITH SOMETHING EVEN REMOTELY INTELLECTUAL.

'PLUNGE IN – JUST BEGIN. I'D BEGIN WITH HIS NOTES, HIS DIARIES – HE NEVER MINCED WORDS THERE. EVEN EARLY – WHEN HE WAS TRAVELING IN FRANCE, IN 1882 – HE WROTE: "SINCE I DISCOVERED SEVERAL YEARS AGO, THAT I WAS LIVING IN A WORLD WHERE NOTHING BEARS OUT IN PRACTICE WHAT IT PROMISES INCIPIENTLY, I HAVE TROUBLED MYSELF VERY LITTLE ABOUT THEORIES. I AM CONTENT WITH TENTATIVENESS FROM DAY TO DAY." YOU COULD APPLY THAT OBSERVATION TO EACH OF HIS NOVELS! THAT'S WHY I SAY HE WAS "ALMOST RELIGIOUS" – BECAUSE HE WASN'T A GREAT THINKER, HE WAS A GREAT *FEELER*!

'TO BEGIN, YOU SIMPLY TAKE ONE OF HIS BLUNT OBSERVATIONS AND PUT IT TOGETHER WITH ONE OF HIS MORE *LITERARY* OBSERVATIONS – YOU KNOW, ABOUT THE CRAFT. I LIKE THIS ONE: "A STORY MUST BE EXCEPTIONAL ENOUGH TO JUSTIFY ITS TELLING. WE STORYTELLERS ARE ALL ANCIENT MARINERS, AND NONE OF US IS JUSTIFIED IN STOPPING WEDDING GUESTS, UNLESS HE HAS SOMETHING MORE UNUSUAL TO RELATE THAN THE ORDINARY EXPERIENCES OF EVERY AVERAGE MAN AND WOMAN."

'YOU SEE? IT'S EASY. YOU TAKE HIS HIGH STANDARDS FOR STORIES THAT ARE "EXCEPTIONAL" AND YOU PUT THAT TOGETHER WITH HIS BELIEF THAT "NOTHING BEARS OUT IN PRACTICE WHAT IT

PROMISES INCIPIENTLY," AND THERE'S YOUR THESIS! ACTUALLY, THERE IS *HIS* THESIS - ALL *YOU* HAVE TO DO IS FILL IN THE EXAMPLES. PERSONALLY, I'D BEGIN WITH ONE OF THE BITTEREST – TAKE ALMOST ANYTHING FROM *JUDE THE OBSCURE*. HOW ABOUT THAT TERRIBLE LITTLE PRAYER THAT JUDE REMEMBERS FALLING ASLEEP TO, WHEN HE WAS A CHILD?

> 'TEACH ME TO LIVE, THAT I MAY DREAD
> 'THE GRAVE AS LITTLE AS MY BED.
> 'TEACH ME TO DIE . . .

'WHAT COULD BE EASIER?' wrote Owen Meany.

And thus – having cut off my finger and allowed me to finish graduate school – he started my Master's thesis for me, too.

This August in Gravesend – where I try to visit every August – Dan's students in the summer school were struggling with Euripides; I told Dan that I thought he'd made an odd and merciless choice. For students the age of my Bishop Strachan girls to spend seven weeks of the summer memorizing *The Medea* and *The Trojan Women* must have been an exercise in tedium – and one that risked disabusing the youngsters of their infatuation with the stage.

Dan said: 'What was I going to do? I had twenty-five kids in the class and only six boys!' Indeed, those boys looked mightily overworked as it was; a particularly pallid young man had to be Creon in one play and Poseidon in the other. All the girls were shuffled in and out of the Chorus of Corinthian Women and the Chorus of Trojan Women as if Corinthian and Trojan women possessed an interchangable shrillness. I was quite taken by the dolorous girl Dan picked to play Hecuba; in addition to the sorrows of her role, she had to physically remain on the stage for the entirety of *The Trojan Women*. Therefore, Dan rested her in *The Medea;* he gave her an especially rueful but largely silent part in the Chorus of Corinthian Women – although he singled her out at the end of the play; she was clearly one of his better actresses, and Dan was wise to emphasize those end lines of the Chorus by having his girl speak solo.

' "Many things the gods achieve beyond our judgment," ' said the sorrowful girl. ' "What we thought is not confirmed and what we thought not God contrives." '

How true. Not even Owen Meany would dispute that.

I sometimes envy Dan his ability to teach *onstage*; for the theater is a great emphasizer – epecially to young people, who have no great experience in life by which they might judge the experiences they encounter in literature; and who have no great confidence in language, neither in using it nor in hearing it. The theater, Dan quite rightly claims, dramatizes both the experience and the confidence in language that young people – such as our students – lack. Students of the age of Dan's, and mine, have no great feeling – for example – for *wit*; wit simply passes them by, or else they take it to be an elderly form of snobbery; a mere showing off with the language that they use (at best) tentatively. Wit isn't tentative; therefore, neither is it young. Wit is one of many aspects of life and literature that is far easier to recognize onstage than in a book. My students are always missing the wit in what they read, or else they do not trust it; onstage, even an amateur actor can make anyone *see* what wit is.

August is my month to talk about teaching with Dan. When I meet Dan for Christmas, when we go together to Sawyer Depot, it is a busy time and there are always other people around. But in August we are often alone: as soon as the summer-school theater productions are over, Dan and I take a vacation together – although this usually means that we stay in Gravesend and are no more adventuresome than to indulge in day trips to the beach at Little Boar's Head. We spend our evenings at 80 Front Street, just talking; since Dan moved, in, the television has been gone. When Grandmother went to the Gravesend Retreat for the Elderly, she took her television set with her; when Grandmother died, she left the house at 80 Front Street to Dan and me.

It is a huge and lonely house for a man who's never even considered remarrying; but the house contains almost as much history for Dan as it holds for me. Although I enjoy my visits, not even the tempting nostalgia of the house at 80 Front Street could entice me to return to the United States. This is a subject – my return – that Dan broaches every August, always on an evening when it is clear to him that I am enjoying the atmosphere of 80 Front Street, and his friendship.

'There's more than enough room here for a couple of old bachelors like us,' he says. 'And with your years of experience at Bishop Strachan – not to mention the recommendation I'm sure your headmistress would write for you, not to mention that you're a distinguished alumnus – of course the Gravesend Academy English Department would be happy to have you. Just say the word.'

Not to be polite, but out of my affection for Dan, I let the subject pass.

This August, when he started that business again, I simply said: 'How hard it is – without the showplace of the stage – to teach wit to teenagers. I despair that another fall is almost upon me and once again I shall strive to make my Grade Ten girls notice something in *Wuthering Heights* besides every little detail about Catherine and Heathcliff – the story, the story; it is all they are interested in!'

'John, dear John,' Dan Needham said. 'He's been dead for twenty years. Forgive it. Forgive and forget – and come home.'

'There's a passage right at the beginning – they miss it every year!' I said. 'I'm referring to Lockwood's description of Joseph, I've been pointing it out to them for so many years that I know the passage by heart: "looking . . . in my face so sourly that I charitably conjectured he must have need of divine aid to digest his dinner . . ." I've even read this aloud to them, but it sails right over their heads – they don't crack a smile! And it's not just Emily Brontë's wit that whistles clean past them. They don't get it when it's contemporary. Is Mordecai Richler too witty for eleventh-grade girls? It would appear so. Oh yes, they think *The Apprenticeship of Duddy Kravitz* is "funny"; but they miss half the humor! You know that description of the middle-class Jewish resort? It's always *description* that they miss; I swear, they think it's unimportant. They want dialogue, they want action; but there's so much *writing* in the description! "There were still some pockets of Gentile resistance, it's true. Neither of the two hotels that were still in their hands admitted Jews but that, like the British raj who still lingered on the Malabar Coast, was not so discomforting as it was touchingly defiant." Every year I watch their *faces* when I read to them – they don't bat an eye!'

'John,' Dan said. 'Let bygones be bygones – not even Owen would *still* be angry. Do you think Owen Meany would have blamed the whole country for what happened to him? That was madness; this is madness, too.'

'How do you teach madness onstage?' I asked Dan. '*Hamlet*, I suppose, for starters – I give *Hamlet* to my Grade Thirteen girls, but they have to make do with reading it; they don't get to see it. And *Crime and Punishment* – even my Grade Thirteen girls struggle with the so-called "psychological" novel. The "concentrated wretchedness" of Raskolnikov is entirely within their grasp, but they don't see how the novel's psychology is at work in even Dostoevski's simplest descriptions; once again, it's the description they miss. Raskolnikov's landlord, for example – "his face seemed to be thickly covered with oil, like an old iron lock." What a perfect face for his landlord to have! "Isn't that marvelous?" I ask the class; they stare at me as if they think I'm crazier than Raskolnikov.'

Dan Needham, occasionally, stares at me that way, too. How could he possibly think I could 'forgive and forget'? There is too much forgetting. When we schoolteachers worry that our students have no sense of history, isn't it what people forget that worries us? For years I tried to forget who my father might be; I didn't want to find out who he was, as Owen pointed out. How many times, for example, did I call back my mother's old singing teacher, Graham McSwiney? How many times did I call him and ask him if he'd learned the whereabouts of Buster Freebody, or if he'd remembered anything about my mother that he hadn't told Owen and me? Only once; I called him only once. Graham McSwiney told me to forget about who my father was; I was willing.

Mr McSwiney said: 'Buster Frebody – if he's alive, if you find him – would be so old that he wouldn't even remember your mother - not to mention who her boyfriend was!' Mr McSwiney was much more interested in Owen Meany – in why Owen's voice hadn't changed. 'He should see a doctor – there's really no good *reason* for a voice like his,' Graham McSwiney said.

But, of course, there *was* a reason. When I learned what the reason was, I never called Mr McSwiney to tell him; I doubt it would have been a scientific enough explanation for Mr McSwiney. I tried to tell Hester, but Hester said she didn't want to know. 'I'd believe what you'd tell me,' Hester said, 'so please spare me the details.'

As for the *purpose* of Owen Meany's voice, and everything

that happened to him, I told only Dan and the Rev. Lewis Merrill. 'I suppose it's possible,' Dan said. 'I suppose stranger things have happened – although I can't, off the top of my head, think of an example. The important thing is that *you* believe it, and I would never challenge your right to believe what you want.'

'But do *you* believe it?' I asked him.

'Well, I believe *you*,' Dan said.

'How can you *not* believe it?' I asked Pastor Merrill. 'You of all people,' I told him. 'A man of faith – how can you *not* believe it?'

'To believe it – I mean all of it,' the Rev. Lewis Merrill said, '—to believe everything . . . well, that calls upon more faith than I have.'

'But you of all people!' I said to him. 'Look at me – I never was a believer, not until this happened. If *I* can believe it, why can't you?' I asked Mr Merrill. He began to stutter.

'It's *easier* for you to j-j-j-just accept it. Belief is not something you have felt, and then *not* felt; you haven't l-l-l-lived with belief, and with *un*belief. It's *easier* f-f-f-for you,' the Rev. Mr Merrill repeated. 'You haven't ever been f-f-f-full of faith, *and* full of d-d-d-doubt. Something j-j-j-just strikes you as a miracle, and you believe it. For me, it's not that s-s-s-simple,' said Pastor Merrill.

'But it *is* a miracle!' I cried. 'He told you that dream – I know he did! And you were there – when he saw his name, *and* the date of his death, on Scrooge's grave. You were *there*!' I cried. 'How can you doubt that he *knew*?' I asked Mr Merrill. 'He *knew* – he knew *everything*! What do you call that – if you don't call it a miracle?'

'You've witnessed what you c-c-c-call a miracle and now you believe – you believe everything,' Pastor Merrill said. 'But miracles don't c-c-c-*cause* belief – real miracles don't m-m-m-make faith out of thin air; you have to *already have faith* in order to believe in *real* miracles. I believe that Owen was extraordinarily g-g-g-*gifted* – yes, gifted and powerfully sure of himself. No doubt he suffered some powerfully disturbing visions, too – and he was certainly emotional, he was very emotional. But as to knowing what he appeared to "know" – there are other examples of p-p-p-precognition; not every example is necessarily ascribed to *God*. Look at you – you never even believed in G-G-G-God; you've said so, and here you are ascribing to the h-h-h-hand of God *everything* that happened to Owen M-M-M-Meany!'

This August, at 80 Front Street, a dog woke me up. In the deepest part of my sleep, I heard the dog and thought it was Sagamore; then I thought it was *my* dog – I used to have a dog, in Toronto – and only when I was wide awake did I catch up to myself, in the present time, and realize that both Sagamore and my dog were dead. It used to be nice to have a dog to walk in Winston Churchill Park; perhaps I should get another.

Out on Front Street, the strange dog barked and barked. I got out of bed; I took the familiar walk along the dark hall to my mother's room – where it is always lighter, where the curtains are never drawn. Dan sleeps in my grandmother's former bedroom – the official master bedroom of 80 Front Street, I suppose.

I looked out my mother's window but I couldn't see the dog. Then I went into the den – or so it had been called when my grandfather had been alive. Later, it was a kind of children's playroom, the room where my mother had played the old Victrola, where she had sung along with Frank Sinatra and the Tommy Dorsey Orchestra. It was on the couch in that room where Hester had spread herself out, and waited, while Noah and Simon and I searched all of 80 Front Street, in vain, for Owen Meany. We'd never learned where she'd hidden him, or where he'd hidden himself. I lay down on that old couch and remembered all of that. I must have fallen asleep there; it was a vastly historical couch, upon which – I also remembered – my mother had first whispered into my ear: 'My little fling!'

When I woke up, my right hand had drifted under one of the deep couch cushions: my wrist detected something there – it felt like a playing card, but when I extracted it from under the cushion, I saw that it was a relic from Owen Meany's long-ago collection: a very old and bent baseball card. Hank Bauer! Remember him? The card was printed in 1950 when Bauer was twenty-eight, in only his second full season as an outfielder for the Yankees. But he looked older; perhaps it was the war – he left baseball for World War Two, then he returned to the game. Not being a baseball fan, I nevertheless remembered Hank Bauer as a reliable, unfancy player – and, indeed, his slightly tired, tanned face reflected his solid work ethic. There was nothing of the hotshot in his patient smile, and he wasn't hiding his eyes under the visor of his baseball cap, which was pushed well back on his head, revealing his thoughtful, wrinkled brow. It was one of those old photographs wherein the color was optimistically added – his tan was too tan, the sky too blue, the clouds too uniformly white. The high, fluffy clouds and the brightness of the blue sky created such a strikingly unreal background for Mr Bauer in his white, pin-striped uniform – it was as if he had died and gone to heaven.

Of course I knew then where Hester had hidden Owen Meany; he'd been *under* the couch cushions – and under *her*! – all the while we were searching. That explained why his appearance had been so rumpled, why his hair had looked slept on. The Hank Bauer card must have fallen out of his pocket. Discoveries like this – not to mention, Owen's voice 'speaking' to me in the secret passageway, and his hand (or something like a hand) seeming to take hold of me – occasionally make me afraid of 80 Front Street.

I know that Grandmother was afraid of the old house, near the end. 'Too many ghosts!' she would mutter. Finally, I think, she was happy *not* to be 'murdered by a maniac' – a condition she had once found favorable to being removed from 80 Front Street. She left the old house rather quietly when she left; she was philosophic about her departure. 'Time to leave,' she said to Dan and me. 'Too many ghosts!'

At the Gravesend Retreat for the Elderly, her decline was fairly swift and painless. At first she forgot all about Owen, then she forgot me; nothing could remind her even of my mother – nothing except my fairly expert imitation of Owen's voice. That voice would jolt her memory; that voice caused her recollections to surface, almost every time. She died in her sleep, only two weeks short of her hundredth birthday. She didn't like things that 'stood out' – as in: 'That hairdo *stands out* like a sore thumb!'

I imagine her contemplating her hundredth birthday; the family celebration that was planned to honor this event would surely have *killed* Grandmother – I suspect she knew this. Aunt Martha had already alerted the *Today* show; as you may know, the *Today* show routinely wishes Happy Birthday to every hundred-year-old in the United States – provided that the *Today* show knows about it. Aunt Martha saw to it that they knew. Harriet Wheelwright would be one hundred years old on Halloween! My grandmother *hated* Halloween; it was one of her few quarrels with God – that He had allowed her to be born on this day. It was a day, in her view, that had been invented to create mayhem among the lower classes, a day when they were invited to abuse people of property – and my grandmother's house was always abused on Halloween. 80 Front Street was feathered with toilet paper, the garage windows were dutifully soaped, the driveway lampposts were spray-painted (orange), and once someone inserted the greater half of a lamprey eel in Grandmother's letter slot. Owen had always suspected Mr Morrison, the cowardly mailman.

Upon her arrival in the old-age home, Grandmother considered that the remote-control device for switching television channels was a true child of Satan; it was television's final triumph, she said, that it could render you brain-dead without even allowing you to leave your chair. It was Dan who discovered Grandmother to be dead, when he visited her one evening in the Gravesend Retreat for the Elderly. He visited her every evening, and he brought her a Sunday newspaper and read it aloud to her on Sunday mornings, too.

The night she died, Dan found her propped up in her hospital bed; she appeared to have fallen asleep with the TV on and with the remote-control device held in her hand in such a way that the channels kept changing. But she was dead, not asleep, and her cold thumb had simply attached itself to the button that restlessly roamed the channels – looking for something good.

How I wish that Owen Meany could have died as peacefully as that!

Toronto: September 17, 1987 – rainy and cool; back-to-school weather, back-to-church weather. These familiar rituals of church and school are my greatest comfort. But Bishop Strachan has hired a new woman in the English Department; I could tell when she was interviewing, last spring, that she was someone to be endured – a woman who gives new meaning to that arresting first sentence of *Pride and Prejudice*, with which the fall term begins for my Grade 9 girls: 'It is a truth universally acknowledged, that a single man in possession of a good fortune must be in want of a wife.'

I don't know if I quite qualify for Jane Austen's notion of 'a good fortune'; but my grandmother provided for me very generously.

My new colleague's name is Eleanor Pribst, and I would love to read what Jane Austen might have written about her. I would be vastly happier to have read about Ms Pribst than I am pleased to have met her. But I shall endure her; I will outlast her, in the end. She is alternately silly and aggressive, and in both methods of operation she is willfully insufferable – she is a Germanic bully.

When she laughs, I am reminded of that wonderful sentence near the end of Margaret Atwood's *Surfacing*: 'I laugh, and a noise comes out like something being killed: a mouse, a bird?' In the case of the laughter of Eleanor Pribst, I could swear I hear the death rattle of a rat or a vulture. In department meeting, when I once again brought up the matter of my request to teach Günter Grass's *Cat and Mouse* in Grade 13, Ms Pribst went on the attack.

'Why would you want to teach that nasty book to *girls*?' she asked. 'That is a *boys'* book,' she said. 'The masturbation scene alone is offensive to women.'

Then she complained that I was 'using up' both Margaret Atwood and Alice Munro in the Canadian Literature course for my Grade 13s; there was nothing preventing Ms Pribst from teaching either Atwood or Munro in another course – but she was out to make trouble. A man teaching those two women effectively 'used them up,' she said – so that women in the department could *not* teach them. I have her figured out. She's one of those who tells you that if you teach a Canadian author in the Canadian Literature course, you're condescending to Canadians – by *not* teaching them in another literature course. And if you 'use them up' in another literature course, then she'll ask you what you think is 'wrong' with Canadian Literature; she'll say you're being condescending to Canadians. It's all because I'm a former American, and she doesn't like Americans; this is so obvious – that and the fact that I am a bachelor, I live alone, and I have not fallen all over myself to ask her (as they say) 'out.' She's one of those pushy women who will readily humiliate you if you *do* ask her 'out'; and if you *don't* ask her she'll attempt to humiliate you *more*.

I am reminded of some years ago, and of a New York

woman who so reminded me of Mitzy Lish. She brought her daughter to Bishop Strachan for an interview; the mother wanted to interview someone from the English Department – to ascertain, she told the headmistress, if we were guilty of a 'parochial' approach to literature. This woman was a seething pot of sexual contradictions. First of all, she wanted her daughter in a Canadian school in 'an old-fashioned sort of school,' she kept saying – because she wanted her daughter to be 'saved' from the perils of growing up in New York. All the New England schools, she said, were full of New Yorkers; it was tragic that a young girl should have no opportunity to entertain the values and the virtues of a saner, safer time.

On the other hand, she was one of those New Yorkers who thought she would 'die' if she spent a minute outside New York – who was sure that the rest of the world was a provincial whipping post whereat people like herself, of sophisticated tastes and highly urban energies, would be lashed to the stake of old-fashioned values and virtues until she expired of boredom.

'Confidentially,' she whispered to me, 'what does a grown-up person *do* here?' I suppose she meant, in all of Toronto – in all of Canada . . . this *wilderness*, so to speak. Yet she keenly desired to banish her daughter, lest the daughter be exposed to the eye-opening wisdom that had rendered the mother a prisoner of New York!

She was quite concerned at how many Canadian authors were on our reading lists; because she'd not read them, she suspected them of the gravest parochialism. I never met the daughter; she might have been nice – a little fearful of how homesick she would be, I'm sure, but possibly nice. The mother never enrolled her, although the girl's application was accepted. Perhaps the mother had come to Canada on a whim – I cannot claim to have come here for entirely sound reasons myself! Maybe the mother never enrolled her daughter because she (the mother) could not endure the deprivations she (the mother) would suffer while she visited her daughter in this *wilderness*.

I have my own idea regarding why the child was never enrolled. The mother made a pass at me! It had been quite a while since anyone had done that; I was beginning to think that this danger was behind me, but suddenly the mother said: 'What does one *do* here – for a good time? Perhaps you'd like to show me?'

The school had made some rather unusual, if not altogether extraordinary, arrangements for the daughter to spend a night in one of the dormitory rooms – she would get to know a few of the girls, a few of the other Americans . . . that sort of thing. The mother inquired if I might be available for a 'night on the town'!

'I'm divorced,' she added hastily – and unnecessarily; I should *hope* she was divorced! But even so!

Well, I don't pretend to possess any skill whatsoever at wriggling myself free from such bold invitations; I haven't had much practice. I suppose I behaved as an absolute bumbler; I no doubt gave the woman yet another stunning example of the 'parochialism' she was doomed to encounter outside New York.

Anyway, our encounter ended bitterly. The woman had been, in her view, courageous enough to present herself to me; that I hadn't the courage to accept her generous gift clearly marked me as the fiendish essence of cowardice. Having honored me with her seductive charms, she then felt justified in heaping upon me her considerable contempt. She told Katherine Keeling that our English reading lists were 'even more parochial' than she had feared. Believe me: it was not the reading lists that she found 'parochial' – it was *me*! I was not savvy enough to recognize a good tryst when I saw one.

And now – in my very own English Department – I must endure a woman of an apparently similar temperament, a woman whose prickly disposition is also upheaved in a sea of sexual contradictions . . . Eleanor Pribst!

She even quarreled with my choice of teaching *Tempest-Tost;* she suggested that perhaps it was because I failed to recognize that *Fifth Business* was 'better.' Naturally, I have taught both novels, and many other works by Robertson Davies, with great – no, with the greatest – pleasure. I stated that I'd had good luck teaching *Tempest-Tost* in the past. 'Students feel so much like amateurs themselves,' I said. 'I think they find all the intrigues of the local drama league both extremely funny and extremely familiar.' But Ms Pribst wanted to know if I knew Kingston; surely I at least knew that the fictional town of Salterton is easily identified as Kingston. I had heard that this was true, I said, although – personally – I had not been in Kingston.

'Not *been*!' she cried. 'I suppose that this is what comes of having Americans teaching Can Lit!' she said.

'I detest the term "Can Lit," ' I told Ms Pribst. 'We do not call American Literature "Am Lit," I see no reason to *shrivel* this country's most interesting literature to a derogatory abbreviation. Futhermore,' I said, 'I consider Mister Davies an author of such universal importance that I choose not to teach what is "Canadian" about his books, but what is wonderful about them.'

After that, it was simple warfare. She challenged my substitution - in Grade 11 – of Orwell's *Burmese Days* for Orwell's *Animal Farm*. In terms of 'lasting importance,' it was *Nineteen Eighty-four* or *Animal Farm; Burmese Days,* she said, was 'a poor substitute.'

'Orwell is Orwell,' I said, 'and *Burmese Days* is a good novel.'

But Ms Pribst – a graduate of Queens (hence, her vast knowledge of Kingston) – is writing her doctorate at the University of Toronto on something related to 'politics in fiction.' Wasn't it *Hardy* I had written about? she asked – implying 'merely' Hardy! – and wasn't it *only* my Master's I had written?

And so I asked my old friend Katherine Keeling: 'Do you suppose that God created Eleanor Pribst just to test me?'

'You're very naughty,' Katherine said. 'Don't you be wicked, too.'

When I want to be 'wicked,' I show the finger; correction – I show what's missing. I show *not* the finger. I shall save the missing finger for my next encounter with Ms Pribst. I am grateful to Owen Meany for so many things; not only did he keep me out of Vietnam – he created for me a perfect teaching tool, he gave me a terrific attention-getter for whenever the class is lagging behind. I simply raise my hand; I point. It is the absence of my pointer that makes pointing an interesting and riveting thing for me to do. Instantly, I have everyone's attention. It works very well in department meetings, too.

'Don't you point *that thing* at me!' Hester was fond of saying.

But it was not 'that thing,' it was *not anything* that upset her; it was what was missing! The amputation was very clean – it was the cleanest cut imaginable. There's nothing grotesque, or mangled – or even raw-looking – about the stump. The only thing wrong with me is what's missing. Owen Meany is missing.

* * *

It was after Owen cut off my finger – at the end of the summer of '67, when he was home in Gravesend for a few days' leave – when Hester told Owen that she wouldn't attend his funeral; she absolutely refused.

'I'll marry you, I'll move to Arizona – I'll go *anywhere* with you, Owen,' Hester said. 'Can you see me as a bride on an Army base? Can you see us entertaining another couple of young marrieds – when you're *not* off escorting a body? Just call me Hester Huachuca!' she cried. 'I'll even get *pregnant* – if you'd like that, Owen. Do you want babies? I'll give you babies!' Hester cried. 'I'd do *anything* for you – you know that. But I won't go to your fucking funeral.'

She was true to her word; Hester was not in attendance at Owen Meany's funeral – Hurd's Church was packed, but Hester wasn't a part of the crowd. He'd never asked her to marry him; he'd never made her move to Arizona, or anywhere. 'IT WOULDN'T BE FAIR – I MEAN, IT WOULDN'T BE FAIR TO *HER*,' Owen had told me.

In the fall of '67, Owen Meany made a deal with Major General LaHoad; he was *not* appointed LaHoad's aide-de-camp – LaHoad was too proud of the commendations that Owen received as a casualty assistance officer. The major general was scheduled for a transfer in eighteen months; if Owen remained at Fort Huachuca – as the casualty branch's 'best' body escort – LaHoad promised Owen 'a good job in Vietnam.' Eighteen months was a long wait, but First Lieutenant Meany felt the wait was worth it.

'Doesn't he know there are *no* "good jobs" in Vietnam?' Hester asked me. It was October; we were in Washington with fifty thousand other antiwar demonstrators. We assembled opposite the Lincoln Memorial and marched to the Pentagon, where we were met by lines of U.S. marshals and military police; there were even marshals and police on the roof of the Pentagon. Hester carried a sign:

Support the GI's
Bring Our Boys Home Now!

I was carrying nothing; I was still a little self-conscious about my missing finger. The scar tissue was new enough so that any exertion caused the stump to look inflamed. But I tried to feel I was part of the demonstration; sadly, I *didn't* feel I was part of it – I didn't feel I was part of anything. I had a 4-F deferment; I would never have to go to war, or to Canada. By the simple act of removing the first two joints of my right index finger, Owen Meany had enabled me to feel completely detached from my generation.

'If he was half as smart as he thinks he is,' Hester said to me as we approached the Pentagon, 'he would have cut off his own finger when he cut off yours – he would have cut off as many fingers as he needed to. So he saved you – lucky *you*!' she said. 'How come he isn't smart enough to save himself?'

What I saw in Washington that October were a lot of Americans who were genuinely dismayed by what their country was doing in Vietnam; I also saw a lot of other Americans who were self-righteously attracted to a most childish notion of heroism – namely, their own. They thought that to force a confrontation with soldiers and policemen would not only elevate themselves to the status of heroes; this confrontation, they deluded themselves, would expose the corruption of the political and social system they loftily thought they opposed. These would be the same people who, in later years, would credit the antiwar 'movement' with eventually getting the U.S. armed forces out of Vietnam. That was not what I saw. I saw that the righteousness of many of these demonstrators simply helped to harden the attitudes of those poor fools who *supported* the war. That is what makes what Ronald Reagan would say – two years later, in 1969 – so ludicrous: that the Vietnam protests were 'giving aid and comfort to the enemy.' What I saw was that the protests did worse than that; they gave aid and comfort to the idiots who endorsed the war – they made that war last *longer*. That's what *I* saw. I took my missing finger home to New Hampshire, and let Hester get arrested in Washington by herself; she was not exactly alone – there were mass arrests that October.

By the end of '67, there was trouble in California, there was trouble in New York; and there were five hundred thousand U.S. military personnel in Vietnam. More than sixteen thousand Americans had been killed there. That was when General Westmoreland said, 'We have reached an important point where the end begins to come into view.'

That was what prompted Owen Meany to ask: '*WHAT*

END?' The end of the war would not come soon enough to save Owen.

They put him in a closed casket, of course; the casket was draped with the U.S. flag, and his medal was pinned to the flag. Like any first lieutenant on active duty, he rated a full military funeral with honors, with escort officers, with taps – with the works. He could have been buried at Arlington; but the Meanys wanted him buried in Gravesend. Because of the medal, because the story of Owen's heroism was in all the New Hampshire newspapers,that oaf – the Rev. Dudley Wiggin – wanted Owen to have an Episcopalian service; Rector Wiggin, who was a virulent supporter of the Vietnam War wanted to perform Owen's funeral in Christ Church.

I prevailed upon the Meanys to use Hurd's Church – and to let the Rev. Lewis Merrill perform the service. Mr Meany was still angry at Gravesend Academy for expelling Owen, but I convinced him that Owen would be 'outraged in heaven' if the Wiggins ever got their hands on him.

'Owen *hated* them,' I told Mr and Mrs Meany. 'And he had a rather special relationship with Pastor Merrill.'

It was the summer of '68; I was sick of hearing white people talk about how *Soul on Ice* had changed their lives – I'll bet Eldridge Cleaver was sick of hearing that, too – and Hester said that if she heard 'Mrs Robinson' one more time, she would throw up. That spring – in the same month – Martin Luther King had been assassinated and *Hair* had opened on Broadway; the summer of '68 suffered from what would become the society's commonplace blend of the murderous and the trivial.

It was stifling hot in the Meanys' sealed house – sealed tight, I was always told, because Mrs Meany was allergic to the rock dust. She sat with her familiarly unfocused gaze, directed – as it often was – into the dead ashes in the fireplace, above which the dismembered Nativity figures surrounded the empty cradle in the crèche. Mr Meany prodded one of the andirons with the dirty toe of his boot.

'They gave us fifty thousand dollars!' said Mr Meany; Mrs Meany nodded her head – or she appeared to nod her head. 'Where's the government get that kind of money?' he asked me; I shook my head. I knew the money came from *us*.

'I'm familiar with Owen's favorite hymns,' I told the Meanys. 'I know Pastor Merrill will say a proper prayer.'

'A lot of good all Owen's prayin' done him!' said Mr Meany; he kicked the andiron.

Later, I went and sat on the bed in Owen's room. The severed arms from the vandalized statue of Mary Magdalene were oddly attached to my mother's dressmaker's dummy – formerly, as armless as she was headless. The pale, white-washed arms were too long for the smaller proportions of my mother's figure; but I suppose that these overreaching arms had only enhanced Owen's memory of the affection my mother had felt for him. His Army duffel bag was on the bed beside me: the Meanys had not unpacked it.

'Would you like me to unpack his bag?' I asked the Meanys.

'I'd be happy if you would,' his father told me. Later, he came into the room and said: 'I'd be happy if there was anythin' of his you wanted – I knew he'd have liked you to have it.'

In the duffel bag was his diary, and his well-worn paperback edition of *Selections from the writings of St Thomas Aquinas* – I took them both; and his Bible. It was tough looking at his things. I was surprised that he had never unpackaged all the baseball cards that he had so symbolically delivered to me, and that I'd returned to him; I was surprised at how withered and grotesque were my armadillo's amputated claws – they had once seemed such treasures, and now, in addition to their ugliness, they even appeared much smaller than I'd remembered them. But most of all I was surprised that I couldn't find the baseball.

'It ain't here,' Mr Meany said; he was watching me from the door of Owen's room. 'Look all you want, but you won't find it. It never was here – I know, I been lookin' for it for years!'

'I just assumed . . .' I said.

'Me too!' said Mr Meany.

The baseball, the so-called 'murder weapon,' the so-called 'instrument of death' – it never was in Owen Meany's room!

I read the passage Owen had underlined most fervently in his copy of St Thomas Aquinas – 'Demonstration of God's Existence from Motion.' I read the passage over and over, sitting on Owen Meany's bed.

> Since everything that is moved functions as a sort of instrument of the first mover, if there was no first mover, then whatever things are in motion would be simply

instruments. Of course, if an infinite series of movers and things moved were possible, with no first mover, then the whole infinity of movers and things moved would be instruments. Now, it is ridiculous, even to unlearned people, to suppose that instruments are moved but not by any principal agent. For, this would be like supposing that the construction of a box or bed could be accomplished by putting a saw or a hatchet to work without any carpenter to use them. Therefore, there must be a first mover existing above all – and this we call God.

The bed moved; Mr Meany had sat down beside me. Without looking at me, he covered my hand with his workingman's paw; he was not in the least squeamish about touching the stump of my amputated finger.

'You know, he wasn't . . . natural,' Mr Meany said.

'He was very special,' I said; but Mr Meany shook his head.

'I mean he wasn't normal, he was *born* . . . different,' said Mr Meany.

Except for the time she'd told me she was sorry about my poor mother, I had never head Mrs Meany speak; my unfamiliarity with her voice – and the fact that she spoke from her position at the fireplace, in the living room – made her voice quite startling to me.

'Stop!' she called out. Mr Meany held my hand a little tighter.

'I mean he was born unnaturally,' said Mr Meany. 'Like the Christ Child – that's what I mean,' he said. 'Me and his mother, we didn't ever *do it* . . .'

'Stop!' Mrs Meany called out.

'She just conceived a child – like the Christ Child,' said Mr Meany.

'He'll never believe you! No one ever believes you!' cried Mrs Meany.

'You're saying that Owen was a virgin birth?' I asked Mr Meany; he wouldn't look at me, but he nodded vigorously.

'She was a virgin – yes!' he said.

'They never, never, never, never *believe* you!' called out Mrs Meany.

'Be quiet!' he called back to her.

'There couldn't have been . . . some accident?' I asked.

'I told you, we didn't ever *do it*!' he said roughly.

'Stop!' Mrs Meany called out; but she spoke with less urgency now. She was completely crazy, of course. She might have been retarded. She might not even have known *how* to 'do it,' or even if or when she *had* done it. She might have been lying, all these years, or she might have been too powerfully damaged to even remember the means by which she'd managed to get pregnant!

'You really believe . . .' I started to say.

'It's true!' Mr Meany said, squeezing my hand until I winced. 'Don't be like those damn *priests*!' he said. 'They believe *that* story, but they wouldn't listen to *this* one! They even *teach* that other story, but they tell us *our* story is worse than some kinda *sin*! Owen was no sin!' said Mr Meany.

'No, he wasn't,' I said softly. I wanted to *kill* Mr Meany – for his ignorance! I wanted to stuff that madwoman into the fireplace!

'I went from one church to the next – *those Catholics*!' he shouted. 'All I knew was granite,' he said. That really *is* all he knows! I thought. 'I worked the quarries in Concord, summers, when I was a boy. When I met the Missus, when she . . . conceived Owen . . . there wasn't no Catholic in Concord we could even *talk* to! It was an outrage . . . what they said to her!'

'Stop!' Mrs Meany called out quietly.

'We moved to Barre – there was good granite up there. I wish I had granite half as good here!' Mr Meany said. 'But the Catholic Church in Barre was no different – they made us feel like we was blasphemin' the Bible, like we was tryin' to make up our *own* religion, or somethin'.'

Of course they *had* made up their own 'religion'; they were monsters of superstition, they were dupes of the kind of hocus-pocus that the television evangelists call 'miracles.'

'When did you tell Owen?' I asked Mr Meany. I knew they were stupid enough to have told him what they preposterously believed.

'Stop!' Mrs Meany called out; her voice now sounded merely habitual – or as if she were imparting a prerecorded message.

'When we thought he was old enough,' Mr Meany said; I shut my eyes.

'How old would he have been – when you told him?' I asked.

'I guess he was ten or eleven – it was about the time he hit that ball,' Mr Meany told me.

Yes, that would do it, I thought. I imagined that would have been a time when the story of his 'virgin birth' would have made quite an impression on Owen Meany – real son-of-God stuff! I imagined that the story would have given Owen the shivers. It seemed to me that Owen Meany had been used as cruelly by ignorance as he had been used by any design. I had seen what God had used him for; now I saw how ignorance had used him, too.

It had been Owen, I remembered, who had said that Christ had been USED – when Barb Wiggin had implied that Christ had been 'lucky,' when the Rev. Dudley Wiggin had said that Christ, after all, had been 'saved.' Maybe God had used Owen; but certainly Mr and Mrs Meany, and their colossal ignorance, had used Owen, too!

I thought that I had everything I wanted; but Mr Meany was surprised I didn't take the dressmaker's dummy, too. 'I figure everythin' he kept was *for* somethin'!' Mr Meany said.

I couldn't imagine what my mother's sad red dress, her dummy, and Mary Magdalene's stolen arms, could ever possibly be *for* – and I said so, a little more tersely than I meant to. But, no matter, the Meanys were invulnerable to such subtleties as tone of voice. I said good-bye to Mrs Meany, who would not speak to me or even look at me; she went on staring into the fireplace, at some imaginary point beyond the dead ashes – or deep within them. I *hated* her! I thought she was a convincing argument for mandatory sterilization.

In the rutted, dirt driveway, Mr Meany said to me: 'I got somethin' I'd like to show you – it's at the monument shop.'

He went to get the pickup truck, in which he said he'd follow me to the shop; while I was waiting for him, I heard Mrs Meany call out from the sealed house: 'Stop!'

I had not been to the monument shop since Owen had surgically created my draft deferment. When Owen had been home for Christmas – it was his *last* Christmas, 1967 – he had spent a lot of time in the monument shop, catching up on orders that his father had, as usual, fallen behind with, or had botched in other ways. Owen had several times invited me to the shop, to have a beer with him, but I had declined the invitations; I was still adjusting to life without a right index finger, and I assumed that the sight of the diamond wheel would give me the shivers.

It was a quiet Christmas leave for him. We practiced the shot for three or four days in a row; of course, my part in this exercise was extremely limited, but I still had to catch the ball and pass it back to him. The finger gave me no trouble; Owen was very pleased about that. And I thought it would have been ungenerous of me to complain about the difficulty I had with other tasks – writing and eating, for example; and typing, of course.

It was a kind of sad Christmas for him; Owen didn't see much of Hester, whose remarks – only a few months before – concerning her refusal to attend his funeral appeared to have hurt his feelings. And then everything that happened after Christmas hastened a further decline in his relationship with Hester, who grew ever more radical in her opposition to the war, beginning in January, with McCarthy announcing his candidacy for the Democratic presidential nomination. 'Who's he kidding?' Hester asked. 'He's about as good a candidate as he is a *poet*!' Then in February, Nixon announced *his* candidacy. 'Talk about going to the dogs!' Hester said. And in the same month, there was the all-time-high weekly rate for U.S. casualties in Vietnam – 543 Americans were killed in one week! Hester sent Owen a nasty letter. 'You must be up to your asshole in bodies – even in Arizona!' Then in March, Bobby Kennedy announced *his* candidacy for the Democratic nomination; in the same month, President Johnson said he would not seek reelection. Hester considered Johnson's resignation a triumph of the 'Peace Movement'; a month later, when Humphrey announced that *he* was a candidate, Owen Meany wrote Hester and said: 'SOME *TRIUMPH* FOR THE SO-CALLED MOVEMENT – JUST WAIT AND SEE!'

I think I know what he was doing; he was helping her to fall out of love with him before he died. Hester couldn't have known that she'd seen the last of him – but he knew that he'd never see her again.

All this was in my mind when I went to the monument shop with that moron Mr Meany.

The gravestone was unusually large but properly simple.

1LT PAUL O. MEANY, JR.

Under the name were the dates – the correct dates of his birth, and of his death – and under the dates was the simple Latin inscription that meant 'forever.'

IN AETERNUM

It was such an outrage that Mr Meany had wanted me to see this; but I continued to look at the stone. The letter was exactly as Owen preferred it – it was his favorite style – and the beveled edges along the sides and the top of the grave were exceedingly fine. From what Owen had said – and from the crudeness of the work with the diamond wheel that I had already seen on my mother's gravestone – I'd had no idea that Mr Meany was capable of such precise craftsmanship. I'd also had no idea that Mr Meany was familiar with Latin – Owen, naturally, had been quite a good Latin student. There was a tingle in the stump of my right index finger when I said to Mr Meany: 'You've done some very fine work with the diamond wheel.'

He said: 'That ain't *my* work – that's *his* work! He done it when he was home on leave. He covered it up – and told me not to look at it, not so long as he was alive, he said.' I looked at the stone again.

'So you added just the date – the date of his death?' I asked him; but I already had the shivers – I already knew the answer.

'I added *nothin'*!' said Mr Meany. 'He *knew* the date. I thought you knew that much.' I knew 'that much,' of course – and I'd already looked at the diary and satisfied myself that he'd always known the *exact* date. But to see it so strongly carved in his gravestone left no room for doubt – he'd last been home on leave for Christmas, 1967; he'd finished his own gravestone more than half a year before he died!

'*If* you can believe Mister Meany,' the Rev. Lewis Merrill said to me, when I told *him*. 'As you say, the man is a "monster of superstition" – and the mother may simply be "retarded." That they would believe Owen was a "virgin birth" is monstrous! But that they would *tell* him – when he was so young, and so impressionable – that is a more "unspeakable outrage," as Owen was always saying, than any such "outrage" the Meanys suffered at the hands of the Catholic Church. Speak to Father Findley about that!'

'Owen talked to you about it?' I asked.

'All the time,' said Pastor Merrill, with an irritatingly dismissive wave of his hand. 'He talked to me, he talked to Father Findley – why do you think Findley forgave him for that vandalism of his blessed statue? Father Findley knew what a lot of rubbish that *monstrous* mother and father had been feeding Owen – for years!'

'But what did *you* tell Owen about it?' I asked.

'Certainly *not* that I thought he was the second Christ!' the Rev. Mr Merrill said.

'Certainly not,' I said. 'But what did *he* say?'

The Rev. Lewis Merrill frowned. He began to stutter. 'Owen M-M-M-Meany didn't exactly believe he was J-J-J-Jesus – but he said to me that if I could believe in one v-v-v-virgin birth, why not in another one?'

'That sounds like Owen,' I said.

'Owen b-b-b-believed that there was a purpose to everything that h-h-h-happened to him – that G-G-G-God meant for the story of his life to have some m-m-m-meaning. God had p-p-p-*picked* Owen,' Pastor Merrill said.

'Do *you* believe that?' I asked him.

'My faith . . .' he started to say; then he stopped. 'I believe . . .' he started again: then he stopped again. 'It is obvious that Owen Meany was g-g-g-gifted with certain *precognitive* p-p-p-powers – visions of the f-f-f-future are not unheard of, you know,' he said.

I was angry with the Rev. Mr Merrill for making of Owen Meany what Mr Merrill so often made of Jesus Christ, or of God – a subject for 'metaphysical speculation.' He turned Owen Meany into an intellectual problem, and I told him so.

'You want to call Owen, and everything that happened to him, a m-m-m-*miracle* – don't you?' Mr Merrill asked me.

'Well, it *is* "miraculous," isn't it?' I asked him. 'You must agree it is at least *extraordinary*!'

'You sound positively *converted*,' Mr Merrill said condescendingly. 'I would be careful not to confuse your g-g-g-grief with genuine, religious *belief* . . .'

'You don't sound to me as if you believe very much!' I said angrily.

'About Owen?' he asked me.

'Not just about Owen,' I said. 'You don't seem to me to believe very much in God – or in *any* of those so-called miracles. You're always talking about "doubt as the essence and not the opposite of faith" – but it seems to me that *your* doubt has taken control of you. I think that's what Owen thought about you, too.'

'Yes, that's true – that's what he thought about m-m-m-*me*,' the Rev. Lewis Merrill said. We sat together in the vestry office, not talking, for almost an hour, or maybe two hours; it grew dark while we sat there, but Mr Merrill didn't move to turn on the desk lamp.

'What are you going to say about him – at his funeral?' I finally asked Pastor Merrill.

In the darkness, his expression was hidden from me; but Mr Merrill sat so stiffly at his old desk that the unnatural rigidity of his posture gave me the impression he had no confidence in his ability to do his job. 'I WANT YOU TO SAY A PRAYER FOR ME,' Owen Meany had said to him. Why had the prayer been so difficult for the Rev. Mr Merrill?' 'IT'S YOUR *BUSINESS*, ISN'T IT?' Owen had asked. Why had Mr Merrill appeared almost stricken to agree? For wasn't it, indeed, his BUSINESS, not only to pray for Owen Meany, then and now and *forever*, but here in Hurd's Church – at Owen's funeral – to bear witness to how Owen had lived his life, as if he were on divine assignment, as if he were following God's holy orders; and whether or not the Rev. Lewis Merrill believed in everything that Owen had believed, wasn't it also the Rev. Mr Merrill's BUSINESS to give testimony to how faithful a servant of God Owen Meany had been?

I sat in the dark of the vestry office, thinking that religion was only a *career* for Pastor Merrill. He taught the same old stories, with the same old cast of characters; he preached the same old virtues and values; and he theologized on the same old 'miracles' – yet he appeared not be believe in any of it. His mind was closed to the possibility of a new story; there was no room in his heart for a new character of God's holy choosing, or for a new 'miracle.' Owen Meany had believed that his death was necessary if others were to be saved from a stupidity and hatred that was destroying him. In that belief, surely he was not so unfamiliar a hero.

In the darkness of the vestry office, I suddenly felt that Owen Meany was very near.

The Rev. Lewis Merrill turned on the lamp; he looked as if I'd awakened him, and that he'd been dreaming – he looked as if he'd suffered a nightmare. When he tried to speak, his stutter gripped his throat so tightly that he needed to raise both his hands to his mouth – almost to pull the words out. But no words came. He looked as if he might be choking. Then his mouth opened – *still* he found no words. His hands grasped the top of his desk; his hands wandered to the handles of his old desk drawers.

When the Rev. Mr Merrill spoke, he spoke not with his own voice – he spoke in the exact falsetto, the 'permanent scream,' of Owen Meany. It was Mr Merrill's mouth that formed the words, but it was Owen Meany's voice that spoke to me: 'LOOK IN THE THIRD DRAWER, RIGHT-HAND SIDE.' Then the Rev. Mr Merrill's right hand flew down to the third desk drawer on the right-hand side: he pulled the drawer out so far that it came free of the desk – and the baseball rolled across the cool, stone floor of the vestry office. When I looked into Pastor Merrill's face, I had no doubt about which baseball it was.

'Father?' I said.

'Forgive me, my s-s-s-*son*!' said the Rev. Lewis Merrill.

That was the first time that Owen Meany let me hear from him – *after* he was gone. The second time was this August, when – as if to remind me that he would never allow anything bad to happen to me – he kept me from falling down the cellar stairs in the secret passageway. And I know: I will hear from him – from time to time – again. It is typical of Owen, who was always guilty of overkill; he should understand that I don't need to hear from him to know if he is there. Like his rough, gray replacement of Mary Magdalene, the statue that Owen said was like the God *he* knew was there – even in the dark, even though invisible – I have no doubt that Owen is there.

Owen promised me that God would tell me who my father was. I always suspected that *Owen* would tell me – he was always so much more interested in the story than *I* was. It's no surprise to me that when God decided it was time to tell me who my father was, God chose to speak to me in *Owen's* voice.

'LOOK IN THE THIRD DRAWER, RIGHT-HAND SIDE,' God said.

And there was the ball that Owen Meany hit; and there was my wretched father, asking me to forgive him.

I will tell you what is my overriding perception of the last twenty years: that we are a civilization careening toward a succession of anticlimaxes – toward an infinity of unsatisfying and disagreeable endings. The wholly anticlimactic, unsatisfying, and disagreeable news that the Rev. Lewis Merrill was my father – not to mention the death of Owen Meany – is just one example of the condition of universal disappointment.

In my sorry father's case, my disappointment with him was heightened by his refusal to admit that Owen Meany had managed – from beyond the grave – to reveal the Rev. Mr Merrill's identity to me. This was another miracle that my father lacked the faith to believe in. It had been an emotional moment; I was – by my own admission – becoming an expert in imitating Owen's voice. Furthermore, Mr Merrill himself had always desired to tell me who he was; he'd simply lacked the courage; perhaps he'd found the courage by using a voice not his own. He'd always *wanted* to show me the baseball, too, he admitted – 'to confess.'

The Rev. Lewis Merrill was so intellectually detached from his faith, he had so long removed himself from the necessary amount of *winging it* that is required of belief, that he could not accept a small but firm miracle when it happened not only in his presence but was even spoken by his own lips and enacted with his own hand – which had, with a force not his own, *ripped* the third drawer on the right-hand side completely out of his desk. Here was an ordained minister of the Congregational Church, a pastor and a spokesman for the faithful, telling me that the miracle of Owen Meany's *voice* speaking out in the vestry office – not to mention the forceful revelation of my mother's 'murder weapon,' the 'instrument of death' – was *not* so much a demonstration of the power of God as it was an indication of the power of the subconscious; namely, the Rev. Mr Merrill thought that both of us had been 'subconsciously motivated' – in my case, to use Owen Meany's voice, or to make Mr Merrill use it; and in Mr Merrill's case, to confess to me that he was my father.

'Are you a minister or a psychiatrist?' I asked him. He was so confused. I might as well have been speaking to Dr Dolder!

Like so many things in the last twenty years: it got worse. The Rev. Mr Merrill confessed that he had no faith at all; he had lost his faith, he told me, when my mother died. God had stopped speaking to him then; and the Rev. Mr Merrill had stopped asking to be spoken to. My father had sat in the bleacher seats at the Little League game, and when he saw my mother strolling carelessly along the third-base line – when she had spotted him in the stands and waved to him, with her back to home plate – at that moment, my father told me, he had prayed to God that my mother would drop dead!

Infuriatingly, he assured me that he hadn't really meant it – it had been only a 'passing thought.' More often, he wished that they could be friends, and that the sight of her didn't fill him with self-disgust for his long-ago transgression. When he saw her bare shoulders at the baseball game, he hated himself – he was ashamed that he was still attracted to her. Then she spotted him, and – shamelessly, without an ounce of guilt – she waved to him. She made him feel so guilty, he wished her dead. The first pitch to Owen Meany was way outside; he let it go. My mother had left my father's church, but it never seemed to upset her when she encountered him – she was always friendly, she spoke to him, she waved. It pained him to remember every little thing about her – the pretty hollow of her bare armpit, which he could see so clearly as she waved to him. The second pitch almost hit Owen Meany in the head; he dove in the dirt to avoid it. Whatever my mother remembered, my father thought that nothing pained her. She just went on waving. Oh, just drop dead! he thought.

At that precise moment, that is what he'd prayed. Then Owen Meany hit the next pitch. This is what a self-centered religion does to us: it allows us to use it to further our own ends. How could the Rev. Lewis Merrill agree with me – that Mr and Mrs Meany were 'monsters of superstition' – if he himself believed that God had listened to his prayer at that Little League game: and that God had *not* 'listened' to him since? Because he'd wished my mother dead, my father said, God had punished him; God had taught Pastor Merrill not to trifle with prayer. And I suppose that was why it had been so difficult for Mr Merrill to pray for Owen Meany – and why he had invited us all to offer up our silent prayers to Owen, instead of speaking out himself. And *he* called Mr and Mrs Meany 'superstitious'! Look at the world, look at how many of our peerless leaders presume to tell us that they know what *God* wants! It's not God who's fucked up, it's the screamers who say they believe in Him and who claim to pursue their ends in His holy name!

Why the Rev. Lewis Merrill had so whimsically prayed that my mother would drop dead was such an old, tired story. My mother's little romance, I was further disappointed to learn, had been more pathetic than romantic; Mother, after all, was simply a very young woman from a very hick town. When she'd started singing at The Orange Grove, she'd wanted the honest approval of her hometown pastor – she'd needed to be assured that she was engaged in a decent and honorable endeavor; she'd asked him to come see her and hear her sing. Clearly, it was the *sight* of her that had impressed him, in that setting – in that unfamiliarly scarlet dress – 'The Lady in Red' did not strike the Rev. Mr Merrill as the same choir girl he had tutored through her teens. I suppose it was a seduction accomplished with only slightly more than the usual sincerity – for my mother was sincerely innocent, and I will at least credit the Rev. Lewis Merrill with supposing that he was sincerely 'in love'; after all, he'd had no great experience with love. Afterward, the reality that he had no intentions of leaving his wife and children – who were already (and always had been) unhappy! – must have shamed him.

I know that my mother took it fairly well; in my memory, she never winced to call me her 'little fling.' In short, Tabitha Wheelwright got over Lewis Merrill rather quickly; and she bore up better than stoically to the task of bearing his illegitimate child. Mother's intentions were always sound, never muddy; I don't imagine that she troubled herself to feel very guilty. But the Rev. Mr Merrill was a man who took to wallowing in guilt; his remorse, after all, was all he had to cling to – especially after his scant courage left him, and he was forced to acknowledge that he would never be brave enough to abandon his miserable wife and children for my mother. He would continue to torture himself, of course, with the insistent and self-destructive notion that he loved my mother. I suppose that his 'love' of my mother was as intellectually detached from feeling and action as his 'belief' was also subject to his immense capacity for remote and unrealistic interpretation. My mother was a healthier animal; when he said he wouldn't leave his family for her, she simply put him out of her mind and went on singing.

But as incapable as he was of a heartfelt *response* to a real situation, the Rev. Mr Merrill was tirelessly capable of *thinking;* he pondered and brooded and surmised and second-guessed my mother to death. And when she met and became engaged to Dan Needham, how that must have threatened to put an end to his conjecturing; and when she married Dan, how that must have threatened to put an end to the self-inflicted pain of which he had grown so fond. That for all his sourness, *her* disposition remained sunny – that she even cheerfully sought the bleacher seats for him, and *waved* to him only a split second before she died – how insubstantial that must have made her in his eyes! The closest that the Rev. Lewis Merrill had come to God was in his remorse for his 'sin' with my mother.

And when he was *privileged* to witness the miracle of Owen Meany, my bitter father could manage no better response than to whine to me about his lost faith – his ridiculously subjective and fragile belief, which he had so easily allowed to be routed by his meanspirited and self-imposed doubt. What a *wimp* he was, Pastor Merrill; but how proud I felt of my mother – that she'd had the good sense to shrug him off.

It's no wonder it was such a tribulation for Mr Merrill to know what he was going to say about Owen – at Owen's funeral. How could a man like him know what to say about Owen Meany? He called Owen's parents 'monstrous,' while he outrageously presumed that God had actually 'listened' to his ardent, narrow prayer that my mother drop dead; and he arrogantly presumed further that God was now silent, and wouldn't listen to him – as if the Rev. Mr Merrill, all by himself, possessed the power both to make God pay attention to him *and* to harden God's heart against him. What a hypocrite he was – to agree with me that Mr and Mrs Meany were 'monsters of superstition'!

In the vestry office, where we were supposed to be preparing ourselves for Owen Meany's funeral, I said – very sarcastically – to my father: 'How I wish I could help restore your faith.' Then I left him there – possibly imagining how such a restoration could ever be possible. I have never been angrier; that was when I felt 'moved to do evil' – and when I remembered how Owen Meany had tried to prepare me for what a disappointment my father was going to be.

Toronto: September 27, 1987 – overcast, with rain inevitable by the end of the day. Katherine says that the least Christian thing about me is my lack of forgiveness, which I know is true and is hand-in-hand with my constantly resurfacing desire for revenge. I sat in Grace Church on-the-Hill; I sat there all alone, in the dim light – as overcast as the outdoor weather. To make matters worse: the Toronto Blue Jays are involved in a pennant race; if the Blue Jays make it to the World Series, the talk of the town will be *baseball.*

There are times when I need to read the Thirty-seventh Psalm, over and over again.

> Leave off from wrath, and let go displeasure:
> fret not thyself, else shalt thou be moved to do evil.

I've had a hard week at Bishop Strachan. Every fall, I start out demanding too much of my students; then I become unreasonably disappointed in them – and in myself. I have been too sarcastic with them. And my new colleague – Ms Eleanor Pribst – truly moves me to do evil!

This week I was reading my Grade 10 girls a ghost story by Robertson Davies – 'The Ghost Who Vanished by Degrees.' In the middle of the story, which I adore, I began to think: What do Grade 10 girls know about graduate students or Ph.D. theses or the kind of academic posturing that Mr Davies makes such great, good fun of? The students looked sleepy-headed to me: they were paying, at best, faltering attention. I felt cross with them, and therefore I read badly, not doing the story justice; then I felt cross with myself for choosing this particular story and not considering the age and inexperience of my audience. God, what a situation!

It is in this story where Davies says that 'the wit of a graduate student is like champagne – Canadian champagne . . .' That's absolutely priceless, as Grandmother used to say; I think I'll try that one on Eleanor Pribst the next time she tries to be witty with me! I think I'll stick the stump of my right index finger into the right nostril of my nose – thereby giving her the impression that I have managed to insert the first two joints of my finger so far into my nose that the tip must be lodged between my eyes; thus catching her attention, I'm sure, I will then deliver to her that priceless line about the wit of graduate students.

In Grace Church on-the-Hill, I bowed my head and tried to let my anger go. There is no way to be more alone in church than to linger there, after a Sunday service.

This week I was haranguing my Canadian Literature students on the subject of 'bold beginnings.' I said that if the books I asked them to read began half as lazily as their papers on Timothy Findley's *Famous Last Words*, they would never have managed to plow through a single one of them! I used Mr Findley's novel as an example of what I meant by a bold beginning – that shocking scene when the father takes his twelve-year-old son up on the roof of the Arlington Hotel to show him the view of Boston and Cambridge and Harvard and the Charles, and then leaps fifteen stories to his death in front of his son; imagine that. That ranks right up there with the opening chapter to *The Mayor of Casterbridge*, wherein Michael Henchard gets so drunk that he loses his wife and daughter in a *bet*; imagine that! Hardy knew what he was doing; he always knew.

What did it mean, I asked my sloppy students, that their papers generally 'began' after four or five pages of wandering around in a soup of *ideas* for beginnings? If it took them four or five pages to find the right beginning, didn't they think they should consider *revising* their papers and beginning them on page four or five?

Oh, young people, young people, young people – where is your taste for *wit*? I weep to teach Trollope to these BSS girls: I care less that they appear to weep because they're forced to read him. I especially worship the pleasures of *Barchester Towers;* but it is pearls before swine to teach Trollope to this television generation of girls! Their hips, their heads, and even their hearts are moved by those relentlessly mindless rock videos; yet the opening of Chapter IV does not extract from them even so much as a titter.

'Of the Rev. Mr Slope's parentage I am not able to say much. I have heard it asserted that he is lineally descended from the eminent physician who assisted at the birth of Mr T. Shandy and that in early years he added an 'e' to his name, for the sake of euphony, as other great men have done before him.'

Not even a titter! But how their hearts thump and patter, how their hips jolt this way and that, how their heads loll and nod – and their eyes roll inward, completely disappearing into their untrained little skulls – just to *hear* Hester the Molester; not to mention *see* the disjointed nonsense that accompanies the sound track of her most recent rock video!

You can understand why I needed to sit by myself in Grace Church on-the-Hill.

This week I was reading 'The Moons of Jupiter' – that marvelous short story by Alice Munro – to my Grade 13 *Can Lit* students, as the abrasive Ms Pribst would say. I was a touch anxious about reading the story, because one of my students - Yvonne Hewlett – was in a situation all too similar to the narrator's situation in that story: her father was in the hospital, about to undergo a ticklish heart surgery. I didn't remember what was happening to Yvonne Hewlett's father until I'd already begun to read 'The Moons of Jupiter' to the class; it was too late to stop, or change the story as I went along. Besides: it is by no means a brutal story – it is warm, if not exactly reassuring to the children of heart patients. Anyway, what could I do? Yvonne Hewlett had missed a week of classes just recently when her father suffered a heart attack; she looked tense and drained as I read the Munro story – she had looked tense and drained, naturally, from the opening line: 'I found my father in the heart wing . . .'

How could I have been so thoughtless? I was thinking. I wanted to interrupt the story and tell Yvonne Hewlett that everything was going to turn out just fine – although I had no right to make any such promise to her, especially not about her poor father. God, what a situation! Suddenly I felt like *my* father – I am my sorry father's son, I thought. Then I regretted the evil I did to him; actually, it turned out all right in the end – it turned out that I did him a favor. But I did not intend what I did to him as any favor.

When I left him alone in the vestry office, pondering what he would find to say at Owen Meany's funeral, I took the baseball with me. When I went to see Dan Needham, I left the baseball in the glove compartment of my car. I was so angry, I didn't know what I was going to do – beginning with: tell Dan, or not tell him?

That was when I asked Dan Needham – since he had no apparent religious faith – why he had insisted that my mother and I change churches, that we leave the Congregational Church and become Episcopalians!

'What do you mean?' Dan asked me. 'That was *your* idea!'

'What do *you* mean?' I asked him.

'Your mother told me that all your friends were in the Episcopal Church – namely, Owen,' Dan said. 'Your mother told me that you asked her if you could change churches so that you could attend Sunday school with your friends. You didn't have any friends in the Congregational Church, she said.'

'Mother said that?' I asked him. 'She told *me* that both of us should become Epsicopalians so that we'd belong to the same church as *you* – because you were an Episcopalian.'

'I'm a Presbyterian,' Dan said '—not that it matters.'

'So she lied to us,' I said to Dan; after a while, he shrugged.

'How old were you at the time?' Dan asked me. 'Were you eight or nine or ten? Maybe you haven't remembered all the circumstances correctly.'

I thought for a while, not looking at him. Then I said: 'You were engaged to her for a long time – before you got married. It was about four years – as I recall.'

'Yes, about four years – that's correct,' Dan said warily.

'Why did you wait so long to get married?' I asked him. 'You both knew you loved each other – didn't you?'

Dan looked at the bookshelves on the concealed door leading to the secret passageway.

'Your father . . .' he began; then he stopped. 'Your father wanted her to wait,' Dan said.

'Why?' I asked Dan.

'To be sure – to be sure about me,' Dan said.

'What business was it of *his*?' I cried.

'Exactly – that's exactly what I told your mother: that it wasn't any of his business . . . if your mother was "sure" about me. Of *course* she was sure, and so was I!'

'Why did she do what *he* wanted?' I asked Dan.

'Because of you,' Dan told me. 'She wanted him to promise never to identify himself to you. He wouldn't promise unless she waited to marry me. We both had to wait before he promised never to speak to you. It took four years,' Dan said.

'I always thought that Mother would have told me herself – if she'd lived,' I said. 'I thought she was just waiting for me to be old enough – and then she'd tell me.'

'She never intended to tell you,' Dan Needham said. 'She made it clear to me that neither you nor I would *ever* know. I accepted that; you would have accepted that from her, too. It was your *father* who didn't accept that – for four years.'

'But he could have spoken to me after Mother died,' I said. 'Who would have known that he'd broken a promise if he'd spoken to me? Only *I* would have known – and I would never have known that she'd made him promise anything. I never knew he was *interested* in identifying himself to me!' I said.

'He must be someone who can be trusted to keep a promise,' Dan said. 'I used to think he was jealous of me – that he wanted her to wait all that time just because he thought I would give her up or that she would get tired of me. I used to think he was trying to break us up – that he was only pretending to care about her being *sure* of me or wanting her permission to identify himself to you. But now I think that he must have sincerely wanted her to be right about me – and it must have been difficult for him to promise her that he would *never* try to contact you.'

'Did you know about "The Lady in Red"?' I asked Dan Needham. 'Did you know about The Orange Grove – and all of that?'

'It was the only way she could see him, it was the only way they could talk,' Dan said. 'That's all I know about it,' he said. 'I won't ask you how *you* know about it.'

'Did you ever hear of Big Black Buster Freebody?' I asked Dan.

'He was an old black musician – your mother was very fond of him,' Dan said. 'I remember who he was because of the last time your mother and I took a trip together, before she was killed – we went to Buster Freebody's funeral,' Dan said.

And so Dan Needham believed that my father was a man of his word. How many men do we know like *that*? I wondered. It seemed pointless for me to disabuse Dan of his notion of my father's sincerity. It seemed almost pointless for me to know who my father was; I was quite sure that this knowledge would never greatly benefit Dan. How could it benefit him to know that the Rev. Lewis Merrill had sat in the bleacher seats, praying that my mother would die – not to mention that Pastor Merrill was arrogant enough to believe that his prayer had *worked*? I was sure that Dan didn't need to know these things. And why else would my mother have wanted us to leave the Congregational Church for the Episcopal – if not to get away from Mr Merrill? My father was not a brave or an honorable man; but he had once tried to be brave and honorable. He had been afraid, but he had dared – in his fashion – to pray for Owen Meany; he had done that pretty well.

Whatever had he imagined might come of his identifying

himself to me? What had become of his own children, sadly, was that they had not felt much from their father – not beyond his immeasurable and inexpressible remorse, which he clung to in the manner of a man who'd forgotten how to pray. *I* could teach him how to pray again, I thought. It was after speaking to Dan that I got an idea of how I might teach Pastor Merrill to believe again – I knew how I might encourage him to have a little faith. I thought of the sad man's shapeless middle child, who with her brutally short hair was barely indentifiable as a girl; I thought of the tallish older boy, the sloucher – and cemetery vandal! And the youngest was a groveler, a scrounger under the pews – I couldn't even remember what its sex was.

If Mr Merrill failed to have faith in Owen Meany, if Mr Merrill believed that God was punishing him with silence – I knew I could give Mr Merrill something to believe in. If neither God nor Owen Meany could restore the Rev. Mr Merrill's faith, I thought I knew a 'miracle' that my father was susceptible to believing in.

It was about ten o'clock in the evening when I left Pastor Merrill sitting at his desk in the vestry office; it was only half an hour later when I finished talking with Dan and drove again past Hurd's Church at the corner of Front Street and Tan Lane. Lewis Merrill was still there, the light still on in the vestry office; and now there was also light shining through the stained-glass windows of the chancel – that enclosed and meant-to-be-sacred space surrounding the altar of a church, where (no doubt) my father was composing his last words for Owen Meany.

'I figure everythin' he kept was *for* somethin'!' Mr Meany had said – about my mother's dummy in the red dress. I'm sure the poor fool didn't know how right he was about that.

The Maiden Hill Road was dark; there were still some emergency-road-repair cones and unlit flares off the side of the road by the trestle bridge, the abutment of which had been the death of Buzzy Thurston. The accident had made quite a mess of the cornerstones of the bridge, and they'd had to tar the road where Buzzy's smashed Plymouth had gouged up the surface.

There was the usual light left on in the Meanys' kitchen; it was the light they'd routinely left on for Owen. Mr Meany was a long time answering my knock on the door. I'd never seen him in pajamas before; he looked oddly childish – or like a big clown dressed in children's clothes. 'Why it's Johnny Wheelwright!' he said automatically.

'I want the dummy,' I told him.

'Well, sure!' he said cheerfully. 'I thought you'd want it.'

It was not heavy, but it was awkward – trying to fit it in my Volkswagen Beetle – because it wouldn't bend. I remembered how awkwardly, in his swaddling clothes, Owen Meany had fitted in the cab of the big granite truck, that day his mother and father had driven him home from the Christmas Pageant; how Hester and Owen and I had ridden on the flatbed of the big truck, that night Mr Meany drove us – and the dummy – to the beach at Little Boar's Head.

'You can borrow the pickup, if it's easier,' Mr Meany suggested. But that wasn't necessary; with Mr Meany's help, I managed to fit the dummy into the Beetle. I had to detach the former Mary Magdalene's naked white arms from the wire-mesh sockets under the dummy's shoulders. The dummy didn't have any feet; she rose from a rod on a thin, flat pedestal – and this I stuck out the rolled-down window by the passenger's seat, which I tilted forward so that the dummy's boyish hips and slender waist and full bosom and small, squared shoulders could extend into the back seat. If she'd had a head, she wouldn't have fit.

'Thank you,' I said to Mr Meany.

'Well, sure!' he said.

I parked my Volkswagen on Tan Lane, well away from Hurd's Church and the blinking yellow light at the intersection with Front Street. I jammed the baseball in my pocket; I carried the dummy under one arm, and Mary Magdalene's long, pale arms under the other. I reassembled my mother in the flower beds that were dimly glowing in the dark-colored light that shone through the stained-glass windows of the chancel. The light was still on in the vestry office, but Pastor Merrill was practicing his prayers for Owen in the chancel of the old stone church; occasionally, he would dally with the organ. From his choirmaster days at the Congregational Church, Mr Merrill had retained an amateur command of the organ. I was familiar with the hymns he was toying with – trying to get himself in the mood to pray for Owen Meany.

He played 'Crown Him with Many Crowns'; then he tried

'The Son of God Goes Forth to War.' There was a bed of portulaca where it was best to stand the dressmaker's dummy, the fleshy-leaved, low-to-the-ground plants covered the pedestal, and the small flowers – most of which were closed for the night – didn't clash with the poinsettia-red dress. The dress completely covered the wire-mesh hips of the dummy; and the thin, black stem upon which the dummy rose from its pedestal was invisible in the semidarkness – as if my mother didn't exactly have her feet on the ground, but chose instead to hover just above the flower beds. I walked back and forth between the flower beds and the door to the vestry, trying to see how the dummy appeared from that distance – angling my mother's body so that her unforgettable figure would be instantly recognizable. It was perfect how the dark-colored light from the chancel threw exactly the right amount of illumination upon her – there was just enough light to accentuate the scarlet glare of her dress, but not enough light to make her headlessness too apparent. Her head and her feet were just missing – or else consumed by the shadows of the night. From the door of the vestry, my mother's figure was both vividly alive and ghostly; 'The Lady in Red' looked ready to sing. The effect of the blinking yellow light at the corner of Tan Lane and Front Street was also enhancing; and even the headlights of an occasional passing car were far enough away to contribute to the uncertainty of the figure in the bed of portulaca.

I squeezed the baseball; I had not held one in my hand since that last Little League game. I worried about my grip, because the first two joints of your index finger are important in throwing a baseball; but I didn't have far to throw it. I waited for Mr Merrill to stop playing the organ; the second the music stopped, I threw the baseball – as hard as I could – through one of the tall, stained-glass windows of the chancel. It made a small hole in the glass, and a beam of white light – as if from a flashlight – shone upward into the leaves of a towering elm tree, behind which I concealed myself while I waited for Pastor Merrill.

It took him a moment to discover *what* had been thrown through one of the sacred chancel windows. I suppose that the baseball must have rolled past the organ pipes, or even close to the pulpit.

'Johnny!' I heard my father calling. The door from the

church into the vestry opened and closed. 'Johnny – I know you're angry, but this is very childish!' he called. I heard his footsteps in the corridor where all the clothes pegs were – outside the vestry office. He flung open the vestry door, the baseball in his right hand, and he blinked into the blinking yellow light at the corner of Tan Lane and Front Street. 'Johnny!' he called again. He stepped outside; he looked left, toward the Gravesend campus; he looked right, along Front Street – then he glanced into the flower beds that were glowing in the light from the stained-glass windows of the chancel. Then the Rev. Lewis Merrill dropped to his knees and pressed the baseball hard againt his heart.

'Tabby!' he said in a whisper. He dropped the ball, which rolled out to the Front Street sidewalk. 'God – forgive me!' said Pastor Merrill. 'Tabby – *I* didn't tell him! I promised you I wouldn't, and I didn't – it wasn't *me*!' my father cried. His head began to sway – he couldn't look at her – and he covered his eyes with both hands. He fell on his side, his head touching the grass border of the vestry path, and he drew up his knees to his chest – as if he were cold, or a baby going to sleep. He kept his eyes covered tightly, and he moaned: 'Tabby – forgive me, please!'

After that, he began to babble incoherently; his voice was just a murmur, and he made slight jerking or twitching movements where he lay on the ground. There was just enough noise and motion from him to assure me that he wasn't dead. I confess: I was slightly disappointed that the shock of my mother appearing before him hadn't killed him. I picked up the dressmaker's dummy and put her under my arm; one of Mary Magadalene's dead-white arms fell off, and I carried this under my other arm. I picked up the baseball from the sidewalk and jammed it back into my pocket. I wondered if my father could hear me moving around, because he seemed to contort himself more tightly into a fetal position and to cover his eyes even more tightly – as if he feared my mother were coming nearer to him. Perhaps those bone-white, elongated arms had especially frightened him – as if Death itself had exaggerated my mother's *reach*, and the Rev. Mr Merrill was sure that she was going to touch him.

I put the dummy and Mary Magdalene's arms into my Volkswagen and drove to the breakwater at Rye Harbor. It was midnight. I threw the baseball as far into the harbor as

I could; it made a very small splash there – not disturbing the gulls. I flung Mary Magdalene's long, heavy arms into the harbor, too; they made more of a splash, but the boats slapping on their moorings and the surf striking the breakwater outside the harbor had conditioned the gulls there to remain undisturbed by *any* noise of water.

Then I climbed out along the breakwater with the dummy in the red dress; the tide was high, and going out. I waded into the harbor channel, off the tip of the breakwater; I was quickly submerged, up to my chest, and I had to retreat to the last slab of granite on the breakwater – so that I could throw the dummy as far into the ocean as I could. I wanted to be sure that the dummy reached into the channel, which I knew was very, very deep. For a moment, I hugged the body of the dummy to my face; but whatever scent had once clung to the red dress had long ago departed. Then I threw the dummy into the channel.

For a horrible moment, it floated. There was air trapped under the hollow wire-mesh of the body. The dummy rolled over on its back in the water. I saw my mother's wonderful bosom above the surface of the water – THE BEST BREASTS OF ALL THE MOTHERS! as Owen Meany had said. Then the dummy rolled again; bubbles of air escaped from the body, and 'The Lady in Red' sank into the channel off the breakwater at Rye Harbor, where Owen Meany had firmly believed he had a right to sit and watch the sea.

I saw the sun come up, like a bright marble on the granite-gray surface of the Atlantic. I drove to the apartment I shared with Hester in Durham and took a shower and dressed for Owen's funeral. I didn't know where Hester was, but I didn't care; I already knew how she felt about his funeral. I'd last seen Hester at 80 Front Street; with my grandmother, Hester and I had watched Bobby Kennedy be killed in Los Angeles – over and over again. That was when Hester had said: 'Television gives good disaster.'

Owen had never said a word to me about Bobby Kennedy's assassination. That had happened in June, 1968, when time was running out on Owen Meany. I'm sure that Owen was too preoccupied with his own death to have anything to say about Bobby Kennedy's.

It was early in the morning, and I kept so few things in Hester's apartment, it was no trouble to pack up what I wanted; mostly books. Owen had kept some books at Hester's, too, and I packed one of them – C. S. Lewis's *Reflections on the Psalms*. Owen had circled a favorite sentence: 'I write for the unlearned about things in which I am unlearned myself.' After I finished packing – and I'd left Hester a check for my share of the rent for the rest of the summer – I still had time to kill, so I read parts of Owen's diary; I looked at the more disjointed entries, which were composed in a grocery-list style, as if he'd been making notes to himself. I learned that *huachuca* – as in Fort Huachuca – means 'mountain of the winds.' And there were several pages of Vietnamese vocabulary and expressions – Owen had paid special attention to 'COMMAND FORMS OF VERBS.' Two commands were written out several times – the pronunciation was emphasized; Owen had spelled the Vietnamese phonetically.

'*NAM SOON* – "LIE DOWN!" *DOONG SA* – "DON'T BE AFRAID"!'

I read that part over and over again, until I felt I had the pronunciation right. There was quite a good pencil drawing of a phoenix, that mythical bird that was supposed to burn itself on a funeral pyre and then rise up from its own ashes. Under the drawing, Owen had written: 'OFTEN A SYMBOL OF REBORN IDEALISM, OR HOPE – OR AN EMBLEM OF IMMORTALITY.' And on another page, jotted hastily in the margin – with no connection to anything else on the page – he had scrawled: 'THIRD DRAWER, RIGHT-HAND SIDE.' This marginalia was *not* emphasized; in no way had he indicated that this was a message for *me* - but certainly, I thought, he must have remembered that time when he'd sat at Mr Merrill's desk, talking to Dan and me and opening and closing the desk drawers, without appearing to notice the contents.

Of course, he had seen the baseball – he had known then who my father was – but Owen Meany's faith was huge; he had also known that God would tell me who my father was. Owen believed it was unnecessary to tell me himself. Besides: he knew it would only disappoint me.

Then I flipped to one of the parts of the diary where he'd mentioned me.

'THE HARDEST THING I EVER HAD TO DO WAS TO CUT OFF MY BEST FRIEND'S FINGER! WHEN THIS IS OVER, MY BEST FRIEND SHOULD MAKE A CLEAN

BREAK FROM THE PAST – HE SHOULD SIMPLY START OVER AGAIN. JOHN SHOULD GO TO CANADA. I'M SURE IT'S A NICE COUNTRY TO LIVE IN – AND *THIS* COUNTRY IS MORALLY EXHAUSTED.'

Then I flipped to the end of the diary and reread his last entry.

'TODAY'S THE DAY! ". . . HE THAT BELIEVETH IN ME, THOUGH HE WERE DEAD, YET SHALL HE LIVE; AND WHOSOEVER LIVETH AND BELIEVETH IN ME SHALL NEVER DIE." '

Then I closed Owen's diary and packed it with the rest of my things. Grandmother was an early riser; there were a few photographs of her, and of my mother, that I wanted from 80 Front Street – and more of my clothes. I wanted to have breakfast in the rose garden with Grandmother; there was still a lot of time before Owen's funeral – enough time to tell Grandmother where I was going.

Then I drove over to Waterhouse Hall and told Dan Needham what my plans were; also, Dan had something I wanted to take with me, and I knew he wouldn't object – he'd been bashing his toes on it for years! I wanted the granite doorstop that Owen had made for Dan and my mother, his wedding present to them, the lettering in his famous, gravestone style – JULY 1952 – and neatly beveled along the sides, and perfectly edged at the corner: it was crude, but it had been Owen's earliest known work with the diamond wheel, and I wanted it. Dan told me that he understood everything, and that he loved me.

I told him: 'You're the best father a boy ever had – and the only father I ever needed.'

Then it was time for Owen Meany's funeral.

Our own Gravesend chief of police, Ben Pike, stood at the heavy double doors of Hurd's Church – as if he intended to *frisk* Owen Meany's mourners for the 'murder weapon,' the long-lost 'instrument of death'; I was tempted to tell the bastard where he could find the fucking baseball. Fat Mr Chickering was there, still grieving that he'd decided to let Owen Meany bat for me – that he'd told Owen to 'swing away.' The Thurstons – Buzzy's parents – were there, although they were Catholics and only recently had attended their own son's funeral. And the Catholic priest – Father

Findley – he was there, as was Mrs Hoyt, despite how badly the town had treated her for her 'anti-American' draft-counseling activities. Rector Wiggin and Barb Wiggin were *not* in attendance; they had so fervently sought to hold Owen's service in Christ Church, no doubt they were miffed that they'd been rejected. Captain Wiggin, that crazed ex-pilot, had claimed that nothing could please him more than a bang-up funeral for a hero.

A unit of the New Hampshire National Guard provided a local funeral detail; they served as Owen's so-called honor guard. Owen had once told me that they do this for money – they get one day's pay. The casualty assistance officer – Owen's body escort – was a young, frightened-looking first lieutenant who rendered a military salute more frequently than I thought was required of him; it was his first tour of duty in the Casualty Branch. The so-called survivor assistance officer was none other than Owen's favorite professor of Military Science from the University of New Hampshire; Colonel Eiger greeted me most solemnly at the heavy double doors.

'I guess we were wrong about your little friend,' Colonel Eiger said to me.

'Yes, sir,' I said.

'He proved he was quite suitable for combat,' Colonel Eiger said.

'Yes, sir,' I said. The colonel put his liver-spotted hand on my shoulder; then he stepped to one side of the heavy double doors and stood at attention, as if he meant to challenge Chief Ben Pike's position of authority.

The honor guard, in white spats and white gloves, strode down the aisle in bridal cadence and smartly split to each side of the flag-draped casket, where Owen's medal – pinned to the flag – brightly reflected the beam of sunlight that shone through the hole the baseball had made in the stained-glass window of the chancel. In the routine gloom of the old stone church, this unfamiliar beam of light appeared to be drawn to the bright gold of Owen's medal – as if the light itself had burned a hole in the dark stained glass; as if the light had been searching for Owen Meany.

A stern, sawed-off soldier, whom Colonel Eiger had referred to as a master sergeant, whispered something to the honor guard, who stood at parade rest and glanced anxiously at Colonel Eiger and the first lieutenant who was serving his first duty as a body escort. Colonel Eiger whispered something to the first lieutenant.

The congregation coughed; they creaked in the old, worn pews. The organ cranked out one dirge after another while the stragglers found their seats. Although Mr Early was one of the ushers, and Dan Needham was another, most of the ushers were quarrymen – I recognized the derrickman and the dynamiters; I nodded to the signalman and the sawyers, and the channel bar drillers. These men looked like granite itself – its great strength can withstand a pressure of twenty thousand pounds per square inch. Granite, like lava, was once melted rock; but it did not rise to the earth's surface – it hardened deep underground; and because it hardened slowly, it formed fairly large crystals.

Mr and Mrs Meany occupied the front right-center pew of Hurd's Church all by themselves. They sat like upheaved slabs of granite, not moving, their eyes fixed upon the dazzling medal that winked in the beam of sunlight on top of Owen's casket. The Meanys stared intently; they viewed their son's casket with much the same strangled awe that had shone in their eyes when the little Lord Jesus had spotted them in the congregation at the Christ Church Christmas Pageant of 1953 – when Owen had basked in the 'pillar of light.' The alertness and anxiety in the Meanys' expressions suggested to me that they remembered how Owen had reproached them for their uninvited attendance at the Nativity.

'WHAT DO YOU THINK *YOU'RE* DOING HERE?' the angry Lord Jesus had screamed at them. 'YOU SHOULDN'T BE HERE!' Owen had shouted. 'IT IS A *SACRILEGE* FOR YOU TO BE HERE!'

That is what *I* thought about Owen's funeral: that it was a SACRILEGE for the Meanys to be there. And their nervous fixation upon Owen's medal, pinned to the American flag, suggested that the Meanys quite possibly feared that Owen might rise up from his casket as he had risen up from the mountain of hay in the manger – and once again reproach his parents. They had actually told a ten- or eleven-year-old boy that he'd had a 'virgin birth' – that he was 'like the Christ Child'!

At Owen's funeral in Hurd's Church, I found myself praying that Owen *would* rise up from his closed casket and shout at his poor parents: 'YOU SHOULDN'T BE HERE!' But Owen Meany didn't move, or speak.

Mr Fish looked very frail; yet he sat beside my grandmother in the second row of right-center pews and fixed *his* gaze upon the shining medal on Owen Meany's casket – as if Mr Fish also hoped that Owen would give us one more performance; as if Mr Fish could not believe that, in *this* production, Owen Meany had not been given a speaking part.

My Uncle Alfred and Aunt Martha also sat in Grandmother's pew; none of us had mentioned Hester's absence; even Simon – who was also seated in Grandmother's pew – had restrained himself from speaking about Hester. The Eastmans more comfortably discussed how sorry they were that Noah couldn't be there – Noah was still in Africa, teaching proper forestry to the Nigerians. I'll never forget what Simon said to me when I told him I was going to Canada.

'Canada! That's gonna be one of the biggest problems facing northeastern lumber mills – you wait and see!' Simon said. 'Those Canadians are gonna export their lumber at a much lower cost than we're gonna produce it here!'

Good old Simon: not a political bone in his body; I doubt it occurred to him that I wasn't going to Canada for the *lumber*.

I recognized the Prelude, from Handel's *Messiah* – 'I know that my Redeemer liveth.' I also recognized the pudgy man across the aisle from me; he was about my age, and he'd been staring at me. But it wasn't until he began to search the high, vaulted ceiling of Hurd's Church – perhaps seeking angels in the shadowy buttresses – that I realized I was in the presence of Fat Harold Crosby, the former Announcing Angel who'd flubbed his lines and needed prompting, and who'd been abandoned in the heavens of Christ Church in the Nativity of '53. I nodded to Harold, who smiled tearfully at me; I'd heard that Mrs Hoyt had successfully coached him into acquiring a 4-F deferment from the draft – for psychological reasons.

I did not, at first, recognize our old Sunday school teacher, Mrs Walker. She looked especially severe in black, and without her sharp criticisms of Owen Meany – to get back to his *seat*, to get *down* from up there! – I did not instantly remember her as the Sunday school tyrant who was stupid enough to think that Owen Meany had put *himself* up in the air.

The Dowlings were there, *not* seizing the opportunity to use *this* occasion to flaunt their much-embattled, sexual role reversals; they had – and probably this was for the best – never had a child. Larry O'Day, the Chevy dealer, was also there; he'd played Bob Cratchit in *A Christmas Carol* – in that notable year when Owen Meany had played the Ghost of Christmas Yet to Come. He was with his racy daughter, Caroline O'Day, who sat with her lifelong friend Maureen Early, who'd twice wet her pants while watching Owen Meany show Scrooge his future – it was Caroline who had many times rejected my advances, both while wearing and *not* wearing her St Michael's uniform. Even Mr Kenmore, the A&P butcher, was there – with Mrs Kenmore and their son Donny, such faithful fans that they had never missed a Little League game. Yes, they were all there – even Mr Morrison, the cowardly mailman; even *he* was there! And the new headmaster of Gravesend Academy; he'd never met Owen Meany – yet he was there, perhaps acknowledging that he wouldn't have been made the new headmaster if Owen Meany hadn't lost the battle but won the war with Randy White. And if old Archie Thorndike had been alive, I know that he would have been there, too.

The Brinker-Smiths were not in attendance; I'm sure they would have come, had they not moved back to England – so firm was their opposition to the war in Vietnam that they hadn't wanted their twins to be Americans. Wherever the Brinker-Smiths were, I hoped that they still loved each other as passionately as they once loved each other – on all the floors, in all the beds – in Waterhouse Hall.

And our old friend the retarded janitor from the Gravesend gym – the man who'd so faithfully timed the shot, who'd been our witness the first time we sank the shot in under three seconds! – had also come to pay his respects to the little Slam-Dunk Master!

Then a cloud passed over the hole the baseball had made in the stained-glass window of the chancel; Owen's gold medal glowed a little less insistently. My grandmother, who was trembling, held my hand as we rose to join in the processional hymn – not meaning to, Grandmother squeezed the stump of my amputated finger. As Colonel Eiger and the young first lieutenant approached the casket from the center aisle, the honor guard came stiffly to attention. We sang the hymn we'd sung at morning meeting, the morning Owen had bolted the headless and armless Mary Magdalene to the podium on the stage of The Great Hall.

> The Son of God goes forth to war,
>   A king-ly crown to gain;
> His blood-red ban-ner streams a-far;
>   Who fol-lows in his train?
> Who best can drink his cup of woe,
>   Tri-um-phant o-ver pain,
> Who pa-tient bears his cross be-low,
>   He fol-lows in his train.

There is a note following 'An Order for Burial' in The Book of Common Prayer – according to the use of the Episcopal Church. This note is very sensible. 'The liturgy for the dead is an Easter liturgy,' the note says. 'It finds all its meaning in the resurrection. Because Jesus was raised from the dead, we, too, shall be raised. The liturgy, therefore, is characterized by joy . . .' the notes goes on. 'This joy, however, does not make human grief unchristian . . .' the note concludes. And so we sang our hearts out for Owen Meany – aware that while the liturgy for the dead might be characterized by joy, our so-called 'human grief' did not make us 'unchristian.' When we managed to get through the hymn, we sat down and looked up – and there was the Rev. Lewis Merrill, already standing in the pulpit.

' "I am the resurrection and the life, saith the Lord . . ." ' my father began. There was something newly powerful and confident in his voice, and the mourners heard it; the congregation gave him their complete attention. Of course, I knew what it was that had changed in him; he had found his lost faith – he spoke with absolute belief in every word he uttered; therefore, he never stuttered.

When he would look up from The Book of Common Prayer, he would gesture with his arms, like a swimmer exercising for the breaststroke, and the fingers of his right hand extended into the shaft of sunlight that plunged through the hole the baseball had made in the stained-glass window; Mr Merrill's fingers moving in and out of the beam of light caused Owen Meany's medal to twinkle.

' "The Spirit of the Lord God is upon me, because the Lord has anointed me to bring good tidings to the afflicted . . ." '

Pastor Merrill read to us. ' " . . . he has sent me to bind up the brokenhearted," ' cried Mr Merrill, who had no doubt – his doubt was gone; it had vanished, forever! He scarcely paused for breath. ' ". . . to comfort all who mourn," ' he proclaimed.

But Mr Merrill was not satisfied; he must have felt that we could not be comforted enough by only Isaiah. My father thought we should also be comforted by Lamentations, from which he read: ' "The Lord is good to those who wait for him, to the soul that seeks him." ' And if that morsel could not satisfy our hunger to be comforted, Pastor Merrill led us further into Lamentations: ' "For the Lord will not cast off for ever, but, though he cause grief, he will have compassion according to the abundance of his steadfast love; for he does not willingly afflict or grieve the sons of men." '

The fingers of my father's pale hand moved in and out of the shaft of sunlight, like minnows, and Owen's medal blinked at us as rhythmically as a beacon from a lighthouse. Then Pastor Merrill exhorted us through that familiar psalm: ' "The Lord shall preserve thy going out, and thy coming in, from this time forth for evermore." '

Thus he led us into the New Testament Lesson, beginning with that little bit of bravery from Romans: ' "I consider that the sufferings of this present time are not worth comparing to the glory that is to be revealed to us." ' But Lewis Merrill would not rest; for we missed Owen Meany so much that we ached for him, and Pastor Merrill would not rest until he'd assured us that Owen had left us for a better world. My father flung himself full-tilt into First Corinthians.

' "But in fact Christ has been raised from the dead . . ." ' Pastor Merrill assured us. ' "For as by a man came death, by a man has come also the resurrection of the dead," ' my father said.

My grandmother would not let go of my amputated finger, and even Simon's face was wet with tears; and still Mr Merrill would not rest – he sent us swiftly to Second Corinthians.

' "So we do not lose heart," ' he told us. ' "Though our outer nature is wasting away, our inner nature is being renewed every day. For this slight momentary affliction is preparing us for an eternal weight of glory beyond all comparison, because we look not to the things that are seen but to the things that are unseen; for the things that are seen are transient, but the things that are unseen are eternal," ' Pastor Merrill said. ' "So we are always of good courage"!' My father exhorted us. ' "We know that while we are at home in the body we are away from the Lord, for we walk by faith, not by sight," ' he said. ' "We are of good courage, and we would rather be away from the body and at home with the Lord. So whether we are at home or away, we make it our aim to please him." '

Then he swept us into another psalm, and then he commanded the congregation to stand, which we did, while he read us the Gospel according to John: ' "I am the good shepherd. The good shepherd lays down his life for the sheep," ' Pastor Merrill said, and we mourners lowered our heads like sheep. And when we were seated, Mr Merrill said; 'O God – how we miss Owen Meany!' Then he read to us – that passage about the miracle in the Gospel according to Mark:

> And when they came to the disciples, they saw a great crowd about them, and scribes arguing with them. And immediately all the crowd, when they saw him, were greatly amazed, and ran up to him and greeted him. And he asked them, 'What are you discussing with them?' And one of the crowd answered him, 'Teacher, I brought my son to you, for he was a dumb spirit; and wherever it seizes him it dashes him down; and he foams and grinds his teeth and becomes rigid; and I asked your disciples to cast it out, and they were not able.' And he answered them, 'O faithless generation, how long am I to be with you? How long am I to bear with you? Bring him to me.' And they brought the boy to him; and when the spirit saw him, immediately it convulsed the boy, and he fell on the ground and rolled about, foaming at the mouth. And Jesus asked his father, 'How long has he had this?' And he said, 'From childhood. And it has often cast him into the fire and into the water, to destroy him; but if you can do anything, have pity on us and help us.' And Jesus said to him, 'If you can! All things are possible to him who believes.' Immediately the father of the child cried out and said, 'I believe; help my unbelief!' And when Jesus saw that a crowd came running together, he rebuked the unclean spirit, saying to it, 'You dumb and deaf spirit, I command you, come out of him, and never

enter him again.' And after crying out and convulsing him terribly, it came out, and the boy was like a corpse; so that most of them said, 'He is dead.' But Jesus took him by the hand and lifted him up, and he arose. And when he had entered the house, his disciples asked him privately, 'Why could we not cast it out?' And he said to them, 'This kind cannot be driven out by anything but prayer.'

When he finished reading this passage, Pastor Merrill lifted his face to us and cried out, ' "I believe; help my unbelief!" Owen Meany helped *my* "unbelief," ' my father said. 'Compared to Owen Meany, I am an amateur – in my faith,' Mr Merrill said. 'Owen was not just a hero to the United States Army – he was *my* hero,' my father said. 'He was *our* hero – over and over again, he was our hero; he was *always* our hero. And we will always miss him,' the Rev. Lewis Merrill said.

'As often as I feel certain that God exists, I feel as often at a loss to say what difference it makes – that He exists – or even: that to believe in God, which I do, raises more questions than it presents answers. Thus, when I am feeling my most faithful, I also feel full of a few hard questions that I would like to put to God – I mean, *critical* questions of the How-Can-He, How-*Could*-He, How-*Dare*-You variety.

'For example, I would like to ask God to give us *back* Owen Meany,' Mr Merrill said; when he spread his arms wide, the fingers of his right hand were dancing again in the beam of light. 'O God – give him back, give him back to us!' Pastor Merrill asked. It was so quiet in Hurd's Church, while we waited to see what God would do. I heard a tear fall – it was one of my grandmother's tears, and I heard it patter upon the cover of the Pilgrim Hymnal, which she held in her lap. 'Please give us back Owen Meany,' Mr Merrill said. When nothing happened, my father said: 'O God – I shall keep asking You!' Then he once more turned to The Book of Common Prayer; it was unusual for a Congregationalist – especially, in a non-denominational church – to be using the prayer book so scrupulously, but I was sure that my father respected that Owen had been an Episcopalian.

Lewis Merrill took the prayer book with him when he left the pulpit; he approached the flag-draped casket and stood so close to Owen's medal that the shaft of sunlight that shone through the hole the baseball had made flickered on the prayer book, which Mr Merrill raised. Then he said, 'Let us pray,' and he faced Owen's body.

' "Into thy hands, O merciful Savior, we commend thy servant Owen Meany," ' my father said. ' "Acknowledge, we humbly beseech thee, a sheep of thine own fold, a lamb of thine own flock, a sinner of thine own redeeming. Receive him into the arms of thy mercy, into the blessed rest of everlasting peace, and into the glorious company of the saints in light," ' he prayed – the light from the hole in the stained-glass window still playing tricks with the medal and The Book of Common Prayer.

'Amen,' the Rev. Mr Merrill said.

Then he nodded to Colonel Eiger and the young, frightened-looking first lieutenant; they matched their steps to the casket, they removed the American flag and snapped it taut – the medal bouncing like a coin, but it was pinned fast to the flag and couldn't fall. Then the colonel and the first lieutenant walked haltingly toward each other, folding the flag – triangulating it, very exactly, so that the medal ended up on top of the package, which Colonel Eiger handed completely into the care of the frightened first lieutenant. Then Colonel Eiger saluted the folded flag, and the medal. The young man about-faced so sharply that my grandmother was startled; I felt her flinch against me. Then the first lieutenant mumbled something indistinct to Mr and Mrs Meany, who appeared surprised that he was speaking to them. He was saying something about the medal – 'For heroism that involves the voluntary risk of life.' After that, the first lieutenant cleared his throat and the congregation could hear him more distinctly. He spoke directly to Mrs Meany; he handed her the flag, with the medal on top, and he said – too loudly: 'Missus Meany, it is my privilege to present you with our country's flag in grateful appreciation for the service rendered to this nation by your son.'

At first, she didn't want to take the flag; she didn't appear to understand that she was supposed to take it – Mr Meany had to take it from her, or she might have let it fall. The whole time, they had sat like stones.

Then the organ startled my grandmother, who flinched again, and the Rev. Lewis Merrill led us through the recessional hymn – the same hymn he had chosen for the recessional at my mother's funeral.

Crown him with man-y crowns,
The Lamb up-on his throne;
Hark! how the heavenly an-them drowns
All mu-sic but its own;
A-wake, my soul, and sing
Of him who died for thee,
And hail him as thy match-less king
Through all e-ter-nity.

While we sang, the honor guard lifted Owen's small, gray casket and proceeded up the aisle with him; thus his body was borne from the church, about the time we were singing the third verse of the hymn – it was the verse that had meant the most to Owen Meany.

CROWN HIM THE LORD OF LIFE, WHO TRI-UMPHED O'ER THE GRAVE,
AND ROSE VIC-TO-RIOUS IN THE STRIFE FOR THOSE HE CAME TO SAVE;
HIS GLO-RIES NOW WE SING WHO DIED AND ROSE ON HIGH,
WHO DIED, E-TER-NAL LIFE TO BRING, AND LIVES THAT DEATH MAY DIE.

There's not much to add about the committal. The weather was hot and sticky, and from the cemetery, at the end of Linden Street, we could once again hear the kids playing baseball on the high-school athletic fields – the sounds of their fun, and their arguing, and that good old American crack of the bat drifted to us while we stood at Owen Meany's grave and listened to the Rev. Lewis Merrill say the usual.

' "In sure and certain hope of the resurrection to eternal life through our Lord Jesus Christ, we commend to Almighty God our brother *Owen* . . ." ' my father said. If I listened with special care, it was because I knew I was listening to Pastor Merrill for the last time; what more could he ever have to say to me? Now that he had found his lost faith, what need did he have of a lost son? And what need did I have of *him*? I stood at Owen's grave, holding Dan Needham's hand, with my grandmother leaning against the two of us.

' ". . . earth to earth, ashes to ashes, dust to dust," ' Pastor Merrill was saying, and I was thinking that my father was quite a *fake;* after all, he had met the miracle of Owen Meany, face to face, and still hadn't believed in him – and now he believed *everything,* not because of Owen Meany but because I had tricked him. I had fooled him with a dressmaker's dummy; Owen Meany had been the *real* miracle, but my father's faith was restored by an encounter with a *dummy,* which the poor fool had believed was my mother – reaching out to him from beyond her grave.

'GOD WORKS IN STRANGE WAYS!' Owen might have said.

' "... the Lord lift up his countenance upon him, and give him peace," ' Lewis Merrill said – while clods of earth fell upon the small, gray casket. Then the stern, sawed-off soldier, whom Colonel Eiger had referred to as a master sergeant, played taps for Owen Meany.

I was leaving the cemetery when she came up to me. She might have been a farmer's wife, or a woman who worked outdoors; she was my age, but she looked so much older – I didn't recognize her. She had three children with her; she carried one of them – a pouting boy who was too heavy to be carried easily, or far. She had two daughters, one of whom hung on her hip and tugged at her and continued to wipe her runny nose on the woman's faded-black dress. The second daughter – the eldest child, who was possibly seven or eight – lagged behind and eyed me with a gawky shyness that was painful to endure. She was a pretty girl, with straw-colored hair, but she could not keep her hands away from a raspberry-colored birthmark on her forehead, which was about the size of a passport photo and which she tried to hide with her hair. I stared into the woman's weary, red-eyed face; she was struggling not to burst into tears.

'Do you remember how we used to lift him up?' she asked me. Then I knew her: she was Mary Beth Baird, our old Sunday school colleague and the girl Owen had selected for the role of the Virgin Mary. 'MARY BETH BAIRD HAS NEVER BEEN MARY,' Owen had said. 'THAT WAY, MARY WOULD BE MARY.'

I'd heard she'd gotten pregnant and had dropped out of high school; she'd married the boy, who was from a big family of dairy farmers – and now she lived on a dairy farm in Stratham. I hadn't seen her since her staggering performance in the Nativity of 1953 - when, in addition to her efforts as the Virgin Mother of Owen's Christ Child, she had contributed those striking cow costumes, the ones with floppy antlers that made the cows resemble damaged reindeer. I suppose that she had not been an expert on dairy cows – or on cows of any kind – back then.

'He was so easy to lift up!' Mary Beth Baird said to me. 'He was so *light* – he weighed nothing at all! How could he have been so light?' she asked me. That was when I discovered that I couldn't speak. I had lost my voice. It occurs to me now that it wasn't *my* voice that I wanted to hear. If I couldn't hear Owen's voice, I didn't want to hear *anyone's*. It was only Owen's voice that I wanted to hear; and when Mary Beth Baird spoke to me, that was when I knew that Owen Meany was gone.

There's not much to add about coming to Canada. As Owen and I had discovered: at the New Hampshire-Quebec border, there's little to see – just forests, for miles, and a thin road so beaten by the winter that it is bruised to the color of pencil lead and pockmarked with frost heaves. The border outpost, the so-called customs house, which I remembered as just a cabin, was not exactly as I'd remembered it; and I thought there'd been a gate that was raised – like a gate guarding a railroad crossing – but that was different, too. I was sure I remembered sitting on the tailgate of the tomato-red pickup, watching the fir trees on both sides of the border – but then I wondered if everything I'd done with Owen Meany was not as exact in my memory as I imagined. Perhaps Owen had even changed my memory.

Anyway, I crossed the border without incident. A Canadian customs officer asked me about the granite doorstop – JULY, 1952. He seemed surprised when I told him it was a wedding present. The customs officer also asked me if I was a draft dodger; although I might have appeared – to him – too old to be dodging the draft, they had been drafting people *over* twenty-six for more than a year. I answered the question by showing the officer my missing finger.

'I'm not worried about the war,' I told him, and he let me into Canada without any more questions.

I might have ended up in Montreal; but too many people were pissy to me there, because I couldn't speak French. And I arrived in Ottawa on a rainy day; I just kept driving until I got to Toronto. I'd never seen a lake as large as Lake Ontario;

I knew I was going to miss the view of the Atlantic Ocean from the breakwater at Rye Harbor, so the idea of a lake that *looked* as big as the sea was appealing to me.

Not much else has happened to me. I'm a churchgoer and a schoolteacher. Those two devotions need not necessarily yield an unexciting life, but my life has been determinedly unexciting; my life is a reading list. I'm not complaining; I've had enough excitement. Owen Meany was enough excitement for a lifetime.

How it must have disappointed Owen . . . to discover that my father was such an insipid soup of a man. Lewis Merrill was so innocuous, how could I have remembered seeing *him* in those bleacher seats? Only Mr Merrill could have escaped my attention. As many times as I searched the audience at the performances of The Gravesend Players (and the Rev. Mr Merrill was *always* there), I always missed him, I never remembered him as he was in those bleacher seats, I simply overlooked him. In any gathering, not only did Mr Merrill not stand out – he didn't even show up!

How it has disappointed me . . . to discover that my father was just another Joseph. I never dared tell Owen, but once I dreamed that JFK was my father; after all, my mother was just as beautiful as Marilyn Monroe! How it has disappointed me . . . to discover that my father is just another man like me.

As for my faith: I've become my father's son – that is, I've become the kind of believer that Pastor Merrill *used* to be. Doubt one minute, faith the next – sometimes inspired, sometimes in despair. Canon Campbell taught me to ask myself a question when the latter state settles upon me. Whom do I know who's alive whom I love? Good question – one that can bring you back to life. These days, I love Dan Needham and the Rev. Katherine Keeling; I know I love them because I worry about them – Dan should lose some weight, Katherine should gain some! What I feel for Hester isn't exactly love; I admire her – she's certainly been a more heroic survivor than I've been, and her kind of survival is admirable. And then there are those distant, family ties that pass for love – I'm talking about Noah and Simon, about Aunt Martha and Uncle Alfred. I look forward to seeing them every Christmas.

I don't hate my father; I just don't think about him very much – and I haven't seen him since that day he committed Owen Meany's body to the ground. I hear from Dan that he's a whale of a preacher, and that there's not a trace of the slight stutter that once marred his speech. At times I envy Lewis Merrill; I wish someone could trick me the way I tricked him into having such absolute and unshakable faith. For although I believe I know what the *real* miracles are, my belief in God disturbs and unsettles me much more than *not* believing ever did; unbelief seems vastly harder to me now than belief does, but belief poses so many unanswerable questions!

How could Owen Meany have known what he 'knew'? It's no answer, of course, to believe in accidents, or in coincidences; but is God really a *better* answer? If God had a hand in what Owen 'knew,' what a horrible question *that* poses! For how could God have let that happen to Owen Meany?

Watch out for people who call themselves religious; make sure you know what they mean – make sure *they* know what they mean!

It was more than a year after I came to Canada, when the town churches of Gravesend – and Hurd's Church, upon the urging of Lewis Merrill – organized a so-called Vietnam Moratorium. On a given day in October, all the church bells were rung at 6:00 A.M. – I'm sure that pissed some people off! – and services were held as early as 7:00. Following the services, a parade then commenced from the town bandstand, marching up Front Street to assemble on the lawn in front of the Main Academy Building on the Gravesend campus; there followed a peaceful demonstration, so-called, and a few of the standard antiwar speeches. Typically, the town newspaper, *The Gravesend News-Letter*, did not editorialize on the event, except to say that a march against mayhem on the nation's highways would be a more significant use of such civilian zeal; as for the academy newspaper, *The Grave* reported that it was 'about time' the school and the town combined forces to demonstrate against the evil war. *The News-Letter* estimated the crowd was less than four hundred people – 'and almost as many dogs.' *The Grave* claimed that the crowd swelled to at least six hundred 'well-behaved' people. Both papers reported the only counterdemonstration. As the parade swung up Front Street – just past the old Town Hall, where The Gravesend Players had for so long been entertaining both young and old – a former American Legion commander stepped off the sidewalk and waved a North

Vietnamese flag in the face of a young tuba player in the Gravesend Academy marching band.

Dan told me that the former American Legion commander was none other than Mr Morrison, the cowardly mailman.

'I'd like to know how that idiot got his hands on a North Vietnamese flag!' my grandmother said.

Thus, with precious little to interrupt them, the years have also swung up Front Street and marched on by.

Owen Meany taught me to keep a diary; but my diary reflects my unexciting life, just as Owen's diary reflected the vastly more interesting things that happened to him. Here's a typical entry from my diary.

'Toronto: November 17, 1970 – the Bishop Strachan greenhouse burned down today, and the faculty and students had to evacuate the school buildings.'

And let's see: I also note in my diary every day when the girls sing 'Sons of God' in the morning chapel. I also entered in my diary the day that a journalist from some rock-music magazine tried to stop me for an on-the-spot 'interview' as I was about to take a seat in morning chapel. He was a wild, hairy young man in a purple caftan – oblivious to how the girls stared at him and seemingly held together by wires and cords that entangled him in his cumbersome recording equipment. There he was, uninvited – unannounced! – sticking a microphone in my face and asking me, as Hester the Molester's 'kissing cousin,' if I didn't agree that it all began to 'happen' for Hester after she met someone called 'Janet the Planet.'

'I beg your pardon!' I said. Around me, *streams* of girls were staring and giggling.

The interviewer was interested in asking me about Hester's 'influences'; he was writing a piece about Hester's 'early years,' and he had some ideas about who had influenced her – he said he wanted to 'bounce' his ideas off *me*! I said I didn't know who the fuck 'Janet the Planet' even *was*, but if he was interested in who had 'influenced' Hester, he should begin with Owen Meany. He didn't know the name, he asked me how to spell it. He was very puzzled, he thought he'd heard of *everyone*!

'And would this be someone who was an influence in her *early years*?' he wanted to know. I assured him that Owen's influence on Hester could be counted among the earliest.

And let's see: what else? There was Mrs Meany's death, not long after Owen's; I made note of it. And there was that spring when I was in Gravesend for Grandmother's funeral – it was at the old Congregational Church, Grandmother's lifelong church, and Pastor Merrill did *not* perform the service; whoever had replaced him at the Congregational Church was the officiant. There was still a lot of snow on the ground that spring – old, dead-gray snow – and I was opening another beer for Dan and myself in the kitchen at 80 Front Street, when I happened to look out the kitchen window at the withered rose garden, and there was Mr Meany! Grayer than the old snow, and following some melted and refrozen footprints in the crust, he made his way slowly toward the house. I thought he was a kind of apparition. Speechless, I pointed at him, and Dan said: 'It's just poor old Mister Meany.'

The Meany Granite Company was dead and gone; the quarries had been unworked – and for sale – for years. Mr Meany had a part-time job as a meter reader for the electric company. He appeared in the rose garden once a month, Dan said; the electric meter was on the rose-garden side of the house.

I didn't want to speak with him; but I watched him through the window. I'd written him my condolences when I'd heard that Mrs Meany had died – and how she'd died – but he'd never written back; I hadn't expected him to write back.

Mrs Meany had caught fire. She'd been sitting too close to the fireplace and a spark, an ember, had ignited the American flag, which – Mr Meany told Dan – she was accustomed to wrapping around herself, like a shawl. Although her burns had not appeared to be that severe, she died in the hospital – of undisclosed complications.

When I saw Mr Meany reading the electric meter at 80 Front Street, I realized that Owen's medal had not been consumed with the flag in the fire. Mr Meany *wore* the medal – he always wore it, Dan said. The cloth that shielded the pin above the medal was much faded – red and white stripes on a chevron of blue – and the gold of the medal itself blazed less brightly than it had blazed that day when a beam of sunlight had been reflected by it in Hurd's Church; but the raised, unfurled wings of the American eagle were no less visible.

Whenever I think of Owen Meany's medal for heroism, I'm

reminded of Thomas Hardy's diary entry in 1882 – Owen showed it to me, that little bit about 'living in a world where nothing bears out in practice what it promises incipiently.' I remember it whenever I think of Mr Meany wearing Owen's medal while he reads the electric meters.

Let's see: there's not much else – there's almost nothing to add. Only this: that it took years for me to face my memory of *how* Owen Meany died – and once I forced myself to remember the details, I could never forget how he died; I will never forget it. I am doomed to remember this.

I had never been a major participant in Fourth of July celebrations in Gravesend; but the town was faithfully patriotic – it did not allow Independence Day to pass unnoticed. The parade was organized at the bandstand in the center of town, and marched nearly the whole length of Front Street, achieving peak band noise and the maximum number of barking dogs, and accompanying children on bicycles, at the midpoint of the march – precisely at 80 Front Street, where my grandmother was in the habit of viewing the hullabaloo from her front doorstep. Grandmother suffered ambivalent feelings every Fourth of July; she was patriotic enough to stand on her doorstep waving a small American flag – the flag itself was not any larger than the palm of her hand – but at the same time, she frowned upon all the ruckus; she frequently reprimanded the children who rode their bicycles across her lawn, and she shouted at the dogs to stop their fool barking.

I often watched the parade pass by, too; but after my mother died, Owen Meany and I never followed the parade on our bicycles – for the final destination of the band and the marchers was the cemetery on Linden Street. From 80 Front Street, we could hear the guns saluting the dead heroes; it was the habit in Gravesend to conclude a Memorial Day parade and a Veterans Day parade *and* an Independence Day parade with manly gunfire over the graves that knew too much quiet all the other days of the year.

It was no different on July 4, 1968 – except that Owen Meany was in Arizona, possibly watching or even participating in a parade at Fort Huachuca; I didn't know what Owen was doing. Dan Needham and I had enjoyed a late breakfast with my grandmother and we'd all taken our coffee out on the front doorstep to wait for the parade; by the sound of it, coming nearer, it was passing the Main Academy Building – gathering force, bicyclists, and dogs. Dan and I sat on the stone doorstep, but my grandmother chose to stand; sitting on a doorstep would not have measured up to Harriet Wheelwright's high standards for women of her age and position.

If I was thinking anything – if I was thinking at all – I was considering that my life had become a kind of doorstep-sitting, watching parades pass by. I was not working that summer; I would not be working that fall. With my Master's degree in hand, I had enrolled in the Ph.D. program at the University of Massachusetts; I didn't really know what I wanted to study, I didn't even know if I wanted to rent a room or an apartment in Amherst, but I was scheduled to be a full-time graduate student there. I never thought about it. So that I could carry the fullest possible course load, I wasn't planning to teach for at least a year – not even part-time, not even one course. Naturally, Grandmother was bankrolling my studies, and that further contributed to my sense of myself as a doorstep-sitter. I wasn't doing anything; there wasn't anything I *had* to do.

Hester was in the same boat. That Fourth of July night, we sat on the grass border of the Swasey Parkway and watched the fireworks display over the Squamscott – Gravesend maintained a Town Fireworks Board, and every Fourth of July the members who knew their rocketry and bombs set up the fireworks on the docks of the academy boathouse. The townspeople lined the Swasey Parkway, all along the grassy riverbank, and the bombs burst in the air, and the rockets flared – they hissed when they fell into the dirty river. There had been a small, ecological protest lately; someone said that the fireworks disturbed the birds that nested in the tidal marsh on the riverbank opposite the Swasey Parkway. But in a dispute between herons and patriots, the herons are not generally favored to win; the bombardment proceeded, as planned - the night sky was brilliantly set afire, and the explosions gratified us all.

An occasional white light spread like a newly invented liquid across the dark surface of the Squamscott, reflecting there so brightly that the darkened stores and offices of the town, and the huge building that housed the town's foul textile mills, sprang up in silhouette – a town created instantly by the explosions. The many empty windows of the textile mills bounced back this light – the building's vast size and emptiness suggested an industry so self-possessed that it functioned completely without a human labor force.

'If Owen won't marry me, I'll never marry anyone,' Hester told me between flashes and blasts. 'If he won't give me babies, no one's ever gonna give me babies.'

One of the demolition experts on the dock was none other than that old dynamiter Mr Meany. Something like an exploding star showered over the black river.

'That one looks like sperm,' Hester said sullenly. I was not expert enough on sperm to challenge Hester's imagery; fireworks that looked 'like sperm' seemed highly unlikely if not farfetched to me – but what did *I* know?

Hester was so morose, I didn't want to spend the night in Durham with her. It was a not-quite-comfortable summer night, but there was a breeze. I drove to 80 Front Street and watched the eleven o'clock news with Grandmother; she had lately taken an interest in a terrible local channel on which the news detailed the grim statistics of a few highway fatalities and made no mention of the war in Vietnam; and there was a 'human interest' story about a bad child who'd blinded a poor dog with a firecracker.

'Merciful Heavens!' Grandmother said.

When she went to bed, I tuned in to *The Late Show* – one channel was showing a so-called Creature Feature, *The Beast from 20,000 Fathoms*, an old favorite of Owen's; another channel featured *Mother Is a Freshman*, in which Loretta Young is a widow attending college with her teenage daughter; but my favorite, *An American in Paris*, was on a third channel. I could watch Gene Kelly dance all night; in between the songs and dances, I switched back to the channel where the prehistoric monster was mashing Manhattan, or I wandered out to the kitchen to get myself another beer.

I was in the kitchen when the phone rang; it was after midnight, and Owen was so respectful of my grandmother's sleep that he never called 80 Front Street at an hour when he might awaken her. At first I thought that the different time zone – in Arizona – had confused him; but I knew he would have called Hester in Durham and Dan in Waterhouse Hall before he found me at my grandmother's, and I was sure that Hester or Dan, or both of them, would have told him how late it was.

'I HOPE I DIDN'T WAKE UP YOUR GRANDMOTHER!' he said.

'The phone only rang once – I'm in the kitchen,' I told him. 'What's up?'

'YOU MUST APOLOGIZE TO HER FOR ME – IN THE MORNING,' Owen said. 'BE SURE TO TELL HER I'M *VERY* SORRY – BUT IT'S A KIND OF *EMERGENCY*.'

'What's up?' I asked him.

'THERE'S BEEN A BODY MISPLACED IN CALIFORNIA – THEY THOUGHT IT GOT LOST IN VIETNAM, BUT IT JUST TURNED UP IN OAKLAND. IT HAPPENS EVERY TIME THERE'S A HOLIDAY – SOMEONE GOES TO SLEEP AT THE SWITCH. IT'S STANDARD ARMY – THEY GIVE ME TWO HOURS TO PACK A BAG AND THE NEXT THING I KNOW, I'M IN CALIFORNIA. I'M SUPPOSED TO TAKE A COMMUTER PLANE TO TUCSON, I'VE GOT A CONNECTION WITH A COMMERCIAL FLIGHT TO OAKLAND – FIRST THING TOMORROW MORNING. THEY'VE GOT ME BOOKED ON A FLIGHT FROM SAN FRANCISCO BACK TO PHOENIX THE NEXT DAY. THE BODY BELONGS IN PHOENIX – THE GUY WAS A WARRANT OFFICER, A HELICOPTER PILOT. THAT USUALLY MEANS HE CRASHED AND BURNED UP – YOU HEAR "HELICOPTER," YOU CAN COUNT ON A CLOSED CASKET.

'CAN YOU MEET ME IN PHOENIX?' he asked me.

'Can I meet you in Phoenix? *Why?*' I asked him.

'WHY *NOT*?' Owen said. 'YOU DON'T HAVE ANY PLANS, DO YOU?'

'Well, no,' I admitted.

'YOU CAN AFFORD THE FLIGHT, CAN'T YOU?' he asked me.

'Well, yes,' I admitted. Then he told me the flight information – he knew exactly when my plane left Boston, and when my plane arrived in Phoenix; I'd arrive a little earlier than his flight with the body from San Francisco, but I wouldn't have to wait long. I could just meet his plane, and after that, we'd stick together; he'd already booked us into a motel – 'WITH AIR CONDITIONING, GOOD TV, A GREAT POOL. WE'LL HAVE A BLAST!' Owen assured me; he'd already arranged everything.

The proposed funeral was all fouled up because the body

was already two days late. Relatives of the deceased warrant officer – family members from Modesto and Yuma – had been delayed in Phoenix for what must have seemed forever. Arrangements with the funeral parlor had been made and canceled and made again; Owen knew the mortician and the minister – 'THEY'RE REAL ASSHOLES: DYING IS JUST A BUSINESS TO THEM, AND WHEN THINGS DON'T COME OFF ON SCHEDULE, THEY BITCH AND MOAN ABOUT THE MILITARY AND MAKE THINGS WORSE FOR THE POOR FAMILY.'

Apparently the family had planned a kind of 'picnic wake'; the wake was now in its third day. Owen was pretty sure that all he'd have to do was deliver the body to the mortuary; the survivor assistance officer – a ROTC professor at Arizona State University, a major whom Owen also knew – had warned Owen that the family was so pissed off at the Army that they probably wouldn't want a military escort at the funeral.

'BUT YOU NEVER KNOW,' Owen told me. 'WE'LL JUST HANG AROUND, SORT OF PLAY IT BY EAR – EITHER WAY, I CAN GET A COUPLE OF FREE DAYS OUT OF IT. WHEN THERE'S BEEN A FUCKUP LIKE THIS, THERE'S NEVER ANY PROBLEM WITH ME GETTING A COUPLE OF DAYS AWAY FROM THE POST. I JUST NOTIFY THE ARMY THAT I'M STICKING AROUND PHOENIX – "AT THE REQUEST OF THE FAMILY," IS HOW I PUT IT. SOMETIMES, IT'S EVEN TRUE – LOTS OF TIMES, THE FAMILY *WANTS* YOU TO STICK AROUND. THE POINT IS, I'LL HAVE LOTS OF FREE TIME AND WE CAN JUST HANG OUT TOGETHER. LIKE I TOLD YOU, THE MOTEL HAS A GREAT SWIMMING POOL; AND IF IT'S NOT TOO HOT, WE CAN PLAY SOME TENNIS.'

'I don't play tennis,' I reminded him.

'WE DON'T *HAVE* TO PLAY TENNIS,' Owen said.

It seemed to me to be a long way to go for only a couple of days. I also thought that the details of the body-escorting business – as they might pertain to this particular body – were more than a little uncertain, if not altogether vague. But there was no doubt that Owen had his heart set on my meeting him in Phoenix, and he sounded even more agitated than usual. I thought he might need the company; we hadn't seen each other since Christmas. After all, I'd never been to

Arizona – and, I admit, at the time I was curious to see something of the so-called body escorting. It didn't occur to me that July was not the best season to be in Phoenix – but what did *I* know?

'Sure, let's do it – it sounds like fun,' I told him.

'YOU'RE MY BEST FRIEND,' said Owen Meany – his voice breaking a little. I assumed it was the telephone; I thought we had a bad connection.

That was the day they made desecrating the U.S. flag a federal crime. Owen Meany spent the night of July 5, 1968, in Oakland, California, where he was given a billet in the Bachelor Officers' Quarters; on the morning of July 6, Owen left quarters at the Oakland Army Depot – noting, in his diary, 'THE ENLISTED MEN ON FAR EAST LEVY ARE REQUIRED TO LINE UP AT A NUMBERED DOOR, WHERE THEY ARE ISSUED JUNGLE FATIGUES, AND OTHER CRAP. THE RECRUITS ARE GIVEN STEAK DINNERS BEFORE BEGINNING THEIR FLIGHT TO VIETNAM. I'VE SEEN THIS PLACE TOO MANY TIMES: THE SPARS AND CRANES AND THE TIN WAREHOUSE ROOFS, AND THE GULLS GLIDING OVER THE AIRPLANE HANGARS – AND ALL THE NEW RECRUITS, ON THEIR WAY OVER THERE, AND THE BODIES COMING HOME. SO MANY GREEN DUFFEL BAGS ON THE SIDEWALKS. DO THE RECRUITS KNOW THE CONTENTS OF THOSE GRAY PLYWOOD BOXES?'

Owen noted in his diary that he was issued, as usual, the triangular cardboard box, in which the correctly prefolded flag was packaged – 'WHO THINKS UP THESE THINGS? DOES THE PERSON WHO MAKES THE CARDBOARD BOX KNOW WHAT IT'S *FOR*?' He was issued the usual funeral forms and the usual black armband – he lied to a clerk about dropping his armband in a urinal, in order to be issued another one; he wanted *me* to have a black armband, too, so that I would look ACCEPTABLY OFFICIAL. About the time my plane left Boston, Owen Meany was identifying a plywood container in the baggage area of the San Francisco airport.

From the air, flying over Phoenix, you notice the nothingness first of all. It resembled a tan- and cocoa-colored moon, except that there are vast splotches of green – golf courses and other pampered land where irrigation systems have been installed. From my Geology course, I knew that everything below me had once been a shallow ocean; and at dusk, when I flew into Phoenix, the shadows on the rocks were a tropical-sea purple, and the tumbleweeds were aquamarine – so that I could actually imagine the ocean that once was there. In truth, Phoenix still resembled a shallow sea, marred by the fake greens and blues of swimming pools. Some ten or twenty miles in the distance, a jagged ridge of reddish, tea-colored mountains were here and there capped with waxy deposits of limestone – to a New Englander, they looked like dirty snow. But it was far too hot for snow.

Although, at dusk, the sun had lost its intensity, the dry heat shimmered above the tarmac; despite a breeze, the heat persisted with furnacelike generation. After the heat, I noticed the palm trees – all the beautiful, towering palm trees.

Owen's plane, like the body he was escorting home, was late.

I waited with the men in their guayabera shirts and huaraches, and their cowboy boots; the women, from petite to massive, appeared immodestly content in short shorts and halter tops, their rubber thongs slapping the hard floors of the Phoenix airport, which was optimistically called the Sky Harbor. Both the men and women were irrepressibly fond of the local silver-and-turquoise jewelry.

There was a game room, where a young, sunburned soldier was tilting a pinball machine with a kind of steadfast resentment. The first men's room I found was locked and labeled 'Temporarily Out of Order'; but the paper sign was so yellowed, it looked like an old announcement. After a search that transported me through widely varying degrees of air-conditioned coolness, I found a makeshift men's room, which was labeled 'Men's Temporary Facilities.'

At first, I wasn't sure I was in a men's room; it was a dark, subterranean room with a huge industrial sink – I wondered if it was a urinal for a giant. The actual urinal was hidden by a barrier of mops and pails, and a single toilet stall had been erected in the middle of the room from such fresh plywood that the carpentry odor almost effectively combated the gagging quality of the disinfectant. There was a long mirror, leaned against a wall rather than hung. It was about as 'temporary' a men's room as I ever hoped to see. The room – which was in its former life, I guessed, a storage closet;

but with a sink so mysteriously vast I couldn't imagine what was washed or soaked in it – was absurdly high-ceilinged for such a small space; it was like a long, thin room that an earthquake or an explosion had turned on its end. And the one small window was so high, it was almost touching the ceiling, as if the room were so deeply underground that the window had to be that high in order to reach ground-level light – scant little of which could ever penetrate to the faraway floor of the room. It was a transom-type window, but without a door under it; as to how it was hinged, it was the casement-type, with such a deep window ledge in front of it that a man could comfortably have sat there – except that his head and shoulders would be scrunched by the ceiling. The lip of the window ledge was far above the floor – maybe ten feet or more. It was that kind of unreachable window that one opened and closed by the use of a hook attached to a long pole – *if* one opened and closed this window, at all; it certainly looked as if no one had ever washed it.

I peed in the small, cramped urinal; I kicked a mop in a pail; I rattled the flimsy plywood of the 'temporary' toilet stall. The men's room was *so* makeshift, I wondered if anyone had bothered to hook up the plumbing to the urinal or the toilet. The intimidating sink was so dirty I chose not to touch the faucets – so I couldn't wash my hands. Besides: there was no towel. Some 'Sky Harbor,' I thought – and wandered off, composing a traveler's letter of complaint in my mind. It never occurred to me that there might have been a perfectly clean and functioning men's room elsewhere in the airport; maybe there was. Maybe where I had been was one of those sad places for 'Employees Only.'

I wandered in the air-conditioned coolness of the airport; occasionally, I stepped outside – just to feel the amazing, stifling heat that was so unknown in New Hampshire. The insistent breeze must have been coming off the desert, for it was not a wind I'd ever felt before, and I've never felt it since. It was dry, hot wind that caused the men's loose-fitting guayabera shirts to flap like flags.

I was standing outside the airport, in the hot wind, when I saw the family of the dead warrant officer; they were also waiting for Owen Meany's plane. Because I was a Wheelwright – and, therefore, a New England snob – I'd assumed that Phoenix was largely composed of Mormons and Baptists and Republicans; but the warrant officer's kinfolk were not what I'd expected. The first thing that I thought was wrong with this family was that they didn't appear to belong together, or even to be related to each other. About a half dozen of them were standing in the desert wind beside a silver-gray hearse; and although they were grouped fairly close together, they did not resemble a family portrait so much as they appeared to be the hastily assembled employees of a small, disorderly company.

An Army officer was standing with them – he would have been the major Owen said he'd done business with before, the ROTC professor from Arizona State University. He was a compact, fit-looking man whose athletic restlessness reminded me of Randy White; and he wore sunglasses of the goggle style that pilots favor. His indeterminate age – he could have been thirty or forty-five – was, in part, the result of the muscular rigidity of his body; and his bristling skull was so closely shaved, the stubble of his hair could have been either a whitish blond or a whitish gray.

I tried to identify the others. I thought I spotted the director of the funeral home – the mortician, or his delegate. He was a tall, thin, pasty presence in a starched, white shirt with long, pointed collars – and the only member of the odd group who wore a dark suit and tie. Then there was a bulky man in a chauffeur's uniform, who stood outside the group, and smoked incessantly. The family itself was inscrutable – except for the clear possession of a shared but unequal rage, which appeared to manifest itself the least in a slope-shouldered, slow-looking man in a short-sleeved shirt with a string tie. I took him for the father. His wife – the presumed mother of the deceased – twitched and trembled beside this man, who appeared to me to be both unmovable and unmoved. In contrast, the woman could not relax; her fingers picked at her clothes, and she poked at her hair – which was piled mountainously high and was as sticky-looking as a cone of cotton candy. And in the desert sunset, the woman's hair was nearly as pink as cotton candy, too. Perhaps it was the third day of the 'picnic wake' that had wrecked her face and left her with only minimal consciousness and control of her hands. From time to time, she would clench her fists and utter an oath that the desert wind, and my considerable distance from the family gathering, did not permit me to hear; yet the effect of the oath was instantaneous upon the boy and girl whom I guessed were the surviving siblings.

The daughter flinched at the mother's violent outbursts – as if the mother had made these utterances directly to her, which I thought was not the case; or as if in tandem with the oaths she uttered, the mother had managed to lash the daughter with a whip I couldn't see. At each oath, the daughter shook and cringed – once or twice, she even covered her ears. Because she wore a wrinkled cotton dress that was too small for her, when the wind pressed hard against her, I could see that she was pregnant – although she looked barely old enough to be pregnant, and she was not with any man I would have guessed was the father of her unborn child. I took the boy who stood beside her to be her brother – and a *younger* brother to both the dead warrant officer *and* his pregnant sister.

He was a gawky-tall, boney-faced boy, who was scary-looking because of what loomed as his *potential* size. I thought he could not have been older than fourteen or fifteen; but although he was thin, he carried great, broad bones upon his gangling frame – he had such strong-looking hands and such an oversized head that I thought he could have put on a hundred pounds without even slightly altering his exterior dimensions. With an additional hundred pounds, he would have been huge and frightening; in some way, I thought, he looked like a man who had recently *lost* a hundred pounds – and, at the same time, he appeared to have within him the capacity to gain it all back overnight.

The overgrown boy towered over everyone else – he sawed in the wind like the vastly tall palms that lined the entrance to the Phoenix Sky Harbor terminal – and *his* rage was the most manifest, *his* anger (like his body) appeared to be a monster that had lots of room to grow. When his mother spoke, the boy tipped his head back and spat – a sizable and mud-colored trajectory. It shocked me that, at his age, his parents allowed him to chew tobacco! Then he turned and stared at the mother, head-on, until she turned away from him, still fidgeting with her hands.

The boy wore a greasy pair of what looked to me (from my distant perspective) to be workmen's overalls, and some serious tools hung in loops from something like a carpenter's belt – only the tools more closely resembled the hardware of a car mechanic or a telephone repairman; perhaps the boy had an after-school job, and he'd come directly from this job to meet his brother's body at the airport.

If this was the most intimate welcoming party from the warrant officer's family, it gave me the shivers to think of the even less presentable members of kin who might still be making merry at the three-day-long 'picnic wake.' When I looked at this tribe, I thought that I wouldn't have wanted Owen Meany's job – not for a million dollars.

No one seemed to know in which direction to look for the plane. I trusted the major and the mortician; they were the only two people who stared off in the same direction, and I knew that this wasn't the first body they had been on hand to welcome home. And so I looked in the direction *they* looked. Although the sun had set, vivid streaks of vermilion-colored light traced the enormous sky, and through one of these streaks of light I saw Owen's plane descending – as if, wherever Owen Meany went, some kind of light always attended him.

All the way from San Francisco to Phoenix, Owen was writing in his diary; he wrote pages and pages – he knew he didn't have much time.

'THERE'S SO MUCH I KNOW,' he wrote, 'BUT I DON'T KNOW EVERYTHING. ONLY GOD KNOWS EVERYTHING. THERE ISN'T TIME FOR ME TO GET TO VIETNAM. I THOUGHT I KNEW I WAS GOING THERE. I THOUGHT I KNEW THE DATE, TOO. BUT IF I'M RIGHT ABOUT THE DATE, THEN I'M WRONG ABOUT IT HAPPENING IN VIETNAM. AND IF I'M RIGHT ABOUT VIETNAM, THEN I'M WRONG ABOUT THE DATE. IT'S POSSIBLE THAT IT REALLY *IS* "JUST A DREAM" – BUT IT SEEMS SO *REAL*! THE *DATE* LOOKED THE MOST REAL, BUT I DON'T KNOW – I DON'T KNOW ANYMORE.

'I'M NOT AFRAID, BUT I'M VERY NERVOUS. AT FIRST, I DIDN'T LIKE KNOWING – NOW I DON'T LIKE *NOT* KNOWING! GOD IS TESTING ME,' wrote Owen Meany.

There was much more; he was confused. He'd cut off my finger to keep me out of Vietnam; in his view, he'd attempted to physically remove me from his dream. But although he'd kept me out of the war, it was apparent – from his diary – that I'd remained in the dream. He could keep me out of Vietnam, he could cut off my finger; but he couldn't get me out of his dream, and that worried him. If he was going to die, he knew I had to be there – he didn't know why. But if he'd cut off my finger to save my life, it was a contradiction that he'd invited me to Arizona. God had promised him that nothing bad would happen to me; Owen Meany clung to that belief.

'MAYBE IT REALLY *IS* "JUST A DREAM"!' he repeated. 'MAYBE THE DATE IS JUST A FIGMENT OF MY IMAGINATION! BUT IT WAS WRITTEN IN STONE – IT *IS* "WRITTEN IN STONE"!' he added; he meant, of course, that he'd already carved the date of his death on his own gravestone. But now he was confused; now he wasn't so sure.

'HOW COULD THERE BE VIETNAMESE CHILDREN IN *ARIZONA*?' Owen asked himself; he even asked *God* a question. 'MY GOD – IF I *DON'T* SAVE ALL THOSE CHILDREN, HOW COULD YOU HAVE PUT ME THROUGH ALL THIS?' Later, he added: 'I MUST TRUST IN THE LORD.'

And just before the plane touched down in Phoenix, he made this hasty observation from the air: 'HERE I AM AGAIN – I'M ABOVE EVERYTHING. THE PALM TREES ARE VERY STRAIGHT AND TALL – I'M HIGH ABOVE THE PALM TREES. THE SKY AND THE PALM TREES ARE SO BEAUTIFUL.'

He was the first off the plane, his uniform a startlingly crisp challenge to the heat, his black armband identifying his mission, his green duffel bag in one hand – the triangular cardboard box in the other. He walked straight to the baggage compartment of the plane; although I couldn't hear his voice, I could see he was giving orders to the baggage handlers and the forklift operator – I'm sure he was telling them to keep the head of the body higher than the feet, so that fluid would not escape through the orifices. Owen rendered a salute as the body in the plywood box was lowered from the plane. When the forklift driver had the crate secured, Owen hopped on one of the tines of the fork – he rode thus, the short distance across the runway to the waiting hearse, like the figurehead on the prow of a ship.

I walked across the tarmac toward the family, who had not moved – only their eyes followed Owean Meany and the body in the box. They stood paralyzed by their anger; but the major stepped smartly forward to greet Owen; the chauffeur opened the tailgate of the long, silver-gray hearse; and the mortician became the unctuous delegate of death – the busybody it was his nature to be.

Owen hopped lightly off the forklift; he dropped his duffel bag to the tarmac and cracked open the triangular cardboard box. With the major's help, Owen unfolded the flag – it was difficult to manage in the strong wind. Suddenly, more runway lights were turned on, and the flag swelled and snapped brightly against the dark sky; rather clumsily, Owen and the major finally covered the crate with the flag. Once the body was slid into the hearse, the flag on top of the container lay still, and the family – like a large, ungainly animal – approached the hearse and Owen Meany.

That was when I noticed that the hugely tall boy was *not* wearing a pair of workmen's overalls – he was wearing jungle fatigues – and what I had mistaken for splotches of grease or oil were in fact the camouflage markings. The fatigues looked authentic, but the boy was clearly not old enough to 'serve' and he was hardly in a proper uniform – on his big feet, he wore a scuffed and filthy pair of basketball shoes, 'high tops'; and his matted, shoulder-length hair certainly wasn't Army regulation. It was not a carpenter's belt he wore; it was a kind of cartridge belt, with what appeared to be live ammo, actual loaded shells – at least, some of the cartridge sleeves in the belt were stuffed with bullets – and from various loops and nooks and straps, attached to this belt, certain things were hanging . . . neither a mechanic's tools, nor the equipment that is standard for a telephone repairman. The towering boy carried some authentic-looking *Army* equipment: an entrenching tool, a machete, a bayonet – although the sheath for the bayonet did not look like Army issue, not to me; it was made of a shiny material in a Day-Glo-green color, and embossed upon it was the traditional skull and crossbones in Day-Glo orange.

The pregnant girl, whom I took to be the tall monster's sister, could not have been older than sixteen or seventeen; she began to sob – then she made a fist and bit into the big knuckle at the base of her index finger, to stop herself from crying.

'Fuck!' the mother cried out. The slow-moving man who appeared to be her husband folded and unfolded his beefy arms, and – spontaneously, upon the mother's utterance – the specter in jungle fatigues tipped his head back and spat another sizable, mud-colored trajectory.

'Would you stop doing that?' the pregnant girl asked him.

'Fuck you,' he said.

The slow-moving man was not as slow as I thought. He lashed out at the boy – it was a solidly thrown right jab that caught the kid flush on his cheek and dropped him, like Owen's duffel bag, to the tarmac.

'Don't you speak to your sister that way,' the man said.

The boy, not moving, said: 'Fuck you – she's *not* my sister, she's just my *half* sister!'

The mother said: 'Don't speak to your father that way.'

'He's not my father – you asshole,' the boy said.

'Don't you call your mother an "asshole"!' the man said; but when he stepped closer to the boy on the tarmac – as if he were positioning himself near enough to kick the boy – the boy rose unsteadily to his feet. He held the machete in one hand, the bayonet in the other.

'You're *both* assholes,' the boy told the man and woman – and when his half sister commenced to cry again, he once more tipped back his head and spat the tobacco juice; he did not spit on her, but he spat in her general direction.

It was Owen Meany who spoke to him. 'I LIKE THAT SHEATH – FOR THE BAYONET,' Owen said. 'DID YOU MAKE IT YOURSELF?'

As I had seen it happen before – with strangers – the whole, terrible family was frozen by Owen Meany's voice. The pregnant girl stopped crying; the father – who was *not* the tall boy's father – backed away from Owen, as if he were more afraid of The Voice than of either a bayonet or a machete, or both; the mother nervously patted her sticky hair, as if Owen had caused her to worry about her appearance. The top of Owen Meany's cap reached only as high as the tall boy's chest.

The boy said to him: 'Who are *you*? You little *twit*.'

'This is the casualty assistance officer,' the major said. 'This is Lieutenant Meany.'

'I want to hear *him* say it,' the boy said, not taking his eyes off Owen.

'I'M LIEUTENANT MEANY,' Owen said; he offered to shake hands with the boy. 'WHAT'S YOUR NAME?' But in order to shake hands with Owen, the boy would have had to sheathe at least one of his weapons; he appeared unwilling. He also didn't bother to tell Owen his name.

'What's the matter with your *voice*?' he asked Owen.

'NOTHING – WHAT'S THE MATTER WITH *YOU*?' Owen asked him. 'YOU WANT TO DRESS UP AND PLAY SOLDIER – DON'T YOU KNOW HOW TO SPEAK TO AN *OFFICER*?'

As a natural bully, the boy respected being bullied. 'Yes, sir,' he said, snidely to Owen.

'PUT THOSE WEAPONS AWAY,' Owen told him. 'IS THAT YOUR *BROTHER* I JUST BROUGHT HOME?' Owen asked him.

'Yes, sir,' the boy said.

'I'M SORRY YOUR BROTHER'S DEAD,' said Owen Meany. 'DON'T YOU WANT TO PAY SOME ATTENTION TO *HIM*?' Owen asked.

'Yes, sir,' the boy said quietly; he looked at a loss about *how* to PAY SOME ATTENTION to his dead brother, and so he stared forlornly at the corner of the flag that was near enough to the open tailgate of the hearse to be occasionally moved by the wind.

Then Owen Meany circulated through the family, shaking hands, saying he was sorry; such a range of feelings flashed across the mother's face – she appeared contradictively stimulated to flirt with him and to kill him. The impassive father seemed to me to be the most disagreeably affected by Owen's unnatural size; the man's doughy countenance wavered between brute stupidity and contempt. The pregnant girl was stricken with shyness when Owen spoke to her.

'I'M SORRY ABOUT YOUR BROTHER,' he said to her; he came up to her chin.

'My *half* brother,' she mumbled. 'But I still loved him!' she added. Her *other* half brother – the one who was alive – needed to ferociously restrain himself from spitting again. So they were a family torn in halves, or worse, I thought.

In the major's car – where Owen and I were first able to acknowledge each other, to hug each other, and to pat each other on our backs – the major explained the family to us.

'They're a mess, of course – they may all be criminally retarded,' the major said. His name was Rawls – Hollywood would have loved him. In close-up, he looked fifty, a gruff old type; but he was only thirty-seven. He'd earned a battle-field commission during the final days of the Korean War; he'd completed a tour of duty in Vietnam as an infantry battalion executive officer. Major Rawls had enlisted in the Army in 1949, when he'd been eighteen. He'd served the Army for nineteen years; he'd fought in two wars; he'd been passed over for promotion to lieutenant colonel, and – at a time when all the good 'field grade' officers were in Washington or Vietnam – he'd ended up as a ROTC professor for his twilight tour of duty.

If Major Rawls had earned a battlefield commission, he had earned his measure of cynicism, too; the major spoke in sustained, explosive bursts – like rounds of fire from an automatic weapon.

'They may *all* be fucking each other – I wouldn't be surprised about a family like this,' Major Rawls said. 'The brother is the chief wacko – he hangs around the airport all day, watching the planes, talking to the soldiers. He can't *wait* to be old enough to go to 'Nam. The only one in the family who might have been wackier than him is the one who's dead – this was his *third* fucking tour "in country"! You should've seen him between tours – the whole fucking tribe lives in a trailer park, and the warrant officer just spent all his time looking in his neighbors' windows through a telescopic sight. You know what I mean – lining up everyone in the cross hairs! If he hadn't gone back to 'Nam, he'd have gone to jail.

'Both brothers have a different father – a *dead* one, not this clown,' Major Rawls informed us. 'This clown's the father of that unfortunate girl – I can't tell you who knocked her up, but I've got a feeling it was a family affair. My odds are on the warrant officer – I think he had sighted her in his cross hairs, too. You know what I mean? Maybe *both* brothers were banging her,' Major Rawls said. 'But I think the younger one is too crazy to get it up – he just can't wait to be old enough to kill people,' the major said.

'Now the *mother* – she's not just in space, she's in fucking *orbit*,' Major Rawls said. 'And wait till you get to the *wake* – wait till you meet the *rest* of the family! I tell you – they shouldn't've sent the brother home from 'Nam, not even in a box. What they should've done is send his whole fucking family *over there*! Might be the only way to win the fucking war – if you know what I mean,' Major Rawls said.

We were following the silver-gray hearse, which the chauffeur drove ploddingly along a highway called Black Canyon. Then we turned onto something called Camelback

Road. In the wind, the palm trees sawed over us; on the Bermuda grass, in one neighborhood, some old people sat in metal lawn chairs – as hot as it was, even at night, the old people wore sweaters, and they waved to us. They must have been crazy.

Owen Meany had introduced me to Major Rawls as his BEST FRIEND.

'MAJOR RAWLS – THIS IS MY BEST FRIEND, JOHN WHEELWRIGHT. HE'S COME ALL THE WAY FROM NEW HAMPSHIRE!' Owen had said.

'That's better than coming from Vietnam. It's nice to meet you, John,' Major Rawls had said; he had a crushing handshake and he drove his car as if every other driver on the road had already done something to offend him.

'Wait till you see the fucking funeral parlor!' the major said to me.

'IT'S A KIND OF SHOPPING-MALL MORTUARY,' Owen said, and Major Rawls liked that – he laughed.

'It's a fucking "shopping-mall" *mortician*!' Rawls said.

'THEY HAVE REMOVABLE CROSSES IN THE CHAPEL,' Owen informed me. 'THEY CAN SWITCH CROSSES, DEPENDING ON THE DENOMINATION OF THE SERVICE – THEY'VE GOT A CRUCIFIX WITH AN ESPECIALLY LIFELIKE CHRIST HANGING ON IT, FOR THE CATHOLICS. THEY'VE GOT A PLAIN WOODEN CROSS FOR THE PLAIN, PROTESTANT TYPES. THEY'VE EVEN GOT A FANCY CROSS WITH JEWELS IN IT, FOR THE IN-BETWEENS,' Owen said.

'What are "in-betweens"?' I asked Owen Meany.

'That's what we've got on our hands here,' Major Rawls said. 'We've got fucking *Baptists* – they're fucking "in-betweens," all right,' he said. 'You remember that asshole minister, Meany?' Major Rawls asked Owen.

'YOU MEAN THE BAPTIST THE MORTUARY USES? OF *COURSE* I DO!' Owen said.

'Just wait till you meet *him*!' Major Rawls said to me.

'I can't wait,' I said.

Owen made me put on the extra black armband. 'DON'T WORRY,' he told me. 'WE'LL HAVE A LOT OF FREE TIME.'

'Do you guys want *dates*?' Major Rawls asked us. 'I know some hot coeds,' he said.

'I KNOW YOU DO,' Owen said. 'BUT NO THANKS – WE'RE JUST GOING TO HANG OUT.'

'I'll show you where the porn shop is,' Major Rawls offered.

'NO THANKS,' Owen said. 'WE JUST WANT TO RELAX.'

'What are you – a couple of fags?' the major asked – he laughed at his joke.

'MAYBE WE ARE,' said Owen Meany, and Major Rawls laughed again.

'Your friend's the funniest little fucker in the Army,' the major said.

It actually *was* a kind of shopping-mall mortuary, surrounded by an unfathomable inappropriateness for a funeral home. In the style of a Mexican hacienda, the mortuary – and its chapel with the changeable crosses – formed one of several L-joints in a long, interconnected series of pink- and white-stuccoed buildings. Immediately adjacent to the mortuary itself was an ice-cream shop; adjoined to the chapel was a pet shop – the windowfront displayed an arrangement of snakes, which were on sale.

'It's no fucking wonder the warrant officer wanted to go back to 'Nam,' Major Rawls said.

Before the oily mortician could inquire who *I* was – or ask on whose authority *I* was permitted to view the contents of the plywood container – Owen Meany introduced me.

'THIS IS MISTER WHEELWRIGHT – OUR BODY EXPERT,' Owen said. 'THIS IS INTELLIGENCE BUSINESS,' Owen told the mortician. 'I MUST ASK YOU NOT TO DISCUSS THIS.'

'Oh no – never!' the mortician said: clearly, he didn't know what there was – or might be – to DISCUSS. Major Rawls rolled his eyes and concealed a dry laughter by pretending to cough. A carpeted hall led to a room that smelled like a chemistry lab, where two inappropriately cheerful attendants were loosening the screws on the transfer case – another man stacked the plywood against a far wall. He was finishing an ice-cream cone, so he clumsily stacked the wood with his free hand. It took four people to lift the heavy coffin – perhaps twenty-gauge steel – onto the mortuary's chrome dolly. Major Rawls spun three catches that looked like those fancy wheel locks on certain sports cars.

Owen Meany opened the lid and peered inside. After a while, he turned to Rawls. 'IS IT HIM?' he asked the major.

Major Rawls looked into the coffin for a long time. The mortician knew enough to wait his turn.

Finally, Major Rawls turned away. 'I *think* it's him,' Rawls said. 'It's close enough,' he added. The mortician started for the coffin, but Owen stopped him.

'PLEASE LET MISTER WHEELWRIGHT LOOK FIRST,' he said.

'Oh yes – of course!' the mortician said, backing away. To his attendants, the mortician whispered: 'This is *intelligence* business – there will be no discussion of this.' The two attendants, and even the mild-looking fellow who was handling the plywood and eating ice cream, glanced nervously at one another.

'What was the cause of death?' the mortician asked Major Rawls.

'THAT'S PRECISELY WHAT'S UNDER INVESTIGATION,' Owen snapped at him. 'THAT'S WHAT WE'RE *NOT* DISCUSSING!'

'Oh yes – of course!' the idiot mortician said.

Major Rawls again tried not to laugh; he coughed.

I avoided looking too closely at the body of the warrant officer. I was so prepared for something not even recognizably human that, at first, I felt enormously relieved; almost nothing appeared to be wrong with the man – he was a whole soldier in his greens and aviator wings and warrant officer brass. He had a makeup tan, and the skin on his face appeared to be stretched too tightly over his bones, which were prominent. There was an unreal element to his hair, which resembled a kind of wig-in-progress. Then certain, specific things began to go a little wrong with my perception of the warrant officer's face – his ears were as dark and shriveled as prunes, as if a set of headphones had caught fire when he'd been listening to something; and there were perfectly goggle-shaped circles burned into the skin around his eyes, as if he were part raccoon. I realized that his sunglasses had melted against his face, and that the tautness of his skin was, in fact, the result of his whole face being swollen – his whole face was a tight, smooth blister, which gave me the impression that the terrific heat he'd been exposed to had been generated from *inside* his head.

I felt a little ill, but more ashamed than sick – I felt I was being indecent, invading the warrant officer's privacy . . . to the degree that a thrill-seeker who's pressed too close to the wreckage of an automobile accident might feel guilty for catching a glimpse of the bloody hair protruding through the fractured windshield. Owen Meany knew that I couldn't speak.

'IT'S WHAT YOU EXPECTED – ISN'T IT?' Owen asked me; I nodded, and moved away.

Quickly the mortician darted to the coffin. 'Oh, *really* - you'd think they'd make a better effort than *this*!' he said. Fussily, he took a tissue and wiped some leakage – some fluid – from the corner of the warrant officer's mouth. 'I don't believe in open caskets, anyway,' the mortician said. 'That last look can be the heartbreaker.'

'I don't think this guy had a gift for breaking hearts,' Major Rawls said. But I could think of one heart that the warrant officer had broken; his tall younger brother was heartbroken – he was much *worse* than heartbroken, I thought.

Owen and I had an ice-cream cone, next door, while Major Rawls and the mortician argued about the 'asshole minister.' It was a Saturday. Because tomorrow was a Sunday, the service couldn't be held in the Baptist Church – it would conflict with the Sunday services. There was a Baptist minister who 'traveled' to the mortuary and performed the service in the mortuary's flexible chapel.

'You mean he *travels* because he's such an asshole that he doesn't have a church of his own!' said Major Rawls; he accused the mortician and the minister of frequently working together – 'for the money.'

'It costs money in a church, too – wherever you die and have a service, it costs money,' the mortician said.

'MAJOR RAWLS IS JUST TIRED OF LISTENING TO THIS PARTICULAR BAPTIST,' Owen explained to me.

Back in the car, Rawls said: 'I don't believe anyone in this family ever went to church – not ever! That fucking funeral director – I know he talked the family into being Baptists. He probably told them they had to say they were *something* – then he told them to be Baptists. He and that fucking minister – they're a match made in hell!'

'THE CATHOLICS REALLY DO THIS SORT OF THING BETTER THAN ANYBODY,' said Owen Meany.

'The fucking Catholics!' said Major Rawls.

'NO, THEY REALLY DO THIS SORT OF THING THE

BEST – THEY HAVE THE PROPER SOLEMNITY, THE PROPER SORT OF RITUALS, AND PROPER PACING,' Owen said.

I was amazed to find that Owen Meany had *praised* the Catholics; but he was absolutely serious. Even Major Rawls didn't wish to argue with him.

'No one does "this sort of thing" *well* – that's all I know,' the major said.

'I DIDN'T SAY ANYONE DID IT "WELL," SIR – I SAID THE CATHOLICS DID IT "BETTER"; THEY DO IT *BEST*,' said Owen Meany.

I asked Owen what had been the stuff I'd seen leaking from the warrant officer's mouth.

'That's just phenol,' said Major Rawls.

'IT'S ALSO CALLED CARBOLIC ACID,' Owen said.

'I call it "phenol," ' Rawls said.

Then I asked them how the warrant officer had died.

'He was such a dumb asshole,' Major Rawls said. 'He was refueling a helicopter – he just made some stupid-asshole mistake.'

'YOU AGGRAVATE HIGH OCTANE – THAT'LL DO IT,' said Owen Meany.

'I can't wait to show you guys this fucking "picnic wake," ' Major Rawls said. Apparently, that was where we were driving next – to the 'picnic wake' that was now in its third, merrymaking day. Major Rawls blew his horn at someone who he thought was possibly inching out of a driveway into the path of our car; actually, it was my impression that the person was waiting in the driveway for us to pass. 'Look at that asshole!' Major Rawls said. On we drove through nighttime Phoenix.

Owen Meany patted the back of my hand. 'DON'T WORRY,' he said to me. 'WE JUST HAVE TO MAKE AN APPEARANCE AT THE WAKE – WE DON'T HAVE TO STAY LONG.'

'You won't be able to tear yourselves away!' the major said excitedly. 'I'm telling you, these people are on the verge of killing each other – it's the kind of scene where mass-murderers get all their *ideas*!'

Major Rawls had been exaggerating. The 'tribe,' as he'd called the family, did not live (as he'd said) in a trailer park, but in a one-story tract house with turquoise aluminum siding; but for the daring choice of turquoise, the house was identical to all the others in what I suppose is still called a low-income housing development. The neighborhood was distinguished by a large population of dismantled automobiles – indeed, there were more cars on cinder blocks, with their wheels off or their engines ripped out from under their hoods, than there were *live* cars parked at the curbs or in driveways. And since the houses were nearly all constructed of cheap, uninsulated materials – and the residents could not afford or did not choose to trouble themselves with air conditioning – the neighborhood (even in the evening) teemed with outdoor activities of the kind that are usually conducted indoors. Televisions had been dragged outside, folding card tables and folding chairs gave the crowded suburb the atmosphere of a shabby sidewalk café – and block after block of outdoor barbecue pits and charcoal grills, which darkly smoked and sizzled with grease, gave the newcomer the impression that this part of Phoenix was recovering from an air raid that had set the ground on fire and driven the residents from their homes with only their most cherished and salvageable belongings. Some of the older people swayed in hammocks.

Screen doors whapped throughout the night, cats fought and fucked without cease, a cacophony of dogs malingered in the vicinity of each outdoor barbecue-in-progress, and an occasional flash of heat-lightning lit up the night, casting into silhouette the tangled maze of television antennas that towered over the low-level houses – as if a vast network of giant spider webs threatened the smaller, human community below.

'I tell you, the only thing preventing a murder here is that *everyone* would be a witness,' said Major Rawls.

Tents – for the children – filled the small backyard of the dead warrant officer's home; there were two cars on cinder blocks in the backyard, and for the duration of the 'picnic wake' some of the smaller children had been sleeping in these; and there was also a great boat on cinder blocks – a fire-engine-red racing boat with a gleaming chrome railing running around its jutting bow. The boat appeared more comfortable to sleep in than the turquoise house, at every orifice of which there popped into view the heads of children or adults staring out at the night.

One of the boat's big twin engines had been removed from the stern and was fastened to the rim of a large iron barrel, full of water; in the barrel, the noisy engine ran and ran – at least half a dozen grown men surrounded this display of spilled gasoline and oil, and the powerful propellers that churned and churned the water in the sloshing barrel. The men stood with such reverence around this demonstration of the engine's power that Major Rawls and Owen and I half expected the barrel to take flight – or at least drive itself away.

By the marvel of a long extension cord, a TV was placed in a prime position on the dry, brown lawn; a circle of men were watching a baseball game, of course. And where were the women? Clustered in their own groups, according to age or marriage or divorce or degree of pregnancy, most of the women were inside the sweltering house, where the ovenlike temperature appeared to have wilted them, like the limp raw vegetables that were plunked in assorted bowls alongside the assorted 'dips' that were now in their third day of exposure to this fetid air.

Inside, too, the sink was filled with ice, through which one could search in vain for a cold beer. The mother with her high-piled, sticky, pink hair slouched against the refrigerator, which she seemed to be guarding from the others; occasionally, she flicked the ash from her cigarette into what she vacantly assumed was an ashtray – rather, it was a small plate of nuts that had been creatively mixed with a breakfast cereal.

'Here comes the fuckin' Army!' she said – when she saw us. She was drinking what smelled like bourbon out of a highball glass – this one was etched with a poor likeness of a pheasant or a grouse or a quail.

It was not necessary to introduce me, although – several times – Owen and Major Rawls tried. Not everyone knew everyone else, anyway; it was hard to tell family from neighbors, and specifics such as which children were the offspring of whose previous or present marriage were not even considered. The relatives from Yuma and Modesto – aside from the uncomfortable fact that their children, and perhaps they themselves, were housed in tents and dismantled cars – simply blended in.

The father who'd struck his stepson at the airport was dead

drunk and had passed out in a bedroom with the door open; he was sprawled not on the bed but on the floor at the foot of the bed, upon which four or five small children were glued to a second television set, their attention riveted to a crime drama that surely held no surprises for them.

'You find a woman here, I'll pay for the motel,' Rawls said to me. 'I've been working this scene for two nights – this is my third. I tell you, there's not one woman you'd *dare* to put a move on – not here. The best thing I've seen is the pregnant sister – imagine that!'

Dutifully, I imagined it; the pregnant sister was the only one who tried to be nice to us; she tried to be especially nice to Owen.

'It's a very hard job you have,' she told him.

'IT'S NOT AS HARD AS BEING IN VIETNAM,' he said politely.

The pregnant sister had a hard job, too, I thought; she looked as if she needed to make a nearly constant effort not to be beaten by her mother or her father, or raped by the latter, or raped *and* beaten by her younger half brother – or some combination of, or all of, the above.

Owen said to her: 'I'M WORRIED ABOUT YOUR BROTHER – I MEAN YOUR HALF BROTHER, THE TALL BOY. I'LL HAVE A WORD WITH HIM. WHERE IS HE?'

The girl looked too frightened to speak.

Then she said: 'I know you have to give my mother the flag – at the funeral. I know what my mother's gonna do – when you give her the flag. She said she's gonna *spit* on you,' the pregnant sister told Owen. 'And I know her – she will!' the girl said. 'She'll spit in your face!'

'IT HAPPENS, SOMETIMES,' Owen said. 'WHERE'S THE TALL BOY – YOUR HALF BROTHER? WHAT'S HIS NAME?'

'If Vietnam hadn't killed that bastard, somethin' else would have – that's what *I* say!' said the pregnant sister, who quickly looked around, fearful that someone in the family might have overheard her.

'DON'T WORRY ABOUT THE FUNERAL,' Owen told her. 'WHERE'S THE TALL BOY? WHAT'S HIS NAME?' There was a closed door off a narrow hall, and the girl cautiously pointed to it.

'Don't tell him I told you,' she whispered.

'WHAT'S HIS NAME?' Owen asked her.

She looked around, to make sure one one was watching her; there was a gob of mustard on the swollen belly of her wrinkled dress. 'Dick!' she said; then she moved away.

Owen knocked on the door.

'Watch yourself, Meany,' Major Rawls said. 'I know the police, at the airport – they never take their eyes off this guy.'

Owen knocked on the door a little more insistently.

'Fuck you!' Dick shouted through the closed door.'

'YOU'RE TALKING TO AN *OFFICER*!' said Owen Meany.

'Fuck you, *sir*!' Dick said.

'THAT'S BETTER,' Owen said. 'WHAT ARE YOU DOING IN THERE – BEATING OFF?'

Major Rawls pushed Owen and me out of the path of the door; we were all standing clear of the door when Dick opened it. He was wearing a different pair of fatigue pants, he was barefoot and bare-chested, and he'd blackened his face with something like shoe polish – as if, after the merrymakers all settled down, he planned to engage in undercover activities in the dangerous neighborhood. With the same black marker, he had drawn circles around his nipples – like twin bull's-eyes on his chest.

'Come on in,' he said, stepping back into his room, where – no doubt – he dreamed without cease of butchering the Viet Cong.

The room reeked of marijuana; Dick finished the small nub of a roach he held with a pair of tweezers – not offering us the last toke. The dead helicopter pilot, the warrant officer, was named Frank Jarvits – but Dick preferred to call him by his 'Cong killer name,' the name his buddies in 'Nam had given him, which was 'Hubcap.' Dick showed us, proudly, all the souvenirs that Hubcap had managed to smuggle home from Vietnam. There were several bayonets, several machetes, a collection of plastic-encased 'water beetles,' and one helmet with an overripe sweatband – with the possessive 'Hubcap's Hat' written on the band in what appeared to be blood. There was an AK-47 assault rifle that Dick broke down into the stock group, the barrel, the receiver, the bolt – and so forth. Then he quickly reassembled the Soviet-made weapon. His stoned eyes flickered with a passing, brief excitement in gaining our approval; he'd wanted to show us how Hubcap had broken down the rifle in order to smuggle it home. There were two Chicom grenades, too – those bottle-shaped grenades, with the fat part serrated and the fuse cord at the pipelike end of the bottleneck.

'They don't blow as good as *ours*, but you can get sent to Leavenworth for sneakin' home an M-sixty-seven – Hubcap told me,' Dick said. He stared sadly at the two Chinese-made grenades; then he picked up one. 'Fuckin' Chink Commie *shit*,' he said, 'but it'll still do a job on ya.' He showed us how the warrant officer had taped up the end of the grenade, where the firing-pin cord is; then Hubcap had taped up the whole grenades in cardboard, placing one of them in a shaving kit and the other in a combat boot. 'They just come home like carry-on luggage,' Dick told us.

Apparently, various 'buddies' had been involved in bringing home the AK-47 assault rifle; different guys brought home different parts. 'That's how it's done,' Dick said wisely – his head still nodding to whatever tune the pot was playing to him. 'It got tough after sixty-six, 'cause of the drug traffickin' – everyone's gear got inspected more, you know,' he said.

The walls of the room were festooned with hanging cartridge belts and an assortment of fatigues and unmatching parts of uniforms. The ungainly boy lived for reaching the legal age for legal slaughter.

'How come *you* ain't in 'Nam?' Dick asked Owen. 'You too *small* – or what?'

Owen chose to ignore him, but Major Rawls said: 'Lieutenant Meany has requested transfer to Vietnam – he's scheduled to go there.'

'How come *you* ain't over there?' Dick asked the major.

' "HOW COME YOU AIN'T OVER THERE," *SIR*!' said Owen Meany.

Dick shut his eyes and smiled; he dozed off, or dreamed away, for a second or two. Then he said to Major Rawls: 'How come you ain't over there, *sir*?'

'I've already *been* there,' Rawls said.

'How come you ain't *back* there?' Dick asked him. '*Sir* . . .' he added nastily.

'I've got a better job here,' Major Rawls told the boy.

'Well, *someone's* got to have the dirty jobs – ain't that how it is?' Dick said.

'WHEN YOU GET IN THE ARMY, WHAT KIND OF JOB

DO YOU THINK *YOU'LL* HAVE?' Owen asked the boy. 'WITH YOUR ATTITUDE, YOU WON'T *GET* TO VIETNAM – YOU WON'T GO TO WAR, YOU'LL GO TO *JAIL*. YOU DON'T HAVE TO BE SMART TO GO TO WAR,' said Owen Meany. 'BUT YOU HAVE TO BE SMARTER THAN *YOU*.'

The boy closed his eyes and smiled again; his head nodded a little. Major Rawls picked up a pencil and tapped it on the barrel of the assault rifle. That brought Dick, momentarily, back to life.

'You better not bring this baby to the airport, pal,' Major Rawls said. 'You better never show up there with the rifle, or with the grenades,' the major said. When the boy shut his eyes again, Rawls tapped him on his forehead with the pencil. The boy's eyes blinked open; hatred came and went in them – a drifting, passing hatred, like clouds or smoke. 'I'm not even sure those bayonets or machetes are *legal* – you understand me?' Major Rawls said. 'You better be sure you keep them in their sheaths,' he said.

'Sometimes the cops take 'em from me – sometimes they give 'em back the same day,' Dick said. I could count each of his ribs, and his stomach muscles. He saw me staring at him and he said: 'Who's the guy outta uniform?'

'HE'S IN INTELLIGENCE,' Owen said. Dick appeared impressed, but – like his hatred – the feeling drifted and passed.

'You carry a gun?' Dick asked me.

'NOT *THAT* KIND OF INTELLIGENCE,' said Owen Meany, and Dick closed his eyes again – there being, in his view, clearly *no* intelligence that didn't carry a gun.

'I'M SORRY ABOUT YOUR BROTHER,' Owen said – as we were leaving.

'See you at the funeral,' Major Rawls said to the boy.

'I don't go to fuckin' *funerals*!' Dick snapped. 'Close the door, Mister Intelligence Man,' he said to me, and I closed it behind me.

'That was a nice try, Meany,' Major Rawls said, putting his hand on Owen's shoulder. 'But that fucking kid is beyond saving.'

Owen said, 'IT'S NOT UP TO YOU OR ME, SIR – IT'S NOT UP TO US: WHO'S "BEYOND SAVING." '

Major Rawls put his hand on my shoulder. 'I tell you,' the major said, 'Owen's too good for this world.'

As we left the turquoise house, the pregnant daughter was trying to revive her mother, who was lying on the kitchen floor. Major Rawls looked at his watch. 'She's right on schedule,' he said. 'Same as last night, same as the night before. I tell you, picnics aren't what they used to be – not to mention, "picnic wakes," ' the major said.

'WHAT'S WRONG WITH THIS COUNTRY?' Owen Meany asked. 'WE SHOULD ALL BE AT HOME, LOOKING AFTER PEOPLE LIKE THIS. INSTEAD, WE'RE SENDING PEOPLE LIKE THIS TO VIETNAM!'

Major Rawls drove us to our motel – a modestly pretty place of the hacienda-type – where a swimming pool with underwater lights had the disturbing effect of substantially enlarging and misshaping the swimmers. But there weren't many swimmers, and after Rawls had invited himself to a painfully late dinner – and he'd *finally* gone home – Owen Meany and I were alone. We sat underwater, in the shallow end of the swimming pool, drinking more and more beer and looking up at the vast, southwestern sky.

'SOMETIMES I WISH I WAS A STAR,' Owen said. 'YOU KNOW THAT STUPID SONG – "WHEN YOU WISH UPON A STAR, MAKES NO DIFFERENCE WHO YOU ARE" – I *HATE* THAT SONG!' he said. 'I DON'T WANT TO "WISH UPON A STAR," I WISH I *WAS* A STAR – THERE OUGHT TO BE A SONG ABOUT THAT,' said Owen Meany, who was drinking what I estimated to be his sixth or seventh beer.

Major Rawls woke us up with an early-morning telephone call.

'*Don't* come to the fucking funeral – the family is raising hell about the service. They want *no* military to be there, they're telling us we can *keep* the American flag – they don't want it,' the major said.

'THAT'S OKAY WITH ME,' said Owen Meany.

'So you guys can just go back to sleep,' the major said.

'THAT'S OKAY WITH ME, TOO,' Owen told him.

So I never got to meet the famous 'asshole minister,' the so-called 'traveling Baptist.' Major Rawls told me, later, that the mother had spit on the minister *and* on the mortician – perhaps regretting that she'd given up her opportunity to spit on Owen when he handed her the American flag.

It was Sunday, July 7, 1968.

After the major called, I went back to sleep; but Owen wrote in his diary.

'WHAT'S WRONG WITH THIS COUNTRY?' he wrote. 'THERE IS SUCH A STUPID "GET EVEN" MENTALITY – THERE IS SUCH A SADISTIC ANGER.' He turned on the TV, keeping the volume off; when I woke up, much later, he was still writing in the diary and watching one of those television evangelists – without the sound.

'IT'S BETTER WHEN YOU DON'T HAVE TO LISTEN TO WHAT THEY'RE SAYING,' he said.

In the diary, he wrote: 'IS THIS COUNTRY JUST SO HUGE THAT IT NEEDS TO OVERSIMPLIFY EVERYTHING? LOOK AT THE WAR: EITHER WE HAVE A STRATEGY TO "WIN" IT, WHICH MAKES US – IN THE WORLD'S VIEW – MURDERERS; OR ELSE WE ARE DYING, WITHOUT FIGHTING TO WIN. LOOK AT WHAT WE CALL "FOREIGN POLICY": OUR "FOREIGN POLICY" IS A EUPHEMISM FOR PUBLIC RELATIONS, AND OUR PUBLIC RELATIONS GET WORSE AND WORSE. WE'RE BEING DEFEATED AND WE'RE NOT GOOD LOSERS.

'AND LOOK AT WHAT WE CALL "RELIGION": TURN ON ANY TELEVISION ON ANY SUNDAY MORNING! SEE THE CHOIRS OF THE POOR AND UNEDUCATED – AND THESE TERRIBLE PREACHERS, SELLING OLD JESUS-STORIES LIKE JUNK FOOD. SOON THERE'LL BE AN EVANGELIST IN THE WHITE HOUSE; SOON THERE'LL BE A CARDINAL ON THE SUPREME COURT. ONE DAY THERE WILL COME AN EPIDEMIC – I'LL BET ON SOME HUMDINGER OF A SEXUAL DISEASE. AND WHAT WILL OUR PEERLESS LEADERS, OUR HEADS OF CHURCH AND STATE . . . WHAT WILL THEY *SAY* TO US? HOW WILL THEY HELP US? YOU CAN BE SURE THEY WON'T *CURE* US – BUT HOW WILL THEY COMFORT US? JUST TURN ON THE TV – AND HERE'S WHAT OUR PEERLESS LEADERS, OUR HEADS OF CHURCH AND STATE WILL SAY: THEY'LL SAY, "I TOLD YOU SO!" THEY'LL SAY, "THAT'S WHAT YOU GET FOR FUCKING AROUND – I TOLD YOU NOT TO DO IT UNTIL YOU GOT MARRIED." DOESN'T ANYONE SEE WHAT THESE

SIMPLETONS ARE UP TO? THESE SELF-RIGHTEOUS FANATICS ARE *NOT* "RELIGIOUS" – THEIR HOMELY WISDOM IS *NOT* "MORALITY."

'THAT IS WHERE THIS COUNTRY IS HEADED – IT IS HEADED TOWARD OVERSIMPLIFICATION. YOU WANT TO SEE A PRESIDENT OF THE FUTURE? TURN ON ANY TELEVISION ON ANY SUNDAY MORNING – FIND ONE OF THOSE HOLY ROLLERS: THAT'S HIM, THAT'S THE NEW MISTER PRESIDENT! AND DO YOU WANT TO SEE THE FUTURE OF ALL THOSE KIDS WHO ARE GOING TO FALL IN THE CRACKS OF THIS GREAT, BIG, SLOPPY SOCIETY OF OURS? I JUST MET HIM; HE'S A TALL, SKINNY, FIFTEEN-YEAR-OLD BOY NAMED "DICK." HE'S PRETTY SCARY. WHAT'S WRONG WITH HIM IS NOT UNLIKE WHAT'S WRONG WITH THE TV EVANGELIST – OUR FUTURE PRESIDENT. WHAT'S WRONG WITH BOTH OF THEM IS THAT THEY'RE SO SURE THEY'RE *RIGHT*! THAT'S PRETTY SCARY – THE FUTURE, I THINK, IS PRETTY SCARY.'

That was when I woke up and saw him pause in his writing. He was staring at the TV preacher, whom he couldn't hear – the preacher was talking on and on, waving his arms, while behind him stood a choir of men and women in silly robes . . . they weren't singing, but they were swaying back and forth, and smiling; all their lips were so firmly and uniformly closed that they appeared to be humming; or else they'd eaten something that had entranced them; or else what the preacher was saying had entranced them.

'Owen, what are you doing?' I asked him.

That was when he said: 'IT'S BETTER WHEN YOU DON'T HAVE TO LISTEN TO WHAT THEY'RE SAYING.'

I ordered a big breakfast for us – we had never had room service before! While I took a shower, he wrote a little more in the diary.

'HE DOESN'T KNOW WHY HE'S HERE, AND I DON'T DARE TELL HIM,' Owen wrote. 'I DON'T KNOW WHY HE'S HERE – I JUST KNOW HE HAS TO BE HERE! BUT I DON'T EVEN "KNOW" THAT – NOT ANYMORE. IT DOESN'T MAKE ANY SENSE! WHERE IS VIETNAM – IN ALL OF THIS? WHERE ARE THOSE POOR CHILDREN? WAS IT JUST A TERRIBLE DREAM? AM I SIMPLY CRAZY? IS TOMORROW JUST ANOTHER DAY?'

'So,' I said – while we were eating breakfast. 'What do you want to do today?'

He smiled at me. 'IT DOESN'T MATTER WHAT WE DO – LET'S JUST HAVE A GOOD TIME,' said Owen Meany.

We inquired at the front desk about where we could play basketball; Owen wanted to practice the shot, of course, and – especially in the staggering midday heat – I thought that a gym would be a nice, cool place to spend a couple of hours. We were sure that Major Rawls could gain us access to the athletic facilities at Arizona State; but we didn't want to spend the day with Rawls, and we didn't want to rent our own car and look for a place to play basketball on our own. The guy at the front desk said: 'This is a golf and tennis town.'

'IT DOESN'T MATTER,' Owen said. 'I'M PRETTY SURE WE'VE PRACTICED THAT DUMB SHOT ENOUGH.'

We tried to take a walk, but I declared that the heat would kill us.

We ate a huge lunch on the patio by the swimming pool; we went in and out of the pool between courses, and when we finished the lunch, we kept drinking beer and cooling off in the pool. We had the place practically to ourselves; the waiters and the bartender kept looking at us – they must have thought we were crazy, or from another planet.

'WHERE ARE ALL THE PEOPLE?' Owen asked the bartender.

'We don't do a lot of business this time of year,' the bartender said. 'What business are *you* in?' he asked Owen.

'I'M IN THE DYING BUSINESS,' said Owen Meany. Then we sat in the pool, laughing about how the dying business was not a seasonal thing.

About the middle of the afternoon, Owen started playing what he called 'THE REMEMBER GAME.'

Owen asked me: 'DO YOU REMEMBER THE FIRST TIME YOU MET MISTER FISH?'

I said I couldn't remember – it seemed to me that Mr Fish had always been there.

'I KNOW WHAT YOU MEAN,' Owen said. 'DO YOU REMEMBER WHAT YOUR MOTHER WAS WEARING WHEN WE BURIED SAGAMORE?'

I couldn't remember. 'IT WAS THAT BLACK V-NECK SWEATER, AND THOSE GRAY FLANNEL SLACKS – OR

MAYBE IT WAS A LONG GRAY SKIRT,' he said.

'I don't think she *had* a long, gray skirt,' I said.

'I THINK YOU'RE RIGHT,' he said. 'DO YOU REMEMBER DAN'S OLD SPORTS JACKET – THE ONE THAT LOOKED LIKE IT WAS MADE OF *CARROTS*?'

'It was the color of his hair!' I said.

'THAT'S THE ONE!' said Owen Meany.

'Do you remember Mary Beth Baird's *cow* costumes?' I asked him.

'THEY WERE AN IMPROVEMENT ON THE TURTLEDOVES,' he said. 'DO YOU REMEMBER THOSE *STUPID* TURTLEDOVES?'

'Do you remember when Barb Wiggin gave you a hard-on?' I asked him.

'I REMEMBER WHEN GERMAIN GAVE *YOU* A HARD-ON!' he said.

'Do you remember your *first* hard-on?' I asked him. We were both silent. I imagined that Hester had given me my first hard-on, and I didn't want to tell Owen that; and I imagined that my mother might have given Owen *his* first hard-on, which was probably why he wasn't answering.

Finally, he said: 'IT'S LIKE WHAT YOU SAY ABOUT MISTER FISH – I THINK I *ALWAYS* HAD A HARD-ON.'

'Do you remember Amanda Dowling?' I asked him.

'DON'T GIVE ME THE SHIVERS!' he said. 'DO YOU REMEMBER THE GAME WITH THE ARMADILLO?'

'Of course!' I said. 'Do you remember when Maureen Early wet her pants?'

'SHE WET THEM *TWICE*!' he said. 'DO YOU REMEMBER YOUR GRANDMOTHER WAILING LIKE A BANSHEE?'

'I'll never forget it,' I said. 'Do you remember when you untied the rope in the quarry – when you hid yourself, when we were swimming?'

'YOU LET ME DROWN – YOU LET ME DIE,' he said.

We ate dinner by the pool; we drank beer in the pool until long after midnight – when the bartender informed us that he was not permitted to serve us anymore.

'You're not supposed to be drinking while you're actually *in* the pool, anyway,' he said. 'You might drown. And I'm supposed to go home,' he said.

'EVERYTHING'S LIKE IN THE ARMY,' Owen said. 'RULES, RULES, RULES.'

So we took a six-pack of beer and a bucket of ice back to our room; we watched *The Late Show*, and then *The Late, Late Show* – while we tried to remember all the movies we'd ever seen. I was so drunk I don't remember what movies we saw in Phoenix that night. Owen Meany was so drunk that he fell asleep in the bathtub; he'd gotten into the bathtub because he said he missed sitting in the swimming pool. But then he couldn't watch the movie – not from the bathtub – and so he'd insisted that I describe the movie to him.

'Now she's kissing his photograph!' I called out to him.

'WHICH ONE IS KISSING HIS PHOTOGRAPH – THE BLOND ONE?' he asked. 'WHICH PHOTOGRAPH?'

I went on describing the movie until I heard him snoring. Then I let the water out of the bath, and I lifted him up and out of the tub – he was so light, he was nothing to lift. I dried him off with a towel; he didn't wake up. He was mumbling in his drunken sleep.

'I KNOW YOU'RE HERE FOR A REASON,' he said.

When I tucked him into his bed, he blinked open his eyes and said: 'O GOD – WHY HASN'T MY VOICE CHANGED, WHY DID YOU GIVE ME SUCH A VOICE? THERE MUST BE A REASON.' Then he shut his eyes and said: 'WATAHANTOWET.'

When I got into my bed and turned out the light, I said good night to him.

'Good night, Owen,' I said.

'DON'T BE AFRAID. NOTHING BAD IS GOING TO HAPPEN TO YOU,' said Owen Meany. 'YOUR FATHER'S NOT *THAT* BAD A GUY,' he said.

When I woke up in the morning, I had a terrible hangover; Owen was already awake – he was writing in the dairy. That was his last entry – that was when he wrote: 'TODAY'S THE DAY! ". . . HE THAT BELIEVETH IN ME, THOUGH HE WERE DEAD, YET SHALL HE LIVE; AND WHOSOEVER LIVETH AND BELIEVETH IN ME SHALL NEVER DIE." '

It was Monday, July 8, 1968 – the date he had seen on Scrooge's grave.

Major Rawls picked us up at our motel and drove us to the airport – to the so-called Sky Harbor. I thought that Rawls behaved oddly out of character – he wasn't at all talkative, he just mumbled something about having had a 'bad date' – but Owen had told me that the major was very moody.

'HE'S NOT A BAD GUY – HE JUST KNOWS HIS SHIP ISN'T EVER GOING TO COME IN,' Owen had said about Rawls. 'HE'S OLD-FASHIONED, BROWN-SHOE ARMY – HE LIKES TO PRETEND HE'S HAD NO EDUCATION, BUT ALL HE DOES IS READ; HE WON'T EVEN GO TO THE MOVIES. AND HE NEVER TALKS ABOUT VIETNAM – JUST SOME CRYPTIC SHIT ABOUT HOW THE ARMY DIDN'T PREPARE HIM TO KILL WOMEN AND CHILDREN, OR TO BE KILLED *BY* THEM. FOR WHATEVER REASON, HE DIDN'T MAKE LIEUTENANT COLONEL; HIS TWENTY YEARS IN THE ARMY ARE ALMOST UP, AND HE'S BITTER ABOUT IT – HE'S JUST A MAJOR. HE'S NOT EVEN FORTY AND HE'S ABOUT TO BE RETIRED.'

Major Rawls complained that we were going to the airport too early; my flight to Boston didn't leave for another two hours. Owen had booked no special flight to Tucson – apparently, there were frequent flights from Phoenix to Tucson, and Owen was going to wait until I left; then he'd take the next available plane.

'There are better places to hang around than this fucking airport,' Major Rawls complained.

'YOU DON'T HAVE TO HANG AROUND WITH US – SIR,' said Owen Meany.

But Rawls didn't want to be alone; he didn't feel like talking, but he wanted company – or else he didn't know what he wanted. He wandered into the game room and hustled a few young recruits into playing pinball with him. When they found out he'd been in Vietnam, they pestered him for stories; all he would tell them was: 'It's an asshole war – and you're assholes if you want to be there.'

Major Rawls pointed Owen out to the recruits. 'You want to go to Vietnam?' he said. 'Go talk to him – go see that little lieutenant. He's another asshole who wants to go there.'

Most of the new recruits were on their way to Fort Huachuca; their hair was cut so short, you could see scabs from the razor nicks – most of them who were assigned to Fort Huachuca would probably be on orders to Vietnam soon.

'They look like *babies*,' I said to Owen.

'BABIES FIGHT THE WARS,' said Owen Meany; he told the young recruits that he thought they'd like Fort Huachuca. 'THE SUN SHINES ALL THE TIME,' he told them, 'AND IT'S NOT AS HOT AS IT IS HERE.' He kept looking at his watch.

'We have plenty of time,' I told him, and he smiled at me – that old smile with the mild pity and the mild contempt in it.

Some planes landed; other planes took off. Some of the recruits left for Fort Huachuca. 'Aren't you coming, sir?' they asked Owen Meany.

'LATER,' he told them. 'I'LL SEE YOU LATER.'

Fresh recruits arrived, and Major Rawls went on making a killing – he was a pro at pinball.

I complained about the extent of my hangover; Owen must have had a worse hangover – or one at least as bad as mine – but I imagine, now, that he was savoring it; he knew it was his last hangover. Then the confusion would return to him, and he must have felt that he knew absolutely nothing. He sat beside me and I could see him changing – from nervousness to depression, from fear to elation. I thought it was his hangover; but one minute he must have been thinking, 'MAYBE IT HAPPENS ON THE AIRPLANE.' Then in another minute, he must have said to himself: 'THERE ARE NO CHILDREN. I DON'T EVEN HAVE TO GO TO VIETNAM – I CAN STILL GET OUT OF IT.'

In the airport, he said to me – out of the blue: 'YOU DON'T HAVE TO BE A GENIUS TO OUTSMART THE ARMY.'

I didn't know what he was talking about, but I said: 'I suppose not.'

In another minute; he must have been thinking: 'IT *WAS* JUST A CRAZY DREAM! WHO THE FUCK KNOWS WHAT GOD KNOWS? I OUGHT TO SEE A PSYCHIATRIST!'

Then he would stand up and pace: he would look around for the children; he was looking for his killer. He kept glancing at his watch.

When they announced my flight to Boston – it was scheduled to depart in half an hour – Owen was grinning ear-to-ear. 'THIS MAY BE THE HAPPIEST DAY OF MY LIFE!' he said. 'MAYBE NOTHING'S GOING TO HAPPEN!'

'I think you're still drunk,' I told him. 'Wait till you get to the hangover.'

A plane had just landed; it had arrived from somewhere on the West Coast, and it taxied into view. I heard Owen Meany gasp beside me, and I turned to look where he was looking.

'What's the matter with you?' I asked him. 'They're just penguins.'

The nuns – there were two of them – were meeting someone on the plane from the West Coast: they stood at the gate to the runway. The first people off the plane were also nuns – two more. The nuns waved to each other. When the children emerged from the airplane – they were closely following the nuns – Owen Meany said: 'HERE THEY ARE!'

Even from the runway gate, I could see that they were Asian children – one of the nuns leaving the plane was an Oriental, too. There were about a dozen kids; only two of them were small enough to be carried – one of the nuns carried one of the kids, and one of the older children carried the other little one. They were both boys and girls – the average age was maybe five or six, but there were a couple of kids who were twelve or thirteen. They were Vietnamese orphans; they were refugee children.

Many military units sponsored orphanages in Vietnam; many of the troops donated their time – as well as what gifts they could solicit from home – to help the kids. There was no official government-sponsored refugee program to relocate Vietnamese children – not before the fall of Saigon in April, 1975 – but certain churches were active in Vietnam throughout the course of the war.

Catholic Relief Services, for example; the Catholic Relief groups were responsible for escorting orphans out of Vietnam and relocating them in the United States – as early as the mid-sixties. Once in the United States, the orphans would be met by social workers from the archdiocese or diocese of the particular city of their arrival. The Lutherans were also involved in sponsoring the relocation of Vietnamese orphans.

The children that Owen Meany and I saw in Phoenix were being escorted by nuns from Catholic Relief Services; they were being delivered into the charge of nuns from the Phoenix Archdiocese, who would take them to new homes, and new families, in Arizona. Owen and I could see that the children were anxious about it.

If the heat was no shock to them – for it was certainly very hot where they'd come from – the desert and the hugeness of the sky and the moonscape of Pheonix must have overwhelmed them. They held each other's hands and stayed together, circling very closely around the nuns. One of the little boys was crying.

When they came into the Sky Harbor terminal, the blast of air conditioning instantly chilled them; they were cold – they hugged themselves and rubbed their arms. The little boy who was crying tried to wrap himself up in the habit of one of the nuns. They all milled around in lost confusion, and – from the game room – the young recruits with their shaved heads stared out at them. The children stared back at the soldiers; they were used to soldiers, of course. As the kids and the recruits stared back and forth at each other, you could sense the mixed feelings.

Owen Meany was as jumpy as a mouse. One of the nuns spoke to him.

'Officer?' she said.

'YES, MA'AM – HOW MAY I HELP YOU?' he said quickly.

'Some of the boys need to find a men's room,' the nun said; one of the younger nuns tittered. 'We can take the girls,' the first nun said, 'but if you'd be so kind – if you'd just go with the boys.'

'YES, MA'AM – I'D BE HAPPY TO HELP THE CHILDREN,' said Owen Meany.

'Wait till you see the so-called men's room,' I told Owen; I led the way. Owen just concentrated on the children. There were seven boys: the nun who was also Vietnamese accompanied us – she carried the smallest boy. The boy who was crying had stopped as soon as he saw Owen Meany. All the children watched Owen closely; they had seen many soldiers – yes – but they had never seen a soldier who was almost as small as *they* were! They never took their eyes off him.

On we marched – when we passed by the game room, Major Rawls had his back to us; he didn't see us. Rawls was humping the pinball machine in a fury. In the mouth of the corridor I'd walked down before – it led nowhere – we marched past Dick Jarvits, the tall, lunatic brother of the dead warrant officer, standing in the shadows.

He wore the jungle fatigues; he was strapped up with an extra cartridge belt or two. Although it was dark in the corridor, he wore the kind of sunglasses that must have melted on his brother's face when the helicopter had caught fire. Because he was wearing sunglasses, I couldn't tell if Dick saw Owen or me or the children; but from the gape of his open mouth, I concluded that *something* Dick had just seen had surprised him.

The 'Men's Temporary Facilities' were the same as I had left them. The same mops and pails were there, and the unhung mirror still leaned against the wall. The vast mystery sink confused the children; one of them tried to pee in it, but I pointed him in the direction of the crowded urinal. One of the children considered peeing in a pail, but I showed him the toilet in the makeshift, plywood stall. Owen Meany, the good soldier, stood under the window; he watched the door. Occasionally, he would glance above him, sizing up the deep window ledge below the casement window. Owen looked especially small standing under that window, because the window ledge was at least ten feet high – it towered above him.

The nun was waiting for her charges, just outside the door.

I helped one of the children unzip his fly; the child seemed unfamiliar with a zipper. The children all jabbered in Vietnamese; the small, high-ceilinged room – like a coffin standing upright on one end – echoed with their voices.

I've already said how slow I am; it wasn't until I heard their shrill, foreign voices that I remembered Owen's dream. I saw him watching the door, his arms hanging loosely at his sides.

'What's wrong?' I said to him.

'STAND BESIDE ME,' he said. I was moving toward him when the door was kicked wide open and Dick Jarvits stood there, nearly as tall and thin as the tall, thin room; he held a Chicom grenade – carefully – in both hands.

'HELLO, DICK,' said Owen Meany.

'You little *twit!*' Dick said. One of the children screamed; I suppose they'd all seen men in jungle fatigues before - I think that the little boy who screamed had seen a Chicom grenade before, too. Two or three of the children began to cry.

'*DOONG SA*,' Owen Meany told them. 'DON'T BE AFRAID,'

Owen told the children. '*DOONG SA, DOONG SA*,' he said. It was not only because he spoke their language; it was his *voice* that compelled the children to listen to him – it was a voice like *their* voices. That was why they trusted him, why they listened. '*DOONG SA*,' he said, and they stopped crying.

'It's just the place for you to die,' Dick said to Owen. 'With all these little *gooks* – with these little *dinks*!' Dick said.

'*NAM SOON!*' Owen told the children. '*NAM SOON!* LIE DOWN!' Even the littlest boy understood him. 'LIE DOWN!' Owen told them. '*NAM SOON! NAM SOON!*' All the children threw themselves on the floor – they covered their ears, they shut their eyes.

'NOW I KNOW WHY MY VOICE NEVER CHANGES,' Owen said to me. 'DO YOU SEE WHY?' he asked me.

'Yes,' I said.

'WE'LL HAVE JUST FOUR SECONDS,' Owen told me calmly. 'YOU'LL NEVER GET TO VIETNAM, DICK,' Owen told the terrible, tall boy – who ripped the fuse cord and tossed the bottle-shaped grenade, end over end, right to me.

'Think fast – Mister Fuckin' *Intelligence* Man!' Dick said.

I caught the grenade, although it wasn't as easy to handle as the baseball – I was lucky. I looked at Owen, who was already moving toward me.

'READY?' he said; I passed him the Chicom grenade and opened my arms to catch him. He jumped so lightly into my hands; I lifted him up – as easily as I had always lifted him.

After all: I had been practicing lifting up Owen Meany – forever.

The nun who'd been waiting for the children outside the door of the 'Men's Temporary Facilities' – she hadn't liked the looks of Dick; she'd run off to get the other soldiers. It was Major Rawls who caught Dick running away from the temporary men's room.

'What have you done, you fuck-face?' the major screamed at Dick.

Dick had drawn the bayonet. Major Rawls seized Dick's machete – Rawls broke Dick's neck with one blow, with the dull edge of the blade. I'd sensed that there was something more bitter than anger in the major's uncommon, lake-green eyes; maybe it was just his contact lenses, but Rawls hadn't won a battlefield commission in Korea for nothing. He may not have been prepared to kill an unfortunate, fifteen-year-old boy; but Major Rawls was even less prepared to be killed by such a kid, who – as Rawls had said to Owen – was (at least on this earth) 'beyond saving.'

When Owen Meany said 'READY?' I figured we had about two seconds left to live. But he soared far above my arms – when I lifted him, he soared even higher than usual; he wasn't taking any chances. He went straight up, never turning to face me, and instead of merely dropping the grenade and leaving it on the window ledge, he caught hold of the ledge with both hands, pinning the grenade against the ledge and trapping it there safely with his hands and forearms. He wanted to be sure that the grenade couldn't roll off the ledge and fall back in the room. He could just manage to wriggle his head – his whole head, thank God – below the window ledge. He clung there for less than a second.

Then the grenade detonated; it made a shattering 'crack!' – like lightning when it strikes too close to you. There was a high-velocity projection of fragments – the fragmentation is usually distributed in a uniform pattern (this is what Major Rawls explained to me, later), but the cement window ledge prevented any fragments from reaching me or the children. What hit us was all the stuff that ricocheted off the ceiling – there was a sharp, stinging hail that rattled like BB's around the room, and all the chips of cement and tile, and the plaster debris, fell down upon us. The window was blown out, and there was an instant, acrid, burning stink. Major Rawls, who had just killed Dick, flung the door open and jammed a mop handle into the hinge assembly – to keep the door open. We needed the air. The children were holding their ears and crying; some of them were bleeding from their ears – that was when I noticed that my ears were bleeding, too, and that I couldn't actually hear anything. I knew – from their faces – that the children were crying, and I knew from looking at Major Rawls that he was trying to tell me to *do* something.

What does he want me to do? I wondered, listening to the pain in my ears. Then the nuns were moving among the children – all the children were moving, thank God; they were *more* than moving, they were grasping each other, they were tugging the habits of the nuns, and they were pointing to the torn-apart ceiling of the coffin-shaped room, and the smoking black hole above the window ledge.

Major Rawls was shaking me by my shoulders; I tried to read the major's lips because I still couldn't hear him.

The children were looking all around; they were pointing up and down everywhere. I began to look around with them. Now the nuns were also looking. Then my ears cleared; there was a popping or a ripping sound, as if my ears were late in echoing the explosion, and then the children's voices were jabbering, and I heard what Major Rawls was screaming at me while he shook me.

'Where *is* he? Where is Owen?' Major Rawls was screaming.

I looked up at the black hole, where I'd last seen him clinging. One of the children was staring into the vast sink; one of the nuns looked into the sink, too – she crossed herself, and Major Rawls and I moved quickly to assist her.

But the nun didn't need our help; Owen was so light, even the nun could lift him. She picked him up, out of the sink, as she might have picked up one of the children; then she didn't know what to do with him. Another nun kneeled in the bomb litter on the floor; she settled back on her haunches and spread her habit smoothly across her thighs, and the nun who held Owen in her arms rested his head in the lap of the sister who'd thus arranged herself on the floor. The third and fourth nuns tried to calm the children – to make them move away from him – but the children crowded around Owen; they were all crying.

'*DOONG SA* – DON'T BE AFRAID,' he told them, and they stopped crying. The girl orphans had gathered in the doorway.

Major Rawls removed his necktie and tried to apply a tourniquet – just above the elbow of one of Owen's arms. I removed Owen's tie and tried to apply a tourniquet – in the same fashion – to his other arm. Both of Owen Meany's arms were missing – they were severed just below his elbows, perhaps three quarters of the way up his forearms; but he'd not begun to bleed too badly, not yet. A doctor told me later that – in the first moments – the arteries in his arms would have gone into spasm; he was bleeding, but not as much as you might expect from such a violent amputation. The tissue that hung from the stumps of his arms was as filmy and delicate as gossamer – as fine and intricate as old lace. Nowhere else was he injured.

Then his arms began to bleed more; the tighter Major Rawls and I applied our torniquets, the more Owen bled.

'Go get someone,' the major told one of the nuns.

'NOW I KNOW WHY YOU HAD TO BE HERE,' Owen said to me. 'DO YOU SEE WHY?' he asked me.

'Yes,' I said.

'REMEMBER ALL OUR PRACTICING?' he asked me.

'I remember,' I said.

Owen tried to raise his hands; he tried to reach out to me with his arms – I think he wanted to touch me. That was when he realized that his arms were gone. He didn't seem surprised by the discovery.

'REMEMBER WATAHANTOWET?' he asked me.

'I remember,' I said.

Then he smiled at the 'penguin' who was trying to make him comfortable in her lap; her wimple was covered with his blood, and she had wrapped as much of her habit around him as she could manage – because he was shivering.

' ". . . WHOSOEVER LIVETH AND BELIEVETH IN ME SHALL NEVER DIE," ' Owen said to her. The nun nodded in agreement; she made the sign of the cross over him.

Then Owen smiled at Major Rawls. 'PLEASE SEE TO IT THAT I GET SOME KIND OF MEDAL FOR THIS,' he asked the major, who bowed his head – and cranked his tourniquet tighter.

There was only the briefest moment, when Owen looked stricken – something deeper and darker than pain crossed over his face, and he said to the nun who held him: 'I'M AWFULLY COLD, SISTER – CAN'T YOU DO SOMETHING?' Then whatever had troubled him passed over him completely, and he smiled again – he looked at us all with his old, infuriating smile.

Then he looked only at me. 'YOU'RE GETTING SMALLER, BUT I CAN STILL SEE YOU!' said Owen Meany.

Then he left us; he was gone. I could tell by his almost cheerful expression that he was at least as high as the palm trees.

Major Rawls saw to it that Owen Meany got a medal. I was asked to make an eyewitness report, but Major Rawls was instrumental in pushing the proper paperwork through the military chain of command. Owen Meany was awarded the so-called Soldier's Medal: 'For heroism that involves the voluntary risk of life under conditions other than those of conflict with an opposing armed force.' According to Major Rawls, the Soldier's Medal rates above the Bronze Star but below the Legion of Merit. Naturally, it didn't matter very much to me – exactly where the medal was rated – but I think Rawls was right in assuming that the medal mattered to Owen Meany.

Major Rawls did not attend Owen's funeral. When I spoke on the telephone with him, Rawls was apologetic about not making the trip to New Hampshire; but I assured him that I completely understood his feelings. Major Rawls had seen his share of flag-draped caskets; he had seen his share of heroes, too. Major Rawls never knew everything that Owen had *known;* the major knew only that Owen had been a hero – he didn't know that Owen Meany had been a miracle, too.

There's a prayer I say most often for Owen. It's one of the little prayers he said for my mother, the night Hester and I found him in the cemetery – where he'd brought the flashlight, because he knew how my mother had hated the darkness.

'"INTO PARADISE MAY THE ANGELS LEAD YOU,"' he'd said over my mother's grave; and so I say that one for him – I know it was one of his favorites.

I am always saying prayers for Owen Meany.

And I often try to imagine how I might have answered Mary Beth Baird, when she spoke to me – at Owen's burial. If I could have spoken, if I hadn't lost my voice – what would I have said to her, how *could* I have answered her? Poor Mary Beth Baird! I left her standing in the cemetery without an answer.

'Do you remember how we used to lift him up?' she'd asked me. 'He was so easy to lift up!' Mary Beth Baird had said to me. 'He was so *light* – he weighed nothing at all! How could he have been so light?' the former Virgin Mother had asked me.

I could have told her that it was only our illusion that Owen Meany weighed 'nothing at all.' We were only children – we *are* only children – I could have told her. What did we ever know about Owen? What did we truly know? We had the impression that everything was a game – we thought we made everything up as we went along. When we were children, we had the impression that almost everything was just for fun – no harm intended, no damage done.

When we held Owen Meany above our heads, when we passed him back and forth – so effortlessly – we believed that Owen weighed nothing at all. We did not realize that there were forces beyond our play. Now I know they were the forces that contributed to our illusion of Owen's weightlessness; they were the forces we didn't have the faith to feel, they were the forces we failed to believe in – and they were also lifting up Owen Meany, taking him out of our hands.

O God – please give him back! I shall keep asking You.

THE END

The Cider House Rules
John Irving

'Bound to make as vivid an impression as *The World According to Garp*' said *Publishers Weekly* of John Irving's magnificent new novel spanning six decades.

Set among the apple orchard's of rural Maine, it is a perverse world in which Homer Wells' odyssey begins. As the oldest unadopted offspring at St Cloud's orphanage, he learns about the skills which, in one way or another, help young and not-so-young women, from Wilbur Larch, the orphanage's founder, a man of rare compassion and with an addiction to ether.

Dr Larch loves all his orphans, especially Homer Wells. It is Homer's story we follow, from his early apprenticeship in the orphanage surgery, to his adult life running a cider-making factory and his strange relationship with the wife of his closest friend.

'John Irving has been compared with Kurt Vonnegut and J. D. Salinger, but is arguably more inventive than either. Wry, laconic, he sketches his characters with an economy that springs from a feeling for words and mastery over his craft. This superbly original book is one to be read and remembered'

THE TIMES

'The Cider House Rules is difficult to define and impossible not to admire'

DAILY TELEGRAPH

'Like the rest of Irving's fiction, it is often disconcerting, but always exciting and provoking'

THE OBSERVER

0 552 99204 6

BLACK SWAN

The World According to Garp
John Irving

'It is not easy to find words in which to convey the joy, the excitement, the passion this superb novel evokes. The imagination soars as Irving draws us on inexorably into Garp's world, which is at once larger than life and as real as our own most private dreams of life and death, love, lust and fear . . . some of the most colourful characters in recent fiction'
PUBLISHERS WEEKLY

'Absolutely extraordinary . . . A roller-coaster ride that leaves one breathless, exhausted, elated and tearful'
LOS ANGELES TIMES BOOK REVIEW

'Like all great works of art, Irving's novel seems always to have been there, a diamond sleeping in the dark, chipped out at last for our enrichment and delight . . . As approachable as it is brilliant, GARP pulses with vital energy'
COSMOPOLITAN

0 552 99205 4

BLACK SWAN